PENTAGON'S HAMMER

TWELVE DAYS TO ARMAGEDDON

PENTAGON'S HAMMER

TWELVE DAYS TO ARMAGEDDON

Fiction

By

T. RANDALL

PENTAGON'S HAMMER – Twelve Days to Armageddon –
Copyright © 2015 by T. Randall. All Rights Reserved.
Graphics Design Copyright © 2012 by Valentino Group. All Rights Reserved.
Nuclear & Biological Warfare – Fiction. First Edition July 2012
First book in a PENTAGON'S HAMMER™ trilogy series.
Revised addition © 2015 – Published by PREMIER TECHNOLOGIES, INC.

Library of Congress Cataloging-in-Publication Data
ISBN: 978-0-9857047-1-1, EPUB
ISBN: 978-0-9857047-8-0, Hardcopy
ISBN: 978-0-9857047-0-4, Softcopy

DISTRIBUTOR:
Ingram Spark Print-On-Demand
Ingram Book Distribution for eBook:
Ingram Book Company
One Ingram Blvd.
La Vergne, TN 37086
http://www.ingrambook.com/default.aspx

Print-on-demand Hard & Soft copy:
Lightning Source Inc.
1246 Heil Quaker Blvd.
La Vergne, TN 37086
http://www1.lightningsource.com/

Printed in the United States of America
First Printing July 2012
10 9 8 7 6 5 4 3

DISCLAIMER

PENTAGON'S HAMMER – TWELVE DAYS TO ARMAGEDDON is fictional in nature, using fictitious names for all characters. Locations and events are suggested possibilities based on the current political state of world nations. The flag depicted specifically for this novel is not intended to deface the flag of the United States, nor is it meant to degrade in any way the honor of the nation and its citizens who have fought many battles under the flag of the Stars and Stripes. The flag, as illustrated on the cover page, is only a reflection of the intense storyline of the novel.

Although the author spent twenty-five years working as a government contractor, and, at times, had access to highly sensitive information inherit to the Intelligence community, it is not his intention to disclose any sensitive or classified materials to the public or to the enemies of the free world.

Where the author has intricate knowledge of organizational and governmental structures in the arenas of intelligence, defense, and science and technologies as described in this book, some information was extracted from public encyclopedia sources.

The author hereby thanks and acknowledges the many sources for their efforts in contributing specific information whether willingly or through the liberties of the Freedom of Information Act.

PENTAGON'S HAMMER – TWELVE DAYS TO ARMAGEDDON, although a work of fiction about the United States defense system, is based on real probabilities. The story could take place at any time, without a moment's notice to the public. To protect the nation and its citizens from the possibilities illustrated in the novel, the strategic nuclear-based defense system was created at the end of WWII. With the de-scaling of the defense system following the Cold War, the nation had become vulnerable to potential foreign attacks. To breach this vulnerability gap in fending off such potential threats, cyber warfare was borne and taken into cyberspace, making the strategic nuclear-based system virtually obsolete.

During the span of the strategic, tactical, and cyberspace defense deployments, an army of dedicated workforce is necessary to design, develop, and implement the complexity of the defense systems. It is this army of experts from government, military, and industry including scientists, engineers, technicians, operations, management, and support personnel that makes the United States a safer place to live. The story was created to acknowledge and thank every one of these experts for their commitment, dedication, and allegiance to the cause of preserving the freedom of a nation. Even though the characters within this book are fictional, every one of us could have played out the role of Alex Bauer and his crew.

ACKNOWLEDGEMENT

Special thanks to:

My daughter, Elsa Margaret
– For planting the seed that turned biography into fiction

My daughter, Nova Jennifer
– For being the tolerant sounding board for her dad

My daughter, Crystal Belle
– For the free-spirited Being that she is.

WEBSITE CREDITS:

http://www.nsa.gov/
http://www.nro.gov/
https://www.cia.gov/
http://www.norad.mil/
http://www.northcom.mil/
http://www.southcom.mil/
http://www.stratcom.mil/
http://www.defense.gov/
http://www.defenselink.mil/
http://www.dhs.gov/index.shtm
http://www.spaceimaging.com
http://www.knox.army.mil/
http://www.commemorativeairforce.org/
http://en.wikipedia.org/wiki/United_States_Penitentiary,_Leavenworth

TERMS/ABBREVIATIONS/ACRONYMS LINK:

http://www.fas.org/news/reference/terms/s.html

PENTAGON'S HAMMER – TWELVE DAYS TO ARMAGEDDON is a comprehensive fiction novel based on the vulnerability of the United States defense system. Extended in volume size over the average novel and, because of the complexity of the plot, many chapters are necessary in the development and subsequently segmented into a number of sub-plots merged into the main story. Making up the chapters are dozens of characters and organizations necessary that are dependent on each other in case of an all-out attack on the nation. In addition, a number of segments, traumatizing the lives of American citizens affected by an all-out attack on the nation, are illustrated.

The story is played out during a twelve day global event involving the United States, North Korea, India, Pakistan, the Pacific Rim, and, on a peripheral scale, Cuba, China, and Russia. The stage was set with 9/11 on the New York trade center, when Islamic extremists successfully carried out the worst terrorist attack on U.S. soil. Years later, following the outsourcing of critical and sensitive programs by the defense department, vital information for the NSA's most critical, and highly classified satellite system, the ASATs (attack satellites), falls into the hands of the adversary.

The adversary, HASAN HAMMAD, principal jihad antagonist to the Unites States and the free world, by manipulating critical satellites is able to puncture the U.S. defense shield. The earliest indication to the breach is detected by TRACY BAUER, NSA Intel strategist, liaison to the Pentagon. In conjunction, ALEX BAUER, father of Tracy, and longtime defense analyst and design engineer with DOD and BMO (Ballistics Missiles Office), a branch of SAC, comes across classified information on EMP and its inherited vulnerability to the nation's strategic defense infrastructure, the Minuteman III and Peacekeeper missile systems.

Whereas EMP, electromagnetic pulsing, is a highly sophisticated process generated by an atomic explosion, it can also be set off through a simple and inexpensive trigger device. What makes it even more detrimental, this science and technology has been hidden from the public eyes for more than sixty years. Through vital intelligence leaks and organizational compromises created by current economic conditions, North Korea, Pakistan, Iran, and the Jihad have gained knowledge for this once closely guarded secret.

Initial attempts by BRIAN HARRIS, NSA operative and longtime friend to Alex Bauer, in fixing the vulnerability in the satellite defense system, fail. It will take days, in collaboration with Tracy and Alex, for Brian to identify the source of the breach. Attempts to resolve the problem for the deliberate intrusion on U.S. airspace prove unsuccessful. The antagonist, manipulating the U.S. defense grid, is setting off a chain of events culminating in a series of confrontations involving North Korea, Pakistan, Cuba, Al Qaeda, and a number of global jihad cells. Due to the complexity of the defense structure, many of our defense and intelligence organizations become intricately involved in the strike, counter strike, retaliation, and reprisal.

In addition to the adventurous nature of Alex Bauer, the novel describes, through realistic means, the workings and interdependencies of the many egocentric, sometimes uncooperative agencies such as the CIA, NRO, DOD, SAC, BMO, DHS, NORAD, DELTA, and SPACECOM, whereas the White House and the Pentagon try to coordinate an effective triad defense for land, sea, and space. Each chapter, within the twelve days of global events is segmented further by describing character, initiative, environment, action, reaction, and resolution with strong character support interdependent of each other presented through the sphere of a global theater.

In the process, the United States comes under direct nuclear attack with the destruction of one major city. Furthermore, the enemy, in the heart of the nation unleashes a series of assaults through chemical and biological means affecting the lives of every citizen across the country. With every defense mechanism rendered ineffective by the initial EMP attack, the nation is brought to its knees resulting in an economic Armageddon effecting commerce, power, utilities, communication, banking, finance, Wall Street, transportation, hospital, emergency operation, law enforcement, national defense, government and the military, not to mention the lives of millions of U.S. citizens.

What heightens the novel's suspense are a number of detailed action packed plots in the wake of the EMP strike involving the potential meltdown of the Tree Mile Island nuclear power plant; the chaotic struggle of cockpit crews and passengers from incoming international flights destined for Chicago's O'Hare airport and unable to land; prison break at Fort Leavenworth, KS, with prisoners staging the takeover at Fort Knox, TN, to gain access to America's gold used to fund the future of the newly emerging nation, The Badlands, played out by gang leader Rusty Norton, and First Lieutenant Duke Wheeler, aka Bad Man, the Enforcer.

In an attempt to defuse the growing threat escalating with each day, the plots lead the reader into hostile territories. What makes the novel unique is the intricate knowledge of the writer in the Intel community, the defense system, and the nation's nuclear strike capability.

LIST OF CHARACTERS

PRINCIPLE CHARACTERS

Alex Bauer – Department of Defense analyst, retired, home base Castle Rock, CO
Brian Harris – NSA Analyst, longtime friend of Alex with romantic attachment to Tracy
Hasan Hammad – Supreme commander, Jihad antagonist and adversary to the free world
Lisa "Liz" Bauer – Specialist, nuclear emergencies, disaster recovery, search & rescue
Scott Brooks – Delta Force Operative, 1st Special Forces Operational Detachment/CIA
Tracy Bauer – Alex's daughter, NSA defense strategist, assigned liaison to the Pentagon

SUPPORT CAST – U.S. SECTOR

Benjamin "Ben" Jackson – Commanding General, NORAD, Colorado Springs, CO
Brodie Elliott – Command Sergeant Major, 1st Armored Division, Fort Knox, KY
Diego Martinez – Brigadier General, Peterson AFB, NORTHCOM, CO, Doug Olson –
Supervisor, Power Station, Three Mile Island, PA
Duke Wheeler, aka Bad Man – Enforcer, Patriots, Badlands, Ex-Penitentiary Inmate
Emmett W. Fletcher – Four-Star General, Flag Officer, U.S. European Command
George Wilmot – U.S. President, the White House, Washington, D.C.
Harry Carter – Chief of Operations, CIA HQ, Langley, VA
Henry "Hank" Foster – Commanding General, Four Star, DOD, the Pentagon
Jack Warner – Chief of Operations, NSA HQ, Fort Meade, MD
Jake Fulton – Chief of Operations, O'Hare International Airport, Chicago, IL
Janet Doe – Passenger, Wife, Ill-fated Intl. Atlantic Flight
Jon Barrister – Director, DHS, Washington, D.C.
John Hanson – Director, NRO HQ, Chantilly, VA
Lewis (Hawk) Hawkins – Chief of Operations, SAC, Omaha, NE
McAllister – Procurement Broker, Offshore Trading Agency, Cayman Islands
Missile Operators – Minuteman III Launch Facility, Cheyenne, WY
Mitchell (Mitch) Kelley – Stunt Pilot, Flight Interceptors, Key West, FL
Nelson Tucker – Commanding General, SOUTHCOM, Miami, FL
Patrick "Pat" Adams – Commander, 15th Air Base Wing, Honolulu, HI
Paul Doe – Passenger, Husband, Ill-fated Intl. Atlantic Flight
Rhonda Hicks – Chief of Operations, NORTHCOM, CO
Russell Wilcox – Unit Leader, Penitentiary, Fort Leavenworth, KS
Rusty Norton – Leader, Patriots, Badlands, Ex-Penitentiary Inmate
Secretary General – United Nations, New York City, NY
Smokey – Gunner, Confederate Air Force, Midland, TX
Sparky – Intelligence Operative, NSA HQ, Fort Meade, MD
Tyler Marshall – Pilot, Aussie, Intl. Atlantic Flight
Wendell Nelson – Commander, Garrison U.S. Army, Fort Knox, KY
Wesley (Wes) Simmons – Pilot, Confederate Air Force, Midland, TX

SUPPORT CAST – FOREIGN SECTOR

Carlos Domingo – Ambassador, Cuban Embassy, Cuba
Cesar Romulus – General, Air Defense Forces, Cuba
Kim Hak Su – Commander, Missile Command, Defense Ministry, North Korea
Miss Lee – South Korean hostess and spy, reporting to the North Korean Ministry

Party Leader – National People's Congress, Beijing, China
Rajesh Chandra – Subcontractor to NSA, responsible for the defense breach, India
Ron, Mike, and Gary – Tech buddies, Intel network, South Korean region
Vladimir Potempkin – Foreign Minister, Russian Federation, Moscow, Russia

SUPPORT CAST – JIHAD SECTOR

Abdul "Omar One" Baser – Plant Chief, REX Chemicals, Islamabad, Pakistan
Amin Madani – Action Officer, Jihad Mission Command, Islamabad, Pakistan
Antarah Radi – Mission Commander, Al Qaeda, Jihad, Islamabad, Pakistan
Bandar Malik – First Lieutenant, Jihad, U.S. Cell Alpha, New York, NY
Hakim Massoud – First Lieutenant, U.S. Cell Central, Denver, CO
Jamuh Faisal – First Lieutenant, Al Qaeda, Jihad, South Cell, Madras, India
Joseph (Yusuf) Hashim – Commander, Jihad, U.S. Cell Alpha, New York, NY
Kazim Rashid – Tribal Elder, Al Qaeda, Jihad, Mountainous Region, Pakistan
Muhab Sadek – First Lieutenant, U.S. Cell West, Sacramento, CA
Rashid Abu – First Lieutenant, Al Qaeda, Jihad, Base Camp One, Yemen
Shakir Murad – First Lieutenant, Al Qaeda, Jihad, Base Camp Three, Yemen
Tariq Amman – First Lieutenant, U.S. Cell East, Washington, D.C.
The Serpent – Code name for the world's feared adversary, Al Qaeda, Jihad, Dubai, UAE

America will never be destroyed from the outside. If we
falter and lose our freedoms, it will be because we
destroyed ourselves.

— Abraham Lincoln (1809 – 1865)

Forgive your enemies, but never forget their names.

— John F. Kennedy (1917 – 1963)

Only the dead have seen the end of war.

— Plato (428 BCE – 348 BCE)

FIELD OPERATIVES

"What am I doing *here*...hellhole of the world," Scott Brooks whispered in the solitude of the desert, "when I could be home stretched out on my private beach...sipping piña coladas...with my woman?" Colorful visions of his dream place had been cropping up more frequently. Who could blame him? They'd been camped out in the same spot for days, dug into this godforsaken dustbowl. Perched on a yellow-crusted hill near the northern fringes of the Yemen desert, their dirty bodies blended in perfectly with the terrain below. They squatted, they crouched—waiting. There was nothing else out here in the wastelands of the Arabian Peninsula but sandy bowls and valleys surrounded by barren hills. The view was the same for hundreds of miles no matter what the direction: searing sun above, burning sand below. Worse, shimmering mirages of sandy beaches and palm trees emerged in the distance. *Are they real,* he'd questioned his own sanity, *or am I going insane?*

"See," a dry cough almost escaped his throat, "what I see?" The thirst and parchedness was choking. There was no response. The optical illusions created by the immense heat kept drifting across his vision, stationary at times, other times in motion. He dared not make a sound when shifting into a more comfortable position. Brooks shot a quick glance in the direction of his combat buddy. *Asleep.*

Over the past few days, both operatives had been on the brink of hallucination. What was supposed to be a mission of hours had turned into days. Skin parched from dehydration, they were out of rations.

Life for the forward spotter was, for most part, boring. It took patience, a lot of it. Appearing high on the psychological hiring profile, it was a prerequisite for getting the assignment. There were other, more imperative qualities needed, but those required training and practice. Scoring skill was one, as in scoring targets—not girls. Planning was another, as were deprivation, isolation, self-discipline; all vital to covert OPS.

It'd been his ambition, what seemed to be ages ago, to become an engineer. He enrolled in college with that in mind. But destiny had something else in store for Scott Brooks. It sought him out right after graduation, when he was approached one day by a recruiter. Being young and adventurous, seduced by the intrigue of it all, he readily accepted. Following a few days' indoctrination, and three months of boring policies and procedures, he'd been sent to a training camp in the Arizona desert along with a number of other new recruits. Training had been tough, but, in the end, rewarding. Because of his concentration skills, he'd rapidly advanced to squad leader. His superiors quickly recognized his potential in matters of targeting, analysis, and combat. Tall, closely cropped hair, rugged in appearance, he projected a muscular physique any person could respect. Size mattered for the perfect fighter.

Right away, it put him in the forefront—with pay to match. There had been Columbia, Kosovo, Azerbaijan, and now this. While in Columbia, between assignments, his buddies and he would take trips to San Salvador for some well-deserved R&R. Once there, he fell in love with the place. Where Columbia had been ravaged by drug wars, El Salvador, at the time, was a haven. "Look no further," he told himself. He'd found his paradise. He bought a lot by the ocean, pristine beachfront property, ocean swells gently washing over the sandy beach; it was all he needed to fulfill his dream. Only twenty miles south of the capital, the purchase had been cheap. One day he'd planned to build a cottage there.

Presently stretched out on the searing desert sand, he could feel the sweltering heat penetrating his senses. Propped on both elbows, a pair of Nikon 10X42 high-powered field glasses clutched between steady hands, Brooks scanned the horizon once more. They took turns—he and his buddy. They kept switching positions between wake and sleep, swapping brief catnaps. They hadn't taken a shower in days. It didn't matter. With intrusions on the body from aches and pain, there was much discomfort in the life of a sniper. Their brains were trained to ignore pain caused by crouching for endless hours in a cramped position with unpleasant sensory input caused by offensive smells emanating from armpits, crotch, and feet—it was all the same. He suddenly felt the unavoidable urge from an under-exercised bladder. He checked the time on the chronometer, his special treat acquired from Switzerland. *Best Omega money could buy.* He elbowed his buddy slumped in sleep next to him. "Take the watch."

"What?" It was an angry grumble accompanied by a bleary-eyed stare.

"Gotta piss," was the soft hiss expelled from between tightly clenched teeth. The sun was beating down mercilessly. The body dried up quick. It was a dilemma. Replenishing fluid frequently was necessary. An unavoidable nuisance factor, the cycle repeated from sunup to sundown. Gulp down a few swallows of liquid…sweat trickling down the face…urge to piss.

His moves were deliberate. Propped on both elbows, he lifted his body off the ground just enough to slide back a few yards. Seconds later he reached the familiar spot. It was dry but the urine stench lingered on. Careful not to make a sound he unzipped and groaned with the relieving pressure. Motion carried in the wastelands of the desert. They'd been watching a camp. Many had sound and motion sensors stuck around the perimeter. One thing they didn't need was attention. Avoiding confrontation was a necessity for survival. The Company didn't appreciate conflicts, especially not from the field. They created political tension, and, not to mention, impeded career advances and caused possible death on the spot.

It all boiled down to one element: "Teamwork—teamwork on the smallest scale." Two bodies, four eyes, four ears, one high-powered sniper rifle, one high-end spotter scope with one to give orders, the other to follow. The two bodies were blended into one human element, an element with only one object in mind—to kill. No mistakes. No regrets. Errors were not permitted. It meant elimination. It led to self-annihilation. Retaliation was swift. It could come by air, by land, or by sea. The result was always the same. Operative lost on mission, a nameless subject reduced to only a number. "Casualty of yet another conflict," the papers would say. Nobody would miss him. The Agency made sure. No kin, no attachment, no connection, all part of the profile for the sniper. It was the profile of a trained killer, legalized by necessity.

"What the hell's that?" he heard his spotter buddy call out.

Immediately, the sound got his attention. Straining upward, Brooks quickly zipped up and edged his way back to the observation spot. It'd come on fast. He caught a glimpse of it. What appeared was a winged torpedo shape racing toward the target they'd been spotting. Dumbfounded, Brooks offered an opinion. "Reaper."

"Reaper?" his buddy asked, "as in death?" It took seconds for the shockwave to reach them. When it did, all hell broke loose. Good thing they were dug in; otherwise they'd been blown away like tumbleweed.

Still breathless from the shockwave, junior surmised, "Hellfire? Took out the whole damned target."

"Air Force held that a secret," Brooks summed up, "even from us." He knew UAVs were used for recon and surveillance. He had no idea about them carrying weapons with the destructive power they'd just witnessed.

"Let's go," Brooks gestured at the blast site. He had to be certain there were no survivors. It took close to ten minutes to get there. Both stumbled through the wreckage looking for survivors.

Thirty minutes later, "Nothing." There seemed to be no life. None was expected after the utter destruction from the bomb carrying drone.

"Call in the damages," Brooks ordered his junior observer.

"What'll I tell 'em?"

"No survivors," Brooks offered. "Camp destroyed."

"What now?"

"We wait." It wasn't the first time Brooks had been left stranded in the fields. It wouldn't be the last either. It all depended on the vigilance of the agency.

Soon, the distant pitch of an unmarked helicopter reached their ears. Bored with the wait, "About time," the spotter muttered to no one in particular. It'd be the end of their mission.

"What took you so long?" Anger showed in Scott's face when the pilot thumbed them into the craft. "Whose idea to leave us stranded out here?"

"Command had you on satellite." The pilot was factual, seasoned and callused. "I got my job," he countered, "you got yours. And yours is done. Enjoy the ride."

CASTLE ROCK (Colorado)

Poised in front of the panoramic picture window, Alex Bauer was fixated by the beauty of this magnificent country. He was undecided about what to do next. In the distance, he could make out early commuter traffic winding along I-25 against the backdrop of the Rocky Mountain range. From this vantage point he could clearly see the white-tipped mountains jut up high above the central plains. Set within a weathered face, two calculating eyes watchfully scanned the horizon. It was a determined face. A face hardened by a lifetime of challenges. The magnificence of the scene jogged distant memories in his mind. One brow furrowed with concern, he'd remembered the peaks much whiter when he first got here, even this time of year. *Something's happened to the climate,* he calculated, *and not just here.* His sister in Austria had mentioned this during their infrequent but lengthy phone calls. With each passing decade, the winters seemed to grow milder, she'd remarked. An avid skier, he had noticed the receding snowcaps in both worlds: the old country where he grew up and the new world he was living in now.

The hour was early yet. Chilled by the brisk mountain air streaming down from the foothills across the valley, he pulled his robe tighter around his waist. Undecided about the day's agenda, he strode to the kitchen where a freshly brewed pot of coffee awaited him. He poured a measure and leisured to the den, his domain. The warmth between his palms gave him a great sense of presence. Holding it up, he studied the colorful contours permanently edged into the white porcelain. He admired the cup. It was a symbol for his accomplishments. It embraced a generation of legacy. "My trophy," he muttered into the quiet of the morning. It was a retirement gift he'd received after twenty-five years of serving the defense department. Prominently displayed was the glorious Pentagon emblem encircled by the communications insignias of the various agencies he'd served. He felt touched by notions of pride and remorse at the same time. One was pride of great accomplishments for his achievements, the other, the notion of remorse he could never share his missions with others.

He was about to pick up the Federal Weekly he hadn't had time to read when the thought of his daughter crossed the mind. Haven't heard from her in ages...have to give her a call...see if she's still planning to come out for the summer.

He got up and took the few strides across the spacious room. Backed against the far wall was an office desk. There, he unlocked the drawer and fished for the well-worn black booklet. It was an address book he kept locked up, just to be on the safe side. It contained information he'd rather keep concealed. Aside from proprietary phone contacts it contained more sinister data. The book also contained codes and passwords. At one time, he'd been able to recall every bit from memory, but with age slowly catching up, he needed the backup. He dialed the number. There was a faint click followed by a trained voice. "Pentagon," it said. "Who would you like to reach?"

"Tracy Bauer, please."

"Just a moment," was the formal, almost mechanical reply. It only took a couple of seconds for her to get back to him. "I have no one listed by that name. Could she be with another agency?"

"It's possible. Could you try the NSA branch?"

"I'll check," was her efficient response. He was placed on hold.

Sitting idle, he suddenly felt the morning chill seep into his aging, but well-toned, body. It seemed to take forever for the operator to return. Slightly annoyed by the wait, he reached for the remote. Impatiently, he switched channels, searching for the morning news. The familiar face of the president caught his attention. He turned up the sound and listened to what George Wilmot had to say. Ever since the invasion of Afghanistan initiated by his predecessor, this president had had a tough time winning back international confidence, not to mention the national trust of his people. Alex felt sympathy for him inheriting the can of worms he already knew was a lost cause. He shifted his concentration to the news.

The U.N. Security Council voted unanimously Saturday to slap North Korea with trade, travel, and other sanctions as punishment for its claimed nuclear weapons test. The president described the U.N. action as a swift and tough message that the world was united in its determination to see to it that the Korean Peninsula remained free of nuclear weapons. He went on to say North Korea had an opportunity for a better way forward and promised aid to the impoverished country if it verifiably ended its nuclear weapons program.

The North Korean ambassador to the U.N. cut in, protesting that Pyongyang had totally rejected the unjustifiable resolution. *If the United States persists in increasing pressure on North Korea,* he maintained, *it would continue to take physical countermeasures, considering it a declaration of war.* With that he walked out of the national assembly chamber. That quickly prompted the U.S. ambassador to point to the empty chair and denounce him.

The resolution called on Pyongyang to end all nuclear weapons programs. It forbade U.N. member nations from engaging in North Korean trade involving nuclear and other weapons of mass destruction. The ban appeared to be directed at the North Korean leader, who had a long, documented record of living a life of luxury while his people suffered the deprivations of a national famine.

Across its border, the U.N. ambassador for China—a strong ally of North Korea—said the resolution sent an unbalanced and destructive message. That "rather than mandating stop-and-search operations, the resolution would…" CNN reported.

"That should shake 'em up," Alex muttered. He was barely aware of the operator's voice cutting in to get his attention.

"Sir, we have located Tracy's office, but there's no answer. If it's urgent, I'll have her paged."

"Please do. I'll hold."

Sitting idle once more, the strong aroma from his favorite roasted beans caught his senses. "Ah, yes," he savored the moment, "Columbian Supreme."

Waiting for the operator, he let his mind drift. He liked dwelling on the past. It gave him a great deal of comfort during the lonely days. And there were plenty of those. Ever since the divorce and his daughters having taken on families and careers, he was plagued by a life of isolation. He had no reason to complain. It was self-imposed. Not so much by the present environment, but rather from a life of conditioning and discipline, much of it spent as a lone wolf. His thoughts drifted back to an earlier time.

It seemed not so long ago when his children were the joy of his life. Because of his travel schedule, he was not always around to watch them transition from infancy to childhood, and then into adults. He tried to make up for it when he was at home.

He vividly remembered his wife's dedication to the family, with the occasional reminder of his priorities between family and job. Whereas her energy was solely directed at raising the girls, his had been demanded by yet another crisis. Many years earlier, while still single, he'd chosen a career with the Agency over becoming a dedicated family man. One turned into a lifelong adventure while the other ended in failure.

Where has the time gone? Look at me now, he thought in the quiet of the den, sitting alone in the chilly morning air. *No family…no friends. If only I could turn back time.* There was much he'd like to have told his daughters, especially Tracy, his favorite. They'd always shared a special connection.

"Sir," the operator inquired once more in her monotonous voice, "would you like to continue hold?"

"Yes." He was growing annoyed. "Give it another minute."

Remote in his left hand, he switched channels again. His thoughts sifted through an endless stream of information for more bad news. *Whatever happened to the good news?*

The familiar voice finally cut into his thoughts, "Tracy," it announced.

"Hey." Jolted to the present, he called out, "How're things at the Puzzle Palace?"

"Fine, Dad." Her voice sounded pleased but rushed. "Been assigned to the Pentagon," she said.

"Why is that?"

"Needed a liaison with the NSA."

"Aside from that," Alex was genuinely curious, "what's happening in your world?"

"Oh, the usual," she remarked. "Analysis, presentations, swamped with meetings."

"Yeah, I know what that's like—had my share. Anything unusual happening?" he inquired offhandedly. It always interested him to hear about his daughter's accomplishments. In a way, she'd followed his career steps. Steps he'd paved for her, he hoped, would make her career easier. All she had to do was confide in him. He could mentor her without her repeating some of the mistakes he'd made. There were not many, but…

"Not much." She sounded casual. "Got my hands full with some stubborn birds."

"Birds?" His interest piqued. He knew she made reference to satellites. Space, satellites, intelligence was her world.

"Got a problem keeping some in orbit…"

"Wait a minute," he cut in, "satellites stay up there for years."

"Typically yes," she agreed, "but not these. KH[1] series—you know."

"I knew it!" Alex exclaimed, but immediately muffled his voice. *Don't wanna compromise her position.* Silent ears were always listening…and recording.

"What's that?" She sounded strained. Her voice turned cautious.

"Oh nothing," he said. "Just thinking out loud." He'd had his suspicions ever since satellite manufacturing had been outsourced to third-world countries.

"Dad," she reigned in his attention, "I'm late for a meeting."

---

[1] Keyhole is a satellite spy/reconnaissance program deployed for military and intelligence agencies.

He knew better than to pry further, especially on a public phone. As far as he knew, *Big Brother's always listening.* He'd never compromised anybody and had no desire to start now, especially not with his daughter.

"Still coming to Colorado?" he asked. It had been years since their last time together.

"As soon as I get a fix on the problem."

"Promise?"

"Promise."

"Okay then. Let me know if you need anything. I'm always…"

"Gotta go, Dad." She abruptly hung up.

"Bye…love you…" His parting words trailed into emptiness.

The receiver had gone dead, leaving him to reflect on their relationship. He could not imagine life without his precious Tracy. At times, he felt like he'd fallen victim to an unintentional dilemma. He'd tried not to have favorites between his daughters. But where a dad had his, a mom had hers. *Maybe someday,* he lingered, *she'll forgive me for not being there.* He felt strangely abandoned. *That's what I get for being so selfish.* His thought reflected deep regrets. To change his frame of mind, he briskly got up and left the room to get dressed.

Despite feeling sorry, he could not stop thinking about the satellites she'd mentioned. They were programmed to stay up for ten years or more. To prevent orbit degradation, they adjusted automatically via self-correcting GPS. *Why should I be bothered?* He tried to push the thoughts from his mind. It didn't work. It was a problem…his problem. "Has to be software related," he finally decided. "Gotta check with Brian."

YEMEN (Arabian Peninsula)

"That will do," the Serpent muttered. His words directed at the computer monitor, he spoke to no one in particular. His upper body was stiffly poised over the control panel in air weighted down by layers of hazy blue smoke drifting toward the exit door. The ceiling fan didn't help much. It only spread the blue-layered haze further through the room. Someone finally shut it off because its grinding noise impaired his concentration. Surrounded by his team, everybody in the room was smoking. The unhealthy practice, largely avoided by the western world, had not yet reached the cultures of the Middle East. Here, for many, smoking was the only recreation.

He could feel their presences. Only an occasional stifled cough was audible. He could see the reflection of faces in the monitor watching over his shoulder. He detected fear. Fear, not of the enormity he'd unleash, but fear of him. And he knew it. Soon, the whole world would share their fears. He'd see to that.

A mean grin cut across his grimly set face. His index finger on the last key, he deliberately paused to let the enormity of his action sink in, before punching down on the Enter button. Satisfied, he expelled a lung full of stale air. His body visibly relaxed. He'd just activated a sequence of events that would change the world as it existed today. The faces still stared at the monitor. Stony faced, they expected some response action, but none followed.

Ready to get up, he briefly paused. His eyes caught a glimpse of his own reflection in the monitor screen. Slightly squinting, he examined the face staring back at him. He hadn't looked in a mirror for weeks. Immediate contempt welled up from his gut. Having spent most of his time in deserts lately, he'd almost forgotten about the scar. Several attempts to grow a beard to partly cover up his face had failed. Eventually, he'd had to admit he lacked the genetic predisposition to grow enough facial hair to disguise the blemish.

Years before, he had been slashed by a knife that sliced his left cheek leaving him scarred for life. It had been an accident caused by a new recruit during combat training. It left his face permanently etched with a scar that many mistook for a grin, although, there was little humor to be found in the cruel life of the Serpent. Shortly afterwards, the recruit had mysteriously disappeared without a trace.

"That's it," he commanded in his usual tone of brutality, "return to your duties." He stood up, promptly turned, and headed for the exit for a well-deserved smoke break. He savored the moment. *It's not every day one gets to mess with the despicable, the infidel.* He was gloating at the thought. It gave him an immense feeling of satisfaction.

Once outside, he propped his body against a boulder a few paces from the complex. His gaze fell on the distant hills. They were the customary colorless scenes of his present environment. All gray. Not a single tree or bush filled the sandy void. Tightly pressed between his lips, deep in thoughts of a better time, he puffed on a cigarette. Pakistan, the home of his youth with Kashmir, Nepal across the border, the snowcapped Himalayas towering in the horizon seemed so distant now.

With eyes scanning the horizon, the present weighed heavy on his body. *Only temporary,* he reminded himself. *Soon, it'll be paradise.* It was an unconditional promise. Confined to this wasteland, he couldn't help it; his anger quickly returned. His mind was filled with contempt once more.

Suddenly, his senses became aware of something advancing his way. It started as a single spot in the distant horizon, then rapidly increased to a menacing silhouette. It passed directly overhead. His eyes caught its full measure. It'd taken on the shape of a winged torpedo. Being a seasoned warrior, on instinct he ducked. Eyes partly blinded by the sunlight reflected off the bright object, he dove for cover. He landed hard behind a nearby truck. A fraction of a second later he felt the impact. A devastating shockwave picked his body up and wildly threw it through the air. Then some fifty feet of tumbled freefall with a muffled thud landed him on hard ground. Half-conscious, half-buried beneath a layer of sand and debris, he wildly shook his head to clear his senses. Eyes finally cleared from sand, he became aware of the effects of the tremendous explosion emitted from the direction of the command center he'd just left.

Unable to breathe freely, his battered chest desperately struggled for air. Both lungs had temporarily collapsed. The lack of air brought him close to panic. Almost at a point of passing out, he was able to force a labored breath of air into his lungs. It took several minutes for him to recover. He pulled himself up on trembling legs. Staggering, his blurry gaze tried to focus on what lay ahead. He carefully patted himself down. There seemed to be no broken limbs. "Allah," he uttered in disbelief, "I'm still alive."

What used to be a desert outpost, Base Camp Three, now was nothing but rubble. He stared at the heap of incinerated concrete and dust. Aside from a deafening ringing in his ears and superficial nicks and bruises from flying debris, he had escaped with only scratches. The bleeding had already stopped from the cuts and was quickly drying up with the desert heat.

There was no sign of life where the command center once stood. The inhabitants, if any were left, were now buried beneath tons of rubble. *I am truly blessed by Allah*, he thought jubilantly. In this desolated place, some fifteen hundred miles from his hometown, Islamabad, he'd survived yet another attempt on his life.

Hope the cause's worth the prize, he thought with faint contempt, *paid for with yet another dozen lives.* Setting aside further empathy after counting his blessings, he had one last thought for his comrades. *May they be blessed into the everlasting realm of paradise.* Feeling somewhat detached, he did not share the spiritual beliefs of the innocent recruits filled by indoctrinated promises. His conviction was more down to earth. It had been westernized many years ago. His dreams were set on the future. The future was here on earth and now. Someone had to change it. And that someone was him, the Serpent, future leader of the jihad.

OUTER SPACE

It was well below freezing. The deep blackness of space was punctuated by the brilliant sparkle of uncountable stars. Then, like ghostly shadows, out of the darkness, in periodic intervals of ninety minutes, silent, menacing shapes of spiked disks came slicing through space. Within each structure, a pair of red and green blinking LED indicators was the only indication of life. Miniscule as they were, they, nevertheless, produced two dimly reflecting light beams repeatedly bouncing off the highly polished interior, not unlike a miniature lightshow. Otherwise, within the complexity of this highly sophisticated body drifting in asynchronous orbit, there was total silence.

Suddenly, an almost imperceptible motion broke the blackness. A click would have been perceived had the satellite been within Earth's atmosphere. At this altitude, in the absence of air nothing generated sound. A miniaturized relay had sprung into action. It closed the contact connection between the power source and transmitter circuits. What followed was a rapid stream of electrically charged atoms set in motion by a ground-based command station. Touching tens of thousands of integrated components on the way, the intelligently compressed instruction set arrived at the programmed target points.

A single unit of a highly sophisticated satellite had just received a string of attack orders. Aside from being stealthy, this unit had a multitude of functions. Its primary configuration was set for ground surveillance to spy on neighboring nations. Undisclosed to the public, its ultimate objective was much more sinister. As result of the programmed instructions just received, the satellite immediately reacted. What followed was an ever so slight change in g-forces. The unit bounced out of its predetermined orbit into the path of a similar space object. Monitored by SPACECOM[2], this motion started a chain of events that would hound every agency and sponsor in the satellite industry for months to come.

---

[2] In 2002, SPACECOM merged with STRATCOM to become the Unified Combatant Command of the United States' Department of Defense to oversee the command's global strategic mission.

YEMEN

Back on his feet, on unsteady legs, the Serpent staggered a few paces in the direction of what, minutes before had been the command center. What was left was a jumble of broken down concrete blocks piled on top of mortar and iron bars, covered in powdered dust. With a wiping motion his hand brushed pieces of debris and splinters from his camouflaged combat garb. His head was still hazy from the explosion, and so was his mind. He needed time to think. Vision blurry from trickles of salty liquid squeezed from damaged tear ducts, he took hold of a jagged iron bar to steady his shaken body.

"Well, they may have tried to stop me, but they're too late. I've already sent the command." The thought made his deep-seated anger return. Between clenched teeth, cussing out the western world, his mind screamed into the desert silence, "Damned all you Infidels! You will pay for messing with Allah's creation." Powerful thoughts of a liberated future entered his mind. It gave him the focus to stay on track. *The only thing that matters is the mission.* And a mission it would be; only he knew its enormity.

After years of planning, now, within reach of his fingertips, he had the means to control an entire constellation of space assets moving in orbit. *What was it again? Well in excess of 10,000 space objects.* But the only ones he was interested in were commercial components such as the TELSTAR, EARLY BIRD, and MARISAT managed by COMSAT and INTELSAT. It would have been extremely difficult to enslave U.S. military assets. The U.S. government had tight control over its own clusters of constellations in Iridium and others, serving covertly as smart and secure switchboards. *Won't matter,* he thought with contempt. They would be rendered inoperative as result of collateral damages to a ground-based infrastructure he'd cause.

With satellite functions limited to a few years' operation patiently floating in standby orbits, to extend their capabilities it was necessary to periodically replace a unit. This expensive, but necessary, element became the determined factor of the mission. It was this constant supply of standby satellites that gave him the opportunity to penetrate American defense grid.

The very thought of the space debris made his blood boil once more. He took a deep breath to calm his nerves. His body slowly began to relax. He was in complete control again. He could think clearly once more to take stock of the present situation. Everything, all of his belongings, however measly, had been buried in the explosion. There was no going back.

He'd made the choice to live as a mercenary many years ago, even with the depravation and hardship he knew beforehand would become his life. There had been small mementos collected over the years to remind him of personal achievements. Souvenirs purchased from bazaars in Athens, Morocco, Afghanistan, and the Philippines, all gone now. Among them were fashionable and expensive items from designers such as Armani, Gucci, and Ralph Lauren. Fashion items could be replaced, he felt, especially when funds were unlimited. *But mementos?* That was another thing. With it all gone, he buried the past, right here and now.

His mind fully functional, he headed for the motor pool—or what was left of it. Most vehicles appeared damaged beyond use, either torn apart by the explosion or flung on top of one other, effectively rendered unusable. Still slightly trembling from the blast on unsteady legs, he tramped through debris of metal and rubber. His eyes darted from wreckage to wreckage searching for radio gear. It did not take long to locate a unit in a partially buried vehicle. He dug up the transmitter and dusted off the controls. Flipping on the power switch, to his surprise, it still functioned. Rotating the dial, he selected a specific frequency. "Shahadah…come in…come in."

Still numbed from the explosion, he jerked back at the sound of his own voice. In the silence of the desert it sounded metallic. His ears were still stressed from the shockwave. Momentarily, he gave up talking. It was too painful.

Brows furled in concentration, he listened for a comeback. Aside from a steady stream of white noise emanating from the receiver, he could make out no intelligible words. *Keep trying,* he instructed himself. "Shahadah…come in…come in." Close to an hour went by. About to give up, a faint crackle caught his attention. Hastily, he fumbled with the frequency dial. *That's it.* The voice came in clear. "Identify."

"Serpent."

"Code?"

"Shahadah."

"Status?"

"Base Camp Three destroyed—no other survivors."

"Proceed to Base Camp One."

"Will do...over." He'd noticed the ignition key stuck in the vehicle he'd leaned against. One hand clenched on the frame, he yanked with the other on the handle with full force. "Come on…come on, you bitch." The door finally pulled open with a creaking sound. Layers of sand covered the interior. The dashboard was powdered over with fine dust. He reached for the key. It turned. The overhead lighting came on. "About time!" he muttered into the quiet.

With a firm grip on the steering wheel he forced his solid frame into the driver's seat, then, in anticipation, turned the key. *Allah,* he beckoned. The engine labored a couple of times, then, with a popping sound, the starter kicked in. The crankshaft turned over. A few more turns and the engine jumped to life. "My lucky day."

Oddly pleased, he pushed the shifter into first. The mud-studded tires tore the mass of metal from the rubble. He gunned the accelerator. The jeep, now freed, burst into motion. He caught his reflection in the mirror. His eyes briefly scanned over his face, checking for damages. *Nothing serious aside from the familiar scar.* Fully energized, he pushed the pedal and sped off into the distance, leaving a trail of dust in his wake.

PETERSON AIR FORCE BASE

Alex Bauer was getting restless. He'd spent the idle time on rudimentary projects, nothing significant. He even tried subcontracting for a while, but got bored with endless meetings, micromanagement, and tedious paperwork. He took the time to build out his own intranet wired within the confines of his home he also referred to as The Castle. It had kept him busy, but only for brief periods. Soon, he felt as if he'd been getting stagnant. Professionally, that was. Doubts encroached on his mind more often than not about the retirement. He wasn't happy. He needed a change. He needed a new focus on life.

Almost a lifetime ago, when Alex entered the United States decades ago he'd applied his trained skills from the old country. It soon became apparent that it wasn't befitting him in his new world. Where his training was in industrial engineering, a new age had taken hold. It was the age of computers and electronics. Feeling inadequate, he went back to school. It proved to be a rewarding move. It provided the foundation for a new career. The career turned into thirty-some highly productive years blessed by prosperity, profiting both employer and employee. Although a "childhood dream" comes true, he never allowed himself to ever become stagnant. After getting to know a program in and out, it would be time to move on. Stagnation in the career, he knew from experience, was the source of frustration and discontent. It was time for a chance.

After putting out feelers with a number of defense agencies, it did not take long to get responses back calling for interviews. One response in particular interested him most. It was from the defense agency that controlled and managed satellite communication. The interview was scheduled for this morning. Alex had not allowed enough time to consider the morning commute, ID check, and parking. Arriving late, it made him tardy to meet up with the head of the agency.

His strides were hastened. *Come on...come on.* Having been assigned a personal escort at the entrance, an anxious glance at the security fellow did nothing to speed up the man's pace. Overweight and complacent, the guard took his good old time. "I'm late," Alex urged the puffing sentry. Painted in customary Air Force blue accented within a dark trim line, the brightly lit corridors seemed endless. His mind was on the upcoming meeting. He'd wanted to get on this program for some time, but somehow never managed to get a foot in the door.

Several days earlier he'd gotten a call to come in for an interview. At his stage in his career, it would be more of a formality rather than getting grilled for the job. He'd meet the new commander in person. Slightly irritated, he checked his wristwatch the shook his head with impatience. It was an obvious gesture to show his irritation that went unnoticed. Ahead, one last turn. His eyes were distracted for a moment, and then it happened. "What the...?" Alex called out.

He'd collided with another visitor. In the brightly lit hallway he came face to face with a tall, good-looking male grasping a Styrofoam cup. Alex could feel the sting from spilled coffee on his skin but ignored it. There was something familiar about him. Their eyes met. There was recognition. *I know this guy.* "You!—*Here?*" Completely unprepared, he'd bumped into a longtime friend.

There was some brief composure on both sides, then the impeccably groomed, grinning face called out, "Alex Bauer!"

Alex wasn't sure whether to shake hands or hug. Instead, he helped him brush off spilled droplets of coffee from a pristinely fitted Armani suit. "Brian Harris!" he shouted in heightened excitement. "What brings you here?" Alex was genuinely surprised. The words reverberated through the hallway. Obviously disinterested, the sentry stood in silence.

"Getting onboard the KE." Brian beamed. They pumped hands.

"What a coincidence," Alex said, "so am I." Planted abreast from each other they practically occupied the entirety of the narrow corridor. They bumped elbows with other passersby rushing to their immediate missions, but ignored the annoyed glances thrown their way.

Whereas Alex had been living in Colorado for ten years already when he was asked to consult on a satellite proposal for Lockheed Martin, Brian had flown in today from Baltimore for similar reasons.

Alex still couldn't believe it—his friend here in town. "Listen," he offered, "I'm late for a meeting. Give me your number and we'll talk in the evening. Got a lotta catching up to do."

"Better believe it," his friend quipped, handing over a business card.

"How about the Lone Star," Alex suggested, "around seven?"

"Steakhouse…North Academy?"

"Right," Alex shot back. Headed in opposite directions, they quickly parted down the hall.

That evening, Alex sat in his favorite restaurant, anxious for Brian to show. While waiting, his eyes darted between the diners and new arrivals in an attempt to locate familiar faces. *Nothing. All strangers.* His gaze moved on. He checked out the establishment. It'd been a while since he ate here last. *Still looks the same.* He gave it a three-star rating for elegance but a five for quality. By Colorado standards, it was a top-notch steakhouse. People in this part of the country placed more value on the quality of the food than on the service. It was a cultural thing dating back to the frontier days. Back then, people were used to roughing it and, after a hard day's work on the prairie; they took pleasure in a plate of wholesome food washed down with a couple of beers. Steak was always first choice. That hadn't changed. Forget about fancy restaurants and stiff-jointed waiters; put a twenty-ounce steak in front of any cowboy and he'd bust his back all day.

"Man, it's good to see you…haven't changed a bit," Brian said. He had pushed his way past busy tables to greet Alex with a heartfelt handshake.

Alex jumped from his seat. "Neither have you." He was envious of his younger buddy. "Still good looking," Alex shot a glance at Brian's left hand and added, "and still unattached."

Besides good looks, Brian displayed two distinct characteristics: all business on the job and all charm once work was finished. Like Alex, Brian was always on the move. He liked travel as well as the challenges it provided. In a way, their character traits were similar and that was probably the reason they had hit it off so well ever since they had met.

Both were seated when the waiter appeared. To kick off the evening Alex ordered a bottle of wine with a buffalo wing appetizer, then studied the menu. Brian did likewise. A couple minutes later they watched the waiter uncork and pour a taste for Alex.

"Fine," Alex approved. He readily accepted the bottle.

Brian inspected the label. "Excellent choice."

The waiter impatiently shifted on his legs. "You ready to order?" He seemed anxious to serve other customers in the now crowded place.

"Think we'll wait." Alex glanced at Brian for approval. "Give us half an hour," he said and waved him off. "So Brian," Alex was getting comfortable in the booth, "what brings you to this part of the world?"

"NSA," Brian replied, "talked me into taking this project. At first," he admitted, "I was reluctant, but when I heard it was Colorado Springs, I agreed." He appeared genuinely sincere. "Thought I might run into you." Lifting his glass indicating a toast, "Cheers," he offered.

"You, too," Brian countered with a smile. "Knew you'd moved here but lost your contact with all the travels."

"Still travel?" Alex could already feel the effects of the wine on his body. He felt completely at ease.

"Never stopped," his buddy responded. "They keep me on the run—one week Europe, the next Asia."

"Reminds me of my days," Alex reflected with a hint of sadness.

Brian reached for the bottle. He tactfully refilled both glasses. "Remember the times overseas?" That statement was sure to kick off the topic for the evening.

"As clear as yesterday—the Gulf, Bosnia, Kosovo," Alex joined in excitedly. He was looking forward to the promise to relive an epic of the past, regardless of how chaotic it may have been back then. Living alone most of the time, he'd often dwell on the past. His brain was filled with memories. Unfortunately, he couldn't share them with anyone other than a close friend, such as Brian, or his daughters. The evening proved to be as he'd envisioned. It was filled with amusement, laughter, delight, hilarity, even sadness and melancholy at times followed by drinks, a hearty meal, and more drinks. *Truly a happy occasion.* Alex savored this special evening, wishing there'd be many more.

Two hours into the evening there was a faint chirp. "Hang on a sec," Brian interrupted. He fished for his Blackberry, then read the message. The pleasant veil he'd carried all evening fell from his face. He turned all business. "State department," he sputtered, "live feed."

"Serious?"

"Could be." His eyes quickly scanned the live broadcast scrolling across the screen. "Check this out." He handed Alex the gadget to read for himself.

"...the U.S. State Department cites seven nations—Cuba, Iran, Iraq, Libya, North Korea, Sudan, and Syria—as state sponsors of terrorism...These nations have long been accused of harboring groups that help terrorists in varying degrees by providing sanctuary for suspects wanted elsewhere, supplying weapons, money, and intelligence, or in planning attacks on foreign contractors...The State Department has issued a worldwide travel caution, urging Americans traveling outside the U.S. to maintain a high level of vigilance and to increase their security awareness. Specific warnings were issued for Turkmenistan, Pakistan, and Yemen."

"There goes travel," Alex remarked, handing back the Blackberry. He quietly assessed the potential political and economic implications. It usually didn't stop there. There was always more to come.

"Wait," Brian said, handing back the gadget, "there's more."

Alex scrolled down on the text. He read the report.

"ISLAMABAD, Pakistan (AP)—Police rounded up hundreds of opposition leaders and rights activists Sunday after Pakistan's military ruler suspended the constitution, ousted the top judge, and deployed troops to fight what he called rising Islamic extremism...The former coup leader, who had promised to relinquish his army post and become a civilian president, declared a state of emergency, dashing hopes of a smooth transition to democracy for the nuclear-armed nation."

"Not good," Alex expressed with deep concern.

"Not good for anybody," Brian agreed.

The news had a sobering effect on the evening. Alex took note of the environment. It had turned quiet through the evening. There were things on his mind he wanted to pass by his buddy. Now would be a good time.

"By the way," Brian also seemed ready to change subjects, "how's the family?"

"Doing okay," he said with faint sadness, "considering the circumstances." He took a brief pause. "Got divorced a few years back."

"I heard."

Alex's expression turned serious. "My fault for not being there for her—you know...work precedence over personal life."

"You know it," Brian agreed. He was shifting in his chair.

"Managed to have daughters." His face brightened at the thought of his precious girls.

"Congratulations."

"Thanks. Lisa's out west doing well for herself. Tracy's with the NSA."

"Really! Have to look her up when I get back to D.C."

"Careful," Alex warned with a fond smile, "I know your reputation."

"Innocent me?"

"You know—irresistible charm and all."

"I'll try not to." Appearing sincere, Brian grimaced.

"Got her employed after graduating Polytech."

"Good school. What's she doing?"

"SPACECOM...liaison to the Pentagon."

"What's the project?"

"KH."

"Interesting..."

"Listen," Alex interrupted. His voice turned subdued. "Something's been on my mind the last few days." He cautiously leaned forward. "Need your opinion."

Pulling his chair closer to the table, in a subdued voice, his buddy said, "Shoot."

"Talked with Tracy a couple days ago," Alex stated. "She made a comment that concerns me."

"Why is that?" Brian's face took on a quizzical look. His interest seemed piqued.

"Without being specific," Alex continued, "she mentioned some satellites behaving erratically. Apparently, SPACECOM's got a difficult time keeping them in sync." He explained further. "Constant need to adjust a cluster from drifting off orbit. Can you think of a reason?"

Brian briefly paused to recollect. "Nothing comes to mind. Birds in orbit have been reliable for years. They're stable. We've had no problems other than occasional maneuvers to adjust for drift, but that's normal. Why'd you ask?"

"Remember," Alex cautioned. His gaze swept over their immediate surroundings. "I worked DIN much of my career."

"You helped build the network."

"Deployed a number of centers worldwide," Alex asserted. "Your organization's one of its subscribers…along with other Intel orgs." DIN was colloquial for AUTODIN[3]. It was the most secure network on the globe. Built at the onset of the Cold War, it provided the U.S. government and military with instant and secure communications worldwide. Being closed circuit, it guarded the secrets of the nation. To work it required a highly classified clearance.

Leaning even closed into the table, Brian encouraged him. "I hear you…go on." "While doing some analysis work…" Alex relayed information he'd come across. It was some disturbing data. It didn't make much sense at the time, but with additional information freed up through the Freedom of Information Act, it all started to make sense. "Let me just say something's brewing."

Brian sat upright. "What do you mean?"

"May not be common knowledge," he spoke quietly, "but the rumors are disturbing. It's a mystery to me why the government keeps such important information from the public. After all," he paused, "these days, people are remarkably informed."

The waiter arrived to check on drinks. "Anything else?" He collected the empty dishes from the table.

"Everything's fine." Alex waved him on.

"Yeah, fine…what are you getting at?" Waiting for the punch line, Brian displayed impatience.

Alex, at times, had an inadvertent way of heightening the suspense. When working in analysis mode, this interruption would break the flow in conversations. "You worked SIOP/ESI,[4] didn't you?"

"Sure did."

"You and I," Alex hinted, "have similar clearances. Can we talk?"

"Can."

"SIOP's been compromised." To let the information sink in, Alex paused a few seconds. He watched an immediate reaction on Brian's face. It displayed disbelief, suspicion, and doubt all at once.

"How'd you know?"

"Keep track of things," was all he confided for the present. His buddy would learn the secrets of The Castle soon enough. Covertly monitoring the skies for his former employees, DCA was the only thing that kept him busy. But it wasn't enough to compensate for the idle time. And, there was too much of it.

"Go on," Brian said. He'd taken several seconds to compose himself…and rightly so.

---

[3] Automatic Digital Network

[4] Single Integrated Operational Plan (SIOP/ESI) is a blueprint that tells how American nuclear weapons would be used in the event of war. The plan integrates the nuclear capabilities of manned bombers, long-range missiles and ballistic missiles fired from nuclear submarines. The SIOP is implemented in case the United States is under nuclear attack or if a nuclear attack on the United States is imminent. It also includes procedures on how to mass evacuate the population from congested prone cities. It is a highly classified document, and one of the most secret and sensitive issues in U.S. national security policy.

Extremely Sensitive Intelligence (ESI) is a special access category with a need-to-know restriction that requires special authorization.

SIOP was a list of highly sensitive issues identifying the nation's nuclear assets, among other things, used against foreign targets. The plan was designed as a massive strike force to include using the entire U.S. nuclear arsenal against potential threats. Initially, it was directed specifically at the Soviet Union and China, but it was later revised into a counterforce strategy with a "No first use" policy to prevent a MAD condition.

"Mutually Assured Destruction." If one side launched their nuclear arsenal, the other would counterstrike with equal force, assuring nothing would survive. "Nobody wins."

"Exactly."

"Don't remember that period well," Brian remarked, "still in school."

"Wouldn't have mattered anyway," Alex assured him, "paradigm's changed. Superpower's gone. Smaller nations acquired nuclear strike capabilities."

"What's the solution?"

"TACAMO."

"TACAMO?"

"It'll have to wait for another time." Alex finished the remainder of his wine. "Getting late… head's spinning. Don't wanna forget my way home," he joked.

"Okay." Looking somewhat deprived, Brian seemed puzzled but didn't press on. Instead, he reached for the check and raised an arm to prompt the waiter for the bill.

"My treat," Alex insisted, taking the bill from his hand.

Brian conceded. "Thanks. Can we get together during the weekend?" He was already moving towards the exit.

Hasting after him, "We can do better," Alex said. "Come by tomorrow. I'll fix us breakfast and show you my place. Afterwards," he suggested, "we could go to the lake for some windsurfing."

"Terrific." Brian sounded enthusiastic. "Miss the days on the lake. I'll be there." He briskly broke off and strode to his rental car.

Hoping he'd get to the hotel without incident, Alex watched his buddy drive off. He knew they'd had too much to drink, but reunions don't happen often. Especially for two war buddies who hadn't seen each other in years. He left the parking lot for the open highway, carefully watching his speed during the thirty-some miles back to Castle Rock.

NORTHCOM (Colorado)

"Home in on two-two-one-four." It was obvious to the operators working the computer monitors that Rhonda Hicks, the boss, was agitated. The team of young cadets was hunched over the flat screen monitors anticipating her next decision or rather, command. Two minutes earlier, another red alert had popped up from a low orbital unit generated some 450 miles out in space. The mouse over identified an orbital drift alert. Red, above other colors, needed immediate attention.

Satellites, one of man's greatest inventions—gift for some, curse to others, depending on their side of the border—drifted in and out of orbit on a daily basis. There was nothing unique about it. Most of the alerts were tagged green and yellow. They were usually cleared through internal self-correcting adjustments and demanded no immediate attention. It was the operator's responsibility to log and monitor all errors. This one was different. It required special attention.

"KE series," the action operator said. He seemed eager to please her. A recent recruit, the specific alert was a first for him.

"Pull up the parameters," Rhonda ordered. It'd take a few seconds. Waiting for the database to search and assemble the record, her gaze touched on the rows of neatly dressed operators performing the monitoring duties. "Space Cadets," they called themselves, the new breed of electronic technicians (ETs) or technology spies. Well-disciplined on the job, wild when off duty: that was them. They knew how to get most out of life. *Unlike me,* Rhonda mulled. Fun, joy, and excitement were part of a distant past; her life had been nothing but career.

Eyes on the big screen, her thoughts were interrupted by the scrolling motion on the monitor. Data had just painted across the display. It was the KE datasheet. She studied it carefully. There was nothing unusual. Just as she started to order an error reset, a new alert popped up.

"Couple others," the young operator called to get her attention. He pointed at the upper section of the computer screen. Accompanied by an irritating sound, a high-pitched alarm, several slow-moving images rapidly flashed on and off, demanding immediate attention.

"Give me a status report…and turn that damned thing off."

Slight smirk on his face, the action operator shouted, "Right!" while executing the next keystrokes. *Here it comes,* she silently noted, *the expected wisecrack.* It never failed.

"NSA must be chasing chicks," he smarted off.

Partially ignoring his feeble attempts at humor, Rhonda muttered into the building tension. "Wiseass. Orbit re-sync," she corrected, "and," shooting an annoyed glance at the young operator, "get me a hardcopy." Regardless of the young cadet's attitude, he reminded her of her own past. Back then, facing only a few floating space objects compared to today, she'd started out the same way. Space events were taken much more seriously. *Today,* she reminisced, *everybody's a comedian.* "Keep tracking," she ordered.

"Whatever," the young muttered out of her earshot. "Not my problem."

Angered by the unprofessional remark, "Quit mouthing off" she responded, "or I'll have you cleaning toilets."

"Sorry." He knew better next time than being a wiseass.

"Get that status yet?" she demanded.

"Just a sec..." He hurriedly rushed to the print station, then handed her the report. "What's that all about?" He shrugged at his grinning buddies nearby.

Rhonda ignored the comments and glanced at the printout. "Give me a global view." She watched the monitor switch to high altitude. By now, other operators had been alerted. Their watchful eyes shifted to the enormous monitors mounted against the mission wall. The new vantage point showed additional objects on display. Positioned in orbit some 22,000 miles out, most were geostationary satellites. Unlike low orbit satellites whose functions were mostly surveillance, these were to broadcast information around the globe. In spite of the multiple alerts, these still seemed stabilized. *No changes there. After all,* she thought with contempt, *who'd mess with anything that high up?* "I'll be in the office if there's a change." With printout in hand, Rhonda abruptly turned and stormed from the control room.

Waiting for shift change, the operator relaxed once more into the comfort of the computer chair. Hoping to save some face by his peers, "Everybody's way too serious," was his final comment.

In the quiet of the office, Rhonda sat at her desk and carefully studied the report. It revealed nothing unusual. Alarms were triggered daily. Some were from residual debris floating in and out of satellite paths others from passing meteors slicing through Earth's atmosphere. Most objects followed a predetermined path today, but some well-established orbits seemed to be changing. Studying the printed report held firmly in her hands, a slight deviation to the general pattern of floating objects caught her scrutinizing eyes. On the surface it looked like a self-adjusted orbital change, but a closer look revealed something else. The software had detected a flaw. An object had broken its calculated path.

Rhonda reached for the optical mouse resting on the desk pad. She used it to scroll across the computer screen. A click on the navigation brought up the Intel portal page. Hesitating, she moved the cursor across the rows of navigation bars. Each was a hot link connecting to a secure Intranet site labeled SPACECOM, NSA, MILNET, NORAD, in addition to others. Some were primary links necessary to the national defense; others were secondary level connections to military organizations. To effectively do her job she'd been given access to all defense related assets. This, however, required the highest security access above Top Secret.

Her software searches on current satellite activities, as well as scheduled space launches, revealed nothing unusual. Nothing new registered from any of the organizational commands. Nor was there a scheduled orbital decay registered from any possibly descending satellites.

Massaging both temples to clear her focus, she worried, "Hmmm." Nothing obvious jumped out at her. Dissatisfied with herself, she glanced at the printout one final time, then tossed it into the HOLD bin. Yet, try as she may, she could not eliminate an uneasy *why do I feel this way?* Her eyes sought out the many service rewards stuck on her office mantel. She should be proud of her achievements. *Why's my confidence faltering after all these years?*

After many years of dedicated service, to this day, Rhonda Hicks was still puzzled about why she was handed the responsibility of managing SPACECOM. It came as a complete surprise. It happened years ago after the last RIF. The change was part of a major reduction in force brought on by severe budget cuts. Jobs of this nature usually fell to a senior level commander or seasoned officer—male, that was. Although huge career strides had been made in recent decades, women still had to struggle to ascend the executive ladder. Even now, she could not entirely shake the sense of inferiority she felt when seated among high-ranking organizational heads during special conferences. At first, it'd taken some time for her to feel acceptance among those equal to her echelon. Now, after having gained recognition not only by making the right decisions, but also demonstrating superior management qualities, she was often called on to do much of the organizational planning and decision making.

The job itself had been created with the inception of the supercomputer. If it were not for these fairly recent technological changes, there would be no space asset tracking. It would be almost impossible for a human being to effectively manage the minute-by-minute changes of all the space objects tracked in orbit. This especially held true with GPS assets. What followed in rapid succession was the creation of the many defense organizations, with SPACECOM being a newcomer. Whereas SPACECOM was a joint space surveillance and monitoring agency, the USAF maintained its own intelligence functions (as did the Army and Navy), tasked with space surveillance, nuclear detection monitoring, and, to a lesser extent, weather reconnaissance.

Amid her reflective thoughts, Rhonda became aware of her own breathing within the otherwise quiet in the office. *Maybe the satellites have settled back into their orbits.* So she hoped, but she knew it was only wishful thinking. *Problems never go away by themselves.*

Her eyes fell on the report stacked in the HOLD basket. Her hand subconsciously reached for it before she reread the printed pages. Again, there was nothing out of the ordinary, only the usual objects floating in space. Categorized, they included active and inactive satellites—spent rocket bodies amid thousands of fragmented debris. The report also predicted when and where a decaying space object would re-enter Earth's atmosphere to trigger the appropriate alert. Her thoughts kept drifting between the present and a successful career of the past.

In that she devoted most of her time to her career, there was little time left for personal life. It was the one aspect she'd always regretted. Routinely, over the course of years, she'd meet people but never anyone special. Most passed through for short assignments with eyes on a long-term field command. For an ambitious officer, that's where the opportunities were, but she lost out by having been born before equal gender opportunity.

In retrospect, Rhonda had always hoped to have a family and children. A dejected feeling came over her as she realized she'd been passed over—socially, that was. Past her prime to start a family, the most she could hope for at this stage in life was a meaningful relationship. *Getting sentimental again,* she cautioned herself.

Her mind had drifted from the duties at hand, but all things considered, she had no reason to complain. *What more could one want from life?* she thought. Her eyes caught her own reflection in the desktop monitor. From her vantage point she looked as attractive as she did in her twenties. Lines in her face did not show unless she stood directly in front of the brightened bathroom mirror. For that, she worked hard to hold onto her shape. Gyms, cycling, skiing, and hiking made sure of that. Sometimes, when on walks, she even prayed she'd meet a man. She missed the touch of a man...the right man...one with pride and integrity, romance and passion. A heartfelt sigh escaped her lips. *Is wishful thinking all I have left?*

CASTLE ROCK

Brian got up early. He looked forward to the visit with Alex. He was anxious to get going. On the way out he stopped by the hotel breakfast buffet to grab a bagel and a cup of coffee. It wasn't much of a breakfast, just enough to keep his stomach from growling. The drive took him north on I-25 toward Denver. Along the way he passed Garden of the Gods[5] on his left. Telltale silhouettes jutting up vertically from an age-old ground, it was the region's landmark. He was struck by the magnificent beauty of the purple rock formation with names like Kissing Camels, Balancing Rock, and Tower of Babel.

Twenty minutes into the drive, a sign announced the next turnoff, "Castle Rock." It was his exit. Brian slowed the rental car on the off-ramp. In the distance to the left he could make out the contours of the Rockies. To his right was nothing but offshoots of the foothills.

Slightly puzzled, he shook the head. "Must have missed the place." He drove ahead at a crawl to find a turnoff. Almost a mile later, mounted within a cluster of railroad ties, he spotted an obscure mailbox. Stylishly encased by pine trees and sagebrush, the design perfectly blended in with the otherwise rocky terrain. Slowly driving on, he made out a construction planted amid smartly-designed landscaping. Not uncommon to this part of the country, he'd been informed, he finally understood what Alex meant by "earth shelter."

Living on the perimeter of the wilderness, inhabitants were not subjected to rigid building codes, and this one was definitely unique. To the surprise of the visitor, the earth shelter completely blended in with the terrain.

Brian took a minute to absorb the surrounding scenery, then parked. Shifting left in the driver seat, he could see the ground below drop off into the valley. Sprawled in the distance ahead were the pristine grounds of the Air Force Academy. To the right, if he craned his neck, he could follow up the steep slope supposedly housing the shelter.

Then his eyes caught a sparkling reflection. "There it is." A huge picture window, fronted by a wooden deck built on top of a heavy entrance door, caught his attention. He suspected it was the garage entrance.

"This," he muttered in the silence of the surrounding, "I've got to see." Stretching his legs on solid ground felt good. Nearby, he became aware of the shuffled sound of footsteps.

Seconds later, a familiar voice sounded off. It was Alex. "Spotted you come up the valley. Thought I'd meet you," he greeted, "otherwise you may have driven right by the place."

Approaching the host, "You'd never suspect a home built into these hills," Brian replied.

Beamed with pride Alex acknowledged the remark. "Purposely designed it this way."

---

[5] Garden of the Gods is a public park located in Colorado Springs, CO. Where it used to be a pristine area used mostly by local hikers and rock climbers, toady it is a popular tourist place. The unusual reddish colored rock formations were created during a geological upheaval along a natural fault line millions of years ago.

"Why, it's a fortress," Brian said, not without admiration.

"Safety reasons," Alex explained, "in case of natural," he gestured to the sky, "or unnatural disasters."

"Tell me about it." Brian lingered outdoors to absorb the surrounding hills.

"When I built," Alex went on, "everybody from the permit registrar to the county assessor was bitching." He, back then, shared a less than popular reputation. "I'm known around here," he paused to lead his buddy up the driveway, "as the Mad German."

"How appropriate." Brian acknowledged a somewhat eccentric Alex, the German he was. It went unnoticed.

"They couldn't get a handle on my design and construction plans, but finally gave me the permits I needed." Brian was let into the domain of his longtime buddy. "Join me for breakfast?" Alex graciously invited the visitor into what he called The Castle. "I'll show you the place after we eat." He held the gate open. "In the meantime," he suggested, "we talk."

The steel door clanged shut. Brian found himself inside a fortress. He marveled at the interior. "How'd you come up with the idea?"

"Always wanted to build my own place," Alex explained, "but the right way. Leaving it up to somebody else always caused me frustration. My biggest gripe was the shortcuts builders used to squeeze additional profits from the client."

"I hear you." Brian had never owned a home and could only appreciate the effort Alex had put into the place. He was somewhat awestruck by the size of the domicile. "Remarkable," he muttered.

"They think," Alex went on, "people are too stupid to notice, but they do. Problem is, most people are too polite to raise an objection or don't have the knowledge to criticize the 'so called experts.' I, on the other hand," he boasted, "notice any detail deviating from the specs."

"I remember," Brian recalled, "trained in industrial engineering." Alex's education, Brian remembered, included training in manufacturing, construction, and processing materials of every kind, make, and shape. "Knew you grew up in Germany but don't remember where. The south," he offered, "wasn't it?"

"Bavarian Alps," Alex replied. "It's why I like it here so much." He steered his guest into a spacious kitchen, offered him a chair by the table, and then set out to make breakfast. Brian watched while Alex prepared the breakfast.

While waiting, he walked the few paces to the picture window. He could feel the freshness of mountain air flowed into his lungs. He marveled the spectacular view, "Truly magnificent."

"How'd you like your eggs?"

"Scrambled."

Alex was a gracious host. There was nothing sloppy about the man. Efficient, well organized, but sometimes a little pragmatic. In between tending to the stove, he slid a plate of hash browns, German sausages, and scrambled eggs in front of his guest. The smell was enticing.

"Give me a minute to fix the pancakes."

Brian was ready for a hearty breakfast, and homemade to boot. "Smells terrific."

Minutes later, Alex, with an encouraging sigh, joined him at the table. "Help yourself."

Brian, savoring a hearty meal, prepared a stack topped with real butter and dark maple syrup on the side. "Ah, yes," he groaned, "the pleasures of a homemade breakfast." Then he added, "Nothing like the real thing. Where'd you pick up fresh produce?" He hadn't tasted farm fresh butter and syrup in ages.

"Plenty of farms around here," he was told and offered a dish of delicious looking strawberries from across the table. "Gotta get up early to catch the produce before it hits the markets." Alex took a bite from his triple stack, then, between chewing the food, said, "Building the place had been on my mind for years. Self-contained shelter provides tremendous cost savings, and what's more," he emphasized, "protection."

"Protection?" The term cut a puzzled look across Brian's face. Apparently, he hadn't thought on those terms. "Getting paranoid in your old age?" Brian was joking but immediately realized Alex could be offended. He shot a glance at his host seated across the table; it appeared he hadn't taken notice. What'd always amazed Brian was his buddy's calm demeanor. Nothing seemed to anger the man.

"Not at all," Alex continued. "Had it in mind ever since I came across some info." He looked up. "You know," he briefly stopped chewing the sausage, "guarded intelligence."

"How's that?"

"Remember SIOP?" Alex picked up on the previous night's conversation.

"Go on."

"People in the '50s," he elaborated, "had the idea of building earth shelters to protect them from nuclear attacks. Not that it would have made much difference. Nuclear fallout would have killed everybody within weeks." Unofficially, the act was to pacify a population ignorant of the dangers from radiation. "Only few scientists knew the true effects."

"I remember," Brian recalled, "the government conducting tests out in the Pacific after WWII." He hoped Alex didn't consider him completely uninformed. Although his scope of interest was broad, it did not quite compare to Alex's knowledge base.

Used to interruptions, Alex continued. "Right. My intention was adoptive for the long term."

"Enlighten me."

"Take famine for instance," he explained further. "It's not out of the question if you believe in global warming or, for that matter, a new ice age. Could go either way. We don't know enough." He encouraged Brian to have more pancakes. "How about a regional catastrophe? What happened with Katrina could happen anywhere."

"Flood in the Rockies," Brian joked.

"Funny, ha...ha—no." Alex paused with a smile. "Starving people will fight to the death for food and survival. I'm more concerned with terrorism."

"How could terrorism affect this place?" Brian turned curious. "Place's surrounded by a wall of defenses." Unknown to the general population or outsiders to the area, Colorado Springs was built on defense. With the Air Force to the north, infantry to the east, NORAD to the south, and the Rockies protecting the west, one would think no force on Earth could break into the area. The only vulnerable spot was from above, but the nation's defense grid had that covered.

"Lateral harm," Alex rationalized. "Threat from terrorism is growing. With worldwide access to dirty weapons, chemical compounds, and biological agents, it's only a matter of time before any of them will be deployed." Control over nuclear matter, in recent years, may have been tightly enforced by IAEA, but that wasn't necessarily the case with unregulated supporting elements just as lethal.

"I see your point," Brian agreed.

"Wanted a place isolated and completely self-contained." The place was directly built into the hillside leaving only the shaded windows exposed. "Could just as easily have enclosed the entire place but couldn't imagine living without sunlight. Besides," he paused with a gesture at the picture window, "who'd deny the spectacular view?"

"Totally," Brian consented. "Must have cost a fortune."

"Didn't come cheap—reinforced composites specially treated against shock waves."

Brian was genuinely impressed. "How long did it take to build?"

"Couple of years." There was a hint of pride in Alex's voice. "Designed the infrastructure using solid I-beams and steel frames. Did a lot of digging and carting dirt with a couple of workers I'd hired."

"What about utilities?"

"There's no electrical hookup. I get power from solar panels. With mobile and satellite for entertainment, don't need phone lines either. Come on," he gestured, "I'll show you around." Receiving barely visitors he didn't get much chance to show off the place. "Place's got three levels," he explained on the way down the hall. "You came in on the first level, the garage. Same floor are utilities for heat, water, power, and waste. Second level holds guest rooms, living room, bathrooms, and kitchen. Top, as you can see, is my domain. Next door's the master bedroom."

"Remarkable."

"Here." He led the way. "My den. Sound system's built into all rooms, as well as central air and heat. Let me show you my favorite spot."

Brian stepped into a huge room. "Jacuzzi!" he exclaimed. One side held the spa, and, elevated off the floor, the other was occupied by a California king size bed. It provided full view into the mountains. He grew more envious by the minute. "Some people sure know how to live," he remarked with envy, noticing to the built-in wine cellar.

"That's not all." Alex gestured for him to follow. At the end of the hall they took the stairway to a basement. Inside, Brian noticed the utility room stacked with latest state-of-the-art equipment. At the far end of the corridor a sign blocked the steel door, "Keep Out."

"Keep out what?"

"Derelicts, misfits, oddballs, and other intruders." With his dry sense of humor, Alex chuckled, then pushed a button. A door slid quietly open.

At the far end of the hall he noticed a steel ladder mounted into the wall. He stepped up to inspect. It led up a darkened shaft sealed by an escape hatch. "Impressive," he readily admitted, "but why the escape?"

"Remember SIOP?"

"How could I forget?" Brian, as well as Alex had worked on the policies for their respective agencies. Where the two differed were organizational procedures. Where one was strategic defenses, the other was surveillance.

"Just recently," Alex explained, "came across information quite disturbing."

"Go on."

"Been monitoring the ether waves…"

"Hey," Brian cut in, "that's my turf."

Alex knew very well the covert organization his buddy worked for. "Yeah," he agreed, "but does your agency share information." There was a halting silence. "Thought so," then continued with his findings. "As I said," his face had taken on that of real concern, "our defense system has been compromised."

Brian was keenly aware of current world events. What he did not expect was anybody outside the Agency to be knowledgeable, especially not a retired contractor. But in fairness, he did not know all of his buddy's activities during the past years and present. He had to feel him out. "Could you be more specific?"

"We're about to be invaded."

What he just heard was an information bombshell he had not expected. He had to somehow defuse it. Aside his organization's echelon members, the president with immediate military commanders all services, the JCS, the information was classified above Top Secret. The nation and its citizens had been shielded from any form of attack threat whether rumored or true, pending or imminent. Releasing this kind of sensitive information could prove extremely chaotic.

"Where'd you get your info?"

"Not important. What's important is the nature and that it's happening."

"Think we're a bit paranoid. Aren't we?" Even though they were war buddies with similar access clearances, he could not allow an outsider to interfere. He had to protect the integrity of his organization. Being an insider, perhaps he was getting pumped for information. To steer the conversation away from all sensitive issues he changed the subject. "What's your next step?"

Alex must have realized he was treading on foreign boundaries. He probably did not want to compromise their friendship. With a dismissive gesture he remarked, "Doesn't look like wind's gonna pick up for windsurf. If you want," he offered, "we could hang out in the spa with a couple of beers."

"Fine with me," Brian heartily agreed. "Amazing what you did with the place."

"As I said," Alex motioned around, "I wanted to build my own place at least once. With all that's going on in the world, it seemed the right time. Besides, I took an early retirement to dedicate myself full-time to the construction."

"What about the job?"

"Formed my own consulting firm. Got the independence I needed. Twenty-five years on defense contracts is enough career for one lifetime." They'd arrived back upstairs. Alex gestured at the bathroom door. "There's an extra pair of trunks in there."

"Thanks."

"I'll get the beer." Alex headed for the fridge. "Meet you in the Jacuzzi."

Ten minutes later, when he arrived at the hot top, Alex had the beer waiting. "Thanks." Brian exhaled deeply as he slowed his tense body into the heated water. "Man," he mused, "this is living." He was content to let the Jacuzzi jets massage his back. "What else have you been up to?"

He was getting comfortably seated in the tub, "Last project," Alex replied, "five years with BeeMoh."

"Ballistic' Missiles Office?"

"Yeah," he remarked, "contracted to work on the Rail Garrison."

"MX Missiles?" Brian shot Alex a surprised glance. "Wasn't that terminated by Reagan?"

"Right," Alex agreed. "Instead, I was given a project with REACT."

"Missiles?"

"Yeah," was his diminutive answer, "quite a challenge."

From what Brian knew Alex had no prior experience in nuclear technology when handed the responsibility of hardening communications and power feeds to the underground Minuteman and Peacekeeper launch facilities.

Adjusting the water temperature, he stated, "Fortunately, I'd been given access to the necessary material."

"Classified…I presume."

"Some. Remember the tests conducted during the '50s at places like Eniwetok, Bikini, and Johnston Island?"

"Vaguely." He was still a youngster when it came to that history.

"At the time," Alex continued, "TRW had the contract to record the test results. If you're interested, I'll enlighten you."

"Yeah…but," Brian beckoned, "sure could use another beer." He wasn't going anywhere. This place suited him just fine. His face said it all: *what more could a man want than soaking in a Jacuzzi with a buddy and view to die for?* "Just like old times," he said, tossing over the empty can.

ISLAMABAD (Rawalpindi, Pakistan)

To the outside world, REX Chemicals seemed like just another processing plant. This one, however, unknown to the uninformed, was for converting chemicals and refining soluble substances. To gain access to the grounds, yellow hardhats were mandatory and worn by employees and visitors alike. The policy was strictly enforced. Through that, visitors could be spotted easily. With them, the hardhats ranged from a cover prominently propped atop a bushy hairdo to a bobbing shell ill-fitted on a balding head. On any given day, a group of visitors was hurriedly rushed in and out without anybody taking the time to properly size the adjusting bands. At times, to the humor of plant employees, it'd only take a slight gust of wind to catch a hardhat and tumble it wildly across the steel-enforced structures and concrete pavements with the visitor giving chase.

Today, one such visitor was a tall, muscular, and deeply-tanned guest. He had quite a few inches of height on the rest of the crowd. He, unlike the others, firmly held onto his hardhat while gazing upwards at the gigantic, neatly stacked forest of silos spanning the immensity of this modern day chemical processing plant.

"…here we have the toxic waste filtration facilities, and over there is…" Eagerly gesturing in the direction of the distant structures, the plant manager informed the group that was the colossal manufacturing plant. By now, as stated prominently on the nametag fastened on his white lab coat, most had identified the host as Abdul Baser. The tall visitor, aside from watching the others tightly clustered around the spokesperson, had been intently listening and watching. This specific visitor made a mental note of their faces. It was a practice he used to record everything in his passage. It'd saved his life on more than one occasion.

To gain access to the plant he'd registered as a member of the foreign trade commission. For that, he could have easily sent one of his lieutenants, but, because of its importance, he needed to check out the facility firsthand. He wouldn't entrust the task to anyone else. The information was too paramount for the mission. Today, his nametag identified him as Aasim Karim, an arbitrary name he'd picked. The next time and place it'd be some other name. Forgers were only too eager to produce permits and visas whenever generous compensation was involved.

The scheduled tour was almost over. There was only one more stop, "The Underground." For that, he'd have to break away from the crowd.

While everybody in the group seemed preoccupied with the tour host, the tall visitor was momentarily distracted. The gadget in his back pocket began to vibrate. He'd been waiting for the call. He fished for it, moving off to the side. A swift flip opened the cover of the sleek iPhone. Squinting against the bright sun he read the text message. "Contact is Omar One," it said. Relaxing once more, he tugged the mobile back into his trousers.

Seconds later he felt a slight tug on the sleeve of his jacket. Speaking in a muffled tone, a voice announced, "Omar One."

He turned to face the tall visitor. Giving him a quick assessment, he responded, "Shahadah." A nod from the darkened face confirmed the contact. He tugged on Aasim Karim's sleeve to pull him away from the crowd. "This way."

With rapid strides he led the visitor toward the nearby service elevator. Once inside, the door shut with a noisy clang. The platform began its rapid descent, dropping several levels below the ground. After a jerky stop, the visitor was led into a completely different world, a world of secrets contained within 25,000 square feet of steel and concrete. They'd arrived at the underground sector for BIO Safety Level 4.

The tall one demanded, "What's this?"

"Research containment ward," Abdul explained, "medical care for patients who may have been accidentally exposed to hazardous agents, or have acquired a highly infectious disease." While handing off further information, the visitor was led along a spacious and lengthy hallway.

The current floor housed a 12-bed research ward in which clinical trials of vaccines and drugs were conducted. In general, the institute was a mix of military and civilian staff including physicians, microbiologists, pathologists, chemists, molecular biologists, physiologists, and pharmacologists. It also included technical and administrative staff to support the research.

Farther down the corridor, a number of patients occupied beds completely isolated from each other through synthetically sealed off insulated chambers. The hurried visitor momentarily paused. He was taking a special interest.

The scene was pathetic to watch; the patients' faces strained in agony. With twitching bodies and jerky limbs, they were attended by what seemed a calloused medical staff. "Casualties of recent bio wars and lab accidents," the visitor was told. "Please follow." Abdul gestured ahead. The tall one was led to an isolation crosswalk leading to the next level. He was steered towards a prominently mounted red and yellow caution sign. "Radiation Hazard," it read. It was the entrance to BL-3.

Level 3 housed an elaborate laboratory complex. It contained an array of isolation chambers occupied by a staff of busy chemists stooped over high-powered micron instruments among endless rows of caged animals bounding energetically within the soundproof glass enclosures. Sandwiched between neatly arranged plates projected onto the micron scope, he was invited to view a variety of deadly bacterial strains. Under the naked eye the plates appeared immaculately clean, if not sterile. Viewed through the microscope, they were, in fact, Hell's Kitchen.

To the visitor, the world of deadly microbes was meaningless. He was indifference and impatience and said so, "Move on."

He was hastened to BL-2, the chemical lab. Immediately, his interest perked. He was attracted to the delivery mechanism. It was here where the lethal bacteria were mixed with a delivery agent. An array of safely contained colorful glass-enclosed cylinders was waiting to be deployed. "What's the status of the agents?" Steel hardened eyes drilled into the host, who was shifting uneasily on his feet.

"We are making progress," Abdul reported. He'd sensed the visitor's mounting frustration. Suddenly he felt threatened. *This man may appear affable but,* he surmised, *surely doesn't act accordingly.* He'd incorrectly assessed the visitor's personality before he'd noticed the circular scar edged into the left side of his jaw.

"How long before I can expect the quantity we need delivered?"

"We are," he was assured, "working around the clock." Omar refused to commit to a specific schedule. "We will let you know."

"Not good enough." The response was unfaltering. It was a direct threat. "I will hold you responsible."

Omar began to sweat profusely. His breath became labored. He almost fainted. He steadied his body against the doorframe before speaking. "There are many factors you must consider."

"No further excuses," was the threatening command. The stranger abruptly turned towards the exit. It was an indication to end the tour.

"Not to worry," was the host's final reply. With a sigh of relief he hastened the unwelcome caller to the exit. He was anxious to put as much distance between him and the threatening visitor as possible.

CASTLE ROCK

In the relaxed atmosphere of the Castle, Brian and Alex were enjoying the day. "You worked missile design?" Brian picked up their earlier conversation.

Alex slid into the Jacuzzi, handing over a fresh can of beer. "Sure did."

"Ah," Brian graciously accepted the iced crusted can, "this is grand." Seeping into his heated body, the liquid felt great. "What project?"

"Missile defense." With the end of the Cold War, missile production was halted by both superpowers. Following the SALT[6] treaty, the U.S. missile system had been scaled down to a minimum, as was the other side's. Although a sizable forces, it still remained active at places like Minot, Grand Forks, and Warren.

"Thought the silos had been dismantled."

"Not at all," Alex insisted. He was emphatic about it. "It's our only assurance to keep abreast of hostile nations. Russia's doing the same, and the Chinese."

"Chinese?"

"Yeah, but," Alex proclaimed. "They keep a pretty low profile. Don't exactly know what they're up to." Years earlier, he'd been put in charge of engineering the last upgrade. It was to become the last major budget spending by the U.S. government on strategic silos. Since then, the missile arsenal had been pretty much held in a dormant, idle state. Officially, to the public's eyes, it had been shut down but could be scaled up for rapid deployment on a minute's notice. Operations and maintenance crews were busy around the clock to maintain and keep the arsenal at a ready state.

"Who's running the show?"

"SAC has watch teams on alert. Variety of communication systems provides the national command authority with virtually instantaneous contact to the Triad."

"Space, sea, and ground-based defenses?"

To meet warhead levels set by START II[7] treaty, the government decided to permanently de-scale the remaining missiles. Where they used to hold multiple reentry vehicles, the new configuration called for a single system. To counter increased accuracy in the Soviet missile system, SAC needed a new missile fitted with the most advanced technology. That led to the commission of the Peacekeeper design. Alex made a motion to exit the tub.

"What about the Peacekeeper?" Brian's curiosity peaked. *This is getting interesting.*

"I'll get to that." Alex panted, getting out of the tub. He quickly toweled off his steaming legs and torso. "I'll make us a couple sandwiches." He headed for the pantry.

"Great." Brian reclined in the soaking liquid with streams of water jets massaging his body. He was completely relaxed.

Minutes later, Alex returned with a stack of smoked ham on German rye sandwiches. Stepping back into the tub, he placed the plate near his buddy.

"Go on," Brian insisted.

---

[6] SALT – Strategic Arms Limitation Talks. An agreement signed in 1979 by U.S. President Jimmy Carter and Soviet leader Leonid Brezhnev after the second round of Strategic Arms Limitations Talks (SALT II), held from 1972-79.

[7] START II – Strategic Arms Reduction Treaty. Bilateral treaty between the United States of America and Russia on the Reduction and Limitation of Strategic Offensive Arms.

"One day," Alex picked up the conversation, "a load of totally antiquated equipment arrived." They were huge cabinets painted in customary Air Force blue. "My job was to strip out and rebuild the guts with retrofitted components." After removing the covers Alex had not been able to believe his eyes. "My God," he'd prompted the delivery guys, "where'd this come from? This belongs in the junkyard!"

"Junkyard?" Brian was equally astounded, hearing about the supposed antiquated systems.

Alex soon learned the purpose for the outdated technology. To survive a nuclear strike, the equipment could not be built with modern day electronics. "We ever get clobbered on U.S. soil the explosion would destroy everything at ground zero. Ensuing blasts would immobilize every piece of electronics in the region. Only parts surviving would be discrete components."

"We're talking," Brian asked, "transistors, diodes, and capacitors mounted on printed circuit boards?"

"Right — anything newer like present day ICs would get burned up by beta and gamma rays." X-rays were lethal to humans but other types of rays did severe damages to hardware. "And that's where our current dilemma lies."

"Dilemma?"

"Hold that thought," Alex begged off. His eyes had picked up a slight motion nearby. His mobile was vibrating. He strained for it but let it drop from his slippery fingers. It landed on the wooden floor with a clang. "Dammit." He had to jump from the Jacuzzi to retrieve it. Brows furrowed at the caller ID, he said, "Gotta take this one." He turned and disappeared into his private quarters.

Almost ten minutes passed before he returned neatly dressed.

"What…?"

"Wanna take a ride?" Alex urged. He was already headed for the stairway.

"Where…?"

"I'll be in the garage." His fleeting words sounded urgent.

Brian had been caught off guard. He hastened to the guest room to catch up. Five minutes later, speculating what was up, he slid into the passenger seat of a sleek coupe.

WARREN AIR FORCE BASE (LCC)

Right hand gripping the handle bar, Brian exclaimed, "Wow! This is a magnet for cops." He couldn't help but admire his buddy's wheels. He had barely had time to jump in and slam the door shut before Alex stepped on it. The deep red BMW was already on its way, fishtailing wildly towards the valley. "Ever get ticketed?"

"Every time," Alex beamed, "but Gov takes care of it."

"Privileged?" He shot an envious look at him. "Must be nice."

"Comes with the territory." Alex had a heavy foot on the road, especially in an emergency call.

"By the way," Brian turned curious, "what's the emergency?"

Alex had immediately recognized the caller. It was his SAC contact. A "Code Red" had gone out to all mission critical personnel. He'd been informed that there'd been a malfunction with some missiles. An exercise scheduled for an early morning test firing had to be scrapped. When the crew on alert was unable to provide a fix, the call was elevated to Tier II, when that failed to Tier III, Alex. He was the last resort. There was no higher level above Alex's skills. Calls of this urgency were rare and required immediate attention.

This morning, Alex was pushing it. The Beemer was speeding north on I-25. "Ever been to a silo?"

"Heck no!" Brian exclaimed. The revelation came as a complete surprise. "That's where…?"

"Today's your lucky day."

"What's the deal?"

Alex outlined his status as support contractor. Since he'd been responsible for the last design upgrade to the system, he was called in to resolve issues the onsite staff couldn't handle.

It'd take a couple of hours to drive the 180 miles to the silo farm. At times, he'd get flagged by radar, but always got out of getting ticketed by flashing his credentials, with a brief explanation about the emergency.

"What can I expect once we get there?"

"Resistance, intimidation, hostility."

"I meant the system." He eyed his buddy with a hint of suspicion.

"Oh that," Alex countered. "Nothing!"

"Nothing?"

Alex saw the confused look on Brian's face. He felt the need to explain, at least the fundamentals. "All right," he offered. "…command and control is exercised from several independent Launch Control Centers."

"What? Missiles?"

"Minuteman and Peacekeeper. Silos," Alex explained, "are staged twenty to a hundred fifty miles from the central support base. Missiles are clustered in wings according to ballistic missiles flight policy. LCCs[8] are buried by forty feet of dirt and concrete extending down a hundred plus feet to protect the capsule….self-sufficient to sustain life for several weeks…small crew operated the system on a twenty-four hour shift…flight of ten missiles remotely monitored with backup of ten more."

---

[8] Launch Control Center for nuclear tipped ICBM missiles.

"What about inside?"

"Launch console, computers, comm equipment, lavatory, and sleeping quarters. Alerts are scheduled periodically to maintain proficiency. Pretty noisy during those times. Missile Crews," he explained further, "although seated only twelve feet apart, communicate by shouting or headphones."

Alex shifted his attention to the terrain up ahead. "That's it in a nutshell."

"What're we looking for?"

"Small barn."

"Something like that?" Brian gestured at the distance ahead.

"Like that." Alex gave a nod. He'd had the building in sight for some distance already. They drove up to what looked like an old farm. Despite its obvious age, on closer inspection, it was well kept up. What made it unusual was the tight perimeter fence, topped by an array of antennas.

"What's with the receivers?" Brian had noticed a forest of transmitters and receivers protruding above ground. "VLF and UHF," he guessed. "Whole damned gamut."

"Spectrum coverage," Alex agreed, "backup for backup with more backup." A command signal could be received from any known transmission equipment in the military's radio and microwave arsenal.

Leaving two tire tracks on the dusty ground, the Beemer slid to a halt. Two sentries popped up out of nowhere demanding ID checks. "Looks like we've been expected." Brian was impressed at the organizational efficiency. Security had been alerted of their arrival miles ahead. Alex flashed his ID. He didn't have to say much. Badge said it all, "SAC," *showcase for the world's elite.*

An escort jeep dropped them off by the service entrance. An access elevator took them below. Seconds later, they faced a blast proof, glass-encased steel door. Two faces from the inside were staring back. The heavy steel retracted with a clang. Six thousand pounds of solid steel slowly widened to allow entrance.

"Bauer," Alex announced, "this is Harris."

Despite his reputation with SAC he had to identify himself. Every visit there'd be new faces. Rotation schedules were frequent at this isolated place.

Thumbing at Brian, "He can't come in," the sentry gestured after checking IDs. Brian did not have proper credentials for the underground LCC.

Alex promptly turned to leave, "If he goes," Alex insisted, "I go."

"Wait up," the sentry called after him. "I can resolve it." He then picked up a phone cradled to the wall to make the call. Seconds later he Okayed both visitors.

"What's up?" Alex questioned the crew commander.

The crew chief came directly to the point. They had a problem. And the problem had to be resolved, *immediately.* He gave Alex a short briefing on the way to the command console.

"Status alarms," Alex was informed, "when initiating the launch sequence." He then led the visitors to an array of flashing indicators blinking away on the master control panel.

"May I?" Alex gestured and eased his frame into the vacated commander's seat. He was given ready access to manage the system, then took a few seconds to reacquaint himself with the switches, indicators, and pushbuttons. It'd been some time since his last visit. Reassured once more, he was in total control of the operation.

His prominent fingers glided expertly over the various test buttons, activating switches, knobs, and keys. To the observer he appeared much like a piano player. The alarms persisted. The command chair was mounted on highly polished rails. Using an extended leg, he shot his body back and forth between computer keyboards and launch module. Each simulation ended with more brightly lit indicators flashing in red and yellow followed by a software-generated alarm painted across the display screen:

"S Y S T E M...A B O R T...S Y S T E M...A B O R T...!!!"

Brian was stooped over Alex's shoulders. He seemed entranced by Alex's every move playing the keyboard. With a few keystrokes, the software executed a series of internal commands, testing connections and electronics, drilling into the various levels of the system. It only took seconds for the software to respond with: "No Error Found."

"Not a damned thing." Alex shrugged. Slightly troubled, he turned to face the launch commander. "What's the chance for a launch?"

"Impossible!" was the venomous response. Uttered with finality, it denied all options.

"Gotta do it," Alex insisted.

The flight commander seemed to squirm by the very thought. "Can't do it."

Alex knew from past experience it'd be almost impossible to get that authorization. Not only would it impact the defense status, but the action would directly reflect on the crew's career performance. The commander's track record would be on the line, but it couldn't be helped.

"I'll take the consequences." He always did. After all, he was getting paid well to do the work. This was not the usual error condition. It called for extreme measures. It meant a test launch. A launch as close to the real thing as could be measurably possible.

"Can't do it." The commander stood his ground. His demeanor indicated the request was ridiculous. "Not a chance."

"As I see it," Alex insisted, "you've got no choice." *Must been a first,* he thought, and worse yet, *orders from a civilian?*

Alex tried to keep his cool. He insisted it was absolutely necessary. "Software doesn't show anything...controls work perfectly...problem's intermittent...probably triggered by life action sequence." He went on, "Could be the vibration. Live launch's the only way. What's your decision? I'll take full responsibility."

The launch officer was fuming. He was in a bind. It showed in his face. Either way he was screwed. "Gotta check with NORAD."

Brian had a chance to watch Alex in action. He seemed highly impressed and marveled at his buddy's knowledge. A pat on the shoulder got Alex's attention. Brian gestured at the rows of racks lined against the back wall. "What's with the equipment?"

Head turned, Alex briefly paused. His gaze followed the direction Brian had indicated. "What equipment?"

"Over there." Brian gestured. Along the perimeter of the capsule was a series of tall, square shaped cabinets, neatly aligned against the back wall. They were painted in standard Air Force blue.

"That's," Alex said with a grin, "the junkyard equipment I was telling you about earlier."

The commander returned. Alex studied the man's approach. He could tell a lot from body language. *Not a happy man.* The man's face was red with anger. Alex didn't care. He was here to fix a problem. *Big problem. If looks could kill,* he thought facing the man, *I'd be a dead man.* He challenged the approaching officer with a smirk.

"Your ballgame." It was a deliberate and vicious response.

He sidestepped to allow the unwelcome intruders to get to the launch console. A hateful look followed his every move. It bordered on rage. The man's career would be over with a failed launch. With forced reluctance the commander slammed his body into the captain's seat to initiate the launch sequence. Alex, aware of the commander's every move, at a ready for the launch, was seated twelve feet away in the secondary command seat.

NORAD COMMAND

Benjamin "Ben" Jackson should have been a happy man. But he wasn't. Not today. Not after receiving an urgent call from the mountain. He had just sunk a birdie on the fifth when his mobile chirped. To be on the course was his favorite pastime. He spent a lot of time here. As a matter of fact, he spent more time on the course than at the station. Aside from the customary conflicts somewhere on the globe, things had been relatively quiet since 9/11. Conflicts were overseas. And he, Air Force General, NORAD, wasn't directly involved. His job was to protect the nation. Air and space was his forte. "Defense," that was. It'd take an act of sheer ignorance for any foreign nation to breach his space. "Let them try," he'd advised his peers on more than one occasion.

He'd achieved what others in the Air Force could only dream of: Brigadier general, the top grade officer in charge of the nation's most prominent authority, the North American Defense Command. He was a tough, no-nonsense man. *The Smoker,* he mused. That's what they called him. Rarely was he seen without a cigar clamped tightly between his lips, unlit, of course. It was an old habit, hard to break, even in the No Smoking zone. To him, it symbolized a reflection of much happier days. The days when smoking was still fashionable. Today, it had become a stigma. A stigma not unlike the position he held.

Ever since 9/11, there had been grumblings about closing the Mountain—*His Mountain.* In recent years, much pressure was exerted from congressional members who viewed the facility as obsolete. *Short sighted bastards,* he'd grumble to himself when reading another negative editorial. It wasn't his fault they'd dropped the ball. He also knew there were much more capable defense commands around the nation's perimeters to handle the ever-growing threat, the threat of terrorism. *Granted,* both of brows furrowed with contempt at Congress, *dated yes, but closing? Idiots!*

The call taking him from the course was priority, initiated by Warren. It didn't indicate an emergency. He was glad about that. Nevertheless, priority was urgent enough to report to the station, the Mountain. He tried to watch his speed, but on this road one hardly ever encountered a radar trap. Emergency calls were common. The police, most times, turned the other cheek for speeders. *What's higher than protecting the nation's safety?* He couldn't think of any other reason. Fourteen hundred feet up in the distance, the antenna farm slowly crept into view. It was hard to imagine the complexity from his current vantage point. Below, the only thing visible was the gaping hole at the base of the mountain. For a visitor, it could just have been another coal mining entrance.

A few miles later, the guard shack came into view. He slowed the vehicle to a stop. As always, he was immediately recognized. The sentries on duty threw him a smart salute. He handed over his ID. With him it was mostly formality but still enforced. Rules are rules, and regulation demanded an ID check for everybody. Seconds later, he was waved on. A short ride through the tunnel brought him to the parking zone. It fronted a set of massive blast doors. Today, as most days, they were open. "Thank God," he muttered. Lightly short winded by the altitude, he briskly headed for a set of stairs leading up the most prominent of a dozen buildings. "Must not be an emergency," he puffed, but wouldn't know for sure until he entered the War Room.

As soon as he entered, he became aware he'd been expected. The place was busier than usual. It appeared his staff was waiting for a decision.

Jackson shot a glance at the array of flat screen monitors neatly segmented into one enormous display. He was about to seek out the heads of his staff to get briefed when he was handed the phone by a staff member. It was the yellow phone. His heart rate shot up. Reserved only for national emergencies, in recent years, it rarely rang.

"Sir." Smartly dressed in a duty uniform, his assistant handed him the phone.

"NORAD[9]," Jackson answered.

"Warren," the caller identified himself, "Missile command." It was a call nobody wanted, especially not him. Not this close to retirement. It was *The Call,* a call always associated with trouble.

"Go." He wished he'd taken the day off. His lower ranking deputy would have been in command. But it was his day off as commands were handed off frequently during quiet times.

"Defense Sector Delta," the voice demanded. "Need launch permission."

Jackson's blood pressure immediately shot up. He knew the sector well. He'd been there several times. But only to host visiting dignitaries interested in seeing the missile system. Just up the road on the Colorado/Wyoming border, it used to be the showcase for MAD. There was a time, just after the SALT II treaty, when Soviet dignitaries demanded access to this, and similar facilities in Montana and the Dakotas. "USSR here?" he'd raged, "The United States? Enemy at his door steps, the world's most critical defense system?" *Unheard off.* But that was twenty years ago. He'd calmed down since quite a bit, until just now, "What's the emergency?" Immediately, visions of gloomy days long past returned.

"Need authorization for test launch."

Jackson exhaled the breath of air he'd held for close to a minute. *Thank God,* he prayed in silence. He was immensely relieved. *Only an exercise.* His heart had almost leaped from his chest. *Pressure's off.* "Whatcha need?"

"Full launch activation."

Again, his heart rate shut up enough causing the face to redden. A simulation launch was almost as bad as full activation. "Let Vandenberg handle it." It meant alerting a number of commands. And he'd be the focus. *Not good. Not good for any career.*

"Can't," the missile commander insisted, "problem's local."

"Listen here," Jackson fumed, "if you can't get somebody confident to fix your missiles, I'll get your ass replaced." *That'll shake them up.* Threatening worked. It always did.

"Sorry, sir," the field commander begged off, "we've tried."

"Then get somebody out there," he ordered, "who knows the system."

"Already did…Bauer's onsite."

"Alex Bauer?"

"Yes, sir."

This takes some serious evaluation. He contemplated a few seconds. Only one person could authorize a Minuteman missile launch: the President.

"Standby," he held off Warren, "will call back." He handed the receiver back to the assistant. "Get me the White House." Minutes later, the president was on the line. "Mr. President," Jackson began, "we have a situation." He briefly explained the urgency of the missile test.

---

[9] North American Defense Command.

The president advised him of political implication if things went wrong. "How critical?" he wanted to know. This was a first since he'd been in office.

"No other options available." Jackson had other concerns. "What about the press?"

"I'll handle that," was the reply. "Just make sure nothing goes wrong." It ended the call.

Jackson was relieved. Stalling the distant command, he ordered, "Standby," then pulled the SIOP folder from the shelf. It listed the latest points of contact information. He yanked the cradle from the base and pushed the primary button on the hot line. Immediately, he was connected with several major commands to give the clearance. Last call went to the LCC commander, Warren Missile Command. "You've got it."

Jackson could already envision the steps and action that followed next. Within seconds, the missile crew received the authorization, a coded message. After verifying the message's authenticity, the mission commander would relay the order to launch. For that, he would unlock a small, red "Emergency War Order" safe located above the deputy commander's control panel. Within the box were two launch keys. Each officer would take one key and insert it into the control console, one at each end. The missile operators, "Missileers," then strapped themselves into the rail-guided console chairs to start the final countdown. As the commanding officer called out the alphanumeric codes, the deputy commander would verify and repeat the message: "Bravo...Bravo...Alpha…Alpha...Lima...Lima...Indigo...Indigo." At the end of the countdown sequence, the officers simultaneously turned their launch keys.

To prevent unauthorized missile launches or test failures, the Air Force employed several fail-safes. For example, both officers had to turn their spring-loaded launch keys in unison. Because the launch switches were 12 feet apart, it was impossible for one person to turn both keys at once. The final command to launch also required a vote from outside of Minuteman— another LCC, or airborne command.

Fractions after the second vote was received, the "LAUNCH IN PROCESS" would commence. In seconds, the silos were hot. Next, explosive gas generators would force the eighty-ton launch doors covering the silos open, the nuclear-tipped missile would lift and begin streaming toward a target half a world away. As each missile blasted from its silo, its upper umbilical cable severed, triggering the "MISSILE AWAY" indicator on the commander's control panel. In seconds, the Missileers would complete their mission. It'd be an awesome spectacle for anyone witnessing the launch. The missiles would take less than half an hour to reach a target on any point on the globe.

WARREN AIR FORCE BASE (LCC)

"Missile Alert...Missile Alert..." The automated klaxon reverberated wildly through the LCC. A fierce sound, it tore on the nerve edges even of the seasoned. For the non-combatant, the untrained, the visitor, it created confusion, even chaos. On top of it, the hellish sound reporting, "Incoming missiles...forty minutes to impact," didn't help dampen the nightmare. Sirens had gone off at the same instant accompanied by half a dozen strobe lights. The pulsating red and yellow radiance shook the underground nerve center into action. Crews scrambled for their assigned duty stations. It did not matter how much experience one had at this outpost, the effects of a warning were always the same; it rattled the nerves.

"Report to stations," the crew commander was yelling at the top of his voice. "DM," he shouted. The deputy missile commander, second in charge, his first live mission, tripped on a trouser leg. It sent him hop-skipping along the narrow corridor.

"On the way," he yelled into the chaos. Running along in haste, he had trouble zipping up his pants. "Come on...come on," he urged himself on, making it to the armored safe mounted into the wall. One hand fumbled with the zipper while the other went for the dial. He needed the codes. In his rush he misdialed the first time. Already he'd wasted thirty seconds. Time was critical, regardless of mission, whether real or an exercise. The crew never knew. It took two more fumbled attempts to finally open the safe. His hand was quivering from nerves stretched to the breaking point. "The codes," he barked. His fingers rifled through the neatly stacked folders. *Calm down,* he instructed himself.

"Top one," the commander yelled over his shoulder.

The DM tore the seal to get to the plastic plates. One he broke himself; the commander palmed the second. It took both hands to break the plastics. From here on, it was up to the commander who initiated the next action call:

"Bravo...Bravo...Alpha...Alpha...Lima...Lima...Indigo...Indigo..." The sequence kicked off a string of letters. "Ballistic Missile Launch..." followed by the alphanumeric coded sequence for current date and target coordinates. Both commanders verified the mission authenticity against the EAM[10] message urgently flashing across the digital alert screen. It was this flashing alert message initiated by the president that authenticated and authorized the final launch order.

Where normally two missile operators would rush to the launch control console, today, Alex, with the permission of the crew commander, occupied the primary seat waiting for instructions.

"Target acquisition?" the commander yelled at the deputy, seated in the secondary chair poised over the control console.

"Three, five, seven," he spat back, eyes fixed on the code.

With almost rehearsed precision, Alex flipped the respective toggles into the ON position. It turned the action stations "Hot." It activated the missile causing today's problem. Next move was up to the crew. Alex had no authorization to initiate the launch.

---

[10] In case of a nuclear attack, an Emergency Action Message (EAM) will be issued in accordance with the Single Integrated Operational Plan (SIOP) from the National Military Command Center at the Pentagon or, if it has been destroyed by an enemy first strike, by the Alternate National Military Command Center - Site R at Raven Rock or by the Boeing E-4B National Airborne Operations Center alerting all missile launch facilities, silos, and military command centers.

"Standby for keys!" The commander and deputy both poised directly behind Alex leaned into their respective consoles. Fingers tightly gripped on the spring-loaded safety locks they were synchronized for the next action command.

Alex was ready. His mind had already calculated the correct sequence. Tensed in anticipation, his focus was on the status board.

"Three…two…one…" the commander bellowed. "Commit Launch Key." The order was prompted by "Verify count sequence." Every pair of eyes shifted to the computer monitor mounted overhead, tense, waiting.

In rapid sequence, a series of computer-generated text scrolled across the screen. The commander called out each command sequence on display. The deputy repeated each step.

LAUNCH ENABLED — Check…BATTERIES ACTIVE — Check…APS POWER — Hot…SILO READY — Check…GUIDANCE SYSTEMS — Check…FIRING SEQUENCE — Check!

Alex, tensely waiting for the last call to scroll across the screen, was mentally recording the sequence. It would determine the outcome of the test. The suspense was nerve wrecking. Despite his usual coolness, beats of sweat had formed across his forehead. The last call could trigger WWIII. There it was…final command:

LIFT OFF…CANCELLED!

Brian, posed a few feet in back, watched in awe.

Ears tuned in on the calls, Alex's focus had been on the status indicators. With the last command executed, his gaze shot at the station printer pumping out paper. Right away, he didn't like the results. Face taut, subconsciously his fingers repeatedly rubbed across his stubbed chin. His face, normally expressionless, now appeared stressed. He vaguely shook his head.

"What's the verdict?" an anxious commander wanted to know.

"Not gonna like it," Alex responded, "nothin' wrong this end."

"What 'ya mean?" the commander sputtered, "nothing wrong!"

"Launch sequence's normal," Alex explained. "System's sound…interface's solid…software as expected. What'd want from me?" He ignored the commander's verbal onslaught that followed. His eyes shifted back to the printout. *There's got to be some anomaly,* he thought, and pulled up the status log. Several minutes went by in silence, then Alex looked up. "Think we got something." His eyes sought out a still-ranting commander. "Problem's," he indicated, "distant end." He knew what was coming but kept his cool.

"That's just great!" It was a vicious response. The commander punched his own palm, then gave the console a kick, growled, "@#$%," and stormed off. It appeared he couldn't restrain himself. He sought out time to calm his rage.

The center had turned silent. Brian shot Alex a quizzical look who only shrugged his shoulders. They waited in anticipation until the commander returned minutes later. It appeared he'd composed himself. In a calculated move, planting his body in front of his civilian opponent, he stared at Alex for the next action. "What's your call?"

Alex braced himself for another onslaught. "Silo." *And there it is.*

A barrage of insults let loose again. "You…@#$%."

Alex didn't like it either but saw no alternatives. He had to get to the root of the problem. The log status pointed to a problem with the silo. There had been an unexpected data entry from the selected launch tube. Apparently, an error registered just after igniting the rocket engine.

"Which means…?"

"Do it again?"

On hearing that, once more, the fuming commander spat out vehemently.

"I'll be gentle." Alex sounded serious but couldn't suppress a sly grin. Even he had a mean streak, but he was smart enough to avoid the piercing stare, or even a punch, from an irate commander. Alex gestured at his buddy anxious to get out of there.

"Thought he's gonna deck you," Brian grinned on the way out while being escorted to the elevator.

"Notify the crew," they heard the commander bark the order.

"Next?" Brian asked.

"Hell's Kitchen!"

"Huh?" Brian seemed puzzled. He mull over the odd response. His face had taken on a bewildered look.

Alex came to the rescue. "Log status isolated the problem to Oscar flight, Silo One."

MINUTEMAN III (Missile Silo)

Both were strapped in the BMW heading east. "Not a happy camper," Brian gestured at the center they just left, "back there." He was still trying to digest the verbal exchange between Alex and the crew chief. As far as he could tell, the system was still in critical state.

Keeping his eyes directed on the road ahead, Alex explained, "Generally, a squadron's responsible is for five flights with ten missiles each, total of fifty missile silos. They're spread over a wide area identified by labels of doom and gloom picked by the mission personnel. Oscar One's east of Cheyenne, WY, near I-80."

After the brief silo illustration, Alex had retreated into his personal shell. His mind appeared in analysis mode, trying to come up with a fix for the issue ahead. To Brian, hanging on to the handrail, it became obvious that this was no ordinary problem his buddy was dealt. The BMW was clawing its way east, cutting corners on the narrow road as it weaved past wheat fields and farming meadows. He finally tapped his buddy on the shoulder to get his attention.

"What?" Alex edged his view to the passenger seat but still kept the fields ahead, checking for landmarks.

Hair tussled by the rushing air, snapshots of his facial profile were exposed across a high forehead. *Still looks well for his age,* Brian envied. "Slow down." Speeding recklessly on the two-lane country road, he was concerned for their safety.

"Not to worry." Alex's face took on a broad grin. "No traffic here."

"Guess not." Brian relaxed. "It's your ticket." About the only traffic on the road were periodic supply trucks and vans bringing supplies to replenish the flight crews.

"Back there?" Brian picked up on the verbal exchange at the launch center.

"Got their attention," Alex mocked through tightly clenched teeth, "didn't I?"

"Sure did—made your point."

It became apparent that Alex set out to prove that the system was flawed. Regardless of periodic simulation test and diagnostic runs, component compositions did change. The test routine remained unchanged. Alex helped push a system to its limits. It was called stress testing.

"What about the silo?"

"Reverse testing." Most test plans never considered that option. He'd been working this concept for most of his career. "It's a model used in mathematics. Why not use it in infrastructures?"

"Clever." Brian had renewed admiration for his buddy. *It's why he's been so successful.*

"How far out?"

Alex motioned at the dashboard. "GPS."

"Right." Brian held his focus on the panel. *Technology, can't live without it.* He kept quiet for the remainder of the trip. He tried to envision the complexity of a missile defense system. Questions popped into his mind about how silos were connected with the launch center. How much shielding was necessary to protect a capsule from a direct hit? How deep did the cables have to be buried to keep tilling plows from slicing through? Where were the weak points? One single fanatic could unleash the destructive powers of a nuclear device.

He tried to imagine the nation with all communication capabilities wiped out. Computers, databanks, electronics, all burned up. Nothing functional. Not even a wristwatch. Banks shut down, along with Wall Street and other exchanges. Cell phones, ATMs, and credit cards would be useless. Air traffic, shipping, ground transportation all would come to a halt not to mention the chaos that would ensue in hospitals, law enforcement, workplaces, and homes. Not even a microwave would work. Life as everyone knew it would come to a halt, at least until equipment could be repaired and rebuilt. But repaired with what? Manufacturing would be out along with commuting. There'd be no transportation other than bike or buggy.

He was slightly winded just from thinking about the ultimate disaster. "Your last project," he finally broke the silence, "with SAC, what was that?"

"Tactical launch console...nuclear hardened...packaged into a suitcase for both Minuteman and Peacekeeper. In other words," Alex boasted, "I built a portable missile launch case."

"Whoa!" Brian exclaimed, totally impressed about the ultimate engineering. "Isn't that the case the president's aid carries around?"

"That's the Football," Alex clarified. "That one contains only the launch codes."

"Right," Brian answered. He tried not to appear more ignorant. He was still overwhelmed by the performance back at the launch center.

"Had a small team of techs," Alex went on, "to lend a hand with blueprints and assemblies." He'd been chosen for his German language skills. The project had required interfacing with Siemens in Germany. At the time, it was the only company that manufactured nuclear hardened components. "Had to persuade management to manufacture new components," he explained. "Radiation suppressors, spark arrestors, power filters...you know. You see," he stated, "up till then we had nothing large enough to filter out EMP[11] pulsing from a direct hit."

"I had no idea," Brian replied, "that Germans were into nuclear technology." It was difficult for him to imagine a foreign nation building such critical components. After all, it involved national security to the highest level.

"Remember," Alex posed the question, "operation Paper Clip? Nuclear scientists recruited during the '40s?"

"Sure do... the Von Brauns, Tellers, and Oppenheimers."

"Right," Alex settled with a grin, "you could say we capitalized on technology by osmosis."

"Funny." He eyed his buddy with suspicion. "It's a side of you I haven't seen much."

"What? I can be funny," Alex insisted. "It's living alone; I lose touch with people. My focus is usually on issues you see and hear on newscasts...political mostly."

"You always focused?"

"Like to get the facts straight before making a decision."

Wish I had his analytical skills. Brian watched Alex slow into a tight turn away from the main road. "We're here?"

"Yep."

"Where...?" Brian could not detect anything remotely resembling a missile silo. He'd expected something like a launch pad or support structure above ground but only

---

[11] Electromagnetic Pulse is a burst of radiation generated by gamma rays and neutron pulsing caused by a nuclear explosion, solar burst, or cosmic rays (such as a supernova).

recognized a slab of concrete halfway buried in the middle of a field. The only gadgets visible were security sensors. Yet, closer up, he became aware of the huge circular blast cover made up of solid steel and concrete, overgrown with sagebrush and weeds. Alongside were a couple air vents with an entry hatch leading down into the silo.

"Follow me." Alex had already jumped out. With quick strides he led the way to the silo hatch.

"That it?"

"That's it." Alex, for a moment, stood indecisive. Seconds later, the decision was taken from his hands. Like a ghostly aberration, two armed sentries appeared out of nowhere, rigidly poised across the path blocking the entrance. Both wore sidearm in addition to automatics—M-16s, safety off, ready to fire.

"Stop," was the imminent warning.

Alex reacted quickly. He lifted both arms into a defensive posture indicating they were unarmed.

"IDs." It was not a request. It was an order.

Alex handed him his credentials. Apparently, they'd not been notified of their arrival. "Damn him," Alex muttered. He should have expected something like this. "Guy at the command center," he grumbled, "giving us a hard time."

"What?" The sentry gave him a warning stare, unsure if the cussing was directed at him.

"Nothing," Alex said. "Command's supposed to notify you guys."

Calls should have been initiated, authorizations granted to avoid unnecessary delays. "Not our problem," Alex assured Brian who'd patiently followed the verbal exchange.

The hatch cover finally opened up. A missile operator stuck his head out. He motioned them over. The sentries backed away then silently disappeared into the hilly terrain.

"Been waiting for you guys," the Missileer said. He apparently recognized Alex from earlier encounters but suspiciously eyes his companion, "You Harris?"

"Brian Harris," Alex gestured at his buddy. "Check with Jackson."

"You're cleared," the Missileer replied. "Got temporary permission from NORAD." He then gestured below, "Follow me." It appeared allowing the extra visitor below was worth the risk. It was not unusual for the silo to receive an occasional dignitary interested in the underground based defense system.

"Awesome." Brian could not contain his surprise. He was overwhelmed by the immediate sight. There, in all its glory, was the most destructive device mankind had ever built, the towering giant of nothing less than a Minuteman III, intercontinental ballistic missile—ICBM[12]. The shimmering giant sat majestically in its silo eight levels deep. Super-cooled stream escaped from its colossal bowels. It'd been sitting there for fifty some years awaiting action. The only action it had seen, aside from routine maintenance, was the occasional technology upgrade.

---

[12] An intercontinental ballistic missile is a ballistic missile with a long range (greater than 3,500 miles) typically designed for nuclear weapons delivery (delivering one or more nuclear warheads). Due to their great range and firepower, in an all-out nuclear war, land-based and submarine-based ballistic missiles would carry most of the destructive force, with nuclear-armed bombers supplementing the effort.

Brian cautiously followed Alex and the missile man down the lofty staircase. *Looks like Hell's kitchen.*

The silo was a self-contained capsule. The only direct connection it had was through miles of buried cables extending out from the LCC. Missile status was continuously checked for readiness by computers running sophisticated mission software with functions to test the interface along with updating launch and flight trajectory. Thousands of parts were patiently sitting at idle waiting for a trigger command. One such command had been issued an hour earlier but failed to ignite.

They were ushered to the command room. Too much time had already been wasted. Again, Alex, seemingly in his natural element, took over the controls. All business—no distraction…last line of defense. With expert motions he set up controls and trigger logs to trap potential errors during the next simulation. It took fewer than ten minutes to set up the necessary system parameters. "Ready," he informed the missile chief. The test could be initiated. The alert was sounded. Brian watched in fascination the many steps with which each Missileer was tasked.

There was some brief commotion. It appeared one crew member was caught at the bottom of the silo when the alarm went off. His combat boots resonated through the silo tube in the midst of the escaping steam as he clambered up the ladder to safety. He barely made it to the safety vault.

The silo chief had already initiated the launch sequence. He'd executed each step as received from the LCC. The only difference from a real launch was the manual steps he and the crew had to perform. It was a built-in safety backup in case the launch center went out of commission.

"Missile away…" was the final call just carried out.

The first visible action for the launch again was close to chaotic. First, there was a grinding sound directly above. Brian jerked his head up just in time to see the blast door fly off. Next, the firing sequence ignited the first stage of the rocket. The ensuing force traversed through the length of the missile body. Vibration filled the entire silo, reverberating up and down the concrete walls. The missile was seconds away from liftoff. It was the critical point for "Go—No go."

This being a test, at the last second the crew commander gave the signal for shutdown. Moments later, the silo was doused in silence. The launch had been scrubbed. This time, it was a planned abort. Brian's ears were ringing. He was poised behind Alex watching over his buddy's shoulders. His senses were bewildered but his eyes followed Alex's every move. Inches away, the diagnostic software returned gobs of coded data. Alex analyzed the continuous streams as quickly as it scrolled across the screen. *Must be genius reading that speed.*

"Ah yes." Alex gestured at the streams of data. His tensed body relaxed into the softness of the chair. "What I expected," he muttered. "There it is." Reading the log's firing sequence, he found a rocket igniter relay had stuck. It did not close the path to one of the rocket engines. "Easy fix," he proclaimed. "Launch could have been catastrophic."

The launch could have resulted in the missile exploding within the silo, a target acquisition failure, or a nuclear detonation someplace within range of the nation's population. "Test results should be enough to save the commander's career," Alex justified, "back at the LCC…Let's get outta here."

Aside from a speeding Alex shaking up the countryside, the drive back to the Castle went uneventfully. The sky over the Rockies had already darkened. After a day of extraordinary events, nighttime had set in. On the way, both enjoyed a deserving dinner at a local restaurant. The iced-down glass of beer felt great. It was getting late. "Listen," Brian barely suppressed a yawn, "Gotta get some sleep…early flight out…director wants me back for a briefing."

Back at the Castle he immediately sought out the guestroom. Alex was still too tense to retire for the day. He poured himself a Jägermeister, neat, his favorite brandy imports from Germany. It always helped settle the mind. Next morning he would be alone again. He felt the loneliness of the place take hold once more. *Have to call Lisa.*

Lisa, or 'Liz' as she was known to her friends, was his eldest daughter. She was his sounding board. *Wish she'd live closer.* He picked up the phone and dialed. There was no answer. Her voice mail took the call. He left a brief message for her to call back. He'd invited her earlier in the year to spend time here, or at least bring her kids during summer break. She hadn't responded yet. Drained and disappointed, he suddenly felt tired. He turned off the lights and made his way down the hall towards the bedroom, hoping for a peaceful rest. Completely satisfied with the day's events, he wished there were more such challenges. After all, it was his life.

Troubleshooting…Analysis…Adventure… His last thoughts gradually made way to a world of dreams and nightmares.

LISA BAUER

"APB…all units…11-80, Silverado & Lincoln…10-78 needed…dispatch 11-85…Code 54." She'd been listening to the static of the short wave as usual when on standby duty. *That's my call,* her brain registered. Her emergency-tuned body went into immediate reaction. She dropped the dishes into the sink and hastened from the counter, wiping her hands dry on her tightly fitted jeans. *Keys, wallet, ID…what else?* A fleeting glance at the hallway mirror reflected a body ready for action. *Something's missing.* Shoes!

Liz grabbed the set of keys from the kitchen counter just before jumping in the vehicle.

"10-4…Unit nine," she was quick to respond. Crouched in the seat, one hand clutching the steering wheel, Liz kicked the shifter into gear and reached for the talk button. "What's the condition?"

"Code 54—Possible 10-54d." What may have sounded as gibberish to another listener, to her was a routine emergency call. The code identified an overturned tanker leaking combustible material with possible dead bodies. Most of her calls were brush fire related that required air support, but in this case, the middle of the city required ground support. Traffic was already backing up. She flipped a switch. The siren cleared the way. Traffic lights were synchronized to allow her passage. Most drivers moved out of the way to allow her passage, but, as usual, there was that resistive driver disregarding the emergency. It forced her to weave in and out around the obstructions while the blaring air horn cleared the rest of the way. *Was it all worth it? The struggle…the aggravation…the frustration?* she asked herself, speeding towards the crash. *It's my calling* was the usual response. It gave her great satisfaction to help others, and to feel in charge. She'd rather give than take orders.

She could feel a buzzing in her jeans pocket. Ready to take the call, she checked the caller ID. "Not now, Dad." *You'll have to wait.*

Up ahead, the person that called the emergency gave her directions to the scene. *There it is.* The overturned tanker was easy to spot. It blocked four lanes of traffic. Commuting drivers and passing pedestrians were already on the scene speculating, as usual, about the cause of the accident. Sliding to a stop, she made three quick calls. The first was to the local police station. "Already on the way," she was told. The second went for an ambulance. Standard call for most accidents; someone always got hurt. The last went out to the Hazmat team. Hazmat, being a federal issue, would take longer to respond. There was generally nobody on immediate standby. Agents and members of that team had to be notified at wherever they held jobs. It was a mix of duty and volunteer assignments.

It took hours to sort things out and clean up the mess. With the help of a crane, the overturned tanker was eventually removed. Street and sidewalks were scrubbed with anti-agents, but not before thousands of gallons of biochemical materials had washed into the city's drainage system. "More irreversible damage to the eco system," she muttered ruefully, "flooding the delta." *As if we need more pollution.* As was usual for a call of this nature, Liz was disturbed by the ensuing contamination. It would take years for nature to cleanse the waste. End result was always the same: damage, cancer, and even death to land, human, and animal life alike. But those were statistics not readily collected. Life went on.

With the emergency taken care of Liz could relax once more. She remembered her dad's message. Reaching for the mobile, she dialed his number.

NSA HEADQUARTERS (Ft. Meade, MD)

The place was bustling with activity. Recent political tensions had intensified in the Far East, Asia, to be precise. Jack Warner, Head of Operations, was comfortably planted in his executive chair. The contours of the seat perfectly fit his body. Presently he was leafing through the morning's briefs. The report would be late. Something must have held it up. It should have been on the president's desk an hour ago. The president was adamant about getting the daily brief on time. It would direct his demanding schedule for the day. Warner's hand reached for the remote. He'd have to check the newscasts. They usually carried events from the previous night. It'd give him a clue.

His eyes were absorbed in the report with ears tuned in to the flat screen TV mounted on the opposite wall. It seemed the remote in his hand had its own mind. It was busy switching channels. Impatient and edgy as usual, he'd been toggling between AP, World News, CNN, Fox, and Reuters for the latest developments. Most of the data was fed by his Intel satellites sweeping across Iran, North Korea, and other global hot zones. Suddenly, his mind registered something. *That's it.* He paused to listen to the report.

"Today, tensions between North and South Korea have boiled over. Shots were fired by both sides, leaving at least two marines dead and wounding more than 13 others. The conflict came to a head when the North fired artillery at an island belonging to the South in the Yellow Sea," the report stated, according to military officials. It was the hot news item for the day on Headline News. There was more…the regime in Pyongyang effectively affirmed that Kim's son Kim Jong-Un would succeed his father as the next ruler of North Korea…The North continues to upgrade its ability to make nuclear weapons… the spokesman for CNN reported.

"This'll definitely strengthen the agency's position," Warner muttered. He was in the habit of expressing his sound verbal skills whether he was alone or had an audience. Everybody on his staff was aware. It set precedence. It was a dominance that had helped him achieve the position he'd obtained with the organization. *Leave the details to the subordinate,* was his motto, *as long as I have control.* He didn't have much of a philosophy on world events. He just processed the news. Politicians and diplomats did the rest.

Warner was still marveling about how the "'net" had developed in just a few years. His focus had finally settled on Fox News, his favorite channel. In the past, he used to have to sift through daily stacks of wire printouts to get the news. It had to be filtered, analyzed, and categorized to compile reports. Despite the effort it used to take, it gave him a nostalgic notion. Life used to be "paced, organized, and structured." Today, the world had turned impatient. Everybody wanted instant updates, especially consumers and newsmongers. He wasn't sure what was driving what anymore—media feeding the consumer or consumers demanding instant news. Lacking visual perception by the individual, the news business morphed into a whole new industry, with management focus on ratings and the bottom line. "Free enterprise," he reminded himself. He wasn't complaining. As long as conflicts endured, so did his job.

The phone buzzed. "Yeah," Warner answered in his callused, impatient demeanor.

"Priority call." It was his secretary. Warner switched to secure and picked up.

"Sir," an impersonal voice announced, "we have a situation."

It jerked his body upright. A "situation" was never good news. It disturbed the harmony. His adrenalin surged. "What?"

"Pentagon office," the voice reported, "problem with KH."

"Who do we have there?" His mind acted fast. He wasn't about to get sucked into interagency issues. He delegated. Hand off responsibility. It was a gambit he'd learned back in college taking business management. It worked every time. It cleared the way to a scapegoat, if necessary.

"Tracy Bauer."

"Get in touch with her. Tell her to get back to me immediately. Also," he collected his thoughts, "get me Brian Harris on the phone." He slammed the receiver back in its cradle. His blood pressure was on the rise. He could feel it surge through his veins. He knew the symptoms well. He used to get alarmed at the dizziness and shortness of breath. It mostly happened during a developing crisis. But then, over the course of several visits to the doctor, he was assured there wasn't anything wrong with the heart. It was simply hypertension. Relieved, he was able to control it with the help of medication. *Thank God for the miracle of modern science.* Kept in the desk drawer, he popped a couple beta-blockers. It gave him instant relieve. He quickly felt the anxiety fade. Distant images of Tracy took hold.

He reached for the remote and turned down the sound. He'd gotten the news he needed for the day. He could sit back and wait for the call. Relaxed once more, he thought back to when he hired Tracy. Several years had gone by but he could still remember.

It was this same office late one morning that she'd walked in for a scheduled interview. Taken somewhat by surprise, he found himself confronted by a stunning young woman with extraordinarily exotic facial features. Immediately, pheromones took hold of his senses.

"Hi," she'd said, reaching out, "Tracy Bauer." Oblivious to her firmly extended hand, he watched her approach the desk. She was about five-foot-six and shapely, very shapely. *Must spend hours at the gym*, he'd speculated. She was dressed smartly, looking very professional. His gaze lingered on her face. *Exotic,* he recalled, *and body and legs to match.* Reminded of social etiquettes, he jumped up from the comfort of the chair, reached for her hand, and invited her to be seated. Much like a statuette, she sat there by the desk, beauty, intelligence, and self-assurance emanating from her presence. Introduction and formality out of the way, their conversation touched on personal anecdotes and a brief summary on her past and how she'd gotten here. He then proceeded to give her a recorded lecture on the agency, the mission, and position she might fit in.

There was a persistent ring. It took seconds for him to realize it was from the present. *Too bad*, he thought. He'd liked dwelling on their first meeting. It stirred up pleasant memories. It was times like these that he wished he were single.

He reached for the phone. It wasn't the voice he'd hoped.

"What's up?" It was Brian Harris on the line.

"I want you back," he informed the caller. "Immediately! Got a potential crisis on my hands. Need your expertise on this one. And," he emphasized, "I'm assigning one of our strategists to you. Let me know when you get in." He briskly terminated the call. The call waiting line was flashing red. He toggled to connect.

"Tracy," the caller stated. Her voice sounded just as he remembered, pleasant, but direct and professional.

"Understand you're assigned to the Pentagon."

"I am," she responded, "SPACECOM."

"Give me the current status on the KH," he demanded. He immediately regretted his harsh tone. Somebody would catch the blame, but not her. Who, was yet to be decided.

"Critical state," she said. "Better alert NORAD to elevate DEFCON[13]."

Mellowed by her assertive tone, he relaxed. *Must be on top of things*, he decided. "I'll handle that. And one more thing," he insisted, "I'll have you work with an analyst…our best. He'll be here in a couple of days. In the meantime," he paused to take a breath of air, "I want you to gather telemetry data for the last three months on the troubled birds. You'll be assigned to him until the issue's resolved."

"Agreed," she promised. "We'll keep you in the loop."

---

[13] Defense Condition – National Defense Readiness for threat levels one through five. DEFCON alerts apply to the United States national defense designated for global readiness. Since the inception of DEFCON, there has never been a peaceful state of DEFCON-5, because, there has always been a war or conflict somewhere on the globe. Level-4 is considered normal. The alert status remains there unless elevated to DEFCON-3 or 2 through various threat conditions. Since the end of WWII, the world has only seen DEFCON-2 one time in October 1962 during the Cuban missile crisis. We are hoping never to see DEFCON-1, since it means all out nuclear war.

PENTAGON (NSA Liaison Office)

He showed up in her office the following day. "Brian Harris and…you are?"

It was a pleasant sounding voice. Her face shifted from the huge flat-panel wall-mounted monitor to face the man in the doorway. *Must be the expert Warner mentioned.* Extending a hand in welcome, she jumped to her feet. "Tracy." She already liked what she saw as he closed the distance—well-dressed, well-groomed, bristling with self-confidence, and, to her delight, a touch of class. Yet he projected a subtle arrogance.

"Bauer, by any chance?" he inquired.

"Why, yes," she responded. "How'd you know?"

"Psychic ability," he said with a smug grin.

"Really?" She was pleasantly enlightened. She took him seriously. "Clairvoyant?"

"I wish," he reluctantly gave in. "Just saw your dad at his Castle a couple days ago."

What a surprise. "Where do you know him from?" She was genuinely elated. "How is he?"

"Says hello and…" he took a deliberate pause to assess her beauty, "you owe him a visit."

"I know…I know," she replied with a hint of apology, "been busy."

She allowed herself a closer inspection. Her eyes gauged the full extent of this man. There was something familiar about him. *I know.* It suddenly came to her. *Dad.* He emanated traits similar to those of her father, whose qualities she'd always adored. Who wouldn't? She idolized her dad. He'd say, "Always act professional," and went on to explain that, "without decent qualities, you might as well forget a successful career." According to him, there were too many bums in the business already, stepping on one another with little regard for individual integrity.

She met him head on. "I've been expecting you. Warner forewarned me."

"Forewarn is a strong tag," he responded as he approached her. With a firm grip he shook her hand.

"Didn't mean it like that." She was quick to correct. "It's just…your reputation precedes your presence."

"Don't believe everything you hear. Know why I'm here?" His cordial voice suddenly shifted. It turned all businesslike.

"To help solve the KH crisis." She gestured at the visitor chair. "Have a seat."

"Okay…what've you got for me?" She watched his gaze shift around the office. *He's assessing my space.* It was obvious. He seemed pleased. He made himself comfortable.

"Here's the thing," she said, matching his professional demeanor. "A couple of months ago," she reported, "I noticed a drift in a satellite group from Iridium Grid Six. By the way," she wanted to make sure, "are you familiar with Iridium?"

"Yes." The response was abrupt. He shot a quick glance at her. He sounded annoyed to even have to address the issue.

"Didn't mean to question your integrity," she corrected herself. Slightly embarrassed for having doubted his expertise she went on. "Since then, we've made a number of adjustments, but none have fixed the problem." They both knew, at this rate, the fuel source would not support the energy drain on the satellites in question for long. A failure could put the entire grid in jeopardy. "To make things worse," she took a quick pause, "for the past few days we haven't been able to upload new software to override the persistent drifts. It seems we've been locked out of the system."

Iridium was the code name for a constellation of 108 satellites put into orbit in the '80s. Iridium had an element count of one hundred eight on the periodic table, thus the name. It provided global communications coverage for military and Intel applications. Initially, it was a highly classified system, but with the end of the Cold War and the onset of cellular phones, the system was transitioned to commercial usage. The typical lifespan for satellites of this type was five years, after which its orbit degraded and it eventually burned up in reentry into the atmosphere. To replace and replenish the spent units to continue uninterrupted communication coverage, periodic rocket launches were necessary.

He seemed deep in thought. "You with me," she asked. It prodded him to attention. She had become slightly annoyed while explaining the problem. He appeared to just be sitting there preoccupied.

"Why—yes." His response was deliberate. "Just thinking."

"You seem disinterested," she charged. "Please talk to me. It's important you follow me."

He seemed irritated at the sudden patronage. He shot an annoyed glance at her then fired back, "Unlike your other peers," he sneered, "did it occur to you some of us have the ability to multi-task?"

"Honestly, no." She immediately regretted her abrasiveness. *What am I saying; I don't even know the guy.* "Sorry."

"Accepted." Appeased once more, he relaxed but held her gaze. "Go on."

"It's important you understand the issue."

"You already said that." His face turned serious. "Is there a problem?"

"No problem."

"Look, lady," he countered, "you may not be aware of certain facts, but I designed the damned grid."

"Iridium?" She hesitated. "I had no idea." Her tension gradually melted. Her initial doubts had disappeared. She got up from the chair and advanced towards him. Poised directly in front, she extended her hand. With a hint of smile, she begged, "Forgive me?"

"Forgiven." Unintentionally, he'd won the first round. "Tried to reset the password through the backend?"

"Using Code Breaker?"

"Apparently you did."

"Tried every tool in the arsenal." She shrugged. "But nothing seems to work. It's almost as if," she returned to her chair, "someone's shut the ports down. So far, every attempt to get into the software's failed. Consensus's to wait for reentry and let them burn up, but that could take months, even years. Besides the potential security risk, public safety is at stake. Another solution's to shoot them out of the sky."

"Not an option." He was adamant. There were ASATs[14] in orbit, but they were not supposed to exist. Any foreign agency getting wind of it could create major political

---

[14] In contrast to communication satellites, and uncommon knowledge to the general public, there was a breed of anti-satellite weapons moving in low orbit termed attack satellites. These ASATs had been secretly deployed for years. Developed during the Cold War as part of space warfare, the purpose of these was to eliminate missiles and other threats initiated by a hostile nation from entering U.S. airspace. That was the official posture within the political realm of the U.S. government. Its purpose, however, was much more sinister. The real reason was

tensions. "Can't afford any more visibility than we already have. You know…public outcry, privacy intrusion, and all that."

"You're right." She reached for a stack of folders from the desk. "Here." They contained up-to-date telemetry data from the satellites in question.

"Let's see what we've got." He sounded reassuring. It eased her fears.

They spent hours going over reams of data. Nothing obvious jumped out at them. He seemed familiar not only with the rows and rows of printed information but also the software that generated the data. Back in the early '80s, he explained, he'd been part of the software development team for the first group of stealth satellites put into orbit. Then, as now, it was still a closely kept secret, even within the general employees at NSA. Only a few individuals had access to programs such as Misty. "Misty" was a new breed of birds designated for stealth in space, similar to what the F-111 and B-2 bombers were to the skies. Virtually undetectable to radar, they were found only in the U.S. satellite arsenal.

"Need to get in touch with NRO[15]," he said, finally breaking the silence. "Gotta get a list of current ASAT assets."

"Should I make the call?" She was eager to please him. Working alongside him for hours, she'd gained new respect. He'd made an occasional comment, but mostly to himself. *Seems to know what he's doing.*

"Better let me handle this," he suggested. "Sensitive issue. Won't get anything over the phone. You know…plausible deniability. I know the deputy secretary. He'll get us the information. I'll be sure to include you in the visit."

She stood up to stretch her legs. A few paces later, she said, "Okay. What's next?"

"That's it." It was more than a suggestion. Apparently, he had had enough reading figures and numbers. His face looked spent. It was not apparent to her but he was exceedingly disheartened. He seemed displeased with himself for not having gotten a fix on the problem. "We both need a break." Thus the first of possibly many exhaustive working days together ended.

"Where're you staying?" She threw a quick glance at his handsome features then collected her personal things, getting ready to leave. He briskly followed her to the exit.

"Arlington Marriott," was a weary reply. "If it wasn't so late," he suggested, "I'd ask you out for a drink."

"Kind of tired myself," she replied. "Take a rain check?"

"Hold you to it," he grinned, "even if it rains." He turned and walked off.

Her eyes followed him as he headed to the carport. "See you tomorrow," she called after him. He briefly turned. There was a hint of promise in his smile. Lighthearted, she slid behind the wheel of her own car and drove off with a quick glance at the rearview mirror to see him getting into his rental.

Back at the hotel, Brian reflected on the day's events. He realized they had accomplished little other than confirming the problem. It was clear he had a tough situation on his hands. This was a critical event. The telemetry had unveiled nothing. The software

---

known to only a select group of scientists and mission defense personnel. ASATs, by design were kinetic energy weapons deployed to destroy any possible threat in space such as foreign satellites and other spy objects.
[15] National Reconnaissance Office

seemed to perform precisely as it was designed. It seemed absurd, not being able to access the most critical satellites in NSA's inventory. Years ago, when he designed the system, he saw to it that it had a failsafe against any unauthorized intrusion. It held true for the front end. It held true for the backend. It was the firewall's job, whether local or foreign, to automatically reject an intrusion attempt such as a denial of service attack. There had been no indication of any such kind. This was more serious. *Must be network related.* It was an assumption he didn't like at all.

On most trouble calls, he'd walk in and out in a couple of hours having solved the problem. *Any problem.* In fact, he'd solved most satellite issues remotely from his laptop. He preferred it that way. He'd rather work in the comfort of his den than commute to the office. There may be no choice this time. For now, he was looking forward to spending more time with Tracy. *I'll have to get to know this woman.* It was the last thought as he drifted off into an exhaustive sleep.

NRO HEADQUARTERS (Chantilly, VA)

"What son of a bitch's responsible for this?" John Hanson, deputy director for the National Reconnaissance Office, yelled into the receiver. The ensuing silence at the other end did little to calm his rage. "I want your ass in here ASAP," he barked at his subordinate. "Somebody's gonna hang. Supposed to be the nation's super-secret agency, and," he bellowed, "can't even keep the simplest task under the lid."

"Sit," he ordered his Chief Information Officer as soon as he entered. The man appeared bewildered. "What do you know about this?" The boss was shouting now. Completely out of control, he tossed the morning's *Washington Post* across the desk. It landed in the man's lap.

"Just read it myself."

"I want you to investigate the leak. Get somebody on it immediately. I'm going to hang whoever's responsible."

"Right away," the CIO stammered. He seemed to take the accusation personally. Slightly disheveled, in a hurry, he left his boss's office. Without having a clue of what he'd just heard, he rushed by the reception desk. "Get me a copy of today's Post right away," he ordered the department secretary, then hurried back to his office. He felt like a beaten dog. His nerves were still shaken when the secretary walked in.

"Here." She planted a copy of the Washington Post on his desk, shooting a sympathetic look at him. She must have overheard the executive's outbursts.

"Thanks." Despite the unpleasantness he'd just been subjected to, he caught a glimpse of her shapely legs. *Wonder if she's married.* He couldn't help it. The distraction had calmed him. He unfolded the stack of paper in front of him. He did not have to read far. In disbelief, he stared at the front page.

NRO launches new stealth satellite! Unidentified sources confirmed that yesterday's Titan IV launch put a next generation spy satellite in orbit. The new KE series is replacing the current keyhole surveillance technology which has been in operation since the eighties. The mission will enhance the United States' space defense in as much as it is a kinetic energy anti-satellite system identified as an ASAT.

The article went on to describe some supposedly "highly classified" design details. *Bad news*, he thought. Unsure what steps to take next, he noticed Brian Harris walking down the hallway accompanied by a young woman. They were headed for the boss's office. *Wonder what* he's *doing here?*

"Brian." Muffled, the call seemed to come from inside the DD's office. Hanson waved them both in. "We've a bit of a crisis on our hands," Hanson charmed, "but I'm glad to see you. And…who's this lovely lady?" His face instantly changed to a winning smile. One hand fumbled with his earpiece. The other gestured to the chairs. "Take a seat." He was busy with a call. "Be with you in a minute."

Tracy had a chance to inspect the environment. One would not have guessed that this somewhat insignificant looking place was the epitome of secrecy. Stealth, gloom, and obscurity all at once emanated from a place way above Top Secret. Taking the headset off and addressing Brian, Hanson said, "What brings you to this abode?" His eyes, nevertheless, were focused on Tracy.

"Tracy Bauer," Brian announced, "working the KH problem."

"May not have to worry about that much longer," he said, turning to face Brian. "You read the paper?"

"Wondered about that," Brian said with a gesture. "Saw the article this morning."

Taking a deep breath, Hanson proclaimed, "Somebody's going to jail." Settling into the plush office chair, his posture shifted into social mode. Focus still on Tracy, he queried, "So Brian, how can I help you?"

Slightly irritated, Brian took notice of the DD testing the social waters. "Got a problem," he stated, "with some of your satellites that doesn't make sense. I was going to ask about the latest hardware in orbit, but," he emphasized with a facetious grin, "I have a pretty good idea after reading this morning's paper." He couldn't help but rub in the leak.

"Yeah…I'm already dealing with that!"

"New generation," Brian wanted to know, "replacing what's in orbit now? And if so, how soon?"

"It'll take a few years," he was assured. "We still have to maintain what's already there."

"Was afraid of that," Brian stressed. "We've been bogged down with some problem birds," he explained. "I need your support to shut them down." There was an immediate reaction. Hanson's face reflected extreme resistance. "It's only temporarily," Brian was quick to calm him, "just to run some tests until I get a handle on things."

"In that case," Hanson said, "no problem. Just let me know when. We can do some maneuvering with other, less critical birds. Can you stick around for lunch?"

"Think so," Brian replied. He shot a quick glance at Tracy. "You up for it?" She nodded in return.

"There's a new sushi place nearby I wanna take you to." Hanson made an urgent gesture at the phone. "Use my conference room," he said, handing each a printed folder from the table, then buzzed the secretary to direct the visitors.

He was anxious to take a call on his private mobile. While he was talking with Brian and Tracy, it'd been buzzing silently in his pocket. Checking the caller ID did not ease the tension. He pressed the return call button and waited for the other end to come alive.

"NSC." It was a brisk male voice. "We secure?"

He was anxious to get the call over with. "Secure. What've you got?"

"Special meeting," the mysterious voice demanded. "Sunday—noon."

"Yes?"

"Annapolis, Rotary Club."

"I'll be there." An ominous feeling crept into the pit of his stomach. *Don't like this one.* He quickly pocketed the mobile and headed for the reception room.

Minutes earlier, the department secretary gestured to Brian and Tracy. "Follow me please." She briskly strode down the hallway with Tracy and Brian in tow. They were led to a brightly-lit reception room. Tracy took note of the environment. In the olden days, a hat stand would have been planted by the entrance door with commemorative picture frames selectively planted around the walls. Today, the room was impersonal with only a wastebasket aside from a table and chairs filling the spacious room. The room was void of windows. Most rooms lacked windows in the building. The reasons were obvious. The NRO being the nation's most secure organization, Intel security was always an agenda.

Tracy took comfort in one of the chairs neatly arranged around a conference table. Brian planted his body adjacent. When the secretary left, Tracy was already leafing through the contents of the folder. Brian was reluctant to pick up his. He knew most of the contents from previous visits. He'd rather study her. And he did. Tactfully, not to distract or attract her attention, his eyes lingered on the contours of her well-toned body. He felt a magnetic attraction towards her. He was looking forward to working with her. He cleared his throat to get her attention. She did not stir. Her focus was on the material. *Well,* he thought, dismayed, *I'll wait 'til later,* and consoled himself with the material.

Rifling through the pages brought back sentiments. He remembered the day, back in the early '80s, when his boss had volunteered him for the KH program. Back then, even the NRO name of this super-secret agency was classified. He wasn't too thrilled by the prospect of sitting in front of a computer monitor, writing software day in and day out. He preferred field assignments--where the action was--but reluctantly accepted. In the end, it worked out to his advantage. As a result, he was rapidly promoted up the ranks, with salary boosts to match. After that, he could name his mission and location of preference. *Not a bad deal,* he recalled with satisfaction.

Shifting his focus to the folder, he found it contained information on the latest in satellite technology and programs. It gave him the information he needed. He made a couple more unsuccessful attempts to get Tracy's attention. One time she looked up to return his smile, but as quickly turned back to the material. He checked his wristwatch again. He became bored waiting for the director to show. He would have rather talked to pass time.

He studied her some more. Her high forehead was almost obscured by full-bodied auburn hair flowing gingerly over her shoulders. *How feminine.* Aside from their brief verbal joust yesterday, her voice was pleasing. *The rest of her? Let's just say it's what men dream about.* His gaze lingered on. He was about to interrupt her concentration again when the door abruptly swung open. It was Hanson. "Let's go," he said hastily, "got reservations for noon."

With brisk paces, he led them to the elevator. Once inside, he pushed the button for the garage level. He seemed anxious to beat the lunch crowd. "It's a twenty-minute ride to Tyson's Corner."

Reaching for her arm, Hanson helped Tracy into the staff car. "Watch your head." Planting his body behind the wheel, he adjusted the rear view mirror. It reflected the beauty of her face. "So, Tracy," he encouraged, "tell me a little about yourself."

TRACY BAUER

Tracy sat in the back of the plush company car. Up front, John Hanson was chatting with Brian. Their voices were muted by the steady hum of the engine. "Traffic's slow today," remarked Hanson casually. He was trying to make headway in the stop and go traffic. "Some days I should just skip lunch," she heard him comment.

"Some have the luxury of telecommuting," she wanted to cut in but thought otherwise. Not being part of the conversation, she quietly pursuit her own thoughts. They were trouble thoughts. Her thoughts were focused on the satellite issues. What puzzled her most was the sudden deflection from their predicable orbits. In space for decades, the birds in question had been the most reliable of them all. Given utmost attention by operations, although most obscure to the general public, the KH had taken over the agency's backbone of operations. It was that of stealth and surveillance over the globe, used to be performed by the CIA.

"You like sushi?" It was the deputy director. She didn't seem to hear him. "Tracy," a voice demanded, "you with the program?" The voice was probing her deeply focused thoughts back to the presence.

She caught his intently staring eyes in the rearview mirror. Shifting her body upright, she caught the full view of his face. "Sorry. Just thinking on the reason I'm here today."

"Why don't you share that with us?" he prodded. "What about it, Brian? You don't mind, do you?"

"Not at all," Brian encouraged, hoping to get to know her better. He'd rather be seated in back next to her. The last couple of days in the office had been filled with work only. This might be a chance to get to know her personally. "Go ahead, Tracy. I'd be very interested in hearing your story."

"Dad had a lot to do with it."

"Tell me about it."

"Got enrolled in the Air Force Academy high school." Both she and her sister received their appointments based on stellar grades, great physical fitness, and the best of references—a father in the Department of Defense. District 20 was the Air Force's showpiece of living and learning. Developed for the Air Force back in the '60s, it was their first organized settlement. Situated just north of town, it sprawled across the foothills of the Rockies, making up the western sector of Colorado Springs.

"One day at Polytech," she recalled, "I received a lunch invitation from the dean."

With a hint of doubt in the statement, Hanson remarked, "Strange request from a dean."

"That's what I thought," she agreed, "but I went anyway." It felt a bit strange getting invited out by the head of the school. She contributed it to the connection with her dad. After all, Polytech was a ready source of young academics sought out by the government. From the quiet of the backseat she illustrated the highlights of her scholastic days. She was briefly interrupted by the occasional comment and question from both Hanson and Brian.

"Compelling story," Hanson muttered. His voice was laced with admiration for her. "I'd sure like to meet your dad." *There's more to this young woman than just a pretty face. I'll have to keep my eye on her. She's got potential.* He'd already formulated a tentative plan for a possible political career for her. *There's always room for someone with both feet solidly planted on the ground.*

"I'll tell him to look you up next time he's in town."

"Sure do."

"I'm impressed," Hanson admitted, "with your progress with the agency."

"Why'd is that?" she asked. "I paid my dues."

"That's right," he recalled, "you were on the frontlines tracking jihad elements. Philippines, wasn't it?"

"Yeah," she confirmed, "among other places."

"Squeamish about raw fish?"

"Could eat it every day."

"You'll get your treat as soon as we're out of this traffic."

CIA HEADQUARTERS (Langley, VA)

Like clockwork, Harry Carter arrived 7:30 a.m. sharp at the Langley complex. The silver-gray Mercedes 500 rolled to a halt in his dedicated space, as it did every morning. He checked the immediate environment, then the mirrors, and stepped from his car. It was a habit. Security and safety were always on his mind. He did not like surprises. His six-foot-three-inch frame impeccably dressed, with a well-groomed self-assuring aura preceding his path, he briskly proceeded to the elevators. There was no wait to get to the office this early in the morning. His staff and the bulk of the employees wouldn't arrive until close to 9:00 am. He punched the button. The door to the vertical lift slid close. He arrived seconds later at his level and stepped out. Immediately, he was greeted by the huge skylight illuminating the hallway to its fullest splendor. The four-story glass-enclosed atrium allowed him to enjoy the outdoors in good weather and in bad. It was a place in which the old met the new, and where the original building, constructed in the '60s, merged with the new complex added in the '90s.

As usual, his gaze struck a number of replicas idly suspended from the ceiling, reminding him of his organization's achievements. Visitors couldn't possibly miss the array of formidable model planes decorating the loft. Spanning sixty years on display were the agency's operations and missions beginning with the *U-2*, the first espionage plane, the *A-12 Blackbird* for its unheralded speed and altitude records, and lately, the *D-21 Drone*, first unmanned recon craft, all donated by Lockheed Martin.

Walking the hallways, one could not help but notice the many sculptures and plaques dedicated to the cause of the CIA, with Kryptos prominently towering over the visitor at the entrance to the new building. This immense S-shaped scroll created by Jim Sanborn remained a puzzle to even the most gifted cryptologists. Although some of the encrypted text had been deciphered by scientists and hackers, the remaining enigmatic messages may never be solved.

Twenty-five paces later he arrived in his office—a modern office, a high-tech office, but not without a nostalgic feeling that crept up the pit of the stomach. It left a yearning taste in his mouth. He knew the reason and didn't like it. He'd become a product of the changing times. "Can't turn back time," he muttered into the impeccably kept hallways, consoling himself.

Carter leaned back in the posh chair, grunting in anticipation of facing another day of world events. From the desktop screen, the prominent splash page reached out at him, "Central Intelligence Agency." The agency's homepage brought him back to reality. As with most mornings, there was no shortage of messages needing immediate attention. The pulsating email icon made sure of that.

As usually, he pulled up high priority messages first then skimmed the headlines for global burning points. North Korea...Pakistan...Yemen...the prominent entries of trouble spots lunged out at him. He had agents everywhere reporting to him and his deputies who, in turn, compiled daily reports summarized and formatted specifically for him. It was these reports he presented to the president and his advisors each morning. Today was no exception. He sighed with relief. *No crisis today.* The remaining low-priority mail reported only routine correspondences between embassies and field agents. There was one thing gnawing at him, nevertheless. Yemen in the forefront of wire and news services had become almost a daily occurrence. Over just a short time it had become the world's current hot zone. *Something's brewing,* he contemplated, apprehensive that his agents had not yet identified the source of his concern.

"Need to give Warner a call." He made a mental note.

NSA HEADQUARTERS

"Come in for a second," Jack Warner called out, "will you?" He then released the intercom receiver button on the office base phone. While waiting, he sifted through the daily stack of briefs in the In-Basket awaiting his decisions. He could remember a time arriving at the office when the basket would be practically empty. In those days, he used to savor the rich taste of Columbian Lite while reading highlights in *the Washington Post*. *A different time and epoch,* he reminisced, *days long since passed.* It was a time he dearly missed.

Today, like any other workday, it had been a quick stop at Starbucks for the daily fix, hurrying from one meeting to another, spending hours by the phone, and commuting through impossible traffic only to be repeated the next day. He hated it. Not so much the job. That part was okay. It was prestigious, loaded with prominence, and had its rewards. What he didn't like was the harried lifestyle the nation's capital had turned into.

"Yes, sir," a young face, seemingly nervous and slightly out of breath, announced a couple of seconds later. Appearing flushed, the kid lingered by the opened doorway, shifting uneasily from one foot to the other. He stood there waiting to be invited in. He seemed uneasy but also eager to please his new boss and closed the distance to the desk with a few halting paces after Warner waved him in.

Warner, prepared for another hectic day, handed over a page ripped off a yellow note pad, urging, "Get a search on the name." The kid leaned in to take the hastily scribbled note. Warner added, "And get me Harry Carter on the line."

The kid was halfway to the door then abruptly halted in his steps. He turned with a blank faced look on his face. "Harry Carter?"

"CIA."

"Right away, sir."

Sparky couldn't get back to his workstation fast enough. It was the place he felt safe. It was the place where he excelled. *It happened,* he cheered in silence while wiping a few beads of sweat from his forehead. *First task directed by the boss himself.* Even though he'd been working with the agency for several weeks, he'd only been given minor tasks, usually handed down by some coworker with more seniority. *Today was the day.* He looked at the scribbled note just handed him. His face took on a puzzled stare. There was only one word written on the piece of paper. *That's it?* Regardless, his jittery fingers went to work on the keyboard reserved only for top-secret entries. With heightened anticipation, eyes staring at the monitor, he'd been dying to get his hands on the system. One keystroke brought up the search window reserved for authenticated and approved entries. With another few keystrokes he carefully entered the alphanumeric characters: s e r p e n t.

He was prepared to take a break for a lengthy search and hadn't expected the immediate action initiated by the computer. Bewildered, he followed the software taking control over the terminal. He'd just entered a portal into the world of intrigue, secrecy, and conspiracy. What he experienced reminded him of a time when he was a kid reading spy novels.

Back then, he'd dreamed one day to become part of the intrigue and secrecy. It had taken him many years of hard-earned grades to get him to this point. His labored breathing reflected his anticipation as he watched the screen. With the stroke of a few keys he had initiated the world's most sophisticated application software ever designed by man. He had just awakened the sleeping dragon. CARNIVORE![16]

Fascinated, he stared straight ahead at the screen. He couldn't help it. It captured his imagination. He almost forgot to place the call. Nervously he dialed CIA headquarters.

At the distant end, Warner switched to secure mode on the second ring then picked up the receiver. He was expecting the call. "Warner."

"Hey...what's up?" It was the gruff voice of Harry Carter bellowing in his usual indiscreet manner. "Heard some bird droppings landed in your lap." The words, arrogant as usual, were followed by an offending chuckle.

"I'm dealing with it," Warner hammered back.

"What did you guys do?" Harry continued harassing, "Talk in your sleep?"

"Not funny." Warner tried hard to keep his cool but had to admit, "Looks like the cat's out of the bag."

"ASATs, eh, and kinetics to boost?"

"Don't remind me." He tried to steer the conversation from the news leak.

"So," the head of the CIA wanted to know, "what can I do for you?"

"Ever come across a Serpent?"

"Not that I know. Why?"

"Name keeps popping up in connection with Al Qaeda. Don't have anything in our database. Wondered if you did. We believe it may be a new leader or task force planning an assault."

"On *us*?"

"Could well be."

"I'll pass it along and get back to you."

"Thanks." Leaving a hint of lingering insolence, the call ended as abruptly as it began. Harry already had hung up. "Tactless bastard," Warner grumbled, watching the young assistant approach. "Got anything?"

"Nothing." The kid seemed nervous, like it was his fault the search had turned up empty.

"Relax." Warner offered with a slight smile when he realized his analyst's nervousness. "Keep searching. Try Jihad, Taliban, splinter organizations...get in touch with DIA and Armed Services Intel. They might have something."

"Will do," Sparky said as he stormed off with a new mission. "This is getting exciting." His heart almost leaped from his chest as he hastened back to the software dragon with visions of spooks, spies, and conspiracies.

---

[16] Carnivore is the name given to a system initially implemented by the Federal Bureau of Investigation analogous to wiretapping. Later renamed to Digital Collection System, it was segmented into three packages including Carnivore, Packeteer and CoolMiner, referred to as the DragonWare Suite.

BALTIMORE (Maryland)

He had overslept this morning. It was probably due to jetlag from the return flight from Colorado. It used to never bother him when he was on constant travel status. Presently getting comfortable, he was sitting in a lotus fashion, his favorite position. It limbered up his body and gave him easy access to work from bed. Momentarily, with hands clasped behind his back, he leaned forward to stretch his well-toned body. He then cracked his knuckles, causing a popping sound. *I'm ready,* he decided.

Leaned over the edge of the bed he groped for the laptop where he'd left it the night before. It was sitting idle on top of the nightstand. While he was asleep, the background software had been busy with updates, security scans, and receiving urgent mail. He popped the lid. *It'll take a few minutes,* he thought. *Coffee time!* He jumped from the bed and lumbered to the kitchen. With a few quick moves he prepared the maker, turned it to Brew, and headed for the bathroom. By the time he finished with bathroom errands, the coffee was ready, and so was the computer. He could already smell the refreshing aroma permeating the apartment.

He was about to settle back in bed, then thought otherwise. Cup gripped in one hand with laptop clutched under the other arm, he strode toward the den and planted his body on the desk chair. With Laptop connected, in a swift motion, he selected the secure homepage then punched the "Enter" button. The screen sprang alive in work mode but the software took a few seconds to crank up. He took the time to visit the bathroom.

Laptop should be ready. He took the few strides back to the den, reflecting on his visit at the Castle. He still felt envious when he thought about the place Alex had built, respecting the effort the man put into the construction and design. *Remarkable place, the Castle.* He, in contrast, preferred modern living. That's why he chose a residence in the high-rise. It was the ideal bachelor pad. He could come and go as he pleased without the worries of gardening, upkeep, or maintenance. He'd let others more qualified take care of those. He wasn't a tinkerer. His time was too valuable for diminutive tasks.

Settled in for another day surrounded by computers, network switches, hubs, and routers, he leaned back in the comfort of his chair, facing the immediate task at hand. He plugged the laptop into the internal network then tuned in on the array of servers staged along one edge of the den, patiently humming away. From habit, his eyes automatically scanned the rows of green LEDs to check for red alerts. It would mean another server or workstation needed attention. Not that he needed all the computing power staged and configured on an internal net. They were remnants of his software development years that he'd acquired when testing out new computer applications as they hit the marketplace. Back then, he was especially fond of Microsoft's technology. *Gates did something right,* he reflected, and so had Apple, Macromedia, Norton, and other well-known software entities that had worked themselves out of garages into the mainstream of high-tech IT.

He fingered the keyboard connected to the KVM switch, preparing to check mail. That's about all he used it for when at home. For work, he preferred the much faster servers. It gave him instant access to all resources, but when on the road, he could live with the shortfalls of the portable. Generally connected through a secure high-speed satellite VPN, it'd provide a portal for the sophisticated software he needed to access. Not that he was oblivious to newly created gadget like iPads, iPhones, or tablets hitting the marketplace; he could not quite get used to all the pop-ups and app offerings intruded into his daily life.

At the moment, his eyes caught a High-Pri blinking at him. A one-word text message was waiting. "Help." He knew who'd sent it. Sparky was new to the agency. Brian happened to be in Warner's office when the newly hired junior analyst had reported in. He took an immediate liking to the kid and had promised to show him "the ropes." In return, he'd get Intel without getting bogged down waiting for search results himself. In short, they'd become dependent on each other. In a short time, Sparky did his name proud. He was swift and efficient but had a lot to learn about the complexity of the agency's operation, but that took time.

"What?" His response was just as brief.

"Need access to DOD Intel databanks."

"How deep?"

"Ultra."

"Be a minute." Brian had ready access to most security levels but this one. This level required special authorization from the Top, the Echelon panel that decided on what, when, why, and who deserved access to the nation's most treasured secrets. It had taken Brian years to achieve the level of trust he needed to perform his work as a top analyst. Warner had been patient and lenient with him. Warner knew he used a lot of shortcuts to gain access to information. He didn't condone it, but tolerated it the same. Brian would never compromise this trust. And Warner knew it.

Brian grew with the agency. Periodically published by the organization, he kept up with policies, changes, and new guidelines. Seared into the minds of members working and living within this super prestigious intelligence community, "Safeguard information," was always at the forefront.

A few seconds passed before the proprietary portal page popped up on the screen. "CARNIVORE—CLASSIFICATION ULTRA." Brian was aware of the sensitivity and possible implications of compromising this highly protected and sophisticated application. He was very familiar with the intricate workings of Carnivore. But Carnivore wasn't always enough for his needs. Sometimes it was required to go outside the agency. He was also familiar with applications other Intel organizations were using. Following 9/11, a new paradigm was created that allowed the many Intel organizations to work together, the DHS. "Interoperability" was the new buzzword—along with "Continuity of Operations."

Along with others who shared his development skills, Brain had been tasked with creating a program that would share sensitive data over the public Internet, "The Wire."

"Challenging," was his initial assessment, "but feasible." It had been no easy task to satisfy the inherited paranoia of the many Intel communities. There had been much resistance—political mostly. Regardless, his team went ahead and developed PowerOne. It'd solved the highly secure aspects of Intel for access, authorization, authentication, and delivery over the unsecured public wire.

"You got four hours," he informed Sparky.

"Thanks. I'll get back to you."

PowerOne was a specially designed application acting as secure portal switch. It allowed foreign and local authorization over the rapidly growing Internet wire. The agency still cursed DARPA[17] for turning the once classified Internet over to the public. But it was the public sector that shaped the Internet as it existed today.

Unknown to anyone, he'd given himself admin access rights on a hidden port using the management portal. This solved two needs. One, it gave him access to all system elements; the other was an ability to create additional accounts. Today, he needed an account for Sparky. He gave him a four-hour access lease—approximately how long he'd need to get back data without attracting too much attention by the in-house auditing spooks. It wouldn't be the first time he'd been caught. But his philosophy was such that "It'd be easier to beg for forgiveness than ask for permission up front." The philosophy worked every time. Where others may have put their job in jeopardy by this philosophy, Brian, due to his indispensable position with the agency, seemed to get away with it unscathed.

---

[17] The Defense Advanced Research Projects Agency is an agency of the United States Department of Defense responsible for the development of new technology for use by the military.

ALEX BAUER

It was the early morning hours. His body, stiffened from the comfort of six hours sound sleep, inhaled the briskness of clean mountain air. It felt great. He stretched arms and legs to get the circulation going. These days it was rare for him to get this many hours of rest. He allowed himself to dwell. *Just a few more moments of luxury.* Then it was up and off to the bathroom, the usual first stop. He was about to pick up the shaver but changed his mind. *Later,* he decided on the way out. There was no hurry. He had nothing pressing for the day.

The hallway was still chilled from the night's coolness. It would stay that way until past sunup. He kept the thermostat low during nighttime. It kept the air brisk while his body was warmed by the quilt. Dressed in his morning robe, he headed for the front gate to retrieve the *Daily Gazette.* Pausing for a moment, he could feel the breeze in its full force drifting down the foothills. He tightened the garment around his body. Back inside, his eyes caught today's headlines: *National Security Leak! Today,* the editorial claimed, *the* Washington Post *announced a breach in the nation's defense posture that could have dire political implications with the international community. The NRO...* the front page went on. It immediately perked his interest. As he read the editorial his keen mind was triggered into action by a faint sound.

He tossed the unread paper onto the coffee table and made his way to the equipment room. A pair of strong legs, kept in shape by several flights of stairs, promptly carried him to the ground level. It was the place he spent the most time in when not in the den upstairs. It was the heart pulse of the Castle. The basement was stacked with latest state-of-the-art electronics connected to the den via remote sensors. The place would be the envy to any software developer and network guru. Poised in front of the array of equipment, his eyes quickly scanned the panels neatly stacked up within the confines of the rack mount. In an electronics age of computer blades and databanks, he'd spent some hard-earned cash on a corporate-like data center. It was an expensive investment but efficient and cost effective in the long run. In reality, he didn't need all this computing power. Working with high-end gear was more of a habit dating back to his development days. Nevertheless, he was proud being able to afford this technological luxury. At the moment, his eyes were focused on the faint blinking. What caught his attention was the red alert indicator from a sensor in the auxiliary rack. The rack housed the front-end equipment interconnecting his castle with the outside world, containing mostly firewalls, isolators, and sensors fed by wireless receivers relayed from the Mountain, as well as space borne surveillance equipment.

Alarms had gone off more frequently lately. As of today, he had not been able to pinpoint the source. Running tests and diagnostics so far had not revealed the source of the problem. As usual, he'd shrug it off to cosmic interference. Today was no different. Irritated more than concerned, he reset the alarms and returned to the den. Back upstairs he noted the morning sun had gradually risen over the eastern edge of the Kansas plains. The welcomed rays cast a warming spell on the room. The warmth felt comfortable on his body.

Adventurer by heart, where the world used to be his home, aside from the occasional emergency assist with the defense system, he felt like a recluse entrapped within the sanctity of the Castle. He dearly missed the days of travel, schedules, conflicts, and escapades, but that was another time, in other places.

In retrospect, it seemed much time had slipped by in a once adventurous life. Lounging in his den, recounting the years, it became clear it really wasn't that long ago. *What's thirty years*?

He picked up the paper to finish reading the rest of today's news, but noticed the call waiting winking at him. He recognized the number. It was his eldest daughter. He pushed the autodial and waited for her to pick up. Four rings later she was on the line.

"Dad." Her cheerful voice chirped from the distance, "you all right?"

"Missed you." She always seemed concerned for his wellbeing. Ever since the divorce from her Mom, the family fell apart. Most times he felt like a stranger to the family. With his daughters pursuing fulltime careers, raising children and tending to husbands, there never seemed to be time for get-togethers. He had to change that.

"That's why I'm calling about." She went on, "I thought, if you're gonna be home I could bring the kids out. They're on school break and bored with me working. Besides, they could use some of the mountain air."

"That'd be terrific. When?"

"Next week."

"Let me know the day."

"Will do. Bye Dad. Love you." She'd hung up.

Alex was overjoyed. *Company at last.*

Another call was waiting. He checked the number. The caller ID announced a familiar area code. He recognized it as D.C. but could not place the number.

With piqued curiosity, he pushed the caller return button.

Brian picked up at the other end. "You saw the news?"

"NRO leak? Just read it. What do you make of it?"

"All hell broke loose around here. Someone's gonna get axed."

"Don't blame them. This is serious stuff," Alex agreed. "Leak like this causes all kinds of tensions, political and otherwise. We'll hear from the Russians and Chinese, that's for sure. How's it affecting you?"

"Saw the director this morning…downplayed the incident."

"What's his take?"

"Trying to save his ass."

"Don't blame him. He's got nowhere else to go."

"By the way," Brian remarked, "was good to see you again. Envy your lifestyle."

"Too quiet most times. Enjoyed the action working together. Like old times."

"Right. Coming this way soon?"

"Haven't planned on it, but owe the daughter a visit."

"Oh yeah," Brian remarked. "Before I forget…Tracy says 'Hi.'"

"You met up?"

"Already work together," he cheered. "Great girl."

"How's she?"

"Find out for yourself," he hinted. "Good reason for a visit."

"I'll consider. Give her my regards." Alex hung up. He felt guilty for having neglected the family, *especially her.* His thoughts briefly touched on his fondness for this daughter. She'd always been his favorite.

In reflective thought, he slowly paced towards the warmth seeping in from the deck. The sun had risen some degrees since he'd left to check the alarm and taken the call. He could feel the heavy wood warm up beneath his bare feet. The deck felt solid beneath his weight. It should. It was redwood he'd shipped in from the coast. *Will last forever. Probably outlive me,* he thought with dismay.

Time had become an important factor in the life of Alex Bauer. He thought often on how much, or how little, there was left. Gauging from the career he'd had and the success he'd achieved, nevertheless, he had no reason to complain. He had lived a dream others would never experience. He was grateful for that. But there was a hint of sadness in his eyes. *Will I live this way for the rest of my life?* A sense of loneliness crept back into his presence as it always did after talking with a distant friend or family member. It was at times like these when he dearly missed company.

ANNAPOLIS (Maryland)

Wonder who'll be there? It was Sunday. Hanson was speculating. He was on the way to a meeting, clandestine as it was. The car slowly edged up the paved parkway. He'd arrived at the Rotary Club. The place wasn't new to him. He'd been here a number of times. It was always in conjunction with a special event or after a political crisis. Today would probably not be different. *Why would it?* He usually looked forward to this, the gathering of eagles. Think tank on the highest order—power brokers of the first degree, that's what it was.

It was no ordinary think tank. This one was aimed at something much greater. It created world policies, solved crises, and shaped the future of society. It was created to manipulate nations on a global scale. Kept super-secret for many years, rumors eventually leaked out. Not everybody could keep a sworn secret. He would know; he had fired a number of employees for this very reason.

Today's meeting, he calculated, would be different. An ill feeling emanated from the depths of his stomach pit. He suddenly felt uneasy. He should have cancelled, pretending to be sick. But that wouldn't fly very well. Today, he feared, his head was on the chopping block.

"Might as well get it over with." He could only hope that more pressing issues would supersede this week's events. Leaks from the government were common, even expected. It was how the game was played, especially when the need for more funding was the issue, but a direct breach by the Agency? That was different. Especially from an agency *that should not exist.*

He let the vehicle roll to a stop in an open parking stall. Stiff-legged, he got out, stretching. The circulation began to flow again. Although he drove in comfort—a silver-colored Chrysler-300—he'd noticed his legs needed limbering up after sitting behind the wheel. He raised his head to check on the sky. *Clear, and blue for a change*, he thought as his eyes caught an airliner streak overhead, leaving burnt exhaust in its wake. It had just taken off from National. With a jerk of his body, he pushed the driver side door shut then briskly walked up the short driveway toward the solid wood-framed entrance portal.

A few paces past the threshold of the posh hallway, he was immediately ushered into a private banquet hall, always reserved for this occasion. Already he could hear muffled conversation coming from inside. Despite his uneasiness, he held his head up high. As always, he was customarily late for the meeting. He did it on purpose. It gave him a sense of authority. His entrance was casually acknowledged by the other members. They expected him to be late.

"Glad you made it," the secretary-elect called out. He briskly invited him over to the only empty chair, right beside him. "How're things at the Palace?"

Ready to acknowledge the panel, Hanson replied, "Hectic as usual," in his typical non-committal manner. His throat felt parched. He reached for a fine crystal carafe filled with clear water. Pouring some water to take a cooling sip, he was unceremoniously interrupted by an angry voice. "You owe us an explanation."

Deliberately, Hanson turned towards the caller a few seats away. There was an angry face staring in his direction, and the face demanded an explanation. "And," he added, following a calculated pause, "better make it good."

"I know…I know," Hanson yielded in defeat. *They have a right to let me sweat*, he thought. The dining hall had turned silent. All eyes were piercing into him. He pulled together all the mental strength he could muster up and stood up to face the unavoidable. With an unsteady hand he reached for a spoon neatly placed next to an untouched appetizer, then tapped on the half-empty glass resting on the placemat. The sound of the clear crystal silenced the room. "I suppose you saw this week's *Post*?"

"Who didn't?" were some angry responses. There were heated grumblings. Accusations were tossed back and forth between members from the various agencies. Pent-up frustrations were being voiced. Everybody wanted to have their say. The session was prone to speculations. The host sat quietly by the table, allowing members to voice their personal opinions. It would serve its purpose. The outburst reminded him of the parliamentary debates on BBC television he frequently watched. Face depicting a somewhat forced patience, he decided, *Agenda can wait.*

"What're you gonna do about it?" Someone finally yelled a demand. It was a member from the Department of Defense. The face staring Hanson down was a familiar one. It was the head of DCA[18], DOD's intelligence group.

"Already taken care." After the last outburst the conference room returned to its usual atmosphere. Hanson regained his composure once more. "Wasn't as bad as I thought," he muttered into the outbursts. *Must be more pressing issues on the agenda.*

"It'd better," was the caller's reminder of the personal onslaught. "Can't afford any more publicity." He was referring to the periodic meetings usually causing leaks to the public. An unavoidable dilemma as it was to the agency, a clandestine meeting always caught the public's eyes.

"Yeah," some members chimed in. "Already too much scrutiny by the paparazzi."

"Won't happen again," Hanson promised. He had played it low keyed. *After all, you don't mess with the DOD. You want to be in bed with the nation's most powerful defense organization.* For the rest of the session he was spared from any further charges. Lunch was being served by impeccably dressed waiters.

Having been reprimanded in front of the echelon panel did not sit easy with him. He'd lost his appetite. He sat back in the chair and barely listened to the rest of the agenda. From his vantage point, he was able to absorb some of the powerful presences. He knew most from the annual meetings held at various places. Among prominent politicians, bankers, and industrialists, seated at the table were the nation's biggest powerbrokers.

Recollecting getting appointed to manage the NRO years ago, Hanson thought, Wonder where my career would be if it wasn't for this institution, and here I am, whether I like it or not.

He didn't agree with some of the policies he'd helped establish, but didn't have much choice, getting outvoted most times. His purpose for being here was mostly for the space assets he provided, without which none of this would be possible. It had taken decades for this panel to gain solid footing. The reason they'd managed to keep the gatherings a secret for so long was still a mystery. Where most programs had taken a public flogging, his had been spared for decades. Unfortunately, the paradigm had changed. The cat was out of the bag, so to speak. Now, with the flourishing of instant media coverage, along with the ever-probing eyes of conspirators, the cloak had been

---

[18] Where DCA (Defense Communication Agency) is responsible for building and maintaining the intelligence network and infrastructure, the DIA (Defense Intelligence Agency) provides the manpower resources.

lifted. Highly alarmed at first, now, accustomed to the visibility, it did not matter anymore. He had to deal with it. The public demanded justification. They had a right to know where their money went.

Soon, he thought, prompting a self-imposed reluctance, *it won't matter.* The next phase of super weapons had already been set in motion, awaiting imminent deployment. *Today,* he suspected, *is the day for the announcement.*

Impatiently tapping his glass to get everybody's attention, the secretary finally interrupted. "Today's session is to activate Cosmic Sentry." There was an immediate silence. He allowed several seconds for the news to sink in then demanded silence.

"Order…order in the room…" The secretary hammered the gavel repeatedly to silence the hall. "To accomplish this objective," he went on, "we're here to divert unnecessary public attention. However," he added, "there'll be harsh consequences," he further urged, "if someone decides to compromise the program." After a brief pause he finished, "Overt or covert."

"What's the plan?" the representative from CINCPAC[19] wanted to know. The other commands were just as demanding for details.

"Cosmic Sentry," the secretary expounded, "will thwart our adversaries with everything we've got." The revelation was a radical move but a necessary one. In recent years, undeclared wars had been initiated on too many fronts. Europe, Asia, and South America were all affected by the escalated surge of terrorist-inspired fronts and demanded justification. Whereas, in the past, the nation had been geared towards a defensive posture, today the tide must turn. A resolution must be called. And that was to take the initiative. The budget for the new weapons had already been approved. The time had come to implement the system.

"Such as?" someone shouted into the confusion.

"We'll throw everything at them," he insisted, "lasers, plasma weapons, pulsed energy, particle beams, you name it." The statement was followed with hollers and outbursts such as, "Why not the kitchen sink?"

He let them have their day. After all, it was the start of a new chapter in the nation's defense. DARPA had been experimenting with new weaponry since the sixties. Results had been slow, but promising in all sectors. For those who remembered Reagan's Star Wars program, the stated technologies back then had been way too premature. "It'll never work," was the general consensus voiced even from the mega-corporations involved in the development, but, in the end, it had proven effective. It'd forced the Soviet Union to its knees. It had ended the Cold War. Fortunately, for many years there had only been one battlefront. Today, battlefronts were everywhere. The paradigm had changed. Al Qaeda, Jihad, the Taliban, and terrorism from other radical factions saw to that. Their rearing heads popped up everywhere on the globe. Cyber warfare was created. It would be here to stay for many decades to come, perhaps for the entire remaining time of humanity. Only time would tell.

"What about the budget?" In the past few years, budget restraints had been a large burden on the nation, and the taxpayers. There were rumblings among the population, and rightly so. The recent acts of aggressions demanded action. The security of the nation was at stake. And so was the safety of the citizens.

---

[19] Commander in Chief Pacific (CINCPAC) is the head for all U.S. Pacific Naval Fleets Headquartered in Hawaii.

"Approved," the secretary affirmed. With a final motion, the meeting was adjourned.

CAYMAN ISLANDS (Offshore)

The man seated in first class isle seat had not made a move since boarding the craft in Dubai. To prevent passersby from making eye contact, he wore dark shades, tinted sunglasses. Even the flight crew could not read the man's facial expressions. Shortly after the takeoff, one specifically had made attempts to get his attention for refreshments and snacks. With a reluctant shrug, she finally gave up. "No, thank you," had been a casual, but firm response. He didn't want to be bothered. He knew what was coming. Superfluous chitchat and he hated it.

The passenger was good looking. Well fitted in an Armani suit, with Tommy Hilfiger shirt and Gucci tie to complement, people often mistook him for a business tycoon. They were dead wrong. He wasn't here on a social outing, or a vacation. He came here on business, serious business, business that would soon shake the world at its foundation.

Two hours into the flight he could feel his ears pop. It was an indication the craft had begun its descent. *Twenty more minutes,* he thought with relief. It took that long for most commercial flights to descend to low altitude, then down and against cross wind for a final approach to the tarmac. The customary "ping" sound got the attention of passengers occupying toilets and sleeping. The overhead No-Smoking and Seatbelt signs had just been turned on. Some kept on dozing in the comfort of the Cayman flight.

The perky stewardess made one final pass up and down the aisle to gather up the yellow landing cards. Haltingly, she leaned over the silent passenger to collect his. *One final move,* he thought, *to get my attention.* His card was blank. Her face took on a quizzical look, but then she shrugged her shoulders and moved on. Passengers around him were getting energized. They craned over armrests trying to catch a peek out the windows. Some were taking pictures. It was mostly tourists this time of year. You could spot them easily. They were the ones garbed in the colorful Tommy Bahamas, Dockers shorts, and Crocs sandals. Some youngsters already wore flip-flops, squirming impatiently in their seats, eager to get to the beach.

Again, he could hear the engines change pitch. Through the shades his glimpse caught the shadow of the jumbo jet skimming across the white-crusted waves breaking against the shoreline. He was gauging the distance closing between craft and ground. The ground effect had taken over his senses. Seconds later, the craft touched ground. It came to a final stop. He quickly jumped from his seat to collect his light luggage from overhead. With long strides, he headed for the exit ramp. He'd beaten the crowd. Customs inspection was short. He'd already slipped a hundred dollar bill in between his passport pages before handing over the document. With a slight nod, the official slipped the bill into his pocket. He didn't even bother to open the passport belonging to a Hasan Hammad. He failed to check the computer. *Another executive in a hurry* may have been his thoughts. They were the routine customers in and out the island, the business elite. Rich, wealthy, and affluent, most had similar traits in common: greed, fraud, and corruption, the products of free enterprise. The island was built on it. Tourists were second-class citizens, a necessary nuisance to appease the local shop owners.

He was first to exit the airport. His strides were aimed in the direction of the row of waiting taxicabs. "Where to?" The driver was polite.

"Hilton."

"First time in the islands?"

"I'm not a tourist." That usually shut them up. Hammad reclined in the comfort of the air-conditioned cab. He barely noticed the view of the serene shoreline. His focus was on the mission. He tried to remember what he knew of this place.

The Caymans were a British-dependent territory located about 500 miles west of Jamaica. This offshore set of islands was outside U.S. borders, which made it ideal for legitimate tourist trade as well as the concealment of less-than-legal activities. As a result, for years, business and tourism had been prolific. To him, it was just another quick trip to check on business. He wasn't interested in the island's beaches or resorts. For that, he had his own place in Dubai, his private sanctuary removed from chatter and noise. Outside of that, and with good reasons, he preferred staying away from crowds.

Ten minutes later they arrived at the hotel. He liked staying there. Akin to an unbiased international atmosphere, people generally spoke multiple languages. He could converse in English, French, Farsi, and Hindi. It didn't matter to him. He was fluent in all. Within five minutes he'd been processed into a hotel suite.

He'd taken a shower, toweled dry, poured a ginger ale, and taken a seat in the comfort of the modern suite. He asked for an outside line.

"Trans-World Global," the operator announced in perfect English.

"McAllister, please."

"McAllister," a suave male voice announced a few seconds later.

"Shahadah," the caller identified himself. "When can we meet?"

"Thirty minutes," came the polite reply. "I'll send transportation."

CIA HEADQUARTERS

Harry Carter hadn't decided whether to call to apologize or to just let it ride. *Screw him,* he finally decided on yesterday's promise to Warner. *Always meddling in my affairs...let him deal with his. Got too much on my plate as it is.* Jack Warner was his counterpart at the NSA. Where the two organizational policies demanded collaboration between each other, the policy was not always upheld, especially in recent years. With similar careers, both rose up through the ranks. During the early days of their careers, they used to socialize with each other at whatever pub was popular among chief executives from the political arena. The places were still there, unchanged. Only the faces kept changing. D.C. had a high turnover in the job department. Every four years, six, or eight, the political climate changed and, with it, the faces.

Carter may have appeared gruff and impatient to the outside world, but he had his reasons. It hadn't always been like that. Working one assignment after another, he used to be friends with many from the organization. He'd enjoyed taking on projects no matter what the conditions, always prepared for yet another quest. Starting out, it'd been a matter of taking what was assigned. Everybody started at the bottom. He'd been no exception. He'd seen the world as it was, at its worst—bare and exposed. Some places he'd preferred over others. That was to be expected. Chasing criminals and villains had taken him to the worst places imaginable. He'd been there: the Bay of Pigs to oust Castro, Watergate and the Democratic National Committee, Lumumba and the Congo, Cambodia and Vietnam, the Soviet Union and its defectors, and Panama and Noriega among others. But that was years ago.

His break into the executive circles came with the end of the Cold War and the subsequent technological shift to remote surveillance. With it, there was no need for "cloak and dagger" anymore. Criminals and spies were chased through the Net using computers. Shortly after, his former job was replaced by Echelon. "IT" and "CIO" were the new buzzwords. He'd jumped at the opportunity. Years later, elected into office, he further developed the CIA's, by insiders mostly referred as "The Company" programs. It became his mission. He'd attained visibility. It'd been fun calling the shots in and around the Beltway. But then, eventually, politics took over. With rank came responsibility. Responsibilities opened up to vulnerability. Vulnerability gave ground to casualties. He almost succumbed to it but caught the trap just in time. Ever since, Harry Carter came first. Protecting his career, he'd developed a personal barrier not many could breach. Nor did they attempt or even desire to do so. Nobody wanted to deal with him. He liked it that way.

Wonder what that was all about, he thought, regarding yesterday's call. *Ought to put a trace on the Snake—or was it Serpent?* He reached for the phone to call the head of his data center. "Put a trace on a 'Serpent,'" he ordered, "with possible connections to subversive factions. And," he cautioned, "keep it in the agency. Don't want NSA to get wind. Same goes for everybody else."

Mutual exclusivity was his mode of operandi. Contrast, resistance, and insulation were assurances to protect his position. *Let them look out for themselves, the DHS, the DIA, and the rest of them.* His life was dedicated to the CIA. He wanted to keep it that way, no matter what conservatives and liberals were saying. Collaboration? *Maybe.* Interoperability? *Screw that.* Consolidation? *Never!*

Getting that off his chest made him feel immensely better. It's good to talk things out occasionally, if only with yourself.

THE PENTAGON

Henry "Hank" Foster, general in charge of the United States Armed Forces, was fuming. He slammed the phone back in its cradle. He'd just had a disturbing call. It was from the head of the Trade Commission. "Never stops," he grumbled. He forced a couple of deep breaths, then ordered his deputy into the office. Between the slamming of the cradle and a chest filled with air, he somewhat calmed down. His gaze swept the room while he waited. His eyes lingered briefly on the plaque hanging on the opposite wall. It always reminded him of his responsibilities. "The Buck Stops Here," it said. It was a phrase first coined by then President Truman. In practice, it didn't have to stop with him. He could just as well pass major issues up the chain, along with the axe. But that wouldn't be him. The reason he was sitting in a Pentagon executive office was for his dependable qualities. It was a privilege not many ranking officers could achieve. It had to be earned. And that took a lifetime. For some, it involved fighting on the frontlines if, by chance, timing was right for a conflict or a war. Occasionally, others got lucky when the fronts were quiet by kissing the right butts.

There was a knock on the door. "Come in, Bart." Hank gestured for his trusted liaison to take a seat. He handed him a folder stamped SECRET. "Check into this right away."

"Sure. What's up?"

"Seems," he expounded, "we've had another breach in contracting policy." His forehead was carved by two vertical lines, giving weight to the issue. "This one looks pretty grim."

"Go on."

"Appears," he motioned at the folder, "contractor's outsourced some super-sensitive project without our approval."

"Not the first time this has happened."

"Yeah," Foster agreed, "but this involves the highest order of defense intelligence. It's affecting national security directly."

"Who's the culprit?"

"One of those 'bandits,' you know," he spat in disgust, "sprouting up all over the Beltway." He made reference to technology firms growing like weeds in and around D.C., all scrambling for their rightful budget scraps.

"What've we got?"

"Get in touch with the Trade Commissioner for details then work with the FBI."

"Sure thing," he acknowledged then briskly stormed from the office.

The general was distraught. *This could get nasty with the news media.* Contemplating the next move, the frown across his forehead deepened. He flipped through the Rolodex sitting prominently on the desk. He was well aware the item was dated technology but kept it on the desk anyway, mostly for sentimental reasons. He just as well could have pulled the address up from the desktop computer, but out of habit always reached for the index cards first. He flipped through the cards to locate a specific address. *That's it.* He punched the numbers into the phone pad.

"Bauer." The voice at the other end was brisk.

"Alex," he announced, "it's Foster. What've you been up to lately?"

"Hello, Hank." There was a hint of joy in the voice. "You still with the Pentagon?"

"Still here," he answered with a fond chuckle. "Not ready for the scrap iron heap yet."

"Haven't lost your sense of humor, eh?" Alex replied. "Happy to hear."

"It's what keeps us young. Right?"

"Isn't that the truth?"

"Listen, Alex." Foster's voice took on an urgent tone. "Could you fly down here to meet? Need you to check into something. I remember," he inferred, "you were involved with this. Unless we keep it under tight wraps, we may have a problem that might get out of hand."

"What can I do?"

"Tell you when you get here. Can you manage the next flight?"

"Just like old times, eh? I'll be there tomorrow."

"Thanks." The general was relieved. "I'll have a badge waiting at the front desk."

Same evening, Alex caught a redeye flight out of Denver. Three hours later he landed at Dulles. The flight had been uneventful. The cabin was sparsely occupied. It gave him a chance to doze for most of the flight. Transfer from luggage hold to ground transportation was swift. Night porters and rental agents greeted him sleepy eyed. The world was cloaked in a state of semi-dormancy. It reminded him on his early on-the-fly career days.

The parking lots were almost empty when he showed up at the Pentagon's doorsteps. It was still early. The morning sun had just broken over the horizon across the Potomac River. Quietly seated in the rental car, he decided, *No use getting inside.* No matter how many times he'd visited here, a feel of grandeur overcame his senses just looking at the sheer size of the complex.

He'd always been impressed by this bustling city within a city. It housed not only the head of every military force, but also every agency and national laboratory one could imagine, from Lawrence Livermore Laboratory to White Sands and DARPA, employing the best scientists and mathematicians in the world, with all branches tied to this place.

The morning silence was broken up by the slamming of car doors. His eyes sought out the disturbance. Commuters started to arrive. He checked his watch for the time. *Should go in,* he decided. With determined strides he made his way to the entrance. Western Sector, the sign announced. A visitor's badge was waiting as promised. In the pre-9/11 days, he would have been directed to the proper office, but today he was assigned an escort. Security had been tightened on all visitors, calling for rigorous in-processing. An escort was assigned and waiting. He followed but paid little attention to the route they took. *Walking the corridors,* Alex reflected on his twenty-five-year career with the DOD, *many famous commanders have walked these halls before me.* He was proud to be among them.

Not much has changed, he took note, in this "no-salute, no-cover" area. Official visitors still showed up dressed as smartly as ever. One last turn and they had arrived at the general's office. There, the escort handed off his responsibility to a receptionist.

"Bauer," he announced to the secretary.

"He's expecting you. Please follow me." She led him to the back office.

Bounding from his chair to greet him, the general bellowed, "Alex! Been ages. How's retirement treating you?" He was beaming at his longtime friend.

"Not retired yet. Still do consulting work for you guys."

"So I hear. Take a seat," he patted his old friend on the shoulder, "so I can fill you in." The friendliness he displayed was a rare occasion. "I'll get right to the point." His face had turned serious once more. "Remember the contractor…the one that developed the Prowler satellites?"

"Sure do." Alex recalled, "I was liaison on the project. What's the problem?"

"Let me fill you in," Foster said, thumbing at the service counter. "Coffee?"

"Thanks. Could use some."

"Cream? Sugar?"

"Black."

Foster handed him a freshly brewed cup. "Looks like someone's compromised the software," he said, picking up the conversation. "Need you to trace the contracting steps from start to delivery. Get me the names, places, and activities from all parties involved, but please," he emphasized, "be discrete about it. We can't let the press get wind. Treat it as a sensitive issue."

"You know me; middle name's 'anonymous.'"

"Never would have guessed." Foster chuckled. "Everybody in this business knows your accomplishments," he boasted with a grin. A phone ring ended the meeting. Foster made a gesture to take the call. "Keep me posted…daily."

"Will do." Unceremoniously, Alex had been dismissed. Foster had already picked up a waiting call. *Too bad.* He'd have liked to socialize some more but thought better of it. *Some other time.* He hesitated a moment before heading for the exit.

Better give Tracy a call, he thought, *let her know I'm in town.* He fished for his mobile and made the call. Considering the time passed since their last visit, *Boy,* he hoped, *will she be surprised.*

NSA LIAISON OFFICE

Brian was already at work when Tracy walked into the office this morning. He could hear her firm strides headed his way. He looked up from the monitor. Her face turned into an immediate frown when she saw him on her computer. It was apparent she didn't like it. He could read it in her face. *Don't like this...nobody uses my station.* "What are you doing?"

"Company equipment." He grinned at her. It pacified her momentary anger.

"How long you been at it?"

"Schedules don't have much meaning. I work when I'm not asleep," he said. *Time for a break,* he reminded himself. A few keystrokes later he got up, arched his back, and stretched his legs. "Want your chair?"

"Just like Dad." There was a reprimand in her tone. "Always taking control."

"Sorry." It just occurred to him that he was a guest infringing on her territory. "Ready to give me a hand?" he urged in a peace offering gesture. He pushed the stack of computer printouts aside then invited her to take the seat. This morning, he was all business. Because of the critical issues at hand, he was forced to put social politeness aside. If he couldn't find an immediate solution for the problem, the space defenses would be in jeopardy. The Pentagon was breathing down the agency's neck. He had to come up with a permanent solution. *Today! Now!* It all rested on his shoulders. He was it—Level III support, last line of defense, final stage for solution. There was nobody else he could consult. It was up to him to resolve critical issue.

"I'm all yours," she replied.

An invitation, he wondered, *or just a business gesture? Women!* He wasn't quite sure what to expect.

"Home in on 13-Alpha," he instructed. "Let's see if we can change the orbit a couple degrees." As she entered the coordinates, he was keenly aware of her female scent. It slightly distracted his senses, watching her take control of the keyboard. An enormous wall-size monitor sprang to life. Dozens of color-coded objects gradually arched across a transparent map. It was a global map slowly panning, synchronized to the time zones. Two pairs of eyes carefully studied their paths. There was no response action.

"Hang on." Tracy adjusted the chair he had moved earlier to fit her comfort position. Again, her speedy fingers worked the keyboard. The distant satellite did not respond. "Alpha One doesn't accept the coordinates." The object had received the command but responded with, "Unauthorized Command...Access Denied."

She tried a few more coordination changes without much success. The responses were consistently the same: Negative.

"Let me give it a try," Brian suggested. He was growing impatient. *This isn't going anywhere.* He was used to commanding his own actions. "Could you get me some coffee?" Her fingers paused on the keyboard. Her head lifted in his direction. She shot him a stare, a quizzical stare. *There's that look again.* "Please," he begged.

She got up to turn the seat over to him.

"Black?"

"Why not? Could use a strong fix." He watched her promptly walk away then edged his body into the vacated seat.

Brian preferred cafe latte first thing in the morning. He'd developed a taste ever since Starbucks had gained popularity. It hadn't always been that way. He'd been spoiled drinking espresso in Italy, but ever since AMA had announced adverse effects on the brain and arteries, he'd tempered his caffeine intake.

He shot a quick glance back over his shoulder to check the room. He did not want anyone close. *Not now.* He was about to access classified software without permission. He had no prior authorization. And probably wouldn't get any, if he'd request it. He could go to jail. He was about to access a backdoor port he'd programmed years earlier. He'd had to use it in the past on several occasions in similar situations. When it came down to the wire, the basics, he was part of a tough breed. He grew up in a different world. It was the world of super users, gurus, and hackers.

As any smart programmer would tell you, "Don't ever corner yourself without a backdoor exit." Without it, you were just another skilled programmer. Given proper tools a hacker could identify the default port and pass code. For the administrator, an imbedded access would most likely remain undetected and remain dormant until the operating system was purged.

Let's see what we've got. His fingers flew across the keyboard much like a pianist playing a concerto. He was in his world. It was the world of stealth, intrigue, and conspiracy. His next actions opened up the gate to the highest echelon of secrecy, privy only to executives of the highest cleared levels, top secret and above.

Because of his systems responsibilities, Brian had access to most of the NSA network tools and utility programs. The tool was Carnivore. As such, it was the most classified of all software applications. It was the tool of all tools. Not only could Carnivore scan network devices to identify open ports, it read information transmissions generated by emails, computers, and communication devices at any point, whether on the public Internet or a proprietary network. Carnivore, also known as Big Brother, in contrast with spook activities, worked to identify subversive nations and, these days, was mostly used to listen in on terrorists.

His fingers, once more, were in automatic mode. They took hold of every key faster than his conscious thoughts could command. Because of years of constant use, the letter patterns were permanently imprinted in his brain. His eyes scanned the negative key responses as fast as they scrolled across the screen. "Ping statistic failures...denial of services...connection timeouts," were most of the rejection responses. He tried other satellite connections but without much success.

Reflecting on the application waiting for another input command, Big Brother was a two-edged sword. Used to monitor subversive subjects by an authorized operator on the one end, it could also be used to monitor an operator's activity, as well as other users within the organization. With this, an automated check and balance was created to keep the good guys "honest" and the villains "in check." Carnivore was a self-perpetuating system. Safeguarded within the underground vaults found in many intelligence organizations, sensitive information was fed to a forest of computer servers, gobbling up every bit of data sent on the wire from any point on the Net. As long as a system was connected to the Net, regardless of wireless or direct connection, Carnivore would know—no matter how many firewalls, routers, and filters were in between.

"No response." More rejections. Brian was beginning to get irritated.

He tried to remember other port IPs he'd used in the past. His otherwise swift fingers hovered on the keyboard.

>C:\Windows\System32\neststat\Milstar\749...

>TCP 12.120.75.256:57856 <Local>…UDP Kerberos:admin-protocol <Foreign>
State: Open. Wait…

That's it…my port. Brian sighed a breath of relief. Kerberos, the multi-headed hound guarding the gates of Hades did it again, just in time.

Tracy returned with a coffee mug in time to see the access response. She was surprised to see Brian manipulating the KH orbits.

"You're a genius!" she exclaimed. "How'd you manage?"

"Had my way with it," he grinned, "kicked it a couple of times."

"I wouldn't be as forgiving." She returned his grin.

"I treat women differently," he stated smug faced. He gratefully accepted the mug she handed him and unintentionally touched her hand. She didn't pull away. He liked the smoothness of her skin. It spawned a feel of pleasure within his tense body.

He sought out her eyes. They lingered for a second, probing the depth of each other. He almost blushed. She finally broke the spell. "Suppose you know how all this stuff works?" She eyed him, slightly suspicious but exceedingly pleased at his progress.

"I should," he boasted. "I developed most of it."

"Hacking days?"

"Some of it." He wouldn't admit to his somewhat darker days of programming and politely ignored the insinuation.

An hour later, barely suppressing a yawn, Tracy finally conceded. "I'm pooped."

Brian got the queue and terminated further testing. "One last thing." He reached for the secure phone to inform NORAD that DEFCON could be reset to the normal level. Next, he called the SPACECOM command center's officer in charge to schedule a mandatory debriefing.

"We ready to clear out of here?" Tracy prepared to leave.

"Hold up." He hesitated.

She turned to face him. "What now?"

"Got to send your dad a message."

"At this hour?"

"Promised to let him know the test results. After all," he explained, "he's involved with the KH." Alex was responsible for the subcontractors. "It's rather important, don't you think?"

"You're right."

AL QAEDA (Base Camp One)

With the destruction of Base Camp Three, primary jihad command had shifted to Base Camp One situated in the middle of the Yemen desert. From the ground-based perspective, as far as the eyes could gage, the terrain was the same: nothing but gray, desolated wasteland. From the sky, the terrain below took on a much different view. The ground appeared like a giant spider web stretched out, reaching from the mountainous ridges to the west across the distant wasteland to the east, connecting up with the many desert dwellings, however small. Despite the vast emptiness, people did live here. For the newcomer assigned to the command center, streams of extremely dry air flowing down from the Arabian Peninsula made life almost unbearable. The Serpent was no exception. Still battered from his miraculous escape, he'd just arrived to take command. The enemy had managed to wipe out every other base of his forces. Being the last remaining refuge, he took command but also had to assume the camp was closely watched from the sky.

The best time to travel was after the air had cooled from the searing sun. He'd arrived during the cool of night on a troop carrier. Assigned temporary sleeping quarters, already filled with the bluish haze of smoke, he stepped outside to absorb the quiet of the night. It always amazed him how clear the skies appeared in the absence of city lights. He immensely enjoyed the view within the calmness of the desert night. The brilliance of the starlight above illuminated the grounds. His gaze swept across the sky in anticipation. "Yes," he whispered between clenched teeth, "right on time."

He knew the schedules for the incessant spy satellites cutting across the sky. Illuminated by the distant sun, they were clearly visible during the dark of the night. Appearing every ninety minutes, he'd plotted their path years ago. Base camp activities were planned accordingly. Their watches were linked to the cycles above. He couldn't help but grin. There had been sheer excitement in the camp as they watched the satellites drift from their standard courses. It'd been his doing. The access port he'd programmed many months ago worked. It allowed passage for digital commands to manipulate the U.S. commercial space assets. Success was assured.

Hours later, his monitors had picked up digital activities initiated via NSA relay stations. He assumed they were counter commands issued in response to his satellite manipulations. His plan was set to initiate the first phase of the attack.

Halfway around the globe in Baltimore, Tracy walked into her apartment and noticed the call-waiting indicator. It was flashing a familiar number. She kicked her shoes off then paused to push the redial button. Her dad answered after the second ring.

"Well, well, keeping late hours, aren't we?"

"No, Dad, working late."

"Listen, I'm in town..."

"You're *here*?" she interrupted. She was taken completely by surprise. She hadn't spoken with him in months.

"Flew in today...Pentagon business. Can we have lunch tomorrow?"

"Actually, Dad, it'll be later today. Already way past midnight."

"You're right."

"I'll make the time, but really need some sleep. Call me late morning. Night, Dad..." She hung up without giving him a chance to start a conversation. She realized that he'd missed her, but she was dead tired. They'd catch up later. She took a quick shower and slipped between the sheets without as much as a bite to eat. She was looking forward to lunch with her father, and the opportunity to spend more time with Brian.

CENTRAL INTELLIGENCE AGENCY

Years ago when the agency started, human beings used to do all the legwork. Today, it was mostly computers. Harry Carter sat at his desk catching up with mail—email that was. There was a lot of it. With the world relatively quiet in past weeks, it gave him an opportunity to answer much of it, important ones anyway. Some mornings, especially close to the weekend, he'd just highlight the entire inbox and hit the delete key. It was that easy to get rid of pending issues…obligations, that was. It gave him the time to contemplate. He tried to imagine a world without data processing machines. Granted, he still had agents dispersed around the globe in embassies, foreign offices, and field locations, but the real intelligence gathering took place internally, through data mining. Only computers could sift through the continuous stream of information satellites gathered from every corner of the globe. It was up to him, with the help of sophisticated software, to make sense out of all. He had final authority for what, when, and who'd be on the distribution list.

Life's been good, he recollected with a sense of nostalgia for the good old days. A hushed knock at the door interrupted his thoughts. It was the department secretary. She handed him a one-page report. It had just come in over the wire. He'd been anxiously waiting for it. It confirmed the recent mission. It simply read, "Mission accomplished…possible survivors…identity not verified."

He wasn't happy. Disgusted, he tossed the report across the table. The mission was *not* accomplished.

It all depended on how one looked at the text. To him, the glass was always half empty. Not that he was a pessimist; it was the result of *somebody screwing things up*. And somebody always did. Nothing was ever flawless. "Gotta do everything yourself," he grumbled. Unfortunately, he wasn't in a position to do that anymore. That's why he had contracted agents. In times like these he wished he could be out in the field, "The front lines." But that was impossible now. It was a life he'd left behind years ago. He verified the data one more time. *Possible survivors. That's gonna bite me in the back.* There were survivors. And survivors were witnesses. And witnesses talked. He couldn't afford that. He cursed in silence, waiting for the next fuckup, then did the unavoidable—called his NSA opponent for confirmation. "May have some satellite video."

After many years of devoted dedication to The Company, Harry Carter had achieved a position as high as anyone could rise in the organization. Unfortunately, he couldn't share the reason for his success readily with anyone, not friends, not family. Where others could openly discuss daily events at the dinner table, his knowledge was shrouded in secrecy. It was something you learned to live with, but didn't necessarily get used to.

Silent gratification was all one could expect when things went well. It could be a thankless job when something went wrong. For most part, his agents performed well. He was grateful for that. After all, where else could you write an analysis of a world event and have it read by the President? Or be called on to brief U.S. policymakers at the height of an international crisis?

While he was taking care of politics, officers in the CIA's Directorate of Intelligence—and there were many—were on the forefront, safeguarding U.S. national interests in a fast-changing world. As Deputy Director for Intelligence analyst, for instance, your challenge was to anticipate and quickly assess rapidly evolving developments and their impact, mostly foreign, both positive and negative, on U.S. policy interests. The intelligence support that the Deputy Directors developed and provided through the "President's Daily Brief" was a core function of The Company. From computer simulations to multi-dimensional maps, graphics specialists drew on their creative expertise to play an active and unique role in supporting the Directorate of Intelligence.

All this was fine and good working for a highly specialized organization, but there was more to it. He'd come to understand years ago the fundamental flaw with the organization. "If it were up to me," he'd ponder, "I'd reorganize the whole damned defense structure," with everybody reporting to him. He knew he could do wonders for national defense, but he had to curtail private thoughts like these. Careers were cut short for making a remark like that in public. It had taken close to a century for the organization to form and develop to its present standing. To change the self-contained hierarchy from the executive level on down would be an impossible task. A more realistic approach was for organizations to work together effectively. And that was where the flaw came into play.

Interoperability between agencies had always been resistive. By its very nature, inherent to the business of secrecy, the notion of concealment implied the absence of communication. The only way to be sure information remained secret was by not sharing it with anyone. Information *was* power, and power was the ultimate goal for any broker…and there were many.

"Sir," his secretary's voice came over the speaker phone, "secure call."

Carter furrowed his brows. He pondered for a second who it could be this time. Calls of this nature were not routine. They always required action. He punched the secure button.

"We have a mission," the faceless voice ordered. "Target base 'Bauer.'"

"Termination?"

"Negative," the voice insisted. "Detention only. Please confirm."

"Detention only…confirmed."

"A dossier's on the way."

"Okay. When…" The phone turned silent before he had a chance to ask when the file would arrive.

He stood up and briskly walked over to the wall safe. Inside, he reached for the black book. Carter thumbed through the pages. He found the information he needed: Tactical Field Office, Arizona. He dialed the number. Two rings later a voice answered, "Brooks."

"We have a mission. Can you handle?"

"Can do," was the distant response. "How soon?"

"Profile's en route," he confirmed. "Special courier."

"Roger that."

The line went dead. He checked the time on his Rolex and briskly left the office. He was late for his favorite recreation: golf.

MADRAS (India)

Rajesh Chandra was sitting in the quiet of his home. He was faintly aware of activity coming from the kitchen. The maid was putting clean dishes into the cupboard. He reclined into the posh of the deep-cushioned couch. *Life's been good to me.* He was at peace with himself. He was reaping the rewards of a busy career, a career that'd brought success and much harmony to his life. Cradled between his palms was a cup of freshly brewed tea. The tea was harvested a thousand kilometers to the south, in Sri Lanka. *And it is a beautiful thing*, he'd comment when in the company of family and friends.

Like most of the affluent in India, he had a flowery way with words. Their language was based on extravagant Sanskrit writing still practiced today. His father, when still alive, would have said, "Do your name proud, my son." His name, Rajesh, was indicative of the title of king. A celebrated title as such bestowed on a boy was guaranteed to have lasting consequences. In keeping with this royal heritage, he learned to hold his head high, even if by name only. In contrast to familiar domicile customs, exercising great patience and understanding, it took him a while before he learned to deal with the unrelenting methods of American industrialists. But, without them, he would still be struggling to carve out a meager living.

Absorbed in thought, he was slightly startled when his mobile phone gave a familiar jingle.

"Yes?"

It was his chief software engineer. "I'm sorry to disturb you so late in the evening," he said, "but I just received a call from our business partner in Virginia. He seemed to indicate we have a software flaw in the satellite system."

"Do you have any more details?" Rajesh wanted to know.

"Not at this time."

"Let's meet at the office." He strained to get out of the comfortable divan. "Make it an hour." Rajesh walked over to the TV, turned off his favorite cultural show, and went to the bedroom to let his wife know. "I am going to the office. I will be a while."

"Well then," she said, nodding in acknowledgement.

It was not unusual to be called to the office so late. Ever since he formed the business with the American partners, working at night had become commonplace, especially at the start of a new project. This time, the project was not new. It had been in operation for years. Why all of a sudden a problem had developed was a mystery. *Guess I'll find out soon enough*, he thought.

Years earlier, after obtaining a business visa, the sought out "Green Card" to foreigners, Rajesh had the good fortune to enter the United States and form a partnership with American business partners. It was a business opportunity for which he'd waited many years. The partnership turned into instant success, mostly contributed to his availability and the patience of his people. *Imagine an industry in which development never stopped.* With established business ties between the U.S. and India--and because the two countries were basically twelve hours apart--a twenty-four-hour workday could be realized. As a workday would end in Virginia, people were just starting in India. With most Indian people traditionally working a twelve-hour day, development took place around the clock. It was one reason why U.S. corporations were so willing to outsource to India. But, of course, there was the cost savings advantage by utilizing cheap labor. The only challenge at times was scheduling a conference call to satisfy both ends. But that did not present much of a problem. Since Indians had a great regard for courtesy, they would rather place themselves at a disadvantage before putting an American colleague into a demeaning position.

His American partners were amazed at the rapid success of his people. "How do you do it?" he was asked on numerous occasions.

"By squeezing water from the rock." It was an age-old adage from Indian culture.

It did not take long for Rajesh to become successful. In just a few years, his company had more work than he could manage.

Unfortunately, with the assault on the World Trade Center in 2001, the good fortune came to a halt. Because of security risks, most green card holders were instructed to leave the United States immediately. What followed was an economic slump. Rajesh, still bitter about the incident and the resulting consequences, returned to his home country, but not without strong business ties. Taking most of his profits to India, he was able to form his own enterprise.

It grew with rapid success. He was able to acquire all the resources he needed very inexpensively. The cost of labor between India and the U.S. was about thirty cents on the dollar, making for considerable profits at both ends. With all these earnings, a person could become quite wealthy in India. And wealth was important to the nation. People there had been oppressed and kept poor for centuries. It seemed the time had finally arrived for the entire nation to share in the success.

With his name becoming an icon in software development, Rajesh had a visitor in 2002. It was shortly after his return. Called into his office through the intercom one day, he was greeted by an old friend. The visitor was Hasan Hammad.

"Looks like you hit the jackpot," was the first thing out of Hasan's mouth.

"Hello, my friend. It has been many years, yes?" Rajesh replied, overjoyed to see his childhood friend.

"I have heard," Hasan remarked with a hint of veiled envy, "that you have become very successful in America."

"I most certainly have."

"Tell me something," he said. "How can I become part of your success?"

"I will tell it to you," was the flowery response, "but first, let us have lunch. Tomorrow, we will discuss some opportunities. Besides," he promised, "we have much to talk about."

The next day, Hasan drove up to Rajesh's software development center. He arrived early and was ushered into a plush waiting hall. The place was alive with activity. He watched as workers, dressed in the customary white garb, rushed in and out of hallways, folders in one hand and bottled water in the other. Summers in India could be extremely hot. He was already sweating from the short walk from his car to the building. Once inside, he embraced the coolness of the air conditioning with delight. He wore the traditional white bleached Kurta, as was befitting the occasion.

Hasan was not used to the heat this far south. He came from the Kashmir region up north, where the climate was cool most of the year, although lacking jobs. His people liked it there. Once they found work, nobody ever left. But jobs were hard to come by, even given the low pay. They were mostly positions supporting the tourist trade. He had higher aspirations, especially after getting involved with the jihad. His thoughts were interrupted by a pretty young office clerk approaching. "Please come with me," she said with a soft smile.

He followed her brisk walk, taking in the sweet aroma of oriental scents trailing her. She was a pretty one. Most hostesses in India were. It was a prerequisite for young women to get a public relations job. It was a longstanding, good business practice, as most businessmen would attest. What better way to break the ice in making a business deal?

"Enter, my friend." Rajesh motioned to a seat while ending a call. "I am glad you came."

"No problem," Hasan said. "You have a beautiful place here." He admired the surroundings.

"I have earned it." Rajesh motioned Hasan down the corridor. "Let me show you around." Walking briskly within the modern, palace-like building, he proudly explained the development process of the company.

They arrived at the far end of the hall. Rajesh swiped his security ID. It unlocked a winged set of doors into a well-organized room. Hasan was taken aback by the chill in the room. Pulling the Kurta tighter, he remarked, "Must cost a fortune to cool this place."

"Technology does not come cheap," Rajesh explained. "This is our computer center," he added. "We store all the servers and communication equipment here except the desktop computers."

Gazing at rows of equipment racks, Hasan noticed servers labeled with cultural names like "Shiva," "Guru," "Swami," and "Dharma." Labeling with individual names, especially prominent ones, was still common practice here. It was a quick way for engineers to identify a specific server while paying tribute to revered entities.

Guiding his guest around the spotlessly sanitized room, Rajesh pointed out some equipment. "On this side, we store the communication racks."

"Most impressive."

"When you have the money, you can get the very best."

"Over here," Hammad was informed, "we have the web farm computers for our clients. Over there are the database and staging blades for the programmers."

"How do you interface with the outside world?"

"We run fiber on the internal network connecting to the national grid. Our speeds are higher than most country's because we can afford the best technology. Let's have lunch," Rajesh suggested. It ended the tour.

"Fine."

Twenty minutes later they were seated in Rajesh's favorite restaurant. "I have a job for you," Rajesh opened the conversation. "I would like for you to head up a project we were just awarded. It is for a satellite program for the United States government. I cannot tell you anything specific until you have decided to accept because it is very proprietary. The parts are built in America but assembled here. We also write the software."

"Really! How did you ever get such an important project?"

"I have close business associates in America. Besides, they have come to depend on our inexpensive labor."

Hasan accepted the well paying position on the spot. "How soon can I start?"

"Tomorrow," he was told. "We are already behind schedule. I need a good manager to oversee the development. You don't have to be a technology expert as long as you can manage the people. Do you think you are up for it?"

"I will make you proud."

It did not take long for Hasan to become familiar with the new environment. Managing was easy. Indians, by nature, were accommodating. They were hard working. They never questioned a superior. All it took was some coordination to make all the pieces fit.

His friend had just handed him the best opportunity he could have hoped for. It gave him the liberty required for the mission. All he needed now were a few trusted engineers on his side. It did not take him long to get the team together but that was years ago.

Tonight, the moon had moved several degrees across its azimuth, illuminating the road Rajesh had to take. He was driving from the outskirts of his home to the office complex in the city. Twenty minutes later he drove up to his dedicated parking spot. A prominent sign above the building illuminated most of the space. It read, "Chandra Industries." The chief engineer was waiting. Rajesh was greeted with, "We have a problem."

"Satellite software?"

"Most possibly."

"Let us go to the lab." With brisk paces they headed towards the main entrance of the towering complex.

SPACECOM (Colorado)

The duty officer was anxious for the shift to end. Slouched over the duty desk, he was about to doze off when the phone began ringing. *That's just great.* He wasn't happy being torn from the solace of slumber. He'd just finished a ham sandwich from the vending machine not five minutes ago. Reluctantly, he forced himself upright to take the call. His hand crept toward the cradle as he tried to shake off his drowsiness. "Duty officer." He listened to the caller but was distracted by a few bits of ham stuck between his teeth. They wouldn't dislodge. He managed to annoy the caller with repeated sucking sounds. Distracted, he scavenged the desk drawer for a paper clip.

"Harris," the caller identified himself, "NSA. Listen," the voice demanded, "we've had some recent issues with a series of satellites."

Finally, the morsel dislodged. He could talk freely again. "You're the one that's been causing the alarms?"

"I'm the one," was the apologetic response. "Just wanted to let you know the problem's fixed. You can lower DEFCON. Confirmation message is on the way."

"I'll notify the XO when he comes in at oh-seven-hundred," he further patronized. "Don't forget to send the confirmation." He wanted to be sure he had the hardcopy in hand. Otherwise, if something went wrong it'd be his neck on the chopping block.

"Will do," were the caller's final words.

"World's going to be a safer place," he muttered with a sigh of relief. Keeping a wary eye on the DEFCON display panel, a few keyboard strokes later changed the status. The prominent flat panel had been sitting at Defense Level 3 displayed in yellow for days. He waited a few seconds for the status change back to green. Level 4 wasn't exactly the peaceful state he'd desired. *It is what it is.* They'd had a difficult time keeping the critical alert state from the public.

Ever since the problem started with KH-13 the panel had been driving him crazy. With each change he'd had to alert JCS, all the defense commands, and call Offutt Air Force Base in Nebraska for immediate alert notification. Offutt, in turn, sounded an alert to SAC flight crews on standby for the mission call. Depending on the level of threat, if an intrusion was detected, they would either scramble a squadron of B-2s or dispatch F-117 interceptors from the nearest airbase to track an unidentified impostor. These days, missile silo squadrons went on alert only on rare occasions. Since the end of the Cold War with the two superpowers in political good standing, ICBM alerts had been relatively rare. Regardless, strategic alert status was kept up at a ready with instant notification. There was always the slight chance for a rogue nation to flex its muscles.

By now, he was wide awake. Night shift had its ups and downs. It screwed with his internal clock. He could never get used to the disruptive sleep pattern. Five days on, two off until rotation change. He turned his attention back to the job at hand. As duty officer, he had to verify the programmed flight path of the KH wings. With another keystroke he refreshed the gigantic status screen. It repainted the flight paths for the orbiting space assets. He took a few seconds to study the programmed coordinates. *Great. No alarms.* He could relax. A few seconds later his mind lost hold again. His concentrated effort to stay on tracking the orbits drifted on to his next assignment. His body gradually relapsed into a slouched position once more. His focus caught the short-time calendar propped in front of him. Almost the entire year had been checked off. *A couple of weeks to go before DEROS.* The "Date of Expected Return from Overseas" calendar, popular for overseas assignments, usually applied to shorter tours of duty overseas, had been readily adopted for CONUS[20] assignments. It served the entire military community.

With the end of the Cold War and the dismantling of many of the ICBMs, this place had grown quite boring, at least until the recent alarms with the KHs.

Regardless of political state, "Space Force Application" maintained a combat-ready force around the clock for the remaining ICBMs. The command was responsible for all components of the nation's strategic triad including land, sea, and space assets with a ninety-nine percent on-alert readiness.

After four years duty at this station, he still pondered what effects that one percent of failure would have on the nation. *That's for my replacement to worry about*, he decided with a sigh of relief.

---

[20] CONUS is the common acronym for "Continental U.S." within the defense community.

OFFUTT AIR FORCE BASE

Lewis "Hawk" Hawkins, mission commander, SAC,[21] took a deep drag on a Lucky Strike. Immediately, he felt the gratifying rush of burnt tobacco pump through his veins. A few hacking coughs later, he reminded himself, for the umpteenth time, "Should really quit smoking." He knew that one of these days he'd have to give up his last remaining pleasure. He wasn't getting any younger and had promised the wife for years to give up this "nasty habit," as she called it. He persistently ignored the negative health reports the AMA put out insisting "smoking could cause cancer." The reports never used to bother him. "Don't believe everything you read," he used to say to her. He wasn't so sure anymore with the prolonged coughing spells he suffered following each cold. He knew he should get that checkup his wife kept insisting on. His personal thoughts were interrupted by the phone.

"NORAD," the voice hammered in his ear. "Cancel the alert. Status is back to Four."

"Roger. Will notify my team," he slurred, somewhat relieved. *Just another test,* came to his mind. Although there had been military overtures in recent days made by a couple of what he considered rogue nations, the globe, from a political perspective, had been relatively quiet. He read the news. He knew what went on in the world. Alerts initiated by NORAD were usually pretty closely linked to world events.

He picked up the hot line. A craggy voice answered on the first ring. "What's the status?"

"Stand down for now. Mission's been scrubbed."

He casually reclined in the commander's chair and propped both legs on top of the desk. Both hands clasped behind his neck was his favorite position. Completely relaxed, he could feel the vibration created by the jet engines slowly winding down. Two F-117s had been on hold on the nearby tarmac. He loved that sound. It mixed well with the acrid smell generated by the turbine exhaust. *I must be addicted to JP4. Better yet,* he shot a glance at the cigarette burning between his fingers, *addicted to all fumes.*

From the desk, he had a clear view of the runway. He loved watching the planes take off and land. It was his life. To the consternation of the wife, he spent more time at the office than at home. It would be his last assignment before retirement. He would sure miss his job. He tried to imagine how it would be like spending twenty-four hours a day in the company of the wife. *I'll find out soon, that's for sure.*

With the tarmac quiet, he let his gaze sweep around the familiar office space. Tacked to the walls were many pictures, plaques, and awards he'd received over the years. His favorite picture had always been the one of the B-2 stealth. Years ago, before accepting the desk job, he was mission commander in one of these magnificent birds. He could still feel the prestige and power surge sitting behind the fly-by-wire controlled majestic wing.

He could still taste the exhilaration of flying the fortress into the stratosphere. A complement of support personnel on the ground made sure the performance of each flight, at a cost of one billion plus, was flawless and without failure. It was the pride and joy of the United States Strategic Air Command.

---

[21] Strategic Air Command - Major Command of the United States Air Force and a Specified Command of the United States Department of Defense. Operational establishment in charge of America's land-based strategic bomber aircraft and land-based intercontinental ballistic missile (ICBM) strategic nuclear arsenal.

Waiting for the next mission alert, that would sound as sure as the sun came up, he pulled his beloved album on Offutt from the desk drawer. Paging through the album with its colorful history, the Hawk once again indulged himself into his favorite subject: Air Force history.

MADRAS (Chandra Industries)

Rajesh was profusely shaking his head. "Why haven't you told me sooner?" He was waving a personnel folder in front of the strained face of his chief software developer.

"We did not know," his chief developer defended himself. "May I point out," he said to justify his position further, "you hired him."

"That is no excuse." Rajesh was mitigating his superiority. "You worked with him."

"I had no authorization to tell him what to do. He reported directly to you."

"Let's not quarrel." Rajesh made the piece offer. "We have work to do. We need to fix this."

Hasan Hammad, the subject of their dispute, had spent the past years managing the satellite project for Rajesh. It was not always easy getting the time off he needed to meet with the jihad mission commanders. But with the age of the mobile phone, he could slip away for short periods without anyone being the wiser. For important meetings he would inform Rajesh, "I'll be on the road a few days." In no time at all, he became the most trusted officer in the company. He seemed to flourish taking care of the tight hardware and software test schedules. The promotion to CIO gave him the license to move freely. Rajesh came to depend solely on him.

Because of the high-pressure schedule, Hammad was able to hire new recruits without delays. He was able to manipulate the direction of the project, but not without outside help. And help readily came from sympathetic sources such as Pakistan, Iran, and North Korea. Each country provided a specific element needed for the mission ahead. He was able to use hardware engineers from Pakistan whereas explosives experts came from Iran. North Korea would play a role later down the road.

It was no easy task to fit the pieces together, but anything was possible when you had the money. There seemed to be unlimited funds. Where the money came from he could only guess. The cost of an item did not matter. All he had to do was ask. Under his supervision, every mission segment was meticulously developed and tested. Years into the program, he could finally relax. He walked into Rajesh's office. "I need time off."

"You deserve it," he was told. "Why don't you take a couple of weeks? I can handle the delivery to the U.S. government. Your job is basically finished. We will line up something else for you when you get back."

"Fine," he said, looking at his employer and childhood friend one last time before heading for the airport where he boarded a flight destined for Islamabad.

Presently, on board a commercial airliner, Hammad sat back in the comfort of first class. The flight was on its way to a new destination. It would be the beginning for a new chapter in his life. *What will be next?* He wondered.

His gaze struck his hands neatly folded on his lap. *Strong hands. No,* he corrected himself, *powerful hands, and under worked.* He made an effort to assess the time he'd spent in India. *What have I accomplished?* It was the first time he'd been able to relax since taking on the project. The flight would take several hours.

The flight attendant appeared from the galley. She steered directly for him. With her trained smile she handed him the tea he'd requested. "Here we are." She lingered a few seconds expecting a response, but, when none came forward, she moved on to the next passenger. He had not even noticed the opportunity she extended. Women meant nothing to him. To Hammad, they were an object of pleasure. There was a time and place for it.

This was not the place. His mind was on the mission that lay ahead. He let his mind drift back to the time it all started.

THE PENTAGON

Alex met his daughter and longtime friend Brian for lunch at the Ground Zero Café. He'd arrived early. The morning had been slow getting started. Earlier, he'd debated whether to visit the Smithsonian, more precisely the Air and Space Museum, his favorite, but decided against it at the last minute. He didn't want to get trapped in beltway traffic and get here late. A waiter had just served the Latte Grande he ordered while waiting for them to show. The place felt crowded. Or was it only him? *Should go out more often,* he reminded himself. Living semi-isolated in his shelter by the Rockies did not help his social life. Talking with Foster gave him a sense of belonging again. At least, he had a purpose to get out once more. Perhaps even travel. His thoughts were wandering. They lingered on his daughter. He hadn't seen her in ages. Her abrupt behavior earlier bothered him. *Could she still hold a grudge for my childhood neglect?* She practically grew up without him, without a father, and so did his other daughter. Thoughts like these bothered him. He felt remorseful. *Enough of that.* He shifted his mind to other subjects.

He studied the people coming and going. A plaque caught his eyes. It listed the names of the people that had perished here. *How long has it been?* He tried to imagine what it must have been like when the Boeing 757 struck the north wing. Horrific, to say the least. Today, no traces were left. The place was business as usual. *Truly,* he reflected, *time heals most wounds.*

Walking in chatting and all smiles, he spotted them immediately when they arrived. *They make a nice couple.* He got on his feet, waving a hand. Tracy spotted him. He was still unsure how to handle the greeting. She took the worry out of him. She was as charming as ever. *I'm making too much of it...guilt, remorse...and all.* She practically jumped at his chest. Her arms clutched around his neck. She planted a kiss on his cheek. *All is forgiven.* "I'm glad to see you, Dad," she said with the customary warmth he so dearly missed. "It's been so long."

"Too long," Alex replied. He acknowledged Brian with a friendly pat on the shoulder. "So," he remarked with the candor of old friends, "you met my daughter."

"You'd asked me to, remember?"

"…what brought you here?" Tracy broke in. She was anxious to get the latest news from friends and family.

"General friend asked me to check into something. Work I did years back."

"How long are you going to stay?"

"Few days..." Alex was interrupted by the waiter. He'd lingered by the table, trying to get their attention. Alex put him off but noticed his impatient demeanor.

"Why don't we order lunch and talk then," he suggested. "Might take a while for him to come back." The lunch crowd was arriving.

"I'll have a BLT," Tracy ordered.

"Same here," Brian echoed.

Alex closed the menu after a brief pause. "Salad's fine with me." The waiter quickly left the table.

"So," Brian started the conversation, "what's up?" He was facing Alex.

"Been tasked to check into some contracts."

"Talk about it?"

"Some," he speculated, "as long as we keep it on general terms."

"Sensitive?"

"EMP, neutron pulsing," he cautioned, "etc…etc…your guess."

"Here we go," Tracy interrupted. She shot a glance at Brian who shifted his attention her way. "Hope you have a couple of hours to spare. You just touched on Dad's favorite turf."

"No problem." He shifted his focus back to Alex. "We'll take the time."

"Here's my rationale," Alex began to explain. "I've been following world events for many years. On the surface, life appears as usual, but that's not the case. Beneath, power struggle's goin' on."

"What do you mean?"

"You may've heard about the New World Order."

"Globalization," Brian confirmed with a light nod. "I'm aware of it, but," he shot a glance at Tracy, "refuse to let it bother me." He wouldn't want her to get a tainted picture of him.

"It's played down politically," Alex continued, "but it's real, nonetheless. Ever wonder why regional conflicts are not resolved immediately and completely?"

"I've wondered about that," Tracy remarked. She had her own view on world events.

"It's big business for policy makers and industrialists to promote and prolong conflicts. Take terrorism, for instance. It'll never be eliminated from the globe. They'll persist. Law enforcement agencies and support organizations are already dependent on it as an industry. That's my assessment."

"I've also noticed," Brian agreed, "a developing pattern."

"Aside from that," Alex continued, "nature's not helping us either, maintaining stability. Global warming on the rise, ice caps melting, ozone layer disappearing, or so meteorologists claim. It may be overstated, but all the pollution created by industry can't possibly help. Westerners learned to clean up after themselves, but developing nations still need to be educated."

"You turn Green Peace?"

"No." Alex felt rebuffed. "Just a reality check. To make things worse," he went on, "on my last project I learned about the real threat. A threat much closer to home. If terrorists ever get their hands on it, we'll be in deep shit."

"Dad!"

"Sorry."

"What're you talking about?"

"Excuse me." The waiter had suddenly popped out of the crowd. He efficiently served silverware with one hand and balanced sandwich plates with the other. His presence faded as quickly as it had appeared.

Alex poked at his salad. "Electromagnetic field effects," he picked up the conversation, "neutron pulsing."

"Don't we control all the planet's nuclear materials?" Tracy's face took on a look of concern. Her hand held her sandwich, poised in the air; she momentarily suspended another bite. Her interest seemed piqued at what he just said.

"We've tried." Alex shrugged. "But lost control. Former soviet states put much of their inventory up for sale on the international markets."

"What can we do to protect ourselves?" Brian showed equal concern.

"Sure you want to get into details?" Tracy cut in. She was growing distraught at all this gloom. She'd rather have talked about her dad's visit and family life.

"Sorry." Alex suddenly became aware of having stolen the center of attention. "Whenever I've got someone's ear," he excused himself, "I get carried away."

"I hear you," Brian said. "Go on."

"It's the only time I can voice my concerns," Alex complained. "Nobody seems worried. Can't talk to the general public, and," he dwelled, "government's pleading ignorance."

"You can talk with us. We've got similar credentials," Brian assured him. He checked with Tracy, who was nodding in assent.

Deferring family interests for the moment, she chimed in, "We insist."

"Let's take a closer look at the technology," Alex picked up the conversation. "It's important to understand the threat, but let me give you some basics first." He briefly highlighted on the science behind EMP. An electromagnetic pulse was an intense energy field that could instantly overload or disrupt electrical circuits, even at a great distance. Modern electronics were especially sensitive to this. Making matters worse, EMP could be produced on a large scale using a single nuclear device, and on a smaller, non-nuclear scale, triggered by a battery or minute chemical agent.

"I thought trigger devices were pretty much controlled and managed by the NRC.[22]"

"One would think." Some nations, including purported sponsors of terrorism, might currently have the capability to use EMP as a weapon for cyber warfare or cyber terrorism. Their primary purpose was to disrupt computer and communication systems.

"How realistic is the threat?" Tracy seemed to get evermore immersed.

"Pretty real—take my word."

"Your concern's starting to make sense," Brian admitted.

"There's more, but it raises several policy issues."

"Like what?"

"One: what are we doing to protect critical infrastructure systems against the threat of EMP? Two: does the level of vulnerability of our civilian and military electronics encourage other nations to develop or acquire nuclear weapons? Three: how likely are terrorist organizations to launch an EMP attack against the United States?"

"Pretty serious issues."

"You're not kidding."

"What's the answer?" Facing her dad, Tracy wanted to know.

"Shielding the infrastructure, air, land, and sea, the whole nation," he emphasized, "but at tremendous cost." The initial action created gamma radiation interacting with the atmosphere. This action generated an intense electromagnetic energy field but was relatively harmless to people because it radiated upward into space. The rays reaching the ground could overload electronic circuitry with effects similar to a lightning strike but much more powerful only fully understood in the '50s with tests conducted in the Pacific.

"Give me an example closer to home."

"If you insist." Alex picked up the thread after munching another fork load from the salad. "Single device detonated at an appropriate altitude, let's say over Kansas, could affect all of the continental U.S."

"Really?"

"Reason is," he detailed out, "that the force can be picked up by metallic conductors such as wire or power cable. It'd act as antennae to conduct the energy shockwave into

---

[22] Nuclear Regulatory Commission - The NRC oversees reactor safety and security, reactor licensing and renewal, radioactive material safety, and spent fuel management (storage, security, recycling, and disposal).

the electronic systems of cars, airplanes, and communication equipment. There's much more," he paused, "but…we'd probably be talking about technology overload."

"Where you getting all this?"

"Used to design countermeasures, remember?"

"Right." Brian recalled similar conversations in the past. "Go on."

"Maybe some other time," Alex cautioned. "Getting into a real sensitive area here."

"You're right," Brian agreed. He seemed eager to hear more but was distracted by his mobile chirping from his pocket. He tried to ignore it, but it kept buzzing. Slightly agitated, he fished for the gadget and took the call, intently listening for a minute.

"Right away." He sounded troubled when the call ended. A concerned frown on the face, he turned to Tracy.

"What?" She was alerted by his look.

"We've got to go, and…you won't like it."

"KH," she confirmed. "Another alarm?"

"That's right," he replied. "Think we need to work this one out of SPACECOM."

"Colorado?"

"Can't get a handle on the platform from this end," he stated. "Need to work it from the control center."

"That means," Alex suggested, "you two could fly back with me…tomorrow?"

"Looks that way." Brian sought out Tracy's eyes. "How about it? Feel up to visiting your hometown?"

She hastily agreed then abruptly stood up, turned, planted another kiss on her dad's cheek, and headed towards the exit. Brian followed closely behind. They had things to do on such short notice.

Alex picked up the check. He squared the bill on the way out. He met up with them by the exit and handed Tracy his departure information for the next morning expecting her to book the flights.

Alex headed back to the hotel. He was humming a tune by John Denver, "Rocky Mountain High." He felt elated to have his daughter and best friend back at the Castle, if only for a few days. Tomorrow promised to be a great start for solving problems.

CASTLE ROCK

They caught an early flight out of Dulles. All three arrived at the departure terminal from different points within fifteen minutes of each other. Tracy had left her apartment in Annapolis, Brian his downtown flat, and Alex the hotel near National where he'd checked in the day before, all headed for 495. Once on the Beltway they'd made excellent time on the toll road to the airport. Commuter traffic hadn't picked up yet, and, besides, they were going against it. City travel could be murder, as all knew well, especially when major links were bogged down from frequent congestions and mishaps.

Alex arrived first. Tracy and Brian each had booked a seat on the Airporter bus service the night before. They just showed up. "Morning, Dad...sleep well?" All were in heightened spirits waiting for the flight to board.

The load was light this morning. Alex sat up front, busy working out a strategy for Foster. Brian and Tracy took seats in back to enjoy some privacy. "Looking forward to Colorado?" Brian asked while getting comfortable in the seat. He barely noticed the hum of the engines. On the contrary, it felt soothing on his body.

"I am...once I get there. Got fond memories of the place," she said, "growing up."

"How long has it been?"

Leaning towards him to close the distance a bit she explained, "After graduating the Academy high school, I went to Polytech for four years and then moved to D.C. Been there ever since."

"Didn't you have an Air Force commitment with the Academy?"

"Not in high school," she explained. "It's true for college. How about you?"

Despite the cool stream of air flowing from overhead vents, he could feel the warmth of her body emanating from her skin. "I've moved so many times in and out the country it's hard to keep track."

"Just like Dad."

"You love your dad," he asked, "don't you?"

"More than anything." Her eyes took on a hint of melancholy. It was more of a veil of sadness. It faded as quickly as it came on. "He's the reason," she said, "I'm sitting here today, next to you."

Four hours later, after a thirty-minute layover in Denver, the party arrived at the Colorado Springs airport. Brian hailed a cab. He checked into his favorite inn, the Ramada near the airport.

Alex led his daughter to the public garage nearby. "Wow." She couldn't help but admire the sleek looking BMW waiting in the stall. "Like your lifestyle. Always wanted one myself."

He fishtailed out of the airport proper to demonstrate the power under the hood. Twenty minutes and forty-five miles later they arrived at the Castle. "Here we are." Alex was panting while stretching his legs. It always took him a couple paces and a few deep inhales to adjust back to altitude. They were at seventy-five hundred feet above sea level. It would take Tracy days, perhaps weeks, to readjust. It was quite a change from

Baltimore. She appeared already winded trying to get the luggage from the trunk. "Let me," Alex demanded. "You go on inside." He collected the luggage. "I'm happy you're here."

"Me, too," she agreed. "It's been too long." She stood by the entrance a few moments to give the place a once over. "Still looks the same," she approved. "Tidy as ever."

With a quick wave of his head, Alex encouraged her to cross the threshold. He carried her case. He led her to the living area. "Care for a drink? Or would you rather unpack?"

"That can wait. Wine would be fine."

They sat for hours, catching up while savoring his favorite cabernet. Alex was interested in her life back east. They also touched on the recent satellite problems without getting into classified details and the reason she was here. He did not want to compromise her position. Even though he held similar clearances, information was categorized as need-to-know. You never knew if Big Brother was listening. He was well aware of their technologies and capabilities. He exercised caution all the time. And there had been incidences of which he'd rather not be reminded.

It was back in his contracting days. Every so often one of his teammates failed to show up on the jobsite. Such an absence would always be followed by a visit from federal agents informing him about a security breach. Everybody knew the consequences of such an infraction, but in the heat of a conversation, for instance, one could easily overlook the sensitivity of the mission. Losing a clearance this way was a career-ending mistake. Accessible to all intelligence agencies, the file went to the central register. It was a sure guarantee the individual would never work or contract for an Intel agency again.

"Great wine, Daddy. What's it called again?" She always enjoyed the brand he served.

"You should know," he offered with a challenging hint. "Only get one vintage. Take a guess."

"Don't tell me…I know—Barons de Rothschild, Lafitte, probably five years old," she volunteered. She'd almost forgotten the guessing games they used to play.

"Good memory," he cheered. He took a few strides across the room to open the windows. He could have turned on the solar-powered air conditioning but preferred the clear air of the Rockies. "It'll cool down in a couple minutes." He'd locked the place tight before going on the trip. Not that this area was prone to crime, but it was a habit he'd acquired from having spent years in tumultuous places where break-ins and burglaries were commonplace. This place was almost as secure as a vault, but you never knew how desperate or determined an intruder might be. "Care for a bite to eat?"

She nodded in acknowledgement aware of him busy preparing lunch. Gazing through the large picture window, she had a clear view into the mountains. She'd forgotten how spectacular it was. Her eyes took in the scene. Her thoughts were turned inward when she realized it'd been years since she felt this relaxed. *Dad sure knows how to live.* She watched him pace in and out of the efficiently organized kitchen, getting things from the fridge. She admired the vigor with which he attacked things no matter how miniscule the task. He seemed focused on every move. *Disciplined training from the old country,* he'd explained on more than one occasion. There, educators placed great emphasis on the industry's philosophy: "Only do something once—but do it the right way." It meant calculating each move before it was executed. This could mean taking additional time in setting things up, but at the end of the day, it would save time and energy. Most people never thought in those terms, but he did.

Her focus shifted to the glass of wine sitting in front of her. The refracted sunrays sparkled brilliantly as they passed through the hand-cut German-lead crystal, cutting into the deep dark red of the wine. Years ago, she recalled, he'd educated her on the nuances of fine wine. Coming from Europe, he appreciated the rich wines from Germany, France, and Italy. Back then, it didn't interest her much. But now she could recognize and appreciate the quality. He taught her well, not only in the ways of wine, but in many other aspects of life. After her mom left, they used to sit up nights, discussing philosophical topics from history and psychology to science and technology, along with many more subjects. She'd affectionately addressed him as her "modern philosopher." He'd always appreciated that. *Perhaps,* she thought, *not many know of his quiet intellect and the unheralded accomplishments of a lifelong career.*

In all her days, she had never met anyone quite like him. She'd always adored her dad. He was her mentor. He was her hero. It was probably the reason why she had not yet had a serious relationship. She was holding out for similar qualities in a romantic partner, and that was not likely to happen anytime soon. Not with her commitment to the career.

Alex broke the spell with a plate of chicken fettuccini accompanied by lightly-salted garlic bread and garden salad, which he'd placed in front of her. "So, what do you think of him?" her dad wanted to know on a more personal note.

"Brian? I really like him."

"Glad you hit it off. Great guy, known him many years."

They enjoyed a relaxed meal and more wine in the leisure of each other's company. They were catching up on several years of separation. She talked about her life, work, and accomplishments, and he told tales from the past. The rest of the day flew by in no time at all.

Watching her suppress a yawn, he suggested, "Take a nap. You probably want to unpack." He had some work to do.

"Right."

"I'm happy you finally made it here."

"Me, too, Dad." She briskly got up to fetch her suitcase.

"You know your way," Alex offered. "Room's still the same since you left. Only check in to clean once in a while."

NORAD COMMAND

"Duty Officer Jones."

"Network security group, please," Alex requested. He was watching Tracy disappear into her room. Waiting for the distant end to connect, he thought, filled with parental pride, *quite a woman she'd turned out to be.*

"Just a minute," was the gruff response.

He wondered what kind of person the voice belonged to. Whenever he was placed on hold, his mind gradually drifted to the far end. He would imagine the environment. It was a mental game he played to occupy the time while waiting. *Probably counting the minutes 'til shift change. Name like that—from the South...Louisiana or Tennessee.*

"NORAD Security." A new voice interrupted his idle thoughts.

"Have an urgent request to access your secure network."

"Verification code?" The communications specialist seemed efficient. It was his job to dole out VPN access codes. He was one of NORAD's man-machine interfaces. Once he issued the secure parameters, it was up to machines to verify, authorize, and authenticate.

Using NATO's standardized phonetics, Alex enunciated his access code, "Charlie-alpha-sierra-tango-lima-echo-romeo-oscar-charlie-kilo," then took a short breath and added the pass code, "Delta-echo-foxtrot-charlie-oscar-november-fiver."

"Request's been authorized...your thumbprint, please."

Alex touched the built-in finger scanner on the laptop then waited for confirmation. It came within seconds.

"Connection confirmed. Access lease's good for three days."

"Appreciate it." Alex hung up. Well, that was easy, he thought. Technology must be getting better at the old mountain.

Using his business credentials, he logged into the secure network. He was ready for the next command, "Strategic Defense Grid." The splash page loaded in seconds. It had been awhile since he'd used the link. *Yep,* he confirmed after securing the connection, *still there.* The computer screen sprang into action. A stream of coded data pumped onto his drive. From there, digitized data was instantly painted onto the flat screen monitor. Sharply defined color images scanned neatly across the screen painting U.S. defense barriers. He needed current information for the report he'd promised Foster.

Alex carefully studied the radar configurations. He'd been here many times in the past. Over the years, with the end of the Cold War, many had been eliminated. Some removed. Others relocated. All because of defense budget cuts, or, in some instances, threat levels shifting in different directions. But the basic core was still intact. The screen provided a clear layout for the various barriers still in place.

The first system painted on the screen was the Distant Early Warning Line. "DEW" was a network of fifty-seven microwave stations along the 70th parallel cutting through Greenland. It gave around three hours advance warning in case of bomber attacks across the pole before they could reach major U.S. population areas. That was when ICBMs tipped with nuclear warheads were carried by long-range bombers on both sides. Since then, attack time with ICBMs had been cut down to twenty minutes. Not a comforting thought, when, in most cases, it'd take that long to make a command decision, providing the command was on alert.

The second line of defense, the "McGill Fence," consisted of a Doppler radar complex for the detection of low-flying craft, a system roughly 300 miles north of the Pinetree Line along the 55th parallel.

Next line of defense was the "Pinetree Line." It consisted of thirty-three radar stations spread across Southern Canada.

The last line of defenses was directed across the oceans. Attacks from the Pacific or Atlantic were detected by the "Airborne Early Warning" aircraft, Navy ships, or offshore radar platforms. So prolific was the defense system, that by the early 1960s a quarter of a million personnel were involved in the operation of NORAD.

Alex was drilling deeper into the classified infrastructure. Confronted with each layer, he had to cope with the more sensitive MIL, DIS, and SCI nets, the heart of NORAD. He dug up the data he was interested in. "Condition Green," the scrolling text announced in likewise color. He exhaled a breath of relief. There was still time. The defense conditions were listed in their appropriate colors. Even though he knew them well, he'd not seen red, ever. *And it's a good thing.* It'd mean doomsday.

Although all equipment in Cheyenne Mountain was put through rigorous inspections through periodic testing, aside from the failed Bay of Pigs attempt and Cuban Naval blockade, on at least two occasions failure in its computer systems had pushed the world to the brink of World War III.

Alex recalled the two most recent incidents well, because they were the direct result of systems malfunctions while his crew was performing careless maintenance on the equipment.

The first occurred on June 2, 1980, when a technician loaded a test tape but failed to switch the system status to "Test" mode. The mistake caused a stream of false warnings to be spread to government bunkers and command posts worldwide.

The second occurred because of a hardware malfunction during a 427M systems upgrade with FTC-31, an automatic secure voice communications network integration project. The Federal Technical Communications program, then responsible for upgrades and integrations, grew out of WWII supporting government programs. The 427M system, a generic term known to the outside world as WOPR, the War Operations Plan Response, was the heart of the project. It provided an interface to the outside world, also immortalized by the film *War Games.*

Alex saw enough for today. He ended his search through the national defense systems. Inquiries from special agencies were sure to follow today's intrusion. But checking his credentials against the security files would sanctify his name. He had good reasons to capture uncensored and unbiased information. He was an additional line of defense. A defense authorized only by Foster.

NSA HEADQUARTERS

As soon as he stepped into the office, Jack Warner was handed the daily folder by his secretary. "Sir, your brief." Immediately, he noticed the pink folder stamped, "Top Secret/SCI." Aside from the daily status reports on global events, it contained a high priority report. Documents of this nature were not an everyday occurrence and were given immediate attention.

Today's folder included highly sensitive data. It was a profile. It hadn't been supplied by an agent. It was generated by a CRAY Jaguar XT4, in conjunction with an IBM Blue Gene supercomputer lurking underground in the deep recesses of the organization.

Technology sure has come a long way since RISSMAN, TELLMAN, XMP, and YMP, he thought. Warner opened the folder. Right away he recognized the automated computer printout. An Intel watch list, it'd been generated by Carnivore. It read:

ALERT STATUS: HIGH
PRIORITY: IMMEDIATE
CLASSIFICATION: EXTREMELY SENSITIVE
TOPIC: INTELLIGENCE SATELLITE
GROUP: KEYHOLE
SERIES: ALPHA
ORDER: POSSIBLE COMPROMISE
LOCATION: PAKISTAN
LINK: AL QAEDA
SOURCE: MOBILE TELECOM
SUBJECT: HASAN HAMMAD
MATCH FOUND:
JIHAD...KEYHOLE...EMP... MISSION...PLAN...TARGET...SCHEDULE...
REPORT: END
NNNN

Scanning over the report with swift eyes, his face turned serious. A deep frown had formed on his forehead. "Why haven't I been informed earlier?" He yelled at the secretary who visibly shrunk from the verbal onslaught. "Is everybody asleep?" He was close to losing it. He shot the brief close and locked the copy up in the safe then dialed the secure number.

"Harris," the other end answered.

He recognized the voice. "Just received an automated report from Big Brother regarding one of your projects. Need you to check it."

"Region?"

"Pakistan."

"Level?"

"SCI. You can use our resources in the Middle East if you need assistance. The report's on the way. Give it your immediate attention."

"Right."

"How long you plan to stay in Colorado?"

"Don't know yet...just had a repeat alarm. We'll be working with SPACECOM out of Pete Field to get a handle. May need all their resources to solve this one," Brian summed up.

"Okay. Keep me posted." With that, the mobile went dead.

Brian had just checked in at the motel when the call came. Rarely did he use a local line. Most were unsecured. The mobile provided secure access on top of authentication and encryption. *Modern miracle*, he marveled. In the past he used to take the page and locate the nearest "Skiff" to return the call. Today, SCIFs were few and far between. They were costly. Only agencies and the successful contractor could put them up and afford to support them.

With his feet propped on the edge of the desk, feeling cozy, he turned to the laptop. He punched a function key to load his favorite application: a client copy of Carnivore. He gave a lot of credit to the guys designing the software. He remembered working alongside the tech-talking UNIX geeks, way back in the 1970s, each coming up with new ideas to incorporate into the software. There were no restrictions on structure and design back then. Software was the result of academic wizards and private gurus incorporating every conceivable idea.

Brian used to watch a couple of guys playing a word game they'd designed. The idea started as simple code breaker programmed years earlier. The objective was to encode and decode words and sentences with specially designed algorithms. The early algorithms were based on the mechanical Enigma machine used in WWII to break the Japanese code. Since then, encryption had become so sophisticated and complex it would take an enemy's supercomputer months to resolve. By that time, events were usually over and rendered academic. Today's codes changed randomly with every input to keep from establishing trends.

He watched the familiar NSA homepage load in the foreground. In back, the computer automatically found a satellite link, connecting with a "secure connection established." It never ceased to amaze him, looking at the screen-wide logo: "National Security Agency—United States of America," with its centrally fixed American eagle carrying a stars and stripes shield. He was proud to work with the agency.

As promised, the document was already on cue. He recognized a name right away. He remembered it from working with an outsourcing firm in India while meeting a number of managers and engineers tasked to put the satellites together.

The name Hasan Hammad stood out. He was one of the outsourcing project managers. It could be a coincidence. I was up to him to find out. He checked his wristwatch. 10:30 a.m. in Colorado. That made it 10:30 p.m. India time.

He pulled up a contact list and placed the name into the search parameters. The search had a response as soon as he'd entered the last keystroke: "Rajesh Chandra, Madras, India." It included the office address and phone contact. Brian dialed the number. Rajesh answered after a few rings.

"This is Rajesh."

"It's me, Brian Harris."

"Hello, my friend," Rajesh answered. The voice sounded cheerful. "How have you been?"

"Busy as usual," Brian responded. "I'll have to come your way again someday."

"We've also been busy, as you probably know. Business has been profitable to us, thanks to your country."

"So I hear," Brian acknowledged. He was happy to hear of the prosperity.

"Our economy is booming with high-tech, you know. We have more work than hours in the day. Everybody is employed. Just keep sending us work," he chuckled, "life has been good for the last five years…"

"I'm happy for you," Brian broke in. "Listen." He would have liked to chat some more but this was too important. He had to cut his former partner short. "We need to talk about something, but it's confidential. Can we talk in private?"

"Can you give me few minutes? I will call you back on a VPN socket. I have your number on the caller ID, yes?" Rajesh replied.

Wonder where the software's gone wrong, Brian thought while waiting for the call. Was it possible Rajesh had something to do with it? Thought I knew the guy. I'll have to put him to the test. Sorry, old fellow, but national security's got priority over personal sentiments.

His mobile rang a few minutes later. He was ready. "Rajesh?" he answered in a somewhat reserved tone.

"Yes, we are secure."

"Think we have a breach in the software."

"But how can this be?" It was a worrisome reply. "It has been in operation for years."

"Problem developed over the course of a couple of months," he informed his business friend. "I've analyzed the application software your people loaded but can't find the problem. I'm not that familiar with the latest version and need your people to check it out. Something's triggering orbital changes in some of the satellites."

"I don't understand…" The words were almost pleading.

"To make things worse, the system's locking out our operators when they access the software console. We've reloaded several times, but the problem keeps coming back," Brian explained. "Looks like something or somebody's manipulating the system."

"As you know," Rajesh offered, "we don't have access to the live birds, but I can get my chief developer on the simulator immediately. Can you send me the latest satellite data? I will need to compare the telemetry readout with our sample code."

After listening to the response, Brian felt a bit easier. He had reassured himself of the sincerity of his business friend.

"I'll get it to you," Brian said.

"Give me a couple of days to get back with you," Rajesh offered. "I will call about the same time. We will work something out."

"One more thing," Brian prompted. "Does Hammad still work for you? I remember him being on the project."

"No. He left. Said he was moving back to Pakistan to be near his family. I can understand that. The family here comes first. Without the family, life is empty. Why do you ask?"

"Oh, no special reason." He was ready to defuse the inquiry. "Just thought I'd ask." It ended their conversation.

Apparently, Brian thought with relieve, *guy's clean. Doesn't know anything about the compromise.*

At least he had something to get the investigation going. He pushed a programmed button, dialing NSA headquarters. Brian relayed the bit of information about Hasan's last point of known contact to start the investigation. NSA itself did not carry out investigations. For that, his agency called on either the FBI or the CIA, depending on the theater of responsibility.

CIA HEADQUARTERS

Harry Carter was mulling over the detention order he had issued days earlier. *What was her name again,* "Tracy Bauer." He hadn't heard about it and needed to check with Arizona. He was about to reach for the phone when there was a brief knock on the oak encased office door. "Sir," the neatly dressed secretary said as she entered. It was her first day on the job.

Harry Carter, from behind his solid cut oak desk gave her a once over. "You new here?"

"First day." Her voice wavered with diffidence.

"Relax," he eased her on then stretched across the desk to reach for the brief she handed him. It was the daily report. He'd been expecting it. It was late again. It used to be promptly on the desk when he came to the office. He gave her a break, *first day.* Otherwise, he'd reprimanded her. Although the delay wasn't her fault, she was the visible interface with his elusive staff.

He noticed the pink cover sheet. He didn't react. After years in office, he had been desensitized to the ever-present crisis situations. He wasn't so sure if things got better with technology. Computers could not reason things out or rationalize a situation. They were only as good as the input provided.

No matter how sophisticated the ECHELON program, Carter thought as he read the day's report, *it's only as strong as its weakest link.* "And that's," he turned audible, "man himself."

"Sir?"

Carter noticed her shifting uneasily from one leg to the other but said nothing. Something in the daily had caught his immediate attention:

    ALERT STATUS: HIGH
    PRIORITY: IMMEDIATE
    CLASSIFICATION: EXTREMELY SENSITIVE
    TOPIC: JIHAD
    ORDER: INCREASED CHATTER
    LOCATION: PAKISTAN
    LINK: AL QAEDA
    SOURCE: MOBILE PHONE
    REPORT: END
    NNNN

Using his special access credentials, Carted thought he better verify the validity of the data. He called up ECHELON. The program came back with additional information. This one perked his interests. Where the rest of the world was relatively calm, there seemed to be heightened communication exchanges between North Korean military commands and foreign embassies.

"ECHELON..." Carter deliberated, "last trusted friend," if only a machine. With all the negative publicity and political distrust in the world, who else could you depend on but a reliable computer application?

Carter noticed the new hire still lingering. She seemed unsure of what to expect. "Tell you what," he offered, "see that folder by the case?"

"The one marked ECHELON?"

"Read it. It'll highlight your duties for this office."

"Thank you, sir," she whispered. Thankfully, she took her exit with the voluminous document clutched under her arm. It was the agency's "Bible."

ECHELON was not only a name given to the application, it also identified the program. Its original design grew out of the Cold War. It was designed to address the need to eavesdrop on the enemy then—Russia and China. But since then the source of the threats had shifted from strategic superpowers to tactical elements, namely terrorist cells. It required fast responsive action—action made possible only with the help of number-crunching machines.

Millions of data bits were collected daily from thousands of communication channels. The channels included landlines, satellites, microwave receivers, and, in recent years, the massive number of mobile phones and iPads, seemingly packed with white noise. The numbers were mind-boggling. Unfortunately, computers did not know the difference between data and noise--until ECHELON. That's where the program shined through. It deciphered the avalanche of white noise. It literally filtered and extracted out any intelligence sought.

Additional needs surfaced quickly, resulting in a number of data-mining enhancements. It made life much easier for those eavesdropping on electronic communication.

In all its complicated intricacy, the American intelligence agency, together with intelligence agencies in England, Canada, Australia, and New Zealand, had established a system of satellites and computer systems that could monitor by and large all electronic communication in the world, including phone conversations, e-mails, telexes, and telefaxes, with a number of other countries affiliated as third or fourth party participants.

Carter contemplated what action to take next. It was an alarming report but not unusual. *Should I keep it with the org,* he asked himself, *or send it on?* It was a mental struggle he was forced into ever since the DHS was established. New policies demanded collaboration with the other intelligence agencies for shared threat analysis and risk management.

"To hell with them," he muttered with distaste, then, in a swift motion, pulled the report sheet from the folder and fed it through the shredder. "Let them do their own work."

ISLAMABAD (Jihad Mission Command)

The Jeep slid to a halt inches from a boom. Thumbing at the passenger in back, the driver announced, "Hasan Hammad," gloating with a confident stare at the sentry. He and his passenger were facing a heavily armed sentry post. Defense towers were staged on both sides along the dirt road. From behind protective openings, Hammad could make out automatic arms aimed in his direction. Slightly annoyed, he patiently endured the routine identity check. Although most of the camp's force knew him by sight, he never expected to receive special treatment, especially when it involved security. He watched the guard make the call to announce his arrival.

The guard scrutinized his ID once more. An armed soldier jumped into the vehicle, flanking the driver. Pointing ahead, he commanded, "This way." They sped across the camp. Thirty seconds later, amid dust devils kicked up by the braking vehicle Hammad was dropped off in front of the headquarters building. He briskly headed for the main entrance. Stepping inside, the interior was sectioned off by divider walls. Wires and cables feeding clusters of computers and comm equipment were running everywhere. It was a typical makeshift structure. No frills. It served one purpose—tactical command and control. At the end of a mission, it could be abandoned quickly or dismantled and moved with little effort.

Gathered in the commander's room, flanked by technical experts, were several group leaders. Apart from being field trained for combat, each specialized in a particular subversive terrorist function. Some had been trained for explosives, whereas others were used for covert operations, all united with one common goal: suicide missions. Since the death of bin Laden, Hasan had rapidly escalated to an authority position. "You survived another attack from the infidels." The commander, Kazim Rashid, boisterous, bearded and uncombed, beamed. In a gratifying gesture, he moved up to proudly pump the visitor's hand.

Nearby, patiently waiting their turns, were first lieutenants from the various tactical camps, voicing personal congratulations.

"Allah was with me," Hammad admitted. The latest attempt on his life, readily publicized by Al Jazeera, Arabic news cast out of Qatar, was received with envy of yet another survival. "Protected again by Allah," were some of the headlines printed. There were even films on YouTube showing the aftermath of the latest attack on his life.

Hammad's personal presence here had become necessary. Today's meeting was to firm up the detailed processes of the mission. Expected to take several hours, it entailed a final round of trial simulations. Every step of the operation had previously been documented, checked, and verified by the mission coordinators in preparation for one final test.

"Quiet," Kazim Rashid, ordered. He took a few steps toward the wallboard. "Everybody take a seat."

"Today," he said in his commanding voice, sensing the heightened tension in the room, "we will conclude simulation runs for mission Shahadah. Scheduled date is set for September 11." The same date was selected as in 2001. It was meant to enhance the infidels' shock effect. Carried out remotely in its entirety, the mission would be a complete surprise attack. All of the target elements had been set in motion for a preemptive strike. "Once the attack is triggered," he stated, "it cannot be recalled." It would be carried out systematically. The mission was to inflict maximum damage on the American infrastructure and its citizens.

...and I will see that it's carried out, Hasan thought with delight. In anticipation of the impending mission, the feel of personal exhilaration had built to a crescendo. Although it was his plan, he quietly sat in back and let the commander have his day.

"As you know," the commander went on, "the mission has been in the planning for several years. Fortunately, to this date," he emphasized further, "we have had no indication of any compromise. For that," he proudly stated, "I must express immense gratitude to everyone on the team for following the protocol." He specifically made reference to strictly adhered coded communications and timed transmissions in-between the incessant satellite orbits. "This last simulation will take six hours, after which," he stated, "you will take your assigned positions. Mission control will be coordinated and carried out from here, Islamabad headquarters. All operatives are expected to be at the ready state by September 9. His delivery was passionate. He handed out the test plans, including a stack of checklists.

"Everybody," he instructed, "open chapter one." Familiar to all, the contents had been practiced, refined, and corrected many times. They had read and reread the plan until each step had been permanently imprinted in their minds. Although it consisted of only six chapters, The Plan contained the mission processes for all segments.

This will be my final time in this room, Hammad thought with suppressed anticipation. He was ready and prepared to execute the mission. Guided by the training commander, the team ran through its paces one final time. In summary, the test illustrated the first phase of The Plan. It was comprised of five major elements: a comprehensive action list for mission personnel; confirmation plus verification for mission progress; checklist for each mission step executed; sequential summary of major group segments for the mission; and final checklist for the entire operation.

"If any segment of the mission is compromised," Rashid emphasized, "tactical commanders will, on the spot," he paused, "evaluate the overall state of the mission. At any point," he further emphasized, "responsibilities can be shifted to backup teams. Calling off the mission," he concluded the directive, "is not an option."

Under his guidance, the final test run took place as planned with interjections such as: "Only coded terms will be used for voice and e-mail communications...The mission depends on our stealth mode of operation...We have been successful in defeating the enemy before and will do it again...Each group will have backup operators standing by in case someone cannot be at his post...All of you have been assigned to your predetermined selected location designated, 'Top Secret.'" He was determined to instill one final fear into the subject recruits. "You all know what the consequences will be if the mission is compromised."

"Finally," Hasan groaned. He sighed with relief as the test runs came to a close. He'd noticed some of the team members, at times, had become weary with the step-by-step dry run. He didn't like that one bit. The mission success depended on each and every one completing their tasks. And that took complete and total dedication. *New recruits,* he decided, *would rather be on the battlefront than sitting in this crammed room.*

It had taken great patience to work through the tedious procedures. Even his thoughts had drifted on occasion. It had taken him to the places he had visited in recent months. Now, with the final test over, his mind turned to his childhood in India and his close friend Rajesh. He wondered what Rajesh would think when he realized his friend had severely compromised honor and friendship. It would not matter. Loyalty was well in the past, overtaken by recent events.

The final practice run was over. Jolting him out of his brief comfort zone, the group commander's voice pierced into his mind. "Hasan… come."

Getting up from the chair, he readily replied, "Right." Feeling slightly troubled, he followed without objection. "What is it?"

"My office." The commander gestured towards the end of the hallway. "We need to talk."

"Okay…"

"The door," Rashid ordered with a slight gesture at the entrance. Hammad kicked it close. "Need you for a special assignment." The commander pulled a pack of cigarettes from his breast pocket and offered Hasan a smoke while taking a seat behind the desk.

"What?" Hasan pulled a lighter from his pants pocket and offered a flame in return.

Spreading out a map on the makeshift table, the commander ordered, "India. Specifically," he pointed at a region, "Madras."

"But the mission," Hammad objected, "on whose authority?" He'd been preparing for years. He could not let this happen. For his plans to succeed, he needed to be on the frontlines.

"Elders." The commander, known only to the most trusted, made reference to the invisible command authority. Although Hasan would be "Commander in Chief' elect to the world, the real authority was the Coalition, tribal chiefs dwelling in and around caves spread along Pakistani's central plateau.

"You'll be back in time."

"What's the mission?" He forced himself to remain calm.

"Termination."

"Who?"

"Possible compromise…your former employer."

The order hit him like a bombshell. He had not expected this. *"Rajesh?"* He momentarily held his breath then exhaled with force. He could feel an internal apprehension build up.

"You will coordinate the mark," the commander stated, "to an assault detachment." He then took a deep drag on a freshly lit cigarette. A puff of blue smoke billowed across the desk into Hasan's face. Smoke never bothered him. What bothered him was the statement of superiority the commander intended to convey. It was clearly a warning sign. "You will meet up with South Cell Madras," the commander said, blowing another puff across the table, "specifically," another puff, "Basil Faisal, tactical field operative."

Have I been compromised? He was on instant alert. Only he knew the real intent of The Plan and hoped the puff of smoke in the face was only a warning not to fail. He was so close to the target date. He could not afford to be exposed. Not now. A few more days of charade and he'd take control. "When?"

The commander turned gruff. "You'll be contacted." He seemed agitated by being questioned. "Should not take more than two days. Pick up your orders on the way out." He briskly got up, indicating the meeting was over.

Hasan was about to object but thought better. He felt regrets for his childhood friend and former employer, but there was no room for sentiments. Not for what he had in mind. He briskly turned and headed for the exit. Striding along the hallway, his gaze struck the wall. The walls of the command building were plastered with posters and articles from jihad missions. They served as incentives to new recruits. They prominently announced credits for their accomplishments. He recognized pictures and articles from places including the 1983 U.S. Embassy bombing in Beirut that killed sixty-three employees. There were many more scores memorializing acts of destruction such as the U.S. embassy massacre in Nairobi, and destroyer USS Cole anchored at Aden, amounting for thousands of casualties.

"There'll be bigger things to come," was his personal, and silent, promise to the cause of Islam. Satisfied with the course of events, he collected his few belongings and headed for the airport. The primary operations plan was about to be set in motion. Shrugging his shoulders, he reflected with casual indifference, "What's a few more days?" Right now, this very moment, he needed to concentrate on the immediate mission: "Kill a friend."

PETERSON AFB (OPS Center)

Brian left early to meet up with Tracy. They were having breakfast at the IHOP on South Circle Drive. It was close to Pete Field where they planned to spend the next few days. From the restaurant window, he had a clear view into the mountains. *Wonder what it's like in winter? Snow drifts? White capped peaks? Slopes? Moguls?* "Gotta try it someday." His thoughts shifted to Tracy. A smile formed on his face. He'd never felt this way. *Could it be love?* He felt like an innocent schoolboy waiting for her to show. *There she is.* His heart skipped a beat. Wearing casual attire, enhancing her beauty even more, he spotted her by the entrance. Her auburn hair caught a trace of the morning rays. *Looks ravishing.* He slid from the booth. He waved her over, almost spilling his coffee.

What's the matter with me? He was annoyed with himself for acting so clumsy. *Take a deep breath.* He forced himself to calm down. *After all, we're only working together. Better cool it.* She wore a bright smile. He didn't know whether to shake hands or hug. She solved the problem by planting a slight kiss on his cheek, then said, "Good to be together. I feel adventurous." He accepted her with delight. "Tell me," she said, directing the conversation while taking a seat, "how'd you like the area?"

"Love it. Not surprised your dad made it his home. There's so much open space. It really gives you a sense of freedom. The Rockies to the west are spectacular. To the north, the deep colors of the Black Forest."

"I like that too," she wholeheartedly agreed. "East, you can see forever across the plains. Kansas. Looking south gives you a feel for the New Mexico deserts."

"Not only seasonal views," he stated. "You get a sense of different worlds."

"Consider moving here?" She was searching his eyes for a sense of direction.

"Haven't given it much thought, but," he gave her an approving nod, "can picture having a home in the hills." Waiting to be served, they discussed the latest satellite problems. Neither could come up with a viable reason to explain the recurring failure.

The waitress approached with decanters in each hand. "Regular or decaf?"

"Regular," she ordered with a bright smile, "cream."

"Regular," he said, "black for me." They watched her pour and quickly move on to the next table. Brian picked up the conversation. He suggested various approaches using additional diagnostic software and data traps.

"May want to work with NORAD on this one," Tracy suggested.

"Not just yet. Let's get outta here." Eager to get started, he paid the bill and led the way. "Day security should be at the desk by now to get signed in," he suggested, "follow me." He took the lead driving. It was a short distance to the site.

Ten minutes later, they arrived at the gate. It took almost an hour to gain access to the secure SPADOC[23] sector. The place had been buzzing for the past few days. Additional intrusion alerts had been triggered since they left Baltimore. Every time a synchronized satellite drifted out of its programmed flight path, an alarm sounded and triggered the status board. The board, comprised of huge LCD display panels, was an impressive sight

---

[23] SPADOC – Space Defense Operations Center. Organization attached with NORAD.

in itself. It covered one entire wall of the space dome. Orbital flight paths painted in high resolution codes were gradually plotting across the screen. Orbital objects could be selected by the operator for detailed visual rendering. These days, it was mostly the KH series on display.

They were greeted by the Officer in Charge of operations. He'd been anxiously awaiting their arrival. "Harris," Brian gestured at his companion, "and Bauer." He beckoned her to step ahead. "Tracy Bauer."

"We've got your dossiers," the officer confirmed. "You're cleared for the building. Sorry for the wait, but," he took a step forward to fasten on ID badges, "we've been swamped with visitors this morning. Hope you can get this problem under control," he urged, "and quick." His eyes lingered on Tracy for a second. Brian noticed the familiar *Wonder if I'll stand a chance with her* stare.

"Sorry about that. We'll take care of it," Brian promised.

"Everybody on command is breathing down my neck. The DEW[24] line's on alert and so are the B-2s. Incident's extremely seriously," he indicated, "never had alerts this close to home," the OIC explained.

"Can you set up an office?" Brian asked.

"We've a space all ready for you," he replied. "We can furnish a desktop computer, if you like."

"That's okay. Be using my laptop. It's got all the tools we need. One more thing: can you get us the latest tracking printouts?" Brian requested.

"Already on the desk. This way," he gestured. He led them to a nearby office then quietly retreated.

"Nice fellow," Tracy was sincere, "despite the critical condition."

"Yeah," Brian agreed. "Not every day you run into somebody with personality."

It took many hours of comparing each line entry with the sample code—the original source code compiled for operational use. What made it even more difficult was the many software patches applied over the years. Worse yet, nobody kept records. Generally, the final software was compiled at the lab and then loaded into the satellite memory as operating system. If at any point the software differed from the source data, the matching tool could identify and flag the specific entry. But not a single discrepancy was found. All seemed to be in order. There was absolutely nothing indicative of a problem, but something had to have triggered the vector jets to cause the changes in flight trajectory.

Brian could sense NORAD command getting more anxious through the day. Tension was building with every hour that went by unresolved. Officials kept calling the OPS center for current status. Extreme pressure was felt by everyone. Ranking commanders stopped by hourly to check on their progress. Brian delegated Tracy to deal with it. She did a terrific job keeping visitors appeased. He couldn't afford to get sidetracked by the constant interruptions. He needed complete focus. "This is a first," Brian remarked at the end of the day. He was shaking his head. He even questioned his ability. His face showed the strain.

---

[24] Distant Early Warning is a system of radar stations in the far northern Arctic region of Canada, with additional stations along the Northern Coast, Aleutian Islands, Faroe Islands, Greenland, and Iceland.

Satellites should stay in orbit indefinitely. Guided by GPS, powered by solar panels, they were launched into orbit expecting to stay there for a minimum of ten years. Many remained much longer.

Tracy had been watching his performance in silence. It was getting late in the evening. He spotted her nearby talking with an officer. The command center was already emptied out for the day. Only a skeleton crew remained on duty. After an exceedingly long duration his eyes finally sought out hers. "Why don't you call it a day." He stretched his back and legs. "I'll stay on for a while."

"You sure?" She seemed weary.

He knew the feeling of semi-helplessness. He felt this way when watching Alex at work. It was the feeling of depending on someone else to come up with a solution. But she did her part. She kept the brass and visitors in check. And that was important to him.

"I insist."

"How about something to eat," she offered. "You must be starving."

"Don't feel like eating much. I'll grab something from the snack bar." He was already headed towards the hallway in the direction of the restrooms.

"In the morning," she called after him in a tired voice while being escorted out by the night watch.

"Dream up a solution." His fading words trailed after her.

On the drive back, Tracy mulled over his last words. She recalled her dad remarking on numerous occasions how he used to solve problems in his sleep. After a day of challenging analysis, he would wake up during the night or the following morning totally aware of the solution. *I should get so lucky.* Thirty minutes later she drove up at the Castle. With the car lights turned off she caught the full breadth of a Rocky night. It was pitch black. The Milky Way was just as she remembered. *Overwhelming.* The sky was filled with countless stars.

There was a rustle by the front gate. Her dad stuck his head out. "Working late?" He'd heard a car drive up and assumed it was her. Her tired face gave her away. "You should take a few days' rest. Enjoy your stay."

"I will," she said, "as soon as we have a handle on the problem."

"Still no results?"

"It's a mystery."

"You eaten yet?" He led her inside. He felt compassion for her. He knew the feel of unresolved issues too well. *Comes with the territory.*

"Not hungry." She parked her tired body by the kitchen table.

He fetched a pot from the cupboard. "I'll fix us some soup. By the way, what tools you using?"

"Mostly Carnivore."

"Tried the software DOD developed?"

"Not familiar with anything new."

"Talk to Brian to get a copy from DISA," Alex suggested. "I can help him with that. I know people there."

"What's the software?"

"Started in 2000 when DISA launched Centaur," he explained, watching his daughter's budding interest.

"Exactly what?"

"Honeynets…data mining and pattern recognition," he explained. "Sophisticated trapping tool…identifies attacks and trends against network intrusions."

"Never heard of it." Her mind wasn't alert enough to follow all he was telling.

"Most people haven't," he said, "still classified."

"I'll talk to Brian," she promised, "in the morning." She decided not to wait for the soup to heat up. "Need some sleep…Night, Dad."

"Sorry," he said. "Pleasant dreams." He was disappointed.

After a few hours of restless sleep, Tracy suddenly bolted upright. Her heart was beating rapidly, and the clarity of her vision astounded her. *Of course—that's it! Has to be.* Beside herself with excitement she reached for the bedside phone. Her fingers nervously dialed Brian's number. "Come on…pick up," she uttered impatiently. *Click.*

"Guess what?" Her voice was elated.

"You won the jackpot," he answered with casual indifference.

"Nooooo," she teased, dwelling on the suspense.

"I give up."

"Listen," she explained, "it came to me during sleep."

"What?"

"The solution." She could not curtail her excitement any longer. She had to share the revelation. "Somebody's accessed a hidden port. You know," she lingered on the momentary silence, "unauthorized transmit command codes on the lowest level." She made reference to the OSI[25] stack.

"You know," he said after a few second's pause, "you may be right." He had thought of that possibility earlier but had shrugged it off as too difficult an intrusion. It would require the most sophisticated programming tools available only accessible by the intelligence community. But, in view of the current issue, it could be the case. "Great job. Can you meet me here?"

"You still on site?" She was amazed at his tenacity.

"Still here."

Ending the call, she said, "I'll be there in thirty minutes."

---

[25] The OSI or Open System Interconnection model defines a networking framework for implementing protocols in seven layers. Control is passed from one layer to the next, starting at the application layer in one station, and proceeding to the bottom layer, over the channel to the next station and back up the hierarchy. It is the standard developed to interconnect with every computer and data processing device. The seven layers the data must travel are: Application, Presentation, Session, Transport, Network, Data link, and Physical (the actual wire).

THE PLAN

It came out of nowhere. The nation had been blindsided. The date will stand as a symbolic icon for all future mankind. Amid a sea of clay and dust, coinciding with the nation's law enforcing call sign 911, the date signified the destruction of the free world. "Twin Trade Center," reduced to a pile of twisted metals. Such was the scene as the world watched that terrifying day in horror.

The Serpent vividly remembered the euphoria. It had consumed every inch of his body and mind. He, among his fellow comrades, had been celebrating for days. Cheers for the nation's leader rippled through the Islamic cause for weeks. The airwaves were buzzing with congratulations. And so was the internet.

Years prior, while the world was lulled into a false sense of security, the Serpent had been busy planning. He always had a plan. Most nights he'd lay awake, body filled with vigor and distant anticipation. He had unlimited sources of energy. Genetically, he'd been created close to perfection. It was the combination, a superior body melded with a brilliant mind into one entity, creating a superhuman. His restless mind was always focused on the next plan of action. There was so much to accomplish. He'd had a vision, and he devoted all his energy to sustaining it.

Ever since the mysterious fading of the once prominent icon, Osama bin Laden, he'd developed an infernal drive to take the leadership. It had become his sole purpose for survival. And survival it was. Most of his waking hours were spent further developing The Plan. It had germinated from the seeds of Islam doctrine and grew from there. He'd never forgiven Osama for his retreat into obscurity. He'd tried to rationalize it time and time again. Osama had the world by the balls. Al Qaeda was well on the way in its quest for world dominance. Although it wasn't the first time; Islam had ruled the world at numerous points on history's arduous pathway. "And now?" The Serpent reflected on his inner feelings. "Dead!" The world had witnessed the once infamous leader getting buried at sea, gone forever. He could not allow that to ever happen again. Not him.

Whereas Osama had laid the groundwork for The Base, he, the Serpent, developed The Plan. It was his creation. The premise was simple; in contrast to having an iconic figurehead, as was the case with most visions, his would rely on obscurity, cloaked by the shadows of darkness. It would be solely based on fear from the unknown.

He'd studied history at its best—and at its worst. What he'd learned was that when exploits were shrouded in mystery, successful endeavors usually followed. Typical examples included the Knights Templar, the Freemasons, and, in modern times, the NSA. Who was behind these causes? Asking that question had proved the key to his revelation.

Where bin Laden had laid the ground rules, he would carry out the cause. He could care less what other nations were doing. It made no difference what other policy makers had in mind. He'd rule the world—the world of Islam. Immensely satisfied, he took measures to make for his immediate destination. A destination not even *he* would know.

NORTHCOM (Northern Command)

As soon as Tracy walked into the control center, Brian announced, "This is what we need to do." He wanted to demonstrate he was on top of things. He planned to use Carnivore to set up filters. "We'll build a trap." It'd reveal the source address to break the barriers. He referred to routers, hubs, and firewalls. With the tools the agency had on hand, no matter how many barriers were in between source and target, he would make the breach by manipulating data packets at their lowest network levels, the machine code.

"Right," she agreed. "By the way," she asked, "you aware of Honeynets?"

"Intrusions trap?"

"Yeah, you got a copy?"

"DISA won't release it."

"Oh?"

"Political."

"Dad's got connections with DISA. Can get a copy."

"We may have to."

Tracy sidled next to him. Despite the endless hours they'd been at the center, she could feel new vigor. She liked the strength of his mind. It emanated confidence. She stood quietly, craning over his shoulders. From here, she could follow the internal workings of code breaking unfolding across the screen on the network level. For that, a simple tool could be used to catch the thief. Brian was using one of the many utility routines for UNIX systems designed years ago by DARPA.

A simple "Whois" query was sent out on the LAN, Internet, or satellite network. The command returned ample amounts of data. It would identify the domain, owner, registration date, location, and contact information on any target or user online worldwide. However simple, it was the most useful tool in their network utility repertoire. If that wasn't enough, there was always trace route or "tracer." It plotted the entire network path from originator to destination, identifying every router, node, network, and server in its path regardless of location, distance, and number of hops.

Of course, hackers also knew these tools. Cyber criminals and terrorists caught on pretty quick. Information spreads rapidly among the cyber community. With that, the NSA was forced to design ever more sophisticated algorithms and crypto codes. On the surface, it was for the benefit of privacy protection for the citizen, but below, it was applied to much more sinister causes. Despite the technology prodding by the NSA, it kept the hackers busy, but did not deter the skilled hacker from encapsulating simple or complex computer commands into undetectable network packet strings.

Those were the rudimentary tools. There was much more sophistication available for tracking information, but that had to be specifically authorized by the justice department. So it claimed. "Anything?"

"Not yet." Brian was busy on the keyboard.

"Gosh," she said in admiration, "you're quick."

"Old school," he commented. "Ever use 'The quick brown fox jumps over the lazy dog's back?'"

"What?"

"Character pattern to test the interface."

"But why 'Dog'?"

"Assimilation," he smiled, "string contains every character in the alphabet. If," he insisted, "you type it often enough, you're bound to pick up speed." With the stroke of the 'Enter' key, he released a stream of unstoppable commands no enemy would be able to block. It executed a series of Java applets that scanned the spectrum of the worldwide net. "This'll take a while. Let's see what the cafeteria's serving this early."

"We'll be back in fifteen minutes," she informed the OIC on the way to the exit. "We're waiting on the software to respond."

"Got you covered." He shot an admirable glance at her and nodded his head in acknowledgement.

The cafeteria was a short trip down the hall. "Not bad," Tracy remarked, taking in another spoonful of scrambled eggs. She was seated across from Brian on cafeteria style furniture. The place was almost empty this early in the morning.

"Military chow's always been plentiful," he recalled with gusto, "despite the volume chefs have to dish out." He was used to chow halls from the Gulf war, Kosovo, and other places more obscure.

"Thought this base was mostly DOD, you know…civil service."

"Used to be," he explained. "Major command change in 2002 revamped the base after 9/11. SPACECOM was replaced by Northern Command."

"How's NORTHCOM[26] fit into DOD?"

"Has complete control over homeland defenses for space intrusion, air, land, and sea, including NORAD."

Thirty minutes later they were on the way back to the control room. The scan results were already posted on the computer screen. One log entry immediately caught Brian's attention. The source identified a foreign-owned IP address. It was registered to somewhere in Pakistan.

Bound from the chair, he exclaimed, "We've got them!" He gave her a heads up. "Why don't you give headquarters a call and tell them?"

What a guy, she thought with delight, *letting me take the credit*. It confirmed her earlier assessment of him. *He doesn't need more fame. He'd establish that long ago.* She dialed the number.

"NSA," the familiar voice of the department head stated, "Warner."

"Tracy Bauer," she identified herself. "Think we've got something for you." She went on to report their progress and findings.

"Outstanding! Send me the data and we'll get somebody on it right away."

"On the way."

"We'll take it from here. Take a couple days off," Warner suggested. "You both deserve it. Many thanks also to Brian." *Click.* The line went dead.

It was the first time in days she could breathe freely. All the pent-up tension melted away from her shoulders. She didn't know how Brian felt but planned to find out. She was looking forward to spending a few days of leisure time with him until they were called up on the next assignment. She stepped up to Brian to inform him about the call, "Warner says to take a few days off."

"Great. Could use a break."

---

[26] The United States Northern Command, located in Colorado Springs, is a Unified Combatant Command of the United States military. Created in 2002 in the aftermath of the September 11, 2001 attacks, its mission is to protect the United States homeland and support local, state, and federal authorities.

"What's the next step?" She hoped for some personal time together. So far, it had all been work. She wanted to get to know the person.

"Should get word back from the field shortly," he suggested. "Probably have agents on the case already. We'll stick around a few days to monitor the network." By "agents," he was referring to the CIA and FBI doing the footwork for NSA, in most cases. At other times it was the DIA, armed services intelligence, or other law enforcement branches within and outside the national borders.

"We don't have to stay here. I can monitor the process from the laptop. We could use your dad's place. He assured me a secure connection with SPADOC."

"Great."

"That'll give us a direct VPN link to the OPS center," he explained. "I'll set up an alert link to my pager. It'll keep us posted in any event."

"Want to get out of here?" Already headed for the exit, taking his arm, she suggested, "Let's take a hike at Garden of the Gods."

"You read my mind."

She watched the tension slowly fade from his face. The out brief with the OIC went quick. They gave him a contact number and where to be reached.

Stepping outside, she was delighted. "What do you know, already daylight." They stood for a few seconds by the exit, admiring a beautiful Colorado sunrise.

GARDEN OF THE GODS

"Morning, Dad," Tracy cheered. She kissed him on the cheek. He was busy in the kitchen preparing breakfast.

"Work? This early?" He was surprised to see her enter fully dressed.

"No, Dad," she said with a smile. "Just got in."

"In?" He put the utensils to rest on the sink. Interest piqued, he threw a curious glance at her.

"Yeah…solved the problem." She relayed the night's events, including an account of their process. She knew he'd be interested on how they traced the defense net intrusion. It used to be his turf. "Agency's already tracking the fields."

"From above?"

"Mostly. Don't have many agents in the Middle East. None in Pakistan."

"I know. Budget cuts, politics, administration RIFs[27]. What's your plan for the rest of the day?"

"Cut some Zzz's," she yawned, "then hike your favorite place."

"Just be careful." He cringed. She could sense he still vividly remembered the incidence with his eldest daughter. "You know what almost happened to Liz."

"I know, Dad. Wake me up in four hours."

Following a few hours of revitalizing rest, Brian at the hotel and Tracy back at the Castle, both met at the park's visitor center. They planned to spend the afternoon hiking God's country.

"Come with me," she called out as soon as he showed up. She led the brisk quarter mile walk to the park. He followed her quick strides. Headed towards a prominent rock formation, Balancing Rock, she pointed it out. "My favorite spot." Hopping from rock to rock he hurriedly followed her. Up the steep incline she went with him in pursuit. It didn't take but a few minutes for them to reach the top. Perched at the edge of the Rock they let their feet dangle over the edge.

"Spectacular view," he admitted.

"We used to come here often." She threw her head back. It cleared her vision from behind strands of auburn hair. Her elevated breathing turned steady once more. "Family was still together then. Used to be our weekend sanctuary. That was before the tourists found out about this place. Now," she said with a hint of sadness, "most locals stay away, especially on weekends."

"Yeah," he settled. His mind appeared absent. He seemed completely absorbed taking in the bizarre sight of the deep reddish landscape. Aside from an occasional echoing call reverberating against the steep walls shouted by an exuberated visitor from down below, the place had a calming aura.

She stole a glance at him. He looked completely relaxed. Her eyes traced the contours of his profile. "Hmm."

"What?" Expecting a comment, his face shifted at hers.

"Nothing." She enjoyed the closeness of his body.

"This is living," he exhaled. He was still slightly out of breath. "Got winded hiking up here."

"Usually takes a couple of weeks to acclimate," she said.

---

[27] RIF – Reduction in Forces. Common military acronym.

With a slight groan he reclined on his back. It gave him a leisurely view of the blue sky. She mimicked his move. Completely at ease, legs dangling over the edge, both watched puffs of clouds shaping images slowly drift across the sky. It turned into a game. Each was guessing the shape the next cloud would form. "Feel like a kid," he muttered into the hushed calmness. "Can't remember how long it's been since I felt this relaxed." An occasional jetliner thirty-five thousand feet up was cutting across the blue leaving lingering contrails in its wake. He seemed at peace with the world. All issues and problems seemed forgotten. "I could live like this."

"What's on your mind?" she whispered.

"Just thinking," he replied. Brief notions of family life drifted across his mind. *Wishful thinking.* From the corner of the eyes he could make out the placid rise and fall of her shapely body. Her breasts were moving with the rhythm of every breath she took. *Wonder what she's thinking?*

"Look at the ridge over there," she broke the silence. Propped up on one elbow, she'd recognized the vertical rock formation. "Kissing Camels. Dad used to take us girls up that cliff."

"Really?" He gauged the drop off. "Pretty steep, isn't it?"

"Some spots we weren't tall enough to reach up the next ledge," she proudly announced. "He used to lift us up and over. Now," she explained, "you need a permit to even get close."

"Rather dangerous, don't you think?"

"Yeah," she agreed, "but tell that to a kid. You know how persistent they can be."

"I can only guess. Don't have much experience with the young."

"Ever think of having some?"

"Never gave it much thought. What about you…the career woman you are?"

"Let me tell you about women," she demurred. "No matter how busy or sidetracked we get, the thought's always on our minds. We look at many a guy cutting across the path. First thing we notice's the looks. Next, attire, behavior, and demeanor, but foremost, potential quality to be a good father. The difference is preconceived image. Some like looks in a guy, others prefer intelligence, heritage, or ambition."

"What about you?"

"Still focused on the career." She shrugged. She'd had private thoughts about him ever since they met. Even having a child by him had crossed her mind, but she had curtailed that thought. She didn't know much about him. A slight movement in the distance distracted her. "Look," she pointed, "climbers." They could make out a couple pulling their way slowly up the cliff trailing nylon ropes.

"Takes guts."

"Take a look over here," she gestured, "Balancing Rock. My sister almost went off the edge."

"What?" He gave her a worried stare.

"I was only a couple years old and don't remember." Her voice sounded sedated. Her eyes took on a forlorn look. "Dad told me. She was about four when, one Sunday, not aware of the drop off, my sister took a running leap. He caught her by the collar of her jacket just as she was going over the edge. From her vantage point, she couldn't see the drop-off between the two rocks."

"What a lucky kid." His expression was genuine. It was filled with compassion. He seemed to cringe at the very thought of freefall. The lower part of his body had tensed up. Slowly, he moved one hand to his lower abdomen to soothe the muscles.

She'd noticed. "You all right?" Her eyes lingered on his for a moment. "Dad still feels guilty every time he comes here."

"Hard to imagine what a parent must feel with a child's life cut short through negligence."

A whisk of wind caught her hair. It was a cooling breeze flowing down the foothills. Her body trembled ever so slightly. "Gettin' chilly. Wanna get goin'?"

He jumped to his feet, preparing to leave. The breeze had picked up force. He was unprepared for the next gust of wind. In an instant he lost balance. To regain his footing, he threw his body back but his feet slipped off. Desperately struggling to reach for a hold, in a panic he yelled, "Tracy!" His hands tried to cling to the edge but the gravel gave way.

Watching his body slip over the edge, panic stricken, she yelled, "Oh my God!" then threw her body forward, desperately grasping for his hands. *Not him too,* she screamed in silence over visions of her falling sister. She caught hold of him. Her fingers locked onto one sleeve of his jacket. Straining against his weight not to let go, she yelled, in sheer desperation, "Hold on!" His body had disappeared below the edge of the cliff. His free hand was struggling in mid-air, grasping for a hold. Groping blindly, it was searching for anything to grab.

"Please," his panicked voice cried from below, "don't let go."

"Here," she yelled, "take my hand!" She strained her body forward to reach his other hand. She was frantic. She could feel her body getting dragged to the cliff's edge. Fear took over her struggling mind. Her foot barely caught on a tree root protruding from the ground. It was enough to stop her body momentarily. It kept her from going over the edge. Exerting one last effort, both of their hands finally locked. Every fiber in her strained against his weight.

"Please God," she silently pleaded, "don't let him die." Her face was ground into the dirt. Her skin broke from gravel scrapes. Bloodstains slowly appeared in the dirt. Her strength was rapidly leaving her straining body. "Help!" she yelled in final desperation but nobody was nearby. She hung on. Her heartbeat was racing. In the struggle, she inhaled dirt. It clogged up her lungs. She coughed up violently. She was on the brink of blacking out from lack of oxygen. Eyes tightly clenched, she held on a few more seconds but felt her strength rapidly fading.

"Don't let go." Another plea from below slowly seeped into her mind.

A slight puff of air brushed across her face. She forced her eyes open. His face had appeared in front of hers. Bewildered, she gazed up. She couldn't believe her eyes. He'd been able to pull himself up on her arms. His struggling feet finally got a solid hold on the edge. One final pull and he threw himself back from the cliff. His battered body landed next to her.

She slowly turned to face him. A short burst of hysterical laugh escaped her lungs. His face looked ashen. She reached out to embrace him then slowly regained her composure. "Thank you, God," she managed to whisper. Silent tears were streaming down her face when she finally stood up on shaky legs.

"Let's get outta here." He tried to get up but collapsed with a cringe. "Dammit, that hurt." He tried the other leg. Supported by her shoulders, he was able to get on his feet.

She helped him dust off the dirt. He winced when she touched the knee. Blood was smeared across the shin. It showed through his torn trouser legs.

His eyes caught her wiping her face clean of dust. He held her by the shoulders. He could feel her trembling, "You okay?"

Her voice was still shaky. Holding onto him, she pleaded, "Don't tell Dad." Slowly, she helped him hobble to the car lot. The park had already emptied out. Taking brief breaks, they caught the last shadows cast across the ridge. The sun was setting behind the fourteen-thousand-foot peaks of the Rockies.

He forced a smile at her. "He'll know from the first look at us," he said, shaking off the intense strain. For the first time, he felt a close connection with her. "Thank you," he whispered, "for saving my life."

CASTLE ROCK

They showed up at the Castle's door in disheveled array. Brian, chafed legs protruding from torn trousers, bleeding forearms, head wounds and swollen ankle, wasn't a pretty sight. He was supported by Tracy whose face was crusted over with dried-up blood.

"What...?" Alex was stunned. His gaze shifted from her face to his. Then back. "I'll call emergency."

Brian reclined with a groan. "Don't think that's necessary," he objected. He was minimizing his injuries. "Nothing's broken."

Alex slid under Brian's arm to help him indoors. With Tracy's help they managed to place him on the couch.

"You sure? What happened?"

"Accident, Dad."

"Tell me."

"Brian slipped off the cliff..." The thought alone made Alex cringe.

"She saved my life," Brian cut her short. "I slipped and she caught my fall. If it wasn't for her quick reaction, I'd be dead."

"Let me take you to the hospital," Alex insisted. "Leg looks nasty."

Tracy was already tending to it. She cut into the trousers to remove some fabric. It made Brian blush. "Don't think that's necessary," he objected again. "Nothing's broken."

"Sure?" Alex carefully took one leg and slowly twisted the foot, then the other. He was watching for a reaction. "You got lucky. Mountains can be treacherous," Alex summed up then focused on his daughter.

He led her to the medicine cabinet. "Let's get your face fixed."

Using cotton swaps dipped in hydrogen peroxide, Alex dabbed the facial wounds clean. "Ouch." Tracy grimaced.

He concentrated on her face. "Might leave a scar," he cautioned. "Your first battle wound."

"Could do without it." She checked the cleaned cuts. "Doesn't look too bad."

"Don't worry. You're pretty enough—regardless." He turned to exit the bathroom.

"Dad." Her trailing words followed him down the hall. "I'll look after Brian."

"You do that. By the way," he informed her, "your sister's on her way."

"What? Great! When?"

"Today."

Thirty minutes later both Tracy and Brian showed up in the living room. Alex looked them over. "How you feelin'?" Once the blood was removed the scrapes and bruises didn't look as traumatic. "Know what you need?" He'd been preparing a sandwich plate by the counter.

"Stiff drink," Brian answered.

Tracy sat by his side. "Me too."

"Coming right up. Make yourselves comfortable." They watched Alex working the kitchen counter. He returned with a decanter. "Jägermeister Brandy," the label stated. An assorted tray with cold cuts and Melba toast followed.

"Trying to get us drunk?" Brian grinned with a broad smile. Alex noticed him rubbing his legs. Both shins and one ankle were bandaged up. And so were his elbows. His body might be battered, but his spirit was lifted.

"Take your mind off the pain." Alex picked up two crystals and handed both a drink. "Salute!" It was Alex's favorite toast. He'd learned that in Italy.

Both Tracy and Brian returned the toast. "Fine Brandy."

"Tell us a story, Dad," his daughter pleaded. "About the Pacific." On and off, he'd spent many years there in the early days of his career when he'd kept up vital communication support for the Pacific naval fleet command. Once he got going there was no stopping him. He liked telling stories, especially when his daughter did the prodding. She particular liked hearing about his flying, diving, and foreign travels.

They spent hours relaxing and in turn telling personal encounters into the night. "Water anyone?" His throat felt parched. He disappeared into the kitchen and returned with a full carafe of iced water.

"Bored you enough?" He broke the sudden silence. Brian and Tracy had been occupied with their own thoughts.

"Getting late," she suggested.

"I'd better get going," Brian said. With Tracy's help, he pulled himself up on unsteady legs and bade Alex goodbye.

Once outside, in the midst of darkness, using one hand he gently caressed her pretty features. "I'm sorry about your face," he whispered. With the other he pulled her body close. They tightly embraced. It was their first kiss. It was a kiss without much passion. It was intimacy, nevertheless. Both were too mellowed from the alcohol.

She released her hold to let him go. "Okay. See you tomorrow?"

"Of course," he assured her. He softly kissed her one more time. "Can't wait."

"Hope you feel better," she responded. "You safe to drive?"

"I'm fine," he strained, getting into the rental car. She watched until the tail lights disappeared around the next bend. Suddenly, she felt the night chill seep through her clothes. It took hold of her body. Her gaze shifted to the starry sky, watching its full brilliance. *How beautiful!* She briefly lingered. In the quiet, today's events crept into her mind. They made her shudder. It was more from the close call than the night chill.

TAEGU AUTODIN CENTER (South Korea)

The communications room was quiet this time of night. *Much like a morgue,* Gary, the comm tech on shift, reflected. Most nights, only a skeleton crew was on duty. Four, maybe five techs at the most, were spread between comm, COMSEC, and the supply room. The complex was spacious. It was well kept. Clean, polished, and organized. The local custodian crew made sure of it. The white tiled floor was scrubbed and polished nightly, two-foot square sections at a time. Despite the rows and rows of equipment cabinet, there was certain emptiness to the room. Overhead neon lighting lit up every space on the floor. When necessary, it provided ample light for the techs to bury their heads inside the equipment. Cabinets were aligned in neat rows stacked with racks of comm and modem gear from floor to ceiling.

Every so often, a COMSEC tech from next door would pop his or her head in to chat or take a trip to the bathroom. Although dressed alike in casuals during night shift, they were a different breed—the COMSEC crew. The lived like hermits, on and off the job alike. It was the mark of the trade. Shrouded in secrecy, most were introverts. It was the result of working with classified data day in and day out. They were the U.S. Intel most trusted. No talk, no leaks, no compromise was their unheralded motto. With access to firsthand information generated by the White House, Intel communities, military commands, and field agents, it had to be that way. A compromise meant the end of the career, if one got lucky. Most times, it would earn years in the stockade, blemished with a criminal record for life.

Tonight, three tech buddies, Gary, Mike, and Ron were assigned the late shift at this secure, stockade-type walled comm center located deep in the remote hills of the Korean central mountain range.

"Hey, Gary," Mike found himself yelling in the direction of his teammate, "gimme a ring on 97—another line failure." Ever since he came on shift some comm links' been giving him fits.

"Roger that," his buddy yelled back from the far corner of the equipment room. Hunched over the monitor keyboard, he swiftly punched in the circuit number. "Line looks good," he shouted back. "Must be equipment."

"Swap it out, will ya?"

"Whatever..."

Mike grumbled. He wasn't exactly pleased with the response. After all, he was the shift supervisor and demanded his orders be followed by the book. *That's what happens when you socialize with the workers,* he thought, slightly dismayed, appreciating the need for the military's rigid rank enforcement.

"Shit!" he heard his other buddy suddenly call out. An array of faulty lights suddenly started blinking all over the status panel. "Don't like it," Ron hollered out. "Do something," he added, "or we'll be in deep shit."

By instinct, Mike punched the intercom button to the COMSEC room. "What?" an alerted voice cut in.

"You guys doing anything?"

"Negative."

Mike was rubbing his bristled chin. He sported a beard but kept it neatly trimmed. He didn't need to make a statement. *Just look cool.* It gave his face a distinguished cut.

Wonder what's goin' on. His eyes impatiently scanned across the status board. He was waiting for Gary or Ron to get back with him.

Anxiously waiting for a result, his eyes darted between the bank of time zone clocks mounted against the far wall and the equipment section. He watched his buddies checking out equipment and connections on remote monitor screens across the room.

"What's taking it so long?" he yelled out for the third time. He'd already taken several calls from field agents demanding why the lines were down. As always, he stalled the callers with the standard reply, "Workin' on it."

"Gimme a break," Gary responded, "workin' on it."

"Hurry up, dammit," Mike shot back. He checked the overhead clock for the umpteenth time. "Almost shift change." He was hoping to get out by midnight. Problems had to be resolved before the next shift took over. If not, the techs had to stay over. It was an unspoken code. Technicians knew failure would reflect on their performance record.

While waiting for his buddies to fix the problem, Mike was monitoring the Intel circuits losing sync with increasing frequency. Mike had a bad feeling about this. He had never seen so much high-volume traffic. *Strange,* he'd puzzled. To his knowledge, there was no major conflict in this part of the world other than the occasional political exchange between diplomatic offices with the North and U.S. policymakers. He wondered where all the traffic was generated. Patching a monitor into the circuit, he recorded the online text scrolling across the screen.

What he witnessed was increased chatter on the secure lines coming from field agents somewhere in North Korea. He reached for the checklist. It identified subscribers for the region. The coded information scanning across the monitor came from multiple sources for the traffic. It identified embassies, military command posts scattered across Korea, and field agents feeding military Intel to the NSA or CIA. Some text was encrypted, some was not. It all depended on the criticality of the information source. While he was reading the live text on the monitor, the line suddenly went dead, and so did a number of other circuits in the region. Bounding from the seat, he rushed over to the panel to patch out and isolate the failed circuits. At first, he suspected total equipment failure, but this happened very rarely with the reliability with which military equipment was built. Swapping out one line after another did not solve the problem. Pushing the self-test buttons on the equipment indicated an "all channel" ready status. "Outage must be remote," he'd finally decided.

Mike acted quickly. He rushed for the hot line and dialed HQs, but couldn't get a connection. Next, he tried the Pentagon. Same results, negative. Every connection he made showed a dead line. *Something big's up,* was his immediate assessment.

The graveyard shift had just made its appearance. Mike informed his relief supervisor about the trouble. "Half the comm links are out. Want us to stay?"

"Don't worry," he was assured, "my crew will take care of it."

"I owe you one," he said on passing then hurried to catch up with his buddies already waiting by the exit interlock. He was dying to have the first beer.

On entering the local tavern, the trio was accosted by a new face in town. She smiled at them as they walked through the entrance and gave them the common greeting, "Yeoboseyo, (Hello)." As soon as they found a table, she came over and introduced herself. "I am Miss Lee," she said. "What can I get you?" Just looking at her pretty young face and body to match, their pheromones began to stir. "We'll have OBs." Oriental Brewery beer was the GIs preferred drink.

Miss Lee was born Lee Min Jin. Surnames in her country were listed first. Only close friends and family members addressed Koreans by their first names. To address someone, everybody else used titled surnames. She had been born twenty-five years earlier in Kaesong, a place just north of the present DMZ. Following the separation from the South in '55, her parents had moved to Pyongyang. Like many families separated by the war, she had relatives on both sides. Only in recent years did the North allow cultural exchanges between the two countries. It was on those days (usually holidays) that families and business people could cross the border for a few days on a special pass. On one such crossing, based on orders she'd received from her party leader, she stayed behind.

Since she held an official passport and used it frequently, her crossing the border was not questioned. Because of family ties to the South, nobody suspected her real purpose.

Assessing the new face, Mike grinned at his buddies said, "Wonder who'll wind up with her tonight."

"I will!" both Gary and Ron exclaimed in unison. They were still joking when she returned with the beer. "Thank you," Ron smirked at her.

"You're welcome," she sang. There was an inviting hint in her smile.

They were sitting in their favorite hangout, the Bat Cave, just outside Camp Walker's main gate. The place was packed like most nights. To place an order you had to shout to be heard. Off to the side, the three tech buddies were smoking a little pot, sipping some OB beer, and making life pleasurable away from home.

In social settings, Koreans were very polite, especially to foreigners. It may not have been obvious at first glance, though. At times, among local settings, there could be a lot of shouting and pushing between friends, couples, and family members, but as soon as things were sorted out, formalities returned. Koreans generally did not take to brawling and fist fights, as was customary with some cultures.

"Can I sit with you?" she sang in her sweet and demure voice then gingerly reached out to pour the beer.

"Sure." They nodded in unison. It was always a pleasure to be in the company of a new girl, especially a pretty one. And pretty she was. Her face revealed a pleasing mix of natural Mongolian features blended in with Western beauty. It was a quality only Westerners could appreciate. In Asia, in many instances, a beautiful face was ostracized and associated with immoral activities. To be labeled "hostess" may have had honorable connotations in the Western world, but in Asia it signaled illicit behavior. When addressing a girl as such, one would be immediately reprimanded with, "I am a business girl." That night, this quality was appreciated.

Tonight it was Ron who wound up with Miss Lee. His choices were to check into a local hotel or stay at her place. Since he'd had too much to drink already, he chose the latter. Most single hostesses were live-ins. The rooms were small but colorful and were always kept clean and tidy. Swaying on unsteady legs, he noticed the room's layout. It contained a bed, a table, a couple of chairs, a nightstand, and a few personal keepsakes, probably from a special friend. He was feeling no pain after four bottles of OB and a couple of joints. Marijuana on base was not legal, but off-base, smoking in small quantities was tolerated. Most locals did not take drugs. Culturally unacceptable, weak narcotics were tolerated with foreigners. A foreigner in this part of Korea was mostly a GI, or, to a lesser extent, a government contractor.

Ron and Miss Lee made out several times. Whereas he was trying to get to sleep, she kept prodding him with questions such as, "Where're you from? Where're you working? What kind of job do you do? What's new in the world and anything unusual going on?"

Feeling good about himself, he boasted a little about work and the critical nature of his position, telling her more than he would, had he been sober, not realizing he was slowly drawn into a compromising situation. What he revealed was information that had shot across the monitors earlier that evening.

This was the information Miss Lee had been waiting for. Looking at the drunken guest sprawled next to her she reached to pick up her mobile phone. She dialed a coded number to place a long-distance call to Pyongyang, North Korea. "Field Command" picked up.

"We have confirmation," she responded.

"Proceed to home base." The connection was terminated.

The information she charmed out of the GI that night was all she needed to complete her mission. It always amazed her how, after a few bottles of OB, young men were so eager to please. They were so easily plied with promises of a good time. After one last glimpse at the snoring GI, she quietly sneaked out during the early morning hours. Her departure went unnoticed by her guest and host. In the dark of night, she headed back across the border into home territory. Her destination was Pyongyang. It was to be her last crossing.

JIHAD DELTA CELL ALPHA (U.S. Sector East)

"Move it…move it, hurry up…get the others," Yusuf commanded his squad leaders. He displayed hurried urgency. "We have the go signal." He'd just terminated a call from the Serpent. "Shahadah!"

"About time." Bandar Malik, his first lieutenant, hurried. He was ready to move. And so was the team. After months of preparation and drills, he scrambled to get word to his team. "What's the destination?"

"I'll explain on the way," Yusuf promised.

Alarms went out immediately. Destined for the airport, members of the team should arrive within the hour. They'd been waiting weeks for this call. The team had been on edge and was getting restless for action. Pent-up battle hormones desperately demanded release. *Good thing it finally happened.* Ever since arriving in New York, the team had been restricted from mixing with locals, specifically the women. Despite growing tempers, women in general, as well as the ladies of the night, had been deemed off limits. It was a necessary precaution. The move curtailed any possibility for compromise. What time remained for social interaction was restricted, keeping to each other. *That,* he reasoned, *was the difficult part.* Quarrels and fights broke out almost daily. The agitators were mostly the new members. They were the fresh recruits hastily hired to support the pending missions. One by one, they had arrived from the various camps. To his dismay, with Malik enforcing the rules, Yusuf had to constantly restrain them from wandering off to the city. Bearded and tough looking in appearances, he knew they'd attract the attention of the law. "And that," he reasoned more frequently as time went on, "I cannot have." The mission was too monumental to be compromised at the last minute.

Today, the problems had been solved. The team arrived energized. Yusuf watched them cram into the sizable van. The little luggage they had was carelessly tossed into the back. They were headed for JFK airport. "Keep the speed down," he cautioned. "Don't want to attract the law." It would not only be the end of the mission. If they got caught, it'd be the end of them. They'd all wind up in U.S. detention, with life sentences sure to follow. He sat back in the passenger seat watching the city skyline slowly pass overhead. It would be the last time. "I'll miss this place." It was here where it all started.

"Slow down," Yusuf cautioned for the third time. He gave the driver a warning stare. "One more time," he threatened, "and you'll be left behind." This shot home. The driver, like the other recruits, did not speak the local language. They were uninformed about the host culture. They had no money. Compensation was promised after the completion of the mission. They did not fear death. They feared lifetime imprisonment. That, to the Jihad, would be the death sentence.

For Yusuf, growing up in a metropolis curtailed by solid family unison was difficult at first. As with many others in his calling, he had been confused by the diversified cultural mix in this mega city. Where, on the one hand, his first generation ethnic family tried to preserve their hereditary Islamic culture, on the other, they had been subjected to local pressure imposed by the changes of time. It was nothing new. Ever since people began migrations, cultural struggles were experienced by nearly all immigrants.

Where most youngsters normally outgrew their subjected vulnerability by this influence, Yusuf had become absorbed, almost to obsession. He not only enjoyed the cohesiveness of this closely-knit organization, but began soliciting new members as well.

Word spread. Somewhere along this path, he met up with one of the movement's leaders. The leader flew in from the homeland, laying out a long-term plan for their cause, as well as lending support for the ever-increasing expense to recruit and shelter new members. The Plan called for identifying personal qualities to build group leadership, not only to promote specific talents, but for combatant skills as well. Some were trained to handle explosives, others to recruit, with some sent to special training camps around the globe, always with the same goal: promote and expand factionary cells.

It was in the late nineties when their cause began to escalate. Everybody knew something big was up, but nobody had knowledge of the details, let alone the complete plan. Rumors were flying. Calls were prolific using the newly invented cellular communications technology. Mobile phones made their tasks so easy. You could be connected day and night to any point on the globe to coordinate tactical planning. Precise timing was critical to the operation, especially when something major was planned such as the mission ahead.

As cell leader, Yusuf followed the news very closely. Over the years, he saw trends develop. Twenty years ago, in the early days, the impact of their operations had been relatively small, but over time they kept escalating into bigger missions, creating more and more fatalities. It seemed the plan had become more demanding with each mission. It was to serve dramatic effects to demonstrate to the world that Islam had become a faction to respect.

Traffic in New York was relatively easy this late morning. The excruciating rush hour usually dominating the commuting force was over. Yusuf studied the mission map in between checking the road ahead. "Colorado State," the map was labeled. The present mission called for closely coordinated timing. His part of the mission was to take some hostages. He was not very thrilled at having to deal with relatively inexperienced recruits from training camps in Algeria and the Sudan, but he had no choice. Orders had to be followed by the book, without question.

An hour later, they departed on a flight for Denver. From there, it would be necessary to acquire transportation that would take them to the final leg of their mission, a place called Castle Rock. He still did not understand why the place would be important for takeover. All he was told that it was home of an important functionary working with the U.S. defense systems. The place or person must be a considerable threat to the jihad mission that could be used as a potential bargaining power.

After a delayed departure from JFK due to a delayed connection flight, to Yusuf's dismay, the flight arrived hours late at the pre-assigned destination. On arrival, each collected their carry-on. The exit process was hastened. A rental van had been reserved for the team at Denver International Airport. Dusk had already set in when they reached I-225. A steady stream of commuter traffic led their way to intersect with I-25 south. They were well on the way when all of a sudden the cab was filled with a blinding flash. At the same instant, the engine quit. And so did the instruments. The surrounding terrain had turned pitch black. The driver shouted some cusswords in his mother language. He swerved violently to avoid colliding with other cars in trouble. It appeared all traffic had come to a halt. The crashing of metal against metal was cascading in both directions, up and down the freeway. Extremely alert, the team jumped from the van. Yusuf held them in check. They were so close. He was worried about not making the rendezvous point in time. With everyone stranded on the freeway, there was no point to hijacking transportation. All was dead lined when all of a sudden this single craft appeared from the sky. It made a crash landing just ahead in the middle of the interstate he thought would be the end of the craft. Moving up close, he overheard the woman talking about her destination. He recognized the names Castle and Bauer. After her short stop, she continued on south. He and his team followed on foot.

It took close to two hours of forced march to reach the destination. "Castle Rock," the sign finally proclaimed, "Next Exit."

With the Shahadah call, other cells had been dispatched to many points with the same orders: take hostages. Tactical Islamic forces had been mobilized not only in the United States, but worldwide. Their function was to secure prominent individuals that could be used as effective leverage in negotiating a powerbase for the cause.

Yusuf had no specific knowledge about the other cells. He could only guess on the magnitude of the operation. Rumors he'd received from the recruits were prolific. Training camps had been expanding everywhere on the globe, but more so in Islamic-supporting nations. *Shahadah must be something enormous.* In the days to come, his conclusion would prove him right.

ISLAMABAD (Primary Jihad Mission Command Center)

Streams of sweat trickled down Amin Madani, the action officer's forehead. It wasn't so much from the moisture-laden air heated by the late summer afternoon. It was more from anticipation. Madani turned to the next page. It contained another segment of the well-rehearsed mission plan. He slowly read the steps to be executed next. They were precise instruction parameters, one step after the next, coordinates to be specific. In the past, he'd used simulated coordination points. Today, it was a new set of numbers. Handed to him by the mission commander, they'd just been retrieved from a secure vault. They were for real. The numbers were final.

To avoid compromising the critical operation currently in progress, the information had been kept highly classified. The codes had only recently been finalized. The numbers were a product of the politically-charged atmosphere from two adversary nations' rapidly escalated tensions in recent weeks.

Antarah Radi, Jihad mission commander, was authenticating the coordinates. Directions were final. Base phone tightly gripped in one hand, he was intently listening to instructions received via European based satellites from some secret base. Clueless as to who was calling the shots, he didn't care. His job was to execute the target points. He checked the time on the wall-mounted clock one final time then briskly turned to Madani hunched over the terminal. "Target Points," he suddenly announced. "Get ready."

Intensely listening, he repeated each instruction coming live over the wire:
One, "TARGET ALPHA ONE — 38° 51' N AND 77° 2' W."

Typing rapidly on the keyboard, the operator entered the precise parameters for the first grid. He dutifully repeated each alphanumeric code.

Two, "TARGET ALPHA TWO — 38° 49' N AND 104° 43' W."

He swiftly executed the next parameters.

Three, "TARGET ALPHA THREE — 37° 37' N AND 122° 23' W."

"Execute target points."
Madani entered a final set of instructions. "It is done." With that, he exhaled a stream of air he'd been holding. It visibly released the tension in the command center, built up for months of preparation.

On the distant end, the day had finally arrived. It was *his day*. By selecting the first target points, the Serpent, from his concealed location, had just set in motion the long awaited plan, Shahadah. The teams were in position. All preliminary steps had been implemented. It was now up to the field agents to follow through. One more parameter had to be entered to execute the plan, but that required patience. Patience he had—but tolerance, no. Unfortunately, the mission required tolerance, and teamwork. He preferred working alone. Especially during critical elements, but the sheer magnitude of this operation required a sizable force. He couldn't be at several places at once and could only hope all stations would follow through with their assigned tasks.

His final instructions were to hold all positions until further notice. One more step was pending. It was the final step. It would trigger the beginning of Armageddon. *My Armageddon.* Pressed tightly between his lips, fingers on the smoldering cigarette, he was in deep thoughts until the burning on his fingers jolted him back to reality. Annoyed by the stinging sensation and the waiting, he tried to imagine the American satellite surveillance center spring into action.

Seven thousand miles away, the Chief of Operations at the Space Operations Center immediately spotted something wrong. Three satellites from the KE series simultaneously drifted out of their orbits. Although the KHs had been giving him ulcers for the past couple of months, trouble with the KEs was a complete different matter. In heightened apprehension he squinted at the status board. *This is ridiculous.* It was getting to be too much. "Fuck this shit." His nerves were on edge. He forced to himself to calm down. "As if there isn't enough on my plate." He suspected NSA was working the problem. Avoiding immediate action, he surmised, "Must be doing more testing."

This judgment call, or lack of one, would prove to have fatal consequences. It would come to haunt him for the remainder of his career. He failed to check on the critical mission plan of the new KE series. He should have known better. The kinetic energy type was the most critical of NORTHCOM's satellite assets. It could have prevented the disaster that followed.

Back at jihad mission command, confirmation arrived less than twenty minutes later. The ring of the phone suddenly broke the silence. Madani almost jumped out of his skin. He quickly ground out his smoke in an overfilled ashtray. Some burned flakes of charred remains landed on the paper. He blew the dust from the manual then flipped the phone to PA for all to hear. He was ready. Instructions quickly followed. They came loud and clear for everyone in the center to witness. They were final.

"Proceed to final step." It was the ominous voice of the previous caller.

Phone clutched in one hand, Madani's other was working the keyboard. His eyes were burning from the bluish haze of the smoke-filled room. He knew the final step by heart but had a difficult time reading the text. His hand was shaking. The suspense was impossible. *Allah,* he prayed in final desperation, *give me strength.* His finger was poised on the enter key. He had to be sure. His next move would release an event that could not be recalled. Beats of sweat were seeping into his vision. He quickly wiped his eyes clear. The plan held the execution code:

Four, EXECUTION CODE — ALL COORDINATES.

As rehearsed many times before, he entered the remaining keystrokes. One character at a time, he executed the second phase of the mission: "S-H-A-H-A-D-A-H." All eyes in the room were glued to the mission monitor. Two seconds later, the screen responded:

"MISSION EXECUTED."

Aware of the smoke-laden room, his eyes sought out the group leader. Allah would finally settle the great injustice he and his countrymen had endured for so long. "What's next?"

"Now we wait." The initial phases of the mission had been accomplished. Radi had no clue what was next. "More is to come," he'd been instructed. *What's another hour compared to a thousand years of suffering*? For now, he was deeply satisfied. In measured fragments, he slowly began to relax.

Four hours had elapsed since Radi had issued step four. Emotions at the command center had been tense. It was quiet aside from an occasional scuffing of boots above the steady hum of the overhead fan. During the wait, it seemed all had been absorbed in their own thoughts. Only an infrequent cough broke the silence. Nobody left the room.

More smoke was mixing with the already stifling air. It seemed nobody cared. When the call finally came, it bound the center into action once more.

This time, Madani was ready. Apparently, what the high command had been waiting for was word from field agents deployed to the pre-dedicated regions. With satellite links down they had to rely on HF radios supplied to each cell. The coordinated effort from the many attack cells had to be acknowledged by each team operative. It was this effort that made the mission possible. He stooped over the mission plan resting in front of him and recorded the time. His hands moved to the keyboard. With one swift stroke, he entered the final sequence of instructions directed by the caller:

Five, "COORDINATES 37° 46' N AND 122° 26' W."

He executed the last mission command. This last command called for an entirely different mission segment. Whereas alpha one, two, and three were a series of preliminary steps involving Kinetic Energy satellites, this command triggered a sequence of actions relayed via special HF transmitters. Directed at an underground silo somewhere in the northern reaches of Asia, the path of the decoded data stream reached its destination with lightning speed. What happened next was up to Allah. All Madani and the mission personnel could do now was sit tight. Either way, results were sure to follow. Jihad commanders would make sure of that. Shahadah had been executed in its entire stages.

OUTER SPACE

One face of the silent bodies was cloaked in darkness. The other was brightly illuminated by sunlight. The three dish and spike encased bodies slicing through North American orbit were in final position. About one thousand miles apart from each other, the bodies had just completed another ninety minute orbit around earth. Panning across high resolution instruments, four hundred fifty miles from the ground, the northern regions of the United States spanned slowly across their optics. For the moment, the highly sensitive equipment was at rest. The latest set of spy images taken over foreign territory had been successfully processed and sent via relay stations to ground receivers.

Minutes went by in silence. Then, an almost imperceptible motion was followed by a silent click. Another set of instruments had just been activated. A stream of digital data transmitted from the Asian continent was being directed to a set of internal receivers. The command string triggered a miniaturized relay into action. The contact connections between the power source and transmitter circuits simultaneously closed on all three satellite bodies. Patiently waiting for years, the ensuing reaction, in each satellite, forced a miniature explosive charge to simultaneously detonate a lightweight neutron-charged device.

What followed an instant later were three compacted nuclear explosions slamming a wall of destructive forces in every direction. Within one microsecond, the KE series Alpha One, Two, and Three satellites circling the globe at low altitude were obliterated. With millions of destructive neutrons released in every direction racing outward, eliminated next was a cluster of GPS satellites orbiting the northern hemisphere. Next, the destruction carried on further to the synchronized communication satellites broadcasting thirteen thousand miles out in space. The forces released enough energy to blanket the Earth below, as well as the surrounding space and beyond. One millisecond later, the forces of ionized radiation, alpha particles, and gamma rays were quickly followed by rapid neutron pulsing, seeking out a path of utter destruction near and far.

Where much of the radiation and blast effects dissipated into deep space, the detonated HEMP[28] charges directed at the ground proved devastating. Affected regions taking the biggest brunt of damage were Washington D.C., Colorado Springs, and San Francisco. The effects were traumatic. Sector by sector, reaching from the Eastern Seaboard across the nation as far as the West Coast, the nation turned dark. All electronics and electrical power across the central belt of the United States, so vital to every day communication and commerce, had been taken out within seconds. In addition, communications to the northern regions of the United States and borders of Canada and Mexico had been crippled.

The visible effects were immediate. Viewed from the space station, whereas the globe had been illuminated seconds earlier, like a curtain swept across, the U.S., coast to coast, turned dark. Aside from black and white noise generated by the explosions, the cohesive airwaves throughout the audible spectrum had instantly been silenced.

Closer to earth, all airborne traffic appeared in serious trouble. Thousands of jetliners, in transit or ready to land, were forced to fend for themselves. For some, the eventual end would take hours, but for others it would take effect immediately.

---

[28] High-altitude Electromagnetic Pulse – Effects of a HEMP device depend on a large number of factors, including the altitude of the detonation, energy yield, gamma ray output, interactions with the Earth's magnetic field, and electromagnetic shielding of targets.

On the ground, power grids, power plants, stations, generators, and distribution systems burnt up, at times with incredible firework displays, in turn affecting traffic, transport, business, emergency, medical facilities, news media, broadcast, and every household. The United States and its population, Civil War and WWII set aside, would experience the first modern day of Armageddon.

The destructive powers affected ground-based electronics and communications, space-based electronics and communications, including the International Space Station. Saved from total annihilation, in part due to nuclear hardening, were the constellation of ASATs, Air Force One and Two, Marine One and Two, B-2 bomber fleet, stealth fighters, missile LCCs, missiles silos, critical military command centers, and submerged submarine fleet. But, with transmitters and transmission lines out, every military and law enforcement unit became isolated islands to fend for themselves.

PAKISTAN (Mountain Region)

In the mountainous regions near the Afghan borders, they were huddled around an open fire burning in the deepest recesses of the cave. Patches of choking fumes drifted up from a kerosene lamp providing additional lighting. Squatted on the ground were a group of tribal elders. They were dressed in loosely fitted Kurta, the customary shirt for the region. Most wore a Kufi, matching headgear. Wearing light slippers to keep their feet from getting chafed, they discussed their next strategy while smoking thin, tightly rolled cigars. A tin kettle was simmering on top of the open fire. It provided hot tea around the clock for the dwellers, as well as the guards posted outside. Their voices sounded subdued. Sound carried far through the dessert night, even in the mountainous valleys of the Pakistani border. The occasional scuffing of sandals broke up the silence between semi-heated discussions.

"Who will be responsible," one voice spoke from the shadows of the cave, "for the inflicted damages on the infidels?" It was an elder making conversation.

"We do not know yet," another replied. "The only knowledge we have is his code name. They call him 'Serpent.'"

"What good is fighting for a phantom? He is not to be found."

"He is in seclusion," a somewhat aging, but yet authoritarian, third voice emerged from the shadows of the cave, "but he is there." The voice belonged to Kazim Rashid, senior tribal elder in the group.

"Al Qaeda needs a commander for their forces," the first voice insisted. "He must be visible. He must take the command."

"It will be decided," Rashid replied with a wave of a withered and aging hand, thus administering the final verdict on the current topic. The elder gestured at a crudely fashioned armoire placed along the earthen wall. It was an heirloom passed down for many generations. It had survived the Afghan war. "Bring me the scripture." He was handed the only reading material in the dwelling. The elder chief carefully leafed through the well-worn book. It was the Holy book. He opened up to a specific chapter. It was his favorite, "Five Pillars of Islam." As with most nights, stooped over the open fire pit to acquire a flicker of light in the otherwise dimly lit cave, he proceeded to read excerpts from the scripture, the laws of Mohammed, hewn into stone, forever.

"Tomorrow will be a new beginning," he whispered from the sanctity of the darkness. Propped onto one hand to support his withering body, suppressing a groan as he got up off the ground, for a moment he stood there stiff legged. It was time to prepare for the evening's prayer, the communal ritual, held at a nearby cove. Daytime rituals had been suspended for most part owing to the ever-watching eyes in the sky. The brief nightly walk gave the elders an opportunity to stretch their weary bones. Aside from a frequent stop to a hidden away urinal pail, the walk provided the only bodily exercise for the day.

PALM JUMEIRAH (Palm Island, Dubai)

"True miracle," the Serpent marveled. Five years ago there was nothing here but pristine coastlines washed over by the ever present desert sand. "Look at it now," he muttered, "paradise of my people." Still under development, it wasn't perfect yet. Construction cranes were moving slowly about, hauling immense steel girders skyward. Cement was poured as fast at the operator allowed. For the observer, it looked like giant cranes pecking away in the sand searching for sea crabs.

From the distance, he observed the greatest construction project ever undertaken by Dubai, *perhaps the entire globe.* Palm Jumeirah…Palm Island, three in all, each shaped in the form of a palm tree. When finished, it would number more than 120,000 residents spending their days on each island made of rock, gravel, and sand. Materials were blasted out from nearby mountains. Sand was dredged from the bottom of the Gulf. Aside from thousands of luxurious apartments and mansions still under construction were hotels, restaurants, monorails, and a water theme park. The most prominent structure, the Trump International Hotel and Residence Towers, would stand tall for ages to come. Other nations in the region, including Qatar and Oman, as well as the Emirates capital Abu Dhabi, were quick to borrow from Dubai's model to develop their own. The region was to become the ultimate dream Mecca for the wealthy, the rich, and the visitor.

The day before, he'd flown in to check on his new home--a colossal mansion just finished. He'd waited several years for it to be completed. The day had finally arrived when he received the call. And just in time. "Great timing," he muttered. It matched The Plan perfectly. His thoughts briefly touched on yesterday's events. Although he had to rely on many operatives, he was satisfied executing initial events. It was only the beginning. There was much more.

The flight had been an unexpected marvel. An A-380 airbus, a newly built jetliner, had provided the comfort of home. Spending much time in deserts, he was not accustomed to all this luxury. *Yes, a shower.* Who'd have thought such frivolous extravagance would have ever been offered on an airliner? The thirty-minute slot allocated to each passenger had been ample time for a shower, a clean shave and slipping into a set of fresh clothes. He had taken advantage of it. He'd felt unclean after killing off his former employer then hurriedly leaving.

Flying west on Egypt Air, the 1,800-plus-mile flight had taken him over the Gulf of Oman. In the distance below, he'd made out the northern tip of the UAE jutting out into Hormuz Strait. Preparing for the final descent into Dubai International, the craft made a lazy circle over the Persian Gulf. Arrival and customs processing had been handled swift and efficient. He'd flagged a taxi to take him the few miles to his new home, The Palace.

The place turned out to be more villa than the mansion he'd expected. Tinted in soothing and trendy earth tones, appropriate for this scorching Arabic region, the first impression it had was one of splendor. Two spires prominently adorned the top of the villa, giving it the appearance of an Islamic mosque. When he entered, the place felt remarkably cool. Supported by a dozen marble columns, it was not surprising given the height of the lofty structure. Somewhat elated, he'd thought of himself as Lord, master of his Palace, ruler of nations—icon for the new base of operation. The place suited him perfectly. *Let them try to take it from me.* He'd chosen the place for its political insulation from the free world. It was to be *their world.* The world of Islam.

Today felt great. He hadn't slept as well in many months. "Could get used to this," he muttered, picking up a copy of The Plan stretched out under the balcony's shady awning. The overhead canopy was rapidly flopping in the brisk ocean breeze. His eyes fastened for a second across the channels of turquoise sea among tightly bunched mansions aligned like a string of pearls. Wealth seemed to be everywhere. Prosperity expanded in every direction. It was the new paradise–paradise for the rich and the affluent. This was the place. It would be his sanctuary away from the battle fields. It would be the place he could relax and enjoy the fruits of his accomplishments without prejudice.

He would blend in perfectly among his brethren, but this time within the modern amenities of luxury. He had enough of desert quarters made up of mud and dirt. Here, in the comfort he deserved, he could leisurely oscillate between dreaming up grand visions and commanding his forces. The Plan was relatively simple. It called for adaptation. Where most of the Muslim population adhered to a strict Islamic doctrine, he, on the other hand, had realized the need for change. Adaptability was the key. "You must grow with a changing world," was his philosophy. He had studied the Koran. He'd searched Christianity and other doctrines for a solution. Then, one day, it had dawned on him. It was a revelation unprecedented in all of Islamic history. The key to world dominance had been in front of him all along. It'd been the key to the world's dominant superpowers for hundreds of years. "Of course...that's it!" It satisfied everybody's needs. "Faith, freedom, prosperity, success," he found himself freely admit, "have to admire the strategy of the infidels."

The reason for their success became clear: "Separation between Church and State." He'd vowed to make it the guiding principle for The Plan.

Already his mind was whirring with ideas. His feet were propped comfortably on a solid oak coffee table. He leaned forward to scribble another note on an office pad. He made a mental note to get a laptop computer. Earlier, he'd placed a call to schedule an Internet service connection. The technician was scheduled to arrive tomorrow to configure the wireless. Reading what he'd written, he contemplated what steps to take next.

Based on the statistics he'd collected, priorities became obvious: World Nations — 250, in total. Minor Islamic Nations — 140, making up 56 percent. Major Islamic Nations — 55, providing 22 percent of the population. From the list, it appeared that almost 80 percent of the world was populated by Muslims, although Christianity, Buddhism, Hinduism, and other minority faiths still held sway in many areas. Much work needed to be done. Eyes focused on the figures, he reached for his mobile. With a swift move he flipped the cover, rapidly tapping the keys, selecting options, address book, and list of contacts. He then jotted down several names with connections to Islamabad, the Cayman Islands, Moscow, London, Frankfurt, and Lisbon. He hadn't even addressed contacts in Africa, Asia, and the U.S. yet. That would come later. He closed out the contact list and placed an urgent call.

"REX Chemicals. How can I help?" the voice answered in broken English.

"Omar One."

Seconds later, the distant voice responded, "Omar One...yes?"

"What's the status of the package?"

The voice was assertive. "Wrapped and ready for pickup," it said. "Need date of delivery and destination address."

"Hold until notified."

"Right," the voice confirmed. "Hold for further instructions."
Click.

CASTLE ROCK

Brian had left for the hotel. Tracy had retreated to the guest room for the night. For Alex, it was too early in the evening to retire. Besides, his other daughter hadn't arrived. He felt mellow after melting off a few pounds in the Jacuzzi sipping brandy. He didn't need to lose weight. He just loved this combination of elixir. His body was steaming when he moved to the balcony. In the cool night air, it gave off streamers of fog. Completely relaxed, he reclined in the folding chair. That way, he hoped to catch a few shooting stars. Some nights, the sky was virtually painted with streaking beams of lights traversing the blackness. His eyes slowly adjusted to the darkness. As usual, the sight of innumerable stars overhead became overwhelming. The only sound he perceived was that of chirping crickets eagerly rubbing their spiny legs together, generating the familiar buzzing sound from an army of tiny creatures. Soon, the chill seeped through his skin. *Time to lock up.* He closed the balcony doors for the night. *Wonder what's keeping her.* He was expecting a call from Lisa. She'd promised to call as soon as she arrived at the local airport.

Most network channels were already off the air for the night. Daytime shows were replaced by all-night promotions and public service programs. Alex kicked back in the comfort of the sofa. He tuned to BBC, his favorite news source. The additional cost for the international news package was worth it. He liked to keep in touch with the world. It gave him an unbiased perspective. Through years of travel, he'd learned that much local broadcast information was distorted. Local news delivered in a foreign nation did not necessarily match that of U.S. broadcasts. One would think in a free society such as the U.S. this wouldn't be considered necessary, but, for some reason, it was. Trade mags such as *Life-Times*, *Stars & Stripes*, and *World News* printed various versions for their weekly distribution and were editorially tailored to a specific region. The same was true with television broadcasts.

A developing story just appeared on the TV screen. He followed it with piqued interest. He knew the areas. He'd been there on assignments.

At least 28 persons were killed and more than 85 wounded in a string of suicide car bombings across Baghdad. Many of the dead were police officers and at least one of the attacks took place in Hurriya, a stronghold of Muqtada al-Sadr and a heavily protected part of the city, surrounded by blast walls and checkpoints. Other attacks took place in Mosul, Kerbala and several other towns in the south. At least 10 persons were killed and 8 more injured in these incidents...

...a firebomb exploded and another bomb was found on the Hamburg to Berlin railway line in the city of Berlin, followed by a bomb found on another railway line in the city the day after. The bombs were designed to derail trains and a left wing group calling itself Hekla Reception Committee said it was responsible. No one was killed or injured in the attacks...

As if, Alex thought with dismay, *people don't have enough problems struggling with their own affairs.* There was more—much more. It seemed no day went by without another terrorist incident—bombings, ambushes, and shooting plots. *Never ends.* The Islamic cause seemed to spread like wildfire. *One good thing,* he thought with empathy, *for the time being, the U.S. seems calm compared with the rest of the world.*

The newscast was interrupted by yet another commercial. *Commercials,* he silently cussed, *idiotic nuisance.* He tolerated them with the news. At times, it was a welcomed break. It allowed him to fetch a snack, a drink, or a trip to the bathroom. But otherwise, he considered them an intrusion into his personal life. He missed the old nostalgic commercials. Now the pounding audio tracks drilling into the brain accompanied by the idiotic casting brought on nausea. His eyes caught the current time on the TV screen. *She should be here already,* he worried once more. He was getting troubled about his daughter and her kids. He'd called her mobile phone earlier and left messages. Since there was no response, he suspected she was still in transit. The central region of the country was sparsely populated and did not have much mobile coverage. He sat back in his recliner and waited, troubled.

NAPA VALLEY (California)

Earlier that day marked two weeks after her dad's urgent call. Lisa had been struggling with the thought of taking a week off from the job. *If I don't do it now,* she finally decided, *it'll be another year.* With the kids on summer break and the fire season coming up soon, *this is the only chance I've got.* It was a spur of the moment decision. *Dad will be happy.* The kids were thrilled not only by the thought of riding a plane cross-country, but also with spending time with Pappi. That's what they called their granddad. He'd insisted on the endearment watching the Popeye film years ago—and rightfully so. It suited his personality. It was his lifestyle. *Ageless and forever young,* she'd say.

Early this morning, Lisa Bauer found herself loading up the kids and supplies in her SUV. She was headed for nearby Napa County Airport, and her private craft, a Cessna 172 Skyhawk. The 360 preflight check went quick. She knew it by heart. Inspect fuel levels, drain fuel sump, and check engine oil capacity. It ended with a visual around the craft by shaking wing struts, rudder, and ailerons for lose connections. She had plenty of fuel capacity with the extra 40 gal auxiliary tank installed behind the back seats. She'd never needed the extra fuel before, but didn't want to take the chance. It'd only taken another five minutes to fill. The kids were getting antsy to get going.

"Mom, I wanna sit up front," her daughter whined.

"No," her son insisted, "I'm gonna sit next to Mom."

Here we go again. No matter what the outing, it was always the same. "No fighting," she insisted. She had to play Mom the Tyrant. "In back, both of you." It was better that way. They could watch the world below from the raised back seats. Besides, it gave her the peace and quiet she'd need for a well-deserved break.

She took a seat behind the controls. With the kids secured in back, she made herself comfortable for the next eight hours. It was an all day trip. Her eyes sought out the panel for one final check: Radio — departure frequency 121.7. Altimeter — ground reference 35 feet, Compass heading — 90 degrees east. Satisfied with the flight check she pulled the mic from the hook.

"APC...LIZARD THREE," she called in.

"Come in, LIZ." The controller responded without delay. There was hardly any air traffic this morning.

"Clearance request on 6R for takeoff," she requested.

"No 18R today?" The controller's voice sounded somewhat surprised.

"Got my own wings."

"Where you headed?"

"East." She was slightly bemused. They were used to her flying rescue missions in the county's Twin Otter off the primary strip. They'd even given her the nickname. Not derived from her real name, but the frequent call requests working rescues. LIZARD THREE happened to be the airport's departure point call sign.

"What's the flight plan?"

"Checked with the desk." She wanted to get going.

The craft lifted off at 75 knots. For the first time in many months, she felt the pressures of work melting off her shoulders. After passing the threshold, Napa Valley faded away quickly beneath the wings. Departure control gave her a weather brief. *Should make good timing,* she thought, climbing to 12,500 ft. It would take her into the wake of the jet stream. Anticipating only one refueling stop at Salt Lake, she should reach the 950-mile distance to the Springs before nightfall. Ten minutes into the flight she reached the preset altitude and flipped the switch to "Autopilot." *What a beautiful day.* The first segment of the flight went without a hitch.

The kids were quietly dozing in the back seats. She sat back and relaxed, as bumpy it was at times, but enjoyable nevertheless. Her view was on the vastness of the country slowly passing beneath the wings. To really appreciate this land, one had to cross the plains by air, rail, or highway at least once. Up ahead, the blue sky beckoned her along. It was broken up only by an occasional cloud formation. At this altitude, the scene only changed slightly for color, hue, and terrain. Miles farther out, she could make out the various mountain ranges to the north, east, and south. The Sierras had just passed beneath them. Her eyes scanned the instrument panel. The indicator held steady at the pre-assigned altitude and direction. Her ears were in harmony with the steady hum of the engine. The pitch of the blades was set at three quarter maximum speed, allowing for efficient fuel consumption.

Soon, the ground beneath changed from rocky terrain to cultivated farmland. *Wonder where I'd land in an emergency.* Her eyes scanned the ground below. The thought of a possible emergency landing was always on the forefront of her mind. Most responsible pilots felt that way.

Her thoughts drifted to the trip ahead. *Dad,* she mused. *Wonder how he's been.* A sense of guilt crept up within for not keeping in touch more often. *Well,* she thought in heightened anticipation, *I'll make up for it.* She was still awed by the amount of knowledge he'd passed on to her. Knowledge that paved the way to a career she totally enjoyed. Take for instance today…this very flight. *Dad was responsible.* Although an avid pilot, he was only qualified for single-engine craft. She vividly recalled his instructions when she took to the skies years ago. "Don't ever lose sight of the horizon…watch the compass…and," he'd caution, "always check the ground for possible landing sites." Where most of his words made sense, she'd always questioned the emergency landing. From this altitude, the ground below was almost imperceptible. She pondered where to set the craft down amid the many rugged mountain peaks. "Hope I'll never find out." He'd persist, "It's not *if* you'll emergency land someday, but *when.*" She wondered what was on a jetliner pilot's mind.

"Oops." It was an automatic response triggered by the feel of freefall. It gave her a brief feel of nausea. She calmed herself. "Not the first time."

"Mom," her daughter shrieked out from the backseat, "what happened?"

"Don't be alarmed," she calmed, "just a bump." The instruments indicated a fifty foot drop. "Only a downdraft, dear." She craned out the window and realized the cause. They just left the Wendover ridge in their wake. Way below, I-80 was guiding her eastward. It's where the jet currents dipped into the Salt Lake Basin. Her son dozed on, unaware of the slight turbulence. Downdrafts could be a frightening experience for someone unfamiliar with flying light craft. They happened frequently. A plane this size responded immediately. Up, and down, most times, but back on course within a couple of seconds. A craft could lose hundreds of feet of altitude in the midst of it, but recovered immediately with the updraft that was sure to follow. *No biggie.* She got them all the time flying over burning forest fires.

Shortly after, he daughter complained, "Mom, I'm hungry."

"Won't be long," she pacified her, "we'll land for lunch." She checked the flying time. "Ten more minutes." The glare from crystallized salt reflected off the lakebed from below much like a mirror. 90 miles ahead, Salt Lake was already coming into view. *Time to check in for landing clearance.* She reached for the mic to make the call.

Refueling went without a hitch. After a quick stop to McDonald's and the restroom, they were back in the air an hour later. Three hours into the second leg of the trip, her son whined, "Mom, we there yet?"

"I'm bored," her daughter complained. They were getting impatient from sitting still for hours.

"Play with the iPod," Lisa suggested, "or read a book." They stayed quiet for the rest of the trip.

"Won't be long now—almost there," Liz announced an hour later. After a late start, she was hoping to still get there by daylight. It became obvious they wouldn't be able to make it. The night's shadows rapidly approached from the east. *It will be dark soon.* She shot an occasional glance back at her children. *I'm glad to have these two,* she thought, watching their serene and patient faces—*couldn't imagine life without them. Better concentrate on the upcoming landing.*

From the darkened cockpit, eyes fixed on the ground below, she could make out the interstate traffic slowly moving ahead. *I-25 should be just ahead.* It was the marker for her to turn south, the final leg. Nighttime had fallen over the country. She switched the overhead lighting on to check the map. The city of Bolder was passing to the left. Ahead was Denver International Airport with its busy air traffic. Landing lights from neatly stacked jetliners indicated their final approach patterns. Beyond lay the fertile plains reaching into Kansas.

The nearest landing to her dad's place was the Colorado Springs airport. He knew they were flying in and had promised to pick them up. Better check in with him. "My mobile," she gestured to the kids. There was silence. She craned back. Both had fallen asleep. She fumbled to get her purse. She'd placed it behind her seat. *Where's that damned thing?* Her fingers were groping on the floor. *There it is.* She touched the strap. She was about to pull the bag off the floor when all of a sudden the world around lit up.

"What?" Her entire body contracted. Her mind was trying to cope with the flash. The brilliance of white lightning had bathed the inside canopy against the shadows of the night. Her subconscious mind recorded the eerie snapshot. The propeller blades were frozen in midair by the strobe effects. Her mind did not yet register the full impact. Her hands reached for the controls. The bag slid from her hand. It tumbled to the floor. Her eyes sought out the instruments. "The kids," her mind screamed out. Her head snapped back once more but there was only dark and empty space. Panic sat in. Only by instinct did her hand reach for the mic. "Mayday…mayday." There was no response. The airwaves had turned silent. Only a high-pitched sound of air passing over the canopy seeped into the craft.

SPACECOM

Headquartered at Peterson AFB, Colorado Springs, CO, the defense command operated the Space Defense Operations Center, Space Surveillance Center, Missile Warning Center, and the Joint Space Intelligence Center. As such, it directed the Defense Satellite Communications System, GPS system, Transit Maritime Navigation System, Fleet Satellite Communications, Air Force Satellite payloads, and the Defense Meteorological Satellite Program, along other activities. Specifically, it kept constant records of the movements of thousands of man-made objects orbiting the Earth. These objects included satellites and the many pieces of space debris left behind from rocket launches.

"Class...class...please," she beckoned. She was clad in her customary government-issued attire. Anxious to get started, she thought, *Chatty bunch,* with growing impatience. It was the beginning of another training session for new recruits just arrived. Not thrilled about pulling second shift she called the class to attention. Reaching for the laser pointer, she announced, "I'm Rhonda Hicks, your instructor." The beam focused on her name written across the wallboard. "You can call me Rhonda." There were a few cheers and catcalls. She didn't like it but let it slide.

Hired by Lockheed Martin, primary contractor for SPACECOM support, it was her responsibility to make sure that future "Space Cadets" received the best training. Most had graduated from the Academy but a few civilians also made the grade. Presently, they were at Schriever AFB, located just a few miles east of Colorado Springs, recruited to the 50th space wing. Grown enormously over the past twenty years, the wing was essential support in air defense.

Her responsibilities expanded likewise in various phases of the program. One thing still bothered her: she never understood why they changed the name of this site from Falcon Air Base to Schriever. She'd liked the old name. Everybody did. It symbolized the mission. Today, it's just another busy place with people rotating in and out weekly.

"Okay, class," she demanded once more. With a practiced move she lowered the retractable wall screen. "To begin," she started this evening's lecture, "you'll see a film about the role and purpose of SPACECOM and," she paused, "please refrain from questions until after the presentation." She'd seen the demo film many times and decided to take a ten-minute break. She liked teaching, but on her terms. Starting the film, not waiting for the screen to come alive, she briskly walked from the room.

Ten minutes into her break, Rhonda was about to return to the class when all of a sudden the break room went dark. "Another brownout," someone said. She paused a few seconds to get her bearing. Emergency lighting had not come on. Her eyes gradually adjusted to the darkness. She then rushed to the hallway, bumping into others rushing for the exits.

"This is no brownout," she muttered in no uncertain terms. From the corner of her eyes, something through the windows had caught her attention. It was an intense flash of light. She pulled her mobile from her uniform. A quick flip opened the cover. "Nothing?" Using cautious strides, she headed for the exit but it was blocked. The doors had been shut tight due to the loss of power. Retracing her steps she tried to use the hallway booth phone. "Dead! No dial tone?" There was one other way out. Emergency exit! Rhonda stepped outside. Dead silence. Except for the nightly cricket chirps the night was unusually quiet.

An overwhelming feeling struck when she noticed the night sky above. It unveiled the brilliance of a starlit sky she'd not seen since college-day camping trips. She could identify the constellations she'd remembered from the training manuals and wondered what could have brought on the complete silence embraced by total darkness. *I was right,* she thought about her earlier assumption, *this is no ordinary brownout.* Despite her anxiety, she couldn't help but admire the starry skies overhead. She stood breathless, scanning the horizon for any activity. There was none. Most of the cadets had gathered around. They were just as much taken in with awe. "Could have been an asteroid," was one comment.

"Naw," another insisted, "meteoroid maybe…re-entry vehicle?"

"Don't think so…I'd know about it." Speculations were prolific among the young cadets.

COLORADO AIR SPACE

Liz was humming to a song. It was a popular tune from late the 70s. *Johnny Cash,* she recalled, *Riders in the Sky.* She was riding a bronco across an ever-widening stretch of prairie. There were hurdles to jump. "You can make it," she reassured herself as she faced the wooden fences. The scene suddenly shifted. She was riding a rollercoaster. "Strange world." It was then that she realized it may be a dream. Cool puffs of air were touching her face. Thinking it was a strand of hair, she rubbed her hand across her forehead. *Ouch.* A burning sensation sprang from her eyes. Her fingers had touched open eyeballs. She was fully conscious but the whistling persisted. *What is this?* Reality suddenly stuck. "Must have blacked out." It came in a flash of recognition. She turned her head toward the sound, but darkness prevailed. Bewildered, she tried to determine the source. Her hand reached out. It touched the cold frame of the plane. She realized the source. Airflow across the canopy generated the whistling sound penetrating her left ear. "This is all wrong."

Her mind had touched on reality. She suddenly knew where she was but refused to accept it. Her brain screamed for help. There was no answer. Her next reaction was to go back to the dream, the comfort of darkness, but her conscious mind dictated otherwise.

Fully awake now, her hands frantically groped around the darkness. There were the familiar objects, instrument panel, flight controls, straps; they were real. "Feels like the cockpit." Her right hand reached behind the seat. She touched a hand. It was her daughter's. Her conscious screamed with panic. It finally dawned on her. "I'm flying."

Horrified by the sheer thought, her body snapped back into the seat. She was facing the front, but all there was more darkness. "Oh my God," terror-stricken she stammered, "I'm blind."

"Mom," a voice called out, "what happened?" It was her son.

"Your sister?" Liz was desperately groping in back.

"Don't know…asleep." Fortunately for her, her daughter was asleep and strapped in the backseat unaware. Fully conscious now, Liz remembered something. Something extremely unnatural had happened. "How long's it been?" She couldn't remember. Time was outside of her realm of understanding. "Horizon?" Her eyes tried to get a fix on her position but couldn't find it.

She forced herself to think, *pull yourself together.* It was then Liz realized she couldn't see. She refused to accept it. "What is happening? Where am I?"

"Here," was the fear-filled voice from the back. She could feel her son frantically grabbling for her right hand. "See the stars outside?" Her left hand desperately held on to the yoke, the craft's control.

"Where?"

Pointing out the window, he yelled, "Down there!" She could not see his gestures. Nor did she see the ground.

Impossible, her mind screamed back at her, *stars are always up. Or?* She did not dare to think the impossible. To fight off further panic she pulled all of her strength together. It didn't help. There was nothing but darkness. *I'm blind,* she panicked again. On the verge of getting sick, she wondered, *But why?* Not letting them know her plight she tried to focus on the hum of the engine. There was no pitch. There was no sound. *Freefall.* It finally dawned on her. "Don't get hysterical on me," she silently screamed at herself. It didn't help. Her face broke into a shallow laugh. Or was it tears? She wiped her eyes with the back of the sleeve. "Ouch!" The fabric had rubbed against her open eyeballs, extended wide in the blackness. Taking a deep breath calmed her somewhat. "Not the first time an engine quit on me."

"Mom," a faint voice complained, "I'm sick." It was her daughter.

"You awake?" Close to tears again, Liz screamed into the blackness.

"My chest hurts."

"No!" her senses demanded, "I won't give in." Still disoriented, she felt a sense of change. It went from a sickening weightlessness to an increase in Gs then back to weightlessness. There it was again. The craft was looping. She could not see it but sure could feel the force. It wasn't the first time she'd felt the sensation. It happened during practice stalls.

The Cessna craft was very forgiving. It was designed that way. If the engine should give out, the craft, by design, turned into a glider. *Almost.* Aerodynamically, it worked this way: the engine quit, the weight of the craft pulled the nose downward into a dive. Fifty some feet later, the wings catch the force of the passing air and lift the nose upward into a stall. This cycle repeats until the craft runs out of space, with the ground its ultimate destination. What helped Liz today was the added fuel tank centered in the midsection of the craft. The balance slowed the motion. It'd gained her time, but time was running out rapidly.

"Come on...dammit," she screamed into the silence. Squinting furiously, her hands were desperately pulling the yoke. She tried to get a bearing, any bearing, but there was nothing but darkness. Her fingers kept groping. They touched a button. Ignition! Her hand pushed down. The engine labored. It cranked, then sputtered a few times. More silence. She tried again...and again. "Do something," she heard a voice scream then realized it was her own.

"Wait...wait," she whispered, "I see something. Stars...can't be...landing lights?" She couldn't make out a pattern, but was euphoric by her sight coming back, even if only faint. "Thank you, God," she whispered. Liz could concentrate on the craft's bearing once more. She tried the engine again....and again. *Flooded*!

With each torque the lights on the ground were spinning faster, and closer. *Like a kaleidoscope.* Almost subconsciously, Liz kept pushing the starter. Suddenly, there was a shudder. The engine caught once. It sputtered. Then it kicked in. Slow rotation at first, but it held. The craft was flying again, but out of control. The lights on the ground were spinning in ever-increasing rotation. She was getting dizzy. *I'm losing it.*

She tried frantically to get out of it. She slammed the rudder right, then left, but the craft did not respond. "Dammit," she screamed. "Why can't I stop the spin?" Panic set in again. Then she remembered. *What was it Dad had said?* "Check the throttle."

Her mind was racing, retracing the events. It was in the midst of the flash when the engine quit. Controls had been almost at max power. A stall was nothing new to her. She'd performed it many times on practice runs, but never with controls at full power. Those were executed by stunt flyers only, but she'd remembered the instructions Dad gave her.

Running out of time, the lights kept rushing up from the ground. She was losing height fast. Her mind was frantically groping for the information. *What was it again?* Pull throttle...stop spin...pull up...level off...accelerate, provided the engine was on. There was a new glimmer of hope. *Is there time?* She could clearly make out the lights rushing in from the ground.

Then, in a sudden revelation, it came to her. *Check the throttle!* Her hand reached out. Immediately, she pulled the throttle to idle. The engine responded. "Great! What next?"

She tried to recall his other instructions. He'd been in power-on stalls. He told them stories when they were kids. She would intently listen. Her mind recalled: low throttle...slam rudder. "Which way?" Opposite of spin! "Good." Level off. "Come on...come on..." The craft was straining with Gs. Push the yoke. "Good." The craft gradually responded. It leveled out. She was gaining speed. *Where's the landing strip?* Her eyes tried to penetrate the darkness. "Wait, I see it...over there."

The craft had drifted off course. The Cessna responded to the controls but not fast enough. *Gotta clear the ground.* She pulled back even harder. More strain on the frame. A sudden thought came to her about something else her dad had mentioned. "Be careful with the controls."

"Why," she'd demanded. "Just remember," he'd said, "there's only one quarter-inch bolt holding each strut to the wing and fuselage. If you're not careful, wings will snap off at 150 knots."

Today, she got lucky. The wings held. She barely cleared the ground after snapping off some outgrown tree twigs. "Come on," she huffed under her strained breath, "pull...pull up, dammit!" The wings barely missed another tree line. Her gaze sought the speed indicator. "Power!" She pushed the throttle all the way. The engine surged. Her confidence was coming back. The craft was gaining altitude under her full control. *Now, she* could concentrate on the landing. She headed in the direction of the landing lights which she estimated were a couple of miles out. "How're you kids?" she called over her shoulder. Aside from the occasional "Ouch" and "Careful, Mom," they'd been quiet throughout the ordeal. *Probably sick. Sick from flying... sick from me.*

"Okay, Mom."

"Fine—now."

She felt relieved. Her eyes scanned the instruments. "Can't believe I dropped twelve thousand feet," she muttered, tremendously elated to be alive. *But then,* she thought, *never had to fly by the seat of my pants in total blindness.* She reached for her bottom. *Still dry.* A brief smile spread over her face. Liz prepared for the imminent landing. *Ninety degrees crosswind...another ninety downwind...final approach dead ahead.* She could clearly make out the landing strip. *Must be emergency lighting.* Full confidence returned, she pulled ten degrees flaps. It slowed the craft. Then it dawned on her. "Why only one runway?" There was no time to contemplate. She prepared for a hard landing. The craft came in hot.

"...and so narrow...what the fuck," she screamed, "cars on a runway?" The wheels touched down with a solid thud. Next thing she heard was crunching. It was an awful sound. It was metal against metal. The craft jerked violently once, then again. The right wing was sheared off. It was a stalled truck sitting along the outer edge on I-25. The left wing followed. It tore into a parked camper to the left and snapped off. She desperately held on to the shaky controls. Her hands barely managed to keep the plane on the road while her mind registered, *Interstate.* She was speeding amid stalled cars stranded along both sides of the highway. From the corner of her eyes she could make out passengers lunging for cover from her fast approaching, crippled plane. With both wings gone, and feet jammed on the brake pedals, the broken-up craft finally rolled to a halt close to a crowd frenetically flagging her to a stop.

Visibly shaken up, she pulled her kids from the back seats to safety. "You okay?" She checked them over. They were shaken but otherwise appeared fine—no physical injuries. *Have to get them into counseling,* she promised herself, after things had settled, *especially her.* "Stay here," she ordered.

Liz had led them under the protection of a nearby tree. She quickly strode back to the craft. There, she noticed a strong odor seeping from the fuselage where the two wings used to be. "Fuel." Now, only two gaping holes remained. Strands of wires were dangling from the torn edges sparkling and bouncing with electricity. The ends were darting from metal to metal. She tore at the insulated ground wire. It snapped, giving off one final spark.

Stunned by her appearance from the sky, stranded passengers approached the craft. They were gazing at the gaping holes amid the fuselage. Heads were shaking in disbelief. "What happened…where you from…the craft?" some bystanders asked.

"Don't know—light in the sky."

"Saw that." Nearby people were pushing close, talking over each other. Most were more concerned for her and the kids' wellbeing than for their own safety. Liz noticed many blank stares especially from a strange looking group crowding in on her. There was hesitation about what to do next. "What's your name?" one asked.

"Liz…Lisa Bauer."

"Communication's out," another remarked. "We're stranded." More people were asking questions. She had no answers.

"Where you from?"

"California. You people stranded?"

"Cars won't start," one said, "but lights work."

"Thank God for that," Liz said. "I used them for landing."

"What now?"

"Head south." Her confidence was returning. "Castle Rock."

"Like this—no wings?" People gestured at the craft. "You crazy?"

She threw her head back in defiance. "I'll try." Striding back to the Cessna, she did not really believe it herself. "Come." She collected the kids. Two caring ladies helped them into the backseats. Liz swiftly climbed behind the controls. Her hands were waving out the window. "Clear!" she shouted. People backed off to clear space ahead. After several labored cranking, the ignition started up. It'd take dual magnetos to start and maintain the Lycoming-320 engine. It gave them the necessary torque to suck the remaining fuel into the engine. *Thank God for auxiliary tanks.* The prop sprang into action. Unstable at first, it then quickly turned into a steady hum. They were on their way. It'd been a true miracle for her and the kids to be alive. "I'll get help," she yelled over the sound of the engines taking on speed.

"Stop." There were shouts from people ahead getting in her way. She ignored them and kept pushing forward. There were more shouts from dazed and stranded drivers. "Stop…stop your…" Words were drowned out by the sound of the speeding craft. People tried to flag her down.

"Out of my way," she yelled through the open window.

"Fuck you, lady." There were more shouts and curses about her and her freewheeling wreck. She kept pushing on, planning to make the last few miles to Castle Rock on tires.

O'HARE INTERNATIONAL AIRPORT

Jake Fulton was running late. Stuck in the evening traffic he was cussing, "Dammit…shoulda left earlier." He contemplated taking an alt-route, but knew it wouldn't gain him time. Most access roads were congested. Traffic volume was compounded by the arrival of international flights, all scheduled to arrive at the same time, it seemed. On top of it, this time of day everyone was in a hurry to get home. People were impatient. Horns were blaring constantly. After all the years jostling for position, he should be used to the city by now. There it was again. *Beep… beep.* He gave the guy the finger. He didn't have to turn to see what make it was. "Damned Beetles." Those irritating European cars with their annoying horns drove him nuts. In between the stop and go traffic, he lapsed into another segment of stupor, people-watching. Evening traffic was murder. "Everybody's in a hurry." People rushed to meet friends, wives, or family for an evening dining out. They all had plans. *Not me.* He was on his way to work.

Jake checked his chronometer again. A showpiece, it was a birthday present from his wife. It had everything built in but a wet bar. "Sure could use a drink." It listed every time zone. It had half a dozen dials running different speeds. There was a calculator, direction finder, compass, and, best of all, it was waterproof to a depth of 330 feet. Not that he'd ever use it in the oceans, but it was good to brag. To him, it was a conversation piece. *Thirty minutes late.* He thought of calling in but knew they wouldn't answer. It was against regulation to take personal calls unless there was an emergency. "Oh well," he sighed, "ten more minutes." Despite his present demise, Jake Fulton considered himself the luckiest dog alive. Thirty years earlier, he slid into a career he'd never dreamed of.

Back then, a good paying job was hard to come by without higher education. He was driving a cab. He couldn't remember why he'd dropped out of high school. He was stupid then, a young kid. It didn't matter now. He'd been given a second chance. *Thanks to President Reagan.* The year was 1981. Nearly 13,000 air traffic controllers walked off the job. Negotiations had failed after they demanded higher wages. In the eyes of the nation, PATCO[29] members were already overpaid. There was not much sympathy from the public, or from the government. Everything with the strike went wrong. To begin with, it was illegal for government employees to strike. Union leaders had pushed too far. The result was massive firing. It was a test case for both sides, government and union alike. The strike was designed to take place during the busiest time of the year for airlines. It affected major carriers like Braniff, Eastern, American, Pan Am, and TWA. As luck had it, the FAA was prepared. They had worked out a contingency plan. It immediately went in effect. Emergency hires went into effect. It worked flawlessly—minor air infringements, yeah, but no accidents. That's how Jake got the job.

O'Hare was the nation's busiest airport. Already overloaded and at maximum capacity, the increase in passenger demand, year after year, squeezed more buildings onto the airport's real estate. There were seven primary air carrier runways, tangentially arranged in 3 parallel sets. A jumble in air traffic design, but it worked…for now.

Ten minutes later, Jake arrived at the parking garage. In long, hurried strides he caught the elevator up the control tower. He was expected. "Sorry I'm late."

"You owe me." It was a common tradeoff between PATCO members.

---

[29] Organization for Professional Air Traffic Controllers.

"What's the load?" He could check the ticket tags but it was quicker to get a cursory status first hand on pending flights.

"Fifteen final…twenty three on hold…fifty plus in flight…I'm outta here."

"Thanks. Have a good one." He checked his staff. *All there.* Jake picked up the pair of binoculars, lifeline with the carriers. He took position in the center of the glass-enclosed platform. It was soundproof. The glass filtered out much of the jet engine noise.

He was shift supervisor. He'd taken over the night shift. There was a crew of seven this evening—one controller per runway set. He could rely on every one of them. His team was efficient. Others were busy by computer terminals directing ground control. They were filing schedules for arrivals, terminals, and departures. Things went smooth like clockwork. He was listening in on pilot-to-tower calls. Most were requesting final approach this time of day. It was one arrival every forty seconds. And that was for each runway. Planes were set up in one hundred foot intervals stacked thousands of feet in the air. Dispatchers were busy with placing landing tickets in front of the controllers. As always, they were stacking up. It was up to the controller to land each plane safely as quick as ground control could handle the load. Jake watched for errors. As expected, there were none. *Time for a coffee break.*

He was just about to fill his mug when his eyes caught a flash of light. It was intense. He spilled some coffee. "Dammit." He stopped in mid track. At first he thought it was some landing lights that'd swept the tower. It happened sometimes when a flight was aborted. The next second, all lights shut down. He rushed back to the lookout. All terminal screens had gone blank. From his vantage point he wasn't sure about the ILS, MLS and TLS[30]. "Holy shit," was all he could stammer, *Blackout.* His heart almost jumped from his chest cavity. He rushed to the phone to call the power station. *Nothing.* The phone was dead. He started to panic. His staff was frantically trying to direct air traffic. "Abort…abort landing," was most of the calls. There was no response from pilots. All communication seemed to have gone silent. Air and tarmac space, in an instant, had turned into a phantom world.

What happened next was an enigma for the history books. With hundreds of craft stacked on approach, and no landing lights or instruments, the pilots had to fend for themselves. To avoid colliding, each tried to hold their altitude. With city lights out, the night was pitching black. Pilots had to revert to flying under manual control. Instrument panels had shut down an instant after the lightning blast. Backup generators had shut down from power failure. Each craft turned into a potential weapon. Hundreds of menacing shadows where on a holding pattern desperately trying to maintain altitude. Pilots and copilots were mentally calculating how much fuel was left. Many flights were international in origin and low on fuel. Others had reserves, but it wouldn't matter. Without navigation, city or landing lights, it was only a matter of time before every plane would run out of fuel. Dozens would attempt emergency landings. The rest would fall out of the sky.

Jake was in trouble. And so was his crew. They all knew it. Everyone felt helpless. Some took to prayers for the pilots and passengers. Unless a miracle happened soon, all knew the results, but tonight, there was no miracle. What followed would be the worst aviation disaster in human history.

---

[30] ILS, MLS, TLS – Instrument, Microwave, and Transponder landing systems.

THREE MILE ISLAND (Nuclear Power Plant)

Doug Olson had a bad day. He had just dealt with another power surge. Where they used be a rare occurrence, in recent years, they seemed to be on the increase. There were many such days. Once content, he wasn't happy with the job anymore. He was drinking more than usual. It affected his health. It affected his marriage. "You should quit," his wife suggested on more than one occasion. "Where will I go?" he'd worried.

The thought had been on his mind more often than not. It was especially bad after the monthly status briefs. He hated them. There, he had to face his superiors, an entire panel, alone. That's what bugged him the most. Not once had they shown any appreciation to him. It was always the same. "Where's your efficiency? Why can't you balance the grid? What are you people doing up here? We promise the customers 99 percent efficiency and what do we get—Fuckups."

He'd just come back from a brief. *Here I am, screwed again.* He was shaking his head in self-pity. Scratching his itchy beard, he thought, *should change my image.* "Might get the respect I need." He'd been meaning to trim it for some time, but never got around to it. He was mulling over the pros and cons of leaving the job. *Naw,* he finally decided, *they need me.* "Might even ask for a raise." The thought bolstered his ego.

Right now, he was pacing in front of the control panels. It was an impressive sight, the switches, the buttons, meters, screens, and more gadgets waiting to give him status. The place was spotless. He kept it that way. It was in the manuals. And so was every other step needed to keep the place in shape. Visitors passing through each week were always impressed. At least that was one dignity they'd left him. "Great place you got here," was a frequent comment, even though everything in the place was dated: the switch gear, the generators, and the connections. He was to impress the visitors, the money people. It didn't matter that the infrastructure was failing. They never saw it. That part was invisible. Nevertheless, it was this infrastructure that kept the nation going, regardless of its condition. It was an "aging giant," and it was alive, barely.

Inside the plant, the steady hum of this aging monster was pressing on his senses. There was a grinding sound. It'd been persistent for some weeks. It came from a nearby generator. He could feel it more than hear it. Packaged within precision ball bearings were highly polished shafts spinning rapidly. On the one end was the switchgear. It carried the high voltage electricity directly to the commutators. On the far end was the DC to AC converter, pushing the load onto the grid. It was that load that was the weakest link. In-between were the moving parts. All were connected by sensors feeding the status board. He treated the board like a chess game. It made one move. He countered, waiting for the next. The game was played day and night. Presently, several flags were blinking at him. It meant several moves. Most were yellow in color. It meant nothing. It was a beginner's move in the game. And the name of the game was load balancing.

Computers did his job most of the time. He was thankful for that. There was a time when the system had been less sophisticated. Then it took teams of operators to keep the grid operational. Now, it was technology, sophisticated software mostly, running on old equipment, a result of dollars and cents, the bottom line. *That's all that counted. I sure don't see any of it.*

He recalled the days of glory when he was on top of it. Prestige had been his incentive then. He had achieved his dream, a childhood dream, driving a nuclear sub. It was the ultimate power trip. "Nuclear," was the buzzword then. He had worked hard keeping his roaster clean. He'd followed the chain of command in perfect accord. "Yes, sir," it was from the bottom of the deck all the way to the top rank, from ensign to commander.

Although the mystery had been shattered early on, he stuck it out for twenty years, in the U.S. Navy. The revelation came during rigorous nuclear power training courses he'd attended. First, it was on simulators, then on training runs. As commander, you had to know every detail of your ship, from navigation to radioactive fuel disposal. From the stern where torpedoes were stored, to mid-ship and the bow where power was generated. It was the heart of the system that attracted him most, the nuclear power plant. It was there that held his imagination captive. Until the day the mystique was shattered. He couldn't believe it. All that mystical power, just to heat water? "That's right," were the instructors words. "All that nuclear power just to heat the water." Water was heated to create steam. The steam drove the turbine. The turbine attached to the shaft. The shaft propelled the submarine forward to submerge. Mystery solved. "That simple."

Doug was about to take a break when reality came knocking. It came on suddenly. It jolted him from his nostalgia trip. It was too quick to react to. His widened eyes followed the sequence as it unfolded. His mind could not comprehend. It was the ultimate game, all moves thrown at him at once.

It grew out of the far left on the panel. From there it progressed through the center panels and sped on to the opposite end with lightning speed. The controls lit up like a Christmas tree. The ensuing sound, the alarms, almost drove him nuts. Sick to the stomach, he watched his staff rush up. It was a feeble effort to save the system. An instant later, the plant shut down. "My God!" he yelled. Little did he know that he'd lost the game to the adversary. Enemy won. Technology lost. "Game over!"

Doug was panic-stricken. In an instant, everything went off the air. What he and his crew did not know at this time was that the EMP strike had taken out the eastern seaboard's power grid. It would be the largest power outage the U.S. had ever experienced.

Acting as antennas, the high voltage power lines had taken the full brunt of the EMP impact. From there, the massive burst of energy was carried along the national power grid. All the electronics equipment and sensors connected either melted into twisted metal or incinerated into heaps of ashes. Transformers, no matter the size or make, mounted along the power stations across the nation blew out like timed explosive charges. The surge reached into buildings tall and small. Inside, fuses short-circuited. Conduits of copper alloy provided a perfect path to critical electronics and appliances, industry, commerce, and household alike. Everything connected to the wire became fried. The results were catastrophic. But that wasn't his major concern. He only had to look out the windows to grasp the magnitude of the outage. There, in full plume, were two of the remaining four containment towers, billowing clouds of white smoke into the atmosphere.

It would be only a matter of time, minutes, perhaps hours, before radiation would start to leak out. Without power to run the pumps to cool the reactors, fuel rods would begin to melt. He and his team knew the results only too well, "China syndrome." Visions from the recent Fukushima disaster crept into his mind. "My God," he prayed in silence, "the fallout." *Doomsday.*

FINAL DESTINATION (United Arab Emirates)

At Dubai, UAE, International Airport, the young, deeply-tanned Western-looking couple, after two weeks of holiday, had just checked through airport security. They rushed for the departure gate. "Janet," Paul, her husband, bogged down with carry-on luggage, charging ahead, offered. "Your boarding pass." Trying not to miss the flight, Janet had passed him on the rush for the gate. As always after enjoying a vacation, both found it difficult to leave a paradise behind.

Today, again, they barely made the flight, but only because the flight was late. Arriving passengers, hurrying to get to their final destinations, were still exiting the gate. In the rush, a tall, immaculately dressed, brown skinned, designer shade-wearing, passenger briefly bumped into Paul hanging on to his jostling luggage.

"Excuse me." Paul, half out of breath, offered a hasty apology.

The stranger, slightly startled, turned to face Paul, accepted the apology with a slight nod, and continued down the exit way. "Nice fella'," Paul remarked to Janet, "friendly smile."

"I don't think so," Janet replied, slightly shaken from the brief, but intense stare the stranger had given her. "You see the scar?"

"Thought it was a grin," Paul, finally able to drop the luggage to take the weight off his shoulders, said.

Turning to take one departing glance at the hurried passenger, Janet muttered, "Don't think so. Gave me the creeps."

Carry-on luggage securely stored in the overhead bin, Janet and Paul settled into the comfort of the somewhat dated, spacious craft. Paul, from habit, picked the airline brochure from the front seat pocket, checking out the craft's specs. "L-1011-500 TriStar," the pamphlet stated. Paul, sharing the brochure with Janet, proclaimed, "Thought they'd been retired years ago."

Throwing him a smug glance, Janet, in the travel business and more up to date on worldly things, corrected him as she sometimes did. "Charter flight. Still in use," she stated.

The flight, late by almost an hour, finally took to the air. Settled in for a long flight, close to 6,800 miles with more than twelve hours to Chicago, their destination, Paul was ready to change the topic. "What's on the menu?" he asked.

"Chicken, steak, and fish," was her answer.

"Steak for me," he indicated.

With the craft steadily ascending, Paul's eyes darted edgily between the Arabian Peninsula slowly panning in the distance below and the overhead bulkhead, hoping the seatbelt sign would turn off. Parched from the airport rush, he was impatient to order his first drink. His eyes sought out the galley. "Where's that steward?" he muttered. He knew it'd be minutes more before the seatbelt sign turned off. To calm his somewhat jumpy nerves, and to occupy time, he spent the next minutes checking out the craft. Looking at Janet for approval, he remarked, "Seat's comfortable. Forgot how roomy these old craft are," he added. Otherwise, he didn't question much else about the craft's parameters such as history, performance, and why the dated craft was still in service.

The TriStar, built between the early 70s and mid-80s, for its time was considered the most advanced and safety conscious craft in the commercially operated travel industry until overcome by a number of fatal crashes, mostly from engine failures and other critical malfunctions causing the death of hundreds of passengers.

With time, traumatic events became blurry, people forgot, and the pain from human losses would be healed. Today, the returning vacationers, including Janet and Paul, within the safety of this once majestic craft, felt secure. The flight, contracted out to "Happy Travels" doing business from Mogadishu, after a refueling stop obtained due to favorable fuel costs in Dubai and after taking on additional passengers, as packed as the craft was, originated in Somalia.

FT. LEAVENWORTH PENITENTIARY (Kansas)

Today, other than periodic upgrades, enhancements, and technology integration to the security of the complex, not much had changed over the past couple hundreds of years of its existence. Inmates were as tough as they came back then. Clustered in tightly formed groups, separated mostly by ethnic and cultural background, all had one thing in common. They were federal prisoners, sent here to do time from minor infractions to severe crimes committed while in the U.S. military.

With that, many inmates, not so much by individual choice, were indoctrinated and trained by the military as hard-core killers. Where killing in civilian life by law was forbidden, in the military, fighting on the frontlines protecting the nation and its people, it was not only condoned, but ordered without subterfuge. In other words, there was no repercussion to a soldier for carrying out the order.

"Watch it," Rusty Norton, a muscular build of six foot two, tough, clad in frayed shorts and combat boots, huddling in one corner of the yard, warned. He was the apparent leader of the gang. "Voices carry." He'd been keeping a watchful eye on the prison guards. The opponent in this case was his cellmate and longtime buddy dating back to their teens. Norton, a relatively good-looking individual, European heritage, adapted street smarts to the city's neighborhood. Unlike many of his present cellmates, he could have had anything he'd wanted out of life, but unfortunate circumstances decided on a rather unfavorable destiny.

Five years earlier, growing up in Southside Chicago, to European immigrants, it was not easy to fend off neighborhood gangs always on the prey for new recruits. Seeking a new leader after the current had been killed in a shootout pressure had kept building from a particular gang. He'd finally decided it was enough. To get away, on a spur of the moment decision, he'd volunteered for the Army.

Following boot camp, excelling in courses on heavy artillery, tanks, and armory, he was assigned to Fort Benning, GA, United States Army Armor School. Planning to make it his career, Rusty Norton was looking towards a long-term, military-oriented future. It was there when his troubles started.

Not willing to readily move, due to a recently met local girl, he missed the reporting date at Fort Benning. Holed in with his girlfriend, overdue by two weeks, he was eventually tracked down by military police at a local motel. Following an Article Fifteen, and short legal process, he was sentenced to five years imprisonment. That's how he wound up here, at Fort Leavenworth. Highly dismayed at the way his life had turned out, initially fending off aggressive inmates, at times with solitary confinement consequences, it'd taken him months to adjust to the prison environment. That was almost five years ago.

Today, ready to bid goodbye to the penitentiary, he was to be released in six months and planned to return to Fort Knox, home to his girl. It was this promise that kept him from getting involved in any kind of foolish schemes like a prison break or otherwise.

It was late afternoon. The sun was slowly sinking towards the western horizons into the plains of Kansas. Rusty Norton was heading off another gripe, as well as planning sessions for, "What to do just in case." As with so many times over the past years, he was negating most of the wild brained schemes. He wasn't about to risk his life or another prison term for others on the not-well-thought-out talks by his cellmates about a possible prison break. Elected leader of the inmate gang, due to popularity, he was too smart to fall into the potential trap periodically set up by the prison staff. Today, like any other day, they were being watched. Huddled near the far corner of the courtyard, throwing an occasional glance at the unit officer for his cellblock, Norton was halfheartedly listening to his long time buddy, his right hand man, better known as "Bad Man" to the inmates.

Bad Man, brute by nature, the bully and tormentor he was, was always on the forefront of causing trouble; he'd earned the title many times over. Presently in the company of Norton, happily occupied with senseless schemes, as usual most inmates avoided the group.

Today's plot was nothing unusual. Bad Man had laid it out many times. It was mostly based on rumors and conspiracies, The Republic, his favorite topic; arguments were heated. If it weren't for his hostile identity and violent disposition, inmates would have laughed at him. But that wasn't the case. Despite the idiotic rumors he created, the obsessive notions he pursued, he was, nevertheless, respected. Many did not believe one word he said. Nobody knew where he was from. He was tight-lipped about the past. Only Norton was privy to the secrets of the penitentiary's most feared inmate.

What people didn't know was that Bad Man had been a member of an underground movement. As a matter of fact, following years of active membership, he'd escalated to the rank of First Lieutenant. The movement, created during the last administration as a result of years of discontent by the common citizen, was so interwoven in society that most shrugged it off as myth and nonsense. "There's no such thing," or "You're nuts," or "Impossible," or "Idiot," were remarks made when he talked about it.

"Bad Man," the unit manager for cellblock C yelled from across the courtyard, "get your ass in line." It was time for roundup. Near the day's roll call time, penitentiary's daily Lockdown Count, the inmates did not move quick enough for the head of the federal inmates. As always, some straggler was challenging the guards on duty for authority, especially the one called Bad Man.

Russell Wilcox, Fort Leavenworth's unit manager and administrative head, like all unit leads dressed in combat fatigues, was pushed to the brink of losing his patience. Like so many times in the past, he'd been waiting for an opportunity to eliminate the penitentiary's most dreaded inmate, but that would take an act of direct assault from the inmate in possession of an assault weapon to justify a death sentence carried out on the spot. It was a dangerous game played by both inmates and guards. As years went on, it seemed the law gave more and more preferential treatment to the inmates. It bugged the hell out of him. Aggravated as hell, he scanned the courtyard for other stragglers. "Fuckers," he muttered to no one in particular, "always pushing the limits." Today was no different for Wilcox, head of all unit sections.

This late afternoon, with the last prisoner and unit staff positioned inside the containment walls and unit officers assigned to each section, Wilcox halted briefly to secure the courtyard gate. From the central hall, core of the detainment block, he was able to watch the section monitors clustered around the building's primary control console. Scanning each terminal, he had a clear view of the clusters of halls. At present, as was usual in late afternoon, waiting to be shut close for the night, cell gates were open to receive the inmates. Unit officers were planted at each section to assure each inmate was inside cell. If not, much like cattle getting pushed up a ramp, the inmate would be forcefully prodded to his respective cells.

If an inmate was not in his assigned living quarter during a count, the staff would take disciplinary action. Disciplinary action would also be taken against inmates for leaving an assigned area before the count was cleared. The inmate must be seen at all counts, even if the inmate must be awakened to do so. The daily lockdown count was in progress.

Satisfied another day of stress and tension had come to an end, Wilcox was about to get up, ready to walk the halls, when all of a sudden the power went out. At first, since all monitors went blank, he suspected a power failure. He gave it a few seconds for backup to kick in. It wasn't the first time this had happened. It wouldn't be the last time either, with the ever-increasing demand on the power grid, but today, power stayed out. Searching for a cause, his eyes caught the gate shutoff controls. His heart jumped a few beats. In an instant, he knew there would be trouble. Inmates with the most severe criminal records in the nation wouldn't let an opportunity like this go by unscathed.

Alarmed by now, but still in control, Wilcox snatched the PA mic from its hook. "Manual!" he shouted. In a state of heightened alert, he repeated the call several more times. "Switch to manual." Nobody seemed to pay him any attention. It was then he realized the PA was out. Ripping the base phone from its cradle, he dialed garrison command. "What?" He was stunned. "Dead too!" From his pocket, he got hold of his mobile and fumbled for the number. "What the fuck's goin' on?" was all he could stammer. "No signal?" Precious minutes had already been wasted to try and contain the inmates.

It was Wilcox's inability to alert command that triggered the next action. A howl, much like a rabid animal's, echoed through the halls. In an instant, he recognized the caller's voice. It belonged to none other than Bad Man. Wilcox knew then he was in trouble. And so was his staff. Fully alerted now, he bounded from the chair, checked the monitors one last time, and, running with big strides, he hastened for the cellblock's main hallway. "Shit." Breathing heavy from exertion and anxiety, he called out, "Where's weapons when you need them?"

Hurrying along the hallways, floors polished to spit shine as usual, he slipped, stumbled, but caught himself from landing on the floor. Angered at his loss of composure, he sputtered, "Get a grip," then carried on. Not to alarm the inmates, he forced to pace himself around the last corner. "No place could they go," he reasoned the rest of the way.

Along with the indoctrination, the rigid training, the repeated exercises, and hand-to-hand combat, detainment administration was confident the Army garrison would be able to contain the inmates. Help was only a phone call away. It would be true if the phones were working. Today, they were not.

As soon as he turned the next corner, eyes widened in panic, his heart stopped. "Too late!"

FINAL DESTINATION (Somewhere over the Atlantic)

Tyler Marshall, one of few TriStar rated pilots left capable of flying the craft, since most former pilots had retired or converted to newer type craft, reached forward to activate the Autopilot. "Take control," he ordered his copilot. Head turned to the right in the direction of the flight engineer's seat, third member of the crew who also doubled as navigator, he seemed busy with maps and monitor readouts getting today's weather. "What's the report?" he asked him.

Airline crews, flying in and out of American airspace, no matter what nationality, or how fluent, were required to speak the English language. Today's crew, contracted from New Zealand, although heavily inflected by the southern hemispherical accent, was native to the northern continent's language. "Jet stream's in our favor," the flight engineer readily indicated. Taking additional time concentrating on the weather currents, he said, "We can ride the Westerly for most of the way, then catch the Polar Easterlies over Greenland…should drop us directly over the East Coast."

Today's flight was no different. With main and wing tanks topped to the maximum, the onboard fuel should take the craft to its destination without a refueling stop. The distance, close to the craft's maximum flying range, at cruising speed for most of the way, should be sufficient to reach the American continent. It's a gamble no American-trained crew would exercise. A foreign crew, not subjected to the stringent and unwavering American air traffic rules enforced by the NTSB[31], due to economic shortfalls, many times stretched the limits.

"Thanks, mate," Marshall confirmed. In a quick gesture, he advised the copilot to input the required data into the onboard computer program.

"Roger," the pilot replied in the brief and customary flight jargon.

After confirming the necessary changes, Marshall, from the comfort of the pilot seat, was ready to get up to leave the cockpit for the first class toilet. As was usual with long flights, he planned to get to know the flight attendants, pace the aisles, and, on the way back, chat with some passengers in first, and possibly business, class.

Janet and Paul, resting comfortably in the business section of the craft, were savoring drinks just served, Paul a dry martini on the rocks, and Janet a glass of vintage French cabernet. "Ahh yes," said Paul, daydreaming and completely at ease, "that's living."

Janet, more interested in keeping up with worldly things, especially travel and fashion to satisfy her somewhat inquisitive mind and to occupy time, was reading one of several copies of trade mags she'd acquired from the overhead magazine bin. Time in the comfort of business class passed relatively fast for the two between drinks, a savory dinner served with more drinks, a recently released film, and a couple of hours nap time. Before long, the cabin lights were back on with the flight crew announcing Chicago, O'Hare, the destination a couple more hours out. Passengers, sleepy-eyed as they were, began lining up at the back of the cabin, getting refreshed.

Paul, drowsy from drinking several glasses of hard liquor, briefly looked up, closed his eyes and briskly went back to sleep. "Ping," the metallic sound indicating the "No Smoking and Fasten Seatbelts" alarm sounded Paul awake. When he opened his eyes, attendants were busy walking the aisles to advise weary passengers to pull up their seats.

---

[31] National Transportation Safety Board.

Paul quickly got up and hastened for the toilets. "Sir," an attendant urged, "please take your seat."

Thumbing at a just vacated toilet, he called after her, "Be just a minute." For Paul, the urge to urinate at the moment took precedence over airline rules and regulations. The business manager he was, he was used to getting his way.

Gripping the handrail due to some slight air turbulence, Paul squeezed one final stream into the toilet bowl when all of a sudden the lights went out. Curious as to why the emergency ones didn't come on, he found himself in the dark. And a pitch-black dark it was.

Shaking off some remaining droplets, he stared into blank space. Not even the mirror was visible. No matter how hard he squinted, the space, as crammed as it was, remained dark. For a second, his space was eerily quiet. Just finished with his business, brushing off the front of his pants to make sure he didn't wet himself, Paul was getting ready to exit when he suddenly turned weightless. His body was whisked off the floor and thrown onto the cabin ceiling. His immediate thoughts, as simple as they were, in an automatic reaction from the impact were squeezed from the lungs. "What the fuck," a cuss escaped his lips.

He didn't know what was up and down anymore. Where the craft was doused in an eerie silence just seconds ago, now it had changed into a screaming pitch. It was almost too much to bear. In a steeply reclined position, he clutched both palms over his ears. It took seconds for him to figure out the source of the sound. "Engines…Dive…Crash." "Janet," he yelled into the dark in sheer panic.

Squeezed into one corner of the toilet, body pushed into heap, unable to breathe freely, he hung suspended. He didn't know for how long. In the dark, his eyes were wildly probed for the exit. His hands were groping for a hold; any hold would do to align his body. His mind, as pathetic as it was, searched for an escape. There was none. In an effort to make peace, he sought out prayer.

Outside the door, in the main cabin, the situation was just as chaotic, even more so. When the craft went into a sudden dive, the passengers were lifted off the floor. Passengers not strapped in were thrown against the ceiling, the bins, the bulkhead, and wherever there was open space. Screams, cries, and whimpers made the scene even more chaotic. The craft had gone into a steep dive. Whatever had not been secured either with straps or fasteners was violently smashed against walls and ceiling. People and things would remain there until impacted into the ground or until the craft regained control. There would be many injuries accompanied with hospitalization. If there were survivors, many lawsuits would follow, but at this moment, that was not on the passengers' minds. All they could do was plead, pray, and hope for an end to the present chaos.

Back inside the toilet, almost at the point of passing out, Paul suddenly felt gravity come back. At first, he thought it was only his imagination, for he had already made peace with his Maker. "Could it be?" his mind registered, clinging to a shred of hope. "It is." Gradually at first, now with added gravity, the craft actually rotated upright to its former flying angle. Once more, Paul found himself resting on the toilet seat. He wiped heavy beads of sweat from his forehead. "Phew." Paul, holding his breath for he didn't know how long, exhaled immensely relieved. He didn't know whether to laugh or to cry; that's how confused his emotional state was. "Janet!" Paul suddenly remembered his wife amid the chaos it must be in the cabin. "My God!" he exclaimed.

Still in the dark, somewhat stabilized, he could hear the steady drone of the jet engines. Ignorant of having messed up the toilet seat, zipping up, he turned and fumbled for the door latch. Groping in the darkness, a cussword escaped his tightly-compressed lips.

Muffled by the insulated door, Paul nevertheless could hear repeated outcries of pain from a number of passengers, mostly women's voices. He finally managed to open the door. As quiet as it was inside the bathroom, stepping out, the situation was different.

Surprised by more black space staring at him another cuss escaped his chest, "What the fuck." Probing with one foot forward, he cautiously took a step into the aisle. Disoriented, unable to see anything, he yelled out, "Janet!"

"Paul," a voice he recognized as his wife's echoed back from a general direction to the left, "over here."

There were many more yells, mostly from people calling for flight attendants to turn on the lights, flash lights, emergency lighting or any light.

Paul carefully groped his way toward the direction of his wife. "Shit...'Scuse me," he offered to someone whose foot he stepped on.

"Sit down," the angry passenger yelled back. "Jerk!"

Moving a little more subtly, bumping his way closer with every step, touching stranger's heads and brushing bearded faces, Paul whispered, "Janet," into the semi-darkness.

"Here," she called, reaching out for him. In between the shouts of angry passengers, men mostly, weeping and sobbing from frightened women, bawling children being scared to death by the darkness, he could barely make out his wife's voice. To Paul's surprise, faint as it was, he could finally see the outline of his wife, as well as passengers nearby.

To get a better vision, he strained his eyes. "Janet," he called out again. *There she is.* He could see now. He also noticed most travelers had pulled down the window shades. It allowed starlight, as dim as it was, to shine through the windows. Squeezing by the last passengers, finally, he was able to drop into his seat. Wiping one hand across his face, he felt the stubbles of a twelve-hour beard scraping across the skin of his palm. Still in disbelief, shaking his head at his wife, he puffed, "What a mess. You alright?"

"Where have you been?" Her voice quivered with fear. Clutching at his arm, her eyes were filled with concern. Janet, the organized and orderly character she was, had been securely strapped into the seat when the craft took a dive.

"Couldn't get out the bathroom," he told her. His eyes sought out hers. "Listen," he said, "I'm gonna go up front..."

Immediately, he could feel her grip tighten on his arm. "Don't leave me," she interrupted.

"Gotta find out..."

"No!" she begged. He could see fear in her eyes. "When you were gone," she said, "there was a flash."

"What flash?" *Women,* he thought to himself, but for the moment said nothing, *so fragile.*

"In the sky," she explained. "I saw it."

"You sure?"

"Sure I'm sure," she insisted. "Why can't you believe me?"

"Sorry," he said, "couldn't see a damned thing in there." What she just said made him wonder. *Flash?* Now he really had to find out. Manager that he was handling projects for his firm, he didn't get to where he was by letting other's decide. It was he who made all the decisions to get the job done. And he was getting impatient. "Where's the damned stewards?" Paul hollered into the semi-darkness.

As disorganized as the cabin was with sobs and whimpers, as frightened as she'd been, there was enough turmoil already without him adding his anger. "Quiet," Janet told him.

Not to get into an argument he kept silent. Undecided what to do or what action to take next, he pressed his forehead against the cool safety glass of the bulkhead. Staring at the ground below, he couldn't see a thing. "Still over the ocean," he muttered.

He could not restrain himself any longer. "I really gotta find out," he insisted. Squeezing by her, he forced his body into the aisle, then, in the dark, pushed his way forward. His aim was the cockpit, or, if unable to talk to the pilot, the galley. "Paul," he heard his wife call after him, "come back." He disregarded her pleas, disregarded passengers he bumped into, ignored the commotion in the aisles with his mind set on only one thing. "Gotta find out what the hell's going on. What son-of-a-bitch caused all this misery?"

FT. KNOX (Kentucky)

Wendell Nelson, garrison commander Army post, Fort Knox, was about to leave his desk when power went out. "Shit," escaped his lips. Momentarily halting in his steps, he flipped the power switch by the door entrance several times. He did not give it much thought since brownouts were not unusual in the region at this time of year. Casually shrugging his shoulders, taking firmly planted strides, he quickly left in the direction of the commissary. He'd promised the wife, on the way home that he'd pick up a package of ribs and suitable condiments to season up the evening's family BBQ. "Let me know when power's back," he instructed Brodie Elliott, his second in command, mechanized infantry, Fort Knox, as he passed the command sergeant major's desk.

"Will do," the sergeant major replied. As second in command, it was his duty to cover base operations whenever the commander left the post. "The Boss," as he referred to his commander, gave him unconditional trust in all of the affairs confined to within the army post's perimeter, at times extending to nearby towns of Louisville to the north and Elizabethtown to the south when his troops got out of hands at some local establishment. "Soldiers will be soldiers," he'd excuse their unruly behavior to local law enforcement whenever necessary to keep them out of jail.

It may not always be ideal for a young Private First Class to get an assignment in the Kentucky Hills, bordered by the Ohio River, fending for social rights among the local male populace. The girls, as with everywhere else in the nation, were pretty as can be, but had to be won over by the somewhat aggressive and insistent young infantry warriors, especially after a few bottles of locally brewed spirits, customary to the region. After all, Kentucky was known for its rich and flourishing heritage in producing superior quality alcoholic beverages.

That did not stop the early settlers from the growing demands of population increase from the eastern shores. As added protection to the local populace, the fort was built. The fort was populated. The Fort, described in historical annals, as many others in the nation, was here to stay.

Fort Knox, bordered by the Bluegrass Region, it occupied the northern part of the state, protecting Kentucky's early majority of the state's population of European settlement. Also notable to the early settlers were large herds of bison and other wildlife. The name "Kentucky" itself meant "meadow lands" in several of the native languages specifically applied to this region and eventually became the state's name.

Much like the Pentagon, protected by layers of security surrounded by layers of barbed wire fences, within this fortification proudly stood the fort. Solely operated by the Treasury Department, Fort Knox had maintained the Bullion Depository since 1937. A highly classified bunker ringed by defenses of multiple alarms, and guarded by Apache helicopter gunships, few people had been inside Fort Knox. After the Fort was built, the gold was shipped in on a special train manned by machine gunners, loaded onto Army trucks, heavily protected by a U.S. Cavalry brigade. Ever since, the Fort has been pretty much off limits to the general population.

Stacked inside massive granite walls topped by a bombproof roof, encased by a seemingly non-breaching moat, its present worth, at current commodity prices, was valued at about a quarter trillion.

It was this valued national treasure that Brodie Elliott was responsible for when the garrison commander left base.

FINAL DESTINATION (In the Cockpit)

Tyler Marshall, just returned from a final check on all three cabin sections, ready to take controls for the initial descent, had just settled in the pilot's seat. Still thirty minutes out, he flipped the overhead cabin alert lighting to the "ON" position for passengers to take their seats. It was right after when a brilliant starburst lit up the cockpit. Stunned, blinking his eyes in rapid succession to shake off darkness, he exclaimed, "What was that?" No sooner had he said that than the craft tilted forward into a steep dive. Marshall, to compensate for the sudden attitude change, immediately pulled back on the flight controls. No matter how hard he pulled, there was little response. The force was too great to ease the controls back to level out.

Eyes focused on the distant ground, which at this time was a black gaping hole, not letting go of the controls, Marshall yelled out, "Need help!" The copilot, hesitant to take control until so directed by the pilot, with their combined strengths managed to right the craft somewhat, but not after losing some fifteen thousand feet of altitude. Both pilots, now hanging on to the controls had sweat profusely running down their faces. "Kill engine three," Marshall shouted into the dark as he watched his copilot groping for the controls.

Marshall, after the blinding flash, deducted that a sudden energy burst must have disengaged the Autopilot. Unknown to him at this time, the aileron and rudder controls had stopped functioning from massive hydraulic failure. Later analysis proved him right on his assumption. With ailerons and rudder out, the force of the third engine mounted onto the vertical tail section above the center of gravity of the craft kept pushing the craft's nose towards the ground. The only way to reduce the force was to disengage the engine. And so he did. It leveled the craft into a steady flight, for now.

As for the earlier starburst, aside from an occasional light beam hitting the pilots sitting by the runway or shuttling for takeoff or landings, Marshall had never seen anything like it in midair. The copilot voiced a similar comment. Eyes widened with a hint of faint understanding, the flight engineer muttered, "EMP strike," into the dark.

"What?" Marshall asked, incredulous.

Recalling long forgotten events, the engineer tried to explain. "Like back in the 50s."

"Instruments are out!" the copilot announced, his voice elevated almost to a high pitch. "All of it."

It was then that the crew knew they were in trouble. Aside from an entire computerized navigation cluster out, without backup battery support there was nothing in the books to get a handle on. If power couldn't be reacquired within the next thirty minutes, a crash would be imminent, but there was one last resort, manual mode. Approach control and emergency support for a possible emergency landing would provide backup for the landing.

In the midst of the darkness, only slightly illuminated by starlight breaking through the windows, eyes gradually adjusting to the ambient, the cockpit crew went to work.

"Flashlights…checklist?" Marshall ordered, "Get 'em."

Groping around the dashboards, side pockets, in back of seats, the copilot finally located both and handed Marshall the items. "Here," he offered.

"Just the list," Marshall said, "you handle the controls."

With the beam from the flashlight focused on the instruments, Marshall and the copilot, with the fight engineer's help, went to work. Marshall read:

"Master Power Switch—SET…nothing. Instrument Panels—nothing. Master Radio Switches—ON. Fuel and Ignition Switches—ON. Altimeters—SET. Auto Flight System (Autopilot)—OFF. Hydraulics, four systems—Checked & ON. Engines, three systems—Checked & ON. Generators, three systems—Checked & ON. Electrical, three systems—Nothing. Fuel Systems, all four—Balanced. GPS and ILS—nothing. Cabin Temperature—nothing. Cabin Pressure—nothing. Landing Gear—UP. Speed Brake Lever—Forward. Flap Lever—SET & Checked."

After reading hundreds more dials and instruments in front, in back, along both sides of the cockpit cabin walls, and many more overhead, with a stomach cramped into a tight knot of anxiety, Marshall concluded, "Nothing." His nerves were on edge, but he was still in control. Nothing else in the craft seemed to be functional. Craning to the right to check with the flight engineer in back he requested, "Status?"

"Not a damned thing," was the equally distressed reply. "Radio's out too," he further remarked. "Can't raise tower control."

"Get an SOS out," Marshall urged the engineer. "Now!"

"Mayday…mayday," the call went over the ether. "Repeat…mayday…mayday." With nerves strained to the breaking point, ears trained to the headset, no one could hear a thing. The airwaves were in complete silence.

"Cabin crew," Marshall instructed the copilot, "inform them. I'll check the controls again. Hand me the light…and," straining to keep calm while instructing the flight engineer, "keep checking with tower control…approach control…flights in the air…anybody. Somebody's gotta listen."

Flashlight in one hand, checklist in the other, there were a number of pages left to check. Marshall kept racing through the checklist while listening to the muffled voices of his crew.

"Oil Pressure—nothing. Avionics—OFF. APU[32]—Check," he muttered into the quiet. Eyes ready to move to the next item on the checklist, suddenly, in a heightened state of exhilaration, he burst out, "Wait a minute." A few heart-gripping seconds went by, then, he affirmed, "I think we've got something."

"What?" the copilot asked, hoping for a miracle.

"Auxiliary power unit," Marshall slapped his forehead in sheer euphoria. "Of course!" Marshall didn't have to explain. A light turned on in the heads of the crew. When the EMP pulse hit, it rendered all of the electrical devices, instruments, and controls ineffective. What kept bothering Marshall was that the craft still kept flying. For all practical purpose they should have crashed by now. By some miracle, nevertheless, the APU had not been affected by the EMP burst. "Could be a number of things," he reasoned. The unit had been shielded and filtered by the surrounding mass of metals. Filled with renewed vigor, he readily announced, "Folks, let's get to work."

In reality, as luck had it, the craft's design engineers, after much debating with contractors, suppliers, and regulatory agencies, due to new government regulations, for the first time in aviation history had outfitted the L-1011 airliner with triple, and even quadruple, backup systems.

That, however, as soon as the craft was forced to change altitude or prepare for landing, would change. And a change in altitude was imminent. Only fifteen more minutes out of Chicago's O'Hare, it was high time for the pilots to bring the craft down.

---

[32] Auxiliary Power Unit – Backup power system.

Since all fuel gauges were out from electrical failure, and fuel must be critically short, the pilots could only estimate the fuel consumption by using flight time and distance computations. The crew prepared for the impending, but inevitable, landing.

FT. LEAVENWORTH PENITENTIARY

Russell Wilcox, adrenaline racing through his veins, bounded through the isolation chamber. It was his last hope to contain the inmates. Little did he know that what used to isolate the prisoners from the outside world today became his death trap. Two paces inside, with a resounding shudder, the steel gate he'd just entered shut tight. Swarms of inmates on both sides of the cage blocked the paths. Dumbfounded, staring ahead past a cluster of wildly threatening prisoners, his eyes caught what appeared to be the remnants of a bloody encounter. It took him several seconds to identify the scene. Sprawled across the hallway floor, flattened by maddened inmates and beaten to pulps, bloodied faces turning purple, already swelling from blows was the cell block's unit leader. There was no turning back. Howling for vengeance, he was forced to meet the prison's most feared adversary, Bad Man. In an instant, Wilcox knew it'd be payback time. Wilcox knew he'd be a dead man. He would be the sacrificial lamb to even the score for the irritated inmates.

"Bring him to me." It was a dreaded command issued by the voice that was so familiar. Torn from the isolation chamber, Wilcox was forced into the containment hall. What the monitors were unable to confirm, now, with his own eyes, he saw the full extent of the clash. What started as an opportunity, soon had turned into a bloody battle. Now the sounds of hundreds of irate inmates echoed through the halls. In accord, exerted under full strength, the heated inmates demanded justice. "Down with the Screws…down with the pigs." Wilcox's only hope for survival was negotiation.

Accompanied by blows to the head and body, he was pulled and pushed in the direction of the gang leader. "Kill 'em," repeated shouts rang out.

With one hand raised, Norton in the lead squelched an immediate attack on the prison's administrative manager. "You know the score."

"Whatcha want?" Mostly a rhetorical statement, an arbitrary question, Wilcox knew precisely what to expect. Following past prison riots he'd witnessed on a number of accounts, two with personal involvements, demands made by the rioters were always the same. Typically, they ranged from better living conditions, increased liberties, less oppression, reduced discipline.

Today, both sides knew better. The demands would be entirely different. The difference was obvious. Brought on by the lack of communication, absence of electricity, prison guards seized, and, most significantly, inmates achieving superiority, the difference became obvious. The bargaining power, negotiating edge, at this time was solely in the hands of the inmates.

Square faced, staring his opponent down, Norton demanded, "What's goin' on?" With power and communication out and remaining out, he sensed something unusual had taken place on the outside. "Where's reinforcement?"

"On the way," Wilcox stalled. He wasn't going to give in without a fight, but also knew it'd only be possible with the help from SWAT[33], or, in this case, the National Guard, if he'd been able to get word out. The way things looked at the moment, there wasn't much hope.

Norton seemed to hesitate, evaluate, and assess his opponent's response. "I don't believe you."

---

[33] Special Weapons And Tactics team.

"Believe what you want," Wilcox insisted. "They're on the way."

Supported by shouts of hostilities from inmates pushing and shoving, moving up ever closer, encircling the administrative head, Norton negotiated, "Tell you what, we can do this the easy way," he paused to let the next words sink in. "Or we do it my way." His head flipped back, "Quiet!" he shouted to calm the inmates down demanding action,

Bad Man, agitated almost beyond control, tightened his iron grip around Wilcox's neck, streams of sweat dripping from his body. "Let me kill 'em...let me kill 'em," he fervently spat at a face almost turned purple.

"Keys," Norton insisted.

Struggling to loosen the grip around his neck, Wilcox replied, "Don't have 'em." He was still furious about getting overpowered by the inmates. He should have known better. The second he rushed around the corner, he'd realized he was in trouble. Trained in combat, being without a weapon was fine when pitted against one or two opponents, but an entire cell block was something entirely different. He and his staff, due to most unfortunate circumstances, had been taken by surprise, overpowered, and subjected to the will of the inmates. And they, at the moment, vowed revenge. They wanted his blood.

Staring Wilcox in the eyes, deliberately shaking his head, Norton insisted, "Have it your way." With that he raised one fist, the gang's signal to move out in the direction of the cellblock's main exit. For now, for whatever lay ahead, the inmates were on the move.

Wilcox and the unit staff, along with the penitentiary's trusted, were quickly collected and herded into emptied cells, were locked up using manual measures, and left in the wake of the prison's guardsmen, at the moment weaponless. Doors were busted open, offices ransacked, resisting prison guards through sheer numbers immobilized, keys collected with one focus: get to the penitentiary's armory. There, normally used by SWAT, waiting to be deployed, was a cache of assault weapons neatly stored away alongside stacks of thousands of rounds of ammo.

Today, for the inmates, a band on the run, it was open season. For whatever came across their path, following years of individual punishment, mercy would not be exercised. The band headed for the nearby town. They wanted food, they needed clothes, and, most importantly, they needed transportation. The mob, minus an armed security detachment left behind to guard the imprisoned units, was headed directly for town, the city of Leavenworth, four miles to the south, embraced by the Missouri River.

FINAL DESTINATION (Final Approach)

The flight crew, up to now, had been doing their best to keep the passengers from panicking. To make things worse after the sudden dive, it was not easy at times, in complete darkness, to attend to the injured to provide first aid. A flight attendant crew of ten, the head, and most senior chief purser took charge between directing his staff, interfacing with the cockpit crew, and keeping angered passengers in check. He kept his staff informed of any changes in the flight plan, which was imminent. After the sudden dive, the chief purser had made several attempts to calm the passengers using the PA. It seemed that the system was not working. Finally giving up, he used word of mouth to keep his crew informed of the current state of emergency. Passengers, as frightened as they were, had been kept from the severe situation the pilots were struggling with, and were encouraged with only positive information, as little as there was.

Back in the passenger sections, the flight engineer, shouting above the furor made the announcement, "Attention please..." He paused to formulate the words. "All passengers please take your seats. As you know, we experienced a power failure affecting the cabin lighting. I apologize for the sudden flight change earlier and for any injuries as a result. Flight attendants will prepare you for the upcoming landing and guide you to the exits after the landing. We need you to stay calm. Thank you."

As usual following a statement of an impending landing, passengers scurried back to their seats. Today, because of the dark and injured, it took longer to settle in. As soon as the last passenger was strapped in, the chief purser disappeared into the cockpit. He took one of the vacated seats behind the pilot. After confirming passengers were secure, he informed Marshall, "Ready. We're gonna' make it, right?"

"Here we go." Marshall, right hand embracing two of the three engine control levers mounted into the center console, left tightly gripping the attitude controls, gradually pulled the engine controls to two-third power. To his relief, the craft responded. Although it took several seconds for the engines to react, with speed reduced the craft kept level.

Body pushed forward, craning into the dark to get a better angle on the windshield, the copilot remarked, "There may still be hope."

"What about the dark?" the flight engineer urged. "I can't see O'Hare." The airport, their final destination, descent path already overshot by fifteen minutes, should have been directly ahead.

Feverishly searching the terrain below, Marshall burst out, "See some lights!" He'd been silently wondering about the shorelines of the Great Lakes. Normally, coming from the north over Lake Michigan, faint lights should have been visible with Detroit already passing to the left below. "Emergency landing lights," he assumed, "we'll see." Still out twenty-five or so miles at about five thousand feet altitude, it'd only take a few minutes more to descend to a final landing approach.

"Try tower control again," Marshall directed the flight engineer, "and check on approach and ground control."

The flight engineer, in the meantime, had tried to raise the airport authorities. No matter how hard he tried, there had been no response. Every effort had been in vain. "Must be a massive outage," he finally deducted.

"Watch out!" the copilot suddenly yelled out in a panic. His face, staring straight ahead through the windshield, was distorted with horror. Marshall, pushing down hard on the left rudder, arms tilting in the same direction, responded almost immediately. What they saw come up from beneath the nose was the shadow of another craft on final landing approach. Because of his quick reaction, an imminent collision was avoided.

There was no indication that a craft was close. With radio frequency dialed into approach control, assuming other crafts on final tuned into the same frequency, the copilot yelled into the mic, "Mayday...mayday!" There was no response. The airwaves remained silent.

"Fall in behind," Marshall instructed the copilot. Marshall, so close to the final landing, was reading the checklist one final time. "Here," handing the copilot the flashlight, he ordered, "Use it," indicating that he should shine the beam through the windshield to alert other flights close by. "I have control." From here on, no matter what it'd take, it was up to Marshall to guide the craft in for the landing. He was ultimately responsible for the safety of the passengers.

"Gotta come in low," he remarked more to himself than the crew. Taking into account flight time and the distance they'd flown, there was only one shot he had for the landing, he assumed. It was no use to check the instruments. They were all out reading zero. Without tower, ground, or approach control in operation, Marshall, to keep the crew informed, would announce every move he made on the controls. In case of any sudden changes he was forced to make, they'd be instantly alerted.

He verbalized the landing sequence. "Flaps." There was no response. He read the next item on the list. "Engine power one fourths." There was a response. Greatly relieved, they all noticed the change in engine pitch. The craft's speed was steadily slowing. Without compass, speed indicators, direction finder, altitude controls, or computer guided fly-by-wire, Marshall had to fly the craft by the seat of his pants. And that, he recalled, due to his age and experience, aside from the mandatory but infrequent simulations, was ages ago. "Landing gear," he ordered next.

"No response," the copilot returned.

"Use manual," Marshall ordered. In case of just such an emergency, the craft had a manual option to lower the gear. It'd take some doing to get the gear down, but it'd be a last resort avoiding a crash landing. 45-degree flaps would be ideal on touchdown from a standard approach. Today, flying on manual, in case he had to make quick corrections, he needed maneuverability. It meant added airspeed.

"Flaps...20 degrees."

With every manual pumping action, they could feel the drag on the craft increased. "Down," after some heightened suspense, the copilot indicated.

"Increase airspeed!" Pushing engines one and two control levers forward, Marshall made an immediate correction; otherwise he'd miss the runway and land short. With the added drag on the gear, the craft had slowed to below landing speed.

"What's the closest runway?" Marshall shot a quick glance at the copilot who hurriedly checked the flight map. Although Marshall had flown into O'Hare many times, he just needed confirmation one last time. With approach and runway lights out, since he could not identify the airport by its usual lighting configuration in the dark, final landing directions had to be made nearly at ground level. Once close to the Chicago shores, he'd have to come in at treetop level.

His eyes were darting between map and ground, with only the pale moonlight reflection over the lake, highly distressed at flying near blind, "28R," the copilot ordered. There was only one shot for the landing. It would be the most direct approach using the lake and shoreline as landing guide. He'd chosen the longest runway at 13,000 feet, two and a half miles in length.

"What's that?" Marshall suddenly yelled out. He saw a flare-up in the distance. All had spotted the event. It happened suddenly. It appeared that some sort of emergency lighting had been hastily arranged. It began straight ahead at the end closest to them; a cluster of lights had appeared, spreading out along a straight pass. Assuming it was runway 28R, Marshall headed directly for it.

Fifteen miles out now at three thousand feet final approach, approximately 175 mph landing speed, he guessed, not to miss the threshold coming in hot, he pushed the craft down for final. The Chicago shorelines directly below, with Belmont Harbor to the left and vague outlines of Wrigley Field ahead to the right, his eyes piercing ahead trying to penetrate the dark, the copilot announced, "Dead center."

Marshall had a difficult time keeping the craft's nose aligned with the fast approaching threshold. Fortunately, the perimeter of the runway, it seemed, had been illuminated by some sort of lighting. "What do you think?" He made an attempt to identify the fairly dim, but visible, light sources.

The chief purser sitting directly behind Marshall hesitated, "Don't know." He, like everybody else in the cockpit, was staring into the dark ahead.

"Here we go," Marshall made the final announcement. "Call the cabin," he instructed the flight engineer for a final time.

"Attention..."

Marshall was barely aware of the flight engineer departing for the cabin and returning one minute later after giving final instructions to the passengers. He was concentrating on the runway ahead coming up fast. Then he spotted it. In an instant, his face contorted. Eyes widened with pupils extended to almost bursting point, he exclaimed, "Good God!" At the same instant, the copilot, chief purser, and flight engineer spotted the gruesome scene playing out directly ahead. Feeling completely helpless, awaiting the inevitable end, the flight engineer shrunk deep into his seat and silently muttered, "God help us." He suddenly realized there was nothing he could do but pray.

FT. KNOX (Kentucky)

Brodie Elliott, command sergeant major in charge of the Fort for the evening, took it in strides. "So," he reasoned, "power's out." Not the first time on his shift. "Big deal." Regardless of the time of day, or night for that matter, it was always his shift. In charge of the mechanized infantry, 1st Armored Division, the base's major occupants, thousands of soldiers strong, Brodie had expected the power services to be back within the hour, but today, it wasn't the case. Not only had several hours already gone by, but the entire town was without power. "Worse yet," he was informed by troops reporting for duty, "everything's out, backup generators, street lights, phones, and," alarming reports from the town came in non-stop, "vehicles! All of them."

To get a mental grip on the situation, he inquired, "Whatcha mean?" He felt like rushing home to check on his family, but didn't dare to leave his post, since the base was his responsibility, and, most of all, the fort with all of the nation's wealth.

"Cheap foreign shit," he cussed when he realized the time on his wristwatch had stopped. Asking soldiers reporting for night duty about the time, he was repeatedly told, "Don't know."

"What's goin' on?" Nobody seemed to know the time. He started to get worried. Hours had gone by with nothing but negative reports. It must have been close to midnight when the Boss, garrison Commander Wendell Nelson, finally showed up.

"Here's the situation," Nelson, slightly short on breath, but otherwise his usual self, said. "Put the base on high alert. And," padding the holster he'd strapped on when leaving home, he emphasized, "check out all available arms. Gonna be a long night."

Base put on high alert meant all personnel, with leave cancelled regardless of status, reporting for duty. Every available security guard, military police, local law enforcement officer, and National Guardsmen had to be alerted. That was no easy task without communication or motorized transportation. Homes were put on alert. Searches for bicycles were initiated. Where located, they were hastily acquired.

"I want," the commander ordered, "checkpoints on every access road and..." brows furrowed with concern, "get a detail out to the air field." Godman Army Air Field, aside a possible breach from the nearby Ohio River, was the Fort's most vulnerable site for a potential attack.

"Right away, sir" Brodie assured the commander, snapping to a salute. Although both commanders, Nelson, commissioned officer commanding the garrison, and Elliott, non-commissioned officer in charge of the armored division, during a normal day operation were less formal with each other, no salute, no salutations, the present circumstances, in view of the armed forces, called for rigid discipline as dictated by military protocol.

The commander's orders, enforced by the sergeant major were implemented at once. By morning, emergency measures were in full swing. Like events dating back to WWI with soldiers on bicycles hurrying in and out the perimeter, some on their kid's bikes, may have appeared somewhat ridiculous to an outsider. The base sprang into action.

"Let's hope," Nelson made a verbal assessment to Brodie, "it's only a local outage." In back of his mind, he was fearful there would be more to it.

Brodie, busy dispatching orders, suddenly halted in mid-pace. "HAM," he burst out. "Somebody," he called out, "rustle up a HAM set." He, as many likeminded ether enthusiasts, although he hadn't used it in years, during phases of crises was very familiar with the benefits of the somewhat-dated technology, replaced by smart phones and intelligent handheld gear. The HAM, not very frequently used, was still the most effective instrument during a severe crisis, strategic, tactical, or otherwise. Dated equipment as it was, it may be the command's only hope for survival. Nothing else seemed to function.

It took days to setup roadblocks through the region, and more to secure shipping lanes and airport facilities. At the end, without effective communication, for all practical purposes, the Fort, nevertheless, seemed secure. So everybody thought.

"Let 'em try," Brodie boasted when someone voiced concern. He had every access leading to the treasure covered, barricaded, blocked out solid. As far as he was concerned, the Fort was protected. Little did he know a menace so big only an effective army could stop it was making its way east, headed his way.

FINAL DESTINATION (Cabin)

In the cabin, "Attention please..." It was the flight engineer, warning flight attendants and passengers to prepare for the landing. "...take your seats and fasten seatbelts," were the final instructions before disappearing back into the cockpit.

Janet, securely strapped in, prepared for the landing and tightened her grip on Paul's arm. Unsuccessful as he was earlier in trying to get some information on the blackout by pestering several of the attendants, he finally returned to his seat with an unhappy grunt. Extremely unhappy, he swore into the dark, "Damned airlines. They'll hear about this." It was a personal promise to Janet to get at least the money back, if not additional compensation for this ill-fated flight. Settled back next to her with mixed emotions, angered at the airline but satisfied that the extended flight was coming to an end, Paul, like the other passengers, prepared for the landing.

"Love you." Wanting him to know how she felt, Janet whispered it in the dark.

Letting her know his feelings, he responded, in his business-like demeanor, "I know." It was the last two words spoken just before the wheels touched ground. Then all hell broke loose. If it wasn't for the seatbelts, he, Janet, and the other passengers would have been thrown clear from their seats.

The first jolt took place a fraction after touchdown. Whatever force hit the landing gear traversed up through the wide-body jet, ripping the gear from its mountings. The craft, suddenly freed from the air drag, barely ten feet suspended off the ground, soared a couple hundred feet ahead at landing speed, and then, almost vertically, with a deafening sound, plunked onto the runway. From here on, the sounds emanating from the ground and cabin were nothing but screeches, shrieks, and screams. In an ever-increasing spinning motion, the craft, on its belly, slithered wildly along the runway much like the contents within a centrifuge. Clinging desperately to whatever was in the reach of their hands passengers inside the cabin were torn from their seats and tossed against the bulkhead.

Paul, ripped from the seat and flung through space, tried to hang onto Janet. Violently bouncing along the fuselage, smacking against seats and bulkhead, not knowing which way was up and down, both, seconds later, landed against the softness of bodies. Pushed against the fuselage, twisting and turning in agony, they were human bodies. Although it had only taken seconds, to Paul it seemed like an eternity before the out of control spinning craft came to a final halt. The cabin suddenly turned silent. Paul, in the middle of the spinning force, had lost his hold on Janet. In total darkness, desperately groping around the space nearby, he touched a body he thought was her. Crawling closer to inspect the contours of the female body he felt was hers, he whispered, "Janet," into the dark. There was no response. Once again, he whispered, "Janet." He thought there was a slight motion followed by a moan. He recognized the sound. It was her. Disregarding his own misery, Paul cradled her in his arms and gently lifted the limb body of his wife off the floor. "Gotta get outta here," he said. Amid the cries and screams of helpless passengers, weighed down with Janet, Paul stumbled toward what appeared to be an exit door. "Gonna get that son-of-a-bitch," he silently vowed again, "causing all this trouble."

He gently placed his wife on the twisted floor. Dimly illuminated by the porthole, he reached for the exit door handle and yanked down hard. It gave way. Adding the full force of his body, he shoved it open. Looking up, he could not believe his eyes. There it was, brightly illuminated by the brilliance of uncountable stars he'd not seen before, the clear sky overhead.

With the lifeless body of Janet in his arms, he took a hesitant step outside on what looked like the outline of the remaining right wing. On unsteady legs, he pushed his way forward on the downward-slanted metal. It appeared the craft, on its final bounce, had come to rest on the right wingtip. Freed from the entrapment of the craft, gently settling Janet's body on the edge, he stooped over to check for the ground. Shaking his head over and over, he could not believe his eyes. Everywhere he looked, there was carnage. From his vantage point, as far as the eye could make out, there was wreckage. Wreckage from dozens, perhaps hundreds, of craft plummeted to the ground.

Heavyhearted, staring bewildered into the night, he became aware of others joining him on the wing. Many were injured. Many more still trapped inside. The night was broken up by cries, his eyes touched the lifeless body of his wife. Her helpless shape urged him back to the present. "Gotta get goin." It was then that his eyes caught a moving object. It appeared out of the dark from the distant end of the runway that the craft had just landed on. It took a couple seconds for Paul's brain to register. "Oh my God." The sight hit him like a sledgehammer. It suddenly dawned on him. "I'm dead," he wailed, "we're all dead!" Nearby passengers, alerted by his sudden outburst turned to follow the direction of his stare. As nightmarish as the present conditions were, the watching faces instantly turned to horror.

Paul was already moving. He hastily collected Janet's lifeless body, pulled her to the wing's edge and jumped to the ground. Eyes darting between his wife's body and the incoming craft, Paul tried not to panic. He collected her lifeless body, threw her over one shoulder, and took off running. He ran like he hadn't run since his high school track days. Afraid to turn around, he kept on running. "Not gonna make it...not gonna make it," he kept repeating, but luck this night was on his side. He and Janet made it. Ignoring the crashing sounds he left in his wake, Paul could only imagine the devastation the landing craft had on the passengers trapped inside, and the remaining ones left atop the wing.

Trapped inside the fuselage, faces he'd gotten to know on the ill-fated transatlantic flight perished in an instant. Barely escaping himself, he slowly turned to get a glimpse of the burning wreckage strewn across the runway and adjacent field. The fuel, what was left in the craft's tanks, exploded with a thunderous sound, adding to the night's carnage. O'Hare, for all practical purposes, after the crafts' fuel had run out, had become the dumping ground for uncountable incoming Atlantic flights. And there were more on final approach...many more.

Mesmerized by the drama unfolding from the sky, barely aware, he heard the faint call of his name. "Paul?" His eyes sought out the sound below his feet. There was slight motion. Squatting down to check her face, with one arm supporting her neck and head, he gently lifted her upper body off the ground. "Janet?"

Gazing at the stars above, she fully opened the eyes. "Where're we?"

Teary eyed, gently squeezing her hand, he muttered, "Safe, we're safe."

PYONGYANG (North Korean Missile Command)

"Status!" The order issued sounded much like a bark from a Doberman. "I demand status," he repeated. The command was given to a team of operators hunched over their respective computer terminals. Kim Hak Su, chief of mission control, was responsible for the nation's national defense sector. Presently, the team was awaiting the ready call from ICBM missile command. Aside from the grinding of his boots, the center was dead silent. Stomping the ground impatiently, he was furious. Every head in the control room was focused on his reaction. There may have been tension in the room, but it did not show in the faces. There were no signs of emotions. If it weren't for the swift fingers moving across the keyboards, the scene may have struck as a routine act. But it wasn't.

He was pacing again. Priming the missiles was taking too long. *Should have been prepared earlier*, he cursed in silence. He also knew that was impossible.

The order to launch took everybody by surprise. It had only been authorized earlier this morning. Irrational, spur of the moment, and unexpected, such was the culture of a nation used to aggression, hardship, and rigorous discipline. It was the result from decades, perhaps centuries, of oppression. To make things worse for this isolated nation in the Asian peninsula with China to the west, South Korea to the south, Russia up north, and Japan across the straights, political sanction was exerted from every possible direction. Self-imposed political and economic trade had been enforced decades ago. Isolated for years, the state was on the brink of starvation. The results were obvious. Trimmed to the bones, but toughened from arduous discipline, it created a nation that could endure any hardship.

"Yes, Comrade Commander," was the unsteady reply from the section leader. The mission display screen immediately switched to Musudan, DPRK's[34] secret underground missile launch center. It had only been recently that the center went operational. More specifically, it was the DPRK's launch pad for their ICBM, the Taepodong.

Kim Hak Su was proud to be the top element in the chain of high command. *After this launch*, he thought, *I will finally get the respect I deserve. I cannot fail or it will be my neck.* His thoughts reflected a string of recent launch failures contributed mostly to equipment malfunctions. But high command did not accept excuses. They demanded justification with fingers pointed in his direction. Today, he was ready, and so was the gigantic tube poised in the silo.

Kim Hak Su, with obvious concern for the delay, planted his body in front of the mission display screen. On restless legs, his body shifted back and forth. "Where's that damned EAM?" The entire mission depended on it. He silently cursed the ministry. Where his team was poised and ready to turn the launch keys, members of the ministry of defense were dragging their asses, as usual.

Unable to conceal his apprehension, he began to pace the floor again. It gave him time to reflect on the course his career had taken. He remembered the expectation his family had for his future. Despite the corporal discipline and training imposed by the state's education, he endured punishment like most of his comrades. It began with the party doctrine taught in early schools balanced with rigorous martial arts training for boys and girls alike. His parents had sent him to the best schools and Dojos in the country. While psychological conditioning was demanding, physical demands were brutal most

---

[34] North Korea - Officially the Democratic People's Republic of Korea

times. Over the years, most of the physical conditioning had waned from his body, but tortured memories from history lessons remained vivid.

Every few seconds he shot a distressing glance at the mission panel. Still puzzled at the turn of events, he'd been unprepared for this. Unbeknownst to him, some political incident must have triggered the alert condition. "Perhaps the Americans finally managed to break the ministry's patience," he deduced, "with their incessant condescending attitude."

He still had hopes that today's launch was only an exercise to be cancelled at the last second. Already, for days, red alerts had been issued to "rattle daggers" at the free world. He could not imagine the head of state would be stupid enough to launch an atomic-tipped weapon.

An hour into the wait, the suspense was killing him. Despite cultural discipline and the absence of emotions, many eyes flinched when the mission panel came alive. "That's it!" The red flashing EAM alert scrolled across the display one Hangul[35] symbol at a time. It contained the launch codes. With shaky hands he reached for the current mission folder. Blurry-eyed, he read and confirmed the message with the launch commander. It took seconds to comprehend. His face took on a stunned expression when he read, "Execute Missile Launch."

The commander was not prepared for this violent act, but with a swift motion picked up the microphone. "Launch Taepodong One." Kim Hak Su had just given an order of immense destruction nobody would be able to stop. Not even him.

Uncertain seconds passed in silence. He was still hoping the mission would be cancelled at the last second or terminated in failure, as it had with recent launches. But that was wishful thinking. And he knew it. Then, they felt it—the tremendous rumbling. The sound was quickly followed by the roaring inferno of a missile leaving the launch tube, even though the silo was almost a mile from the center. The sight was awesome. Farmers harvesting rice crops nearby threw away their tools and fled to nearby shelters. Somewhat secure, they marveled over the fire-spitting spectacle exploding out of the ground and slowly rising to the skies. Only a few personnel in the government knew its destination. For better or for worse, the warhead was on its way to destruction.

The Taepodong was the latest achievement in North Korea's nuclear arsenal. Despite its early stage of development, it had been termed an ICBM missile with nuclear strike capability at a range of 10,000 km. It would reach its destination in approximately forty minutes.

Kim Hak Su could already envision the rejoicing of his people when news leaked out about the preemptive strike against the Western oppressors. The country would be in celebration for days. *What euphoria it will be.* For the moment, he was caught up in the excitement.

"Comrade, sir," one operator asked. "What now?"

"Now," he instructed, "we wait." The contrail created by the speed of the missile left a visible trace in its wake. Individuals who spotted the flight wondered about this phenomenon streaming rapidly towards the eastern seas.

---

[35] Hangul – Korean alphabet symbol.

FINAL DESTINATION (Cockpit)

Minutes earlier, on final approach, the craft was ready to touch down on the barely illuminated runway. "Pull UP...Pull UP!" Completely panic stricken, both the copilot and the chief purser yelled in unison.

Marshall, suddenly aware of the wrecks blocking the approach, had already reacted. Using his right hand, he forced the speed levers forward. With the left, he pulled back hard on the flight controls. Right foot slammed on the rudder controls, the craft, under its full weight, kept pushing forward towards the ground. It took several seconds for the two engines to respond, barely enough to clear the wreckage, but not enough to not slice through the mangled fuselage from a previous flight. Ever so slowly, the craft responded. The nose came up. With the craft slowly gaining altitude, the crew left the awful grinding sound from metal tearing into metal behind.

Marshall, desperately gripping the controls, yelled out, "Not again!" With the craft under his control, he'd felt it first. Seconds before, barely missing the ground, nose in the air to gain precious altitude, the jetliner suddenly jerked. He knew the symptoms. "Number one's out." From here on, only one engine was left to carry the craft through the air. What made the situation worse, it was the left engine that had quit. It just ran out of fuel.

In the split second decision Marshall had to make, right after the landing abort, for a second he had a clear few of the airport complex below. What he spotted was the only alternative for a landing and that was Runway 14R, immediately to the right. Being the second longest runway in the airport's configuration, almost 10,000 feet in length, it would be the only choice. To reach the threshold, he had to take the craft a couple of miles out, followed with a steep right bank for final. With the engine failure, out of all things on the wrong side, the remaining engine pushing against the upcoming turn, he was unable to guarantee the landing.

"Need more rudder," Marshall shouted into the dark. Leaving 28R in his wake and with it the illuminated tarmac with crashed and burning wreckages, the craft entered the darkened airspace ahead once more.

The copilot, waiting for final instructions, immediately reacted. His right foot slammed down hard on the right rudder controls. "Thanks for triple backups," he silently prayed. The controls responded.

Marshall, now on crosswind, with the copilot aiding with maneuvers, got ready to align the craft for final approach. Still a couple of miles out, eyes penetrating the dark, he could only guess at airspeed, altitude, and distance. The ground ahead, lit up by burning wreckage, provided a vague view of the landing spot. To keep the craft somewhat stable for final, he had to come in fast, faster than normal landing speed. Getting closer by the second, he finally spotted the threshold. Marshall, hands and arms cramped up barely able to move the controls, hoped the fuel would last another minute. "Tanks gotta be dry," he muttered, followed with, "Hang on, mates." It would be his final command. What followed was beyond his control. The craft, crossing the threshold, sliced though fuselages and wings spread across the runway and surrounding fields. From there, it bounced several times before smashing against a heap of wreckage.

An eerie quiet followed. The crew, momentarily cowered in the dark collecting thoughts, was immensely relieved at having survived the landing. With one flip on the latch, Marshall popped the window open to his right. A stream of cool Chicago night breeze swept across his face. He could even smell the freshness of ozone seeping into the cabin. Taking a deep breath, just about to get out of the seat, he watched it come. From the blackness of the sky, its silvery contours illuminated by the moon, a silent silhouette appeared. It bore directly down on them. Frozen in horror, unable to alert his crew in time, face contorted in agony at what would come next, lungs filled with fresh air, Marshall let out a final scream. It went unheard. The sound was drowned out by the tearing sounds of metal tearing into metal from the jetliner landing on top of his beloved, reliable workhorse of many years, ending the last of the remaining TriStar L-1011.

For the crew, dedicated to a lifetime of flying passengers safely around the globe year after year, the world had turned silent. Forever.

THREE MILE ISLAND

It was late at night when Doug Olson and his crew finally took a break. He knew everyone was exhausted to the limits. It showed on all of their faces. Despite the hopelessness, he thought they did a terrific job bringing the system under control, if only partial. There was still much to do but that had to wait until the next day. The disaster earlier that day may have caused damages to the power plant beyond repair, but there was one positive outcome. It brought him and his crew closer. *As a matter of fact,* he thought with admiration for his crew, *they had become interdependent as a cohesive unit.* Sure, there were the many simulation tests conducted periodically executed with precision in the past. But those were conducted under controlled conditions. But today was different. Their immediate lives depended on each other.

"Let's get some rest," he suggested. He did not have to say more. Most had already collapsed on cots kept at the facility for emergencies. There had been times in the past when the cots had been used. Olson recalled the one time the plant went into critical. But that was many years ago. To prevent it from happening again, additional safety features had been implemented. "Oh my God," his mind screamed out at him. A terrible thought had just struck at him. It even shook up his crew.

"What?"

"The other plants." The magnitude of today's events just hit him. Completely isolated and cut off from the world, he had no information on the rest of the country. At first, when some tried to get in touch with their families, they couldn't. Phones were out and so were mobiles. Eventually, some of the wives got worried and showed up at the plant. They were sent home with a promise to be reunited once power was restored.

"NRC[36]," he blurted out. "Gotta get a hold of them." It occurred to him that it wasn't going to happen tonight. All he knew was the commission was located in Rockville, MD., and the drive would take hours even if he could get a vehicle to start. But so far, they had all been dead lined. That fact alone still puzzled him. "Only thing," he'd surmised at the crew earlier, "EMP strike."

The revelation alone, if true, would be too traumatic for him to cope with at the present condition of exhaustion. That had to wait until tomorrow. He could not find a volunteer crew tonight to even make an attempt to take to the road. Aside from the several wives earlier, there had not been any other visitors or phone calls. "Guys," he shouted over to where his crew was resting, "any of you got HAM equipment?"

One came forward, "I do." But he refused to make an attempt to get it. It would mean trekking home and back on foot he had no energy at the moment. "First thing in the morning," he promised.

Doug tried to get some rest himself but the thought of his nation in peril kept him awake. He took the time to form an action plan for the next day. There was much to do but how to go about would be an almost impossible feat. All he knew it had to be done. Doug was taking stock of what he knew.

According to the NRC, there were 104 commercial reactors in operation in the U.S. of which 69 were pressurized water reactors and 35 boiling water reactors operating from 65 nuclear power plants. All in all, there had been ten "close calls" over the past three decades of which any one of these had the potential of a meltdown. Most never made the news for obvious reasons, "not to alarm the public."

---

[36] Nuclear Regulatory Commission.

But those were nothing even close to today's accident. Even if he could get hold of the NRC, "then what?" They all were helpless unless power could be restored. For that, his plant needed to operate. He realized here that there would be no outside help. It was up to him and his crew to get the plant back in operation to prevent the meltdown. He also realized there were concerns much greater than his plant. The entire nation was in jeopardy. Although he could clearly envision the magnitude of the disaster, but the public backlash he dared not think about. With a meltdown throughout the nation, it would mean the end of future nuclear power plants and with it his beloved technology, and job.

Doug finally dozed off hoping he would never wake up into what would sure be a world of chaos and anarchy.

MADRAS (India)

As was customary this time of year, it was another sweltering day in India, but not for Rajesh Chandra. Surrounded by comfort, he was sitting at his home office desk in the quiet streams of central air conditioning. Since his business success, it did not matter where he performed the work. With affluence came comfort, especially in a nation like India. Presently, he was going over the test analysis data Alex had provided. He liked working at home rather than at the modern, but impersonal, office in the center of the city. Same as the super modern office structure, he did not cut corners when building his home. Bathed in sheer elegance, every room had a personal touch. The Jungle Den, as he called his sanctuary, was his favorite retreat.

On entering the exquisitely carved wooden doorframe, flanked by a matching pair of six-foot tall elephant tusks, a visitor's view would immediately be touched by nature's splendor from an assortment of selective paintings. They were no ordinary paintings. They had been expressly designed to blend in with the decor. Each wall depicted another landscape populated by the grandness of tigers, elephants, and other wildlife grazing among the lush forest jungles of India. It was a personal reflection of the past he was so desperate to preserve.

Admiring the various landscapes made him feel happy. It reminded him of days when his country was still untouched by technology and conglomerates. Unfortunately, it was only a matter of time before all this would diminish, eventually lost in the ever-expanding population growth rapidly infringing on India's landscape and wildlife. *Was it all worth it?* The tradeoff was personal. He had achieved prosperity beyond his dreams. *Am I happier?* "No." *Not until technology can be curbed to coexist alongside nature's miracles.* He took a few moments to reflect on the unfortunate changes his country was going through.

It was not so long ago when his country was a hunter's paradise. From all corners of the globe, the wealthy came to hunt big game. It was mostly the British. Back then, the human mindset reflected very much a colonial ruling. Hunting, for the affluent and the extreme adventurer, had been looked upon as a feat of courage. Until the seventies, people thought there was an endless supply of wildlife. It was not until conservationists in the West presented disturbing statistics to the World Council. Nobody believed them until these proud creatures started to disappear at an alarming rate.

Rajesh, like many others in India, resisted world pressures for some time but eventually gave in to common sense. What nobody realized was the rapid population growth that had taken hold of the nation. In just a couple of generations, the growth had multiplied exponentially. When Rajesh grew up, he remembered an Indian population of a few hundred million. Latest statistics indicated it had reached over one billion.

"Impossible," was the general response. Nobody believed the figures. Voices were screaming, "Political maneuvers," accusing the government of manipulating statistics for their own gain. Birth control would be the only solution. It was unthinkable in Indian society not to have multiple children. The more boys a mother bore, the greater the chances were for carrying on the family heritage. It gave the family power. People could not rely on the government for support. It's why family government was created. It was the birthright of the primitive. Unthinkable, to be limited to only three children, but that was something for the next generation to worry about. It was thoughts like these that kept him awake many a night.

For now, Rajesh Chandra was content with his achievements. He was a successful businessman and a good provider for his family. Seated comfortably at the solid Oakwood table, he evaluated the piles of computer printouts one more time. He was reluctant to make the call. There was nothing he could tell them. He considered putting off the call to Alex until tomorrow, but remembered the urgency. His former business partner was waiting for a solution. He checked his watch. According to his calculation, it should be early evening in Colorado.

Pride and responsibility got the better of him. He picked up the fashionable phone's receiver to place the call, but had second thoughts. He hesitated. He placed the receiver back in its cradle. He wanted to make sure the figures were correct. He gazed at the hand resting on the wireless mouse. One click with the index finger pulled up the simulation software on his laptop. He had to take another look at the data. The results were the same, "No errors." *I should be happy,* were his immediate thoughts, but a nagging feeling still persisted. *I must find something.*

He had made the promise to his business partner. A thought had just occurred to him, *the application stack.* It was his last option. He would have to resort to the basics. With a swift move of the mouse, he clicked on the application icon then sat and waited. It took a few seconds for the simulation model to load.

He checked the data one last time, but this time from a sourcing perspective. Ten minutes into the analysis he spotted something. "Strange," was his initial reaction as he probed further. Then, all of a sudden, it hit him, causing a gagging feeling in his throat. It confirmed the intuition he had. Somebody had tampered with the software but, how could this be? The proof, nevertheless, was there, right in front of his eyes.

With unsteady hands he reached for the phone. He dialed the number.

"Bauer," Alex answered after a couple rings.

"Hello, my friend." Rajesh used the friendly approach to diffuse any tension. His voice was not the cheery one from two days earlier. "Wish I had good news," he started, "but we have confirmed your suspicion."

"What," Alex sounded concerned, "what have you found?"

"Somebody," he prodded his way through a maze of guilt, "has tampered with the software, definitely."

"You sure?"

"I do not know how this could have happened, but Hasan," unloading some of the responsible burden, he suggested, "was responsible for the development. He must have been aware of it."

"Let me talk to him," Alex insisted. At the moment, unable to comprehend a reason, he needed a rational explanation.

"Unfortunately," Rajesh excused the former employee, "he is no longer here."

"Can you have it fixed right away?"

"Of course," Rajesh assured his friend. "I have my programmers already working, but that's not all."

"What's that?" Alex wanted to know. His voice was heightened with concern.

"It is…" Rajesh tried to explain the find and warn Alex about a specific hardware change he had uncovered, but for a moment was distracted by a shuffle coming from the door. Expecting his wife, he turned in the direction but instead stared into the glaring face of his former employee. Eyes widened by the unexpected recognition, he dropped the phone. "What," he stammered, "you have come back?" It was all he could muster. Still in disbelief, he jumped from the comfort of his seat to greet his former employee, Hasan Hammad.

"Not for long." It was a calculated statement. It was an alarming statement.

"I do not understand," Rajesh stammered again. Picking up the phone, he was trying to make sense out of this unexpected situation. A second person, an accomplice, entered the room.

"Put the phone down," Hammad ordered. A few paces later, the intruder was alongside Rajesh. It was a grim face turned killer face.

"Hasan…what is this?" A chill ran through his spine.

Hammad gestured at the receiver. "How much have you told him?"

"Told who?"

"Don't play ignorant," Hasan reprimanded his former employer. "You are not stupid. You must know about the hardware fix by now."

Rajesh was momentarily distracted. It came from the entrance. The frame of a third accomplice had appeared. Followed by a slight nod, the intruder shot a quick glance at Hammad. "It is done," the man said.

"What have you done?" Rajesh yelled out in anguish. Panic-stricken, he pleaded, "My wife?" He suddenly realized the intruder's purpose. Extreme anger well up within him. Overpowered by the ominous feeling, he called out for his wife. There was no answer. Only a lingering silence prevailed. He abruptly turned to face the enemy. He made one last attempt to reason. "Please."

The next move was sudden. It came from behind. A blunt object in back of the head, the barrel of a weapon forced his head to face his former childhood friend. It would be the last face he saw in this life. It was not the face he remembered. It was a mask-like grin that would remain with him for eternity. Next, the lightning flash from a silencer seared his hair. It did not register with his brain. He never heard the explosive sound of the .45 caliber cartridge crunching through his skull. Neither did he feel the impact of the bullet rapidly expanding within his brain matter.

"Sorry, my friend." Hasan took a last look at his former partner and friend. "It had to be done." He turned and briskly walked from the room, followed by his accomplices. Striding down the hall, he passed by the living room. There, he noticed the wife's lifeless body sprawled along the plush flowery carpet. Blood was squirting from a gashing wound in her throat. It quickly turned the flowery garden into a scene of weeping indignation.

"Two less capitalists," without so much of a hint of emotion Jamuh Faisal, first lieutenant, South Cell, Madras, India, commented. Sprawled nearby was the dead body of the maidservant. Faisal sneered at both then quickly departed for the next assignment.

Despite the immediate mission that lay ahead, Hasan Hammad felt slight remorse for his former employer and childhood friend. *Can't just wipe away all memory,* he thought with regrets, *no matter who you are.*

CASTLE ROCK

Ten thousand miles away, Alex was intently listening to Rajesh when Brian and Tracy walked in. He gestured to the balcony, indicating he'd join them as soon as he was off the phone.

"…yes, my friend," Rajesh, at the distant end had just confirmed. "I have some bad news."

"What's that?"

"It seems somebody has tampered with the software…"

"How's that possible?" Alex reacted. A surge of anger welled through his body.

"I will come to that." Rajesh sounded as composed as ever. Nothing seemed to shake him up. Alex remembered working with his people. They were not only courteous to the point of annoyance at times, but had the ability to defuse arising conflicts. It was a cultural thing. Patience seemed to be their virtue. "We did a data analysis comparing the original source code. Somebody manipulated the host data layer. The port address had been reset. The default port had been reassigned. It permitted an unauthorized intrusion. The system has been compromised."

"What's your fix?" Alex demanded immediate justification. This was serious. He knew the consequences. It could be disastrous if the enemy got hold of the satellites. His stomach turned into knots just at the thought. *We may be too late already.*

"We have a temporary fix until new software can be loaded," he proceeded to tell Alex. "It is…" Unexpectedly, his sentence was cut off. The line had gone dead.

"Rajesh? What's happening? Rajesh?" Alex kept repeating, but there was no answer, even after dialing back several times.

"What's going on?" Brian asked as soon as Alex joined them on the balcony.

"Looks like we have a fix for the problem," he assured him, "but the line went dead before I could get the details."

"Called back?"

"I did, but he never picked up."

"What could have happened?" Brian was likewise concerned. "You tell him how critical it is we get the data?"

"I'll send an email to get the fix to us right away." Alex hastened indoors for his laptop.

In the serenity of the evening, on the balcony, Tracy and Brian were enjoying each other's company. On the interstate, glittering streams of headlights were snaking their ways along the distant valley basin. An occasional meteoroid could be seen shooting across the darkening sky, leaving a brilliant swat of crystal particles in its wake. Denver, twenty miles to the north, and Colorado Springs to the south were giving off the pale orange glow typical for a city. Tracy was resting against Brian. She probed his arm. "Still hurt?"

"Hurt? Not anymore," he assured her. "It's itchy."

"Means it's healing." His body had taken a severe beating, but after a lengthy shower followed with a stiff drink, his spirits had lifted. Together, they savored the scotch Alex had prepared. It had mellowed both. They were listening to the chirping song of crickets when Alex joined them back on the deck.

"Sent him an urgent message," he said.

"Priority?"

"Flash." Alex was gloating.

"You authorized?"

"Who cares?" A grin cut across his face. "Probably the only time I'll get away with it."

"What's next?"

"We should hear back soon." Alex seemed distracted. "Always been good calling back." After a brief silence, he murmured, "Wonder what's keeping her."

"Liz?" Tracy wondered, equally concerned.

"Promised to be here." They passed the evening chatting while waiting for her to arrive.

"Be nice to have everybody here." Several days earlier, Alex had asked her to spend a couple of weeks with him. It was the kids' summer break. He was looking forward to a long overdue family reunion. "So," he was facing both of them, "tell me about your day."

"Wished I'd had climbing gear," Brian replied. He seemed to want to avoid talking about the afternoon's incident.

"It's not that easy," Alex explained. "You gotta have a special permit. Have to take a course to qualify."

"Maybe I will."

"What's your next move?" Alex wanted to know. He was interested in Brian's plans with the KE issue. Brian was about to elaborate alternatives but stopped short, mouth agape, "What…?"

For a split second the night had turned into the brilliance of daytime. Immediately after, it turned dark again. This time pitch black. All three faces shot upward to identify the source. With eyes penetrating the blackness, there was none. Instead, they were drawn to an unforgettable splendor. Their focus became mesmerizing. Neither Tracy nor Brian had ever experienced such brilliance. In contrast, Alex had remembrances from an earlier childhood. There is was, the Milky Way, the cosmos in its fully expanded splendor. Awestruck, their views lingered. It took exerted willpower to break away from this overwhelming grandeur.

"What the hell was that?!" Brian reacted first.

Tracy was still dazzled. She moved up close to Brian. A chill went through her body. She clutched his arm. "What do you think?" Her face had taken on a frozen gaze. "Dad?"

"Don't know yet—but sure will find out." Alex abruptly turned, taking long strides towards the staircase. "Stay here," he ordered, "I'll be right back." He was headed for the comm center located in the basement.

"What do you think?" Tracy wondered. She still carried a stunned look on her face. "Power outage?"

"Not a chance. You saw the flash. That was no ordinary lightning. Besides," he reasoned, "where's the thunder?"

They had witnessed the greatest strobe light effects any of them had ever experienced. For a split second, it seemed all life had frozen. Their eyes had perceived the same effects, a forest of shadows plotted against the landscape. Shrubs, brushes, trees, and home all were brilliantly lit, casting deep, dark shadows onto the ground like a huge surrealistic landscape painting. It happened so fast that there was no time to react. The scene was followed by an eerie silence. Where there had been traffic snaking along the distant valley below, now everything had turned dark. "Listen," Tracy urged.

Out of the silence, from the distant valley, grew the muffled sounds of metal crashing against metal. She craned her body over the rail to get closer to the sound. Her pupils widened to penetrate the darkness. Her vision sought out the north, and then the south. Both orange glows had disappeared. Getting over the initial shock, she suggested, "Think it was a meteoroid." Brian suspected something much more sinister. "Don't think so." He had been in deep thought. After a pause, he said, "I think it's related to the problems with the satellites."

"You think? What's keeping Dad?" Tracy had been waiting for her dad to get back, then thought otherwise. "Follow me." She pulled Brian along. It was dark inside. She rifled through the kitchen drawer for a flashlight.

Brian spotted the light by the counter. "Here," he offered. With him in tow she headed directly for the basement. "Control room," she explained. To their surprise, the emergency lighting in the hallway lit up. The utility door was partly opened. She lingered by the entrance to adjust to the light. Alex seemed to be staring at a pile of computer printouts.

"EMP," they heard him mutter, "had to be."

Tracy took the few strides towards her dad. "What makes you think that?" She wavered. "How come the lights are on?"

"The house?" He seemed bewildered. "Backup power—hardened the whole damned place," he replied. His voice trailed off into preoccupied silence.

"What…when…why?" Tracy stammered. "What do you mean, hardened?"

"Antennas on the roof." Alex tried to focus on her question. His mind was on the sensor data. "Only connection to the outside. It'd taken gamma and neutron hits. That's why the lights went out."

"What about electricity?"

"Generators. Interface's filtered to ground. Heavy-duty spark arrestors," he explained, "just like the silos. Take about any force other than a direct hit."

"Phones?"

"Wireless." He made a mental note to check the HF antenna on the hill first thing in the morning. *Probably fried.*

"If what you're saying is true," she challenged, "the whole country could be without power."

"You saw the valley?"

"But we don't know." She hoped he was wrong about the EMP.

"Take a look." He handed her the printout. She stared at it. She tried to make sense of it. Mostly numbers, there were lines and lines of data. It was the status readout generated from some of the equipment, mostly particle sensors. The data suggested strong electromagnetic interference, accompanied by a tremendous power surge. He was surprised the system had held up. *Must have done the job well.*

Alex checked his wristwatch but it had stopped. *Thought so.* He wondered why Liz hadn't arrived.

"What?" Tracy said. She noticed the lines deepen on his forehead.

"Your watch," he asked, "is it working?"

"It's dead."

Brian shot a glance at his. "You may just be right," he agreed, "about the EMP."

Alex just had a thought as to why his daughter hadn't called in yet. He was supposed to pick her up at the airport. "Dammit," he cursed, "totally forgot."

She was supposed to call in on her final leg. He fished for the mobile, but wasn't surprised. "Out."

Tracy followed his move. She checked hers. "Mine's dead too." In the silence, they could hear the generator humming in the equipment room. It had kicked in a second after the power loss. The house had power. But what good would it do with the rest of the nation in a total blackout?

"Let's get back upstairs." There was not much else they could do down below. He led the way back to the deck.

The night had turned quiet again. An evening chill had set in. Tracy pulled her coat tighter around her shoulders. Many more stars were shining their brilliance. "This is beautiful." Despite the alarming situation, Tracy felt a twinge of romance. She sidled up to Brian. The distant valley had silenced. There were no more crashing sounds. The wrecks apparently had settled on whatever spot they had landed.

"Must be total chaos down there," Brian wondered. "Maybe," he suggested, "we should look."

"May not be safe," Tracy worried. "Better wait it out 'til daylight."

Alex was immersed in his own thoughts. He imagined drivers edgily shuffling around cars, speculating with others about what had happened. Eventually, some informed serviceman would come up with an acceptable explanation. It would be passed up and down the disabled interstate: "EMP effects." People working at NORAD would be aware of the technology although they had never experienced the effects of such an explosion. With the end of the Cold War, nobody had imagined ever having to experience such an effect.

"Liz," Alex urged. "We should start looking for her." He was getting extremely worried. "She should be here by now."

"Look where?" Tracy was just as concerned for her. And so was Brian. "Better stay put."

"Listen," Alex broke in. "No use for you to go anywhere tonight. Might as well stay close to home in case she shows up…and Brian," he suggested, "you take the guest room."

"Appreciate it."

Alex appeared to get busy. "I wanna see what's happened in the valley. I'll try to make it over to Pete Field."

"I'm coming," Brian insisted. He was on his legs.

"Me too." Tracy wasn't going to stay here alone.

"You stay," Alex ordered both of them. "Somebody's got to be here when they show up." He shot a pleading look at his buddy. "It's settled." He quickly turned and hastened for the garage.

"Be careful," Tracy called after him.

Alex grabbed a jacket on the way out. Below, at the garage, he tried to start the Beemer. "Dammit," he cursed. There was no response. The ignition was dead. Only the headlights worked. The instrument panel stayed dark. "Figures!" He slammed the door shut and headed for the other vehicle. "Hope it'll do better."

He purposely kept a Jeep Wagoneer in the garage. It was for backup transportation. It was one of few vehicles not dependent on electronics other than the starter and ignition. But that could easily be overcome with a jump-start rolling down the driveway. "Why would anyone want to buy an old clunker like this?" he remembered the car salesman saying years before, amazed when he was looking for a rugged backup vehicle. It paid off. The engine started with the first crank. "Good choice," he congratulated himself. Not knowing what to expect down the valley, he drove off in a hurry.

PACIFIC RIM (Hawaii)

"Used to be paradise," Patrick 'Pat' Adams grumbled. He was frustrated. "Stuck in traffic again." He reached for the controls in his Subaru rental to turn the air conditioning up another notch. "Ahh," he puffed with delight, "much better." It was still early in the morning but beads of sweat were already forming on his forehead. Swells of heat emanating from the freshly tarred H-1 didn't help much either. "Gotta get outta here," he labored in the dampness of morning, "and soon."

He recalled H-1 the first time he'd set wheels on the road. It was sparsely traveled back then. "How long has it been?" Almost forty years. Then, it had connected Honolulu with Barber's Point on the west end. That was about it for paved roads on the island. On a day off, he used to joyride around the island in the open Jeep. The trek was easy. It carried him past Diamond Head on the eastern end, headed north to Waimea Beach and back home across Mililani Town, the island's grand tour.

Pat Adams, Commander 15th Air Base Wing, stationed at Hickam, was dwelling on happier times. He recalled his first assignment to PACAF[37]. A young fighter pilot just out of training, he'd had high hopes for a promising future, full of piss and vinegar. Since then, he'd seen many changes. Where Waikiki at one time was a place of leisure for the occasional tourist, it'd become a crowded Mecca for sunbathers, himself included. He didn't like it any more. He was tired of the endless streams of visitors chatting in every possible language. Everything had changed. Until recently, this had been the place he'd planned to retire. Now, he wasn't so sure. Much of the excitement he used to feel had vanished, especially after the family broke up. He was looking forward to his next, last assignment on CONUS before retiring.

"Traffic's getting worse each year," he grumbled and stepped on the gas to advance another few hundred yards. "Now what?" He was shaken out of his daydream stupor by the chirp of his mobile. The number on the readout didn't make him feel any better. It was an emergency call tagged by the 999 prefix. This was never good news. Trouble always followed.

"15th Wing Command," the voice connected.

"What's up?"

"Emergency, sir." The caller was obviously troubled. "Need immediate action."

"Now hold on, junior." He forced the caller to calm down. To those young whippersnappers everything was an emergency. He knew. He'd been there once. "Don't get excited."

"PAC early warning picked up possible ICBM launch," junior puffed, "northern perimeter."

Adams had been aware of the recent missiles testing by North Korea and wasn't very alarmed. "Probably just another test launch."

"We thought of that, sir," the poor kid stammered, "but the launch was registered by both Osan and Elmendorf."

"Do we have a flight path?"

"All indications point to the U.S. West Coast, sir." The airman sounded sincere.

"What about NORAD?" Adams demanded. He was getting worried himself. "Could it be? Impossible." *No fool would be reckless enough to launch a nuke.* "No way," he determined, *not on us.*

---

[37] PACAF – Pacific Air Forces.

"No confirmation from there. Seem to be asleep this morning."

"Who gave the alert?"

"Priority call…seventh headquarters, Osan. Couple minutes ago."

"Confirmed?"

"Couldn't. Taegu comm lines are down."

"Checked DIN backups?"

"Working on it, sir."

In a semiconscious move, one hand rubbing across his chest, he ordered, "Sound the alert for an E-3 AWACS[38] and scramble two F-15Es. Have them armed with AMRAAMS[39]. Keep this channel open. I'll call back in a couple minutes." He could feel a slow burning sensation in his abdomen. His ulcer was welling up again. "Damned this traffic," he cursed. *It'll be another twenty minutes to base.* He let go a desperate moan. "Don't need this now," he pained, "just when I was rotating out of here." *Here I am, probably worried about nothing…should be lying on the beach.*

He'd just moved to the Hale Koa to spend the last month in transit quarters. The nice thing about moving was you got some time in a hotel while the movers were packing up household goods. He'd always liked the hotel. It was the last sanctuary in Waikiki still fronted by a pristine beach. All the other hotels had lost their sandy access to the waters in the seventies when the Japanese built their mega structures on what used to be the beach. Hell, they even had to haul in megatons of sand from the North Shore to cover the coral rocks just to give the tourists a few feet of beach. *That's what I mean by change.* His thoughts were filled with regrets for the old days. He felt sorry for himself…for his family…for the locals, for what used to be paradise.

Hoping to calm the burning in his chest, he popped a few more Tums. Up ahead, just above the horizon, his eyes caught a motion. It was the dome-covered E-3 taking off in the distance. Immediately following were two F-15s in pursuit. *Right on time,* he thought, shooting a glance at the chronometer strapped on his left wrist, then picked up the mobile from the center console where he'd tossed it a couple minutes earlier.

"Any additional data?" he checked with the OPS officer on duty.

"Flight trajectory's got the trace—target destination, central coast, California."

"What's the ETA?"

"Thirty minutes."

"Has anyone else confirmed?"

"Only Elmendorf, Sir. We should get a fix from the E-3 as soon as it reaches altitude."

Adams was worried now. He almost hit the guy in front of him. "Idiot," he yelled out the window. Capable of Mach-3, he doubted the F-15s would catch up with the ICBM, but it was all he had to intercept. There was nothing better available out here. Hawaii was only a monitoring outpost for the mainland and didn't have a defense strike force. Alaska got a fix but its interceptors failed because they couldn't catch up to a missile flying Mach-8. Only an Aurora could catch up but, officially, they didn't exist. Any hope for a counterstrike would have to come from a Tomahawk. But there were no subs in these waters that he knew of. The Polaris base out at Guam was too far off to be of any help.

---

[38] Airborne Warning and Control System is an Airborne Surveillance Platform used to command and observe aerial combat.

[39] Advanced Medium Range Air-to-Air Missile.

What a mess. This time, we're really caught with our pants down. He realized the connection was still open. "What does satellite data indicate?"

"There's no data," the OPS officer responded.

"Why not, dammit?"

"Link's down."

"Get it up," he hollered. "Dammit." He was getting angrier by the minute. He still hoped the whole damned thing was a false alarm. *How can they let this happen? Who the hell is responsible? Are they all asleep?* Many questions raced through his mind. He wasn't concerned so much about the immediate crisis at hand. What concerned him more was the lack of strategic planning. *Somebody's got to hear about this,* he promised himself. Millions were spent on think tanks each year to protect the nation against all possible treats, billions more on experimental counter-measures. *What the fuck. Whole Pacific flank's exposed to whoever wants to mess with us.* He was irate by now. *Maybe I should cancel retirement and shake up these assholes.*

"Hickam Air Force Base, Hawaii." He'd just passed under the prominent sign overhead. Adams drove up to the gate shack. A quick flash of his ID gave him immediate access to the base. He gunned the engine, headed for the parking plaza. Rather than taking his usual strides, he ran up the stairs. He made it to the office just as the E-3 flight reached mission altitude. "We've got visual," the AWACS commander reported.

"What's the position?" Adams demanded.

"Fifty degrees north," was the reply, "by one hundred seventy east."

"Dammit. Way out of our reach. We'll never get there."

"Recall?"

"No," he ordered, "hold your position." *Just in case there's a change in flight path.* "Standby…I'll advice."

"Roger that."

Deeply troubled, Adams headed directly for the comm center. It was a short walk to the adjacent building. There was nothing else he could do. Landlines with CONUS were down. And so were the links with satellites. *What a mess.* He'd never experienced anything like it. *Entire comm grid down all at once?* "Everybody's asleep but us? Impossible!" As soon as he entered the comm center the frenzy became obvious. His crews were hurrying along the rows of panels patching in and out equipment. He pulled a senior tech aside. "What's the status?"

"Checking for life circuits, sir."

"Try Offutt on HF. If there's no response, VHF and UHF all commands. Gotta wake somebody."

"Right away, sir." He watched the tech scurry off.

Visions of nuclear holocausts crossed his mind. Images from the 50s, his first Pacific assignment, were still vivid in memory. He was present during many of the initial atomic tests conducted on remote islands. *God help us if this is for real.*

SPADOC

"What the hell…?" It was the SPADOC officer on duty. He swallowed the rest of the words. His mouth had gone completely parched. His heart almost leaped from his chest. "Can't be," he stammered. The situation had escalated from alert to most critical. Utterly confused, he took a few frantic paces in different directions, first here, then there. He was on the brink of panic. Then it dawned on him. "The Book!"

In a last ditch effort he sprinted for the shelves. *Where's that damned thing? Somebody's misplaced it.* His face began to turn purple. His over-inflated lungs had stretched to bursting. With a hissing sound, he let go of the air. He'd forgotten to breath.

They'd prepared for this moment through periodic training, but always with the knowledge that it was just another exercise. "Simulation practice," it was called. This was different. He had no practice scheduled for today. In complete denial, his mind registered, "This is for real." What had shaken him up was the red flashing "EAM" alert pulsing across the status board. And the insane sound. "Somebody," he shouted in desperation, "turn that damned thing off." There were only three distinct choices for the alarm: simulation test, system failure, or imminent attack. That was it. No other options.

It felt like minutes had gone by when his senses finally got hold of his straining body. In reality, only seconds had gone by. He forced his body to move. "Do something." It was a direct order. There was nobody else nearby. It was up to him. He needed instructions. His eyes caught the hot line. He yanked the phone from the cradle. His sweaty fingers lost their grip. With a clang, it landed on the floor. He reached for it and clamped the receiver between chin and shoulder. It freed up his hands. He could hear the familiar pulse dial clicking out a series of numbers. Automatic calls were being triggered alerting Air Force, Naval, Space, JCS[40], and the White House. Officers in charge of their missions were immediately connected to the emergency call via secure pagers. Aside from the call, each mission by now had received an alert "FLASH" backup message across the wire. Simultaneous alerts were made to coordinate the next move. It would be initiated by the highest commands, the president and the JCS.

In just a few seconds, critical mission forces including military, space defense, and nuclear subs had been alerted. The JCS had been connected with the president. They were waiting for him to come online. There was no time for anyone to get to the White House command center. Decisions had to be made on the fly via live conferencing. As Commander in Chief, the president was the ultimate decision maker. The clock had ticked down to 30 minutes, the time remaining before impact.

The Officer in Charge finally spotted the book. It was an emergency checklist. He yanked it from the shelf. A few paces later he landed in front of the alert panel. On unsteady legs and with a trembling body, he fumbled through the list. His fingers were slippery. *Don't panic, not now,* he cautioned himself. In desperation, he was leafing through the pages, searching. He didn't know where to begin. All he could make out were capitalized flags. ALERT, WARNING, IMMEDIATE and MISSION jumped into his face. As OIC it was his responsibility to initiate the mission. It was his duty to coordinate. He sensed company. Staff members had gathered around. They were crowding. They eyed him with expectations. *There's no time to read,* he finally decided. "Here," he ordered his subordinate, "you read."

---

[40] Joint Chiefs of Staff are Generals representing each branch of military services.

The checklist was an excerpt from SIOP. The Single Integrated Operations Plan had been developed decades ago. To cope with national emergencies of this nature, over time it had been refined over and over to reflect an ever-changing climate. Political climates were subject to changes much like the weather. And so were new threats. Following an EAM alert, the plan spelled out every single step to execute, from start to retaliation.

His eyes were darting to initiate an action. The alert panel stared back at him. To no avail, he still struggled with the situation. Relentlessly ticking away, his eyes caught a glimpse at the world clocks overhead. "Dammit," he shouted into the receiver, "where's the president?" Sudden anger welled up within him. "I need more time." *What idiot expects to make an epic decision in twenty minutes?*

By now, everybody on defense duty had been alerted. NORAD facility engineers went into action. Calls were made to alert other critical personnel. The tunnel gate was still open. It allowed entrance for mission critical personnel to reach their stations. In ten minutes it'd be shut. After that, no one would go in. No one would come out.

"We're screwed," the OIC slurred. His subordinates were staring at him. They expected action. There was none. With a shrug of his shoulders, he abruptly turned and stormed out. He headed for the war room. There, computers were already busy plotting the source and trajectory of the imminent threat. The results were continuously updated on the huge display screen. The arc plotted the flight path. It traced back to a source in North Korea. The target was still being computed. "Incoming," the animated voice announced on the PA, "ten minutes to impact." Mechanical, the voice showed no emotions. *At least,* the OIC reckoned, *it's safe in the mountain.* Then it suddenly struck him. "My family!" It was a cry of desperation. He was panic-stricken once more.

THE WHITE HOUSE

Aside from a couple subdued voices it was quiet in the Oval Office. Still early in the day, George Wilmot, President of the United States, dressed in his morning robe, was in hushed conversation with the first lady. She was already dressed up for the day ready to receive early visitors arriving soon. As first lady and emissary to the White House, it was her principal function to make visitors feel comfortable. Only the presidential aid would pop in occasionally to see if something was needed. This morning, the president and first lady were making plans for where to spend the upcoming holidays. Her choices were the Bahamas or Hawaii, his preference, as usual, was Camp David. He preferred it there. Within a thirty-minute hop via the presidential helicopter, it was close by. That way, he was within easy reach of the White House staff if an unexpected crisis should develop. And crises were never far off. There was a brief, but forced knock at the solid wooden entrance door before it suddenly flew open. The president and first lady didn't have a chance to respond with the customary "enter" or "come in."

"Mister President." It was the head of the secret service. Flanked by several agents, all seemingly short of breath, the team appeared extremely urgent.

Unceremoniously, the president was ordered, "Sir, please!" The agents took hold of his arms and ushered him toward the exit. The president's face took on an inquisitive look. Confused, the first lady shot a fleeting look after her husband. Her facial expression took on an alarming glare quickly followed with anger at the sudden interruption. She rebuffed the intrusion. "Please," two agents were already by her side. She was whisked from the comfort of the divan. Both were quickly heralded out of the comfort of this spacious and semi-private presidential domain. The agents were courteous, but firm. "No objections! No options!" Both were rushed under tight escort along the corridor.

"What?" Wilmot immediately realized that something sinister must have developed. Mentally, he was already dealing with the situation. The first lady still struggled with the rude intrusion on her privacy. Wilmot, after being informed on several occasions over the past few days about the satellite incidences, had a subtle foreboding.

"Marine One's on the way," he was advised. The presidential helicopter would arrive in a few minutes. It had been dispatched from nearby Andrews AFB, where it was stationed. "You'll be briefed en route." Standing by the front lawn, this early in the morning, there was a chill in the air from the nearby river, the Potomac. The first lady, still angered by the sudden disruption, waved a secret service agent to attention. "He needs to change," she insisted.

"On board," she was informed. There was a set of complete garb available for just such an emergency.

Marine One touched down on the lawn. "This is serious," the president shouted at the first lady over the chopping pitch made by the rapidly descending craft. As soon as the wheels made contact with the ground, the president and first lady were ushered on board. They had been given no time to pack. Any alternate command destination was supplied with the necessities of living. The given inventory ranged from personal garments to sustainable rations of food and supplies, not only for the president and staff, but for the JCS and a team of agents as well. Additional amenities could be supplied once the presidential party had arrived, providing the supply line was still accessible.

"Raven Rock?" the president inquired.

"Not this time," he was told. It was usually him making important decisions.

"Yes?" George Wilmot expected a reply.

"Insufficient accommodations," he was further informed, "Mount Weather." It took a few seconds for the president to absorb what was just said. "Evacuating all essential leadership," he was further advised.

The Mount Weather Emergency Operations Center, during peacetime, was a civilian command base located in Virginia. It was operated and maintained primarily for the Federal Emergency Management Agency. In case of a pending or imminent national disaster, things changed drastically. Then the base was designated as major relocation site for the highest level of political and military officials. It took on a major role in U.S. government policies within the continuity of operations plan.

Located in the Blue Ridge Mountains, the base was located near Berryville, fifty some miles from Washington, D.C. This underground facility within Mount Weather, had been used once before by the former president and his immediate staff during the September 11 attack. The success of a relocation depended on how much warning the White House had before an attack. Today, the president, his family, and his immediate staff were scheduled as the first wave of the evacuation. Congressional staff members and other high profile officials would have secondary priority depending on the availability of emergency transportation.

By the time additional transport out of Andrews became available, it may become too late for this contingency. Forty minutes of alert did not allow for much lead-time to notify, direct, and evacuate any component, even under the most ideal conditions. For all practical purposes, each action element was forced to fend for itself.

NORAD COMMAND

Benjamin "Ben" Jackson, Brigadier General, North America Defense command, had just finished dinner at his residence. To somewhat relieve the pressure on his expanded gut from another well-served meal, he unbuckled his belt. Still dressed in uniform pants, he didn't feel like changing yet. The wife motioned him from the table. She needed the space he occupied to clean off dishes and silverware. Reluctantly, a groan escaping his throat, he pulled his six foot three frame from the chair and strolled to the deck. He was about to reach for a set of sunglasses but decided against it. Squinting into the sun, he decided, *another couple of minutes, and the red orange disk will be gone.* The sun would have disappeared behind the Cheyenne Mountain crest. With a thud, he planted his stuffed, but otherwise solid, body into his favorite launch. Facing the foothills, he took time to contemplate. His thoughts generally centered on the mission, his accomplishments, and what was ahead.

Ben Jackson's life had been handed him on a silver platter, more or less. Unlike most of his peers, Air Force Academy graduates, he accelerated through the ranks through inherited disposition. Aside from a better-than-average IQ, commanding presence, and solid character, he came from a long line of career officers dating back to the Civil War. A command position during the Vietnam and Gulf wars, compounded with several other conflicts, only solidified his position. Unless there was a major blunder on his behalf, he was in the saddle for life. *And,* he judged with an apt smugness, *can't see how that'd possible.*

He was slightly surprised when the wife joined him on the deck. "Must have dozed off," he muttered at her. She nodded to confirm. It had turned dark in the meantime. "What time's it?" he asked.

"About eight…here," she said, handing him a glass of wine. It was their daily ritual to spend the evening together. It gave them an opportunity to catch up on daily events and relax for the evening. Topics generally touched on politics, his mission, and her charity activities. Today had been just another uneventful day.

He was about to get up to change into casuals when all of a sudden the sky lit up. "What the hell!" he stammered. In a reflex action, he turned to his wife to confirm what he just witnessed actually happened. She appeared just as dumbfounded. It was a sight neither of them had experienced, ever.

"Let's go inside," she suggested, "can't be good."

He lingered on. Once his eyes adjusted to the immediate darkness and he craned the neck upwards to the heavens, he was struck in awe. "My God," he whispered into the silence, "there is a heaven." Reluctantly, he broke away from the marvel to fish for his mobile. Minutes had gone by. Somewhat surprised, he wondered why no one was calling. He was sure others had witnessed the spectacle as well. He pressed the programmed button to connect with his command but there was no dial tone. He also noticed the phone was dead. "Dammit," he cussed into the night, "forgot to charge it." It wasn't the first time the batteries had gone dry. Still in awe, he hastened inside but crashed against the glass doors. "Dammit," he cussed again. His wife, he realized, had closed the French doors on him. "Where are you?" he called for her in the dark. "Where're the lights?" He realized then the house was doused in darkness.

He was groping for the base phone then spotted a feigned flicker in the hall. She'd appeared with a candle in hand. "Electricity's out," she said.

In the dim light he located the phone and dialed the mountain. "What the hell?" This had never happened in his entire career. "Phone's out too," he said. Both took on a perplexed look. Reaching for the uniform jacket where he'd tossed it a couple hours ago, he said, "Gotta get on base."

"Can't you stay?" Her voice was faltering and her face showed concern.

"Gotta find out what's goin' on!" he insisted on the way to the carport.

"Hurry back," her words trailed after him.

Ready to speed off, the car wouldn't start. He cussed some more then realized the ignition was dead. There was no click from the starter. Then it dawned on him. "This is no coincidence." Home, vehicle, light in the sky, and phone power out simultaneously? Not likely. He jumped from the car and headed for the wife's SUV. Same there...no power. "Can't be," he stammered. An ominous thought had struck him. "EMP!"

Inside again, the wife was surprised he hadn't left. Slightly winded, he explained, "Engine's out." He watched her face turn from concern to fear. He was about to explain his hunch about the blackout when he spotted headlights drive up. He hurried to the carport to meet the visitor. Surprised to see a military Humvee[41] sprawled across the driveway, two of his staff jumped from the vehicle. "Sir," one demanded, "we need you at once."

He was quickly whisked off headed for the Mountain. At first, he wondered why the vehicle was still operational then realized it'd been shielded by fifteen hundred feet of granite. Ten minutes later, they arrived at a heavily guarded tunnel entrance. Two minutes more, speeding through the tunnel, the Humvee slid past the blast doors. While Jackson, amid his staff, hastened towards the command center, he took note of the heavy doors slowly closing off the tunnel entrance. "This," he motioned to his aids, "is not a good sign."

As soon as he entered, Jackson bellowed, "I need an answer, and...I need it now."

"Phones are down," a voice yelled from the office. "And comm links," somebody else voiced from the command table. Downlinks had stopped feeding data to the computers. Equipment was sitting at idle. The satellite status board had gone inactive as well.

Jackson turned to face his staff. He could feel the air laden with uncertainty, even fear. He made an attempt to stay calm, but was close to panic himself. What gave it away were his dilated pupils set in a tense stare. His eyes darted between the faces gathered around and the set of global clocks mounted against the wall. "Less than twenty minutes," he bellowed. "After that, we may all be dead."

He shot another glance at the status board. Alert condition still indicated DEFCON-3. *Maybe not all's lost,* he thought, but an ominous feeling of doom silenced his mind. He rushed to the intercom to inform his personnel. "Now hear this," his voice boomed, "except mission commanders, everybody stays at their duty station."

Following a brief pause, he added, "In my office," and gestured at his command staff.

---

[41] High Mobility Multipurpose Wheeled Vehicle (HMMWV), better known as the Humvee, is a military 4WD motor vehicle produced by AM General based in South Bend, Indiana.

WARREN AB (Underground Missile Command)

EAM message in one hand, mic in the other, the missile officer jumped to action. He dropped the mic to free up the hand but tripped on the waxed floor as he rushed to the safe. He had just pulled the hardcopy from the printer. "Come on...come on," he yelled. The outburst was directed at himself. His fingers were sweaty. They were slipping from the rotary dial. It took several tries to unlatch the lock. Finally, he felt the slight click. *That's it.* Nerves on edge, he yanked the handle open. His hand went for the first folder marked "Emergency Action Codes—Top Secret." He tore open the envelope. It revealed the plastic encased tags. Using both hands he broke it in half and handed it to his commander who verified the message. "Authentic," the commander yelled.

"Not good people...not good," the missile officer resounded. Body trembling, he turned to face the launch crew. All he saw were pale faces staring back at him.

At the LCC, procedures required that every EAM must be authenticated by the use of a code. The code must be valid and up to date. Two missile officers on duty then pulled the red framed laminated cards carried around their necks to verify the code's authenticity against a matching card from the safe. If there was a match, as was presently the case, the silo crew, or crews in case of multiple launches, alert and on standby, were directed to launch.

At the silos, prior to launch, a PAL code must be inserted into each nuclear device to activate its warhead. If the Permissive Action Link codes were not entered, the weapons would not be armed. At this point, each missile would have been programmed for a predetermined target.

"People," the commander howled, "we have a match. This is not a test—it's for real." His team, primed and energized, flew into action. They had been drilled for just such an event many times. "Launch missile!"

Although no one on the crew ever expected an actual launch, each knew precisely what to do. The next moves would be the most crucial. It would test the individual's ability. Expected to be carried out without fail, each crewmember must set aside individual concerns and creed. Because of conscious feelings and personal concerns, the human element was still the weakest link in the system, more so than machine initiated. In the past, to prevent potential failure, numerous options had been implemented from totally automated to machine controlled launch. The element of failure, whether from human indecision or equipment malfunction still prevailed. Once the missile was launched, it could not be cancelled. It could not be recalled. For now, the launch was a combination of man, machine, and electronic initiation where the human element had one last option to opt out, but that would have unimaginable consequences for the preemptive strike. It could mean the annihilation of the nation—our nation.

Years ago, when manned bombers were called into flight to carry a missile to its destination, the mission could be recalled. A missile fired from land-based silo or from the submarine could not. Today, here and now, the United States had been committed to nuclear war.

At the mountain, NORAD command, the only consolation Jackson had was access to an arsenal of nuclear assets no other nation outside of Russia had. For now, as far as he could tell, the once adversary superpower was not involved. Not yet.

ALTERNATE COMMAND CENTER (Mount Weather)

"What's happened?" The first lady was trying to get the president's attention. It proved a waste of time. Each time he turned to face her there was another interruption by the staff. She finally gave up and focused her attention on the ground rapidly passing beneath the craft. The world outside was gradually turning to dusk. She was squinting through the portal windows to make out something, anything. *Like someone's turned off a switch.* Despite the crowdedness in the cabin she felt alone. It was relatively quiet inside the craft. Voices were filtered by the hum of the turbojets. The pilot was pushing the craft toward their destination at maximum speed. Only the immediate White House staff was present. Members from various commands in the Pentagon would follow. Loaded onto transports on whatever could be commissioned out of Andrews, destination Blue Ridge Mountain, they would not be far behind. The first lady shifted her view up ahead. Slowly creeping into sight were the shadows of Shenandoah Valley. "Sure hope the kids are all right." With a distracted nod, George Wilmot acknowledged his wife's comment. He'd been on the HF radio with his commanders since they left the White House grounds.

Finally, he turned his head in her direction. For a moment he released the push-to-talk button on the headset. "Should be." A week earlier, the kids had left for France on a family exchange with the head of that country's leader. Because of the satellite blackout, communication was not yet established with Europe.

"Look." The president gestured out the window. He made a gesture to distract his wife from personal matters. He could read from her face how painful a thought the uncertainty was, the separation from the children.

A few miles ahead, coming into view was the clustered complex of Mount Weather. The complex was easy to spot from up here. Brightly lit halogen beams illuminated the secret grounds. She could make out the outlines of the complex. On getting closer, she could see details. *What a shame*, she thought. The construction had removed a sizable chunk from the beauty of the mountain range. As was the case with many military facilitates, the area was restricted to all air traffic. The occasional hiker and weekend vacationer, curious what was behind the unsightly security fences, was turned away by the sentries stationed on and around the post. Heavily armed, they were courteous, but firm. Five minutes later the craft settled down on the helipad.

The full extent of the complex became obvious after the party set foot on the ground. Immediately ahead were protruding water towers, customary to an isolated facility such as this. Generating water pressure to several underground reservoirs, they were necessary to supply close to a thousand inhabitants with fresh water. Carried by a slight breeze from the sewage treatment plant nearby, also noticeable was the smell of methane. Security was intense. Despite immediate recognition, even the president had to submit to a credential inspection. Escorted by heavy security, the party was hastily let below. A few paces later they entered an underground city comparable, perhaps even more extensive, to the NORAD complex. Aside from a modern operations center housing the most sophisticated communications equipment, the complex contained an array of living quarters and dormitories, cafeteria and hospital, a water purification system, power plant and general office buildings.

The primary function for this facility, under peacetime conditions, was to play out political and military simulation games. Today, it became the nation's most important crisis management center. Essential to the center was immediate access to information. In case of a potential communication meltdown, such as the nation was facing presently, backed up and archived on thousands of data storage banks were kept the nation's and civilians' most critical records.

As soon as George Wilmot entered the OPS center, he demanded, "What have we got?"

"Satellite's out," the chief of staff informed the president. "Whole damned network."

CASTLE ROCK

They were propped against the rail of the deck watching the tail lights disappear into the valley. "Thanks for staying," Tracy whispered. Despite the looming threat, she felt safe with Brian by her side. "Hope nothing happens to him." Although she knew her dad's strength and drive, it was her prerogative to worry.

"He can look out for himself." Brian tried to pacify her concerns. He knew his buddy's capabilities. He'd always admired him for it. After all, he was an adventurer at heart. It was getting chilly out on the deck.

"I'm really worried about Liz and the kids." She slightly trembled despite the warmth generated by his body.

"They'll be fine." Feeling compassionate, he thought, *what else can I say?*

Enjoying the feel of intimacy, they were quiet for a while.

He broke the silence first. "Sure could use a drink." Brian felt some brandy would calm her nerves. "Think he'd mind?"

"Not at all." She felt something warm would drive the chills from her body. "I'll get some." She pulled him inside and closed the balcony doors. "Have a seat."

He was comfortably resting on the sofa when she returned a few minutes later with the drinks along with some snacks balanced on a serving tray. "Here." Handing over a glass she sat next to him. "Cheers," she toasted. "Think it's serious—the blackout?"

"Could be—depends on how people react."

"Only takes a small trigger to create panic," she agreed.

"This is different from war." Brian's voice echoed her concern.

"Why's that?"

"Nation at war," he rationalized, "people will help each other. Not sure how they'll behave here."

"Suppose so."

"We could have many localized pockets fighting for dominance. Remember what happens at riots—people shooting and looting."

"Don't remind me," she agreed, "bad scenes."

"Could happen here." He shifted his body to face her. "We should be safe here."

"Hope so."

"Your dad made provisions for just such a possibility," he told her, "but only for the immediate family…didn't know the neighbors." To emphasize what he'd just pointed out, he tugged on her arm and gestured for her to follow.

He led her to the underground shelter. "Last time I was here, he showed me his gun collection." Hidden behind a family portrait, Brian knew where to locate the keys to the cabinets. He strode over to fetch them. "Here." A quick turn unlatched the cabinet door.

"Wow." She was awestruck. There, placed on the shelves, was an assortment of handguns of various calibers. She made out target pistols, revolvers, semi-automatics, and more sophisticated automatic weaponry. Some she recognized, others looked more like things from the future. Also neatly tugged away were throwing knives, daggers, and machetes. She fingered some. They held a distant familiarity. "From his martial arts days."

"I was just as impressed," Brian agreed, picking out several of the weapons. He handed her a .45 semi. "Know how to handle this?" He tugged a Beretta, compact model

PX-4, into his own belt. Primed with confidence, he reached for a couple boxes of fitting ammo. "Think we're prepared?"

Minutes later, they were back comfortably seated on the living room couch. She poured him another drink. It had its effects on his body. She caught him trying to suppress a yawn. "Getting tired," he indicated with an excusing smile.

"Me too." She propped up her feet. "You take the guest room," she offered, "I'll get some towels."

He followed her down the hall then stepped inside the room. *What a day.* He wished it'd turned out differently. *Here I am with a beautiful woman, but have to worry about intruders.* Looking tired, she came back with a stack of towels balanced between her hands. "Guess you're ready for bed too?"

She gave him a peck on the cheek. "See you in the morning." The guest room door closed behind her. *Would have liked to spend more time with him,* she told herself, *but there's always tomorrow.* Back in the quiet of the living room, she suddenly felt sleepy herself. *Guess I'll hit the hay.* Several minutes later she was sound asleep.

Quickly getting undressed, Brian flopped on the guest bed. His tired mind tried to recount the day's events. They were too blurry. It only took minutes for him to find sleep.

Tracy didn't know how much time had passed since she fell asleep. She woke up startled from a persistent banging. It took her seconds to realize it came from the front door. *Liz,* was her first thought. Hurrying from the warmth of the couch, on the way out, she grabbed a housecoat from the closet. Pulling it tight around the waist she rushed downstairs. There, she lingered a moment by the front door. She could hear voices. Muffled sounds seeped through the solid wood.

Expecting Liz she called out, "Who is it?" No one answered. "Who is it?" she called out a second time. She hesitated a moment then slowly turned the lock. It unbolted with a snap. Anticipating her sister and kids, she opened the door. To her surprise, emerging from the recesses of the dark, she came face to face with two uniformed men. They looked official. They were flashing badges. "DOD," it said on their IDs, identifying them as agents.

Face set in a courteous smile, one said, "Excuse us." A stint of concern crossed her weary mind but dissipated as quickly as it had set on. *Anything can happen on a night like this.*

"This is the Bauer residence?"

"Maybe..." She hesitated then thought better. "If you want Alex, he just left. What do you want?"

"You Tracy?" the second man asked.

"Yes." They knew her name. Still guarded, she wondered, *How dangerous could it be?*

"In that case," the spokesperson demanded, "you'll come with us."

She was confused. "What did I do?" Their demeanors changed in an instant. Their faces took on a mask of menace. One lifted from his holster what she made out to be a Glock-29.

"What do you want from me?" she yelled out. Greatly alarmed, she quickly retreated back inside. It was too late. She didn't move fast enough. They jumped her from both sides. She struggled. It was of no use. Tightly gripped around her waist and arms, they overpowered her. One forced her forehead back with one hand, the other pressed a soaked cloth over her mouth and nose. She identified the smell, *Ether,* and panicked. There was only one reason for the ether, abduction. "Help...help me." Her muffled cries went unheard. She tried to struggle free, but instead, watched the world rapidly turn black. She whimpered into unconsciousness.

"Let's get the hell out of here," one agent said. They lifted her limp body into a waiting limo. Gunning the engine, the driver sped off into the dark.

Upstairs, in the guest room, aware of noises coming from below, Brian briefly woke. Undecided, he lay there not knowing whether it was a dream or if Tracy's sister finally had arrived. He hoped she had. Since it had turned quiet below, his foggy mind assumed it was their arrival and promptly dozed off again.

SHAPE COMMAND HQs (Belgium)

In the early morning hours, ever since the airwaves over the Northern United States had gone silent, SHAPE[42], the central command NATO military forces Europe, was in a state of high alert. Being eight hours ahead of Washington, D.C., a new dawn in Europe had already broken when the EMP strike occurred over the north American continent.

It wasn't often that Emmett W. Fletcher, four-star general, flag officer, U.S. European command, was called to action so early in the morning. A man of his statue, commanding all of Europe's armed forces, had certain privileges and obligations bestowed, most of which were diplomatic functions. Sought as most powerful functionary representing not only the United States of America, but the Netherlands, U.K., Germany, Belgium, Turkey, Spain, France, and Italy as well, his function on the European continent was all-encompassing.

SHAPE, NATO's principle command, historically dated back to the WWII postwar era, in keeping up with political and global changes, and was initially directed by Dwight D. Eisenhower, with Field Marshall B. Montgomery instated by the North Atlantic Council in 1950, as Deputy. SACEURO[43] was created. Since then, in recent years, a new NATO force structure had been created and transformed from a once military entity to a reorganized power unequaled in Europe. Capable of rapid deployment, through its High Readiness Forces, NATO's missions not only included peacekeeping and international security, but combating transatlantic terrorism as well.

Fletcher, unceremoniously shaken from a well deserving sleep following another long night's social event, wasn't the happiest man. Arriving at the HQs, he was faced with a beehive of activities, most of them pending his decisions. Taking a brief glance at the stack of communiqué, he ordered, "Get Izmir, Naples, and Madrid on the phone. And...see if you can raise USSOUTHCOM[44]." Although Fletcher had the entire European continent in his command, he rarely made a decision without his principle ally, the United States, but today, he was on his own. The Pentagon did not respond to any of his queries.

Contemplating what steps to take next, Fletcher ordered the secretary, "Conference, twenty minutes." To inform his commanders on such short notice was highly unusual. Today, with the entire U.S. continent out of reach, nothing made much sense. It gave him enough time to develop a strategy.

Twenty minutes later, according to schedule, notepad in hand, he marched into the conference room. Taking a firm stand on the pedestal, he faced his subordinates, whoever had shown up on such short notice. Fletcher grimly faced the audience.

"This is what we have," he began, checking the notepad items he'd jotted down. Without interruptions, other than taking note of late arrivals, he relayed his personal memorandum into action items. Given the highest priorities for establishing communication, he ordered his commanders, "Embassies—get in contact with Moscow, Beijing, South Korea, India, and Singapore." Taking a few seconds to collect his

---

[42] Supreme Headquarters Allied Powers Europe.
[43] Supreme Allied Command Europe.
[44] U.S. Southern Command, Headquartered at Miami, FL.

thoughts, he added, "I want high alerts go out to CINCLANT[45] 2nd, 4th, 5th, 6th, and 7th Fleets." He initiated, "Already informed the 4th." The configurations he'd just listed, he thought, *should take care of most of the waters*. Broken into task forces, it stood for the following:

Second Fleet, assigned to the Atlantic theater, had operational responsibilities from the North Pole to the South Pole and from the shores of the United States to the Mediterranean.

Fourth Fleet, responsible for U.S. ships, aircraft, and submarines operating in the U.S. SOUTHCOM area, encompassed the Caribbean, and Central and South America and their surrounding waters. Its primary mission in recent years had been to direct counter-illicit trafficking, shore security, and bilateral and multinational training.

Fifth Fleet, assigned to the Middle East, had responsibilities including the Arabian Sea, Gulf of Aden, Gulf of Oman, and the Red Sea.

Sixth Fleet, assigned to the Mediterranean, was the major operational component of Naval Forces Europe. The principal striking power of the Sixth Fleet resided in its aircraft carriers and modern jet aircraft, its submarines, and its reinforced battalion of U.S. Marines on board amphibious ships.

Seventh Fleet, established in 1943 to combat the advancing Pacific forces in WWII, was the largest fleet with 60 ships, 350 combat aircraft, and 60,000 Marine Corps personnel. Many of the ships operated from Pacific-based island locations such as Guam and Japan.

Commander Fletcher, today, caught in the midst of a massive communication blackout over the North American continent, it seemed, had his mission cut out for him. Rather than playing political figurehead as usual for SHAPE, he was forced to command what to his sphere of operating theater, for all practical purposes, was as of yet an unidentified, invisible enemy.

---

[45] Commander in Chief Atlantic.

PALM JUMEIRAH

Another day had just broken. An early riser, the Serpent stepped from the shower and took the few paces to the washbasin to fetch a fresh bath towel from the rack. He lingered on in the luxury of the bathroom. Like the rest of the mansion, there was lavishness everywhere. His thoughts briefly touched on the harsh life he and most of his brethren had endured. "You better," an inner voice reminding him, "keep the dream alive." It was, after all, his dream. It was he that made it possible. Thinking back, it seemed a lifetime, but the dream had turned into reality. All he had to do is execute it. *Just like Hitler, Stalin, and more recently, Saddam Hussein, with one difference.* A furtive grin crossed his face. *I'm going to live to enjoy it.*

Preparing to shave, the mirror held his reflection. He looked at a well-developed body and was proud of it. He paused a few seconds then grabbed a bathrobe and moved on to the living room. His gaze caught the laptop computer carelessly tossed by the coffee table the evening before. The world was waiting for his next command.

For the first time in as long as he could remember, he felt a sense of freedom. The morning air touched his skin. The distant sound of waves across the breakwaters beckoned him. He dropped the bathrobe and took the few paces towards the fashionably designed wooden deck. It was lofty up here, to say the least. As soon as he stepped on deck he felt the full breeze. It came sweeping in from the expanses of the gulf. It brought with it the first warmth of day, as every day did in this tropical place. *Does it ever rain? Suppose not. After all,* he dwelled, *it's still a desert.*

Dressed only in briefs now, his skin had dried in just a few seconds. The sunrays felt just as great. In the distance, his gaze caught a few sailors expertly handling their craft cutting in and out the sandy channels. "Must get one," he muttered. "I could get used to this," he marveled. "What am I thinking? This *is* my life." And a paradise it was. It would come to be his sanctuary. A private abode, removed from the havoc he was about to unleash. Here, he'd be safe. The place was far enough removed to the south to be unaffected, for whatever may happen. "Lucky bastard," he thought of himself, thankful for this marvelously designed tropical paradise. It would be the seat of his reign. He would be ruler, the "Ruler of Nations."

A light breakfast was waiting at the table when he stepped inside. He savored a few bites of dates, fruits, and orange juice prepared by his house staff. Neatly folded by the table, his gaze fell on the daily news front page headlines.

Yesterday late, extending through the entire northern reaches of the continent, the United States experienced a massive blackout.

Newscasters and political analysts went on to describe the current state of the nation, speculating on the source of the event, projecting the immediate impact it would have on trade and economics. *At this time,* the story went on; *only fragments of news are available.* It was the information he needed. It brought him back to the present. Pressing actions were pending. He reached for the mobile to dial a number.

"Trans-World Global," the operator announced in perfect English.

"McAllister." He could have delegated the task to one of his commanders, but thought it better to handle it himself. There was no room for slipups. There was no slack built into the Plan. Time was the critical element. So far, there had been no errors. And he made sure there wouldn't be any.

"McAllister," a voice responded seconds later.

"Shahadah," he identified himself. "What's the status with the craft?"

"Ready as scheduled." The reply was firm.

"Range?"

"Five thousand-plus nautical miles."

He quickly calculated the flight path the craft was supposed to carry. *That'll do.* He needed assurance the purchase was safe. "Traceability?"

"None," the voice slightly wavered, "almost."

There it was again. He hated the word. "Almost doesn't count," he fired back. "I need a guarantee." It was essential the craft could not be traced to him, at least, not until after the event. What happened afterwards would be academic. "Crew?"

"Will have to get back to you."

"Cockpit only." He was getting frustrated. He had no tolerance for incompetence.

"Yes, sir."

The A-330 Airbus was the most efficient craft for his purpose. The order had been placed some months ago. Delivery was delayed again and again. He did not have the luxury of time. He needed the craft now. To make it happen, he had to grease many palms to rush the purchase through. The craft was only needed for one mission.

Airbus had become so popular with recent travel that the Hamburg-based manufacturer fell behind schedule. The promised new A-380 and A-400 supercargo models had been delayed until next year. He'd been forced to purchase the A-330 but not without challenges. The craft's markings had to be altered. Registration and delivery route needed changing. To cover up all traces, there was third party on top of third party.

The order had been handled from the Caymans via the London office, with eventual delivery for the craft out of France. Unfortunately, a purchase had been more difficult than a lease. It left a paper trail he couldn't afford. So far, as luck had it, his office had not received any inquiries from the despicable ITC commission. *Good sign,* he reasoned. The craft had been registered for cargo. Regulations were less stringent there. He wasn't interested in the number of passengers it could carry. The only thing that mattered was cargo space.

"No records available on the purchase." McAllister called back within the hour. "Checked it out myself."

"Have it ready for delivery." *Click.* He turned the mobile off.

PETERSON AIR FORCE BASE

The Mountain, was his first thought, but when Alex spotted the stranded vehicles up ahead, he quickly decided against it. *Gate's probably locked tight.* The trouble started as soon as he headed for I-25 southbound. He eased off on the pedal. They'd partially blocked the on-ramp. They saw him come. Stranded vehicles were everywhere. *Careful,* he cautioned himself. *If this is what to expect, I don't want to be around when the mob hits.* People were banging on the vehicle. Foot on the pedal, he kept pushing on. They were chasing after him. They tried to get answers. "Hey…what the hell…come back here…give us a lift, jerk…"

Probably can't figure why my wheels are still running. This could get ugly. Disabled vehicles lined the road as far as he could make out. Fortunately, traffic wasn't heavy when the blast hit. It appeared driver and passenger-formed clusters had turned into mobs. One ahead rushed up. They blocked the road. He'd been boxed in. Banging on the side, someone yelled, "Open up." He ignored their demands. Cautiously, he bent over to reach under the front seat. His fingers fumbled for an object. *There it is.* The cool shape of steel felt comforting in his hand. On the way out he'd stopped in the basement to collect his favorite weapon, a revolver, the .357 long barrel. Thankful for his foresight, he deliberately pulled it from under the seat. His eyes were on the mob. Placing the weapon on the center console in plain view, his move was calculated. It paid off. The crowd backed away from the vehicle. He inched the Wagoneer forward, out of the jam, then gunned the engine.

Feeling relatively safe in the Wagoneer, Alex kept up the speed. At times, he had to weave in and out between disabled cars. He gave the traffic ahead ample warning. Lights flashing and horn blasting, people ran clear. He couldn't help but feel sorry for the stranded. There was nothing he could do without putting himself in jeopardy. He kept on pushing south toward Pete Field.

Without streetlights, the route looked eerie in the depth of night. Shadows crept up ahead, he'd never noticed, passing off to both sides of the piercing headlights. Where there should have been fueling stations and street lighting brightly illuminating the path, he could make out nothing but deep darkness. Once he turned onto Route 24 east, it turned even more sinister. It took another ten minutes to get to the gate entrance. Two armed guards appeared from the darkness of the shack. Staring at the barrels of M-16 automatics, he slammed on the brakes. "What's the rush?" one sentry asked menacingly.

"Isn't it obvious?" Alex sounded off.

"Nobody gets in."

"Need to speak with base command." Alex was annoyed at the guards barring the entrance. He was on edge.

"ID." He watched the sentry edge towards the window. Obviously, he'd spotted the firearm by Alex's side. The sentry's knuckles tightened around the barrel stock. "What's this?" He nodded at the seat.

"What's it look like?"

"Wise guy, eh?" Taking a step backwards the sentry shouted, "Step out!" His motion was emphasized by the automatic. Alex's eyes darted from sentry to sentry. *Act of intimidation.* He knew they followed procedures and the next would be shoot to kill. He eased his frame from the vehicle and handed over his identification. "Here."

He felt reluctant to submit his DOD credentials. He wasn't about to let go of his lifeline with the organization. It'd been known for some hasty sentry to confiscate an ID. His eyes closely followed the guard. *Phones must be out,* Alex deducted. They normally checked in with HQs to verify with the database. The sentries stepped off to the side. He heard them mutter.

He gestured several times, denoting his urgency. It proved useless to convince the wiry MPs. Finally, after minutes on hold, they waved him on with a warning. "Stay on track."

His nerves were agitated by the delay. When he finally arrived at the command center building, to his dismay, he encountered a similar situation to the one he'd just left. The entrance was barricaded by heavily armed military police.

Critical mission personnel had arrived almost continuously. After power and phones failed, many headed for base. Some came on bikes, others rushed on foot. There were even a couple skaters. People needed answers. They knew it'd be the only place that could provide some security in case it'd turn into a national emergency. Many officers were accompanied by family members. Some were turned away, especially the lower ranking soldiers.

It appeared all electronic systems were out, including emergency and security. After minutes of deliberation and convincing, Alex finally gained entrance to the building. As soon as he stepped inside, he noticed command and control in a state of emergency. At this point, everybody was speculating.

Currently he sought out the commander in charge. It was still unclear who that may be. Several present recognized him from years of association with defense projects. He was approached with, "What brings you here?"

"Have an idea," he volunteered.

"Yeah? Speak up, man."

He took a stand. Alex tried to get people's attention. "Any senior commanders present?" Because many had showed up in civilian clothes, Alex could not recognize rank. Many had no candles on hand dressing in the dark.

"That'd be me." A stern-faced personage pushed his body forward. "Diego Martinez, "Commander—Space Surveillance.""

PALM JUMEIRAH

Growing more impatient by the minute, the Serpent sat and waited. His eyes shot a glance at his wristwatch. The infrequent motion gave away the present state he felt. He'd expected something by now. *Where is the call?* There wasn't much he could do but wait. *Or is there?* He took the wait to recapture each and every step of the past days he had carried out to assure nothing was missed. Finally, after his emergence from a life in obscurity, he came a long way in just a short time. *How long ago? More than a decade.*

Where most recruits found themselves in the front lines, he'd worked out of tactical command centers. In support of its missions, all for the same cause, "Islam," Jihad had created many cells worldwide. Unfortunately, some had recently been exposed in various countries, mostly Europe. It'd been a warning call. *Our strategy must be altered,* he kept insisting. Nobody paid much attention until comrades began to disappear at alarming rates. It was not until he submitted a draft plan to the supreme leader and his inner circle of advisors that they'd paid attention. They finally had taken notice of him.

Being an avid history buff, he could see certain parallels between the cause of jihad and those of other nations. *Mein Kampf,* spelling out guiding principles by the not-too-distant ruler Adolph Hitler, and his own subjugation with years of oppression was not that different.

To prevent such grave repeats, self-serving cells were structured all around the globe. The results were clusters of well-trained recruits specialized in the various skills to support a network of independent fighters. Cells were purposely kept small not to attract attention. While keeping financial support and logistics obscured, small groups could be managed effectively for tactical movements. That way, no large support or monetary transaction from sympathetic sponsors was necessary to inadvertently alert the ever-present tentacles of intelligence.

Where's that call? He was losing patience. He wanted the world to know he meant business and the sooner the better. It was time to reveal himself to the world, who he was. He'd worked hard to get to this point. *The time is now.*

Impatiently pacing the floor, waiting for the call, he mentally catalogued the current infrastructure and forces at his disposal. Fortunately, cells in the United States were still operating undetected. Aside from a structured independence, one cell was responsible for coordinating schedules and support locations. Another was for tactical operations and more, for reporting mission results. Most consisted of groups of trained mercenaries disguised as ex-servicemen living in the U.S. Many had been there for years. One cell in particular was of utmost importance. Dormant for many years, it operated out of New York. It was this cell, Cell Alpha, currently dispatched to the central region of the U.S. that he was awaiting the call from. The dispatch would assure him that the odds would fall and remain in his favor. The action plan called for taking hostages. Not just the ordinary hostage. It was individuals of prominence detrimental to the U.S. government. They were individuals potentially damaging to the successful outcome of The Plan.

Hostile cells located in the U.S. were nothing new. With the onset of the Cold War, Soviet cells on American soil had been prolific. Whereas some had been exposed, others were recalled, and more remained dormant. Spies, they were called...Embassy Staff.

The political climate back then was different. Terrorism had not been an agenda. The focus was purely on intelligence work and spying across borders. It was not only the

United States against the Soviet Union; all nations did it. It was a necessity—a necessary evil. Although kept predominantly obscured, it provided each nation with political leverage. The more one knew about the others, the better one could be prepared to secure the nation. It served one purpose—and one purpose only, protecting national wealth. But that came with a high price tag and sometimes with embarrassment and humiliation.

With the end of the Cold War, the political climate changed. The ambience moved from strategic to tactical. Suddenly, hostile cells proliferated, with roots based mostly in Islamic-friendly nations. Modern terrorism was born. The United States and other nations of the free world were being infiltrated, subtly at first, then more prolifically with time. It all happened while the global economy was thriving. Wealth began to spread through many repressed nations. In turn, cultural changes took hold, severely affecting secular factions. The results became very visible. Anti-sentiments grew. Plots were contrived resulting in damages and casualties. The modern world suddenly became unstable. It was a world we learned to accept. Just as with crime, terrorism was here to stay. Operating beneath the fabric of society, cells germinated everywhere. There, they stayed until called into action. Such was the present state.

Still pacing the floor, the waiting became intolerable. The Serpent desperately needed confirmation. He needed confirmation on the satellite status, as well as the pending missile launch. He was fidgeting with his mobile. His fingers were flipping its cover, open—close, open—close. Every few seconds he redialed Yusuf's number. *Nothing.*

Other than the rustling of wind gusts sweeping across the deck, it was the only sound in his space. He grew more restless by the minute. He became aware of the clapping of the cover and stopped his involuntary action with a shrug. He had initiated the blackout. It had been on his orders. He could not afford any compromises by calling around the globe. So he waited.

Another hour went by. He could not contain himself any longer. He dialed the mission center for New York. "Nothing?" No connecting sound. He was dumbfounded at first but quickly recovered. To be certain, he redialed. Again, the same result. It suddenly dawned on him. With a smacking sound he slapped his forehead. "How stupid—of course!" he exclaimed. "Satellite's out." *What else could it be?* The mission was under way. That was the signal. "No signal." He suddenly felt elated.

"The battle has begun." He'd taken the war into space. The waiting was over. He jumped to his feet and headed for the pantry. There, he opened the cupboard and select a packet from an assortment of tea. "Time to celebrate." He poured himself a cup of the finest tea from Sri Lanka that he'd saved for just such an occasion. Taking the first sip, a feeling of heightened greatness surged through his body. It was the feeling of control. It was the feeling of power. He had just elevated himself to supreme leader, leader of the new world order. The balance of power had shifted. It had shifted from the capitalistic power brokers to a new faction, Islam. The Serpent was contemplating his next move. The initial phase of The Plan had been set in motion. It was up to the cells to carry it out. His present concentration was focused on the United States of America. Forces on the eastern seaboard, the central plains, and Pacific Northwest had been activated. Others would soon follow.

PETERSON AIR FORCE BASE

The casuals people wore washed into the gray of the surroundings in the semi-darkness of the command center. Gaunt faces everywhere projected shadows against the walls. He could read it in their expressions: *Who's this guy giving orders?* Alex was an outsider. Most people here did not recognize him. Facing Alex, the brigadier projected his usual commanding posture. "What have you got in mind?"

"Let me shed some light." Alex conveyed his theory about the possible cause for the blackout. He also conveyed the potential threat of a secondary attack. His could see the general's tension mount.

"How'd you know?" he fired back at Alex.

"I've got monitors." Alex didn't want to disclose more than was necessary. Much of what he was doing in the privacy of the Castle was classified. People didn't have to know. He was reporting only to Foster, his personal contact at the Pentagon.

"So does NORAD."

"Can't get word out," Alex gloated, "can you? Billion dollars' worth of receiver farm sitting on top of the Mountain…gate's shut tight…transmitters are down…no phones."

"What are you," the general huffed, "wise guy?"

"Let's be realistic," Alex suggested. "What've we got?" In a few short sentences, Alex played out his theory.

"You're nuts!" the brigadier shouted. An assault on the United States infrastructure, communication, power, and otherwise seemed impossible to the man. "No nation's that crazy."

With more and more people pushing their way in by the minute, the center had become packed. Many disregarded the "No Smoking" policy. It didn't matter. It helped calm the nerves. The smoke had already permeated into his sinuses. Alex had to sneeze. "Excuse me." The smoke burned his eyes. Conditions like these wore at his tolerance, but he had to make concessions. After all, it wasn't his space.

Angered by Alex and his insanity, the brigadier spun around to face the crowd. "Any word?" He seemed desperate for action. "Any contact with other commands yet?"

"Nothing," his deputy replied in the negative. "All lines are dead."

"For all practical purposes," Alex spoke up, "you're on our own until…" He did not finish the sentence. There was a sudden change in the atmosphere. It came in the form of a flash. Not the lighting kind, but one causing as much turmoil. It was a flash message, more specifically, an EAM. The message panel had sprung into action. It was fed by buried landlines. Pre-satellite cables, not used for decades, had picked up the signals. The EMP had triggered the alert and status boards. Pulsating red lights amid an insanely sounding alarm were flashing across the many faces. They were stunned faces at first, but quickly turned chaotic. All eyes in the room, fixated on the display panel, shot to the source of the alerts, waiting. Then it came, boldfaced text scrolling letter by letter:

"EMERGENCY ACTION MESSAGE…TRAJECTORY SOURCE PYONGYANG, (NORTH KOREA) 39° 2'N - 125° 41'E…TRAJECTORY TARGET SAN FRANCISCO, (CALIFORNIA) 37° 37'N - 122° 23'W…OBJECT IDENTITY ICBM TYPE TAEPODONG…ESTIMATED TIME OF IMPACT…40 MINUTES…"

The initial shock on the faces deepened. They were followed by outcries. "I have family there…my sister…cousins"—the natural reaction of worry about loved ones.

"Quiet, everybody…listen up, people!" the general boomed in his commanding voice. He was waving a half-chewed up cigar in front of Alex. It gave off a stale smell. Alex gagged but quickly composed himself.

Despite periodic attack drills in the past, nobody was prepared for this. It has always been, "We'll deal with it when the time comes," hoping it never would. Today was the day. The minutes were ticking away rapidly.

Alex felt for the people. He wasn't completely surprised. He'd watched people react in crisis situations before. They did better one-on-one. Here, they had to rely on electronics in a condition that nobody knew. On top of that, it wasn't up to him to respond to a national crisis situation. He wasn't in charge. That was up to the commanders. They got trained to think for emergencies. They were conditioned. It didn't stop here. In case of an attack, the buck could always be passed up the chain of command all the way to JCS and the president. They were the ultimate decision makers. But today, they were out of reach. No communication with the other commands or the White House could be established. At this point, nobody in the nation knew if or when the next attack would come. Any spot in the nation was vulnerable from another incoming ICBM. For all practical purposes, all missile silos were targets, including the Mountain. Alex knew he had to take out the source of the attack.

Today, the crisis was localized to each unit. Maintenance techs, struggling on both ends of the spectrum, were trying to get something working. Anything! It wasn't easy without ready spares on hand. They were destroyed with the rest of the electronics. Alternatives were suggested, but that would take time. It suddenly dawned on him. "HAM," Alex called out, "anybody?" Logistics personnel acted immediately. They jumped into action. Alex saw them head off to scrounge for gear, hoping there was any left in this complex.

"Thirty minutes to impact." It was the automated voice recording announcing the impact time. Alex stepped away from the crowd. He needed a quiet spot. He had to think. There was still time. His mind was churning. *Think,* his consciousness yelled. *Got to be something I can do.* It came to him in a flash. His hands shot up toward his head. He smacked both sides of his temples. "That's it." He quickly sought out the brigadier. "Got something!"

"Shoot." There was a hint of hope in the brigadier's voice.

"Uh…got a plan," Alex urged, "but need your help."

"You got it."

"We don't know the status of our missile bases." Alex plainly stated the fact. "We don't know the conditions of our defenses. There's no word from the national command center, or the White House. Nobody can get word out because of the blackout."

"Man," the brigadier was stomping the floor, "get to the point."

If there was a glimmer of hope, Alex needed to act fast. "I need access to the base armory."

"What for?"

"Years ago," Alex explained, "I built a portable missile case. It can launch."

"What do you mean?" The brigadier's face lit up with new hope.

"I can launch the missiles remotely."

"Get to it," the brigadier ordered, "and," he gestured at his deputy, "take them with you." He snapped his fingers at some sentries. "You…you…go with him."

Hopping into a military jeep, they had to jump-start the vehicle. Two sentries pushed with the driver kicking the clutch the old fashion way. But it worked. The engine turned over after a few sputters. Alex sat next to the driver, flanked by the guards. Seconds later they were off to the armory. The wheels squealed on the tarmac, leaving black tire marks on the way. The driver was headed for the munitions bunker. It was clear across base. Minutes later, mounds of raised bunker clusters ahead came into view.

Moments later the vehicle skidded to a halt. A guard unlocked the heavy steel-gated armory. The place was dowsed in darkness. Someone fetched a flashlight from the jeep. Alex was already inside, joining in with the search. "Look for an aluminum case," he yelled, "should be two." It took only minutes before someone shouted, "Got something."

Alex watched him pull up the silver-coated case labeled in large bold lettering, "PEACEKEEPER." He recognized the case immediately. "The other one," he shouted. "I need the "MINUTEMAN."

The peacekeeper, he'd decided, was too compound a system. With its multiple warheads, it was much more complex. He grabbed the case, hopped back into the jeep and rushed back to SPADOC command. Arriving, he tossed the case on an empty floor space. Somebody plugged the AC adapter into an empty outlet fed by the emergency generator. Not completely understanding what would develop next, curious eyes were staring at Alex. The room was packed. There it was again! The automated voice announced, "Ten minutes to impact."

Alex shot a glance at the world clocks mounted against the wall. *There's still time.* It was no coincidence the clocks still worked. They weren't just kept for nostalgic reasons. The command had retained the old style, manual controlled, round faced clocks popular for so many years. They would, and had, withstood the EMP surge.

"Wish I had a display screen," Alex puffed. A monitor would trace the path and timeline from start to impact. Although it'd taken close to twenty minutes to get the case, connect the interface, and prepare for launch, he boasted, "Not bad timing, eh?" Ten more minutes left to launch. If he wasn't able to take out the source of the attack, they could all be doomed.

Alex stooped over the opened case. He was undecided. He had designed the case with its complex controls but couldn't remember the launch sequence. "Checklist!" He needed the checklist. He had to override all automated procedures with manual action codes. Frantically, he unlatched and lifted the control panel to get inside the electronics. He lucked out. There it was, amid the bundles of wires, transmitters, and relays, the Bible of destruction—the "Doomsday List."

Alex slammed the panel back in its case then expertly fingered the control switches and knobs. He had to be sure they were functional. He assumed most radio receivers were out in the missile grid, but hoped the surface antennas from the LCF[46] were still intact. He briefly poised over the panel. "This is it." Anticipating faces were watching him. He flipped the power switch. There was a definite hum. "Great!" There were cheers and applauses. Alex felt like he was being crowded. People were craning over his shoulders to get a better view. He could feel the pressure poking him in his back. Someone stepped on his leg. He turned around. "People," he demanded, "give me space."

His eyes flew over the checklist. Long held dormant information came back to him. He remembered. He had chosen Warren AB because it was closest to home. Only a hundred seventy-five miles up the road, near Cheyenne, WY, the transmitters should

---

[46] Launch Control Facility - Underground command center connected to remote missile silos.

reach the base. He threw the LF-7 switch into the ON position. Months ago, due to mounting political pressures, Launch Facility-7's guidance system had been programmed for Pyongyang. If that didn't work, several launch options were available from other bases, but that took time. Missiles would have to be retargeted. The incoming missile would have detonated long before.

"How do we know it'll work?" the commander worried. He shot a glance at the wall clocks. "Time's running out."

"We don't," Alex confirmed. "Only got one shot." There would be no interaction with the launch tube. It was a one-way command string, one last act in desperation. That's the way EAM worked. Failsafe! No human interaction. No confirmation. "All we can hope for is that the missile technicians are on alert." They were the ready force. Alex was the ultimate trigger.

Because he seemed to be the one with answers, Alex had been given full control. Mission personnel were crowding him, speculating. They'd heard of the launch case, but had never seen one. An officer pushed forward. He'd identified himself. "Missile Action Officer. Need a launch code!" He was adamant.

"Not this time," Alex responded. He sensed an immediate reluctance. He hoped the man's action wouldn't wind up in a standoff. He stared the officer down with all the defiance he could muster up.

"Wait," the officer demanded another delay, "only the president can give the order."

"Not today!" Alex was furious at the unexpected delay. "The reason the case's been built," he replied, "was for an emergency like now…override the system."

"What if you're wrong?" More objections, more delays.

Alex shot one last glance at the clocks. He had to activate. Time was getting really critical. Once the incoming missile detonated, there was no telling how it would affect the launch.

The brigadier quickly intervened. "I take full responsibility." He practically spat the words at the officer.

"You're the better man." Reluctantly, the Missileer backed down. He took a step back.

"Time will tell. We ready?" Alex insisted.

The brigadier nodded in final confirmation. "Let's do it. Hope the missile crew's on alert."

Alex knew missile crews. He also knew their behavior. They followed orders. They were on constant alert. It was their job. "They'll know."

"How do you know?" someone asked. *Another idle concern.*

"It's in SIOP." Alex tried to explain but thought otherwise. *Not now.* He pushed the button. It was impossible to authenticate the EAM. The current state of blackout was enough to shoot for immediate retaliation. "Hope to God my assumption's right," he whispered. There was no reaction. It was a silent launch. Immediate disappointment reflected off the many faces. Alex stood up. "What did you expect?"

"It didn't work!" someone yelled out, terrified.

Alex remained passive. "Action's on the other end." After a brief pause he urged the brigadier, "Send a team to Warren! We need confirmation."

"Will do." The general did as suggested. "Get a team up there."

For now, there was nothing more that could be done. Not even waiting around would help relieve tension and anxieties. On the Pacific coast, for better or for worse, people were on their own. There was no way knowing if the hostile missile had detonated. They'd have to wait until some comm link was established with the west. HAM operators would be the first to report. Alex decided to leave. "Gotta take care of personal matters," he informed the brigadier, but promised to be back. With a quick salute, and a "Thanks for the help," he turned to exit, hoping to make it back to Castle Rock without incidence.

Squinting, he stepped outside. It was daylight already. Rubbing a hand over his face, he could feel beard stubble scraping against his skin. Back on the road, the long lines of stranded vehicles on I-24 and I-25 were slowly thinning out. Assisted by the drivers, mechanics had already started to work under the hoods. He caught school busses farther up the road. They were packed with passengers headed for town. *Somebody's got the right idea.* "School buses, huh." *Simple means of transport still work.*

NAPA VALLEY

Annette stepped through the front door. She needed to check on the present environment hoping today would be more promising. It wasn't. The eerie quiet after yesterday's power outage that befell Napa Valley was still prevalent. It promised to be another bright sunny day. Even this early in the morning, the skies were clear and blue. On the distant horizon to the west there was the usual checkerboard pattern blotting out the blue. A mystery to the local populace, most times the pattern appeared without a visible source. It'd been like this for years. Daily weather reports didn't even report it, or they just completely ignored the phenomenon. Either way, people had gotten used to it. This was California, fast-paced, multi-cultural, carefree-spirited, supported by forty million residents, all seeking a slice of comfort in life. Except for those darned checkerboards, today was as beautiful as any other. What did they call it? Chemtrails.

With Liz and the kids' gone visiting Colorado, Annette felt deserted and lonely. Her life had been dedicated solely to bringing up first the daughters, then, in recent years, the grandkids. Divorcing Alex had left a deep scar. It couldn't be helped. After ten years of marriage she'd finally gotten tired of waiting. "Although," she reflected in the quiet of the home, "he'd been a great dad, a righteous man, and a tending husband, whenever he was home, but," she thought with deep regrets, "he'd been gone too many times."

For the children's sake, and her needs, he'd been, and still was, a stranger. To this day, she still had no clue what he did for a career. He never talked about it. She brought up the subject on several occasions, but not once would he reveal his job, or confide about his travels. He was always off to some foreign land somewhere in Europe or Asia. "Gov business," he'd short circuit the subject, "can't talk about." It gnawed on her because she was aware of the illicit pleasures those places could offer a foreigner, especially when one had money to spend. She deliberated long and hard on those lonely nights before making the difficult decision. She had finally had enough. But that was many years ago. This morning, she wished they were a family.

Annette recalled the events from yesterday. She was an early riser. Her plan for the day was organizing the kid's rooms then shampooing the rugs. They hadn't been cleaned in some time. It wasn't easy to tell them, not to use their rooms because the carpet was wet. There had to be a much stronger reason. She couldn't think of one. So today was her chance. The kids were gone. She got busy.

It'd taken most of the day to give the home a once over, a clean bill of health. It'd taken a lot of energy out of her, and, at the end of the day, she was completely exhausted.

It was early that evening. She was taking another run with the vacuum to speed up the drying when the cleaner shut off in a burst of sparks. At first, she thought the plug had come off, but after a repeated check, she realized it was the power. "Brownouts starting early this season," she reasoned. *Time to finish up anyway.* On her way to the kitchen, her eyes caught the clock on the countertop. It too had stopped working. She picked it up and shook it a couple of times. "Strange," she muttered. The clock usually plinked at her in periodic intervals, but not today. It had gone completely blank.

She put the appliance aside to clean her hands. The water from the faucet only came out in a trickle. *Odd,* she thought, *that's never happened.* A couple handy wipes took care of her soiled hands. She moved the few paces to the refrigerator and opened the door, but it only returned darkness. "Oh well." She knew it would come back within the hour. That's how long a brownout usually lasted. She wasn't worried. The food remained cold for hours. "Water could be a main break," she reasoned.

She had worked up a sweat all day, but wasn't very hungry. There was always freshly-squeezed lemonade in the refrigerator. She poured herself a glass. It felt cool inside her heated body. *What now?* She hastened to finish up. With power out, further cleaning would have to wait until next day. She placed the dishes in the sink and sauntered to the bedroom. She briefly halted by the window to watch the sun set in the west, trailed by brilliant color changes. *Gonna be dark pretty soon.*

Guess I'll check the email. The laptop lid was open as usual but the screen had gone black after the power had drained. *Battery's dead.* "Today's not my day," she rationalized. Without the hum of the refrigerator the home was quiet. She stepped out to collect the daily mail.

On the way back to the house something odd struck her senses. It was the absence of sound. "Wonder what's going on?" *This is no ordinary blackout.* There was something else she'd noticed. Her gaze moved skywards. The sky normally washed out by the city lights was almost black. *Unbelievable!* She marveled. *Never seen this many stars.* She rushed back inside and carelessly tossed the mail by the kitchen counter. She fetched a kitchen chair then went back outside, but this time to the backyard.

It was an eerie quiet. Aside the brilliance in the sky, the immediate surroundings was pitching black. It was a little frightening. There were shadows she'd never noticed. The grounds, normally familiar to her, had turned into a strange environment. She felt uneasy in the darkness, but the fence gave her some comfort. She thought about this for several minutes then began counting stars. There were too many. It felt overwhelming. Outside the fence were sounds she'd not heard before. They were sounds of the night normally drowned by the city traffic. Quickly, she moved back inside.

"Where did I put the flashlight? Kitchen drawer." Her hands fingered through several drawers. They touched familiar objects—forks, knives, spoons—but no flashlight. *Must be in the garage.* By now, day had turned to night. *Too dark to find anything without a light.* "Candles." *Where are they? Never there when you need them.* "I know!" It dawned on her. *Utility closet.* She cautiously felt her way along the hall. "Ouch." Her head bumped the wall. She had reached the end. Her hands fumbled for the doorknob. *There it is.* Inside, her body strained to reach the shelves. Nothing she touched felt like a candle. Her heart sank. Then, she felt a familiar object. "Radio." Groping along the hallway, she cautiously made her way back to the kitchen.

Her pupils had completely dilated in the dark of night. In the glimmer of starlight seeping through the windows, the eyes gradually adjusted. Cabinets, table, and chairs slowly appeared out of the darkness. She switched the power on to the radio. *Nothing. Need batteries.* Her mind searched for all possible places where they could be. *Kids,* she concluded, *used them all up.* Annette thought to rummage through the children's rooms to try and locate some batteries, but after stepping on the wet carpet she quickly thought otherwise. *Too messy...I'll wait until morning.* Reluctantly, she succumbed to her predicament.

After she realized there was nothing to do but sit and wait, loneliness sank in even deeper. She felt helpless for the first time in years. She needed to talk with someone. *House phone.* There was no tone. *Mobile?* Pressing the "On" button the screen came alive. *Great,* she sighed with relief but quickly realized there was no signal. Her excitement was short lived. There it was again, the uneasy feeling reaching up from the pit of her stomach. A chill went through Annette's body.

Cautiously, she moved between rooms to check the locks. Both front and rear entrances were secured. She could breathe a little easier. "Tomorrow," she promised herself, "I'll be better prepared." She made a mental note of what items must be on hands, provided the power was still out. With a glimmer of hope, she prepared for bed but peace did not come easy tonight.

ARIZONA DESERT

What is this place? Tracy felt oddly disturbed. Her eyes stared straight up. The ground below her back felt firm, but not cold. Reaching overhead, she stretched both arms. Strangely enough, a slow moving scene came into her vision. It was made up mostly of puffed up layers of clouds. She blinked a few times to clear her eyes. Her breathing became strained. She found herself in what seemed to be an open field. The chopped beating of helicopter blades slowly edged into her vision. *Where's the fuselage? What about the sound?* The scene suddenly broke. Tracy slowly gained consciousness. Then it dawned on her. She was having a vivid dream.

She could feel the blood pressure racing against her temples. Her fingers touched her head. She slowly forced her eyes open. It took a while for her mind to connect with her eyes. The hazy veil finally cleared from her vision. Straight up, she stared at the whirring blur of a ceiling fan. *What is this place?* she asked herself.

Her eyes strained around the room. It was small. The walls were whitewashed. Many notes were scribbled on them. The room had a tall ceiling. Except for the toilet commode against one corner the room was barren. Soiled from years of use without cleaning, it looked nasty. On the far side was a door. With only a small rectangular window in the center, it appeared solid.

Her back felt tight. She reached behind to feel around. It felt like canvas stretched over some framework. Her skin felt clammy. She eased her body up on one elbow. Her blouse was soaking wet. She'd been sprawled on a cot ever since being dumped here.

What happened? How long have I been here? She pulled herself completely upright. Her feet touched the floor. She was on solid ground once more. It gradually came to her...the agents...the force...the clinical smell only seconds before blacking out. Anger welled up. She jumped to her feet. *Wrong move.* Her body slumped back onto the cot. *My legs.* Both soles prickled with pain. It was a strangeness she hadn't felt since childhood. Her hands reached down to gently rub her calves. It helped getting the blood circulating. She finally managed to get up on unsteady legs. Her mind was clearing up. She began assessing the place.

She noticed a slat of light beaming down from a small opening by the ceiling. It brightened the place. Her body stretched out to reach the opening. *Too short.* She jumped but could not leap high enough. She sought out the door. "Locked."

Locked in? Had she been kidnapped? *But why?* Obviously, they wanted her alive. She forced herself to think clearly. "I'm the analyst." *I should come up with an answer.*

From the hall, footsteps slowly approached. They stopped by her door. There was a snap of the lock. The door opened with a sudden thud. "Sleeping beauty's awake?" A set of gauging eyes was probing her. He carried a plate in one hand.

Defiantly, she stared back at him. Her mind was calculating. Immediately, she sensed trouble. He was dressed in combat fatigues designed for desert operation, similar to what soldiers wore in the Gulf war. The boots he wore were dust covered with fine sand. *Desert Rats* came to her mind. Right handed, she deducted from the position of his holstered weapon, armed with a recent Glock model issue. Two sets of eyes were gauging each other, his scanning her body. "What am I doing here?" she demanded. Her stare took on a defiant mask.

With a voice to match, his response was firm. "Don't ask. Just shut up."

"How long have I been here?" she challenged.

"Twelve hours," he replied, handing her the plate.

"What's this place?" She refused his gesture.

"Here's something to eat." He placed the dish on the edge of the cot.

"What's going to happen?"

"Don't know. Up to your dad," he said without showing any emotion.

"Why? What's he got to do with anything?"

"Everything," he stated on the way out. *Snap*—Again, she was locked in.

"Got some Aspirin?" She called after him. His footsteps faded down the hall. There seemed to be no imminent threat. *What did he mean by "everything?"*

Tracy smelled the plate—ham sandwich. The smell made her nauseous. Her head was still pounding. Restless and irritated, she slid the plate onto the floor. *Got to do something.*

She grabbed hold of the cot and dragged it over by the window. The frame made a screeching sound. *Quiet, dammit,* she scolded herself. Determined, she planted her feet onto the cot. The plan was to catch a glimpse of outside. Her body wouldn't stretch high enough to reach the ledge. She caught her breath to gauge the height then had an idea. *This might work,* she thought. She tilted the cot on its end. She climbed up on its edge. It held her weight.

Her hands wedged onto the edge of the windowsill. She held on. With one pull, she caught a glimpse. *What is this place*? Her heart immediately sank. "The desert?"

Tracy was dismayed. She tried to figure out why she had been taken prisoner. The last thing she remembered was being confronted by the agents. This couldn't happen to her. Not certain how this would turn out, she knew Dad would make every attempt to rescue her. And so would Brian.

Something else she remembered: Dad leaving for the base. She wondered what went down…something to do with her being here. She thought back to when the trouble began. She should be able to make some sense out of her present predicament. Her mind was churning with facts. She tried to come up with a rational answer. But nothing came to mind at the moment. At this point Tracy was unaware that a nuclear exchange had taken place. Body resting against the wall, she sat on the floor. Her eyes sought out the tray of food placed on the floor. She decided to put something in her. A few bites made her feel better. For now, Tracy nibbled on the sandwich, thought up more alternatives, and waited.

PYONGYANG (North Korea)

The command station was doused in eerie silence. Kim Hak Su was keenly aware of the stillness. He was waiting. They all were waiting. *Stay calm,* he kept telling himself. Immense tension had been building ever since the missile launch. It had been a monumental act. There had never been an equivalent action since the signed armistice in '53. After millions of casualties, it had stopped the fighting but without ever achieving peace. His nation was, and still is, at war. To break the waiting, again and again, he reached for his timepiece. His fingers swept gently across the delicate glass cover. He adored the watch. It was the only possession left from a happier time. It was a precious heirloom he'd inherited from his grandfather. Most other valuables had been sold off long ago, a penalty paid to survive another day, week, month, in a once glorious and thriving nation. Today, he promised, glory would follow victory once more.

In between pacing to gather some rational thoughts, he made periodic stops. It was a subconscious motion. The pressure was not only on him alone. He could see it in the many surrounding faces, comrades lingering in wait. Zero hour had come and gone. The wait had become almost unbearable. His nerves were balanced on a razor's edge. There was a sudden ring of the phone. His body turned rigid and then dashed into action. It was the call they'd been waiting for. He sprinted to pick it up. The voice from the distance sounded hollow. It had an unfamiliar echo but the words were clear. "Mission successful."

He repeated the two words out loud. Hands flew up immediately. Like a lion's roar, the center broke out in unison. Outbursts of this kind were rare in his restrained culture. He hadn't experienced such joy since attending the last political mass demonstration many years ago. Now, he could relax. For better or for worse, the die had been cast.

The call confirmed the nuclear impact through foreign agents stationed along the coastal regions of central and northern America. Weeks before, a sortie of agents had been dispatched to the United States. Once they had arrived, they'd acquired tactical gear used in survivable communication. It was a challenge to locate dated HAM equipment. Most stores only carried digital gear, but that wouldn't work after an EMP burst. Several sets had eventually been located at government surplus stores.

Kim Hak Su still had the receiver in his hand. He felt triumphant beyond measure. His index finger kept repeatedly flashing the interrupt button. He was trying to reach the base operator. Finally, a voice answered.

"Defense Ministry."

He practically shot the words across the wire. "Target destroyed." Immediately, he could hear ecstatic cheering on the other end of the line.

"Excellent," the head of the ministry came back, "well done."

Kim Hak Su dwelled on the praise. He wanted it to last. It was the first time the ministry had acknowledged any of his actions. Praise and tribute were a novelty in his society. Personal notions were not customary in his highly disciplined culture. He very much savored this once in a career moment.

Members of the ministry for the defense forces were elated. There was profound cheering at first. It was quickly followed by festive celebration. Champaign bottles, purchased from France for the anticipated occasion, popped open across the halls. Bottles were passed around the ministry in ample amounts. Unlike the nation's ruling class, it was not often that the ministry had an opportunity for celebration. In recent decades, most of the festivities had given way to economic pressures. The once proud nation had been driven into extreme poverty.

The sense of duty brought the minister back to reality. He had to make the call. He was light-footed and slightly swaying from the effects of the alcohol. He made the call and reported the success of the mission to his ruler. It would be a day for the history books.

Euphoria did not last long. The phone rang again shortly after. Somebody picked up. It was a call for the minister. He was handed the receiver. He listened intently. Seconds later, his face turned ashen. The glass filled with champagne dropped from his shaky hand. He had just been informed of another EAM message the launch center had received, but this one from the nation's own defense command. He felt sickened. His body began to tremble. He barely managed to replace the receiver. Nobody noticed his reaction. He quietly left the celebration. He felt deep anguish as he paced to his private chambers. Several minutes later, a muffled shot echoed through the halls of the ministry. Nobody heard or took notice of this terminal, and last, personal act by the minister of defense.

Minutes earlier back at the missile launch center, the EAM flash message was scrolling across the Nixie Tube readout, a device similar to Time Square. Printed in brilliantly red bolded lettering, it forced everybody in the command center into action. It would be a last act. There would be no time for retaliation.

"EMERGENCY ACTION MESSAGE..."

"TRAJECTORY TARGET PYONGYANG (NORTH KOREA) 39° 2' N - 125° 41' E"

"TRAJECTORY SOURCE CHEYENNE (WYOMING) 41° 9' N - 104° 49' W"

"OBJECT IDENTITY ICBM TYPE MINUTEMAN III..."

"ESTIMATED TIME OF IMPACT 40 MINUTES..."

"Impossible." Kim Hak Su was overtaken by utter disbelief. He immediately called the ministry back. He alerted its members of the new threat. "It is imminent!"

"What do you mean?" The voice screamed from the receiver.

"We are under attack."

"How much time?"

"Less than forty minutes."

"I will have your head," the voice promised, "if you are in error."

Kim Hak Su hung up. He did not want to hear the verbal onslaught he knew was coming. There was no question the alert was real. *They must have misjudged the Americans.*

What happened to their democratic policy? "It is our Leader's fault." He felt repugnance. Panic stricken, Kim Hak Su tried to think of what action to take. The counterstrike would most likely be directed at this facility. He would be annihilated with everybody else in the Pyongyang region. The center could not withstand a direct impact. It was never designed to withstand a direct ICBM hit. The system had been built for regional confrontations, mostly with neighboring nations like Japan.

How much time do I have? He thought, panic-stricken. Can't just sit and wait for the next forty minutes. "What am I to do?"

He realized the predicament he was in. There was absolutely nothing he could do but wait for the inevitable. "Thirty minutes to impact." The timepiece already had ticked away ten minutes. He was not prepared for the end. There was no exercise and practice to prepare for imminent death. He could not erase the thoughts and fears from his mind at facing the end. There was no sense in thinking ahead. Just like the present, it would only hold fear and panic. To seek comfort, only the past was left. He sought out a quiet spot. Cowered on a well-worn chair, he waited for the inevitable. He was deeply in thought about what once was a rich and prosperous nation filled with ambition, hope, and dreams.

His deepest thoughts touched on his family. They were the early memories after his daughter was born. Those were happy days long past. Unlike him, she saw no childhood. No family life of her own. Her family was the party. All discipline. *No joy. No play.* In deep regret, he thought of his beloved daughter before the functionaries came and took her away. That was long ago. He only saw her again one more time. Not long ago. She was a pretty girl, his daughter. Just like her mom whom she never knew because childbirth had taken her young life. He was heartbroken then. But he thought, someday, that he'd be reunited with his daughter, until today. Now, all hope had vanished.

He felt so sorry for what could have been, and never was, a happy family for his one and only daughter, born Min Jin. He hoped she was safe somewhere in the south.

The end came with a blinding flash. For one split second, his eyes widened in horror. Then, darkness fell—*eternal darkness.* His mind did not have time to register the immense heat of the total destruction. There was no brain matter left to perceive the deafening explosion that followed, incinerating every living organism at ground zero. The world of Kim Hak Su had turned dark and silent, forever.

CASTLE ROCK

Faint streamers of daylight were drifting over the distant horizon. Alex was headed north on I-25. His mind was still captured by the night's events. "What if I'm wrong?" The feeling of guilt gnawed away at him. He tortured himself, perhaps unnecessarily.

"Castle Rock." The traffic sign came up fast. "Dammit," he swerved violently, "almost missed it." *Gotta get some sleep.* He suddenly felt tired. The events of recent days were catching up to him. One more turn. Thank God. There it was. *My sanctuary.*

"What the hell!"

He slammed on the brakes. Not believing his eyes he jumped from the car. There, parked in the driveway, sat a wingless plane, fuselage battered in on both sides. "Liz!?" He was struck by an ominous feeling. It jabbed at his heart. "The kids."

He fumbled for the keys. With shaky fingers, the front door lock opened with a snap. His senses were on edge. He rushed up the stairway, headed for the living room. Winded, he braced himself against the doorframe to catch a breath. There they were, all three sprawled on the sofa. His daughter stirred when he stepped up.

"Liz! What...?"

She jumped onto her feet and, with outstretched arms, flew into his arms. There was only joy on her face. He had to brace his tired body against the doorframe. Still shaken from the sight of the wreck, he almost lost balance. "Dad!" she yelled. "You won't believe what happened."

"I...you..." he stammered.

"Got clobbered by lightning."

"The kids...the plane?"

"Kids are fine," she insisted. "Plane," she explained, "you saw it."

"I'm happy you made it." Alex squeezed her so tight she could hardly breathe. "I missed you." He felt tugging on his sleeves. There they were, by his side. He reached down to lift up his granddaughter. "Had a good flight?"

"Scary." One word said it all. His grandson nodded in agreement.

Must have been horrific on them. Alex turned to his daughter. "Where were you when lightning struck?" He was still dazzled by the sight of the craft. "Can't believe you made it."

"Saw the flash just west of Denver," she said, "thought it was a meteorite."

"What did you do?"

"Lost power and instruments...engine quit...went into a stall...dove...dropped twelve thousand feet."

"How'd you ever manage?" He knew the feeling of involuntary freefall too well.

"I remembered your instructions," she said, squeezing her arms tightly around his neck. "Thank you, Dad, you saved my life and the kids'." She planted a kiss on his cheek. "You need a shave."

"I know," he said. "I've been out for a couple of days."

Upstairs, in the guest room, Brian stirred. Muffled sounds seeped into the room. He rubbed his eyes to clear his head. It was still foggy from the evening before. He lay there trying to make out the voices below. He felt slight pressure build up. His bladder finally forced him to his feet. He headed for the bathroom. The mirror reflected an unkempt, disheveled face. He swallowed hard to clear a parched throat. *Sure could use some coffee.* Unceremoniously, he reached for his pants, then jumped into the trousers and hobbled out the door. The voices came from the living room. He headed in that direction.

"Morning, everybody." He entered with a cheerful greeting. "Daughter finally made it?"

"Liz," Alex introduced the woman. "How'd you sleep?"

"Terrific." He extended a hand to greet her. "Lisa?"

"Friends call me Liz."

"Okay, Liz," he replied with a smile. "This place's so quiet I slept through the night. Tracy around?"

"Thought she'd be with you," Alex said with a slight twinkle in the eyes.

"Haven't seen her since I went to sleep."

"I'll check," Liz offered. They could hear her open and close doors. A minute later she reappeared. "Not in the house."

"Where could she have gone?" Brian was slightly worried, but put the thought aside. She was an adult. *And pretty independent.*

"Don't worry." Alex remembered her habits. "Probably out for a jog; she's an early riser."

"Very independent," Liz agreed. "Can I make breakfast, Dad?"

"No objections here."

She got busy in the kitchen. Alex helped her with the dishware and the ingredients. Coffee was already percolating, "Just like old times." He recalled the times when there was a woman in the house, his wife. He dearly missed them, his wife and daughters.

His stirring thoughts were interrupted by Liz. "Where were you so early, Dad?"

"Went on base," he said, "to check on the blackout." With her arrival he'd temporarily forgotten last night's events.

"Should have come along," Brian said. His was shaking his head in dismay. "What'd you find?"

"Take a seat," he offered his buddy, "you'll need it."

Alex pulled up a chair. "Let me fill you in what's happened." He caught a lung full of air. It allowed him full focus on the previous night's events before he told them what had happened. He illustrated the events from start to finish. They kept interrupting with shouts of disbelief and astonishment.

"*What*…you launched a nuke!?" Brian exclaimed. "That's incredible." He could not believe the bombshell Alex had just dropped. Neither could Liz. The kids were trying to make sense out of their granddad's story. *He must have gone mad.* They stared at him.

"You can't be serious," Liz said.

"Believe it," Alex insisted. "Still needs to be confirmed but after talking with Rajesh, I believe it started with an attack on our satellite system. But that wasn't all." He watched their eyes switch from doubt to amazement, from being dazzled to being overwhelmed.

"That's incredible!" Brian exclaimed again. He was unsure whether to believe his buddy or not. "Why didn't you call?"

"Couldn't." Alex stated facts. "All transmission's out. EAM alert went off with an incoming ICBM, but," he stated, "we couldn't confirm." Recalling the night's events, suddenly, the full weight bore down on him. He was still in doubt over the launch's effectiveness.

"False alarm?" Brian seemed in denial. "Possible?"

"Too late for that—couldn't be verified," Alex affirmed. "All indications pointed to an attack aimed at the West Coast from someplace in Asia." Alex did not want to be specific. He avoided mentioning San Francisco. Liz's mom and husband were out there.

"My God," Liz couldn't help it. A scream slipped from her lips. Her hands went for her mobile. "Mom!"

"Don't," Alex gestured. He tried to be supportive. "Links are down. The strike disabled satellites and relay stations." He watched his daughter slowly lose her so legendary composure. "Couldn't even raise NORAD or The Pentagon."

"What?" Brian yelled out. It was mostly from spilled coffee. He'd accidentally spilled it on his thighs. He jumped up from the chair to rush to the kitchen sink. There, he quickly splashed cold water on his lap. He was exasperated. A large wet splotch had formed on the trousers. "Unbelievable. You launched without the *president*?"

"I had to!" Alex saw doubt reflected in their faces. "You don't believe me?" His actions must seem impossible to them, or any other person for that matter.

Both Liz and Brian carried a stunned look on their faces. "What's next?" Brian asked.

"Don't know…nobody knows. We'll head for base after Tracy shows up."

"Wonder what's keeping her?" Brian said. He was getting worried. He hadn't seen Tracy since the evening before. "I'll go look for her."

"Where you gonna start?" Alex asked. As always, he was realistic about things. "Tracy's a strong woman. She'll manage." His calming words relaxed the tension around him. He was dealing with his own pressure. He still felt the weight of the night's action on his shoulders, then suddenly remembered, "HAM set."

He rushed to the basement. They all jumped to their feet and followed. The kids were curious. They had never seen his domain. There was equipment everywhere. "Oh," Liz's son noticed, "computers. Can we play?"

"Please don't touch!" Alex cautioned. "I'll set up some games."

They watched him rummage through the closets. "Here it is." He blew at the gear and wiped a layer of dust from the top. The power turned on as soon as he plugged it into the outlet. "Grab the extension cord," he gestured at Brian then led the way back upstairs, headed for the deck. "Now for the signal."

Liz watched her dad stoop over the set, fumbling with the dials, "Is it working?" Watching him brought back fond memories. She remembered him playing with the set many times. She'd climb on his lap to pull on those shiny knobs and switches.

Both she and Brian were hovering around the set. They were crowding him. "Just like old times." He grinned. He couldn't suppress a smile thinking of the days with his daughters fighting for air time.

Today, with everybody using iPhones and iPads, the "now generation," he suspected, wasn't even aware of this dated communication mode. *Probably never even heard of HAM and what it stood for.* As he'd remembered, there were even hardened OSCAR (Orbiting Satellite Carrying Amateur Radio) satellites put in orbit for just this purpose.

He let the set scan the spectrum. The frequencies were rapidly scrolling across the digital readout. Seconds later the scanner had a lock. There was chatter. It came from multiple sources. Voices were already reporting on the blackout. Fragmented reports came in from across the nation. Ether traffic was especially heavy in California's southern coastal regions.

"The Bay, the Peninsula?" There was no news reported from the central or northern part of the state.

Could it be? A once thriving metropolis, Silicon Valley, gone? Alex still would not disclose to his daughter the missile's true destination. He was afraid she'd panic. Shortly after, she did.

Not long after getting on the airways, they received distress reports. It confirmed their worst fears; the City by the Bay had been hit. Also, relayed reports via Pacific islands indicated that North Korea experienced a nuclear explosion near their capital city. In addition, Hawaii and Japan confirmed aftershocks recorded on their seismic sensors pinpointing northern Korea.

Alex put the set on auto scan. With ears trained on the set, they were chatting to catch up with family news. An hour had gone by when he thought he heard his call sign. "Shh, quiet." Working the volume dial, he cut in. "That's us." After several more scans he could make out the faint signal from NORAD. Apparently, they were transmitting on short wave from Cheyenne Mountain.

"CQ…CQ…Castle One."

Alex responded, "Come in."

"Hold one." Several seconds went by before there was a reply.

"You Bauer?" Alex recognized General Jackson's voice.

"Yeah," Alex replied. *What now?* He wondered.

"Want you up here immediately." This was not a request. It sounded like an order.

"What's happening?"

His question went unanswered. "Make it quick." Jackson had already gone off set.

For a moment Alex was undecided. "Got my own problem," he muttered, then changed his mind. He had a lot of data to analyze recorded on his monitoring systems. He shot a fleeting glance at Brian, then at Liz. "You may wanna stay put," he suggested. She wholeheartedly agreed. Liz already planned to use the HAM set. She wanted to reach the family in California.

"Let's get going then," Alex urged at Brian. He kissed Liz goodbye and gave each kid a hug on the way out. The Wagoneer, again, proved to be a reliable workhorse. *Thanks for that. How'd I get around without these wheels? How does anyone get around? Where's Brian?* His buddy had fallen behind. *There he is.*

Shaking his head, Brian was perched by the wingless Cessna. "Incredible!" He seemed perplexed. "What's with the wreck?" On Alex's calling, he jumped into the passenger seat. His face was a question mark.

"Liz." With a grin on his face, Alex was already rolling down the driveway. "Don't know how she did it." He was shaking his head. "Her and kids came out alive."

"What happened?"

"After the EMP strike…" Alex explained her plight on the drive up to the Mountain.

NORAD COMMAND

"Nothing, sir," the operator reported. His frustration level was on the raise. Already, for hours, he'd been trying to raise other commands. The line was dead no matter how much effort he wasted. There was nothing but dead quiet. It couldn't get any deader. No static, not even line noise. He silently cursed his superior. *On the one hand he gives me orders, and on the other I get no results. What the hell am I supposed to do?* He felt like pulling out his hair. The normally respectful operator felt like screaming but held his tongue. It could mean the end of his career. Being a peon in the hierarchical structure of the military, he was trained only to take orders.

"Keep on trying," Ben Jackson, Commander in Chief, NORAD, demanded for the nth time.

"Yessir, right away, sir," the young operator acknowledged without hesitation. He hoped to get through this grave situation alive without cutting short his young career. He really liked it here. Whenever he sat with his buddies over a few beers, he called it the "Fortress." He could taste the next round already. It would be at Cowboy's, his favorite place in town. It was the local hangout for a thirsty serviceman.

"The girls?" Someone would always want to know.

"Pretty as they come," he'd brag. Ever since getting assigned to the world's most prestigious duty station, he'd been the envy of his peers and his family. "Cheyenne Mountain," he'd boast, "best of the best." When prodded further, he'd tell them some of the details of the facility. "Military's defense sector, nation's security blanket, and so on."

For better or for worse, the North American Aerospace Defense Command was the nation's semi-secret, eight hundred pound gorilla. Protecting both U.S. and Canadian interests, it overshadowed the Colorado Springs and Manitou areas. Constructed in 1961, the complex provided air, water, and power for its eight hundred plus personnel on duty. To assure short-term survival, a month's worth of food was kept on hand.

It helped to show off a little. Still being a low-lifer, it made him feel important. He knew precisely how much or how little he could disclose. He'd Googled the Mountain many a time. Whatever was in print, he could talk about.

"Almost there." The tunnel entrance was just ahead. They had made excellent timing. Other than clusters of stranded vehicles there was hardly any traffic today. A guard post blocked the tunnel entrance. Alex applied the brakes. The vehicle skidded the last ten yards to a halt. Today, the tunnel was heavily armed blocking their path. Their automatics were leveled directly at the Wagoneer, ready to unload a magazine full of ammo.

"Nobody gets past," one sentry commanded. Alex leaned close to the window. He wanted to explain. "Turn back." It was a direct order he did not dare refuse not when staring down the barrels of several M-16s.

Alex refused to budge. *Idiots,* he muttered under his breath. He was angry. He hadn't come all this way just to be turned back by some idiot guardsmen. Especially when he'd been ordered here. Brian remained in his seat, also staring down the sentries, but stayed quiet. There was already enough tension on the ground. With hands raised, Brian's gesture indicated no confrontations with the guardsmen.

Alex finally forced the initiative. Ignoring the blockade, he jumped from the jeep. The sentries immediately tensed into action but held their triggers.

"Listen," Alex yelled at them, "we're expected."

"Who says?"

"Your commander," he fired back, "that's who."

"IDs," one demanded. Alex understood their indecision. Without a direct link to check with command, the decision would have to be made locally. It was easier to turn a potential threat away than allow access to this highly secure facility.

From a sentry's perspective, everyone approaching the tunnel was a suspect enemy. They had orders, "Shoot to kill." Warily, Alex handed his credentials to the sentry. One guard approached their vehicle with caution. The others held their position. He could read the guard's expression: *What should I do?* He seemed caught up in a quandary. *ID looks real, but I have my orders.* There was no way to check it out without a phone. Today, there was no communication. The massive gates to the mountain had been shut hours ago.

"Well," Alex prompted, "somebody make a decision!" The sentries stepped aside. They quietly discussed their plight. Then two approached.

"What do you know?"

"About what?"

"The blackout."

It became obvious they had been kept in the dark. Nobody seemed to know much about what had caused the massive outage. There were questions among the soldiers. Eventually, rumors surfaced about a nuclear attack, but nobody had any specifics. *Communication's out, that's for sure.* Alex gave them a brief highlight of what had transpired earlier, about the strike and counterstrike. It seemed to satisfy their concerns.

Brian was ordered into the back seat. Two guardsmen slid in beside them, one in front, the other in back. "Let's go." Each had a .45 semi leveled at them. Alex pushed on the accelerator. The vehicle jerked into a darkened tunnel. He sped along the bright yellow painted lines leading into the depths of the mountain. It would be a quarter mile to the complex. A minute later the Wagoneer slithered to a halt. All jumped from the vehicle. There it was, the "Gates of Hell," legendary entrance to the mountain. There were three in all, each leading into a separate sector. All were closed, locked down tight. One sentry approached what seemed to be the main gate. Using the butt of the gun, he rapidly banged against the ten-ton steel door. The hollow sound reverberated up and down the steel plates. He continued the banging several more times.

Idiots. Alex snickered. He shook his head then turned to the trunk of the Wagoneer. There. He reached for a tire iron.

"Here." He tossed it to the guard. "Use Morse."

Years ago, he read in some manual, that as last resort word could get across heavy steel plates using Morse code.

Staring at the flatiron, the sentry seemed baffled. "What's Morse?"

Alex grabbed the iron back. He could read the blank stare in his face. *Why would he know the code?*

Alex still remembered it. It was a prerequisite for getting a HAM license. With a firm grip, he tapped against the heavy steel. Dot...dot...dot...dash...dash...dash...dot...dot...dot! SOS, the most common symbol for crisis, was recognizable by most communicators. The sound reverberated to the other side. He could only hope somebody was on watch. Several attempts later, there was a faint response. Dot...dash...dot, dot, dot...dash, dash...dot...dot, dash…dot…dash…dash, dash…dash…dash, dot…dot…dash! "READ YOU." There was definite intelligence.

"Hey!" They were communicating. Several minutes went by without further response. Then there was a thud followed by motion. The gate slowly opened. Several armed uniforms beckoned them in. The sentries handed off their responsibility. Alex and Brian followed in close accord. Brian seemed impressed. He'd never been here. Just now he realized the extent of the famous complex. Led to central command, his eyes took in the passing scene. Alex explained the various sectors. He'd been here a number of times.

Housed within were elements of NORAD, SPACECOM, and AFSPC. The actual operations complex was a series of buildings. Up to three stories tall, there were fifteen in all. With buildings mounted on a bed of 1,000-pound steel springs to protect the structure from earthquake or nuclear explosion, they allowed for horizontal sway in any direction to filter out shock.

Immediately they were led to the missile warning center, the War Room. As soon as they entered, they faced a stern but engaging Jackson. Alex accepted his outstretched hand. "Bauer…Alex." He thumbed at his buddy. "Brian Harris, NSA."

"Listen up." Jackson lifted a cigar from tightly pressed lips. "We have a situation." The man was a tough-looking commander. Planted on solid ground, barrel chest, he boasted an elaborate fruit salad clipped below his left lapel.

He was addressing Alex directly. "I understand you were the one that launched one of our nukes." Alex wavered. He was going to justify his action, but, to his surprise, there seemed to be no need. "We here," the general said, "appreciate what you've done."

"Thanks, but…"

"Follow me." Alex and Brian were directed to a spacious conference room. Dressed in various uniforms, representing all services was a mixed audience, waiting. Seated around the table were what appeared to be senior officers, each in charge of a specific mission. Also on hand were a few contracting personnel, probably consultants to special programs. They had been trapped here for hours. *They'd rather be with their families,* Alex could read on their faces. As soon as they entered, the assembly had turned to Alex and Brian. He spotted mostly empty stares. Must be speculating: *Who're these guys?* Their stares cleared up when Alex was introduced.

"Ahh, yes, *the* Bauer," were some of the comments.

"Been assessing damages." The general motioned to the table. He then turned to address Alex. "I understand you're the experts."

"Know missile defenses," Alex replied. He gestured at Brian. "He's the expert on satellites."

"Glad to have you here." Jackson appeared sincere. "Okay," he motioned Alex to speak, "enlighten us."

Alex, in his deliberate demeanor, turned to address the table. He briefly gave them an account of his analyses, his theories, and assumptions for the past couple of days' events. He also illustrated his ad hoc missile launch. In turn, he was rewarded with deserving praise. In conclusion, he asked, "What's your assessment?" He did not expect much. There were some opinions, but nothing concrete.

Once again, it was the general's voice booming. "Reports!" he demanded. "I want a report on what systems are down, what can be repaired, and how long it'll take to fix." He shot a quizzical glance at Alex then continued. "I can't put enough emphasis on the critical situation. We've never been this vulnerable since the invention of the nuclear weapon. We don't know the steps our enemies will take next. For all we know the Chinese, Russians, and Iranians may jump on this opportunity to get their licks in."

He was catching his breath. "HAM operators are getting preliminary reports. All indications lend to a hostile strike on San Francisco, recorded with our counterstrike on North Korea." He acknowledged Alex with a nod. "Let's see how many military and government agencies we can raise."

Brows furrowed into two vertical cuts, he ordered, "Alex, you'll coordinate." His stabbing eyes scanned across the conference table. "Any objections?" He'd been consistently ignoring Brian. "Listen up, people," he huffed, "I want a list of our defenses, locations, contacts, and alternates. Find out the flight status of all our planes, military and civilian. Get to it."

He pulled Alex aside. "I need an assessment on all transport assets that can be immediately repaired. Also," he paused to catch another gulp of air, "get in touch with Texas and see if the confederate fleet can be mobilized. Those old WWII planes don't have much electronics on board and should be operational. National Guards have to be alerted in all states. I want a report every hour. Also, see if you can raise anybody at TACAMO.[47] Let's get hopping."

There were several components to the TACAMO system. Elements were strategic communications based at Tinker AFB, a flying air reconnaissance squadron, the U.S. Navy airborne sectors, as well as a West Coast alert base at Travis. For the East Coast defenses, an alert system was staged out of Patuxent River, MA. Created in 1961, the Atlantic TACAMO was also fitted with VLF transmitters trailing wire antenna to communicate with the fleet's ballistic missile submarines.

Alex immediately went to get started. "Why don't you help out with the confederate fleet?" he suggested to Brian. He was apologetic to his buddy. "I know," he said, "he keeps ignoring you."

"So—you've noticed?"

"Well, yeah." Alex felt embarrassed about Brian being completely ignored by the brigadier. "Must be some personal conflict he's got with the NSA."

Alex joined a group in the War Room. The sight was impressive to anyone. Visitors were awed by the presentation. Huge display panels covered most of the walls. In addition, banks of flat panel displays were sprawled across OPS desks fed by racks of computer and comm equipment securely locked away. It was the showcase for command and control, the world's foremost C4 system. Today, the screens were blank. No Intel was fed to the rows of equipment. Downlinks were dead, taken out by the blast.

Jackson joined Alex in the War Room. Impatient as ever, he gestured at the primary display panel. "I need this thing up and running," he demanded, "Now!"

He turned to Alex. "Ideas?" He waited for him to respond.

"Based on the OPS criteria..." Alex started out but was cut short.

"Don't give me that crap," the brigadier countered. "I want facts," he insisted, "and I want them now!"

---

[47] TACAMO is a U.S. military term literally meaning "take charge and move out." It also referred to a system of survivable communications links designed to be used in case of nuclear war for maintaining communications between the decision-makers (the National Command Authority) and the triad of strategic nuclear weapon delivery systems for land, air, and sea.

"Right." Alex took no offense. He was used to dealing with commanders. "Here are the facts: communications, satellites, mobiles, radios, and transmitters, all down. Power, telephones, cables, wires, all fried from east to west."

"That means…" the general interrupted, "transportation's out."

"Right." Alex confirmed. "Every craft has to be scheduled for repair and so do ground control systems. Land transport and maritime shipping's disrupted for the same reasons."

"Somebody needs to contact Naval Fleet Headquarters," the general urged. He flagged over one of his subordinates. "Alert subs out on missions," he bellowed. "Get to it."

"They'd be tuned in on ELF and VLF," Alex suggested.

"Right," he reiterated, "need to get a fix on the subs—immediately!"

"We can assume," Alex continued, "nuclear arsenals and silos are still intact. LCCs are probably operational."

"Then," the commander complained, "why don't they respond?" He waved the chewed cigar through the air then jammed it back between his lips.

"They may not have been able to receive mission calls," Alex suggested. He felt a tug on his shoulder.

"Let's go," the commander ordered. "Can't get anything done here."

In the interim, Brian was busy at the command's primary comm room. It was impressive. The room was spacious. It housed every conceivable electronic gear available in today's market. It was stacked with transmitters, receivers, amps, and spectrum analyzers. Although mil-specs hardened, it was all rendered useless at the moment. There was no input from anywhere. Already, somebody had dug up a set of HAM equipment, connected it to the antenna feed, and put power to it. Brain had taken the lead. His first priority was to get in touch with the CAF[48]. The signal generator sprang into action. He hoped the signal would be received. His best chance to make contact was to the south. It did not take long. The static noise was interrupted by a voice, marginal at first, but quickly gaining strength.

A young airman was operating the transmitter. He suddenly jerked his head at Brian. "Confederates?" He looked dumbfounded. He thought there was a mistake. "Confederacy's been out with the Civil War." So he thought.

"Make the call." Brian insisted.

The HAM operator was perplexed. He'd never heard of a confederate air force. With the little he knew, Brian gave him a short lecture. He had been fortunate to catch an annual air show the confederates had held. It was quite impressive to watch these old war birds take off and land. On the outside they'd appeared large, but once inside, it was as crammed as it could get, especially with the B-17s, B-24s, and the B-25s, with their narrow catwalks from the cockpit to the tail end of the crafts. Visitors would exit rubbing their heads after getting bumped by the metal frame around a tight corner.

---

[48] Confederate Air Force. In 1961, based in Texas, the CAF was chartered as a nonprofit corporation in order to restore and preserve WW II-era combat aircraft. Since then, the CAF continued to grow and included not only medium and heavy bombers such as the B-17, B-24, B-25, and B-29, but a wide range of fighters and fighter-bombers as well. With 9,000 members and a fleet of well over 160 craft representing more than 60 different types—including planes from foreign countries—the CAF now ranked among the largest aerial forces in the world. In 2002 it changed its name to Commemorative Air Force to accurately reflect the present purpose of the organization.

Brian further explained why it was so important to get the fleet in the air. Dating back to the 60s, this specialized air force started when a group of WWII pilots and air buffs began collecting these obsolete, but yet magnificent, craft. While the majority of the craft had been severely damaged or destroyed by the war, many were still serviceable.

Many had been decommissioned and stripped of instruments and armament. Most of these proud warriors were scrapped or abandoned. No one, not even the Air Force or Navy, was making attempts to preserve the historic aircraft that had changed the world.

PALM JUMEIRAH

As he did most mornings while residing at his Mansion, first thing was a trip to the balcony. He stood there, on the lofty balcony of his mansion, his body swaying with the breeze. This morning was different. The world seemed brighter. It could have been his current mood. With yesterday's success, he had reasons to be elated. He had a sudden urge to shout. "Shahadah is alive." The Serpent was shouting from the top of his lungs. It was a feeling of great exhilaration brought on after the successful attack on America. The words were carried away swiftly by the prevalent winds for the area. He had been waiting for the call, the call that never came. He did not need it anymore. Confirmation was all over the foreign news networks. Since the early morning hours, BBC and others carried the news with similar headlines:

"The United States of America, leader of the Western world, experienced a nationwide blackout. At this hour," the news went on, *"no information has been forthcoming. All attempts by outside nations to contact America have failed. It is a great mystery. No group has come forward to claim ownership of an attack. A heightened state of alert is in effect by many nations. Members interviewed from the United Nations have disavowed any knowledge but declared the world in a state of extreme emergency."*

Immediately, political analysts and so-called experts were on the airwaves speculating about possible causes. Since no other country experienced the blackout, it was assumed that it must have been either a massive power failure on a national scale, or some other internal infrastructure disruption.

"The world is mine!" Wildly shaking his head, he was laughing out loud. It helped to clear his mind and wipe away the pent-up frustration. He wished he could have his friend here to share the exhilaration. *Yusuf, we did it!* But his friend did not hear him. His friend was on the front lines. "This calls for celebration." He took several deep breaths to slow the adrenaline then made his way to the pantry. There, he selected a packet of the finest tea the Indian soil could produce. He missed having company, especially during a joyous time such as today. He was about to make a call but thought otherwise. Connections would be down at the destination. Instead, he returned to the shady loft of the deck to enjoy the tea. His strides took him past his personal library. His eyes caught the vast array of books neatly stacked on the shelves, then swept through the titles of celebrated works. He selected a copy of his favorite reading. It was a book from the historical section, entitled "History of Islam."

Ever since childhood, the same question kept gnawing on his consciousness. The Serpent could not understand why the free world was persecuting Islam. From his point of view the Islamic faith was not much different from Western ideology. The difference, he'd learned later on, was that the Western world had many religions whereas Islam had only one faith, with one supreme power—Allah. It was this simplicity that attracted him.

After he and his childhood friends were separated, he had gone into semi-seclusion, even denial. The carefree life he once knew had come to an end. It'd turned confusing. On returning to Pakistan, he had lost the sense of belonging. It was not until the day he joined Al Qaeda that a purpose of being gradually returned. There, he had met many likeminded recruits huddled together in tight groups, passing the time between mission rehearsal and combat training. Life at the camps had been demanding for the body and the soul. Outside of an occasional improvised game of soccer in between satellite passes, there was hardly any recreation in the middle of deserts and on mountaintops. Training camps in Pakistan, hidden away in isolated valleys, camouflaged by the rocky terrain, were numerous. Only top leaders knew of their existence, but no one person knew every location. To keep security tight, camps were divided into cells commanded by group leaders, each trained for a specific mission.

New missions were constantly created based on changing world politics, but the overall purpose remained the same: world dominance through Islamic ideology. The justification lay with the Islamic cause itself. It had been suppressed ever since the fall of the Ottoman Empire. To understand the underlying behavior, one had to get an understanding of the Islamic history. By the same token, what possessed a country to harbor such idealists-turned terrorists could only be gauged by understanding the leaders of such nations. Many were self-elect through one coup d'état or another. This seemed a prerequisite to discipline and manage such a diverse culturally extreme nation.

After climbing ranks to colonel, he had been groomed for military leadership. It was then that he took full opportunity to study the leadership of such a complex world. It became clear that position was determined by two basic principles. One was gained from the position of strength through political training, scholastic achievements, and popular vote by the people; the other through individual strides driven by personal ambitions. Since his path had already been set, he'd chosen the latter. It was the foundation for his potential dictatorship.

It was here that he took reign over the politically charged resources. It gave him the necessary power to build and support his ambitious future, a future that would create a world dominated by Islam.

CASTLE ROCK

Liz was on the HAM set. "CQ...CQ...CQ...Castle Rock—this is Castle Rock—come in, please." For hours already she had tried to raise northern California. "Anybody—anybody out there?" In between calls she'd take few-minute breaks to check on the kids. They were busy nearby. There were no toys, not even a ball. After the divorce when Mom moved on, Dad never had children around. He'd missed out on a lot by not raising them. He knew it. Now, the house was cheerful again. Even if only for a short while.

Thoughts were still fresh on her mind about their almost tragic end. She considered herself and the kids too, the luckiest girl, to have come out unharmed. It suddenly occurred to her how much she'd missed this place. In a way she envied her dad. *We could like it here, especially the kids.* They were playing chase in between hide and seek. "Mom," her son just stopped to take a breath, "I wanna play a game."

"Let's check if Pappi has games on the computer." There were none. It was getting late anyway.

"Sorry, kids," she said. "Get ready for bed."

"But Mom…" Now the arguments started.

Suddenly, there was banging. It seemed to come from below, the front door. Cautiously, she moved towards the sound. The pounding was persistent. She couldn't imagine who it could be this late at night. She became aware of her isolation. Liz tried to ignore the pounding, hoping it would stop. There it was again, *bang…bang…bang.* There was something else, muted, muffled voices. She couldn't make them out. Her ear was pressed against the wood. The only sound was a slight hum coming from the generator in the basement. It fed the hallway lighting. She switched it off. The hallway was doused in darkness. Her eyes slowly adjusted to the dark. "You stay here," she ordered her kids. Her eyes caught a slight movement. It was the doorknob. She reached for it. Fingers pressed against the cold metal, her body suddenly contracted. There was resistance. With the next banging she could feel vibrations though the door. It was getting to be too much. "What do you want?" she yelled out but immediately regretted it. *Stay quiet, stupid!* she chided herself. It was too late. They knew somebody was home.

"Let us in, please," the voice begged. It persisted, "We have injured. Need help."

"Go away." She was torn between caution and reason. Trained in first aid, she wanted to help, but her instinct told her to exercise caution. Remain put. Stay safe. She was confronted with a dilemma. She didn't trust anyone knocking on doors in the middle of the night, especially not a night like this. Her heart was torn between common sense and empathy. *Turn them away,* her mind kept telling. Tonight was different. She'd seen the endless rows of cars stranded on the interstate. *There must be injured from the many collisions.* Despite her better sense, she finally gave in. The deadbolt snapped. The gate opened.

In an instant, Liz realized it was the wrong move. As soon as the deadbolt retracted, the door flew open. Her body slammed against the frame. The door had been pushed open with overwhelming force. All dressed in black, in spilt a group of masked beings acting aggressive and vulgar. They were shouting at her in a foreign language. She could not understand what was said. Two of them lunged at her. Her arms were clutching the doorframe. She fiercely struggled for balance. Her body was ripped away. It left bloody smudges on the wooden frame.

"Shut your face," one shouted. He spoke English with a slight accent. *Definitely Middle Eastern,* her mind registered. He seemed to be the leader. Her body was pinned in from both sides. She struggled to free herself. A fist slammed her into her face. In an instant, she was stunned. There were more shouts…commands. *The kids!* she panicked.

Her body was tormented by the intruders. Her mind tried to make sense. "What do you want?" she screamed out. The response was another hit in the face. This time it was with the butt of a rifle. Her body buckled. The blow forced her to the knees. *Strange,* she thought, *didn't feel a thing. That should have hurt.* With vice-like grips she was forced to the ground. One pulled a set of tie wraps. Her hands and ankles were being tied. Her body was dragged up the stairs. Her head slammed hard on the banister. She became aware of warm, sticky blood trickling down her forehead. Blood seeped into one eye, then across her mouth and down her chin. There was a mask facing her. She spat at it. She was awarded with another blow to the head. The mask came off. Eyes stared down at her. She expected evil. But there was only hatred. Passionate hatred, it was. "Anybody else in the house?" his lips demanded. It was a voice broken in a heavy Middle Eastern accent.

"Just kids…please don't hurt them." She was begging. Footsteps were swiftly moving through the house. They had found them. She tried to struggle off the floor. One boot landed hard in her rib cage. It pinned her to the ground. She struggled wildly…more shouts…another blow. Liz, through swollen eyelids, watched the Castle being taken over by the attackers. Seconds later she blacked out.

Liz had no idea how long she was out. She struggled but couldn't move. Rigid plastic strips cut into her wrists and ankles. It hurt when she struggled to free herself. She thought about her children. A feeling of guilt came over her. *Dad will be furious.* She hoped he'd come back soon. He'd know how to handle them. He would not have given in to the intruders. She drifted back into unconsciousness. She was dreaming.

It was Dad and her. They were in the gym, the workout room below. She was young then, and aggressive. "You're a tough chick," he would praise, "powerful kick." They were sparring. They both wore the Gi, the Kung-Fu uniform. She wore hers with pride. It was befitting. Besides, it looked good on her body. "Tradition," he'd say. It was a scene played out from the past. He taught her how to protect and defend. He was experienced. Earned in Korea, he had the belts to match.

After the sparring, they'd sit in the lotus position. He'd tell stories. "Ancient philosophy," he'd say. He had many stories. She'd sit and marvel. *How could anyone experience so much?* She reminded herself that he was an adventurer by heart. He was proud. And so was she. The sparring continued.

"Ouch," she huffed, "that hurt." Her hands flew to her side to protect against the next blow. It was too late. She had taken the kick. Now it was her turn. Her fist went out. She countered with a punch to the face. His head snapped back to avoid the punch. His face melted under the force. It'd changed. It'd turned into a stranger. She backed off. Her body froze. It was then she realized it was a dream. There was another kick to her body. But this time it was real. It took her breath way. She moaned. She forced her eyes open. They met the stare of the stranger. She remembered.

"Open," the voice demanded. She had been dragged to the safety room. It was barred. They demanded entrance. She thought quickly. "I don't know," Liz pleaded. She added, "We're only visiting. You'll have to wait until the owner comes back." She was defiant. It didn't work. It earned her a blow to the face. This one hurt. She didn't want to think about her face, how swollen or battered it might look. He abruptly turned and left. She was alone again with her tormented thoughts about the kids. She quietly relinquished herself to the assaults. There was nothing she could do. *Hope Dad's coming back.* All she could do now was sit and wait while this gang had its way with her, and the Castle.

NORAD COMMAND

The Mountain... Refuge for the privileged, domain for the fortunate. Alex felt confined, trapped within the granite walls of Cheyenne Mountain. He was barely listening. He still carried the burden from the previous day. Ever more, though, his mind was on Tracy. *Hope she's back by now.* He, along with the commanding staff, had been busy for hours. Special action teams were formed. Somewhat disconnected at first, it'd proven effective. "Think tanks on-the-fly." The thought brought a grin to his face.

The brigadier caught the personal notion. "What's funny?"

"Nothing." Alex turned serious. "Just thinking."

The brigadier was in and out the command center checking for progress and new ideas. His firm steps echoed through the halls. He was desperate for a solution. He'd just called for another summary meeting. It was the third time this morning. "Anything—anybody?" He wanted some answers. Several spoke up, mostly uniforms. They called for retribution, vengeance. They were mostly stating facts. Nobody had a concrete solution. Reports slowly trickled in from the West Coast. It enraged them even more.

Alex kept his cool. He was one of few civilians here. Grossly outnumbered, he waited his turn until addressed by the general. He reported only to him. The system was broke. It was broke on many fronts. It was one thing to fix broken down equipment, a damaged link, or system. It was another to mend a nation. For that, it'd take a miracle. But that wasn't going to happen.

The only substantial aid on hand was the "SIOP," the Bible of survival. Copies of the single integrated operations plan were passed around. It was the baseline for survival. It spelled out simulated scenarios for every possible national emergency. But who had the time to read? "Evacuation," the brigadier complained, "that's all I hear."

"Sir," Alex interrupted, "it's the basis for SIOP." The architects for the plan had been thorough. The manual had been revised over and over to accommodate proven situations as they were identified. One recent contributing factor had been Katrina. It was the aftermath of a catastrophe like this that made up a large part. Although theorists could think up many scenarios, when it came down to specifics, only an actual situation could provide detailed facts. As with the current disaster, books would be written. It would become part of history, just like 9/11.

Aside from the seasoned brigadier, Alex spotted mostly young faces. Action officers, that's what they were. Not much experience, strategic or tactical, or, for that matter, technological. *Perhaps,* Alex postulated, *the answer is in the past—wait a minute.* It was there where Alex found the solution. "Of course!" Problem solved. The rest would be easy. All he had to do was put the pieces together.

Alex audibly cleared his throat. He was excited. "Listen up." The command center turned quiet. Most eyes turned to what he had to say. The brigadier stopped pacing the floors. He motioned for Alex to go ahead.

"Some of you," he started, "are too young to know." He took a few paces to collect his thoughts. "Others may have forgotten, but," he affirmed, "we used to have reliable communication." Many heads perked up. People paid attention. "It's called WATS[49]."

---

[49] Wireless Autonomous Telemetry System. The Wireless Autonomous Telemetry System, as it was known, had been used successfully during WWII and the pre-satellite era. Voice links then were configured through mechanical switches connecting calls. Communication was carried on strictly via landlines. The system, over

Alex briefly outlined the system.

"I remember," and "Yeah," were comments made by some of the "old hands."

Although disabled many years ago, Alex knew that much of the dated components were still packaged away on storage shelves. As a matter of fact, entire equipment racks were still available. Most had been packaged up vacuum tight to prevent rusting. Disposal action was a cumbersome task. Nobody wanted part of it. The result was antiquated components and legacy systems piling up in storage. It was the military way, "Just in case."

The brigadier planted one foot in front of Alex. "Let's get to it!" Alex knew what needed to be done. "You're in charge."

Alex assumed that maintenance crews were already at work switching over to backup systems. The trick was to locate workable components to fix interface connections, but, as was the case with catastrophes, human ingenuity was quick to respond.

"Somebody check the antenna farm," Jackson yelled at the crew, "and where's that HAM set?"

---

decades, had become obsolete with the invention of electronic switching and wireless. It remained, however, as backup for field operatives for some time afterwards.

MOUNT WEATHER

"Try NORAD again," the president demanded. George Wilmot was restless. Absorbed in personal thought, he rubbed his chin. Unshaven and unkempt, he felt the two-day-old stubble. At the moment, he didn't give a damn what his staff thought about his appearance. He hadn't slept in days. Shaking his head, he paced the floor. With deep furrows cut across his forehead, he was concentrating on a way out. There wasn't one.

He finally voiced his thoughts. "What's the matter with you people?" He couldn't contain himself any longer. Staring at his policy makers, he pounded on the table. "We've spent one point four trillion plus dollars on defense," he gesticulated, "and look at us!" His eyes scanned across the many faces seated around the conference table. He detected hints of excuses but the faces remained silent. He didn't want excuses. He had no tolerance for incompetence. They knew that. He was a man of action. He wanted results. But today, there weren't any. The commander in chief, along with the heads of military organizations, was kept in the dark. They were isolated from the rest of the world. "It wasn't supposed to be this way," he grumbled. He was pacing again. "People need me. They need us."

"Mister President," the JCS chairman insisted, "with due respect," he paused to face the president, "we are all in the same predicament."

"What about NORAD?" Wilmot demanded. "It's supposed to be the pulse of the nation. Best sheltered spot on the globe, unbreakable fortress, safe against any intrusion. For all we know," he warned, "the enemy's already on our doorsteps." He was pacing the floor again. "Look at us now. Trapped like cavemen."

"What's your wish, Mister President?"

"Get recons out," he ordered, "NORTHCOM, SPACECOM, Pentagon, anybody, everybody, just get some action. I can't just sit around and wait for better times. For all we know," he protested, "Doomsday's here already."

"We don't have trained forces on hand," the JCS chairman replied. "We've only got limited staff. You know that, sir." He felt insulted. It reflected in his voice. "Mostly for your own protection."

"Then," the president suggested, "commission 'em. Make them earn their pay. They've all been on the front lines." The president was serious. "Hell," he said with finality, "get some combat gear," he insisted, "I'll be out front."

"You can't mean that." There was grumbling among the staff. A few nodded in agreement. Others kept quiet. Individual emotions could be read on the many faces. "Most of us," the chairman called out, "don't have the training." He seemed to be getting upset at the thought of individual combat. He was trying to protect his staff. Many were close to retirement. You couldn't send these men out to fight. The very thought was absurd.

"As I see it," the president said in a final effort to get the men motivated, "we've got no choice." At least there would be action. Doing something would be better than just sitting around and waiting, hypothesizing what was going on in the nation. "Do something!" was his final order. He abruptly turned and stomped out the room. He was headed back to his private quarters. He needed a shower, a shave, and whatever else the bathroom was used for. He suddenly realized how tired he was. He was in dire need of sleep.

NORAD COMMAND

"…standby—we've…!" The HAM operator shouted. He swiveled the chair he was seated in to face the general. "Got something!" He was exuberant. He twisted the dials to raise the volume. They could hear faint voices, garbled at first, then coherent.

"Raise the signal strength." The brigadier was back in action. Backed by communication, he could think clearly again. Justification was first on the agenda. "Somebody's gonna' get the axe." He'd dump blame on somebody or his name wasn't Ben Jackson.

It was a strategy he had used many times in his career. Don't give 'em a chance to point fingers, *especially not in my direction.* There would be enough of that to go around later. *Cut charges off at the root.* He wasn't about to be the scapegoat for the NORAD command no matter which direction the onslaught would come from. And there'd be plenty, once the news wires were up again. With NORAD on the chopping block several times due to budget cuts, Jackson was at a disadvantage, pitted against new space-based defense programs. He had to protect his turf at any cost. He had to justify his position.

"Already maxed out," the operator defended.

"Then give me another frequency dammit, I want a signal—*Now.*"

There had been no news from the Castle. Alex had expected some word from Liz, but the operator logged no call signs from her.

Alex watched his buddy approach. "You square with the general?"

"Pain in the ass." Brian was agitated. "Thinks he's God."

"He's got the right."

"Blames the NSA for all the mess," Brian said with a frown of disgust cutting across his face, "insult after insult for the last hour." His face changed to concern. "Hear from Tracy yet? I'm worried. Let's get outta here."

"Can't," Alex hinted at the general, "wants me to stay. Why don't you take the Jeep and check on the house?" Alex urged. "Call me on the HAM. Here." He tossed him a set of keys.

Brian caught the keys in midair. "Right—see you in a couple hours." Brian seemed relieved to get away. He made a quick exit before Jackson got hold of him.

"Ready for action?" The brigadier seemed to have taken a liking to Alex. Not waiting for a response, he pulled Alex toward the conference room.

The room was filled with people. As soon as the general walked in they got busy. Alex picked up a copy of the OPS plan. He handed the general a copy.

"That piece of crap?" Jackson was furious. He tossed it in the air. The document landed by the trash can. "Any other bright ideas?" Jackson was agitated. Most avoided his stare. "I want action." Expecting a response, his eyes wandered from face to face. "What've you people been doing? Don't just sit around. Somebody else might nuke this place. We may not have much time." He shook his head in disgust then sought out Alex.

"Okay, then," Alex started off. "With the Soviets disbanded, we don't have a strategic superpower to deal with anymore." He was addressing the panel. "Threat's turned tactical. All terrorists now."

"Absolutely." Someone from the command threw out the remark.

"Who's DCA?[50]" Some hands went up. Alex made a mental note. "CIA?" Additional hands went up.

"NSA's here," Jackson pitched in. He leaned into the table but didn't see Brian. "Where's that twerp?"

"My buddy had to leave." Alex eyed the brigadier. "Most knowledgeable head in the Agency." Alex wanted Jackson to know he felt insulted.

"Figures," The brigadier shrugged his shoulders, "couldn't take the pressure."

"You're pretty hard on him." Alex stared at him.

Jackson ignored the remark. He'd turned to a senior staff member. "Anything from the White House?"

"Still checking."

Alex faced the most senior DCA. "What do you have on terrorism…and counter?" The agent handed out a stack of folders. A prominent office symbol covered the neatly bound documents, "Defense Communications Agency."

"What we have," the agent responded, "is data compiled over the past ten years. It's a list on the most recent attacks and our counters…or lack of."

"What do you mean 'lack of'?" Jackson shot back.

"Seems our attackers keep one step ahead," the agent explained. "They're getting sophisticated in their operations and weaponry.

"What's the current status on tracking?"

"Global black market on uranium sales and materials sold out of Islamabad."

"What's this place?" Jackson wanted to know.

"Kahuta."

"Underground base, hardened," said Alex. "Heard of it." A stack of printouts were promptly passed around the table. They were recent surveillance photographs previously taken from satellites. From the support structures above ground, the place looked sizable.

The CIA gave a brief description of what they had on the place. "Uranium processing systems from Europe. Enough weapons grade material for several bombs. Production's up. Korea, Iran, and Islamic states are buying up supplies as fast as they hit the markets. Jihad's their biggest customer."

"Okay, what do we do about it?" Jackson chimed in. He put the finger pointing aside, for now.

"We've got a coordinated effort with the CIA and NSA," the DCA rep advised.

"How's the material tracked?"

"Field agents infiltrated Jihad."

"How can we get to the processing facilities?" Jackson insisted.

"One warhead won't do the job." The voice belonged to a nuclear physicist. "Penetration depth of our warhead's not powerful enough. We've got nothing big enough in our arsenals."

"What's the targeting status of your nukes?" Alex gazed at the brigadier who shrugged his shoulders. "Anybody?"

"Trained at the most hostile targets." SPADOC command provided the information. "Here's the target list." A second set of charts was passed around marked "Top Secret—

---

[50] Defense Communications Agency – Intelligence branch to build, manage, and support the DOD infrastructure.

SCI." The list identified places familiar to most: Islamabad, Rawalpindi, Karachi, Baghdad, Basrah, Mosul, Teheran, Abadan, Tabriz, Damascus.

"This is insane!" Alex exclaimed. He shook his head in denial. "We can't just wipe out the entire Middle East." He stepped back to compose himself for the next approach. "We've got to approach it surgically."

"Why?" a senior SAC commander interrupted. "It'd be a first step toward world peace."

"Don't think so," Alex argued. "It'd trigger nothing but hostilities."

"What options do we have?" someone else came forward.

Alex was getting more frustrated by the minute. "I won't have any part in this madness." He was angry. He was about to reprimand the speaker but was distracted by someone entering. It was Jackson's aid. He whispered something into the general's ear. It even got Alex's attention.

The general stepped forward, "Alex," he said, "we've got to talk. Follow me." He quickly led the way to his office.

"What's happened?" Alex sensed immediate alarm.

"Just got a message."

"What?"

"Daughter's been taken hostage.

Alex was shocked. "Says who?" He wasn't sure he'd understood.

"Can't tell you," Jackson insisted. "But," he emphasized, "if you want to see your daughter again, I suggest you cooperate."

"Whose demands?"

"Cant' tell you."

"Traced her to Arizona. That's all I have."

Alex was outraged and he said so. "I'm leaving," he said. "Screw you people." His exit was blocked by sentries on duty.

Jackson caught up. "Warned you, didn't I?" the general grumbled. He was stern-faced. "We're at war. There's no time for empathy. We've got to act…and act fast." He took a steadfast stance. "Better be with me one hundred percent."

"You people are mad!" Alex abruptly turned and stormed off. Brian was by his side. They didn't get far. The exit was blocked by security. Their weapons were drawn. Alex backed down but not without resisting. "I need time to think."

Jackson was losing his patience. "We don't have the time." It was a warning shot at Alex. "You cooperate…now!" Alex was sandwiched in by security. He was led along the corridor back to the War Room.

Back in the conference room, Alex strained, but quickly composed himself. He slowly advanced to the podium. He stepped up to face the assembly. "May I have your attention, please?" he beckoned. The room turned quiet. "I want to briefly summarize the talking points to propose a course of action. But," he cautioned, "we've got to be rational. In summary," he said, "we must assume that San Francisco was a pre-emptive strike. We also have confirmation that our counter strike was successful." He took a brief pause then continued. "I am not proud of my actions." Alex rationalized the point. "I'm a peace-loving person."

"Nobody will hold you personally responsible," Jackson assured him. He stood up and advanced on the podium. He motioned to Alex to get off. "Listen up," Jackson was saying. "One Minuteman wing is aimed at four of the most hostile nations. Each warhead is in a ready state to deliver a payload."

Alex could not let that happen. "Just one minute," he objected. He tried to reason again. "We're not the aggressor. In case you don't remember, we're a democracy."

"Don't give me that crap," the general spat out. "We may not have a second chance. It's my call that we move now."

Alex still protested. "Only under extreme duress," he insisted.

"We voted and stand fully behind you. The quicker we take action, the safer the nation will be."

"All right," Alex finally agreed. "But," he insisted, "military targets only. After that," he persisted, "you're on your own." The missile wing was reprogrammed with target acquisitions for Kahuta and Pyongyang, so he was told. For now, it was all he could do to prevent an all-out nuclear holocaust.

ARIZONA DESERT

The room was sweltering. "Let me outta here!" Tracy was banging against the steel door. "What're you doin' to me?" she protested. Her shouts echoed against the walls, lost at the end of the hall. She was going stir crazy. In between infrequent checks by her capturers, she was left on her own. Nobody ever talked. They were hardened faces, with bodies of steel, it seemed. They only stopped to drop off food twice a day and to collect the dishes. Left on her own, her mind was running out of ideas. The same thoughts repeated over and over. It almost seemed that the creative mind in her had been shot down. She couldn't think straight. "Who could?" her conscious mind responded, "When captured and locked up?"

She could hear footsteps approach. "Finally!" They stopped outside her door. The little glass window opened. Two piercing eyes stared at her. "Whatcha want?"

"Something to read," she demanded, "and..." The window shut close with a clap. She was alone again. Several minutes went by before the footsteps appeared once more. The lock retracted and in he stepped, wearing boots, shorts, covered in a hat. It was one of those floppy hats popular in combat. In his hand, he carried a couple of magazines. He casually dropped them on the cot.

"Thank you." Tracy was grateful. "Where're you from?" She tried to make conversation. She desperately needed to talk. But there was no answer, only a grunt. He stepped out. The steel banged close again. His boots shuffled back down the hall. *At least,* her mind cheered her on, *something to read.* Her happiness dissipated when her eyes fell on the cover pages. "Playboy, Hustler," they read.

"What am I gonna do with this?" she yelled after him. Some pages were well worn. Others were smeared with dirt.

She spat at them, tossed them on the floor, and then picked them up again. *What the hell,* she thought, *it's better than nothing. Place's a pigsty already. More filth won't matter.*

Despite her disappointment at the lack of meaningful material, her fingers leafed through the dirty pages. She'd never opened one of these, especially not material for men only. The nudes didn't do anything for her. There were some funny anecdotes, though, especially the write-ins, the personals. She got a kick out of reading them. "How dumb." She couldn't imagine anyone being so preoccupied with sex. She had no idea about problems men struggled with to maintain a healthy manhood.

The mags did one thing for her. They distracted her from her present environment. Her thoughts fastened on Brian.

It was this man of late that had captured her imagination. She became absorbed. With happy thoughts about him, she felt she could endure the present misery. Hope settled in on her confusing environment.

NORAD COMMAND

"Anything?" Alex kept checking for status. Maintenance crews were busy setting up equipment. When Brian left earlier, he did not get far. Sentries had stopped him on the way out. Besides, the gates had been shot tight once more. For now, his only option was the HAM radio. He was testing the castle link. "No word yet." It took ingenuity and resourcefulness from all hands to configure the underground backup system. First, the buried landlines feeding the antenna farm had to be tested. Next was the comm gear. Built in the '40s, sitting idle for decades, internal electronic guts needed testing. What made it worse, the outdated "cannon" connectors were not compatible with modern electronic gear. Interfaces had to be stripped, cut, and soldered up to provide a path to the command computers. Fortunately, most processing computers still functioned. Fourteen hundred feet of granite pretty much had shielded the equipment. Only the interfaces connected with the antenna farm were destroyed by the blast.

Alex, out of habit, kept checking his mobile. He'd seen others doing it. *Can't believe we've become slaves to the gadget.* Who would have known twenty years ago that the mobile phone would have such a momentous impact on their lives?

Alex repeatedly shot a glance at ZULU. The time zone clocks indicated a new day in Europe. The Mountain was eight hours behind. They'd been working intensely through the night. Jackson made his presence aware whenever he could. "How we doin'?"

"Running final tests, sir." Wyoming, Montana, and Dakota were online. The warheads were reprogrammed for the new targets. "Wyoming's our best bet. Signals for Montanan and Dakota are marginal, can't depend on them."

"Still on time?" Jackson had set 0600 hours for the launch. If things went as planned, they should be able to fire the missiles. It was close to launch time.

"On time."

"Mission control," Jackson ordered. Alex followed on his heels.

He would run final checks with Wyoming from there. The place was packed. Jackson was shouting out commands as soon as he walked in. The usually unlit cigar stuffed in one corner of his lips now was lit. Alex noticed the pungent burn of tobacco but only made a silent comment. *Disgusting.* It seemed not that long ago when he had enjoyed an occasional cigarette, or pipe, for that matter, but that was back during his college days.

A woman in her forties approached. Alex took note. Appraising her shape, he muttered, "Not bad looking." She planted herself in front of the brigadier. Alex watched her dressing him down. Something must not have sat right with her. She addressed the brigadier directly. "No smoking!"

He deliberately turned to face the interruption. Highly agitated, he sneered at her, "Lady, today all bets are off. You're lucky to be alive. So don't give me that crap about procedures." He knew it was a "No Smoking" zone. He'd enforced the rule years ago.

"But..." the lady protested, getting cut short.

"We're making history here. What's your name, anyway?" his voice resonated through the now silent-turned room. He checked her nametag. Everybody was aware of the reprimand. The aura seemed in her favor.

"Rhonda Hicks," she insisted, "Station Chief, SPACECOM." She held steadfast, staring him down. Abruptly turning on his heals, he stormed off. He appeared miffed because she hadn't addressed him with the proper reverence. Sir would have been the appropriate salutation.

"I like her spirit." Alex grinned at Brian. "She's got spunk."

"Got my vote," Brian agreed.

Alex sidled up to her. He spoke quietly. "Took balls to do what you just did."

"The general?"

"Exactly."

"Don't get me wrong," she started, "I respect rank, but rules are rules."

Her voice carried a pleasant tone. Alex studied her face. *Pretty woman.* "I'd like to have you on my team."

Her gaze was challenging but quickly followed with a smile. "What team's that?"

"Shakeup," he grinned, "once we get through this mess." He'd noted a twinkle in her eyes. *Not bad a woman,* he'd decided, *got something going for her, credentials and all.*

She offered her hand. "Chief of Operations, SPACECOM." They shook. "I'd like that."

"I'll..." Alex tried to assure a personal connection but was interrupted by the general's booming voice.

"On deck!" Jackson was getting ready to pass judgment. He cleared his voice. His eyes scanned the many faces assembled in front of him. "This," he started, "is the most critical time in NORAD's existence." His voice carried across the command center. "There can be no errors." He shifted on his feet. "Once we launch," he continued, "we'll be on our own. Gate's gonna be shut tight."

"How long?" Concerns voiced by the crowd seemed justified. "My family...my relatives." It was an unavoidable act. Everybody assigned to the mountain had known the consequences. To accept them was yet another story.

"You all knew the penalty when you joined the command." His words were harsh. The day everyone dreaded had finally arrived. Nobody ever expected it. *We'll deal with it when the time comes* had been the general consensus. "Let's get this over with!" *The time was now.* "Final status?"

"Set on our end." It was his chief of operations. "Sir!"

"What about Wyoming?"

The mission chief took command. "Alex?" He'd faced his direction.

"I think," Alex responded, "we have a solid connection."

"What do you mean *think*? You aren't sure?"

"Link's tested fine, but," he wavered, "I've got no control over the silos." Communications between the launch center and the missiles were generally reliable. The system had been up in ready state for decades, waiting—ready at a minute's notice. For that, they were tested periodically, not only live systems, but the standbys as well.

"What about delivery?"

"W-70 warheads—combination fission-fusion." The weapons chief stepped forward. For the general to understand, he felt he had to give details. He gave a brief explanation. "The W-70 warhead causes fission that, in turn," he elaborated, "releases neutrons that absorb the ensuing radiation burst through fusion. Resultant neutrons are absorbed by air. A neutron bomb doesn't radiate beyond the blast zone. It's designed to wipe out city life within a narrow range but leaves the infrastructure in place without having a thousand years of radiation to deal with."

"Clean weapon," Jackson couldn't let the opportunity pass without a derogatory remark, "Right?"

"Dirty!" Alex felt he had to correct him. *Nothing was clean about nuclear destruction.* He stepped back to let the other sections report their readiness.

CASTLE ROCK

"Ouch," Liz moaned in the quiet of darkness, "Ahh." It was the sound of air escaping. It took a second for her to realize it was her chest making the sounds. She gulped for air. It slowly filled her lungs. There was pain. *Broken ribs,* she rationed, *or cracked, at least.* She forced her eyes open, but only one responded. The other was shut tight, swollen from a punch to the face.

Darkness surrounded her. Aside from the occasional shuffle of footsteps, it was quiet for most part. There was something else, subdued voices. She lifted her head to focus on the sound but could not make out the words. They were foreign words, a language she didn't understand. *Farsi likely,* she reasoned. *What do they want from Dad? Why this place? How was he involved?* They were questions she couldn't resolve. There could be more to his life than he'd admit. She knew he'd been involved with defense. But that was his job. *Or was it?*

She'd find out soon enough. "Hope I'll still be around…the kids!" Her mind was thrown into panic again. She hadn't heard or seen them. *How long has it been?* She couldn't remember. "Hey!" Hoping to get some attention, she yelled into the dark.

There were footsteps. They stopped. The door swung open. It crashed against the wall. "Cheh?"

Propped up on one elbow, Liz forced her upper body up. She winced with pain. "My kids—I want my kids." The butt of the rifle came down on her but stopped inches short of her forehead. The man gripping it changed his mind. Perhaps it was pity from her battered face, perhaps something else. She didn't know. He looked her body over. There was no desire or cravings in his eyes. It was just the cold stare of ignorance. *Must not speak English,* she thought. Liz's confidence was bolstered. Her poise returned despite the horrific videos of beheadings she remembered seeing on YouTube.

"Kids," Liz beckoned. Pleadingly, with one hand raised, she repeated, "Kids." His face took on a quizzical stare. He shrugged his shoulders. Liz repeated. It suddenly seemed to dawn on him. "Kids!" A grin came over his face. "Kids, okay." He was getting ready to leave when she called out, "Toilet."

Again, there was a lack of understanding. Liz had to repeat the word several more times, making gestures of urgency, before it sank in. He motioned her to get up. "Follow," he said, then led her by the arm to the restroom. With a swift motion he cut the strap from her wrists.

Liz was thankful. There was momentous relief from her bladder. She remained quietly on the commode, deliberating her plight. *What can I do?* she asked herself. She stood up and quietly slid the window open. It was dark outside. There were no sounds. She thought of calling for help but dismissed it. There were no neighbors in the immediate vicinity. Besides, a jump would have damaged or broken her legs. There was impatient thumping on the door. "Open."

"Just a minute." Liz ran the faucet to cool her face. The cold water felt soothing on her swollen eye. She cleaned off smudges of dried blood. The knocking became more persistent. "Alright," she called out, "coming." Liz opened up and was forced back to the living room. "Kids," she gestured in the direction of the bedroom. She poked at her chest and then at the door to indicate her desire. He turned his head to check on his comrades. There were subdued voices from below. It seemed quiet in the house. He nodded in the direction of the kids' room and motioned her to follow.

They were sound asleep. "Thank you," she whispered at the intruder. He led her back to the living room. Wrists tied behind her back, she was forced to the floor once more. He left and shut the door. Darkness returned. She stared into the darkness hoping her dad would come back soon. She could not shake a feel of evil foreboding for what would happen to them all.

NORAD COMMAND

"That's it for me." Alex jerked his head at Brian. He wanted to leave. For his part, the mission was over. He did not count on the brigadier. Immediately, their exit was blocked by sentries. "General's orders." Their response was clear. "Nobody leaves." They'd been trapped again. His mind was on Tracy. All he wanted was to get her back. He was worried sick.

"Stay," they were ordered. Alex had been chosen to coordinate the launch. They held him to it. Right from the start he had a feeling that he'd wind up the scapegoat. *Let it be a damned civilian,* he could bet were the general's thoughts. They'd picked the outsider.

Alex could refuse. He evaluated the odds and considered the consequences. His daughter was the prize.

"You ready?" His thoughts were interrupted. He could feel the brigadier's stare on him.

Alex shot a glance at his buddy indicating, "You with me?" He got a nod in return. In either case, Brian would be by his side.

The brigadier handed him the mic. "The ball's in your court." Alex did a voice check. The PA hadn't been much in use since the '80s. There was a slight crackle and a click. It seemed to work. Alex checked the ZULU clocks. With the automated launch system out, he had to use the manual procedure. "Fifteen minutes to countdown."

"Warren," Alex initiated the launch sequence with Wyoming, "come in." There was no response. The air remained silent. "Wyoming," he tried again several more times. Nothing. He tried the backup sites. There was sound. They both responded.

"Grand Forks…ready on standby."

"Malmstrom…ready on standby."

"Where's Warren?" Jackson demanded. "Gimme that." He ripped the mic from Alex's hands.

"Warren—come in," he yelled, "Warren," more urgent each time, "come in." He repeated several times over but did not get any response.

He was furious. "What's going on?" he demanded. "Bauer!"

"Sir?"

"What's our alternative on the strike zones? Warren's dead."

"It'll take hours to program the backups." Alex saw a slight glimmer of hope that the launch might be aborted. He hated the very thought of a pre-emptive strike.

"Dammit," Jackson cursed. "Don't have the time." His already agitated face turned irate. "Get your ass up there," he steamed at Alex. "Get me a report."

"What?"

"Get your man and check on Warren." He was red faced. He waived him on and stormed off. "And I mean now."

Alex was stunned by the general's outburst. He called on Brian. "What do you think…you ready?"

"It's a two hour drive under the best conditions," Brian protested. Flanked by two sentries, they were ushered from the mission center. "MPs," the IDs indicated. The motor pool was the destination. There, a military type Humvee was waiting, ready to gun the engine. It fishtailed towards the gate. To let them through, it took several minutes for the blast door to open. The driver sped the vehicle out of the tunnel toward I-25.

Alex and Brian were in back. Alex had an idea. "Let's see if we can raise some wings."

"What do you mean?"

"Wings, you know…things that fly."

"Doubt there's any. Besides, who's going to pilot?"

"You are." Alex commanded the driver to head to nearby Peterson Air Force Base.

"Can't do that," the MP protested.

"Why?"

"Orders—Wyoming. You heard the general."

Alex felt he had to educate the MP about the critical situation. "If you haven't heard," he urged, "we're in a state of emergency. The sooner we get there, the quicker we're safe. The nation," he emphasized, "you, and everybody else."

"Can't…"

"You heard the general. I'm in charge." It took intelligent persuasion for the sentries to finally resign. By the time they reached the I-25 onramp, he headed east for Pete Field.

Ten minutes later, the Humvee skidded to a halt. Flanked by military police, the jeep was immediately waved through.

"Where to?"

"See the hangar over there?" Alex gestured.

Seconds later the Humvee pulled up. Dozens of crafts were sitting on the tarmac. Not one of them could take to the air. "Electronics and instruments are out," they were told by maintenance crews busy with repairs.

They'd have a better chance inside the hangar. Damages would be less. Steel acted as conductor. It would have filtered much of the damaging rays to ground.

"See the choppers?"

"What!" Brian exclaimed. "I'm not checked out in an Apache."

"Look at it as riding a bike," Alex grinned, "you know the saying."

"Yeah but…" he protested, "these things are loaded with sensitive electronics. Probably out of commission anyway."

"Well then…" Alex spotted a Bell TH-67 with the canopy open. It was being repaired. "Could you handle that?"

"Trainer?"

"Wanna give it a try?"

"Steal it? Are you crazy?"

"It's called 'borrow.'" There was no one around at the moment. Alex had already slid behind the gunner's seat. "Come on," he urged his buddy, who was reluctant. With a shrug, Brian slid behind the cockpit seat. He flipped a few switches. The instruments worked. He took a few seconds to absorb the once familiar surroundings then grinned at Alex. He seemed elated. "This is great."

"Well?" Alex urged, "Ignition." The damned thing actually kicked in. Puffs of blackened dust shot from the exhaust. The rotor, making a grinding sound, labored, but after a few seconds gained rotation. "Take it up."

"Hey you!" There was a sudden shout. "What's going on?" One of the maintenance crew came running. Dressed in yellow overalls, he appeared out of the billowing exhaust smoke. He was furious. It had taken seconds for him to realize what he was about to lose. "Hey you!" he yelled in the direction of the MPs. The two guards were by the hangar entrance taking a smoke break. Alarmed by the call they came running.

"The chopper!"

Alex leaned out the canopy. He yelled over the engine noise, "Just borrowing it!" There was no time for confrontation. The skids came off the ground. Brian aimed for the hangar exit.

In desperation, the mechanic jumped on the skids. "Gimme that!" he yelled. His hands were grappling for the controls. He was dragged along two feet off the ground.

"Watch me," Brian shouted over the roar of the engine. He had gotten wrapped up in the moment. After clearing the exit gates, Brian jerked the chopper a few feet off the ground. The action caused the mechanic to lose his grip. He slipped off. His body ended up rolling along the tarmac. His curses were muffled out by the engine. Brian forced the turbo to full speed. The MPs tried to cut him off but the craft had already gained altitude. Shots they fired after the chopper went wild not causing any damages.

Brian adjusted the headset. "I'm surprised this thing's working."

"Maintenance must have swapped out the damaged parts." It came as no surprise. Most military parts were wrapped in static resistant plastics. Critical parts were meticulously kept stored in antistatic containers. It was standard military policy for handling and shipping parts.

Brian was getting the feel for the controls. "Direction?" he shouted into the pitch of the rotors. The craft rapidly gained altitude, leaving a hot exhaust trail in its wake.

"North," Alex directed, "across the Black Forest, then intercept with I-25."

WARREN MISSILE COMMAND

Brian was flying the chopper low.

"What's the strategy?" Brian wanted to know. "Got a plan?"

"Nope. Gotta wing it." For most of the flight, his thoughts had been on the environment ahead. Technically, crewmembers could launch a nuclear attack with or without approval from higher authority. As many as fifty missiles could be illicitly fired unless "PAL[51]" foreclosed this option. Military personnel, maintenance airmen, and civilian contractors who possessed proper security credentials could be granted access to the silos. He shouldn't have any problems getting in with his credentials. He wouldn't force a launch, Alex promised himself, or aggravate any resistance by the center. He wasn't thrilled with the launch anyway. For all he knew, they might be refused access. *I could care less.* He wanted to get this over with to search for his daughter.

At present, in layman's terms, he explained the workings of the last obstacle to Brian. There was little in the public record that discussed how PAL worked. It wasn't surprising. Remarkably little was published about technical details on nuclear weapons design. Much more had been published about the so-called "physics package," the payload, than the control aspects. It may have been because fission and fusion, in the abstract, were natural processes that could be studied by scientists around the world. With a little intelligence, someone could even reinvent the atom bomb. "It's been done." In contrast, a PAL was an engineering article with many possible design choices. Furthermore, the design of a PAL was based on cryptography, and cryptography had always been shrouded in secrecy.

"Cheyenne's coming up," Alex warned. He oriented his view. He could barely make out I-25 below. "Take it down to tree level," he suggested. The landscape was still too dark to recognize from their present altitude. The rolling hills of the Cheyenne landscape panned into view. "Base should be a few miles ahead. See that?" Alex pointed off into the distance. "Staff Circle. Head for it." A minute later, the craft roared past a housing cluster. Ahead, an empty stretch of farmland gradually slid into view.

"What do I look for?"

"Concrete block," he was instructed, "middle of nowhere."

---

[51] Permission Access Link is a mechanical safeguard system invoking final launch authorization.

CAYMAN ISLANDS

McAllister was not happy. Ever since the Shahadah call he'd been on edge. *Who does he think he is?* His innate Irish pride had been touched by being ordered around like a water boy. He had a notion to cancel the deal. He didn't need to put up with this nonsense. He expected to be treated with respect like any executive of his standing. *But,* he considered, *the profit is great.* It was the driving factor. It kept him quiet.

He'd given it one last chance. Because the customer had not been satisfied with the previous arrangements, he'd been forced to cancel the original A-300 order. He'd spent hours on end locating a new source for an untraceable Airbus. With orders backlogged for months on end awaiting deliveries, it'd been difficult to close a new deal. *Why all the secrecy?* he'd wondered.

Finally, he'd arranged a deal by bribing one broker enough to make it worthwhile. They'd slipped one customer order. To lose all tracks, the new deal had been rerouted through several obscure corporate entities with additional bribes tendered. He didn't care. *It's not my money.* He just wanted the deal over with, but the final bid hadn't been cheap. Since money was no object, the order had been satisfied.

The intercom was buzzing. He picked up. "Yes?"

"Sir." It was his secretary. "There's a call for you."

He'd anticipated the call. Unsure what to expect, he answered, "McAllister."

"Shahadah." It was the voice he hated. "What's the status?"

"Ready for delivery," he prompted.

"Traceability?"

"None."

"Have it ready for departure," a slight hesitation later, "Twenty-four hours."

"Affirmative. Twenty-four." *Click,* the call was over. Greatly relieved, he exhaled. "Thank God, deal's done." Hoping never to hear from this mean fuck again, he decided to take the rest of the day off. "Think I need a vacation," he expressed on the way from the office with a sense of accomplishment, but choices were limited when spending life in a tropical vacation place. He just knew he had to get away from his place of work, the place of tension, for a while, and headed straight for his favorite massage parlor.

WARREN MISSILE COMMAND

"NORAD…NORAD…come in," Brian repeated into the headset mic. "Bell One." There was nothing but static. Several minutes went by. Then, amid the static, was a response.

"Bell One, go."

"Finally," Brian acknowledged. He switched to talk mode. The response was intermittent. Words were broken up and barely audible above the rotor noise. He couldn't understand what was being said. "Repeat," he demanded. Words finally came through more legibly.

"Must have raised the signal level." Alex followed the dialogue on the headphone dialed into the on-board frequency.

"Any response from Warren?" Brian yelled into the mic.

"Nothing." The next order was clear. "Investigate…take by force…if necessary."

"Can't do that," Alex cut in. The last order made him furious. "We will *not* use force." His left hand stretched out to reach for the instrument knob. He turned it off, breaking communication with the Mountain.

"Hang on," Brian interrupted. He'd been scanning the horizon. "I think we've got something." He craned forward for a better view.

"That's it," Alex confirmed. "Take it down." A few seconds later the helicopter flared out. They had landed fifty yards from a squat concrete building.

"That's it?" Brian asked, curious.

"That's it." Both jumped form the cockpit. Alex led the way. Hunched forward to clear the rotor blades, Alex hastened towards the complex.

Brian hurried to catch up behind Alex. "Sure is quiet," Brian remarked. Somehow, without a weapon, he felt exposed. Dawn was rising over the eastern horizon. The early morning light threw long shadows on the wheat fields. A whispering breeze flowing across the sea of chaffs made them roll like gentle waves. Both men moved with caution. They were checking the surroundings for signs of life. They came up to the shack. It appeared empty.

"Freeze!" A sharp command bellowed out of nowhere. It broke the silence like a whip. Both froze. In an instant, they were surrounded by several armed guardsmen with gun barrels pointed at their faces. There was more shouting.

"Stop! Up…hands up," the leader commanded. "Hands up, I said." His rank indicated that of a sergeant.

Brian immediately reacted. With hands in the air, Alex countered, "We're NORAD." Firm hands appeared from the shadows. They took hold of their shoulders. They were getting frisked for weapons.

"IDs," the sergeant demanded. Alex handed over his pass. "What about him?" Brian was under scrutiny.

"He's with me."

"What are you doing here?"

"NORAD command sent us." Alex briefly laid out the last few hours in the mountain. He emphasized the critical state the nation was in.

"Okay—relax."

They were hurried to the elevator shaft. Alex needed information. "When was the last shift change?"

"Been overdue."

"Thought so." Alex had a suspicion that something below wasn't right. "Okay, take us down."

"Don't have clearance for below." Top security had no authorization for the launch center. Their responsibility was to keep the terrain above secure.

"I'll take responsibility." That defused the sentry's reluctance. Alex didn't know what to expect below and needed support. "I need you below. Right?" He turned to Brian who agreed with a supportive nod.

They fronted the elevator. Impatiently, the sergeant pushed the button. "Nothing." There was no response. "Of course! Electronics are out." He turned and gestured to an emergency exit. It was their only choice. Panting, he led the way. "Should be eighty feet down."

Their rushing footsteps sounded hollow on the concrete and steel. Alex was counting. Twelve steps per level followed by a ninety degree turn, then another twelve steps. Several turns later they turned the final corner. "Ninety six," he'd counted. They had landed at the outer blast door. The sergeant motioned for Alex to step up. With M-16s aimed ahead, the sentries remained on guard.

"Red." The ID reader blinked at him. "Good," he said, "the blast didn't reach here." He swept his ID. There was a flashing "Invalid Entry" response. Alex was puzzled. "Should work." He tried again with the same response.

"Only one way in?" Brian was shaking the head. "There's got to be another option."

The sergeant stepped up. With the butt of the automatic, wildly, he started banging. The sound reverberated through the shaft. He hammered several more times but there was no response. The team was puzzled. Alex stood quietly for a moment to decide on the next step. A decision had to be made. "But what?" Then it came to him, "Shaft."

RAWALPINDI (Pakistan)

The Serpent was moving again. Phase Two, the second act of his Plan, was time critical. He was accompanied by several of his lieutenants: Rashid Abu, First Lieutenant, Al Qaeda, Jihad, Base Camp One, Yemen; Shakir Murad, First Lieutenant, Al Qaeda, Jihad, Base Camp Three, Yemen; and Antarah Radi, Mission Commander, Al Qaeda, Jihad, Islamabad, Pakistan. They had just arrived at the Pakistani capital and were rushed to their immediate destination, the uranium production plant. There, waiting for their arrival, was the local escort. They were led to the underground elevator. Seconds later it stopped four levels below. "Hazard Level IV," the sign read. Stepping off, he was quickly whisked along the lengthy hall to a dorm. A staff of scientists did their best to appear busy. Lab coats prominently displayed the company logo, "PINSTECH." Helpful hands expertly forced his body into a protective suit. The helmet was ill fitted, the gloves and boots likewise.

He wanted to make it quick. He never liked this underground location; it felt like a trap. Stepping back into the hallway, masked faces were scurrying in and out of corridors. Everywhere he turned was another concealed face he couldn't read. The uncertainty bothered him. The protective garments didn't help. It was steaming hot inside. He was flopping around in oversized booties. He'd already tripped several times. *No wonder we are behind schedule.* He was ushered to the first production facility. Steel reinforced, concrete encased, the facility was huge. Thousands of cylinders stared at him much like silver-shiny demigods humming in unison. He stared at one of many gas-centrifuge reprocessing plants Pakistan had acquired for making weapons grade nuclear fission materials. "Production has fallen behind," he was told. From what he could make out, processing stations were only sparsely occupied.

"What's the production level?" he demanded from the plant manager.

"Fifteen kilotons, sir," was a strained response. There was fear in his face. His voice faltered as well.

"A month?" the Serpent asked.

"Year," the voice quivered. As production manager, he had control over production, but not raw materials delivery. Acquired through illegal markets, they came in only small quantities.

"Not good enough!" the visitor screamed at him. "Double the yield."

"We're at maximum production," the escort whimpered, "sir."

"Then get more centrifuges." His orders were clear. "Your output is barely enough to pack three weapon heads."

"We have no funding," the manager insisted. He was physically shaken. His lips moved in silent prayer. They were praying for this uninvited menace to disappear.

"I want a complete report on your operation," the Serpent demanded, "in two hours." His lieutenants in tow, he abruptly turned and stormed from the production area.

How can we compete with Israel and India, he thought with disgust, *with this lazy staff taking coffee breaks every hour?* He did not take into account the recently implemented demands by the detested IAEA[52] commission to protect workers from maximum exposure levels to radiation. He was still infuriated at having to comply with regulations forced on the nation to avoid international sanctions.

---

[52] IAEA – International Atomic Energy Agency.

I will have to shake this place up. He was determined to do so immediately. "The Plaza," he directed when they reached the surface. He felt dirty. He needed a shower stop. He was looking forward to the capital's foremost hotel accommodations. Twenty minutes later, he and his escort stepped into the cooling atmosphere of the hotel lobby.

WARREN MISSILE COMMAND

The atmosphere down here was stale. The staring eyes of the sentries were shifting between Alex and Brian, waiting. Alex's brows were furrowed. He was deep in thought. He searched for an alternative. His mind called up the deepest recesses in the brain. He could not recollect information he did not have. It was long ago and he had not been part of the construction of this or any of the other launch facilities. There had been some blueprints he'd viewed during the last design phase. A slight glimmer of knowledge slowly emerged. "I should know," he muttered. *What was it again?* The sentries kept banging against the outer blast door of the capsule.

Brian had been silent for most part. Watching Alex, he could read the frustration in his friend's face. "Escape hatch?" he suggested. There was not much he could contribute to the mechanics of nuclear missile silos and their intricate workings. He'd spent most of his career within NSA working satellites. But today, they were dead, wiped out by an enemy. His job, for all practical purposes, was eliminated, if perhaps only temporarily. It was only a matter of time before the agency would rebuild. Providing there was a budget.

"No good," Alex replied. "It opens only from inside."

"How about a demolition team?" the sergeant offered. He was guessing. His team remained quiet.

"No time," Alex gestured. "Follow me…I've got an idea."

"You…you," The sergeant ordered two of his men, "cover the exit." The rest quickly joined Alex and Brian to climb back up the stairway. Considerable time had been wasted. Alex shot a glance at his wrist. It was an automatic gesture, a habit hard to break. The time hadn't moved. It was frozen by the EMP. "Anybody's got the time?" They all checked. Not one watch was ticking. Most sentries were unaware their timepiece had stopped.

"Upstairs," Alex ordered.

"Where?" The sergeant was curious.

"Airshaft." Alex sprinted his way up. He took two steps at a time. "It won't be a joyride." The answer had come to him. He'd suddenly recalled an escape route. Back in the fifties, when the facilities were built, air exchange had not been perfected. That science came with the space flights. To be sustained, an underground bunker needed a fresh air supply. When Alex reached topside, he was out of breath. The others were also gasping for air.

"Airshaft?" Brian had an ominous feeling. He was eyeing his buddy. "What's below?"

"The capsule." Alex sounded reassuring. His breathing had caught up.

"Another adventure," Brian groaned under his breath. He'd arrived last.

The sergeant waved them on, "This way." He led the group to the air intake shaft. It was located at the far end of the perimeter fence. Right away there was a problem. The lid would not budge. "Need a wrench," he said. "Be right back." The sergeant turned and headed for a nearby vehicle. He returned just as quick carrying a wrench in one hand, screwdriver in the other. He went to work on the grill.

They watched him wrestle with the rusty fan nuts holding the cast iron grill in place. Beneath was the shaft. "Dammit," he cussed. His fingers had slipped and the rusty nut had gashed his hand. Droplets of blood were seeping onto the concrete.

"Let me." Alex had more patience. He had the experience. Industrial engineer by trade, he'd tackled many rusty bolds. Without WD-40 on hand, it had to be brute force. One bolt after another broke off with a crunch, but it didn't matter. It'd be a one-way route. Finally, the bolts were off. It took all hands to lift the heavy air fan from its mounting. Groaning sounds filtered through the early morning hours as the fan toppled to the side.

"What's next?" Brian wanted to know. His quizzical eyes were staring into the gaping shaft.

"Don't worry," Alex cautioned, "it's only a ten foot drop," he threw a sheepish grin at his buddy, "once you reach the capsule." He stepped up by the edge.

"Wait," the sergeant called out. "Take my .45." He handed Alex his sidearm but kept the M-16.

Alex turned back to face the opening. "Here we go." With a quick step, arms outstretched above his head, he jumped into the dark. Above, they caught the trailing yell, "Geronimo!"

The sergeant followed with his men, one by one, in rapid succession. Brian lingered by the edge. He was waiting for any sound from below. It remained silent. "What the hell." He decided and jumped.

Alex felt himself in freefall. It only lasted a few seconds. He braced his boots against the shaft to slow his fall. From between his legs, he caught a glimmer of light rapidly rushing up. Alex tensed his body. A second later he landed. It was a hard landing. His back took most of the fall. Air was squeezed from his lungs. It sounded much like "Fuck."

In a reflex action, he rolled off to one side and inhaled hard. He strained his body on one elbow to check his location. He had landed in back of some launch racks. His head turned to the ceiling. There was a sucking thud. The sergeant had landed on the same spot. One by one, the sound was repeated several more times. Two guards piled on top of each other. They were cussing. "Quiet," Alex cautioned. Brian made the last entry. His pupils were wide. He also landed on one of the men that couldn't get out of the way fast enough. Alex offered him his hand. "You okay?" He pulled him to his feet.

"What a rush," Brian muttered. He'd forgotten to breathe and was sucking in air.

"You got that right," the sergeant admitted. He had a bloody nose. He'd hit his face on the butt of the automatic when he landed.

Alex gave a sign of caution. The section appeared empty. He was surprised there was no one in the equipment room. Once inside, he whispered, "I know the place." He'd been in the capsule before. He took the lead. "Follow me." Carefully, he eased his way ahead.

With the leveled .45 in his right hand, he cautiously led the way in the direction of the control center. He had to duck several times to clear the cable way. Above their heads was a mess of interconnecting cables and wires supported by cable trays. He pressed forward along rows of comm and computer equipment. With extreme caution, the team slid toward the central section. Alex stepped from behind the rear bay. The massive launch console popped into view, but that wasn't the only thing his eyes captured.

"Cover me." Alex gestured at the trailing sergeant.

"How many?" Brain whispered in back.

"Only make out two."

"Should be four," the sergeant whispered back.

Alex thought to split the team but there was only room for single file. He inched his way forward. The room finally opened up. All at once, they came face to face with the scene. It was bloody. Two lifeless bodies were slammed over the launch panel, each on the opposite end of the rail. On closer inspection, one body still held a tight grip on the trigger key, ready for the launch.

"Wonder what happened," the sergeant whispered.

"I can guess." Alex had an idea why there were the dead bodies. "Moral conflict." He pushed his way past them toward the blast door. The sergeant ordered two of his men to cover them. The others closed up the rear. Alex headed towards the main entrance way. One hand raised, he gestured in that direction. It was there they spotted the two remaining missile officers. Ready to fend off intruders, they were poised by the blast door. Both held their sidearm aimed at the sentries hammering away on the other side of the shaft entrance. The airmen were trapped from both sides. At the moment, they were unaware.

"Sarge," Alex gestured ahead. The sergeant took the lead. Alex and Brian moved to one side of the center. The sergeant and his team inched towards the missile officers. The airmen were flanked in from both sides. "Drop 'em…drop 'em! On your knees."

Alex and Brian had stayed back. They both turned observer for what unfolded next. "Just like the movies," Brian whispered. Ahead, simultaneously, both airmen's heads turned. They seemed stunned. Each face reflected utter surprise, and quickly turned into fear. They exchanged rapid glances. Cast by laser points, red dots bounced across their foreheads. Poised on knees, fingers on triggers, the sergeant and his men were ready to fire. One missile officer dropped his weapon. With a clang, the blue steel landed on the floor. The sound reverberated through the hallway. There was momentary silence.

The second airman hesitated. Spotting the intruders his face had turned to rage. The assault team read the signal, but the airman fired first. Two more shots were fired in rapid succession. Flashes of starlight exploded from the airman's barrel. To Alex and Brian, the next scene happened in slow motion.

Slightly ahead, to their right, the sergeant stood up to full height. His body appeared frozen rigid. His face took on a perplexed look. His eyes slowly widened. He tried to talk, but only managed a gurgling sound. One hand reached for his throat. The automatic dropped from the other. It landed on his boots. Blood was squirting from his finger's grip. His main neck artery had been cut by the bullet slicing through flesh. He would live, but only until blood pressure to the brain ran low.

Alex's focus was on the shooting airman. He saw him poised against the steel door. His gun was pointed at the nearest target, the sergeant. The airman's eyes reflected his intention to kill. With nowhere to hide, he'd squeezed the trigger.

His eyes had also registered the flame of fire released from another angle. One bullet was sent his way. It was from the .45 semi Alex had fired. Alex saw an instant reflex. The airman had changed aim in his direction. His face grimaced in agony when the bullet hit. His body slammed against the steel frame. There, it slowly collapsed in on itself. His life expired, leaving in one last audible breath.

Brian was already tending to the sergeant. He pressed his hands hard over the cut artery, but it was of no use. The sergeant struggled for air. His limbs flailed. To keep his body down, Brian kneeled on his chest. There was one more attempt, one last struggle to live. It was his last. The sergeant was dead.

With the sergeant gone, Alex felt he should take charge. In a quick move, he kicked the airman's gun into a corner, yelling, "Open the blast door!"

Unsure, the airman resisted until Alex shoved the barrel against his temple. Reluctantly, he gave in. He entered the digital code. With a solid clang, the sealed entrance latch gave way. The capsule's eight-ton, blast-proof, steel-and-concrete, pneumatic-controlled door slid aside. The two sentries locked in the stairwell rushed in. Hesitantly, they stepped across a brightly painted yellow sign marking the floor, "No-Lone Zone."

They were in the LCC's ultra-high-security zone. Alex knew no one person was allowed to step across. Anyone crossing that line had to be accompanied by at least a second person. There was no exception. It was a safeguard enforced by the missile command to detect any erratic behavior or sabotaging attempts. Launch control officers carried side arms and were authorized to shoot to kill to guard the space.

"What happened here?" Alex forced the airman in the direction of the control room. He stepped over the dead sergeant. Brian and the sentries followed. The body was pulled out of the way.

"Conflict of commitment," the airman gestured at the two senior officers slouched in the launch chairs. Alex motioned to the sentries. They pulled the two dead missile officers from the blast seats.

Alex stared at the airman. "Go on," he demanded.

"Got the launch order," the airman confessed. "Next thing you know," he gestured at one body, "deputy cracked." Tears crept into his eyes. His jaw quivered with emotions. "My buddy…didn't turn the key…shot by the chief—killed instantly." He was sobbing. "I'm sorry."

"Why didn't you open the blast door?"

"Thought you were the enemy."

"Do we look like the enemy?" Anger welled up inside Alex. *Useless killing over what?* "Keep an eye on him," he ordered the MPs. He wasn't completely convinced he'd been told the truth. Alex didn't want this violence. Visions of Tracy flashed through his mind. She was the reason he was here. If it wasn't for her abduction, he'd have refused this insanity from the onset. He had no choice about the bloodshed. The Missileer had been trained *not* to think. The MCCC, the DMCCC, the BMAT tech,[53] all killed. An *entire launch crew out of commission…and for what?*

Distraught over the killings, Alex approached the launch console. There was work to do. He took a seat in the vacated commander's chair. "Brian," he gestured, "take the far end."

"What'd I do?" Overwhelmed at the sight, Brian approached. His eyes seemed confused by the many rows of LEDs and switches staring up from the console. He took the vacated seat and watched Alex slide his railed chair into a comfortable position. He adjusted his.

"When I give the order, turn the key." Alex reached for the mic mounted on the overhead frame. With his left he turned the selector knob to UHF. "NORAD Command…Bell One…come in."

"NORAD here…." The crackling voice responded almost immediately. "What took you so long?" It was the abrasive voice of the brigadier.

"Ran into resistance."

"You in position?"

Alex scanned the controls on final time. "In position."

---

[53] Missile Combat Crew Commander, Deputy Commander, Ballistic Missile Analyst / Technician.

"Commit launch sequence," the brigadier ordered.

Alex flipped a few switches. "Stand by." From the overhead storage bin he pulled out the checklist. He needed precise instructions. Although he'd done it under simulation only, it'd been awhile since he last initiated a launch sequence.

Across the Wyoming planes, the dedicated missile flights, the silos, had been put on alert. Each silo had its own crew. They had already been alerted and on standby hours ago. Towering menacingly in their respective tubes, the dedicated flights had been armed. Rushing for final checks, hurried boots skipped up ladders two, three steps at a time. Liquid helium was steaming out profusely from pressurized main intake valves. The hissing noise from the steam permeated through the shaft. It was to aid the initial firing. Ready for deployment, the giants assigned for destruction lay in wait.

"Five minutes to countdown." 175 miles to the south, the people at NORAD had switched to PA. They were waiting for the next command from Alex. The brigadier was surrounded by the staff. The entire mountain crew had gathered at the command center. Anxious faces were filled with anticipation. The air was musty and tense. They were waiting for the final moments. There were questions in the faces, questions without answers. "Is this a new beginning...or the end?" The decision would depend solely on the reaction from the other nations.

There it was. The voice they'd been waiting for. It was Alex, ready for final countdown. Burning eyes were focused on the world clocks, watching the last minutes tick away. It was broken up by nervous coughs. Some watchers forgot to inhale. The GMT finally reached the sixty-second marker. The voice of Alex picked up the final countdown. It was relayed over UHF antennas on top of the mountain, rerouted to the makeshift cable connections, and finally fed into the PA system. In place of the MCCC and BMAT, it was Alex and Brian on the controls at the distant end.

Alex deliberated each step as spelled out in the doomsday checklist. He led the final countdown. Brian acknowledged each step:

Surface Warning Control...hot! Launch Keys...ready! Circuit Breaker...set! Operation...initiated! Launch Keys...committed! Batteries...charged! Power...active! Silo...ready! Guidance System...go! Engines...fired! Lift off!

"Bert," the farmer called to get his son's attention, "let's roundup the stock." He and his son were chasing several stray cows. They had been grazing this field for days. It was time to get them back to the barn. The rancher was anxious to get back to the farm for breakfast.

Suddenly, the son's eyes caught a movement. It came from a barren patch in the middle of the field. The movement was followed by the sound of an explosion. A swishing sound quickly followed. They were sounds he'd never heard. Awestruck, he and his dad stopped dead in their tracks. Next, rapid action unfolded in full view. The boy was petrified. "Look," he screamed at his dad, "Diablo!"

What they heard was the sound of the silo lid tumbling through the air. It had been energized by a concentrated explosive charge. With a loud thud, it landed next to them. It was followed by a swishing sound similar to a torpedo leaving its tube. Highly compressed air lifted the missile from its tube. Once the missile cleared the silo, for a moment, it hovered weightlessly. A second later the three Thiokol solid-propelled rocket engines ignited. There was a tremendous flash followed by an explosive sound. Billowing flames shot out in all directions. The force knocked both witnesses off their feet. They sought refuge alongside the concrete-encased silo cover. The two just missed getting incinerated. Burning fringes off their clothes, the flames passed inches above their bodies. The roar was deafening. The sound could be heard for miles. The first nuclear-tipped ICBM fired live from a U.S. silo was on its way to destruction.

"What does it mean?" the boy yelled at his father. His dad got up, brushed the dirt from his trousers, then put an arm around the boy's shivering shoulders. The boy was terrified. He couldn't pull his eyes away from the roaring body just lifted from hell. Then, astonishment seeped into his searching eyes. There it was, unfolded in its entire glory, the American flag. Painted prominently alongside the shiny flank, it was followed by gigantic lettering, "LGM-30G."

"Never thought I'd ever see one of them monsters in my lifetime," the farmer muttered.

"What does it mean?" the boy insisted. Dormant for decades, he'd never been told of the immense destructive powers lurking beneath the soil.

"It was long ago," the farmer explained, "a young GI once told me." From beneath furrowed brows, he tried to remember. "Think the 'L' stands for silo launch, 'G' means it's a ground attack."

"What about the 'M', Dad? The 'M'?" The boy jumped with excitement. He never knew how smart his dad was.

"Missile…guided missile," he was told.

"What about…?"

"Son," the farmer finally succumbed to the quizzing, "too many questions." Uncertain what to expect next, they cowered in silence. Little did he know, the 30G was the most recent guidance system, implemented long after the GI had explained. Also, unknown to him was that four hundred fifty more Diablo were sitting dormant nearby, patiently waiting to be deployed.

"What does it mean, Dad?"

There was no further explanation from Dad as to the destination or the end result for the immensity of its destructive powers. Shaking his head, the father tenderly embraced his son's shoulders. "Don't know son…just don't know."

RAWALPINDI

Currently checked in at a downtown hotel, the Plaza, with his commanding staff nearby on the same floor, the hot water stream beating on his skin felt invigorating. It energized his body. He enjoyed taking long showers. After many years in training camps, the Serpent finally enjoyed some of the finer virtues in life. A clean shower was one. An occasional prostitute was another. There were not many. Life as a devout Islam called for sacrifices. He was going to change that. "If not for me, then for my people." His thoughts shifted to more pressing needs. He needed an urgent assessment from all of the current resources supporting his mission. He could not trust the figures in the reports he'd been getting. *As a matter of fact,* he decided, *need to visit the places in person. That'll shake them up.*

For the free world, it was extremely difficult to estimate the number of nuclear weapons in Pakistan's arsenal, ever since the securities breach at the Los Alamos laboratories. It was there that Pakistan obtained nuclear processing technology with the help of German engineers and Chinese assistance. Outside experts estimated the number of manufactured weapons to be between 24 and 48 nuclear warheads. Their somewhat dated design was relatively simple but very labor intensive; that's what his problem was.

Getting dressed, he listened to the latest broadcasts. Most every primetime station carried news about the assault on the American nation. There was much speculation. Analysts and so-called experts were making prolific contributions. "If they only knew," he cherished. He slipped his watch onto his wrist, another rare luxury he afforded then called one of his lieutenants to attention. "Where's the reports?" They hadn't arrived yet. He checked the time. He was getting impatient. "Coffee," he called out, "and be quick."

"Right away."

Seconds later, a cup was served. He picked it up, took a savoring sip, and moved to the window. Twelve stories below, city traffic was snarling in and out of commuter lanes. The annoying blare from auto horns, so customary to this part of the world, did not reach up here. The suite he'd reserved was quiet.

He was about to make a call when his eyes caught a dark object streaming across the sky. At first, he thought it was an aircraft. But then something registered. What made the object unusual was its shape. It had no wings. Extending several miles out, it left a contrail in its wake. He squinted to get a sharper vision then suddenly identified the object. His subconscious immediately registered, *Missile.* "Allah…" He tried to alert his lieutenants. In desperation he yelled out, "Take cover!" It was too late. An immense pressure wave had taken over their space. The call went unheard. There was too little time for the warning to reach their ears.

An instant later the entire wall collapsed from the intense force. The breaking sound of shattered glass and smashing debris filled the room. His ears popped as the glass incinerated. This was quickly followed by intense pain. It all happened too fast. Next, he felt the pressure change as the air was sucked rapidly from the room. His hands flew up to protect his face. He could feel clusters of particles imbedding deeply into his face, arms, and chest. Then, with unbelievable force, in rapid succession, he felt more changes. It was a series of explosions hammering against his body.

First, it compressed his body almost into extinction, then, waves later, with a crushing sound he was hurled violently across the room, landing hard against the wall. Almost on the brink of unconsciousness, the room fell silent.

Trying to collect his senses, he repeatedly slapped his hands against his ears to stop the insane ringing. They came off wet. He looked at his palms; they were smeared with blood. Immediately, he called for his aids. There was no answer. Sprawled on the floor against one wall, he'd just experienced three tremendous explosions set off in rapid succession. They seemed to have come from the direction he'd just been, the nuclear processing plant he'd visited not thirty minutes ago. Still dazed, he pulled himself out from beneath the rubble. Consumed with rage, directed at the Americans, his archenemy, he screamed out, "Damned infidels!" His brain registered only silence. His eardrums had burst. "There will be consequences!" Pure hatred emanated from his bloody, hazed-over gaze.

WARREN MISSILE COMMAND

With the missile away, his mission was over. Alex couldn't wait to get out of the launch center. "Let's get out of here." Brian hastened after him. He seemed just as anxious to leave the place. It was high time to head back to the Castle. Debriefing NORAD was first. Locating Tracy would be next. The former he could do while in flight.

Brian was already headed for the Bell Trainer. Thirty seconds later the craft lifted off. The ground below the canopy rapidly rushed away, merging with the terrain ahead. The roar from the chopping rotor blades was filtered out by the headsets. Inside, it was quiet. Occupied with his own thoughts, Brian was at the controls. He was shaking his head in bewilderment. *Launching a nuke?* He never thought he'd ever see a live launch. Today, he'd been part of it.

Alex checked the instruments for heading and altitude. I-25 had just come into view. It was the pathway back to the Castle. The chopper leveled out. It adjusted to cruising speed.

"Thought about a plan?" Brian interrupted his thoughts.

"Tracy? No." Alex had no plan. Not yet. He'd thought about it on and off but with today's activities, there had just been no time for personal issues.

"What do you think?"

"Got a few options," he said. "We could let the FBI track her. Have the CIA handle the cause. Or, we hunt her down. They're the options."

"What's your choice?"

"Don't have to tell you. You already know."

The talk channel came alive. Brian was scanning the terrain ahead. He spotted the source. He gestured below. "Look at that." Alex followed his gaze. A continuous stream of tow trucks was hauling off the many vehicles stranded up and down the interstate.

"Condition's slowly getting back to normal," Alex pointed out, "traffic-wise anyway."

Twenty minutes later the castle came into view. The wingless craft sitting in the driveway was easy to spot. Brian flared out by the helipad. He carefully eased the chopper over the landing pad. He hovered for a few seconds. Alex thought someone would have showed on the balcony. He'd expected a welcome. The place appeared lifeless. "I don't like it." His intuition took hold. "Place's too quiet." Brian closed the final few feet. With a firm bump, the helicopter settled down on the deck. Both jumped out. "You go ahead." Alex waved him on. "I'll check out back."

"Back?"

Alex already scrambled up the side of the hill.

Brian headed for the entrance then stepped over the threshold. "Tracy?" he called. "Liz?" He took a couple more paces. "Odd," he muttered. The place appeared empty.

He didn't see it coming but sure felt the impact. The back of his head seemed to explode. He more felt than heard the crunching. There was no pain. Brian's body was thrown forward. He slammed into the doorframe then stumbled to the floor. What he didn't see was Liz cowering in the corner. She was gagged and bound. Several shadows stepped into the dimly lit room. They were talking. The words were from another country. Then, quiet unconsciousness embraced his bewildered mind.

Outside, Alex scrambled up the cliff. It was a steep approach. He tumbled upward on all fours. His feet kept slipping on the grassy gravel mix. He kept pushing on. His aim was straight up, to the escape shaft. When he built the place, he had made sure there was a backup exit. Not that he'd expected to ever use it. It was just smart design.

Short on breath, he finally reached the top. Twenty paces to the left he spotted the familiar iron-clad escape hatch, but from years of neglect it was dirt covered. Stooping on both knees, he brushed it off. The latch unlocked with a snap. Small flakes of rust broke from the hinges when he forced the hatch open. It came open with a slight squeak. He paused a second to listen. *Should've heard from Brian.* Watchfully, he stepped on the ladder and climbed down the shaft. On the bottom, he paused for sounds. He didn't hear anything besides the slight hum of the generator. He cautiously entered through the safe room.

Alex watched his own shadow glide along the short hall. Silently he pressed on. He reached the door to the residence. He pulled it open just a crack. Muffled sounds seeped through from inside. They were voices he didn't identify. Beads of sweat framed his forehead and brows. They trickled into his eyes. They were burning from salt. He hastily wiped them dry. Cautiously, he stole his way along the hall. The sounds grew louder. And so did the pounding in his temples. His apprehension grew.

He still couldn't make out a word. Alex fingered his belt. The MP's .45 semi was still tucked inside. He lifted it from his waist and cocked the shaft. The cold steel cooled the palm of his hand. He felt secure. The weapon pointed steady he moved to the living room just ahead. He was ready to enter but was startled by a sound came from behind. It was the bathroom door. It had suddenly opened. Alex whirled on his heels. He came face to face with a stranger. Immediately, he recognized the intruder as Arabic.

Startled by an unexpected face in the hall, the assailant instinctively reached into his jacket. He pulled a combat knife, staring at Alex then began slashes wielding the blade. Alex jumped back and out of the knife's range. He'd been on guard for the attack. For now he had the advantage. He had the gun.

"Drop it!" Alex hissed with a strained voice. He hoped not to attract more surprises.

The intruder shouted something in a foreign language. To Alex it sounded like Yusuf. It alerted his comrades. Alex had lost the advantage for surprise and jumped forward. With a blow from the .45, he hit him in the temple. It momentarily stunned the intruder. Not giving him a second chance, Alex spun around and dropped him with a frontal kick to the lower chest. There was a cracking sound from broken ribs. The assailant's legs buckled. The same instant, Alex wrestled hold of the knife. He twisted the assailant's wrist.

The intruder winced in agony. The knife toppled to the floor from his broken wrist, but he was fighting back. He had the stamina. Experience, however, was on the Alex's side. One more kick to the groin and the assailant's body buckled over, the wind knocked from both his lungs. There was no air left to yell for help. Quietly, Alex slid into the darkened living room.

There was motion at the far end of the room. Alex caught the danger. It was suddenly on him. He came face to face with what seemed to be their leader holding a weapon trained on him. Alex was facing a standoff. The two assessed each other. Two hardened faces stared at each other, fewer than ten feet apart. There was a halting, a gauging—frozen in silence. Youth was on the one side, years of experience on the other. The leader moved first. Releasing a stream of bullets at Alex he leaped into the air off to one side. There, he landed by the bookcase. He had gone for cover.

Alex had his gun trained on him. It stayed with the target. Finger on the trigger, it pumped out a series of singly fired bullets. He'd hit something. The target went down with a crash. The air was filled with a howl. It was a cry of pain. Alex didn't understand the words. There was a groan. He followed the sound. Yusuf had crawled behind the bookshelf. Blood was oozing from his leg.

Alex had fired from a lowered position. He was kneeling on one leg. His focus was on Yusuf, waiting for his next move. Unexpected, there was a sound behind him. Then he felt something, a stinging blow to the back of his head. He jerked around and ducked to the floor. His eyes found the source. There it was, a second target. He pulled the trigger. The shot found its target, the chest of his attacker. In a violent motion, the body jerked back then collapsed to the floor, mortally wounded from an exploded heart.

Alex reached up. He felt the back of his head. It was wet and bloody. Blood trickled down in back of his neck. He at wiped it with his sleeve. It came back bloodied. Blurry eyed, he shook his head to clear his vision. His mind was still functioning. It had been a glancing blow. He let out a sigh of relief. *One more battle scar.* A second later he was on Yusuf. Gun trained on the wounded, Alex spat at him, "Don't move if you wanna live."

It hadn't been his intent to kill. He needed the survivor for interrogation. There was a shuffle. On shaky legs, Liz approached. She reached for his bloody scalp. "Dad," she said, "You're hurt!" During the fire exchange, she'd managed to free her tied wrists and ankles.

Alex shook his head. "Grazed only."

She hastily scrambled upstairs to check on her children. They were safe.

Ten minutes earlier, on the floor below, Brian had been stunned by a blow, but was shaken into consciousness when the shooting started. *Alex!* His mind was still hazy. Two assailants guarding him moved into action. They hastened for the hall. There was the sound of additional shots from above. Brian heard the scream when one assailant went down. A weapon tumbled down the stairs. It was an assault rifle. Brian rushed for it. Two intruders remained. Brian saw one cowered by the stairway. He checked the weapon. It was armed. Aiming, he fired in rapid succession. His target buckled over, mortally wounded, and slid to the floor.

Another target moved into his vision, rushing towards him. He fired. The body sailed down the remaining stairs. It landed lifeless at the base. Brian stepped over it then met up with Alex. They did a quick room to room search. All bodies were accounted for. They could relax.

Either dead or wounded, the intruders lay sprawled on the floor. Yusuf and one of his lieutenants were tied up by Alex. Brian checked the other bodies. "Dead," he confirmed after checking their pulses.

Liz was rushing in. "Dad!" She spotted him. "Let me help. Where's your first aid?

"Upstairs, in the bathroom," staring at her battered face, he gestured, "you could use a few bandages yourself."

Yusuf was propped against the wall. He had a shattered knee. Blood was oozing from one arm. His shooting arm. Another comrade, sprawled out on the floor, was wincing with pain. He was having difficulty breathing. Yusuf was fuming with rage. His entire cell had been immobilized. To make things worse, they were being held hostage by the detested infidels. *There'll be consequences.* He blamed it on the inexperience of his comrades. He wasn't looking forward to the interrogation and torture that was sure to follow. Wracked with shame at failing his mission, he silently swore revenge.

Alex was busy with the HAM set. He called NORAD base, requesting a pickup for the captives. Thirty minutes later, a military detachment arrived to collect the terrorists. Reports were called in to confirm two wounded and three dead. The dead were collected and zipped up in body bags. The others were whisked away to an undetermined base hospital for possible surgery and treatment. Internment and interrogations would follow. For the sake of the nation, it was important to identify other cells dormant and operating in the U.S.

THE HUNT

There had been no news from the West Coast about the condition of the family. Liz hadn't been able to raise her mom and her ex-husband. Although there was chatter on the airwaves, it was only on the HAM set. All other communication was still out, including TV broadcasts, radio transmission, and emergency channels. It would be many weeks and perhaps months before those systems could be restored.

"Dad," Liz was tending to her dad's head wound, "You're so lucky." She appeared strained. "I'm worried." Her usual self-confidence had been compromised.

Alex understood her concerns. "Mom, Tracy?" He could feel her breathing. Light puffs of breath touched his face while she was applying a gauze patch. It reminded him of Annette, his wife, her mom. *How long has it been?* He didn't remember. She handed him a mirror. "Another inch and you'd been dead."

"Nice dressing, real professional. Thanks. Now," Alex gave her a tender look, "let's fix you up." After cleaning her face and patching up broken skin with band-aids, he tenderly brushed his fingers across her face, inspecting the swelling. "You need rest."

"We all do. How long since you've had any sleep?"

"There'll be time later, Liz." Alex wanted to comfort her. But not right now. He needed her full attention. He needed her full support. He took hold of her hands. Slightly alarmed, her eyes focused on his. "Can you manage the place by yourself?"

"But, Dad…your head." She shot a worried gaze at him. Concerns for his health filled her eyes.

"I'm fine—I'll get the FBI or a couple MPs from the base to stay with you."

"Where're you going?"

"Got bad news." He watched a shade of fear grow in her eyes. "Tracy's been kidnapped."

"Oh my God!" Her fear turned to shock. "Is she all right?"

"Don't know." He tried to restrain his rage. "But I'll find out—I promise."

She understood the urgency. "I'll be okay—just bring her back." Droplets of tears appeared in her eyes. They left two shiny trails down her youthful skin. It'd be inconceivable to her for something to happen to her younger sister. Despite their separation across the nation, they'd kept in touch with each other. Not so much in frequency, but emotionally and spiritually. They had the psychic connection. *Telecall*, they'd termed it and giggled. Liz was the psychic one. She'd inherited the gift from her grandma, who was always predicting things.

Brian stood nearby. He felt regretful and unsure how to console her. He had his own scrapes and pains to deal with.

Alex turned to him. "You all right?" He was concerned about Brian's battered face.

"I'll live." Brian felt his face, arms, and knees. The skin wasn't broken. Injuries he'd sustained to the head were internal. Aside from the bruised head he seemed okay. Although she had sustained considerable injuries herself, Liz checked him over. She was concerned for him.

Alex stepped up, "How you doin?" He gave Brian an assuring pat on the shoulder. "Feel up to a trip?"

Brian gently pushed Liz aside. "Lead on."

"Let's get goin' then." He was already in the hallway. "We'll need tools." Alex headed for the basement.

"Tools?" Brian quickly understood then hurried along. Down below, he watched his buddy, busy in the gun cabinet. Alex pushed a hidden switch. The cabinet made a scraping sound. A hidden panel moved aside. Into view came a weapons cache only Alex knew about.

Brian was flabbergasted. "You could start a war with these." His emotions were reflected in the face. "Never expected this arsenal," he said, lifting a Kalashnikov from the rack.

"Remember Vietnam?"

"Vaguely…still in Kindergarten."

"Packed in with household goods, back then," he motioned, "you could send these legally."

"I had no idea." Alex had done an earlier tour back then when trophy taking was not yet restricted by the government postal service.

Brian was truly amazed. He fingered the weapons. The AK-47 felt comfortable in his grip. His eyes wandered along the cache. There were a couple M-16s. An Israeli UZI stashed alongside a high-powered rifle and an assortment of handguns and hunting rifles.

"Nobody does." Alex sounded matter of fact. He fetched a duffel bag from the bin. "Collector of evil instruments," he said. "That's what I am."

"Yeah," Brian agreed, "but, at times like these, they come in handy."

"Here," Alex said, tossing him the bag. "Take what you need."

Brian filled it with items he was comfortable handling. The UZI, a couple of handguns, several boxes of ammo, and a combat knife. "What's next?"

"You're next." The arsenal gate shut with a clang.

"What do you mean?" His face held a quizzing expression.

Alex motioned to exit. Brian briskly followed him upstairs. They found Liz in the kitchen. She was busy making sandwiches. It was lunchtime for the kids. Alex strode over to her. He planted a kiss on her cheek. "We're out of here." The kids sat hungry by the table. Alex gave each a hug. "Take care of your mom."

"I will," each promised.

The sound of their voices lifted his mood. *Kids,* he thought, *spirits of the future.*

"Here," Liz handed Brian a bag of sandwiches, "you'll need them." He was grateful. He was hungry. He hadn't eaten since the previous day.

Minutes later, Liz and the kids stood by the deck. They watched the chopper take off from the nearby platform, waving goodbye.

"Where're we headed?" Brian was leaning into the instrument panel. He was adjusting the altimeter with one hand and flipping switches with the other. Seconds later they were lifting off, leaving a hot trail of streaming turbine exhaust in their wake.

"South."

"How far?"

"'Bout three hours."

"Arizona?" Brian guessed. He was punching in the coordinates.

"Absolutely."

"What's there?

"Desert mostly." Alex was evasive. "I've got an idea where she might be. Know the area pretty well—used to visit Huachuca on several projects."

"Clandestine?"

"Electronics testing…proving grounds—Army security," he shouted through the accelerating turbo sound. His voice was barely audible over the roar of the Lycoming T53-L-703 turbo-shaft driven engines going at full speed. "Mostly border interdiction."

"That's it?"

"There's more." He tried to recall information on the area. "DELTA training camps, along with other OPS, covert mostly, out by the desert fringes."

"How'd we find it?"

"Infrared." They'd be checking for ground activities much like satellite sensors.

"Desert's a big place."

"I know the general region."

"I'm still not clear."

"Gunships in and out in a couple of spots," he hinted, "mostly unmarked."

"Got it." Brian understood. There had been rumors for some time, especially with the Intel community. "It'll be a couple hours."

"What about fuel?" Alex was concerned. He had failed to check on the fuel level. Finding a fueling station along the way would be almost impossible.

"Plenty on externals—topped at close to 6,000 lbs." Brian set the controls to cruise speed. Alex watched him touch the swelling on the back of his head. *Must still feel tender, but the bulge's slowly fading.*

"Let me have one of the sandwiches."

Alex rummaged through the bag Liz had prepared.

"Here." He handed him the wrap. *Should eat something,* he thought, but he was too tired. He could hardly keep his eyes open. "Let me know when we get close to Tucson."

With the steady beat of the blades, Brian too had difficulty keeping his own eyes open, but the thought of Tracy kept him going.

CIA HEADQUARTERS

The clock, prominently mounted on the wall, jumped ahead another minute. It was a timepiece carried over from the old building. Aside the solid Oakwood desk, it was the only legacy left from the golden days. It carried a rich history, if it could only talk. It was a time when the organization flourished, a time when the nation's security was a solid core. A core of soldiers depended on footwork. The clock registered close to 9:00 a.m. EDT. A hat stand was planted by the entrance. It had lost its usefulness. It used to be, not that long ago, weighted down with cloaks and daggers. Now, it was not even used for hats and coats. Nobody wore them anymore. Today's agent was dressed in casuals. The laptop was his weapon. Covert wars were fought with the stroke of the key. Although there were agents still in the field around the globe, they were mostly contracted instruments managed closely by the department heads, the DDIs.

Deputy Director of Intelligence, of counter Intel, of operations, that's what they were. Highly specialized, there were many.

At present, the personages seated around the solid oak table were subdued in light conversation. They were waiting. They were waiting for answers. They'd been waiting for the DI to arrive. Usually the first in the office, today he arrived late. He finally entered to join the conference. Harry Carter took the seat at the head of the table. "Any word from the field?" He came right to the point.

"Nothing…nothing…nothing." The responses were all negative, unanimously. The world had turned silent. Many of his contacts were employed with overseas embassies. Others were operating from troubled spots in foreign countries. Few had infiltrated within aversive and subversive groups played out across the globe. They were nameless, faceless. Officially, they did not exist. Unofficially, they were the field agents. The force was sizable, but scalable to fit world events.

Despite the technological advances in remote surveillance, specifically from satellites, the field agent was still necessary. He worked to gain personal information that a satellite could not. Where a field of vision from the satellite was mostly vertical from above, the agent's, was horizontal on the ground.

"Comm status?"

"Nothing yet." The director for operations spoke. There was no need to make up excuses. "May have been too close to the strike zone."

"Can we get a fix on the last position?"

"NSA's assessing internal damages," he explained, "we're on standby to get first option."

"What's the status with ECHELON[54]?"

"Inconclusive data," one DD informed the table, "without live feeds."

"Give me data," the DI demanded, "something…anything." It wasn't the first time information was lost, or didn't make it to the office. It wouldn't be the last time. But this, being totally kept in the dark, was unacceptable. "Do something," he demanded, getting up from the table. Taking quick strides, he paced back to his office. The hallways and offices he passed were all empty. With transportation out and personal vehicles inoperative, most didn't make it to work. Only employees living close by showed up.

---

[54] ECHELON, developed by Lockheed Martin decades ago is a system to get access to all-important political movements in hostile and allied territory alike, and to keep an eye on all-important economic developments.

Right now, he had to deal with more pressing things. There was the issue with the DELTA team to which only he was privy. ECHELON may have been the sophisticated program to date, but there were things too secret to share with computers.

Back at the office, seated in front of the flat screen, Harry Carter contemplated what to do next. The screen in front of him was sitting idle. Powered by an internal battery only the flash page was visible. It stared back at him. "ECHELON," it prominently displayed. Today, the company's most effective tool had been rendered inoperative. He tried to find a means to initiate action without it. There wasn't any. There was no fallback. Technology had completely taken over the organization's life. It was directing every facet of his life, his staff, and the nation.

"Dammit," he cursed. He just realized that there was no way to get in touch with Arizona.

MOUNT WEATHER

"Where do we stand? What's the status? Any word from the VP?" the president inquired. He was addressing the JCS, his current advisory panel. Meetings these days were called together impromptu. They were urgent, but set in a casual atmosphere. With the present state of the nation, Mount Weather was just another island, isolated without effective communication. So far, the only link established was via amateur radio. The network of HAM operators in the nation was growing with each day.

They were all present. Seated around the spacious table were the nation's most important crisis functionaries. From the president to the Secretary of Defense, the commanders of the Unified Combatant Commands and Joint Chiefs of Staff, the entire chain of command was present. Each gave a brief.

Presently, the Chief of Air Force spoke. He presented the state of the air and space defenses. It was brief. "Only thing flying is the Confederates."

The Chief of Armed Forces didn't have much to contribute. "National Guard has been called up around the nation. Army units are joining up as fast as word can get to the posts."

The Chief for Naval Warfare leaned into the table. Under the current circumstances, he had the largest burden to carry. With the air defense grid disabled, the nation relied on his submarine fleet. And he couldn't get word out in the oceans. The ELF and VLF systems had been disabled with the blast. Antenna farms located around the eastern perimeter were incinerated. The nation was isolated from the fleet.

"So let me get this straight," the president summarized, "we're fucked." It wasn't often that he resorted to cussing and foul language. But today, the causes justified bad language.

What the staff did not know at this point, due to the lack of information flow, was that on many points across the nation people were making strides to reestablish themselves. Work crews were frantically scrambling to repair damages. There were many. There was much to do. Combined with a line of support services, food supply chains and emergency services were first on the list. Next were vital infrastructures such as power, water, law enforcement, transport, and government. Mundane things such as conveniences, social media, and leisure would be last.

For now, many had to fend for themselves. The entire nation had to become involved. Without secured borders, intrusion was a constant threat. First, there were the basic needs that needed fixing. The day began with getting up at dawn. A simple thing like the customary showering became a challenge. Without electricity, darkness was embracing many chores. What used to be a subconscious convenience had become a difficult chore. Candles were used by whoever had some on hand. Only hours after the blackout, stores had quickly run out of supplies, especially in the cities.

Prior to the attack, over the years, there had been ample warning signs. Unfortunately, for obvious reasons, the threat had been kept a secret. It was mostly the smart ones, the concerned, or perhaps the fearful, that had the foresight. It was they, that had stocked up and kept current on survival equipment. Few were the fortunate who had purchased survival kits and rations to be stored away in cellars, bins, and cupboards. The survivalists, the "Preppers" as they called themselves, were only a small percentage of the population. In view of the current situation, they were the weirdoes, the oddballs, the outcasts. They were considered the eccentrics, but "Who are the smart ones now?"

To get the basic life back would be slow going. Most struggled to survive another day. Many perished from getting attacked for their saved provisions. More yet from the diseases that followed. Starvation would come later. For days, fires kept on raging, especially out west. It took much effort to get them under control. Clashes broke out. Fighting was everywhere. People were killing each other, always for the same reason, to survive another day.

The National Guards were called out. It took days, sometimes weeks, to squelch the fighting, to reestablish order. Metropolitans took the biggest brunt. Refrigerators were emptied first. The cupboards followed. Children went hungry. They became demanding. The same was true for pets. When food ran out at the home, people began marauding. First, it was family members on the prowl. Then, neighbors formed small groups. When protecting the residence and neighborhood failed, many took to the hills. Nobody trusted anyone. Many carried guns. People died for simple things. First it was for monetary things, then for scraps of food.

Some regions were less affected by the disaster. They were near the borders and the seaboards. Up north, near Canada, people could hunt. Game was there for the taking. Along the Gulf coast, there was fish and seafood, but not without its challenges. Fishing ships' navigation needed repairs. Starters had been disabled. Instruments were out. Navigation was limited to the sun and the stars, but the people survived.

Store owners across the nation had closed shops for fear of looting. The first few days were chaotic. It stayed that way until National Guardsmen showed up. They were heavily armed. Carrying armor, they got the respect. They established order. Despite posted warnings, many store windows were broken. Much of the merchandize was looted regardless of its usefulness. Television sets disappeared first, then refrigerators followed with high priced items. *What good would it do without electricity?* People didn't necessarily think. They just looted.

Outlying areas relying on emergency and support were abandoned. Help never came. Red Cross, FEMA, and TSA got organized, but it took days and weeks to reach some areas. With communication out, the population was on its own, isolated to the various regions. In those regions, local leaders emerged. Initially, they formed loosely-knit groups, then more cohesive units. Depending on their strength, the local population would fall in line to their demands. It would take time before organized commerce would reemerge once more, in some areas, perhaps never. There were rumors of roaming renegades banding together. Many had taken advantage of the chaotic situation. They had no plans other than spreading fear among the local population. One such place, rumor has it, was the Badlands. People were fearful.

Over time, unless subdued by the National Guard or army units, some would gain momentum. Without effective communication, armed forces were operating with limited capacity. However limited in applications, radio and microwave, the foundations of communication, were repaired first. It only worked by line of sight. Ineffective over the horizon, long haul circuits had to be established for that. And that took time. Until then, every guard, emergency, and military unit operated on its own.

NAPA VALLEY

Annette woke startled. She had another nightmare. It felt suffocating beneath the blanket. Sitting upright to catch her breath, she tossed it from her body. Curious why it was so quiet, she lingered by the edge of the bed for a few seconds. Her gaze wandered to the bedroom window a few feet ahead. Twilight was just breaking over the eastern slopes of Napa Valley. The room was still bathed in darkness. Growling from emptiness, she clutched her stomach. Her night garment felt damp. It felt like she'd been in a battle. *Dreams are supposed to last only seconds.* So the experts claimed. The gown proved otherwise. It was drenched. She felt soiled. She needed a shower. With one swift pull over her head, the garment landed on the floor. She felt better. Her hands groped for her housecoat. It wasn't there. She lingered. Her eyes caught the full reflection of her body in the mirror. She had time to examine it. There was no rush. She wouldn't go anywhere. Despite her going on fifty, she could still admire her shape. "Must have done something right," she muttered in the semi-darkness, "but what a waste."

Annette tried to reason things out before making the next move. It'd become a habit since the blackout. She had already made a few mistakes. It cost her valuable resources. In just a few days her life had drastically changed. Spontaneity had all but evaporated. Her senses had turned cautious. Ready to lay back down to wait out the darkness, she had the sudden urge to pee. Gradually, she felt her way to the bathroom but immediately backed up. "Ugh, nasty."

Annette had developed the habit talking to herself. She felt more secure this way. The voice kept her company. It calmed her nerves. She'd been on edge for a number of days now. Last night was the first time she got some sleep. It was sound, but the nightmare was something else. The lid on the commode was closed, but the smell from two days of waste permeated through the small room. She pulled one sleeve from the coat over her nose. It didn't help much. From habit she flushed but the stopper dropped back with a metallic clang, "Still no water." The tank was dry from the first flush. "Should I?" She couldn't bring herself to open the toilet lid. The water from the tank had lasted only one flush. The tank had failed to fill again.

Without electricity to drive pump stations, no water would flow through the city pipes. Decades ago, they used to be fed by gravity from elevated water tanks, but modernization thought it unnecessary. Powerful pump stations replaced the unsightly tanks that used to make up a town's façade.

Undecided what to do next, Annette stood there in the dark. "I could use the other bathroom." She'd thought about it already yesterday, but couldn't bring herself to soil that one too. Since Liz's divorce from her husband a couple of years ago, it was her daughter's and the kids' who she shared the house with. But she desperately had to go.

Relieved and exhausted, from habit she reached back to flush the tank, but immediately jerked her hand back. "The water!" She was close to panic at the thought of losing the only water source left in the house. She had lost already precious water from the tank in her bathroom. "Must do something about that," she reminded herself, "as soon as it turns light."

She felt guilty for messing up her daughter's bathroom. She felt around for the toilet paper, "Empty." She shook her head. "Kids." Again, slight panic tugged at her senses. "Get a hold of yourself," she reprimanded herself, "this isn't the end of the world." Her words echoed on the walls of the small room. Her eyes had adjusted to the darkness. She could make out the outlines of the appliances. "Great." She was relieved to see the night shadows slowly give way to another day. With her bottom bare, she stood up to use the panties to clean her butt. "Phew." She felt unclean no matter how much she wiped. "It'll have to do."

Her stomach made more noises since her intestines had been emptied. *Vicious cycle,* she thought in the quiet of the room. Normally, she would not think of the body's necessities, but standing in the semi-darkness, alone, strange thoughts emerged. "I eat," she thought, "gotta go again." Trapped between urges and reasoning the urges won. *They always do.* "Enough." She knew what had to be done. She closed the lid and turned for the exit, leaving the nasty smell behind. The thought of brushing her teeth crossed her mind, but discarded it when her gaze struck the sight of her hands. "Unclean." *Have to use soda.* Yesterday, she used some club soda she'd located in the cupboard. First, she had considered using the water from the toilet tank, but hadn't quite muzzled up enough courage. "Maybe later, after the soda runs out." For now, she preserved the only water source left for emergency use. *What emergency?* She didn't know.

She felt better now after a change of clothes and a few bites of stale bread. It'd been mostly peanut butter and jelly on white, or a carrot stick washed down with a can of warm soda. The overhead cupboard shelves in the kitchen still contained open packages of various brands of cereal, but she hadn't had a taste for any of those. "Wonder how long that's going to last?"

Minutes later, Annette found herself rummaging in the garage. *There it is.* She located the tool she was searching for, the shovel. With a sigh of relief, Annette opened the backdoor and stepped out. She lingered, undecided where to dig. She needed a hole to replace the toilet. "But where?" The answer came when she spotted the tree by the corner. It was an apple tree. It hadn't bore much fruit in recent years. *Maybe this will help.* Despite the gravity of her current predicament, a smile crossed her face. "Fertilizer." The shovel proved useless. The hard-packed ground resisted the tool. She had to find something else to dig through the hardpan. Luckily, she found the pickaxe her son-in-law had purchased. He'd dug some postholes when he built the fence a few years back. It was a heavy tool. Hardly strong enough to lift the damned thing, she managed after a few tries. It took more than an hour of digging. "That's it," she decided, "deep enough." She tried the position. Close to the tree, she could lean back to use the trunk for comfort.

Satisfied, she grabbed the tools and returned to the garage. Her gaze struck the neighbors' house. Yesterday she tried to make contact, but nobody answered. "I'll have to try again." She didn't know the neighbors other than through the casual hello or she could have called out their names. *What a waste,* she thought. *Years of living next door and I don't even know their names.* "California living," came to her mind. *Nobody knows the neighbors.* "Transient lifestyle...everybody on the move...all the same." She longed for the days when people knew each other, especially neighbors. She longed for a change. She needed someone to talk with. *This is as good as any time.* With that thought she strode next door.

Annette knocked on the front door. The sound carried further than she'd expected. The usual city sounds were still absent. Only an occasional dog bark could be heard in the neighborhood. Nobody answered. She knocked repeatedly with the same results. There was only silence. With a shrug of her shoulders, she was ready to return to her home. Her eyes caught something. She thought there was movement behind the window curtains. It was a shadow motion but retreated as fast as it had appeared. *Probably scared*, she thought, *just like me.* She couldn't blame them but called out loud, "Come on, people!"

Discouraged, she returned to the safety of her home.

CAYMAN ISLANDS

The desk manager wore a courteous smile. "Welcome to the Islands." It was the typical greeting in this part of the globe. It was the Caribbean, off shore, a tropical paradise. The friendly face behind the desk was set within a bronze-tinted tropical tan. The skin was slightly moist from the humidity-laden air prevalent to the subtropical region. As most of the hotel staff, he seemed proficient in dealing with guests. "We have your suite ready," he prompted. Handing the guest a welcome package across the counter, he flagged down a porter lingering by the hotel entrance.

Hammad had just picked up the briefcase off the floor when the desk manager got his attention. "Sir," he called over the counter, "you have a visitor." Slightly startled, Hammad halted in his tracks. He was suspicious of the unexpected delay. *Who'd know I was here? Has this trip been compromised?* With deliberate caution, he sought out the object of the disruption. His eyes fell on a rather distinguished looking gentleman. Led by a smartly dressed usher, he purposefully made his way across the lobby.

Close up, Hammad made eye contact with the stranger. The gentleman reached out to shake hands. "Carlos," he introduced himself, "Carlos Domingo. Pleased to make your acquaintance."

"Yes?" Hammad did not like unexpected encounters. They usually spelled trouble. He slightly backed away to gain breathing space. Expecting an explanation, he waited.

In a diplomatic way, "Sir," the stranger asked, "could we talk in private, perhaps your room?"

Hammad sized up the stranger. He was searching for any signs of danger, but nothing obvious projected. In contrast, the visitor seemed well bred. Distinguished, eminent even, one might say.

"Please follow me." The porter, patiently waiting close by led the way to the elevator. As usual, it was quiet inside the shaft. Visitors, once inside the vertical transport mode, projected the usual trend of solemn, silent, and self-conscience mannerisms. The only sound perceived going up and coming down the elevator was an occasional clearing of the throat. Aside from a glance, assessing others, most averted eye contact with other passengers. People acted like they were attending a wake. *Why is that?* Hammad pondered in silence.

They had arrived at the room. "Please," Hasan courteously invited the visitor into the suite. He handed over the expected tip and dismissed the porter who hastened back towards the elevator.

The door slammed shut with the familiar closing sound in hotel hallways. "You must be curious," the visitor started, "who I am." Invited by Hammad, he'd taken a seat by the sofa.

"Carlos Domingo," Hammad replied, "you told me." It was more of an impolite gesture than an acknowledgement.

"I represent the Cuban government," he explained. "More specifically, I am an ambassador."

Hammad was not impressed. He scrutinized the visitor more closely. It seemed the ambassador was expecting more of a welcoming, attendant, or perhaps courteous reaction. Nevertheless, he stirred his curiosity. *Ambassador…Cuban? What would this underprivileged island nation want? Marxist on top of it. I shall have to hear this.* He took a seat on the sofa, giving the visitor his full attention. *At least,* he decided, *I'll listen to what he has to offer.*

"It has come to our attention," Domingo started out, "that your nation is about to make certain advances." He took a brief pause to assess any reaction. When none came forward he continued, "Our intelligence services have reported an impending attack by your people on the United States. If," he cautioned, "this is true, we," he paused again to stress the importance, "we, Cuba, would like to offer our support in this affair."

"How could you be of service?" Hammad was slightly bewildered but did not show any signs. *How could they have known?* Curiosity spiked, he could deny any such allegation and cut the visit short, but needed to find out more to what the ambassador had to offer. It was not every day that a country extended assistance. Nevertheless, representing Jihad, he would appreciate any help he could get. He decided to take the chance. "What is your offer?"

"We have," the ambassador presented in his polite, deliberate, diplomatic demeanor, "military air and ground support at your disposal." He let the importance sink in. "If you so desire."

Now that, Hasan evaluated this monumental gesture, *is a bombshell.* He could hardly suppress a mounting emotion welling up inside. An emotion he had not felt in ages. His eyes brightened at this mammoth revelation. *Could it be,* he dwelled, *an island revolt against the most powerful nation on earth?* His immediate thoughts touched on the biblical legend where David slew Goliath. The island had tried once before and almost succeeded, but had rebuffed. With Fidel Castro at its head, the administration then was a hard-hitting one. That was back in 1961. Today, the world's most powerful nation had been weakened, weakened to its core, economically as well as politically. *There might just be a chance.*

"I will consider it," Hammad decided after a brief evaluation. He had to re-engineer his plan. It would impact scheduling as well. "I will be in touch." The visitor got up and headed for the exit. He left as mysteriously as he had appeared.

With a feeling of great elation Hammad picked up the house phone. *One more call,* he supposed, *should finish this trip.* He was anxious to return to his domicile, his domain, Palm Jumeirah, Dubai, where he felt secure. He had accomplished more than he'd set out. So far, the trip was a complete success. *Now,* he pressed, *one more critical aspect to complete the loop.*

"McAllister," he requested when the office secretary picked up.

HAVANA (Cuba)

Carlos Domingo was happy. Very happy. He had obtained the objective he'd set out to complete. It was not every day that Cuba could gain a political advantage. As a matter of fact, as a nation, Cuba had been on the brink of evaporation. It had disappeared into obscurity decades ago. Ever since '61 when Khrushchev pulled out the intercontinental missiles during the Cuban standoff, the island had withered away from world economics. Without an end in sight, it had become a nation desperately fighting to stave off poverty. This could be their opportunity. An opportunity to gain back a time of flourishing and prosperity, as it had once enjoyed. The roaring twenties, with its free trade exchange, non-stop entertainment, dance, song, woman and wine. *Once more?* Distant but sad values from a glorious past beleaguered the ambassador. He was on his way to see the minister of the armed forces, responsible for the army, air defense force, and naval paramilitary units numbering close to fifty thousand, ready for deployment...any deployment.

It was still early in the morning. The air was relatively cool against the morning sunrise. It wouldn't stay this way for long. Once the sun climbed towards the noon zenith, the daytime heat would press on the land. It would be another steamy type of weather found most days on this tropical island.

The ambassador hurried across Havana Square to reach the ministry of defense building. He had an early meeting with Cesar Romulus, head of the Cuban air defense forces. He wouldn't want to be late. Men of this stature were known to be intolerant to tardiness, ruthless, one might even say. Achieving status within the upper crest of society, in many Latin countries, bestowed the ultimate in lifestyle, especially when the position was held for decades, practically spanning one adult career. The only means such a position would be vacated was by death or through revolution. Either way, the end was terminal. He had met with the head on several occasions. A feeling of uneasiness had always been present. One was "walking on eggs," as the Americans would say.

He'd been expected. As soon as he entered the building, he was ushered up the elevator into the command dominion. Security was tight as expected. After all, packed with employees shrouded in secrecy, it was the nation's hub for military and defense forces.

"Ah, yes," Cesar Romulus extended the invitation to enter. "Mr. Ambassador," he gestured, "have a seat." With calculated deliverance, he invited the guest to the small conference table by the window.

Carlos Domingo savored the moment. He was offered a cup of locally grown coffee, rich in aroma and dark roasted in color, accompanied by the customary cigar always present in a balsa dispenser. The finest the world had to offer, in cigars as well as coffee. He took his time to open the conversation. In island tradition, unlike in the western business world where "time wasted was missed opportunity," a meeting was always preceded by the customary personal anecdote. Presently, there was a light conversation between the two, centered mostly on cursory island chat. Opening conversations deliberately avoided political issues, in that it might damage one's career. Personal sentiments were generally in alignment with the current administration. Criticism would mean political suicide with the career cut short. Therefore, everyone agreed with the head of an organization.

"So," Cesar Romulus encouraged the ambassador, "what do we have?" He seemed to hear about the diplomatic encounter the ambassador had with the leader of the new Islamic movement.

"As we have expected," Domingo asserted without reservation, "the new leader for the jihad faction would welcome our support." He went on to describe the initial encounter he had with the leader. He also indicated that time was a critical element. The jihad forces were staged for an imminent aggression, not only on the neighboring super nation, but other world nations as well. "We must prepare our air defense and land forces in the most expedient manner," he urged. "We do not have much time, a week, perhaps days only."

"Impossible," Romulus responded. He was physically shaken. "We cannot ramp up our forces on such short notice."

"It is imperative we do," Domingo insisted. "This is a onetime opportunity. We may never have another chance." It could mean an internal coup d'état, a military takeover, to align the armed forces under one command. Anything would be better than sustaining the economic demise the nation had suffered for fifty some years.

"I will be in touch." Romulus dismissed the meeting.

Domingo shot an approving nod in Romulus' direction and quietly left the office. He felt triumphant. "Cuba shall live again."

CUBA (Air Defense Forces)

Cesar Romulus was taking stock of his air, land, and sea inventory. He only had a few hours to respond. Beyond that, there may not be another chance to rescue the nation and his people from economic collapse and extreme poverty. He was very receptive to the fortune just handed to them. He was also aware of the potential for failure, and the enormous impact it would have economically, if successful. The decision pressed down heavily on his shoulders. *What if I fail? What if the forces are reduced to nothing?* These were some of the concerns he had to consider. To draw a parallel, he only had to compare the present military strength of his nation with the pre-dawn Bay of Pigs invasion. *Now,* he thought with great pride, *there was a success story.*

Then, the enemy had been defeated. But he was young, a lieutenant in rank. National decisions were made by his superiors. Now, the same weight was placed on *his* shoulders. It was his responsibility and his alone. He was pacing the floor. The window of opportunity had opened, but only for a brief moment. *The odds,* he calculated, *aren't exactly in my favor.* The thought provoked an ominous foreboding. Only he knew the true status of his forces. The public had been blinded for too long. It was the result of strict political censorship.

In all, the modern Cuban air force consisted only of approximately 230 fixed-wing aircraft[55]. Although, there was no exact figure available, Western analysts estimated that at least 130 of these craft, spread out among the thirteen military airbases on the island, were still in service. But that was when the air fleet was maintained to its full strengths.

All one had to do was take a look towards the west from the military air field outside San Antonio de los Banos, southwest of Havana, and it revealed what appeared to be MiG-21s, MiG-23s, and MiG-29s left out to rust in the tropical heat. It looked like the jungle was overtaking some of this once mighty fleet of the Cuban air force.

Cannot be done, but, against his common sense, Cesar Romulus made the ultimate sacrifice, *it must be done.*

It was not until late in the day when he called up the ambassador. His mind and emotions were still wavering, despite the final judgment. He wanted positive assurance, at least a de facto check. *Political collaboration,* that's what he needed, at the outset if the attack turned out to be failure. He did not want to be singled out as sacrificial victim. He was too close to retirement. In retrospect to the present ultimatum, he should have retired years ago. He could kick himself for staying on the force. *Too late now.* He made the call.

It seemed Ambassador Domingo had been waiting for the call. He picked up on the first ring. "Yes?"

"You'll have my support...but," he was about to deliver the true state of his forces, then thought otherwise. *Wouldn't matter,* he worried, *he'd be overruled. In case of failure, they had their scapegoat.* And he knew that.

"What?" Domingo had detected the uncertainty in the general's voice.

"Never mind," Romulus appeased him, "I shall set the force in motion." He reached for the receiver to press the flash button. The line switched over to Holguin HQ, Eastern

---

[55] Recent assessments had the ground forces as 8,000 strong with 31 combat capable aircraft and a further 179 in permanent storage. The 31 combat capable aircraft were listed as MiG-29s, MiG-23s, and MiG-21s. There were also assessed to be 12 operational transport aircraft plus trainers and helicopters still in operation.

Command, to alert his sea and air defense forces. The morning would bring the news to the public. *God only knows how they'll react. There'll be demonstrations, riots, perhaps even a coup.* The enormous impact of his decision sank in with full force. *I must alert internal security,* he reminded himself, *immediately... and the armed forces.* The thought of Cuban's military ground forces somewhat eased his anxiety. They were still the most formidable in the Central American region. *Perhaps,* he decided, *it's not a bad choice after all.*

SOUTHCOM HQ (Miami, FL)

The United States Southern Command, located in Miami, Florida, was one of ten unified combatant commands in the United States Department of Defense. It was responsible for providing contingency planning and operations in Central and South America, the Caribbean, Cuba, their territorial waters, and the U.S. military resources present at these locations. USSOUTHCOM was a joint command of more than 1,200 military and civilian personnel representing the United States Army, Navy, Air Force, Marine Corps, Coast Guard, and several other federal agencies managed by two deputies to the commander, one military and one civilian. Furthermore, it was responsible for ensuring the militarization of the Panama Canal and canal area.

As result of an extensive defense department reorganization plan, Nelson Tucker, four-star commanding general, SOUTHCOM, had just recently been assigned this command. He readily accepted with the notion that the southern defense was a relatively quiet sector. Based on past political accounts, outside of minor border infractions along the Central American perimeters, such as trafficking, mostly drugs and to a lesser degree illegal aliens, he did not expect any major conflicts. Just in case a rogue nation in the southern hemisphere might think of starting something against the United States, all defense elements necessary were in place. He'd made sure of that. It'd been his guarantee against any unexpected infringements on his last and final assignment.

"Sir," the harried secretary paced across the spacious room in the direction of the uniformed, high-ranking officer at the far end corner sprawled across the edge of the table, "wire just came in."

"Where'd you get that?"

"SUBLANT," she replied, "secure."

Submarine Force Atlantic sector, the U.S. submarine fleet assigned to the Atlantic region, also had jurisdiction over Cuba, Central, and South America. With satellite communication out, the fleet had several backup communication capabilities. Today's communiqué, most likely sent using VLF transmission, was probably initiated by a sub sitting off the coast of Cuba.

Patiently waiting for him to finish reading, she lingered, expecting a follow up task. In disbelief, he shook his head then shifted to face her, still planted by his desk. "That's all." He had a second thought. "Wait," he called after her, "get me the Pentagon."

What he just read didn't make much sense. It was an Intel watch list. Or, more accurately, a report flagged as high priority, immediate action required. Apparently, an intelligence branch had picked up an increase in communication out of Cuba. The chatter had emerged with full force early that morning. What made this so highly unusual was there had been no military exercise or joint war game scheduled in that region. *Something's definitely asunder.*

Tucker needed confirmation from the JCS, who may, or may not, have some intelligence on any unscheduled activities in the southern command sector.

Not expecting the phone to ring, as it'd been silent for days, he picked up the secure line connecting with the Pentagon.

"Foster," the voice announced when the line went active.

"Yeah," Tucker proclaimed in his generally southern-intoned inflection, "finally back on the air?"

"Took some doing," Foster proclaimed. "Using landline backup for now," he explained, "'til we get satellites back in the air." Working day and night, installation crews from coast to coast were busy making connections on both ends, and many command places in-between.

"You people got anything goin' on down here I should know about?"

"Nothing…nothing that I'm aware of." Foster had been in meetings since he'd arrived at the office this morning. He hadn't had a chance to read the morning's correspondence. "I'll get back to you," he promised. Just about to hang up, he had a thought. "Check with Eglin," he suggested, "they might have something."

"Will do," Tucker fingered the intercom button. He ordered his secretary to make the connection.

"96th Air Base Wing," the base operator announced, "please state your business."

"Tucker, SOUTHCOM," the general identified himself. Abrupt, concise, to the point, his was an arrogant disposition. He expected all command units within the southern command to recognize him by name. It may have been a somewhat selfish notion, but that's the way it was with military. Self-centered, egotistical, arrogant, but always proud. That's what made him a commander. "Get me ISR."

"Yes, sir!" was the prompt response. "Just one minute, sir." It took fewer than thirty seconds to locate the Intel branch of the air base wing.

"ISR.[56]"

"Anything going on across the straits I should know about?" He was referring to the Florida Straits and Cuba, ninety miles south of the Keys.

"Funny you should ask," the Intel agent disclosed, "Been picking up heavy comm all morning. Don't know exactly what to make of it."

"Any Intel?"

"Foreign office's got nothing yet. DOD's got an alert out. CIA's checking data. That's all I know."

"Keep me posted."

"Will do."

"Probably an exercise," Tucker muttered. Relaxed once more, he reclined in his chair to watch the sea traffic in the distance meander past his vision. From his vantage point, beyond the horizon, he could almost make out Cuba. *Somebody forgot to notify us. Damned embassy.* He snorted under his breath. What puzzled him though was the lack of sea traffic, generally called into action for simulation combat deployment.

It was not long after when the phone rang. "Tucker," he answered. "What's up?"

"ISR Liaison," the caller identified himself. It was the same agent he'd spoken to earlier. "Got some Intel for you," he proclaimed. He was skipping the customary formality.

Must be urgent, Tucker presumed by the caller's tone of voice. "I'm listening."

"Cuban's air defense units have been put on high alert," he was told. "Active fighter units' leave has been cancelled. Reserve units recalled up for immediate duty."

"What's it mean?"

"Not sure at this time," he was told before the call terminated.

---

[56] Intelligence, Surveillance, and Reconnaissance is an integrated intelligence and operations function defined by the Department of Defense as activity to synchronize and integrate the planning and operation of sensors, assets, processing, exploitation, and dissemination systems in direct support of current and future operations.

The news was upsetting. He needed current information. He knew just who to call the dialed the number.

RUSSIAN FEDERATION (Ministry of Foreign Affairs)

"Foreign ministry." It was the foreign minister's secretary taking the call. She was somewhat surprised to receive an official call directly from the Cuban embassy. Relations with this inconsequential nation had been strained for a number of years. Ever since the reorganization after the fall of the USSR, Cuba had become insignificant to the federation. It had become a minor trading partner for specialty items, such as sugar and tobacco products.

With the fall of the Soviet Union, national federation focus had been principally directed first at reestablishing the economy, then at gaining international recognition, economically and politically. With the collapse, most of the seasoned organizational heads had been either retired or sought employment otherwise. On the forefront, new elects were running the once so powerful soviet nation. Most ministries and federal services reported directly to the prime minister, who then reported to the president, collectively referred to as the "Presidential Bloc."

The caller identified himself as Carlos Domingo, Cuban emissary. "I wish to speak with the minister directly." There was a deliberate pause. "In private."

"Please hold," was her response. "I will see if he is in." It was a trained, customary response. Of course, any secretary and office manager knew the whereabouts of a superior. If he or she was available may be subject to personal interpretation. Today, the minister was available.

"Potempkin." Vladimir Potempkin made an exception, taking the call. Normally, he would have handed the caller off to a deputy, but because of his secretary's urging, he took the call. Carlos Domingo was direct, but also discrete.

He conveyed yesterday's highly politically charged development between a possible Jihad and Cuban coalition alliance. He also expressed extreme urgency and made a personal appeal to the federation for possible assistance and support. He further illustrated the time critical element associated with the planned course of action that required an immediate decision. He would not be rebuffed or put on hold. It was either "Da" or "Nyet." Unfortunately, it was neither. He was politely asked to standby. "Somebody will contact you within the hour."

Potempkin quickly realized the importance of the call. This could be a political shift with enormous implications. It would be cause for both endorsement and resistance, perhaps even hostility, but a challenge, nevertheless. On the one hand, a proponent of the old regime, he welcomed the opportunity, but on the other hated the prospect for possible national upheaval. Things were going so well. "Damn the Cubans," he finally decided.

Whether the Russian public was up to another major conflict may yet be seen. It was not up to him to make the decision. This was too important a call for one individual. The cause of action would acutely involve the nation. It would be up to the president and his advisory staff, but that took time.

To prevent any possible ambitious overtures, such as experienced by the old regime, the federation was ruled through strictly enforced policies. The new Russia was structured and ruled by the people, and for the people, in an apt democratic fashion.

Potempkin could have quietly ignored the caller and then pleaded ignorant. Perhaps from a faint yearning for power, perhaps from a waning legacy from an empire lost—it could have been a number of things—against his better judgment he made the call. He called for an urgent audience with the minister of defense. *Let him deal with it.* It would be a political decision, more so than an economic ruling. He left it to history to record his judgment call.

DELTA FORCE (1st Special Forces Operational Detachment)

"Damned phones," Brooks, commander, DELTA Force One, kept cussing at the headset. Frustrated, he hammered the receiver against the wall several times. It's been days since the phone quit working. He had been trying to make a call for several days now but could not raise anybody. What made it worse yet, power was out as well. And so were mobiles. Days ago, they'd been forced to switch to auxiliary. Diesel fuel was running low. Earlier, he was getting ready to make the fifteen-mile run into town. They needed restocking on food anyway. The H-2 SUV was dead as well. Trying to get the vehicle going, he'd put his team to work. "How you doin' out there?" he shouted through the open window.

"Workin' on it."

The air inside was stifling. Not even the slightest breeze was felt. For a moment he stared out the window. He squinted. He used a soiled T-shirt he'd abandoned days ago to wipe his forehead. It cleared his vision. He could see it now, the town, shimmering in the distance, but from experience he knew it was only rays reflected by the heated sand. *Gray shadows,* that's what they were, *Mirages.* The town was much further off.

"Goin' to be another scorcher." In the middle of the desert, it was the norm. He was startled when the phone rang. It persisted. *Should I pick up?* He had to. "Fuckin' calls," he swore. "What?"

"...send detainees...interrogation...expect brief." He thought he'd recognized the caller but could not understand a word. The call reminded him of the early days on field assignments. Back then, always accompanied by a delay, you'd have to shout your lungs out to be heard. *There it was again. Damn echo.*

"What?" he yelled into the receiver.

"...switched to backup...landlines...HAM..."

"Breaking up," was his final word. They probably couldn't hear him either. Mounted against the bunker wall, he slammed the receiver back on the hook. The only thing he got out of the call was gibberish. If the conversation made any sense at all, he'd have to fill in the gaps. "Expect arrivals for interrogation...brief on its way...special courier." Most of it was guesswork.

"Damn calls," he cursed again. *Satellite must be down. What else could it be?* He and the team had no knowledge of events that had happened over the past several days. He had no clue that voice satellites in the northern hemisphere had been knocked out. That command centers had reverted to backup landlines for communication. The signal he'd received was bounced through a satellite relay in the southern perimeter, still in operation. It was a commercial unit placed in orbit paid for by the Mexican government. The desert site was just above the horizon to the north. The damaging EMP rays had not affected much close to the southern border. Airwaves were only quiet in the northern sector of the continent.

There had been quiet times before. It hadn't bothered him, or the team. Things usually started to happen with a conflict somewhere on the globe, mostly some foreign nation. Then the team got busy. There was a specific reason to be way out in the desert. Attached to a tactical unit out of Sierra Vista, AZ, he was the operative leader. Making up the DELTA team, there were several others besides him.

Scott Brooks liked the desert. Surrounded by dust and heat, he felt at home. With nothing but sagebrush, tumbleweed, and the occasional cactus tree, it took a special character to accept this harsh environment. To him, compared to the deserts of Arabia where he spent his first missions during the Gulf War, this place flourished with vegetation and wildlife. At least around here were some interesting places to visit on the days off.

A history buff, he particularly liked Tombstone and Bisbee. Dating back to the mining days, at both places there was a rich American history. Today, much of it had been preserved. He visited often, especially on weekdays when it wasn't crowded with tourists. Any day of the week one could get a feel for the place. He liked to mingle with the citizens rather than the tourists offloaded by the busloads.

In retrospect, the earlier calls may have been an alert. He thought about the possibility of another upcoming interrogation. As usual, it wasn't going to be a pleasant experience for either interrogator or detainee. Interrogation methods used today were different from old torture. In the past, aside from the water boarding popular these days, a variety of devices were used from wheels, splitters, and crushers to Chinese water treatment. In today's world, more humane measures were in place.

Depending on the ferocity of a subject, to extract information could take weeks or months. It didn't matter to the team. They were paid to wait it out. Eventually, the subjects would break down. *It never failed.* What followed was usually incarceration at a camp like Guantánamo or the Salt Pits in Afghanistan.

To him, it was just another job, but a job necessary to preserve peace and freedom for the nation. He walked down the hall to check on his most recent visitor, Tracy. *She is a looker, that's for sure.* He wasn't sure why she was sent here. His instructions were specific, detainment. He didn't care. If only temporary, somebody wanted her out of the way. His strides were interrupted by a shout. "Chopper!"

ARIZONA DESERT

Alex was in a sleep of exhaustion. "Think we've got something," Brian shouted. He slapped Alex on the shoulder. "Wake up." Brian had been at the controls for the past two hours. "Check this out." Once he'd cleared the Rockies up north, he took the craft down to four thousand feet. It gave him a clear ground view. Unlike shaking up their guts with up and down drafts over the Rockies, it'd been a smooth ride ever since.

"What?" Alex stirred. His mind was still foggy from the deep sleep.

"Take a look." Brian pointed at the infrared display. "Activity." The sensors identified several subjects.

Alex locked his eyes on the infrared display. He squinted to get some definition. There were several subjects, some moving with others stationary. Two were bent over what seemed to be a vehicle; others were inside what looked like a bunker.

"Anything on Tracy?"

"Not sure," Alex determined. "Take it down."

"Roger." It took only seconds to touch ground. Brian switched the rotor off. "What now?"

"Act like we own the place. Let them think we're with the agency." Alex was already headed for the bunker. "Let's go," he shouted. The turbo was slowly grinding down. Hunched forward to clear the drooping blades, Brian was close behind. The men on the ground stopped their work. A few were guarding the bunker. They were dressed in boots, combat fatigue, and wearing white T-shirts. Mostly unshaven, they had pulled their sidearm. The tallest one stepped up. "Let's see some IDs."

Alex carefully lifted his wallet from his back pocket. He flashed his ID. Their attention shifted to Brian.

"...and you?" the tall one demanded. He was assessing Brian.

"Right," Brian complied. He pulled his badge from his wallet.

"DCA...NSA...what're you doing here?" He was grunting with distaste.

Alex ignored the order. Instead, he snapped back, "Who are you?"

"Brooks—DELTA."

"We've got a pickup," Alex demanded. They were staring each other down.

"Let's see the orders." The immediate tension had been diffused, for now. Much of the initial apprehension seemed to have faded from the team. Some moved to the building. There, they squatted in the shade.

Scott had made a wrong assumption. He had let his guard down. He connected the visit with the previous idiot calls. *Probably what HQ had been trying to tell me.* His focus shifted to the NSA agent. He watched Brian reach for his back pocket.

On cue, both Alex and Brian pulled their weapons. "Here's my ID!" Brian yelled. He had fallen into a defensive position. Alex promptly shoved his .357 in Scott's face. Brian shifted to cover the team. At first, the DELTA team was stunned. It only lasted a fraction of a second before they went into action. They cocked their weapons on the two intruders. Being trained killers, somebody only had to flinch for them to fire.

"What the hell?" Scott's face had changed expressions. In a split second he calculated his odds. Experience was on his side. The same went for his team. Although the situation was serious, Scott suspected the intruders were bluffing. Otherwise, they would have shot already.

"Looks like," Alex spoke first, "we have a standoff." He had a serious smirk on his face.

"Arizona standoff," brazen-faced, Brian chimed in, "just like the OK corral."

"What do you want?" Scott demanded. Taken by surprise, he was angry at himself. His face gave away his emotions. *I look like a fool...a novice.*

"My daughter," Alex snapped. He was serious now. He would get her at all cost.

"Figured that," he shot back, "when I recognized Bauer on your ID." Scott was unwavering. "You can't have her."

"We're not leaving without her," Alex was adamant. "I want to see her right now."

"If anyone's giving orders," Scott shot back, "it'll be me." Staring down Alex, he slowly moved up. Brian closed up tight.

"Stay where you are," Alex spat back. He knew someone would go down if they started shooting. It would defeat his purpose for being here. He wanted his daughter. Alive. *Try it the diplomatic way...might be able to reason with this guy.* "Listen," he explained, "we're on the same side, just different bosses."

"Go on. I'm listening."

"In case you haven't noticed," Alex thumbed to the north, "we're at war. And I don't mean the agencies."

"Whatcha mean?" Scott demanded. In discerned curiosity, trying to make sense, he was frowning.

"You haven't heard?"

"Heard what?"

Alex suddenly had the notion these guys may be in the dark. Ignorant of events, they could have been stranded out here in the remote desert. "Why'd you think nobody calls— has anyone contacted you the last couple days?"

"Now that you mention..."

"Nuclear exchanges, North Korea...Pakistan...California."

"You're kiddin', right?" His face changed from bold to surprise. The expression was genuine. He slowly lowered his semi. He wanted to hear more.

"As sure as we're standing here," Brian affirmed. He seemed just as interested in diffusing the standoff. "All comm's out."

"That explains a couple things." It was one of Scott's teammates making the comment. Their grip on their weapons slowly relaxed.

"Come inside," Scott motioned. His offer seemed genuine but still guarded. "No funny business," he warned, "'til we sort this out."

"Right." Both Alex and Brian agreed. Weapons tucked into their belts, they were escorted into the bunker. Scott led the way. Guarded, the team closely followed. The shelter was surprisingly cool. The concrete kept the heat out. Humidity was almost non-existent here in the desert. It was relatively comfortable. Scott cocked his head towards the end of the hall. They followed. He paused in front of a cell. It was a steel cage, typical to the detainment block. He released the bolt. With a clang, the gate retracted.

"Daddy...Brian!" Tracy cried out. She was overjoyed at seeing familiar faces. "You came!"

"They don't call me 'Explorer' for nothing," Alex replied.

Teary eyed, Tracy flew at her dad.

He braced himself. He felt her weight jump up on him. *Like the little girl I remember.* She clung to his neck. Then her hold relaxed. Her gaze struck Brian.

"Brian." Her face was filled with excitement. Their eyes locked in tender embrace. "I'm so happy you're here."

Scott broke the happy reunion. "Okay." He was impatient. He had no tolerance for sentiments. It was an emotion unfamiliar to him. It wasn't so much a lack of it. He'd never had the experience. His life was centered on facts, facts alone.

"We'll figure out a strategy," Brian assured him. "We're all troubleshooters."

Scott led the way. They gathered in the interrogation hall. It was the largest room in the compound. His men pulled up chairs. Scott motioned the visitors to take seats. His men squatted on the floor nearby. They were just as curious to hear more. It affected their families as well.

"What's the national situation?" Scott was curious. He wanted to know details for what had happened over the last few days.

"Last we knew," Alex explained, "Northern California's devastated. San Francisco took a nuclear hit from North Korea."

"What?" Tracy was dumbstruck. "What about Mom? Liz, the kids?"

"Liz made it safely. So did the kids. Don't know about your mom." Tracy turned silent.

Alex offered some encouraging words. "She'll be fine." He continued. "We retaliated—wiped out their capital—knocked out a nuclear plant in Pakistan. He could see the astonishment in their faces.

"Communication's out east, central, and west, and so are electronics. Satellite's got knocked off. No airlines. No commercial transports, nada."

"The chopper?" Scott had been listening patiently. "How did you get in the air?" It seemed unbelievable. He had to test them. For all he knew this could be a ploy to get to the daughter.

"Fast maintenance," Brian cut in, "and slight persuasion." His hand slapped the semi in his belt. "Crew swapped out the spare panel when we came along."

Explanations seem credible, Scott determined. "What about navigation…GPS?"

"Out. Fly by the seat…did it in 'Nam," Brian broke in. "No landmarks there."

"Look," Alex picked up. He intentionally turned to face the DELTA leader. "We have a chance to work things out together. It's been a struggle between our agencies for too long. It was okay when we had different fronts, but now," he reasoned, "we have a common enemy."

"Terrorists?"

"That's only part," Alex said. "There's more. Terrorism is the visible enemy. The other's invisible," he stressed, "but more perilous."

"What do you mean?" Scott was curious. His mind seemed piqued. His team's faces came alive. They wanted to know more. This was something new.

"You guys are all action…and that's great for the *job* you're doing." Alex put emphasis on job. He didn't want to offend them. "But you're not paid to think."

"Got it," Scott agreed, "that's for the guys at the Palace." He saw the irony.

"Damned right…and," Alex voiced, "who do you think they are?"

"Enlighten me." Scott had been around long enough. There were rumors. He'd never paid much attention. He was all facts but still interested. *This guy looks like he knows what he's talking about.*

"Self elects. Think they own the world. One purpose only."

"What?"

"Been around for eons. Only names change. Call it dynasty, call it royalty, ruling power, all the same. One purpose only—dominance." Alex paused. He shook his head in dismay and continued. "Dominance over a group, a region, a nation, the globe, it's all the same. Democracy has no provision in their constitution. The consequence?" He paused. "Rule by stealth, covertness, concealment, secrecy, clandestine, hidden agenda, all the same, only difference is the labels. CIA, NSA, DOD, Wall Street, Central Bank. Give 'em money, give 'em power, the result's control. It's an ever-growing organism. They make the decisions."

"I agree."

"Everybody's striving for the top, but only few make it. It's not a matter of skills and talent. It's inherited power."

"That means you and I are powerless?" Scott and his team had been listening intensely. Expressions on their faces had shifted from curiosity to anger. None had ever thought on those terms.

"More or less," Alex claimed, "we're pawns. Only chance we'll have is as a team."

"I'm with you. What'd you suggest?"

"First," Alex suggested, "let's break out of here and get some food. Think we all could use a decent meal." He'd had been ignoring a growling stomach.

"Know a place over at Bisbee," Scott offered, "think you'll like it."

"What's keeping us?" Brian urged. He felt famished. He pulled Tracy towards the exit.

"What's the status with the Humvee?" Scott sought out his maintenance guys.

"Forget it," Brian said. "We'll hop over on the Bell." Minutes later the rotor was kicking up dust devils as the craft lifted off. Brian headed for the town. It was a chance they had to take. "Town may be in chaos."

Getting ready to land, Brian spotted an aviation tank near the local airstrip. He took the chopper down. It took a while to locate a manual hand pump, but they got it working. He was able to top off the fuel tank. Scott, in the meantime, went in search of some HAM equipment. Surprisingly, his team found a set in an old mining office. Prominently on display, mountains of coal were still part of the downtown landscape. It was the town's signature. It was the very reason that attracted tourists to visit the place year after year.

Alex hoped the city had been spared disorder. It was far enough to the south. He was proved right. Circulating among the population had been only rumors. Like many other places, somebody, somewhere, had dug up a set of HAM equipment. At a time like this, it was the survival tool. It would give the town the ability to connect with others. Word gradually spread. It would only be a matter of time before the rest of the nation was connected.

A few hours later, Alex, Brian, and Tracy left the DELTA team. Updated on current events, Scott promised to keep in touch. Someday, they might come to depend on each other.

CASTLE ROCK

Two hours into the flight, the Colorado team was well on its way home. There was some turbulence skimming across the southern Rockies, but Brian seemed to have the craft under control. He tried to stay as low as possible. At times, for safety, he was forced to skirt some peaks miles out of the way. Flying at fifteen thousand feet, the air was almost too thin for unaided breathing. There were no oxygen masks on board.

Alex and Tracy were seated one row back. The sound from the rotor was a steady drone. They were able to talk privately. Tracy was recounting her ordeal with the abduction. When she learned of her dad's difficult decision with the missile launches, she felt partially responsible. She wanted him to know. It was her fault for his forced action. "Sorry, Dad," she said. Her voice was filled with regret. "I screwed up."

"Don't worry." He reached for her hand to give her assurance. *It's been so long since I held her hand.* There was nothing to forgive. "It wasn't your fault." It'd never been his character to put blame on anybody. His nature was geared toward analyzing and resolving. It was a policy he'd learned from his dad. *Don't come complaining—unless you have a solution.* He'd been disciplined to this rule in the service, in business, and in personal life.

"It was," she insisted. She felt drawn to him. She suddenly realized how distant they had grown. Close to tears, she put her hand on top of his. She felt comforting strength emanate. Her eyes fell on Brian seated on the controls. *Looks so confident.* The swelling in his face had faded, turned purple, from the battery. She felt safe settled between these two men. *Fighters,* she realized, *that's what they are.*

They had just left Pikes Peak in their wake. It was Colorado Springs's rocky landmark. The craft skimmed over the last of the foothills. Brian made a final course correction. He was headed for Pete Field. "Let's see how diplomatic you are." He'd turned around to face Tracy. His face carried a broad grin.

"What's he saying?" Tracy perked up. Questioningly, her eyes fell on Alex.

"The chopper," Alex wore a sly grin, "we didn't exactly borrow it."

As soon as they touched down, the results became obvious. MPs were swarming in on them. Seconds later, all three were cuffed and whisked away to the nearby military HQ.

NORAD command was waiting. They'd been notified of their arrival. Infuriated, the brigadier showed up thirty minutes later. "What are you doing to me?" he snapped. "Stealing my equipment?" Alex suspected it was mostly an act. Saving face was a commander's prerogative.

"Had to make a decision," Alex justified his action. "Got my daughter back, didn't I?" He gestured at Tracy. "Nobody got hurt."

"I don't blame you." The brigadier shot a glance at Tracy. "I would have done the same." There was a hint of admiration. "Under the circumstances." He squared Alex. "You're forgiven—this time, but don't let it happen again." Stern faced, he added, "It'll be on your record."

"Don't worry," Alex settled without remorse. He drew a serious face to pacify the Man, but knew he'd do the same again given similar circumstances. They were released and freed to go. "Listen," Alex said to the brigadier, "we still need the Bell."

"Can't have it." The response was clear. "And that's final."

They headed for the Jeep where Alex had left it. Filled with action, it seemed like days had passed. The rescue attempt could have gone either way. Somebody could have been trigger-happy and begun shooting. The outcome could have been disastrous. He was pleased with the way things turned out. So was everybody else. He could see it on their faces. Tracy and Brian seemed content. For most part, they kept quiet.

From here on, they made excellent timing. Most of the wrecks on I-25 had been cleared. Thirty minutes later, Castle Rock came into view. It was an easy landmark. A driver could spot the prominent rock formation miles ahead. The huge, flat-topped mountain was how the nearby town got its name. After another five minutes, they drove up the Castle driveway. *That's how my place got its name.*

Unceremoniously, the damaged craft Liz had driven up in was casting ragged edged shadows onto the driveway. Tracy gasped at the sight. "What…?"

"Your sister," Alex grinned, "made a grand entrance."

As soon as they walked through the door Liz went flying into her sister's arms. "Where were you?" she screamed, overcome with emotion. It was an affectionate moment. "I was worried."

"Got rescued," Tracy stammered. Her gesture at Brian and Alex said it all.

"You've got to tell me everything."

"I need a drink," Tracy answered. "I'll tell you a story you won't believe."

"I've got one for you," Liz promised.

The rest of the day was occupied with happy chatter. *Just like old times. Love it.* Alex treasured the moment.

Alex parked his weary body by the HAM set. Alex had his HAM set to auto scan. This way, he could monitor not only the nation, but scan across the globe. Every few seconds it would lock onto a signal. Voices from distant ends would identify the call, exchange local reports. Many calls also served as relay hops. Each broadcast would forward important messages. *This is my world.* It was a world Alex understood best. He'd helped create it. He savored the moment, although it wouldn't stay calm for long. A troubled thought just hit him. "Radiation." It tore him from the comfort zone he'd just enjoyed. Fear driven, he jumped from the chair and headed downstairs. Like a sailor in a submarine, he almost flew down the stair rails. His aim was the lowest level.

"How could I have missed it?" He blamed himself for spacing out on such a monumental effect. His eyes sought out the fallout sensors. "Thank God," he gasped, "no alarms." *Not yet.* The bank of sensory equipment had not yet registered the radiation fallout. Satisfied for the moment he returned upstairs. He headed for the deck; he needed to cool down.

He felt the mountain breeze drifting from the slopes. It cooled his body. It calmed his mind. His gaze went upward, to the sky. *No clouds yet.* He sighed with relief. *People out west aren't this fortunate.* Clouds out there were lethal, packed with neutrons. *Deadly ones.* "Wonder when it'll get here?"

"CQ…CQ…CQ…Castle Rock. Come in…come in, please." Alex's ears perked. It was his call sign.

"Castle Rock."

"NORAD command," the voice identified its source. "Report to Mount Weather ASAP." Alex recognized the comm OPS' voice.

"What?"

"Mount Weather wants you."

"Who? What about transportation?" Alex, at the moment, was reluctant to leave his sanctuary. Here, he felt secure. He'd have to find an excuse.

"Got that covered," the voice instructed. "Pete Field...on hold...urgent...craft's on standby...over and out."

"Can't..." He was about to resist, but the transmission had already cut off. He had no choice. "That's just great!" They had put the burden on him. *Mount Weather wants me?* He knew, in case of a national crisis, it was the alternate command center for the president.

Under normal conditions he'd have jumped at the opportunity. An invitation to the seat of the nation would be an honor, but these were not normal times. *This can only mean trouble.* Regardless, he had to go. He instructed Liz to monitor the airwaves while he was gone. Tracy helped him pack an overnighter. He asked her and Brian to take care of the place. "I'll be in touch," he promised on the way out. The next minute, in his reliable workhorse, the Wagoneer, he drove off into the valley.

The sisters spent hours catching up telling their recent adventures. Liz recaptured her frightful experience with the ill-fated flight, interrupted with outbursts from Tracy like "Crazy...can't believe it...lucky, sis...the kids?"

Tracy relayed the kidnap, the little she remembered. She'd been immobilized unconscious with drugs for much of the time.

"What're we gonna do?" Tracy was worried. She was concerned. "About Mom?"

"Gotta get back to California." Liz, as much as she liked this place, missed her mom and husband. Although Liz and her husband had separated, he was close to the kids. He needed to see them. "As soon as possible."

"Don't think it's a good idea to leave now." Tracy's suggestion was obvious. She was concerned for their safety. "I think you should sit tight. For a few days, at least," she cautioned, "'til we hear something positive from the West Coast. Brian?" she called on him, "what do *you* think?"

"Absolutely," he agreed. "Wait 'til your dad gets back. He'll have news."

"Hope so."

"We'll come along." Brian was trying to boost her confidence. "I want to see what San Francisco looks like."

"I don't know..." Her words trailed off.

Tracy could read it in her sister's face. Her mind was on Napa Valley. She'd always been close to Mom. From the safety of the Castle, they could not imagine what it must be like on the outside world, especially the populated coast.

They agreed to stay put at the Castle, for now. Liz spent most of the remaining night with the HAM set. Following hours of searching, the set responded. She was finally able to get word to her mom through her husband. He'd been assigned to coordinate a rescue team. As luck had it, the base operator recognized Liz's call sign. She promised to be home as soon as transport was available.

The kids enjoyed the space of the Castle much like their mom had as child. As child, Liz had been free to roam the grounds. Today, in contrast, the outdoors was not safe. Too many marauding looters were on the prowl for unlawful opportunities. For now, the kids played computer games Alex installed on one of his servers. Since they were not allowed to leave the premises, it kept them occupied indoors.

PALM JUMEIRAH

The Serpent had just returned from the Cayman Islands. He was elated by the unexpected encounter he had with the Cuban ambassador. He pondered the opportunity. The very thought of the offer brought a historic fact to his mind. "What was it Hitler had shaped?" *Axis... recorded into history, it will be another East—West axis.* "Remarkable! Incredible!" A windfall he had not expected. Military support from a most auspicious source, at that. "Perhaps," he contemplated in elevated optimism, "I can get additional support from their allies, the Russian Republic." *What a thought,* he lavished. "Improbable maybe, but not impossible." With such thoughts in mind, he casually advanced to the lustrous and his most favorite spot in his world, the spacious and lofty deck outside his domicile.

It was breezy this morning. Onshore winds had picked up as they usually did with sunrise. As soon as the first rays struck the sandy islands, as was customary for the tropics, the heated land pushed the air upwards, thus creating the updraft. The cool air from the ocean followed right in the air current's wake, providing a comforting breeze for most of the day. As night began to fall, the cycle revered itself in the opposite direction, thus creating the offshore winds. The Serpent had just taken an extended shower to wash off the grime of travel. Dressed in a freshly ironed Kurta, the airy garb of his day, he went to fetch his mobile. It slipped from his still moistened fingers when he opened the cover. "Dammit," the cussword slipped from his lips as the phone slithered over the balcony. Bending over the rail, he watched it tumble through the air to smash into tiny pieces when it hit the ground. Watching it break, his concern for traceability quickly faded.

He hastened to the wall safe. There he selected another unit from an assorted array of a dozen cellular devices, all registered and charged for immediate use. He still marveled at the technology of instant communication at one's fingertips. He pushed the programmed speed dial.

"Yusuf," the speed button indicated. His most trusted lieutenant. There was no answer, even after several tries. "Of course," he surmised after some agonizing moments of worry, "the blackout." He assumed that New York cell met with success, but he couldn't be sure.

The Plan, his Plan, would have to be amended. Although it did not change the original operation, it would merely supplement his forces to shift the balance of power. With that, his chances for success had just multiplied by several factors. *Incredible,* he reflected, *air and ground assault forces at my disposal.* He glanced at the brief presented by the ambassador he'd just collected from the coffee table. It contained a concise inventory of the current Cuban military assets.[57] Completely unexpected, he'd just gained hold of sixty some aircraft. "Sizable force," he grinned, "Not bad...not bad at all." It changed the original strategy. It would be in his favor. It tremendously increased his odds. "And," he stated, "it is all mine." He knew precisely the direction he had to take.

---

[57] MiG-21 Fishbed, Fighter, (4); MiG-23 Flogger, Multi-role fighter, (24); MiG-29 Fulcrum, Multi-role fighter, (3); Mi-8 Hip, Attack helicopter, (4); Mi-17 Hip-H, Attack helicopter, (8); Mi-24 Hind, Attack helicopter, (15); Antonov An-24, Cargo, (4); Antonov An-26, Cargo, (3).

LEGACY FLIGHT

As soon as Alex arrived at the Pete Field, he met up with what appeared to be a seasoned veteran waiting by the tarmac. There, in its full glory, was a B-17, a "Flying Fortress" bomber, one of those enduring work horses from World War II. The man seemed older than him. *By a generation,* he guessed. Having waited impatiently for an hour, the pilot said, as he reached out a hand, "Must be important. Don't know who you are."

"Bauer," Alex responded with a firm shake, "Alex."

"Simmons," the pilot offered, "Wesley. Call me Wes, last of the diehard Pilots, CAF."[58] Donned in a well-worn greenish flight suit, he gestured toward the plane. "Climb on up." In a heavy Texas drawl, he added, "First time in one of these?" His head had already disappeared through the open bomb bay. Alex followed the narrow ladder into the fuselage.

"Sure is," Alex shouted above the roar of the engines, "didn't know you still flew them." He caught up with the pilot. "How'd you get this off the ground after the blackout?"

"Call from Mount Weather," Wes said. "Urgent to get my fleet in the air." Almost buoyantly, he shrugged. "Only few in operation."

"But the blast?"

"Swapped out instruments. No big deal, we do it all the time."

As soon as they stepped on board, the copilot revved up the engines. "Strap in." Wes motioned at the flight engineer's seat while sliding into the cockpit. Alex adjusted the set hooked by the seat. He could hear the copilot taking instructions from the base. "Runway 17 Left. Clear for departure."

"Roger," The copilot acknowledged. There was ample room on the runway to accommodate this bird. Alex watched the copilot make the departure adjustments. He set the altimeter at 6,184-foot altitude, dialed the departure frequency to 124.0, and then released the brakes. The blades were spinning at full speed. Gradually, the craft gained speed and left the ground way before the end of the 13,500 ft runway. For the moment, the airwaves were quiet. Simmons picked up their earlier conversation. "Problem's keeping them in the air."

"Oh?"

"Can't find trainers," he yelled over the drone of the four engine craft. "To train new pilots."

"Shame."

"There's still interest keeping up traditions," he elaborated, "but without trainers, we're a dying breed."

"Know the feeling," Alex agreed. At times, he felt the same way.

"Wanna take the tour?"

"Lead on." Alex gladly accepted. The craft was still ascending. It'd take a while to reach cruise altitude. The pilot led the way up the bomb bay. Alex tried to keep up. He swiftly paced along the narrow catwalk, but at every turn he bumped his head on the

---

[58] In its glory days the Confederate Air Force was the showcase of WWII craft. Located in Midland, TX, the CAF was chartered as a nonprofit Texas corporation. Its whole purpose was to restore and preserve World War II-era combat aircraft. Over the years, the CAF fleet grew to a fleet of over 140 flight-worthy craft of all kinds including medium and heavy bombers, such as the B-17, B-24, B-25, and B-29 Super Fortress.

framework. They passed the rear turret gunner's glass dome. It was there he realized how crammed the craft was. The fuselage, despite its size, was packed with instruments. Today, most of it was for show.

"These still function?" Alex gestured at the .50 caliber machine guns. Menacingly mounted on turrets, they looked oiled and shiny in their fullest glory.

"Keep all parts fit," Wes pointed out, "but it's not easy to find spares." He squeezed his way farther down the catwalk. "In most cases," he elaborated, "got to build new parts."

"Must cost a fortune?"

"Not cheap," he agreed, "that's for sure, but, it's worth it watching the veterans and kids having fun at the air shows."

Alex, as a kid, vividly recalled these WWII flying fortresses, relentlessly forcing people on the ground to rush to air raid shelters. He used to watch the endless formations of B-17s and B-24s flying up from North Africa to drop their loads.

Perched on the narrow walkway, hanging on to the right .50 caliber machine turret mount, trying to hold his balance amid the bucking and shaking from the craft, Alex caught a glimpse out the window presently closed. No matter where he turned outside the cockpit, air drifts were passing through the fuselage. The view, some fifteen thousand feet below, was spectacular.

Simmons, squeezing by Alex to get back to the cockpit, bumped into him. "Sorry," he said. "Gonna be like that most of the way."

"No problem," Alex assured him, "just keep 'em flying." He turned around to follow Wes. "Don't wanna crash in the middle of nowhere."

"Yeah," the pilot replied, "especially with rumors goin' around about the Badlands."

"Badlands?" Alex asked curiously.

"Prison break," Simmons remarked, "at Fort Leavenworth. They've taken over most of this part of the country."

Reflecting on such a potential danger, Alex imagined all sorts of implications. "Don't tell me that," Alex replied. After getting back from the trip, he promised himself, "Gotta' check into that."

"Here," Wes shouted over the engine noise, handing over a pair of earplugs. They were back in the cockpit. Alex watched him take hold of the controls. Set to cruise at 15,000-foot altitude, the craft was headed east for the nation's capital. It was bucking like a bronco.

Slightly perturbed, Alex shouted, "Blast must have disturbed the atmosphere!" The instruments looked blurry.

"The bumping?"

"Yeah."

"Get that all the time. It's the tradeoff of these fly-by-cable crafts. You people," he inferred, "flying modern jetliners are spoiled." He handed Alex a thermos. "Keeps from spilling. This is," the pilot went on, "the old days where coffee's served in a thermos." The bottle looked like it had its share of dents, but the coffee was piping hot.

"I suppose," Alex replied, "with sick bags all used up."

"Back then, yeah," he said, "not now. People don't get sick anymore, even with the bumpy rides. I think," he explained, "it's mostly a mass phobia in the early days of flying."

"You may be right there."

Simmons reclined in the seat and handed off the controls to the copilot. He looked like he was getting ready to nap. Alex inserted the earplugs. It muffled out most of the drone. He was left with his own thoughts. It didn't take long for him to fall asleep.

Six hours into the flight Alex woke. He could feel his ears pop. He craned out the window. The craft was descending on Dulles. He hardly believed his eyes. The place could have well been a scene from WWII. There were crashed planes all over the field. Apparently, dozens of jetliners had been on final approach when the EMP pulse struck. The ones with enough fuel were diverted north and south for whatever airport the crew had chosen. Without communication it had been a shot in the dark. Some never made it.

Today, Wes's assortment of bombers was stacked up ready for takeoff and landings. There was a landing jeep busy shuttling the craft. It carried a "Follow Me" sign mounted in back. The craft was on final approach. It touched down with a thump. The pilots applied the brakes. The squealing sound carried loudly through the spacious belly of the B-17.

"Thanks for the ride." Alex beckoned and shook hands. "Hope we'll do this again someday."

"Keep watch for air shows," Simmons motioned, "we go around the country all year, but after this," he shrugged his shoulders, "don't know when that'll happen again."

"Keep up the spirit," Alex encouraged him. He was saddened by this vanishing bit of history. The transportation that would take him up to Mount Weather was waiting. "Watch your head," the chauffer cautioned.

THE CASTLE

It was still early in the morning. Brian was wrapped in a housecoat warding off the morning chill. "Liz up yet?" he asked, joining Tracy on the deck. She was enjoying another spectacular sunup.

"Still asleep," she said, "probably spent most of the night on the air."

Brian could have left with Alex for the East Coast but decided otherwise. He wanted an opportunity to spend time with Tracy. The agency hadn't ordered him back yet. He wanted to be alone with her, at least until they had a chance to test their relationship. Until now, it had been work and drama only. "Beautiful," Tracy whispered in the quiet of the morning, "isn't it?"

Brian took a moment to respond. His gaze lingered on her. His eyes took in the beauty of the woman leaning next to him against the rail. "Yeah," he agreed, "I'm looking at it."

Her face turned to him. She smiled at the hinted promises and took the compliment further. "We work well together," she said, "don't you think?"

It'd been days since their lives had taken a dramatic turn. He studied her features while she talked. *Here I am,* he mulled, *with the most beautiful woman in the world, talking about work.* He felt the urge to embrace her. *Wonder what it'll be like.* He imagined their bodies' embrace. He ached for her. His thoughts may have reflected in his face. She caught his stare. Her eyes locked on his. There was a twinkle in them. "What?" Her face broke into a warm smile. "I know that look."

"What look?" He suddenly felt exposed. The desire he had a moment ago slowly retreated. He felt unsure again. The tension over the past few days still had a grip on his emotions. A couple of drinks would have helped with breaking the emotional barrier. *Stop rationalizing,* he scolded himself. It was a barrier he had put up after the last disappointing relationship. *Was it worth it?* He'd questioned then. He'd been content for years traversing the globe, chasing after conflicts. It was a carefree life he totally enjoyed. Relationships were hard. He knew that only too well. *But then, this is a special woman. At least,* he decided, *I'll have to give it a chance.*

She closed the distance on him. He could feel her shoulder pressed against his. She reached for his hands. "What's the matter?"

He could feel the warmth of her body flow through the fabric. It was at this moment he decided. His worries faded. "Nothing," he said softly, "just thinking."

Tracy had wanted him ever since they met. "Follow me," she whispered. She took his hand and pulled him along the hall toward the guest room. "Used to be my room," she said. Stepping across the threshold, she ignored the disheveled bed he'd left earlier. Although Alex had remodeled it years ago, there was still a feminine touch to the décor. He lingered by the entrance for a moment, not sure what steps to take. "Close the door." Her voice was cheery, inviting.

Men can be so insecure, she thought. But she understood. He was out of his comfort zone. She'd been in similar situations. This was her zone. She was expected to take the initiative. "Come here." Her hands reached out for him. Still unsure, he slowly moved up. They kissed, tenderly at first, then with full passion. They embraced. She unbuttoned his shirt, then his trousers. He helped her undress. She tossed the housecoat. The negligee was next. It slipped to the floor. She stepped out of it to move closer.

His eyes had followed her every motion. There she stood, full figure, in front of him, in the nude. "What a body," he whispered.

Her hands slowly pulled the belt from his trousers. He stepped out of it. It freed his body. He helped with the T-shirt and the shorts. He stood in front of her, stripped naked. Her arms reached up, caressing his chest. Then she pressed her body tight against his. She felt the enormous surge of power rise from his body. She could feel his muscle tense. Their lips touched again. They were burning—burning with desire. Her body pressed against his more. Her body slid to the floor. She pulled him down on top of her. She wanted all of him. She wanted all the firmness of which he was capable. Their bodies came together, melting into one—one body…one mind…into the world of ecstasy. For the moment, time stood still.

MOUNT WEATHER

The smartly dressed marine carefully checked Alex's credentials. Several times, his eyes shifted between the ID and the face staring back. Finally satisfied, he motioned to the glass cage and handed the visitor off to an aide who gestured Alex to follow. He was briskly led to an elevator then underground. Arriving several levels below, they stepped into a lengthy corridor.

Alex kept close pace. There were more guards. He was ushered into a spacious room. Bewildered, Alex hesitated for a moment. He had to catch his breath. His eyes swept across the room. There they sat: the nation's elite, policy makers over the nation, over life, and over death. *Remarkable.*

He had arrived at the lowest level in the nation's alternate command center. The center was run and managed by the National Security Council. This was the first time ever used by the president and his advisory staff. It was designed to protect its occupants and to conduct secure warfare with the outside world. They would monitor and deal with the crises at home and abroad as long as necessary.

The president was just about to address a member of the JCS. "Why…"

The aid, with Alex in tow entered the command center. He cleared his throat to make their presence known. The president turned at them. The center became hushed. Most eyes shifted on Alex. He could read their expressions. *Who's the civilian?*

"Mr. President. Alex Bauer here to see you." The aide formally introduced Alex.

Alex stepped up to accept the President's extended hand. "Honor to meet you, Mr. President." He received a firm shake. He responded equally.

"Yes—have a seat." Wilmot gestured him to an empty chair.

With a polite smile, Alex took the seat.

"Listen," Wilmot said. He was addressing Alex. "I invited you for a reason, but," he gestured at the panel, "bear with me for a minute."

"Yes sir."

"By now," the president turned his attention back to panel, "much of the world knows we're in a state of emergency. We've got offers from all over the globe to lend assistance, especially Japan and Europe. I strongly advise we accept."

"Wait just one doggone minute." It was John Hanson, head of the NRO, strongly protesting. He was red faced with anger. "I refuse," he went on, "I refuse to expose our vulnerability to a foreigner…any foreigner."

"We may have no choice." Wilmot calmed the speaker. "How do *you* propose to fix our damaged infrastructure?"

"It'll take time but," Hanson calculated, "it'll minimize exposure."

"That may be true," the president agreed, "but we don't have the time with every nation juggling for world leadership…and believe me," he emphasized, "there'll be many."

"That's something we need to talk about," Alex interrupted. He saw many eyes land on him. *I should have stayed quiet. Don't need this attention.* It was too late.

"What do *you* have to say?" It was Hanson, the head of the NRO. He'd leaned forward to get a clear shot at Alex. His face, his demeanor, said it all. It projected arrogance.

"I called him here," the President interrupted him. "I want to personally thank him for saving the nation."

"What for?"

"He's the one that saved the nation. Go ahead Alex. Speak."

"Mister President," he began, "I've got information about a new threat on the nation."

"What…Where…When," Hanson demanded. "How'd you get info we don't have." His arrogance surfaced once more. He seemed personally insulted.

"Hunch mostly."

"Hunch?" His face became distorted. He bolted from the seat with fury by the utter nonsense he'd just heard. "You nuts?" He leaned into Alex directly facing him. "This country isn't run by hunches. If you don't have facts then keep your mouth shut."

"Hanson!" the president shouted at him. "Stand down." Highly infuriated, he sat back down but not without staring Alex down.

"Go on," the president encouraged Alex to continue.

Alex knew he should not have used such a frivolous word as hunch but he could not disclose his sources. He had a standing agreement with Foster for keeping his sources contained from the outside world. He was directly reporting to Foster and no one else. He had to honor the agreement no matter what. After all, it was Foster that had funded the independent monitoring equipment setup at the Castle connected directly to the antenna farm on top of the Mountain.

"This is not over," Alex continued. "Jihad is mounting more attacks on us."

"You are sure," Wilmot replied. "Can you be more specific?"

"Chemical…Biological…Dirty bombs…I'm not sure. All I know is it's one of it."

"Got proof?" Hanson demanded. "What's your sources anyway?"

"Can't tell you." Alex could see the fury rising again in Hanson. He chose to ignore him then faced Wilmot once more. "Take my word for it Mr. President. Only a few days out."

"What's your recommendations?"

Without effective defense, communication, and military, the country had no chance. "Put your commands on highest alert," he suggested, "that's all I can offer."

Avoiding another outburst by Hanson or anybody else, Wilmot decided to end the exchange. Reminded by the real reason Bauer was here, he stood up, took the few strides to Alex and extended his hand, "On behalf of the nation and my staff," he offered, "I want to sincerely thank you for all you've done. Keep doing what you have been doing and keep in touch." It ended his visit.

"Thank you for listening, Mr. President." Alex briskly turned to the exit. His gaze swept the room one final time. *Not much hope here.* He hurriedly left the room, barely aware of the president's words addressing the Joint Chiefs of Staff. "Why…" The rest of the words quickly faded as Alex was escorted from the room.

CASTLE ROCK

Brian was perched on the deck. His body was spent. His nerves relaxed. A couple of hours had passed since making love to Tracy. His mind was on her, her body, the lovemaking, the future. His eyes were trained on the distance. He craned forward to get a closer look. Clutched between his hands were a pair of field glassed he'd borrowed from Alex. He was straining one eye first to adjust the primary focus, than the other to sharpen the focal point. He had clear focus. *Perfect.*

He propped both elbows on the rail. It relaxed the tension in his arms. Tightly pressed to his face, he could feel the 30x70 DAKAR field glasses weigh on his wrists. He panned the terrain to find the field of interest he sought. There it was. The glasses needed one final adjustment for distance. He focused, watching with intensity. Then a shadow fell on his face. He became aware of Tracy's presence. She had moved by his side. She put an arm around his shoulders. He could feel her sweet breath next to the ear. It broke his concentration. "Morning, gorgeous." His eyes sought out hers. Tenderly, she gave him a kiss. "Missed you."

Slightly distracted, he pulled free.

"What's the matter?" Tracy, appearing rejected, said.

He handed her the glasses. "Take a look." He immediately became aware of her saddened tenderness. "I'm sorry," he apologized.

It took her several seconds to focus in on the scene below. She finally got a clear fix on the valley. "That's odd," she observed, "dozens of people…maybe a hundred…maybe more."

"Let me." Brian took the glasses back. He adjusted focus, then zoomed in on the distance. He could see it now. Clusters of people had set up camp. There were tents. Many people had gathered in the once sparsely populated setting. "Could be a camp ground."

"Dad never mentioned it."

"Tent city in the makings," he suggested. The thought did not help the already tense situation. From what he knew, people living in this part of the country were pretty well established. They were settlers dating back to the pioneering days. Most inhabitants owned guns and always had some kind of survival supplies on hand. For most part, they were self-sufficient. Strangers were eyed with suspicion. *That's what makes it strange.* "Neighbor could be in trouble."

"You may be right."

Brian knew from experience that you didn't just walk onto somebody's property. Chances were you'd get shot. Clint Eastwood came to his mind. Who was it, Dirty Harry, that coined the phrase "Make my day." This law was very much in effect in Colorado. People understood there'd be no legal repercussion to the owner if an intruder got killed in or on the property. As result, there were not many break-ins and burglaries in this part of the country. He studied the scene. His concentration was distracted by a pleasant smell. It drifted out from the kitchen. Liz was preparing breakfast. Her face popped out by the door. "How'd you like your eggs?" and "Bacon or sausage?"

"Scrambled…sausage," Brian ordered without taking his gaze from below.

"Mine too," Tracy echoed.

Liz paused for a moment. Her interest was piqued. "What's going on?"

"Watching a gang." Brian speculated, "Could be travelers on I-25, stranded with the blast."

"Can't blame them," Liz said and disappeared back inside.

"What's unfortunate," Tracy was sharing her thoughts, "is that every one of us could get caught up. Banding together," she offered, "best chance to survive."

"Breakfast's ready." It was Liz calling. Both sauntered inside. She invited them to the table, gesturing. "Have a seat." Breakfast was delicious. The topic of conversation centered on this morning's activity in the valley. Liz readily agreed with their assumptions and chimed in with her own comments from time to time.

Liz was well aware of people getting caught up in emergency and disaster conditions. It was her business. Working years in search and rescue out in California gave her firsthand experience on how to deal with emergencies. People got hurt. Some needed help. They demanded attention. Survival, in many cases, was dependent on immediate treatment. In this case, it would be supply and demand. Based on the past day's events, from what she'd deducted, the demand was there, but the supply was lacking. Likewise, it'd be the cause for many disruptions across the nation.

Liz watched Brian attack the scrambled eggs framed with half a dozen sausage links, sided by a stack of pancakes.

"Nothing's better than a homemade meal." It was a hearty comment. It was obvious he enjoyed her cooking.

Her thoughts were on the people in the valley. She knew food supplies were stored to capacity. Dispersed throughout the country, ready to be deployed by organizations like the Red Cross, they were maintained in huge warehouses. To gain access, without effective command and control, was the challenge. "We should help these stranded people."

"Not a chance." Tracy was adamant. She wasn't willing to open the Castle's door to just anybody. She'd learned her lesson. "As far as I'm concerned," she insisted, "people out there're on their own." Brian wholeheartedly agreed.

Liz respected their opinions, but it wasn't good enough for her. She had an eternal desire to help. Given the current circumstances, this was a rare opportunity. It was her time. She was called to action. Years ago, in 2005, she wished she'd had that chance for Katrina. There was much suffering. However, she couldn't break away at the time from raising the children. This was her opportunity. She had a plan.

They were finished with breakfast. Liz got up and collected the used dishes then headed for the kitchen. Brian and Tracy picked up their earlier conversation. "What's that?" he startled.

"Think it was the front door." Tracy was already on the deck. "Liz," he heard her call, "where you going?" Her voice held an alarming tone. He quickly joined her on the deck then called out, "Wait, don't...don't do it!" It was too late. She'd already disappeared beneath the underbrush. Headed for the valley, she was out of range. Brian picked up the field glasses. He followed her trail.

Minutes later, she promptly appeared amid the people in the distance. "Foolish girl," he said, shaking his head.

Extremely worried, Tracy said, "Hope she's all right." Both kept a lookout.

GROUND ASSAULT

Liz was aware of the risks she took when she left the safety of the castle. Headed for the valley, her steps were firmly grounded. She was determined. It didn't take long for her to make contact with the first band. Already, she could smell danger. They were clustered in small groups. Tucked inside belts and trousers, she was surprised how many were carrying handguns. She tried to blend in among the groups to get information. She needed to find out what had developed. *Stay cool,* she reminded herself. *No reason to haste.* She'd been in intense surroundings before, but they were mostly accident related she could control.

Here, it was desperation. People were unpredictable. She was on edge. Her senses were tuned in on what was said. She overheard conversations. People were plotting. Tents had been set up in clusters. Some appeared guarded. There was no laughter. Most faces looked grim. Guarded caution was all around.

She wasn't quite sure what to do next. *Get back to the castle or push on?* Liz had to find out. She spotted what appeared to be a leader. A tall, rugged looking figure was giving orders. Unkempt, bearded, he perfectly fit the role. Crowded in by a mob, he seemed to be the organizer. Everybody close by carried a weapon. She cautiously moved ahead and approached the group. Immediately, she was spotted. His stare singled her out. She was a new face. It gave her away.

"What do you want?" the tall one demanded. His weapon went up. It was pointed at her belly. It made her cringe. She froze in her steps. Her stomach tightened into a knot. He moved up close. Step by step he approached until he was face-to-face, only inches away. She sensed his tactics. *Scare me into submission. I know your type.* Bully, opportunist, brute, beastie in nature, always got his way. *The Alpha Wolf.* She sensed the animal instinct emanating from his muscular body. She could smell it.

"You people stranded?" She forced herself to stay calm, but outnumbered and outgunned, her voice wavered slightly. She wasn't quite successful in suppressing her fear. He must have sensed her uneasiness.

"Where're you from?" He spat the words at her. She watched his eyes scanning her body. The face took on a wide grin. It was lecherous.

Mostly an act, she reminded herself, *to impress his peers.* She knew enough psychology. Act of dominance, that's what it was. She pulled herself together. "I wanna help."

"Wiseass," he responded, "eh? We've got all the weapons to take whatever we want." His goons were impatiently milling in the background. They wanted action. "We help ourselves."

"It isn't right." Her confidence was coming back. She boldly stood her ground. "People get killed. There're other ways."

"People always die."

"That's not necessary," she pleaded. She was watching his reaction.

"...and, *Miss* Nightingale," he replied, "what do you suggest?" He was moving even closer. He promptly took hold of her hand. "What do you think," he sneered at his cohorts, "like her spunk?"

"I'm in the business of helping people," she offered, "survive."

"So what?"

"I have contacts."

"Go on."

"Organizations that manage food and equipment stored around the country—you can trust."

"Don't trust anybody," he snarled. "We've got the guns and people here have the goods." To emphasize his position he gestured across the farming property they had acquired.

"You'll get killed. Ever hear of the 'Make My Day' law?" She was defiant.

"That's only in flicks." He sneered back at her. "No such thing."

"Don't have to believe me," she suggested, "ask around." He seemed uncertain about his next move. *Won the first round,* Liz reminded herself. He stepped aside with several of his cohorts. She could hear their muffled discussion. She wondered if she'd been able to convince him. Minutes later he came back followed by his armed goons.

"Don't think so," he stated with finality. He was poking her chest with the barrel of the rifle. "Where you from anyway?"

Her self-assurance was faltering. She pointed in the direction of the castle.

"What's up there?" he demanded. He shoved her forward in the direction she'd indicated. With a clenched fist, he waved his band on to follow. From here, the castle was obscured by scrub oak and pine trees. He pushed her ahead, up the hill.

"Don't wanna go there..." She made an attempt to warn him. It was a bluff. At this point she didn't know how Tracy and Brian would react.

"We'll see about that," he cut her short. "Nobody's telling me what..." he started to say, but was cut short by an intense sting on his leg. Dirt and gravel sprayed his face as the same time.

"What the fuck?" he yelled. In an instant he sought cover behind a tree. Immediately, the gang scrambled in all directions. He took aim. He leveled his rifle at her but was undecided. "You tryin' to get me killed?"

"I warned you," she insisted. "You'd be dead," she said, "if she wanted to kill you." Liz had gained her full confidence back. *Not so tough after all?*

"Who's up there?" he demanded. "Who's 'she?'" He was rubbing the gash in his left leg where the bullet had grazed him.

"Forces," Liz warned, "armed with weapons."

"I don't believe you." She saw rage well up from his crazed face. His pride was hurt. Liz saw the reflection in his eyes. He was used to taking whatever he wanted. "We'll take them out." He motioned to the gang. "Up the hill." They swarmed out.

"Won't get far," Liz called after them. It was another bluff. She'd hoped it would deter them. He didn't buy it. She winced in pain when he rudely grabbed her arm. She pulled free. It left red welts on her skin. Rudely, he pushed her ahead up the hill. He was using her body as a shield. "We'll see," he sputtered. He kept shoving his human shield towards the castle.

Well up ahead, the castle had come into view. "Let her go." They all heard a warning. The voice came from above. They could not make out a face. It was Tracy's voice. Her body was lodged flat against the deck.

When the confrontation started, Tracy and Brian had rushed below to pull out two of her dad's high powered rifles from the rack. Stacked up nearby, Brian had grabbed several boxes of ammo. They hurried back up on deck just in time to ward off the approaching force. Tracy had crouched low on one edge of the deck. She had propped the rifle on the deck support. Brian perched at the opposite end. Liz's captor was centered in the cross hair of her scope. Brian covered the others. He was slowly moving the sight between the closest bodies. The war at the castle began when Tracy fired the warning shot at what seemed to be the leader.

Next, in rapid succession, shots were exchanged on both sides. The heavy oak wood planks making up the deck held out well. Tiny splinters of wood, picked out by bullets, shot across her face. "Take that—and that." Tracy squinted and let go another round.

It didn't deter them. The force kept advancing. Her aim was to immobilize. She sought out a leg, then an arm, then a torso. The results were obvious. They were followed by screams. More of the forces moved up. Fire was returned with increasing fervor. The castle was under attack.

"What do you wanna do?" Brian yelled out in the midst of the rampage.

"We can hold them," Tracy yelled back.

Brian was counting the odds. "There's too many." He'd been in battle before. He'd been trained at the war college. It may have been many years ago, but it was still vivid in his mind. *If you're overpowered, move your line of defense.* In most cases it was a retreat. In this case, it would be a move inside and down one level, until there were no more levels. One side always lost, unless there was a standoff. It wouldn't be the case here. *Somebody will get the idea to start a fire. Smoke us out. It would mean the end.* The rampage went on. Bullets kept flying in both directions. With every minute, the distance was shrinking. The attack was overwhelming. The enemy was closing in.

"Liz!" Tracy was worried. Her sister was nowhere to be seen. She hoped she was able to find shelter when the shooting started.

Brian felt it first. It was pressure waves pushing against his rib cage. They followed with increased succession. Sound followed a few seconds later. Both could hear it now. It was the beating of rotors. He stuck his head up, searching for the source. "I'll be damned."

He spotted it first. "Tracy," he called out, "above." He gestured to the sky.

Surprise showed in her face, then recognition. "Dad?"

An instant later, her surprise transformed to wonderment. In a sudden surge, Brian and Tracy saw what many others only felt. It was the impact from two solid beams of projectiles seeking their targets. A wall of fiery bullets from twin mini guns, mounted on side pods of a Cobra helicopter, was streaming towards the many targets, seeking out death and destruction. *Don't know how you pulled it off,* Brian grinned in admiration, *but you did it.*

The craft blended in with the terrain. The Cobra hovered low on top of the hill. It still held the camouflage from an earlier epoch, the Vietnam War. Alex let go another burst of fiery destruction. Whenever he spotted explosions from expended cartridges on the ground, he took aim and released the trigger. The major battle was over in five minutes, but sporadic fire exchanges continued for another twenty. After that, the valley turned quiet. In full view, the craft slowly descended. It sat down on the helipad. Alex jumped from the cockpit. His gaze fell on the terrain below. He could hear the wounded weep. He could feel the sense of death.

He watched Brian scramble up the hill. Tracy was right behind. They had left the safety of the castle. Brian faced Alex. "How'd you pulled it off?"

"Pilot gave me a hand." He gestured up the hill. The pilot was still by the craft. His hands were on the triggers of the mini guns. It was his craft. He didn't plan to lose it to some rebellious crowd. He watched and waited until the fight was over.

"Dad," he heard a familiar voice call out. Liz had stepped from a cluster of trees near the Castle where she'd sought cover. He remembered telling her stories about the destructive powers of which this oddly shaped craft was capable and delivery power from the mini guns. She must have remembered when the Cobra appeared in the sky and sought cover. She rushed up to greet him. "You saved us."

"Just in time, eh?" he boasted, appeasing her.

"Gotta go, Dad," Liz indicated the valley, "wounded."

With the fighting ended, Alex made his way inside. Tracy and Brian caught up with him. They gathered on the deck. From there, they could watch Liz tending to the wounded. "Her world," he marveled, "got to be a calling." He'd never had the drive or the desire to be a Samaritan.

Alex gave them a brief account of how he acquired the Cobra. When he arrived at Pete Field after the presidential visit, he needed a ride. At the hangar nearby, maintenance was just getting ready to take the craft on a test flight. After some pleading and begging, the pilot finally gave in.

Ten minutes into the flight they spotted the ground fire in the distance. They seemed to come from the direction of the castle. Immediately, Alex was alert. Out of sound range, he made the pilot circle the field. It became obvious that a serious confrontation was underway. The pilot descended to treetop level. They joined the battle. Outnumbered by the renegades, with the help of the mini guns, it made the odds even. It took only a few bursts from the 1,200-rounds-per-minute guns to discourage fighting. *Even in Vietnam,* he recalled, *odds were always in the favor of the guns.* It had proven effective on the battlefields. It was proven again now.

Without transportation and medical facilities, for the severely wounded, help may be too late. Liz treated the light casualties herself.

"You did well." Alex expressed his gratitude to all of them for protecting his personal fortress. Constructing the castle the way he did had paid off. He was proud of his daughters, especially Liz, who had displayed exceptional courage by taking on the renegades. The event had brought them together again into a solid family bond.

FORT LEAVENWORTH

Whether through sheer luck or just plain coincidence, the break was a success. Leavenworth, the town, thrown off guard by the power blackout, was taken without much resistance. Local law enforcement, modest as it was, had been no match for the thousand raiding, looting, and marauding members of the prison gang. The gang, during the first couple of days, was very much left to its own whims. Disorganized, disorderly, and undisciplined, rape, pilfering, and raiding was foremost on the gang's agenda. Some of the former inmates split up in different directions. They sought out life in the country independently. Some went east with others headed north and south. Soon word filtered back that an entire group had been wiped out near the Rockies.

Following days of rioting and vandalizing unfortunate citizens, in the process using up the town's resources, the gang was eventually brought under control by Norton, but not without him having to prove his superiority. Always by his side, Bad Man, his dedicated lieutenant, would have eliminated anyone that came in between him and Norton. Consequently, and they all knew it, the fight for authoritarian dominance was more or less for show. It provided a break in the daily routine of binging, raping, and looting.

In between the fighting, Norton and a group of close followers took the time to hammer out a strategy. Suggestions were flying, propositions were made, and votes were cast; they finally agreed on a clear path to forge ahead. That path was Fort Knox. "Why the Fort?" were some of the objections. Most members were aware of the fortification. Their concerns were for the heavily guarded military units, stationed on the fringes of the Ozarks, surrounding the Fort.

"Two reasons," they were informed by Norton. "One," he elaborated in his characteristic manner, pounding one fist passionately against his chest, a gesture he used to emphasize his fitness, "gold." Following an extended pause to let the hollers and cheers subside, he continued. "Two," he continued, "military armament." There were more hollers and cheers. He then commenced to tell the uninformed that at one time, not so long ago, he'd been assigned and stationed at the post's first infantry division. That was all it took to convince the gang on the direction they had to take.

On the planning end, the ultimate goal was to topple the existing government. Once the members heard about that idea, there was no stopping. The gang went wild. The move east was on.

The next day, after one last night of fear-instilled celebration, with Norton, thanks to his inequitably gained popularity, elected leader, and his right hand man, Bad Man, self-elected lieutenant, the force went on their way, pushing eastward towards their immediate goal, the promised land of untold wealth, Fort Knox.

Although Bad Man, the enforcer, through instructions from Norton, kept the undisciplined forces in line for most part, it wasn't an easy thing to keep the supply lines going. Logistics for feeding and housing the advancing party had not yet been worked out. To make things worse, the gang of derelicts, one-time inmates at Fort Leavenworth, grew rapidly in size and force, becoming a menace to any opposing power. As word spread about the planned takeover, taking advantage of the present disarray the nation was in, and forming a new government, new recruits eager to join were added along the path. Although this stretch of the nation wasn't very populated, there was a reason people had moved into this area. It was to get away from the general society, a society entrenched in technology, greed, and corruption, long out of control. Folks, now with a distinct promise ahead, were only too happy to join up.

The convoy east initially was basically a band of outlaws on foot. Taking frequent breaks it was moving at a foot soldier's pace. Along the way, after adding vehicles after many on-the-spot repairs, the convoy started to pick up its pace. Vehicles such as SUVs, pickups, and semi-trucks, abandoned after the EMP strike, were readily available. What most needed was a short-circuited jump-start to get them going. Used as transport for the troops, the convoy made steady headway.

What lay ahead of Norton and his forces was anybody's guess. Not much information from the east came their way. It seemed the whole world had stopped functioning. Every town they passed faced the same issues. Refrigerated food ran out or became inedible from getting spoiled. Families, the ones with enough foresight, were out hunting. Wildlife was plentiful in this part of the country. Rabbits, pheasants, antelope, and many other critters would feed the families for months, perhaps years, to come. The problem was water. Farmers, especially in the outlying areas, were overrun by townsfolk trying to get their hands on water and whatever else they could round up. Outnumbered and outgunned most times, they generally gave in to the demands to save their lives.

To make his plan work, Norton had to reestablish former contacts. Being imprisoned for almost five years, he wasn't quite sure of the whereabouts of his former connections, but there was one he thought might still be in place, a former friend and buddy, commanding sergeant major Brodie Elliott.

He and Brodie went back a long ways. Presently, with forces moving ahead along I-70 east, Norton momentarily dwelled on the past. Aside from a disciplined family environment, he recalled, there was the no-end-in-sight drudgery of school. As child, it seemed, time was at a standstill. It'd take forever, an eternity, to reach another birthday, a holiday, or, best of all, school break.

In later years, among other recreational activities, he and Brodie took up hunting. Duck hunting mostly. One thing led to another and before long, school came to an end, and so did childhood. What followed, he was afraid, would be family responsibility, raising kids, and in general, a life filled with obligations. He wasn't singled out for this, he realized, but that was life. And he didn't want any of it. He decided to join the army. But, the army wasn't the only organization he'd linked up with. There was a group he tremendously enjoyed. Periodically, its members would get together for picnics, BBQs, and, most importantly, shootouts. On those occasions, he'd get awards. Awards were sizeable. They'd range from a few packs of ammo to a specially engraved handgun, or, perhaps, the ultimate prize, the .30-06 Springfield hunting rifle. The organization to which he'd belonged, and still did, was the NRA, the backbone of the nation. And that's where he sought out the immediate future.

FT. KNOX (Kentucky)

Brodie was waiting. He was ready. He just didn't know ready for what. "But," he'd comment to the troops, "as sure as the sun comes up in the morning, something's gonna happen." It may have been intuition, it may have been a sixth sense he'd always felt he'd been gifted with; a hunch it was for certain. Little did he know how right he'd be. The next morning, just after sunup, the attack came. From the distance, the sound was unmistakable. It was a roar advancing on a broad front from the west. A choking smell, carried east by the jet stream, preceded it. Then, minutes later, the attack came in the form of a semi-truck flanked by clusters of SUVs and pickups crashing through the several sentry layered perimeter fences. The strategy was well placed. The Fort, regardless of Brodie's hurried preparations, had been blindsided by surprise. "Commence fire," he gave the order using a bullhorn from the upper walls of the fortress, the Fort's best vantage point.

"Whoever's leading the attack," Brodie reasoned with Wendell Nelson, garrison commander, "must be well informed."

Nelson realized in seconds that it was too late to stem off the advancing forces. After crashing through gates and fences, the convoy halted and hordes jumped from SUVs and truck beds. It was too late to call out an effective command to his troops. Wild, indiscriminate shooting had already begun as he watched the scene from forty feet on top of the fortification. It was a maddening sight. Without power, unable to use effective communication to coordinate the ensuing battle or call up reinforcements, both sides were waging war on the fly. Mobile as the advancing forces were, they were clearly at an advantage.

Bullhorn in one hand, sidearm in the other, Nelson tried his best to direct his troops. "Front lines...hold your position...left flank, watch out...rear guard, move up..." were some of the commands he issued. At the end, an hour into the fighting, his efforts were to no avail. He was losing too many of his soldiers. Although blessed with an entire armored division at his command, his tank force was no match for the mobile vehicles the patriots had in their control. The white flag came up. In clear view, tightly gripped between both hands, Brodie waved it to stop the battle.

What else but a Humvee, civilian version, speedily drove up to a stop in front of Brodie. It seemed to be the popular command vehicle in any fight or battle situation. For all practicality it was. From a moral, just, and perception perspective, the Humvee projected an image of prowess and superiority. It was built for just that purpose, to intimidate, bully, and harass, as many owners would attest.

Out jumped no other than his old time childhood buddy. "What?" Brodie stammered, "You!" He almost couldn't believe his eyes. "Rusty?"

Jumping from the vehicle with Bad Man in tow, Rusty Norton, legs firmly planted on solid concrete, replied heartily, "The one and only."

"I can't believe it," advancing a few paces, Brodie wavered, "I thought you were at Leavenworth."

"I was," Norton fired back. A sly grin crossed his face when he explained, "But, as you can see, I'm out."

Brodie sidestepped to let his superior pass. "Wendell Nelson, Fort Knox," he introduced the garrison commander.

Wendell Nelson, fuming and outraged at Norton and at the one called Bad Man, at his men for failing to stem off the attack, and at the military for keeping him in the dark, but mostly at himself for not being better prepared, demanded justification. "Get off my land," he roared.

"Let's not be hasty," Norton, trying to maintain a balance, suggested. "I've got a proposition for ya."

"Not interested," Nelson, not the least bit interested in what this band of hoodlums had in mind, nevertheless queried. He was infuriated. "Not now, not here…my quarters, two hours!" Off he stormed.

Brodie, face clearly reflecting his thoughts, silently stood by. He and Norton went back a long time. He thought he knew his buddy. He still couldn't believe the stunt he just pulled, taking the Fort by force, and out of all places, Fort Knox, the nation's supposedly most fortified army post. He couldn't help it. The thought brought a broad grin to his face. *Never thought he had it in him,* he mused. *This'll make history.*

"Didn't know you had it in you," Brodie, still amazed at his buddy's surprise attack, wondered. He was pacing alongside to keep up.

"What?"

"Commanding an army," he declared with a hint of admiration, "ragtag as it is."

"You haven't seen anything yet," Norton replied. "Wait 'til you hear the plan."

"Can't wait…where are we headed?"

"Command vehicle," Norton gestured at the Humvee parked by the main gate, "I'll fill you in."

Both spent close to two hours catching up. Not much could be said about the past other than one spending close to five years imprisoned with the other building an army career. Much of the time was spent laying out the plan, as Norton had stated. The more Norton revealed the details, the more intriguing it became. Brodie, more bewildered by the minute, just kept on shaking his head. Despite a hardened career as command sergeant major, in charge of an entire armored division, he was amazed at the genius of his former buddy. "Let me get this straight," as incredible it sounded, he wanted clarification one more time, "you're planning a coup, a takeover," he stress the unbelievable again, "a coup d'état, on the entire nation, the United States of America?"

"The one and only."

"Have you gone mad?" Brodie could not believe his ears. "You'll never pull it off."

"Think about it." Taking time to let the enormity sink in, Norton squarely faced his buddy. "Nobody's home. Has anybody been in contact with you, or, more importantly, have you been able to reach another command?"

"Come to think of it…"

"There you go."

"Alright!" As incredible as is sounded, Brodie finally surrendered to the plan. While listening to Norton describe the plan from a high-level approach, Brodie made brief mental notes evaluating each phase in its pros and cons. It sounded solid. It made sense, but there were many other factors involved beyond their two relatively minor forces. Taking into account was the entire armed forces of the nation, not to speak of the National Guard, law enforcement, and other military and militant units. Several issues Brodie tried to reason out, but were immediately shut down on all counts. Norton wouldn't allow any room for resisting. "It'll work," was the all-purpose reply.

"Tell me again," Brodie, clearly amazed, repeatedly shaking his head—at times in agreement—demanded. "I don't wanna miss anything."

"Here it goes." Norton illustrated the action plan as a three-phased approach once more. "First," he explained, "the Badlands.

Despite being slightly irritated at having to repeat himself, he nevertheless commenced. "We must get complete control over the central part of the U.S. Once this part is in our hands, we can proceed to the next step."

"Which is?"

"Form a new charter." It would be phase two.

As incredible as it sounded, Brodie was fascinated. He was finally convinced Norton really had not gone made. Committing himself, "I'm in," he promised.

"Phase three," he further explained, "rebuild the nation, and rebuild it my way."

BADLANDS

What Rusty Norton had in mind was the piece of land presently comprised of the Great Plains. This prominent piece of land was situated west of the Mississippi River and east of the Rocky Mountains in the United States and Canada. It was a broad expanse of flat land, much of it covered in prairie, steppe and grassland. The area covered parts of the states of Colorado, Kansas, Montana, Nebraska, New Mexico, North Dakota, Oklahoma, South Dakota, Texas, Wyoming, and extended into the Canadian provinces of Alberta, Manitoba, and Saskatchewan with the Canadian portion of the Plains known as the Prairies. Much of the region, at one time, was home to American Bison herds until hunted to near extinction during the 19th century.

In general, aside from the extreme weather conditions, the prairies supported abundant wildlife in mostly undisturbed settings, but civilization had transformed much of the prairies for agricultural purposes. Historically, the Great Plains were under the dominance of the Plains Indians, whose tribes included the Blackfoot, Crow, Sioux, Cheyenne, Arapaho, Comanche, and others. Eastern portions of the Great Plains were inhabited by tribes who lived in semi-permanent villages of earth lodges, such as the Mandan, Pawnee and Wichita.

Today, modern civilization had taken hold of most of the Plains, with mostly productive farmers populating the region. Following the EMP strike on the U.S., the land had reverted back to the days of the settlers. This time it was not the pioneering settler with trying to cultivate the land in mind. This time, it was the marauding band of ex-convicts taking advantage of the open, mostly unprotected plains. It was this open expanse of prairie that attracted the convicts, now known as "The Patriots."

And so, the "Badlands" was born.

CASTLE ROCK

"We stay together. Agreed?" Alex stressed the point several times. "No matter what."

"We know, Dad," Liz acknowledged. Earlier, she recounted yesterday's events in detailed glory. There were many wounded to care for. Dozens were dead. It was not an easy scene to see citizens caught up in battle in the homeland. Only a few days ago many were driving home from work—a reminder to all to never underestimate the capability of the ordinary man, given an adverse circumstance.

"Don't know what to expect out west," Alex picked up on yesterday's events. "Best chance we have to stay safe is as team."

"Agreed."

"Okay then," Alex was already headed for the shelter, "let's get some tools together."

"Tools?" Curiously, Tracy followed on her dad's heels. Brian had a pretty good idea. Liz was busy cleaning up the breakfast table. They were up early after a few hours of exhausted sleep. Alex had rousted them up at dawn and got the team ready. *His Team. The Castle Team.*

The evening before, they'd agreed to make their way out west. They wanted to check up on Liz's mom and husband. They'd also drop the kids off at home. Afterwards, all were anxious to see the devastation the bomb had caused in the Bay Area.

Alex collected an assortment of firearms. It'd filled two duffel bags. He handed one to Brian and locked up the Castle. Minutes later, the team and kids piled into the Wagoneer. They headed for the air base. A few miles out, in the distance, they could already see air traffic takeoff and land. The WWII craft were a majestic sight. The olive-colored war birds looked magnificent in the air. One could hear and feel the engines roar well before the craft came into view. The Pratt & Whitney were pushing pressure waves in all directions. It was awe-inspiring. A few miles farther, the gate shack came into view. They were waved through without much delay. The sentry had recognized Alex from recent encounters.

Minutes later, they were at the departure counter. "You Harris?" the desk sergeant wanted to know.

"No," Alex indicated Brian, "he's Harris."

Brian was handed a slip of paper. "Message for you." Scribbled on it were three short words, "Report to HQ." His face immediately dropped. One word summed it up: disappointment. "Guess I'm overdue." He sought out Tracy. "Gotta head back east."

"But why?" Her disappointment was obvious. Over the past couple of weeks Brian had become part of the family. Now this? They'd miss him. They'd all been prepped for the trip out west.

"Agency needs me." He pulled Tracy aside. "I'm surprised they've not contacted you."

"Oh," she stressed, "they will." Tracy briefly reflected on her life back in Baltimore. It seemed so distant. The last few days had been filled with excitement. Brian had turned rudimentary life into an adventure. She'd miss him. He had captured her heart. Her eyes sought out his. She reached for his hands and slowly pulled him to a quiet corner. Alex's gaze followed them. He respected their privacy.

"I'll miss you," Brian whispered. He pulled her close. They kissed, gently first, then with passion. His eyes were closed. She gazed at his handsome face. *I think I'm in love.* She could feel the warmth of his body flow into hers but kept quiet. Private thoughts filled with passion flowed through her mind. *Damn the agency.*

"How will you get there?"

"Somehow," he sounded assuring, "but I'm more concerned about you."

"Don't worry," she said, "I'm with Dad."

"Let me know how things turn out…and come back soon."

"I will." She abruptly turned to hide her tears. "Bye."

Alex managed to get seats on a Hercules. For the past few days, it'd been flying rescue missions out of Pete Field. Today, it was scheduled for Travis, departing momentarily. Travis, an air base located west of Sacramento, was the transport connection point to support the many military facilities in the Pacific and Asia.

"Not much of a craft," Tracy remarked, getting seated. The young airman made sure they were strapped in securely. He confirmed the cabin's readiness with the pilot, who made one final check on the passengers before takeoff.

"Hercules may be dated," the pilot assured Tracy, "but the engines are reliable. It'll get you there safe. Enjoy the ride."

The craft took off. From there on, the team had to shout over the drone from its four engines, turboprop driven Allison T56-A-15 power plants. Most of the craft was configured for cargo, but a dozen seats up front carried the team and troops to their missions. Although the C-130 had been commissioned decades ago, many were still in use. There were hundreds still flying missions in one capacity or other. Many were submarine hunters; others transported cargo and troops. It was the military's workhorse.

The flight was bumpy, especially crossing the Rockies and again descending over the Sierras. There were no windows in the craft. The seats faced the rear. "For safety reasons," the pilot had explained. He checked on them occasionally to make sure nobody got sick. An hour into the flight, the airman served sandwiches and coffee. Near the cockpit was a small bathroom they could use. Liz and Tracy talked. The kids were taking naps. Alex was recalling the past few days' events. Although they had been action packed, he wasn't very happy with the outcome, or what's awaiting them.

After close to a three-hour flight, the craft landed at Travis AB. The engines were winding down. The exit ramp opened with a grind. With a solid thud, it came to rest on the tarmac. The team stepped out into a bright, sunlit day. Alex reached for a pair of Ray Ban glasses. A thought struck him. *Protection gear.* He hadn't anticipated protection against radiation. It'd completely slipped his mind.

There was a great deal of activity at this western port. Military planes were taking off and landing almost continuously. Aside from the confederate fleet, they were mostly C-130. The base looked like a scene from WWII. No modern jetliners were present. Those craft were still grounded. Instruments had to be fabricated and installed before they would take to the air again.

The craft's loadmaster directed them to the shelters. The place looked like a war zone. To accommodate the increased traffic, auxiliary tents had been set up. First step was to get protective gear. Radiation suits were on hand, they were told, but the supply was limited. Alex negotiated for three sets. There were no kid sizes available. They were told, toward Napa, that the air was not contaminated. The kids should be safe. Along with the radiation suits, Alex checked out a dosimeter. It was a handheld thermo-luminescent unit. "Detects radiation exposure," he was informed. Alex tested it. At the moment, the gage indicated, "Safe Zone."

"Don't know how long that'll last." There was concern in all of the faces.

"Guess we'll find out soon enough." Liz worried about the kids. They all did. "Jet stream's been in the state's favor," they'd been told, "it'd dipped to the south." Their route would be to the north of the radiation belt. NNSA[59] had set up a tactical command post. Alex was handed a hand drawn sketch. It indicated the general patterns and drifts of the radiation spread. It closely followed the jet stream. With the air safe, at least for the moment, they carried the head gear clutched under their arm. Each suit was fitted with a badge dosimeter to detect radiation. Worn like a patch emblem sewn onto one arm sleeve, it was a gamma-sensitive strip. It'd change color when exposed to deadly rays. "Keep an eye on it," they'd been told, "it'll save your life."

Next stop was the "Motor Pool." It took some time to locate the Chief of Operations. The place was busy. Everybody rushed to a mission.

Alex considered stealing transportation again, but Liz thought it too risky. "Not safe with all the military police." National Guardsmen were also close by. Most were in transit to the various trouble spots in the state. "Better not," she reasoned. The last thing anyone wanted was to get jailed. More likely, they'd be shot.

National orders had been issued by FEMA[60] to shoot looters on the spot. Alex was put off several times, but eventually connected with a master sergeant. "I've family in the Peninsula," he told Alex, "but can't get away." Every hand had been recalled for emergency duty. He'd been assigned to Travis. And that's where he'd stay, for the time being.

"Here's the address." The chief handed Alex a slip of paper. The note was hastily scribbled to "My Wife." In exchange for getting ground transportation, Alex promised to stop by to check on the family. He was handed the keys to a Humvee, H-1 military version. The vehicles were built to handle well in rugged terrains. They were simple, but well designed. Soldiers loved them. It didn't take much of an effort to keep them up. Repairs were quick. Some had burned out wiring from the EMP hit. Others needed a new starter. Damages were minor. As part of military hardening, many had been shielded with copper mesh and component filters. Radio, navigation, and computer equipment had received the same protection. The on-board computers were heavy, but sophisticated, designed for real time battle management.

"Good lucky," the chief called after them.

"Best suited vehicle for the trip." Alex couldn't have hoped for better. The vehicle had been fueled to the top. Military instructions were clear: "Always ready for dispatch."

Liz had been impatient to get going. She'd urged Alex on. He was just about to hop behind the wheel when his eyes caught a face he thought he'd recognized. "Can't be." He

---

[59] National Nuclear Security Administration – Part of DOE's national security organization for nuclear disasters. Also maintains the nuclear weapons stockpile and database information on nuclear weapons materials for the U. S. government.

[60] Federal Emergency Management Agency is an agency of the United States Department of Homeland Security. Its primary purpose is to coordinate the response to a disaster occurring in the United States that overwhelms the resources of local and state authorities.

shook his head. He took a second look. *It's him.* "Look who's here," he pointed in the direction.

"Who?" Tracy turned.

"Brooks," Alex said with a grin, "your favorite guy."

"Better not!" She exclaimed. She still had an axe to grind with him. "We should leave." She did not want to face this brute. She'd put the kidnapping incidence behind her. It wasn't a pleasant memory. *Now this?* But he'd spotted them already.

"Well…well…well," he proclaimed, "what a small world. Fancy meeting you here. Whole Bauer clan." Carrying a broad grin on his face, he came strolling toward them. "Where you headed?"

"Napa," Liz stated, "home."

"You must be Liz," he said, "pleased to meet you." He extended his hand through the open window. Liz accepted his handshake. She had no grievance with him.

Tracy made no attempt to acknowledge the guy who'd detained her in the Arizona desert for days.

He recognized her in the backseat. "Hi there." His grin broadened. "Still angry?"

She turned away. "Damn right."

"What're you doing here?" Alex was still surprised at the unexpected encounter. He should be furious with Scott, but didn't feel the anger. *Like any soldier,* Alex reminded himself, *he lives taking orders.*

"After you left," he explained, "got orders to the West Coast. Agency's been tracking possible terrorist activities."

"Specifically?" Alex's curiosity got the better of him.

"Illegal movement, chemical agents, possible nuclear materials," Brooks explained. "We normally don't care unless it makes its way into the country."

"What's your action plan?"

"Headed for the coast—San Francisco," he stated, "to work with NNSA."

"Might catch up with you," Alex replied. He appreciated his candor. *Tough, yes. Ruthless maybe, but a soldier, nevertheless.* He'd associated with Brooks' kind a number of times. They were a hard-core breed, but dedicated and dependable once you got to know them. *Would give the shirt off his body.* "Gotta go," Alex urged, with a promise to keep in touch.

Five minutes later they were on the I-80 onramp headed west. They made good headway. Traffic flow was unusually light. Alex felt elated. He was back on mission status. He was driving full out within the safety of this remarkable vehicle. He could feel the instantaneous power surge whenever he stepped on the gas pedal. The vehicle sat firm on its tracks like it was hugging the road with gigantic claws. It felt like sitting inside a light battle tank.

"Strange," Liz was making conversation, "only military vehicles on the road."

It was an hour's drive to the valley. The closer they got to their destination, the more traffic they encountered. Emergency and rescue vehicles were patrolling the roads.

"Let's head for Napa first," Alex suggested. Everyone agreed.

ATLANTIC AIR SPACE

The A-330 Airbus was headed west. It should reach the eastern fringes of Canada momentarily. Next stop would be Denver. From there, with Yusuf in command, it'd continue to the Pacific coast to initiate the next phase, the ground attack. He, the Serpent, would stay on to take control over the city, followed with taking over the nation. It'd be the political seat for the new order. *His order.* Denver would be capital city of Islam…the new seat for the cause of Jihad. *His cause.*

On his orders, the craft had been converted into an airborne command center to be used for the next phase of operation. He had it fitted with the most sophisticated equipment available on the market, but the craft was not hardened against EMP. It didn't matter. The blast was over. The craft held most of the comfort and conveniences found in modern jetliners. It even provided a shower and a couple of sleeping quarters for the command team. A section of the cargo hold had been reserved to house computers and comm gear. The passenger section was converted into the command center. It was from here that he directed the pending assault.

"Yemen Central." The voice on the other end sounded crystal clear.

"Standby." He wasn't surprised at the voice quality. Distance wise, not counting the time lag up and down, the satellite was about eight thousand miles from home base, but that was miniscule with sophisticated software making the necessary adjustments. From there, the signal bounced across a couple of satellites to reach his current location, seven miles above the Atlantic approaching the U.S., in his airborne command post.

"Hold for instruction." The Serpent was frustrated. Yusuf and the New York cell were overdue. Regardless of the blackout in northern America, he should have received some word from New York tactical. The team had been on its way to their target destination, but that was already more than forty-eight hours ago. He made allowances for the blackout, but by now he should have heard something. He was agitated, but not worried yet. With the many facets required to play out the battle plan, not every element was one hundred percent successful. But, he needed coordination and synchronization for the plan to work. Time was critical. He had to make a decision.

The computers received continuous updates from many of his commands. Most were from small, tactical support groups stationed in Jihad-friendly nations. Few were from strategic centers organized and managed by his trusted lieutenants. Most of those were located in hidden caves and obscured facilities disguised in the forms of warehouses, cargo ships, and legitimately registered off-shore business entities, secure from the ever-prodding tentacles of law enforcement.

Although frustrated about the lack of word from Yusuf, the Serpent felt confident. He was in control of "Big Bird," the codename for the airborne command. He was anxious to meet up with Yusuf, his deputy commander. The pickup point was Denver; the direction the craft was headed.

NAPA VALLEY

The Humvee approached a turnoff. The sign came into view. "Hwy-12 Napa." Alex turned onto Jameson Canon Road. It would connect with Hwy-29, their destination. A twenty-minute scenic drive followed. Lush green rolling hills, covered by grape bearing vines, rolled along the panoramic view. Before long, they found themselves amid Northern California's most famous vineyards. Artful signs announced family-crested names as they passed by, one by one. One could not help but notice Clos du bois, Coppola, and Robert Mondovi, the finest in the region.

Alex had instructed Liz to check the dosimeter frequently. "Still safe," she periodically announced. Twenty minutes later they arrived at Liz's home. It was a small stucco-built home customary for the region. A three-foot lattice fence provided some privacy. It mostly kept stray dogs from entering the yard. "Mom," Liz called out. There was no answer. She became worried. Her car was sitting in the driveway where she'd left it. Testing the engine, it was disabled. On entering, the place was empty. All the windows were shut. Inside, it was stifling hot. "Pew," the kids called out. "What a stink." They rushed for their rooms but did not linger long. The air was too smelly.

To be sure, Liz checked the dosimeter. There was an alarming crackle. The needle jumped wherever she turned, but the arm patches indicated safe zone. Apparently, the detonation in the bay left traces of radiation. At least there was not enough to wear the suits. The air was hot enough without having to wear the bulky protection.

"Let's go to the police station," Liz suggested. "Jim works there. He can tell us where the shelters are."

The station was not far off. Liz checked with the desk sergeant. Her ex had been assigned to a sector north of town. "What about my mom?" She was told to check with the emergency shelters.

It took fewer than thirty minutes to locate her. They spotted her by the service line. Red Cross had set up shelters to serve food and water to the local residents. Her mom was busy handing out rations to the injured. Most local residents were still residing in their homes. It was just food they didn't have. And water. The reservoir pump station had been disabled by the initial blast. It didn't matter. The water was probably unsafe to drink. Radiation fallout had polluted much of the region's water supply.

"Mom!" Liz exclaimed. "So glad you're alive! Here," she pushed her kids ahead. They were overjoyed to hug grandma. Then it was Liz's turn for a hug.

Over Liz's shoulder, Annette spotted Alex. *This is awkward. How long's it been?* Twenty years, since she'd seen him or talked to him. "Couldn't get word out," she said.

It was Tracy's turn to greet her mom. She had waited nearby to take her turn. She felt like a stranger and a bit jealous towards her sister as she watched them embrace. *But then,* she thought, *they've been together the years I've been away.*

Alex lingered nearby. He didn't pay much attention to what was said. He saw flashes of memories from another time. It was long ago. Unsure how to approach her, he hesitated. He was buying time. Finally, he came face to face with the woman he once loved, the woman that gave birth to his children. She solved his hesitation with, "It's good to see you, Alex."

"You too." He gave her a fleeting hug. "We were worried when the house was empty."

"Ran out of water and food."

Alex studied her face. *She looks good for her age.* His gaze swept across her body. His eyes captured her full contour. *Still shapely.* He was happy for her. *Always took care of herself.* Years ago, when they split up, he'd sincerely hoped she would meet someone that would appreciate her more than he did. She'd needed the things he hadn't been able to give, like a fulltime husband, personal attention, romance, and love. Theirs had been a marriage of convenience, for different reasons. Where he wanted a travel companion, she was looking to a homebound marriage. He'd thought anybody would jump at the opportunity to see the world. *Not her.* It turned out a disappointment for the both of them.

"Mom," Liz interrupted, "where's Jim?"

"The country." Liz's ex was a policeman. "There've been break-ins." When the National Guard arrived in the valley, police, firefighters, and rescue personnel had been assigned sectors of responsibilities as directed by SIOP. The emergency plan went into effect nationwide. FEMA made sure it would be enforced under the direction of the DHS. In this part of the state, casualties had been relatively light. It was different in other parts where the population was heavy. Besides the initial blast casualties, many more people had been killed, mostly from looting. Killing looters was a senseless act, but sometimes necessary to maintain order. Psychologists never had been able to completely solve the mystery of what drives people to such drastic measure as stealing useless items. Televisions, refrigerators, microwaves, what good were they without electricity? People didn't think. They just react to a windfall ending with deadly consequences.

"Mom." Liz turned serious. She faced her mother. "I need to go to the Bay Area. They need help."

"I understand."

"I'll leave the kids with you."

"Don't worry about them."

"Not sure when I'll be back."

"They'll be safe."

"Listen." Liz sought out her kids. "I want you to stay here. Grandma will take care of you for a while."

"But…"

"No buts." Liz was stern about her decision. She had to be determined.

"When will you come back?"

"I don't know," she wavered, "you can come and visit when it's safe. Right?"

"Guess so." Disappointment showed in both faces.

"Be good now." *Children,* she reflected, watching them saunter off, *they can be so demanding.* But they were good kids. *And smart too. Must have done something right.*

"Dad," Liz urged, "can we stop by the station?" She wanted to tell her ex that the kids were safe.

"Okay," Alex replied. "Let's get going." He felt uneasy in the present surroundings. He was angry with himself for not trying harder to keep the family together, and even more so for not keeping in contact. *What's a family for?* he asked himself. *My creation, my responsibility.* He'd failed miserably. *I'll never make the same mistake again,* he vowed, *letting a job come before my personal life.* "Too late now," he muffled. He'd never get a chance for another family. *Not in this life.*

Liz came to his rescue. "Bye, Mom," she called out.

"See you soon." Tracy placed a kiss on her mom's cheek. She promised to return. She also promised to do better with keeping in touch.

Ten minutes later, the party met up with Jim. He'd been assigned to the northern perimeter of town. It'd been relatively quiet in this section. St. Helena and Calistoga were mostly home to residential wine growers. After the nuclear strike on San Francisco, many refugees were sent here from Oakland and Berkeley. They arrived in troves to settle at the temporary shelters. Wounded were delivered non-stop. Many would die in a short time, some from radiation poisoning, and others from diseases. Their time was counted in hours and days. Those were the lucky ones. Survivors badly burned would be subject to extreme suffering. There would be not enough skin to cover the severe burns. Medicine still had a ways to go to perfect lasting skin grafting.

Back on the road, Alex and his party were headed for what used to be the jewel of the West Coast, San Francisco, City by the Bay.

WEST COAST

"Dad," Liz was giving directions, "take 29 South." Alex was driving.

Tracy enjoyed the scenery from the backseat. "Nice country," she remarked. They had just gotten on their way.

"Wanna be on 80," Alex suggested. "Don't we?"

"Intersects in Vallejo."

Either way, it was a scenic drive. Headed south for now, twenty minutes later, the highway intersected with the interstate. They were on the final leg to the bay. To accommodate the passengers, the Humvee was roomy enough, though nothing like the commercial version. The military issue was configured with only the basics. There was no luxury here. It was designed to carry troops. That was it, olive drab in its glory. The standard army color. It was meant to be a reliable workhorse.

"What's the reading?" Alex was aware of the danger they were sure to encounter the closer they got to the city.

Liz took another reading. "Still safe." Ever since they left Napa, the crackling sound was increasing, but it was still in the safe zone. She sounded confident. She was experienced. It wasn't the first time she'd had to use the gadget on Hazmat. Hazardous materials were part of her business. In many instances it was the cause of fires, especially with overturned semis leaking dangerous liquids. Liz was pointing out landmarks. "American River's to the right." Its waters were feeding the bay. "San Quentin's up ahead."

"Prison?"

"The one."

"What's the body of water to the left?" Tracy pointed out. She'd not been in this part of the state. "It's pretty here."

"The bay."

"So, that's it?" She admired it. "The infamous San Francisco Bay."

"Yeah." To one side, sprawling Berkeley came into view. On the other, Oakland, with its high-rise business district, was just beyond. A cluster of road signs came up all at once: I-580, I-780, I-880, and I-980. Several expressways merged into a maze of traffic. The brightly painted lettering stood out prominently against the green-colored signs. Traffic bottled up immediately. Trucks, utilities, and emergency vehicles, mostly military and FEMA, jostled for position. To complicate things, a sign announced a traffic jam up ahead. I-80 into the city seemed to be blocked. Traffic had backed up for miles. "Dad," Liz alerted him, "stay to the left. I know a bypass." He swerved to avoid colliding with other motorists. The Humvee fishtailed into the outer lane. They all hung onto the straps.

"Dad," Tracy cautioned from the rear seat, "slow down."

"Getting sick?"

"Yeah," she protested, "there's a sign."

"What sign?"

"A warning," she said, "I couldn't read it. You're going too fast."

"Sorry, girls."

He'd remembered Tracy as child. She'd always demand to sit up front to avoid motion sickness. The sisters used to fight over the seat. He had to swerve again. "Crazy bastard." The vehicle barely cleared the I-580 onramp. The right tires scraped against the concrete encasement. The metallic sound of a lost hubcap echoed against the ramp. Many more hubcaps were scattered alongside the road, crushed from prior scrapes.

Alex pushed on. He stepped on the pedal. "What's the reading?" For a second, he'd taken his eyes off the road to check with Liz on the radiation level.

"Dad!" Liz yelled out. "Watch out!" Her eyes reflected sheer horror. She'd braced herself. Her hands clutched the door handle. She had spotted something ahead. That something was a sheer drop-off. It was the edge where the bridge ended.

Alex saw the horror in her eyes. He reacted instantly. The instant he saw her panic he slammed on the brakes. It was on pure instinct, even before his eyes caught the danger. "Dammit!" he yelled out. The brake force threw him into the steering wheel. His head snapped forward. "Dammit…dammit…dammit," he swore several more times. His eyes latched on the sight his daughter had caught a split second before. His face turned ashen.

The Humvee had spun out. It slammed into the embankment from the panicked stop. The vehicle bounced off, then slithered to a grinding stop. He heard it now. Both front wheels were spinning freely. Hanging over the broken up edge, the vehicle was on the brink of tipping into the abyss below.

"Nobody move." Everybody in the vehicle froze. Breathing had stopped. The weight of the Humvee hung in balance. Just a slight shift would push it over the edge. To their horror, 220 feet below were the muddy green waters of the bay, rippled with white spray whipped up by the afternoon breeze. They were held in balance for what seemed like an eternity. The cab was bathed in complete silence. Alex dared not move, not even his head. He stared straight ahead then slowly shifted focus to his daughter.

From the corner of the right eye, he made out the ghostly reflection of Liz. Her eyes were locked on his. They were filled with fear, but also determination, even a glimmer of hope. Ever so slightly, she threw him a nod. It was for her sister trapped in back. He understood.

"Tracy," Alex whispered, "you're gonna have to trust me."

"Dad?" There was an ominous sound in her voice. It was filled with fear.

"Everybody…jump on my command." He watched his daughter tense up, ready to jump. "Wait," he cautioned. He paused a few seconds to gather the next words. It would mean life over death. "Liz and I jump first."

"No!" Tracy screamed out.

"You move first," he ordered, "we all die."

"I'm by your side," Liz promised.

"Only need one second," Alex prompted, "you can do it."

"Dad," Tracy protested, "I can't."

"We all open the doors," Alex paused a few more seconds. "Tracy," he reminded her one last time, "on the count of three."

"Let's do it! Three…two…" Three doors flew open simultaneously. Two bodies peeled out from the front. "Tracy!" Alex yelled, but she was frozen on the seat. Liz saw her sister immobilized. Alex saw Liz roll off the pavement then jump to her feet. She rushed for the rear door and yanked her sister's body from the vehicle.

Alex had moved in on the driver side. The vehicle still clung to the balance. Then, in slow motion, it tipped forward. Shaving against the edge, the frame gave off a grinding sound as it tilted and slid over. They watched in horror as it disappeared into the depths below. Alex and Liz crept up to the jagged edge of the bridge. They carefully edged their way back to safety.

"You all right?" Alex forced himself to stay calm. His nerves were on edge but he didn't let it show. Immense guilt swept over his face. He knew the feeling well.

"No." Tracy was shaken up. She was mad at him, at them both.

He reached out for her. She pulled back, sulking. "I just wanna see if you're hurt." He was inspecting his daughters. There were scrapes but nothing serious.

"Man," Liz groaned, "that was close."

"I'm sorry." Alex was begging.

"I know, Dad," Tracy admitted. She had calmed down somewhat. "I'm mad at myself. I could have killed us all."

"Don't give it a thought," he said. He nodded at Liz who gave her sister a hug. "Not your fault the bridge's out. We're alive."

Alex beckoned them away from the sheer drop. It was dizzying this close to the edge.

The full magnitude of the disaster slowly sunk in. From their vantage point they could see the empty span of what used to be the Oakland Bridge. Some parts were intact. Most of the connectors were gone. The vertical trusses that held up the platforms stood out like ominous skeletons. Steel had been twisted by the immense pressure wave. Cables that had held up the bridge through weather and storm for eighty years had snapped. Cable strands were drooping into the sea below much like gray spaghetti. It appeared that some of the steel girders were still intact, but many sections of the road had collapsed into the bay, taking with them countless cars and passengers. It might never be known how many people had perished on the bridge alone.

The immediate break ahead had taken out a few thousand feet of asphalt, girders, and steel. The next solid span was anchored on Yerba Buena Island, a couple miles ahead. It was the half way point connecting with Treasure Island. The immediate drop where the Humvee had fallen off was terrifying. There were other tire marks on the asphalt. "We're not the first," Alex deduced. "Others have gone over." He shuddered at the thought. And so did his daughters.

"That's it?" Liz couldn't believe their trip ended this way. "What now?"

"We walk." Alex had gained his confidence back. He was inspecting the terrain below. "We can make it to the shore." Their journey had come to an abrupt halt in the middle of the onramp. It was impossible to climb down. The ramp was supported by huge vertical columns many feet high. Alex was checking the remaining highway for debris. "We need a barricade."

There was nothing useful. Not even the usual road debris was present. That had been swept clean with the blast. Liz suddenly jumped in the middle of the roadway. She was wildly waving both arms. In succession, several vehicles were rapidly approaching. They had probably had similar ideas about using the bypass. Their speed was excessive. "Stop...stop!" she yelled at the oncoming vehicles. Her warning calls were ignored. She jumped out of the way and knew what would come next. Death.

From the vantage points of the drivers, they were unable to see the abrupt end of the highway. The highway here was on an upslope. Alex and the team watched in horror at what happened next. The two lead cars shot straight out in the air. They saw the occupants' faces change from exhilaration to sheer panic when they realized the road had ended. The screams were awful. The next driver was luckier. He had sense enough to slam on the brakes in time. He slithered to a halt just before the drop. Lives had been spared. Alex pulled the shaken driver and passengers to safety.

Alex discussed a barricade with him. The driver was reluctant to give up his vehicle. Alex insisted. The driver eventually relented. Fifty feet back, using the warning sign from the trunk, they used the vehicle to build a blockade. It was only makeshift, but it should give enough time for a warning. Alex invited him to join his team. The driver was grateful. They stayed there to alert more drivers headed for the open bay. Thirty minutes later there was enough of a barricade to block the bridge. Some of the drivers stayed behind to alert others. Alex felt satisfied enough to continue the trip.

The road had ended for them, but not the trip. The goal was to reach the other side of the bay. He suddenly remembered the counter. "Radiation!" In the midst of the turmoil, he'd forgotten the immediate danger. They had no suits. The protective gear was lost with the vehicle.

The sisters had been resting against the containment rail. They were talking with occupants from other cars. The noon sun was beating down on them. "What's the reading?" Strapped around her neck, she'd saved it. The sunlight was too bright to see the readout. Shielding the screen, she squinted to get a reading.

"Elevated," she yelled back, "but in the safe zone."

Alex exhaled a sigh of relief. "I wanna go on." Liz insisted.

"What about you, Tracy?"

"I'm with you."

"Okay then," they agreed. "Just have to find a way." Alex had studied the terrain below. There was prolific sea traffic leaving the Oakland shores. Ships below looked like miniature toys leaving crested swells in their wake. He spotted what looked like a loading ramp. "We'll try it there," he gestured. There was much human activity. It was a loading dock from the old days. That was before the shipyards had been built. Now, the shipyard was gone. The tall cranes had toppled over and much of the warehousing was destroyed.

"Let's go." Alex was anxious to get going.

They were forced to back track on the highway at least a mile. There, the road gradually met with solid ground. They used the remaining girders to climb down from the onramp to the sloping hill below. From there, they hiked past the mangled shipyard, cranes, and loading docks toward the waterfront by the Oakland shores.

They made their way towards the water's edge. There was more activity the closer they got to the shore. Vessels, ferries, and many private boats were lending their help to the rescue missions. Most came from the mainland marinas out of Berkeley, Benicia, Stockton, and as far away as Sacramento. There, the contamination was lessened with distance. People were spared the shockwave from the initial blast, but not exempted from radiation. "I wonder," Tracy had been silent during much of the march, "what's the effect from radiation?"

"Depends on distance," Liz explained. She had studied radiation effects as part of her job.

Alex had always been proud of his daughter's accomplishments. Although he'd designed the last nuclear protection into the missile systems, he'd never lingered much with theoretical results. For him, the cause had always been the front line: impact, force, and destruction. It was up to physicists, chemists, and researchers to study the latent effects. "Give us some idea," Tracy prompted.

Moving on, they discussed possible effects. Liz illustrated some example figures to visualize what was to come. "Know anything about rems and rads?[61]"

"REM's the symbol for Roentgen, 'Roentgen equivalent in man or mammal,'" Alex offered. "Isn't it?"

"Right," Liz picked up, "RAD's a…unit of measure." She described some of the latent effects of radiation poisoning. "Here're some figures: visible symptoms appear at one hundred rems. Typical effects are nausea with vomiting setting in within three to six hours after exposure. The symptoms include loss of appetite, malaise, and fatigue that could last up to four weeks.

"At two to four hundred rems, illness becomes increasingly severe. The onset of initial symptoms may include hair loss, malaise, fatigue, diarrhea, and hemorrhaging with uncontrolled bleeding of the mouth, tissue, and kidney.

"Still higher, mortality rises. Death occurs weeks after exposure as a result of infection and hemorrhaging. If treated, recovery takes months to years but does not preclude death."

Another mile would take them to the docks. Little remained of the once famous landmark silhouettes. A few miles across the water, clearly visible were Treasure Island, Alcatraz, and San Francisco. The full extent of the mass evacuation became obvious. From across the waters, victims arrived non-stop from the city. Many were wandering aimlessly on weakened legs. Their eyes seemed glazed over. These were people that had been removed from the epicenter far enough to survive immediate terminal damages. They had received first-degree flash burns. The burns were similar to severe sunburns. They were left to fend for themselves. There was not enough shelter space to accommodate them until more facilities became available. They were waiting to be transported to outlying cities such as Stockton and Sacramento.

The less severe were second-degree burn victims. Their skin had peeled off leaving raw patches of flesh exposed. The pain must have been excruciating. It reflected on their faces. Fluid had collected under the remaining skin, oozing from puffed up blisters. They would survive. Their skin would eventually regenerate without much scarring.

Heartfelt, Liz said, "This is so tragic." She had a difficult time keeping her voice steady.

"Look," Tracy noted, "people still have their eye sight." They seemed to be searching for family and loved ones.

"It wasn't a ground explosion," Liz informed her, "altitude detonation."

"How can you tell?"

"Retina only burns off when looking directly into the explosion. Unless you looked up when the bomb went off," she explained, "eyesight won't be impaired…only temporary flash blindness from bleached out retinas."

"Similar to what happen to you over Colorado?"

"Right."

"What about the poor souls over there?" Tracy gestured to what seemed to be a cluster of makeshift shelters.

---

[61] REM - Roentgen Equivalent in Man (or mammal) - is a unit of radiation dose for the effectiveness of radiation to cause biological damage. The RAD is the unit of absorbed radiation dose. An acute whole-body dose of under 50 rems will produce nothing other than blood changes. 50 to 200 rems may cause illness but will rarely be fatal. Doses of 200 to 1000 rem will likely cause serious illness with poor outlook at the upper end of the range. Doses of more than 1000 rems are almost invariably fatal.

"Most won't survive. They'll be gone within days, weeks at most. Some may live for several months, maybe years, but their bodies will be eaten away by cancer."

"There's no hope for recovery?"

"There's always hope," Liz insisted. "Individuals respond differently." Cells were capable of repairing a great deal of genetic damage, but the repairs took time and could be overwhelming to the victim.

"I've heard enough." Tracy was getting nauseated by the thought of what lay ahead.

"Let's move on," Alex reminded them. They had arrived at the waterfront. The Department of Energy had set up temporary headquarters by the loading docks. The first NNSA tent city was up. Others would be quick to follow around the peninsula. Vessels of all sizes arrived and departed from both directions. The sick and the wounded were rushed to temporary emergency shelters where staffs of medical teams attended to their wounds. To minimize the spread of diseases and further contamination, the dead were collected and taken to isolation hangars. Only specially trained rescue units had access to the corpses emanating lethal doses of radiation. Outgoing were tons of supplies.

Temporary shower stalls had been erected to wash off radiation dust. Despite the intense pain on exposed flesh, showering was mandatory. On many burn victims, patches of loose skin were hanging from body parts. Most clothing items had been torn from bodies and incinerated by the blast. The dying and dead were wrapped in bed sheets. That, at least, kept the flies from the open sores.

Power generators were on their way but it'd take days for them to arrive. Interstate transportation, if moving at all, was slow. The power infrastructure in the northern part had been destroyed, with local equipment and transformers having burned up. Foreign nations promised help, but, due to the lack of communication, were slow to respond. Help was expected from Japan, South Korea, China, and as far away as India, but it might not arrive for weeks.

The docks were packed with people and equipment. The team was shoved and elbowed but tried to stay together as a group. NNSA teams barely managed the heavy flow of arriving victims.

Alex took the lead. "We need to get to the city." They were directed to the departure docks. National Guardsmen were standing by to block unauthorized personnel. Local law enforcement was directing traffic. Firefighters were handling emergencies and burn victims. Search and rescue teams dispatched to the city still uncovered blast and fire casualties. The place seemed relatively well organized despite it being only a few days since the attack. The next stage was to move the operation into the city, but contamination levels were still too high.

"How do you decontaminate an entire city?" Rather rhetorically, Tracy posed the question.

"Can't." Alex recalled the many tests following WWII the military had conducted in the Pacific. "Have to wait 'til radiation filters from the air."

"Could take years, decades, and even centuries," Liz suggested, "depending on the fission material. The city, most likely, will have to be abandoned."

"People find ways to rebuild." Alex was practical. "Might take some time to clean up but they always will." The scene reminded him very much of Germany, his homeland, after the war. "We need to get IDs." Issued by NNSA, all mission teams wore badges. Asking a passing member, they were directed to an office nearby manned by military guardsmen. Inside the makeshift tent, Liz submitted her ID. It was a state license from

California. Handed protective gear, she was immediately accommodated by the desk sergeant. The rest of the team was rebuffed. Due to lack of rescue and medical experience, they did not qualify.

"Here," Alex protested, "my orders." The piece of paper had no pull with the sergeant. It'd been issued by the DOD. His orders were clear. They had to come directly from NNSA.

Liz was attached to a rescue unit, scheduled for the next boat across the bay. "Dad," she said, handing over the dosimeter and two extra radiation suits she had somehow coaxed from the desk sergeant, "I've gotta go."

"We'll catch up," he nodded, "somehow."

Off she went, waving goodbye from the departing vessel.

"Let's go," Alex pressed.

"Where?" Tracy looked dismayed. "Steal a boat?"

"Thanks," he grinned back, "for the suggestion…may not have a choice." The harbor was busy with sea traffic. They could make out many boats getting loaded, but not all were attended.

"You're not thinking," Tracy objected, "what I think you're thinking?" The thought of adventure ignited a sense of excitement.

"It's not like stealing for personal gain," Alex reasoned. "Look at all the boats over there." He was already on the move. She hastened after him. He checked a number of vessels, unoccupied at the moment, then spotted something. "That's the one." It was a streamlined powerboat. "Owners probably on lunch break." His eyes caught the ignition key. "Hop in," he gestured.

The craft started right up. "Get the rope." He pushed the throttle. They sped off, not only leaving swells of crested waves in their wake, but an irate owner running to the dock. Furiously shaking a fist, he'd dropped a load of supplies in the process. "Not happy." Alex couldn't suppress a grin. "What's the radiation scale?"

Tracy checked the counter. "Elevated, but still safe."

Despite the tragedy ahead, it was a thrill to ride in the speedboat. Once they passed Treasure Island, the city skyline came into clear view. "Everything's gone!" Tracy exclaimed.

Alex watched her face. It greatly saddened him. "People will rebuild," he consoled her.

"Dad!" she suddenly yelled out. "What're you doing?" She almost got flung overboard. She clung on the rail for dear life.

"Sorry." He swerved to avoid colliding with a cluster of dead bodies floating in the water. There were many, bobbing among the debris. To cool their burning flesh, people must have jumped in, but keeping afloat took a lot of energy. A short while later exhaustion would take over. There was no return for the desperate. The ship docks were too high above the water for the swimmer to climb back up.

Most had drowned. "Salvation," he grieved, "better than enduring the slow decay of the body." Exposed to a lethal dose of gamma rays, cancer spread quickly. "What's the reading?"

"Oh my god," Tracy exclaimed. The reading had exceeded the safe level. Alex saw the fear in her eyes.

Alex cut the engine speed to idle. Hurriedly, he helped Tracy slip on her protective garment then did the same. They were not the standard, white-colored protection suits. These were fashioned from camouflaged, sealed, one-piece materials, light in weight.

Aside from the bulky headgear, it was mostly the breathing unit causing discomfort. The temperature inside the suit was uncomfortably hot but it provided the protection the body needed.

It had taken more than thirty minutes to navigate across the bay. To keep from colliding with floating debris and dead bodies, Alex was forced to reduce their speed. They finally made it to the city's edge. He beached the boat near what used to be the AT&T Ball Park. The once prominent sports park was all but gone. Only remnants of the infrastructure remained. It stuck out much like the Roman Coliseum. As soon as the boat beached, Alex jumped from the rail onto a wooden plank. What may have been a sandy beach many years ago, now was a brown, murky water front. The solid wood kept him from sinking into the muddy beach. "Get the bags," he ordered, "we may need them."

She tossed him one and carried the other. "Damn heavy," she grumbled. Loaded down with weapons, the strap was cutting into her shoulder. Regardless, she jumped from the craft and landed in the muddy sand. A step later she tripped over a body partly buried by the tide. "Daddy!" he heard her yell out.

He abruptly turned. Halfway buried in mud, her headgear had been pulled off by the fall. He dropped his bag to rush to her aid. He pulled her from the sludge. Her eyes were caked with mud. Gently, he wiped her face clean. He could see terror in the eyes, petrified at having been exposed to the radiation. He hastily collected the headgear. It was covered with mud. He picked it up and shook off the water and dirt, "Dosimeter?"

She stared at her empty hand. "Dropped it." Terror returned to her face. The murky water almost came up to their knees. Alex stooped down. The water was up to his face. His hands frantically groped for the gadget. His fingers felt something solid. "Got it." He turned it on. There was crackle. It sounded alarming. The meter reading pointed to the Hot Zone.

Tracy caught a glimpse of the reading. Devastated, she exclaimed, "550! I'm sorry, Dad. Am I going to die?" Her breathing had stopped. She was choking for air. He needed to calm her down. He put a hand on her shoulder then pulled her close. "You'll live." He watched the intense fear slowly fade from her face.

"You sure?"

"Sure," he comforted her. "But," he warned, "you've got your dose for the year." Exposure to 500 plus rads was not lethal but was about the maximum dosage a human body could bear over a one-year period. Radiation was accumulative and stayed with the body for life. In the distant future, Tracy would be more susceptible to cancer. *She'll have to deal with that when the time comes.* Alex kept this thought quiet. He didn't want to alarm her any further. "You ready to go on?"

"I think so."

Leading the way in the direction of Mission Street, he pressed on. They passed many bodies, decay having set in days ago. Fortunately, the headgear filtered out most of the putrid smell. Otherwise, it may have been too much for her to bear.

Alex checked the direction. "Can't make out the financial district," he said, saddened. He'd strolled this section on many a day in the cool shadows of its buildings.

They couldn't make out where Russian Hill, Coit Tower, or Telegraph Hill used to stand. "The city's famous landmarks," Tracy noted with regret, "gone." The view of a barren and hilly contour was the only sight left what used to be one of the nation's most beautiful waterfronts. "Look" she pointed, "most of the wharfs are gone."

He took a moment to identify landmarks on the waterfront. There weren't any. "Must have been the view early settlers saw," Alex's voice was stressed, "on their way to the Klondike." Back in the mid-1800s, outside a few shacks and hastily erected warehouses surrounded by a fleet of steam ships anchored offshore, there was nothing along the waterfront. The devastation was overwhelming.

MOUNT WEATHER

"...why wasn't I briefed on Korea? What's their ICBM capability?" The president was outraged. For once, he was pounding on the table. His gaze was intense. He was glaring at the Joint Chief of Staff, Air Force. Bauer's interruption the day before did nothing to calm his rage, only delay it. He was well aware of the public demands. Nuclear disarmament he'd proposed in first place. It was the reason he'd run for office. It'd been his platform. *What has happened to me?* A sign of disgust swept across his face. *Have I become one of them?* He'd promised to do *his people* right.

To solve just one issue Alex had proposed would have satisfied him and his administration. During the last term in office he had tried his best to resolve each crisis point. And crises they had been, every one of them. *Too late now.* He'd wasted two terms on the damned war in the Middle East that wasn't even his. "Damn you." He let go another flurry of insults.

"We didn't expect the Taepodong," the JCS Air Force snapped in his defense, "ever to reach the mainland." His eyes sought out the head of NRO.

To make him less visible, the DI shrank back in the chair. "Our data's outdated," was his excuse, "without an effective budget." He shifted responsibilities. As part of defense budget cuts, funding had been slashed year after year like in many other departments.

"Now we know." Wilmot stabbed his finger at the assembly.

"Hell," the JCS Air Force insisted, "you all saw their launch failures."

"July 4th fiasco?"

"That's right," the DI confirmed. "They were calculated failures. The purpose," he indicated, "was to drive home a statement to the West."

"They tried several times to launch the damned thing." It was the AF defending the military's position.

"We believe the tests were purposely aborted but," the head of the CIA chimed in, "we have no proof. We've got no agents at the NKPR."

"Then let's change that," the President ordered. "We can't let anybody else catch us with our pants down."

"It's easier said than done."

"...and," Wilmot deliberated, "why's that?"

"No budget."

"Where's all the money that Treasury allocated going?"

"Iraq, Afghanistan..." the JCS Air Force justified. "You should know."

"Let's not quarrel," Wilmot insisted. "Let's focus on the issues at hand."

"Agreed."

"I want damage control," he demanded, "and I mean political."

"Here's our latest assessment." The DI, Director for Intelligence handed out a stack of folders. "We believe the Chinese are secretly supplying the North with weapons."

"How do we know?" The president's face turned curious. He had his chin propped up on his palm waiting for the answer.

"Our strategic site inspection's been neglected with the recent terrorist activities," Wilmot was informed. The U.S. counterterrorist surveillance assets had been on global base camps. In the meantime, funded from the economic boom, the Chinese had been building up their military forces. "But we're not sure," he reiterated. "For all we know, they're supporting North Korea with nuclear technology."

"What's your assessment on that?"

"We have to assume the bomb dropped on San Francisco was in the neighborhood of fifteen kilotons. It's got the Chinese signature."

"What are the other nuclear capable countries doing?" the president demanded, "or are we in the dark there as well?"

"Don't trust the Russians. India's got the capability, but they've been observing the non-proliferation treaties. Don't know the state of Israeli weapons and can only guess what Iran's doing. Here's a list." The DI tossed a stack of folders in front of Wilmot. It contained the latest information on worldwide stockpiles, compiled from data mined statistics. To underscore his point, he tossed additional folders across the table. The statistics were clearly outdated. "Here," he said. The folder included the current inventory for the world's nuclear powered arsenals.[62]

"Not a comforting picture," the president admitted. "What else?"

"We need records from ex-Soviet states. Several are trading illegal weapons materials."

"We still leading the pack?"

"Don't know," the JCS Air Force grumbled, "after last week's attack." He was full of despair. He needed a much stronger position on their global posture. With satellites out, his Air Force and other services cut to the bare bones, the nation was extremely vulnerable to foreign attempts.

"Watch out for the Chinese," Wilmot warned. Despite recent advancements in science and technology, and economic collaboration, the ancient distrust and suspicion was still very much alive. "Mark my words." The emergency session was adjourned.

---

[62] Nuclear powered missile assets.
United States: Missiles 5,735, warheads 9,960, dated 1945, type Trinity.
Russia: Missiles 5,830, warheads 16,000, dated 1949, type RDS-1.
NATO – United Kingdom, 200, 1952, Hurricane; France, 350, 1960, Gerboise Bleue; China, 130, 1964, 596; India, 70, 120, 1974, Smiling Buddha; Pakistan, 30, 52, 1998, Chagai-1; North Korea, 2, 10, 2006, Taepodong; Israel, 75, 200, 1979, Vela Event.

THE CITY

The full effects from the blast and radiation became obvious the closer they got to ground zero. The immediate destruction from blast, thermal radiation, and ionization were clearly visible. Alex checked the terrain. He was looking for signs of emergency shelters. His pace was measured to assure their safety. The thermal suits slowed their progress. The headgear was cumbersome on their shoulders. Their voices were muffled under the visor shields. The breathing tank made hissing sounds. It hampered communicating. Words became distorted. They had to be repeated at times to be understood.

"Hard to imagine the destruction..." Alex tripped on an object he'd stepped on. He kicked it out of the way. It was a human remains partly covered up by dust drifts.

"What?" Tracy had missed most of what he said.

"I said," he repeated, more pronounced, "it's hard to imagine the destruction unless you see it firsthand."

"This is horrible." Tracy was sick to her stomach. "Isn't anyone going to collect the corpses?"

"Search and rescue's busy."

"But," she protested, "the dead, the bodies, the smell?" The stench of decaying bodies was overpowering.

"You haven't seen anything yet." Alex, the expert he was in nuclear technology, and to lessen the psychological impact, thought it'd be important for her to know what would lie ahead. He gave her a brief account.

Based on the casualties and infrastructure destruction they'd seen between the Oakland shores and downtown San Francisco, Alex was able to make a pretty educated guess on the destructive power of the explosive device.

"Probably," he estimated, "15 kiloton, Mark 1...Little Boy-type bomb, like the one used against Hiroshima."

"You sure?" Kilotons and megatons didn't have much meaning to her, nor did fission and fusion. What mattered was the utter destruction such a device left in its wake.

The estimates he took came from data collected by TRW during the early nuclear tests in the Pacific and the survivors they'd witnessed on the Oakland shores. Those were the ones that had to bear the suffering. People on the city ground were more fortunate. They'd been incinerated with the blast. It was cruel to think on those terms, he realized, but in the face of human suffering, it would be a blessing. Also, there were the recent nuclear tests disclosed by the U.S. intelligence committee. According to the reports, in defiance of the "agreed framework" for nuclear test bans imposed by IAEA, "North Korea was pursuing both uranium enrichment and plutonium reprocessing technologies."

"Not a very promising future," she said, "is it?"

Marching on, they were forced to make frequent rest stops. The noon heat was grueling. It took effort not to tear off the helmet. Alex made an attempt to distract his daughter from all the devastation. He explained some of the basics of neutron effects and thermal destruction. Most of the horrifying scenes were concentrated within a one-mile radius. There, rarely had a life been spared. Farther out, up to five miles away, victims were injured to various degrees ranging from third-degree burns to a lesser degree similar to sunburns. Visible signs to the various degrees were shredded clothes with skin and hair stripped from the body.

"What're the effects here?" They were still close to the shoreline.

"Way over the lethal dosage," he estimated. In between brief rests, Alex gave her a brief description. It amounted to frightening figures. "Above 1,000 rems," he explained, "rapid cell death caused severe diarrhea and intestinal bleeding, with death within hours." In the range of 1,000 to 5,000 rems, the onset time dropped to five minutes. Death was certain. Therapy was only to relieve the suffering.

"That the limit?" Five thousand units of radiation seemed enormous. She'd never heard these figures.

"There's much more," Alex explained. There was a time when the information was a closely guarded secret, for the good of the population.

The U.S. military assumed that 8,000 rads of radiation from a neutron bomb would immediately and permanently incapacitate a soldier. It was the ultimate weapon every aggressive nation desired. It was the reason for the prolific black market trade.

"Annihilating soldiers," she lashed out, "is it?"

"Not this time." Alex sensed her frustration. He made a mental note to stay away from frightening topics. The environment they were in was damaging enough to the mind. "Terrorist acts are mostly focused on civilians, causing destruction where it will hurt the most—family, children, and loved ones."

"Where do we go from here?" Tracy was dismayed. She was anxious to get away from the destruction. The heat inside the suit didn't help either.

"Let's track your sister down," Alex suggested, "then we'll leave."

"Okay." They pushed on. They passed the Mission district, then crossed Market Street. To their right were the ruins what used to be The Plaza. Farther down was Pier One. The main terminal had been torn apart by the blast. Pacific Heights, or what was left, came into view. Most of the terrain ahead was barren. The city was still smoldering in many places. Black smoke was everywhere. It could be seen billowing in columns drifting slowly to the east, toward the Oakland shored. Occasionally, a burn victim would stop them, asking for directions to the nearest shelter. Rescue vehicles would stop to pick them up. The dead were collected mostly by national Guardsmen. Their armored trucks would take the victims to makeshift shelters where the bodies could later be identified.

"Let's find the shelters."

"Where'd we look?"

"Upwind," Alex suggested. "Golden Gate Park, that's where they'd be." He led the way, seeking out signs. It wasn't easy. Most street signs had been ripped from the poles. Into view came Sansome Street. A couple of blocks up were ruins that used to be the Levi Strauss campus. What once was a beautiful park now only mountains of red brick remained. Alex stumbled on a partly buried sign. He stooped down to retrieve it. The lettering was burned crisp and barely visible. "Ice House," it read. "Another landmark," he mourned, "gone forever."

To the left was a steep hill. Alex remembered a shortcut he'd take during his contracting days in the city. It connected with Telegraph Hill. A stripped stairway still intact stared at him. Alex led the way up to where Coit Tower used to be. He tried to count the number of stairs, but lost count in between taking breaks. Both had to make frequent stops to catch a breath. Inside the heated suit, climbing stairs became laborious. *Three hundred eight.* He thought he'd remember. Reaching the top, from the new vantage point, they had a clear view over the city. The sight to the north and west was breathtaking. That wasn't the case looking east. There, the full force of the devastation became visible. It was a city laid to waste.

Overhead, white puffs of cloud streams drifted in from the ocean. Tracy checked for radiation. The air was clean. They had reached the upwind part of the city. For now, they could remove the protection.

"Think the city's going to recover." Tracy had doubts. Without the headgear, they were free to move again.

"It'll recover." Alex had hopes. "May take time, but this is a tough breed." The city was built by pioneers. Despite numerous destructions and devastations, it had recovered a number of times before. There were still visible marks from one recent example, the quake in 1989, when parts of the city had been destroyed.

"Sure hope so."

"It'll rise again," Alex assured her, "like a phoenix out of the ashes. After all," he proclaimed, "it's the city's symbolical mark for survival." They made rapid progress without the cumbersome suits. There was one more hill to overcome, the Pacific Heights. From there, some miles ahead, Golden Gate Park became clearly visible. An hour later they arrived. What used to be a lush green, naturally-preserved park was now completely packed with tents. They had arrived at the shelters.

EMERGENCY SHELTERS

A few hours earlier, Liz had been subjected to similar trials of courage. After crossing the bay, the boat had docked by Pier One. There, the new arrivals were picked up by the National Guard. She'd been seated in a troop carrier. Headed westward, a grisly scene unfolded. Twisted metal remains protruding through the rubble stood out like gigantic monuments. Fires were still smoldering, slowly consuming what was left of the once beautiful city. There wasn't much left either along the waterfront. The docks by Pier 39, where the sea lions used to sun, were empty. Their happy barking had been silenced.

Twenty minutes into the drive, they'd arrived at Golden Gate Park. National Guardsmen guided them on to a nearby shelter. Set up as a temporary command, it housed the NNSA field team. From there, Liz had been assigned to the trauma center. It was a section for newly arrived victims. The sight was horrendous even for an experienced firefighter like her. She thought she'd seen it all. But this was much more.

Dozens of huge tents had been hastily erected. The site was chosen for its space, but also for being upwind, free from radiation. Inside the tent, the air was relatively cool. The white fabric reflected much of the sunlight. It kept the temperature tolerable for medical staff and patients alike. To allow doctors and nurses easy access to each patient, hundreds of cots were set up in efficient rows. Shower stalls had been installed for the new arrivals. Each arrival had to be scrubbed free of contaminants. For these poor victims, it was a terrible experience. Regardless of burn severity, they were scrubbed down with chemicals to wash off radiation. It was pitiful to witness the agony.

"This is going to hurt," Liz warned a badly burned victim. The patient yelled out in anguish.

She'd been busy with patients since the minute she'd arrived. Working search and rescue, she'd seen many burn victims, but never to the extent caused through nuclear devastation. She had to keep her emotions in check. "I wouldn't want to live so badly burned," she voiced to a Red Cross worker.

"It'll take years of therapy, and much suffering," was the response, "but at the end, they'll be thankful to have survived."

"I don't know," Liz muttered.

"Take a break," the head nurse suggested, "you've been working hard."

"Thanks." Liz quickly headed to the nearby break room. Her thoughts were on her kids and the family.

"Dad—Tracy!" She had spotted them by the entrance. "You made it."

"Just wanted to make sure you're safe." Alex stated.

The sisters linked arms. Watching them, Alex was proud of his daughters, especially Liz, who'd demonstrated such unselfish devotion to helping others. *It's people like her,* he thought, *that keeps the planet in balance.*

"Liz," a passing nurse called out, "need your help here."

"Coming," she yelled back. She had hoped to spend more time with Tracy and Dad, but ailing patients were waiting.

"Lady wants to talk to you," the nurse gestured to the recovery room. She hastily disappeared towards the rear of the overcrowded shelter. Emergency vehicles had just delivered more victims.

"Be right there." Liz's face turned professional once more. "I'll stay here for now. You go on." She gave her sister a hug and her dad a departing kiss on the cheek. "Don't know how long…I'll keep in touch." Her voice trailed off.

"You know where to find me," Alex yelled after her.

"The Castle." Her words quickly faded.

"Let's get out of here." Alex let the way. He never could understand what drove a person to such dedication for helping others. *True Samaritan.* Tracy swiftly followed.

Liz regretted not being able to spend more time with her dad and sister, but her duty, was set in the immediate environment. It consumed all of her energy.

"Lisa…?" She located the patient that had asked for her.

"Yes." There was a familiarity about the woman searching her out. Liz couldn't make out the face under the blood-crusted skin, but the voice sounded vaguely familiar.

"Don't you remember?" The voice was weakened from pain.

"Let's take a look." Liz reached for a clean towel to wipe away a layer of baked-on ashes. "What's under this grime?"

"It's me." The face grimaced with pain. "Nancy." She made a feeble attempt to push the towel from her face. "St. Leo's."

"San Jose—right! High school," Liz recalled. She gently squeezed the woman's hand. "What're you doing here?" With the ashes gone, she recognized her former schoolmate.

"Visiting the city." Her wheezing voice was interrupted by coughing spells. "Was at the wharf when the sky burned…what happened?" Liz inspected the poor girl's blistered face, arms, and hands. "It hurts so much." Her body was severely burned. She was covered with a linen sheet.

Liz gently tried to lift up the woman's head but was stopped with a painful "Don't." She understood.

"The city was struck by a bomb," Liz explained. Her voice faltered. "You don't know?" *How stupid of me,* Liz thought. She immediately chastised herself about assuming she would know. *One second you're walking down the street thinking about a happy day in the city, the next, you're swept off your feet burned beyond recognition, not knowing what happened.*

"Am I dying?" Nancy lay there in agony, asking the question she already knew.

"Tell me a story," Liz encouraged her. She was distracting the poor girl's mind from the intense suffering amid the misery of this place.

"I was watching the barking seals at the Pier," she began, "when I saw this beautiful shape high above unfold. It was huge. Red and white stripes painted on the body with blue stars…just like the flag."

"Have some juice," Liz offered. She felt heartbroken.

"It hurts to drink." Her voice was weakening. "How beautiful…I thought…greeting card for someone dear…but it wasn't," she whispered between coughing up brackish blood. "Like a flower…pedals opened up…blossomed into brilliant colors…then…the light switched off…everything went dark. Now," she continued, "I can see again…but, eyes hurt so much."

"Here's something for your pain." Liz wiped dark splatters of blood from Nancy's chin. Her lung tissue was rapidly deteriorating from radiation. Trickles of blood were squirting up with every cough. Liz reached for the syringe to inject a shot of morphine into a barely visible vein under the scorched skin. Seconds later, the girl slipped into unconsciousness. "Rest in peace, dear Nancy," where the last words she'd ever hear in a life cut short. She'd never see flowers again. Liz hastily left to attend the next patient.

On that fateful day, what Nancy and others had witnessed was the bomb. It appeared out of the skies above, slowly descending from high altitude over Fisherman's Wharf. Gliding down in complete silence, it had been suspended by a drop shoot brightly painted in the colors of the American flag.

At a thousand feet, the bomb went off. It detonated with horrific results. Everybody below, ground zero, immediately incinerated. Spectators at a distance that had followed the descent of the bomb were blinded permanently as soon as the flash reached their eyes. The result was burned off cornea and vision nerves. Others, faces not directed upward, received an indirect x-ray flash. It caused temporary flash blindness.

Outside ground zero, clothes were torn off bodies from the initial pressure wave. Skin, along with hair, lips, fingers, and ears, was incinerated by the intense heat. A second wave followed. This one was generated by the ground effect. It combined with the first wave. The result was a Mach effect sweeping out for the next few miles with devastating results.

Days later, when rescue arrived, many survivors were still in shock. They did not feel the pain for some time. When it finally set in, it was intense. Unconsciousness followed in many instances because the pain was too much to bear. It would take weeks just to get initial casualty figures. It would take months and years to get a final count because of the latency effects from radiation exposure.

Rescue efforts were taking place around the clock. DHS, NNSA, FEMA, CDC, and the Red Cross set up command and support posts near Ocean Beach. Contamination and fallout there was minimal. With the air currents drifting in from the ocean, the fallout cloud spread across the bay and inland, where it settled as radioactive dust over Oakland, Pleasanton, and the Tri-Valley. From there it drifted on east over the Sierras to eventually dissipate through precipitation in the distant Rockies.

The present count of casualties was already into tens of thousands. With a daytime population in full swing when the bomb exploded, the city center held masses of commuters. The business sector along Market Street took the biggest hit. The explosion took out an entire business population, executives and workers alike. Luckily, most of the city dwellings were located west of Pacific Heights. That section of the city had been protected from the blast by the many hills. Everything east including the marina, North Beach, Russian, Nob and Telegraph Hills, Chinatown, Market Street, Embarcadero, and Union Square, had all but disappeared. Restaurants, supermarkets, and stores were destroyed, and with them it incinerated inhabitants of high-rise apartments, city dwellings, and office buildings. What the blast had not leveled, the ensuing fires did.

Decontamination equipment, scrubbing agents, and support teams were slow to arrive owing to the lack of effective communication. Search and rescue teams at the drop zone wore heavy radiation protection. They continued looking for survivors. Victims beneath the rubble of collapsed buildings would be located when the rebuilding began. Latent radiation effects might last decades before a final death count would be established.

It was not the first time this city by the bay had perished. Nor would it be the last. It seemed it would take a major event such as this to bring the city to its knees. The city would spur life again as with good soil, but this time will be shaped by technology and progress.

FORT MASON

Not sure what to do next, Alex suggested, "Let's head for Pacific Heights." They had accomplished what they set out to do, view the aftermath and check on Mom. It was an experience that would stay with them for a long time. There was much to do, for both of them. Alex, in the immediate future, would have more work than he could probably handle. Tracy was ready to get back to the agency, and Brian.

"Why there, Dad?"

"Best view in the city."

It'd take over an hour's hike to get there. The terrain was hilly. As long as they stayed along the coast they were safe from radiation. In duffels slung over their shoulders, they carried the suits. Each was absorbed in their own thoughts. Alex had flashbacks to the wars in which he'd been involved. Tracy's mind was on more recent events; she missed Brian. Every so often they would stop and turn. The higher they went up the hill, the more they saw of the destruction. It had been especially heavy by the piers.

Pier One, closest to the epicenter, had been completely eradicated. The farther out they went, the lesser the devastation became. Close to Pier 39, the far end by Ghirardelli square, some structures were still intact. To the distant east they could make out the frantic activities of the rescue effort. "Here," Alex offered, "take a look." He handed her the field glasses.

Despite the current conditions, the view was spectacular. In this part, not many dwellings had been touched by the blast. Only slight damages were visible, mostly at the highest points. There, rooftops had been peeled off by the shockwave. To the east, heavy smoke was still billowing up. Fires were being fueled from the many gas leaks. Gas lines were still the largest cause for city fires. PG&E was short on personnel to tend to all the shutoff valves around the city.

They had reached the northern edge of Pacific Heights. Exhausted from the lengthy hike, Tracy beckoned, "Need a break." They dropped the heavy bags. Alex rested against a stone wall. Nearby high-rise buildings blocked the sun. He was facing north, taking in the magnificent view. The ground they had walked dropped away into a steep slope. Below, it merged with the waterfront by the marina.

"I'm beat. How're you doing?"

"Fine."

Fatigued, she hopped on top of the brick wall Alex rested against. She tugged legs into a lotus position. Her mind drifted three thousand miles east. "Wonder how Brian's doing?"

"Miss him?"

"I do."

What a change, he mulled, *life without phones. What peaceful existence.* "Where would progress be?"

"What?"

"Nothing," he said "just thinking." His eyes scanned the distance ahead. Below, traffic was heaviest around the marina. From this vantage point, the view extended from bridge to bridge, or what was left of them. Straight to the north, a few miles out, one famous landmark still stood Alcatraz. It had withstood time and events more than once. It would still be there after the city was gone.

Tracy gazed to the west. The ocean appeared calm in its deep blue hue. Shifting to the south, her eyes took in a sea of gray-colored rooftops. Farther out was Daly City. A few miles more, and there was San Bruno with SFO Airport nearby.

Suddenly, her eyes caught movement out of the Pacific. "Bird sailing in the breeze?" She kept watching. *Frigate maybe.* It slowly descended towards the coast. *Couldn't be— way too big.* It finally dawned on her. *Aircraft.*

"See that?" Tracy hopped from the wall. Excited, she gestured south.

"What?" Alex shifted his view in that direction.

"Jetliner," she indicated, "just disappeared behind the hills."

"Impossible," Alex insisted. "There's no traffic."

"But," she insisted, "I saw it."

"What'd it look like?"

"No markings."

It was doubtful, but he'd always trusted her judgment. He'd been looking for an excuse to get away from here. *I'd rather be someplace else than tripping over dead bodies with nothing but the stench from decayed flesh.* This would give them a sense of direction. He'd been contemplating their next move. His sense of adventure, once more, kicked in.

"We could check it out." Alex stirred.

"No wheels," Tracy reminded him. "Remember?"

"Got an idea," he proposed. "You probably won't like it."

"What?" Her face perked with curiosity.

"See the fort down there?"

She shifted her focus. "Yeah."

"Fort Mason."

"So?"

He was collecting both duffels. "Most likely place for the command post. Let's go." He felt new strength surge through his body. His mind was renewed by venturous thoughts. He was already calculating time, distance, and action. The cluster of red roof tiled structures was easily visible from here. Fort Mason would be the most likely place to make connections. Getting back home would take a few steps.

It was mostly residential areas from here on. Traffic was sparse up here. Rows of cars were parked along the streets. Most were disabled. For most of the way, they strode along Fillmore Street. Whatever little traffic there was would be pedestrian. Most habitation had been moved from the area, evacuated, mostly for safety reasons. Lombard Street was just ahead. Once they'd crossed that, it wouldn't be much further.

"I was expecting sentries and roadblocks," Tracy wondered.

"National Guard." Alex explained. "Probably not enough of them. Takes time to recruit and dispatch the qualified."

"You hear that?" Tracy called a warning. They both heard it: a rumbling sound, coming on fast. The cause was suddenly upon them. It came barreling down on Union, intersecting with the street on which they'd been walking. One last block and it was in sight, an old, battered pickup manned by a bunch of thugs. It slithered to a halt, blocking the way. All were armed, some with rifles; others waved semis. Alex and Tracy were curious, but stayed on their course. It was a mistake.

The gang jumped off the flatbed. "Where you headed…what you got there?" It was the leader. Using an M-16, he gestured at the bags they were carrying. Alex held steadfast. It wasn't the first time he'd had to deal with hoodlums. The members were slowly closing in. They seemed determined to take whatever came across their path. Any item worth bartering would be their aim. "Got money?"

Most of their focus was on Tracy. Alex took a chance. There was no way he'd turn his duffel over. It was the only protection he had. Gauging from the present encounter, he'd sure need it in the future. Using one hand, ever so slightly, he used the momentary distraction to slide the bag's zipper open. Tracy took that as her cue. With an almost imperceptible nod, her eyes sought out his. He understood. "Here." She initiated the next move. It was sudden. In a quick motion, she tossed her bag to the leader. It landed with a metallic clang. All their eyes were distracted by the bag. Alex gradually reached into his. With a quick jerk, his hand came out holding the assault rifle. He leveled it on the leader. The man froze. Surprise in the eyes, he wavered. The gang backed away a few feet. Alex motioned at the bag resting on the ground a few feet ahead. Tracy cautiously advanced to collect it. The gang's weapons were leveled at both of them. They hesitated from shooting. Their leader had motioned a sign of caution.

It was obvious he needed time to assess his options. He was calculating the standoff. The pause would not last long. The answer came in the form of a gun flash, followed by a shot. It came from the driver of the pickup. He'd been watching the exchange from across the roadway. The shot was aimed at Alex. It missed its target. The bulled had entered the duffel. The bag had shielded him. Alex let go of the trigger. Unlike the distant shooter, his bullet found its target. The body directly in front shuddered with the impact. The leader slowly sank to his knees. He collapsed onto the ground.

Tracy jumped for cover. She yanked a .45 from her bag and started shooting. The targets were on the run. Some sought cover behind property walls, others headed for the pickup, all returning fire. The sound of bullets ricocheting resounded between the high-rise buildings. Most of the shots went wild. Tracy and Alex held steadfast. Both had sought cover on the ground. Their aims were deadly.

The standoff only lasted a few seconds. The exchange that followed took minutes. The pickup finally sped off, leaving the wounded behind. Alex disarmed them. Their leader was stretched out, dead, on the ground. Alex collected his weapon then motioned to Tracy. "Let's get outta here." They marched on feeling euphoric about having survived the deadly encounter. Alex shook his head with a grin. "Where'd you learn to shoot?"

"You taught me, remember?" She didn't tell him about the many practice hours she'd taken when first joining the agency. Carrying a weapon was not the organization's policy. She'd taken it on herself to become proficient. Target shooting developed into a sport with her. *Today,* she thought, greatly satisfied, *it'd paid off.*

"Girl, I'm impressed," Alex admitted, "and proud." He promised himself not to let that happen again. Nothing could be taken for granted, especially not at a time like this. Next chance they had, he'd have to discuss some basic strategies with her.

"We make a great team," Tracy agreed, "don't we?" A hint of pride swept across her face.

They walked on. To the left, Crissy Field came into view. The city's popular beach, it was sandwiched between Fort Mason and the historic Presidio. "Bay Street," the next street sign announced. The Marina District was next. It'd be their destination. They took a turn to the right. Another few blocks and they'd arrived.

"There it is." Alex gestured ahead.

The fort bustled with traffic. Soldiers hastened in and out. Vehicles brought in new arrivals. Returning vehicles would deliver more wounded to the Oakland shores. The main gate was clustered with vehicles. "What have we here?" Alex was tempted to acquire one.

"Better not." Tracy objected. "They're needed." It was mostly emergency and personnel carriers for law enforcement and the wounded.

"Okay then…let's get inside." He was already headed for the entrance. She followed. "FEMA," painted in white, the sign announced. Once inside, there were more signs stuck over doors indicating various offices. Everything looked temporary. *Tactical,* came to his mind. His eyes searched around the hall then fixated on one prominent sign. "NNSA," it read. Most people were not familiar with the organization. It had only recently been created. "In here," he gestured. If their services were needed, this would be the place.

It hadn't taken much to turn this historic landmark into disarray. Electronics, equipment, computers, and a lot of cables were thrown across the floors wired together in every direction.

"Been only a few days, and you guys are already back in business?" Alex addressed what looked like the man in charge. He fit the profile of the seasoned operator. No nonsense character: commanding, demanding, and short on courtesy. Without uniform and nametag to identify rank, Alex let intuition guide his mind. In this office, members wore civilian clothes. The NNSA was a public branch.

"Who're you?" Suspicious eyes were gauging both of them. "Where're your IDs?" He was seeking out security. They were nowhere around. Dozens of staff members rushed in and out this temporary center. Their mission was tactical, mostly investigations. His agents were busy tracking new leads.

"Wanna report an incident," Alex said. "You people might be interested. Tracy?"

The man shot an impatient look at her while she gave him a brief account of their earlier sighting about the craft arriving from the Pacific. "Could be urgent."

"Could be nothing." It was a factual statement. "Cloud, bird, debris." The man didn't seem impressed.

Under normal conditions that would be acceptable reasoning, Alex thought, *but with the nation on alert it is another matter.*

"I think you need to check it out." Alex put it politely but firmly, nevertheless.

"Don't have the people," was his hasty, reply. "Now," he beckoned, "excuse me." He'd already turned to handle another calling. "Got things to do."

It was a realistic response, but Alex wouldn't be put off. "Hey," he called out, "you deaf?" That got his attention. The agent abruptly stopped his pace and turned.

His face turned to anger. "I told you," he doubled back, "I can't spare anybody."

"What about us?" Alex pointed out. "Hello?" He indicated Tracy and himself.

"What about?" the man questioned. "What're your qualifications?"

"Bauer," Alex offered in a persistent undertone, "guy who triggered the launch."

That got his attention. He slowly moved up to face Alex, "You 'The' Bauer?" His face had turned incredulous.

"One and only," Alex stated.

"Listen," the man said apologetically, "sorry for not recognizing you. You know," he excused, "emergency and all."

"I understand," Alex calmed him, "Just wanna offer our help."

The man's flushed face rapidly shifted between the two unexpected visitors. "In that case," he suggested, "follow me." He gestured toward the spacious hallway. They quickly followed his rapid strides. "In here," he said. They entered the tactical room. He was about to disturb the person already occupying the desk when Alex called out, "You...here?" It was a rhetorical response, not a question. "Who knew our paths would cross again so soon." It was Brooks.

"You know each other?" It was the agent's turn to be surprised.

"One would think so." Alex nodded at his daughter. "Right?" Tracy had recognized her capturer on sight, but had kept quiet. Her look said it all. She'd rather not get involved with any of his plots. She still carried a grudge. There was something sinister about him and the DELTA Force that she'd rather forget.

"In that case," the agent suggested on his way out, "you work together."

"Take a seat." The DELTA agent invited Tracy over. He offered her the extra chair, but she declined. Alex took a position near a table. His butt found a rest against the edge. "What've you got," Scott asked, "that brought you here?"

Alex gestured at his daughter. "Tell him."

Tracy briefly described the incident with the unmarked craft. It immediately captured Scott's attention. It was the very reason he'd been dispatched here. Others from his detachment had been ordered to the East Coast on similar reports. Just prior to the blackout, the agency had identified possible illegal shipments of highly toxic substances into the country. Suspect was radiation, biological or chemical. Specifics had not been available. Accounts of radioactive substance shipments had been reported from countries under investigation. They were reports mostly from former Soviet bloc nations. He'd been put in charge to track illegal shipments through the Pacific corridor.

"Why don't we do this?" Scott suggested. "You come with me," he said, then gestured at Tracy. "She can stay. Team's late...should have been here by now."

"You okay with that?" Alex liked the idea. That way, they were both helping the cause. *Me on the frontlines with her safe back here.*

"I'm not staying." Tracy was adamant. "I'm coming along." She felt her energy would be better utilized on the road or back with the organization. The Agency was still operating in the dark; they would need all possible help. If not, then General Foster could probably use her support. "I'm going with you."

"I'd rather you stay." Alex tried to persuade her again, but knew how hardheaded she could be. "It's safer here."

"I'm going with you," she insisted. She picked up the duffels, slung them over her shoulder, and headed for the exit. "Try to stop me."

THE CHASE

"What's the quickest way to SFO?" Scott was driving. "Been here as tourist," he offered, "once." He'd been issued a Humvee. It seemed to be the popular transportation of the day. Alex sat in the passenger seat giving directions. Tracy sat in back. The walk had taken much of her energy. She was hungry. She felt dirty. She needed a rest, but kept quiet.

"A bath would feel so good," she groaned.

Alex used to contract in this city. It was back in the '90s when Silicon Valley was the hub for IT. Business was thriving back then with Fortune-500 firms lining Market Street from the piers to the Mission District. He knew the area well.

Presently, they were headed east on Bay Street. It was slow going with rescue vehicles weaving in and out. "Make a left." The next intersection was with Van Ness Avenue, a major artery through the city. Surprisingly, for most part, the road had been cleared. Vehicles were still tossed and piled on top of each other, but mostly along the sidewalks. Wrecking crews were at work directed by the National Guard. Firefighters were blocking off sections that were still smoldering.

It would take forty plus minutes providing there were no major obstacles. One mile ahead, the 101 onramp came up. "South," Alex directed. It would take them to the airport. Aside from an occasional grunt, Scott stayed quiet for most of the way. He followed directions.

Getting close to their destination, Alex had a thought. "Next exit." The vehicle swerved onto the 380 expressway. It led uphill.

"Why?"

"Best view into the airport. I think we should check it out." It ended further objections. "Glasses," Alex beckoned Tracy in back. She rummaged through the duffel for a pair of field glasses and passed them up front.

He trained the pair on the distance below. A couple of miles out, the view on the airport became clear. Many jetliners were jumbled up in between terminals. Most pilots had been forced to abandon the planes when the electronics failed. Where available, passengers had used emergency exits. Many wound up injured, jumping ten to twenty feet to the tarmac. Others, afraid of radiation, spent days crammed in seats within the sealed craft. The first days, from the impact nearby, radiation had spread wide. Eventually, all made it out. Passengers en route had not been so lucky. Alex adjusted the focal point. It gave him clear view of the airport's complex.

"Make out anything?"

"Not yet." He was probing the terminals. *Nothing.* "Wait. Think I've got something." He spotted what appeared to be a jetliner with activity. A crew was unloading cargo.

"Tracy," he handed her the glasses, "take a look."

"Yeah," she confirmed, "that's what I saw—Airbus 330."

"Right." Alex shouldn't have doubted her.

"Let's check it out." Scott had already spun the vehicle around. He sped off in the indicated direction.

"Head for north field gate." It was a secured cargo area. It'd take them to the end of the tarmac where he'd spotted the craft. Minutes later, Scott approached the checkpoint. Flanked by a unit of guardsmen, the boom had been lowered. All carried sidearm leveled at the vehicle. The Humvee was flagged to a stop. Scott hit the brakes. The vehicle slithered to a halt, almost colliding with the lowered boom. The team came face to face with uniforms. The group appeared to be members of the National Guard, but the uniforms seemed ill fitted.

"Something's wrong." Alex faced Scott who'd come to the same conclusion. Tracy watched from the backseat.

"What's the rush?" one called out. He spoke in broken English. Scott stared at Alex. He shot back a guarded glance. Tracy was alerted by the foreign accent.

"No flights," the man gestured. "Airport closed." He and others in his squad planted themselves across the barricade.

"We're expecting visitors," Alex replied, "saw the craft land." He gestured in the direction of the Airbus sitting on the tarmac. From here, they could hear the whining sound of jet engines running idle above the sounds of the wrecking crews at work. "Besides," he gestured at their weapons, "what's with the AKs?"[63] The remark brought on an immediate reaction.

"Take cover!" Scott shouted the alert. The instant his warning echoed out, the foreign squad jumped into action. They let go the first round into the Humvee. A hail of bullets ricocheted off the vehicle. Scott went into action. He kicked the shifter into reverse then punched the pedal hard. The engine gunned and rapidly gained distance. Seconds later he slammed on the brakes. The vehicle skidded to a halt. "Take the wheel," he yelled at Alex. He had already jumped from the front seat to the back. There, he popped the skylight open to get to the weapons platform. The Humvee was fitted with a .50 caliber machine gun.

Expertly, he cocked the safety off, pulled the trigger, and let go a burst from the 800-rounds-per-minute barrel. The enemy's AK-47s were no match.

Alex reversed the shifter and gunned the engine. The jeep flew forward at maximum speed. Five seconds later, the vehicle crashed through the gate. The boom splintered into pieces. It hit some of the guardsmen running for cover. The Humvee flew past the guard shack. Scott spun the turret around and aimed at the shack. Tracy took cover. She cowered low in the backseat, seeking protection from the hail of flying projectiles. Alex slammed on the brakes. The vehicle skidded to a stop.

"Take this," Scott shouted, "rag heads!" He was pumping lead into their attackers. Bullets were flying from both directions until magazines were spent. The firing exchange lasted only a couple of minutes. It turned silent. Alex shot a quick glance at Scott. He knew the next move. Alex floored the pedal. The jeep shot forward toward the shack. With a crashing sound, the Humvee slammed into its target. Shattered glass and pieces of wood pierced through the air in different directions. The attackers were exposed. From here on it out would be hand-to-hand combat. Two inside the shack were killed by the crash. Several were wounded. Two attackers had remained unscathed. They had sought cover behind the debris. Crouched nearby, ready to fight, their bodies were poised for assault. Both carried combat knives.

Alex and Scott had already jumped from the vehicle. Both sought out the target nearest. The fighting did not last long. Scott, the trained killer, quickly overcame his

---

[63] First developed in the Soviet Union by Mikhail Kalashnikov, the AK-47 is a selective-fire, gas-operated 7.62 mm assault rifle. It remains the most widely used and popular assault rifles in the world because of its durability, low production cost, and ease of use.

opponent. The attacker was no match for him, perhaps a new recruit. Unlike Scott, he seemed unskilled and inexperienced in combat.

Alex was holding off his opponent. Both struggled for survival. Scott came to his aid. He snuck up from behind like a deadly shadow. One arm reached around the attacker. Viselike, it clamped down on him. The free hand slit his throat. Alex backed off when the body went limp. He let the professional finish the job. Tracy watched from the inside. She had to turn away. Cutting a throat was nothing she wanted to see. She'd seen enough of that in hostage films taken by terrorists. Dying from a slit throat was a most horrifying thought.

Scott spotted a box left by the attackers. He inspected its content. "Alex," he called out, "get a load of this." It was a set of SINCGARS[64].

The gear was a lifesaver. It may have been dated, but the tactical radio system would do the job. Alex checked the equipment. He couldn't help a grin. No matter how often he'd used this gear, it always reminded him of the butter churner at his grandma's place. Part of the gear was a manual battery charger.

Alex motioned Tracy from the vehicle. He watched Scott wipe his blade clean on his trouser leg. His face was without emotion like nothing unusual had just happened. *There goes a true killer*, he thought, *sure glad he's on my side.* Scott was already headed for the Airbus. Alex and Tracy followed. Within the shadows of the many disabled craft, they quickly gained ground. Their focus was on the ground crew struggling with a container. The bulky load seemed heavy. Without electric power, it took all hands to unload the equipment. It gave the team the chance to move up without being detected.

They got close enough to the Airbus to hear the voices. Commands were shouted. "Language's," Alex suspected, "Arabic." The voice belonged to a commander shouting out rapid orders. A bulky crate was lifted from the cargo hold. It was hastily loaded onto a waiting truck. As soon as its cargo was secured, the vehicle sped off. It headed for the exit gate. The foreign squad prepared to board the craft. Two were headed for the cargo hold. The rest boarded the mobile passenger ramp.

"I'm getting on." Scott had already jumped onto the loading ramp. "Wished my team was here," he muttered.

"Say no more," Alex whispered. He was closing up, lifting his daughter up onto the platform. For a moment she resisted. "You wanted to come." She challenged him, but quickly moved ahead. They disappeared into the cargo hold, tossing their bags nearby. Muffled sounds were nearing. It was the commander's voice. He issued final orders. Rapid footsteps approached the entrance. The ramp was removed. The door slammed shut. The cargo hold turned dark.

It took several minutes for their eyes to adjust. Ominous shadows cast by the cargo slowly came into view. They could hear the engines revved up. The whining sound of jet blades increased to a high pitch. From here on out, the three trapped in the hold were forced to communicate through shouting. The cargo space was not insulated against sound. It carried the full effects from the jet engines. They felt the craft in motion. It made a sharp turn, seemingly headed for the runway. They could only guess which direction it moved. "Going to get cold in here," Alex shouted. "Better find something."

---

[64] Single Channel Ground and Airborne Radio System, currently used as Combat Net Radio by U.S. and allied military forces.

He was already searching. *Should be plenty of covers around.* He spotted a stack of shipping blankets by the crates.

"Where do you think we're headed?" Scott asked.

Alex had been mulling over the possible destination. He carefully recorded each turn the craft made. After leaving SFO, the craft made a couple of 360 degree turns. That was a first clue. It was the normal takeoff pattern to gain altitude to clear the Sierras. The craft was headed east.

"Let's check the load." Alex motioned to the rear. He was already striding toward the crates. "Should give us a clue." He rummaged through his duffel. There would be a crowbar, and a flashlight. His fingers searched for the object. *Here it is.* He motioned to the crates. "Hold this." Scott took the light. The brightly circled beam cut through the dark like a knife. There were two containers—same size as the one that had just been unloaded. The content was anyone's guess. There were no markings. That alone was suspicious. The lids were nailed shut. Alex probed the edges. They gave way to the crowbar. The lid came off with a squeak. He tossed it to the floor. Scott helped with the unpacking, and the crate revealed its contents.

"What's this?" Scott stooped over the crate. Tracy moved up close. Reflected by the light beam, they stared at the dimly-lit complexity. Their eyes glanced at what looked like an array of glass cylinders. Scott reached for one. Filled with liquid, they were mounted neatly, arranged into one stack.

"Careful," Alex cautioned. He leaned in for a closer inspection. There were traces of wires connected to a miniature control panel. It gave a digital readout. There was a series of fixed numbers. The digits were frozen. *Not active yet.* Alex exhaled with a sigh of relief. For the time, they were safe. "Could be anything," Alex suggested.

Scott had never seen anything like them, and neither had Tracy.

"Hazardous either way," Alex speculated until he spotted the symbol. It was a yellow colored triangle. It had been prominently painted on what appeared to be the power source. "Most likely radioactive..." he guessed.

"Biological, maybe chemical," Scott added. They moved to the other crate. It revealed identical contents. "What we have," Alex deducted, "is lethal cargo."

"Three in all," Tracy added, "including the drop-off at SFO. Anything we should do?" She was worried. The thought of being surrounded by death and destruction made her shiver.

"What do you think?" Scott asked. He lingered by the cargo.

"One thing we know," Alex theorized, "gonna be a showdown." He got inquisitive stares from both Scott and Tracy.

"Showdown?" Tracy shook her head. "What do you mean?"

"The past few days," Alex theorized, "have only been an act, a diversion."

Scott was rubbing his face. "Could be right." He was feeling his stubble.

Tracy's face cast a shadow of uncertainty. "Nuclear attack," she said, incredulous, "only a distraction?"

"Let's get a close-up look." Alex jumped onto the crate's edge. He carefully slid into the wooden box. "Hold this." He handed her the flashlight.

"I don't believe it." Alex gestured at the contents. A shadow of recognition swept across his face. He leaned in closer. The components looked familiar. He'd seen it before. They revealed a chemical charge, triggered by some kind of timing device. Color-coded, three isolated vials were neatly connected together. They contained liquid substances. "Chemical or biological," Alex suggested.

"Dirty bomb?" Tracy moved up. She was fixated on the apparatus mounted within the jumble of colorful wiring.

"My thought exactly." Alex frowned. His greatest fear seemed to materialize. He'd hoped never to see such a device. He always suspected technically advanced nations were only experimenting with newly invented destructive devices. Producing such mortal substances for warfare? "Unthinkable."

"EMP blast," Scott conjectured, "distraction only to gain access to U.S. soil?" He was talking to himself. "Crippling the nation's only been the initial step?"

"What's left?" Alex stared at him. "With satellites out, defense grid down, transportation out, the nation paralyzed…your guess."

Scott's face grimaced at the thought. "We'd better do something." He was used to fights, battles, and wars, but an invisible enemy? That was beyond his theater of expertise.

Alex motioned at Tracy. "Try the set."

She pulled the gear from the bag. The compact transmit/receiver pack could be a lifesaver.

"Try UHF," he suggested.

She fiddled with the set. "Battery's dead."

"The crank."

"Crank?" Tracy questioned. She rummaged through the bag. Her hand pulled out an unfamiliar item. "What's this?"

"Before your time." Alex showed her how to crank the handle. "Can't get a signal." There was distant static. It proved the set was working.

Scott helped. He pulled out the retractable antenna. "Still nothing."

"Need to get it outside." Alex was pacing the cargo hold. The craft's body was blocking the signal. "Here." He handed Scott the flashlight. "Landing gear."

Scott gave a nod. He seemed to know what to do. The built in screwdriver removed the screws. The cover came off with a sucking sound. Pressurized air escaped the fuselage. It gave them access to the wheel shaft. A beam of sunlight cut through the opening, illuminating the darkness. Tracy handed Scott the set. The opening was large enough to pass the radio through. The static cleared up immediately. The set went into action, scanning for active channels. It locked onto a channel. It was the atomic time broadcast out of Boulder. Scott was looking for a voice. Then, faint chatter came over several frequencies.

Alex recognized some call signs. "Wait." DCA was broadcasting. On the ether was the Pentagon's intelligence agency. Scott adjusted the set. He locked in and handed Alex the mic.

He pushed to talk. "DCA…DCA…come in…come in." He kept repeating. Finally, there was a faint response.

"Identify." The voice demanded.

"Bauer," he responded, "get me Foster."

"Hold one." There was a pause. Several minutes passed. Then the set came active again.

"Alex?" It was Foster. It was the familiar voice he'd hoped for. "Where are you?"

"Need you to do something," Alex cut in. "Notify NNSA…dirty bombs on board."

Alex briefly described the plight the nation was in. He expressed extreme urgency.

"What's the target?"

"Don't know," he replied, "tracking." He had a second thought. "One more thing…alert Sandia…need experts to identify the substance."

"Will do." While they were communicating, the craft's descent went unnoticed. The wheels suddenly dropped out beneath Scott, who'd been squatting on the wheel's hydraulic arm. He lost his balance and tossed the radio. Alex caught it with one hand. With the other he reached out. Scott struggled. He was still on the tire, clinging to a rapidly extending frame. The force of the rushing air tore at his body. Alex tossed the set to Tracy. His free hand grabbed onto Scott. Alex strained to pull him back into the craft, just in time. The shady contours of the fuselage rapidly expanded against white concrete. A second later, the craft touched down on the runway. The tires spun up creating thick clouds of smog. Scott rolled onto the deck. He was safe.

Tracy noticed the open crate. "Dad. The lid!" Alex and Scott quickly nailed it back on the crate.

Henry "Hank" Foster was not yet convinced of what he'd just heard from Alex. Although it'd been years since he'd actively been associated with the one-time most-trusted civilian contractor with the DCA branch, with all that'd been going on the past few days, he had his doubts. Should he alert defense organizations, law-enforcing agencies, the National Guard, get the entire nation alarmed—possibly looking like a fool—or just let it slide until he had more information?

Hastening back to the emergency meeting he'd been called away from, he decided, "What the hell. Gotta trust the guy."

"Loosen up," he announced the second he walked into the high level meeting. "Something's come up." After he got everyone's attention, Foster briefly explained what Bauer had relayed to him. "Get the word out."

"I know the man…I trust the guy…" were some of the immediate comments, giving Foster added assurance against his previous doubts.

Reps from each organization were immediately dispatched to contact proper authorities wherever possible. In some instances, with the entire communication backbone disabled, it took days to disseminate the information, as critical as it appeared. Word eventually made it to what now seemed distant reaches from the East to the West. The terrorist alert went out to alarm the FBI, CIA, CDC, NNSA, National Guards, and local law-enforcing agencies in every state wherever possible.

Once the information was received in the field, a manhunt went into effect as the nation had never before experienced. It would remain in effect for weeks to come. At this time, unknown to Alex, he had achieved his objectives.

EXPOSED

The craft touched down with a rumble. Alex was in the wheel well before it came to a full stop. He crouched to get a look. A city skyline popped into view. It looked familiar. There was no other place like it in the U.S. "I know the place." They had landed in the midst of downtown Chicago. He'd been in and out this airport a number of times. Scott confirmed it. From their perch, they made out approaching footsteps. A set of boots and legs marched into view. "Quick," Alex warned. Both hopped back into the fuselage. Inside, the team sought cover behind the cargo crates. The door flung open with a thud. Bright sunlight dowsed the entrance port. A loading crew jumped on board. Another container was removed. It was quickly loaded onto a cargo truck.

Two of the unloading team lingered. Busy with the cargo door, they seemed to be searching for something. The frame was closely examined, but nothing must have seemed out of place. Chatting in a foreign language, they made for the exit, unaware of six eyes intensely watching from behind the remaining cargo.

The exit shut once more. Except for the glow seeping through the wheel wells, the cargo hold turned dark again. Minutes later the craft took to the air. It continued on its easterly path.

Watching her dad and Scott in action gave her a feeling of security. *We make a good team. Well coordinated.* The apprehension she'd had for Brooks earlier slowly waned. She was not without admiration watching combatants in action. Her thoughts touched on Brian. *Wished he was here.* She missed him.

The craft had reached cruising altitude once more. "Don't have much time," Scott warned. To Tracy, aside from being a man of action, he appeared dejected, out of place. He hadn't the patience to hide in a hold. Agitated, he was pacing the floor.

Tracy moved to the well opening. The radio set kept her occupied. The scanner was searching for frequencies. The antenna would pick up the signal.

Alex began pacing the fuselage as well. He motioned to Scott. "Check for an opening." Scott joined the search. "There's got to be an exit." Both were tapping the walls.

Scott located one up in the ceiling. It was a connecting panel to the cabin above. He called on Alex to support him. He tried to force the handle. It didn't budge. "Locked," Alex panted. It could only be unlocked from the cabin side.

Frustration showed in both faces. They discussed their options. Unexpectedly, there was sudden movement. It came from above. The lever had shifted. Highly alarmed, both retreated. "Tracy," Alex yelled out, muffled, "take cover."

The panel popped open. It left a rectangular opening. The team hurried for the shadows of the remaining crate. A patch of light dimly illuminated the hold. A pair of legs extended. A body followed. It landed hard on the cargo floor. A second pair followed close behind. Two trained bodies had landed on the deck. They were armed. Their every move was being watched.

With alert eyes, the newcomers moved up. They cautiously approached the remaining crate. They appeared hesitant. "What gave us away?" Scott whispered.

"Radio set," Alex whispered back, "interference." With extreme caution, he moved to the far end of the crate. Scott was positioned at the near end. Sandwiched in, Tracy was protected on both sides. She held her breath. The crate shielded them. Two sweeping beams of light penetrated the darkness.

Alex felt the adrenaline pump through his veins. He could almost feel it flow through his arteries. The jet engines put out a steady drone. It filtered out most other sounds in the hold. The newcomers inched their way up. Pausing after every stride, their approach was deliberate, hesitant. One motioned towards one edge of the crate. The other provided cover. It was a silent command. Using extreme caution, he slowly advanced. There was no reason for anyone other than them to be here, but there had been the alarm. It had to be checked.

Scott was ready. His body was poised to strike.

A face slowly appeared at the edge of the crate. Eyes were probing the shadows. They were guarded eyes. The pupils suddenly widened. They turned to surprise, then recognition. He had spotted Scott. His body retracted with a grunt. He raised his weapon but not in time.

Scott had already lunged. He moved with great speed. His aim was precise. The thrust of his knife found its target. Without making a sound, the blade sliced through the heart. The intruder collapsed. His body slid to the ground. One life extinguished. His fight was over. It'd taken only seconds.

Alex had been watching Scott's swift attack. He caught the new reflection of a shadow. The second attacker advanced on his side. He was prepared. A shadow cast across the edge of the crate. He recognized the shape of an arm clutching a weapon. Then the face appeared. The gun leveled at him, then his face, but before the trigger was pulled, the body sank to the floor. It collapsed in silence. It had been terminated by Scott who'd circled around the crate. His approach went unnoticed by the attacker. His focus had been on Alex. A second life had been extinguished. The incident was executed in complete silence. Tracy appeared from the shadow of the crate. Her gaze was fixated at the dead bodies. It lingered on their faces. "Only boys," she whispered. "Never had a chance."

"Get the weapons." Scott, the trained killer, turned professional once more. He moved swiftly. "Give me a hand." With combined force, they edged the crate beneath the opening above. He seemed in his world. His was a world of action. He did what he knew best, stealth and kill. He'd already squeezed through the opening above. Alex clambered behind. "Stay put," he motioned. A reluctant Tracy stayed behind. She tried to follow but was rebuffed.

"Men," she protested, but gave in.

Alex caught up near the galley. He turned a corner. The cockpit door was just ahead. Scott had moved in that direction. The sound of foreign voices lingered in the air. They came from the rear. Scott pressed on. Alex followed. They poised next to the cockpit entrance. Scott moved the handle. It gave way. "Unlocked," he motioned.

Why wouldn't it be? Almost humorously, Alex had a mental notion. *No need for protection.* They were all terrorists.

Scott indicated ahead. Using great stealth, he pried open the door and slid through. Alex was directly behind. Both bodies tensed for the action sure to follow within seconds.

"Chi?" The pilot turned and gasped. His brows merged into a single line. There was utter surprise in his face. He shot a glance at the copilot. There was equal surprise reflected there. In one motion, Scott lunged forward. He covered both pilots with the automatic he'd taken from the dead jihad below. To his immediate right, Alex spotted a third person. Busy with flight instruments, his back was turned. *Navigator,* he presumed.

Alerted by the unexpected sound, the head slowly turned. The navigator glanced over his shoulder. Aiming at his face, Alex leveled his weapon. An instant later, he received the shock of a lifetime. "You?!" was all he could muster. "How…?" Alex stammered.

The face in the crosshairs became distorted. It cringed from recognition. Alex held steady, although it took seconds to regain his composure. He had come face to face with Hasan Hammad, former employee of Rajesh, his Indian partner. In an instant, he'd recognized the true face staring back at him.

Unable to conceal his shock, Alex stared at the most unlikely person he'd ever expected.

Three feet distant, Hammad had been equally surprised. He grimaced with disgust, changed to loathing, then took on rage. "You!"

"Shut up," Alex spat at him. His gun was leveled, jammed into the adversary's ribs. Alex was catching his breath. He regained his composure. "You guys never know when to quit." He motioned. "Get up." Then he spoke with deliberate firmness. "Your luck has run out, Hasan Hammad. Give up!" Alex shot a quick glance at Scott. He'd covered the pilots, holding them in check.

Hammad slowly lifted his body from the seat. "I think not." His response was calculated. Alex missed the cue. His next move was unexpected. "I will end the mission now." Alex did not anticipate his actions. Too quick for Alex or Scott to react, he'd pulled a weapon from his waistband.

In rapid succession, Hammad took aim at the pilot and pulled the trigger. The bullet exploded in his head, splattering blood across the instruments. The body slammed forward into the controls. The next shot ripped into the copilot. It tore half of his face off. More blood splattered across the canopy.

Scott was unable to react fast enough. His eyes had followed every motion. The scene played out like a cheap movie. Followed by an unexpected reaction, there were the deafening gunshots. It tore into the first skull. The right temple squirted blood. The pilot's body jerked forward. It slammed into the controls. The motion dislodged the Autopilot. Dead weight on the controls, the craft was forced to maximum speed. Immediately, the craft went into a steep descent.

The next frames shifted to the copilot. He had taken the bullet in the base of the skull. The force threw his body into the instruments. Then a third shot rang out but missed its target. The bullet was intended for Scott. It penetrated the cockpit shell. Instantly, air was sucked from the craft. Log books and lose papers slammed against the opening. They partially blocked the escaping air. Distracted by the unfolding events, Hammad had disappeared from the cabin.

Seconds later, both Scott and Alex were swept off their feet. Their bodies were tossed through the air. Both struggled to get solid footing first then sought a hold, any hold. Hanging on in desperation, their bodies turned weightless. The craft had gone into a sheer dive. They were in freefall. Scott was struggling for a solid hold. Grappling for the dead pilot's body, he was desperately trying to remove the dead body from the captain's seat.

Still more frames later, Alex struggled with the copilot whose body had gone limp. If there was any chance to recover the craft, he needed to free the chairs. Straining against the controls, he struggled for life. The craft was rapidly descending. The Airbus headed directly for the ground. The turbines were pushing at full speed. Muscles strained against gravity, Alex finally managed a firm grip. In desperation, he hung on. Knuckles turned white, he gripped the controls then slowly pulled back. The fuselage strained under the craft's weight. His head was spinning. *Or was it the ground?* Spinning like a kaleidoscope, it rushed in rapidly. His mind was racing for a sense of direction. He tried to steady his focus. Then it came to him. He vaguely remembered. Long ago, he'd been in a similar situation.

It was his early flying days. Back then, flight was simple. He was in a single engine Cessna. He'd stalled out. It wasn't the first time. He used to practice the stalls. Not this time. The craft had gone into a spin. No matter how hard he'd tried, the controls did not respond. It'd rapidly lost altitude. Then he had spotted it. It was a mistake only a novice pilot would make. The throttle was stuck at full speed. He'd forgotten to pull it after the "power on" stall. Just like the first time he'd practiced, he yanked back the throttle. He regained control over the craft ever so slowly. That was twenty some years ago.

Today, now, the cabin was rapidly losing pressure. Exhausted strength combined with thin air made him dizzy. Through the mental haze, he noticed the throttles. They were set at full speed. *Of course!* Struggling with the controls, he needed help. To negotiate all sets of levers, he needed another set of hands. "Scott," he called in desperation, "I need you!"

With both sets of hands strained against the controls, using their combined strength, they slowly managed to pull the craft out of the dive. It leveled off then slowly gained attitude. The wide body gradually stabilized. It became manageable. Next, Alex reached for the mic. "Mayday…mayday…" he shouted over and over. His fingers were dialing through the range of frequencies. There was no response.

"You fly?" Scott beckoned. He'd strapped himself into the pilot's seat. Beads of sweat trickled from his forehead. His eyes were pleading, hoping Alex could fly this fortress.

"I can," Alex wavered, "on autopilot." He wasn't sure about the next move. Mind churning in desperation, his eyes were fishing for a solution. He knew the flight was programmed in the onboard computer; the checklist, however, he did not find. It must have gotten lost in the dive.

"This thing okay for now?" Scott gestured at the instruments. The Airbus had regained level flight. He checked the fuel gauges. "Low." They were faced with yet another test. Soon, they'd run out of fuel.

"We need help." Alex faced a real challenge. There were instruments he'd never seen. He pushed Autopilot. The circuit reconnected with the flight controls. It stabilized the craft. Then, his eyes spotted the checklist. There it was, lodged against the cracked windshield. A sudden thought struck him. "The radio." It would give them the link.

"I'll get it." Scott had already jumped from his seat. They both knew where they'd left it: the cargo hold. "You're on your own," was his immediate advice.

Aside from flying, Alex would have to watch the cabin. "Check on Tracy," he called after him. During the crises just overcome, he'd completely forgotten about her. *Hope she's okay.* He could hardly imagine the trauma she'd gone through, freefall, alone in the dark hold, slammed against the bulkhead. The feeling of falling through the air was bad enough, but in total darkness, it'd be traumatic. *Hang on, girl.* It was up to Scott to resolve that conflict. Somebody had to fly the craft. And for now, it was him.

"Watch Hammad," Alex yelled after him, "he's like a snake."

It's been minutes since Scott had left the cabin. Alex kept checking the entryway. *What's taking him?* It seemed to take forever. He was afraid Hammad might return. Then he spotted movement by the entrance. It was Scott. *Thank God.* Slung over one shoulder, he carried the radio set.

"Tracy?" Alex motioned.

"Gone." Scott locked the entrance shut. He took up position by the door.

"What?" Brows furrowed into vertical cuts, his gaze turned into one big question mark.

"Wasn't there," Scott repeated. It was apparent that he didn't appreciate being questioned.

"You mean," getting alarmed, his lips quivered with concern, "she's been...?"

"Don't know," Scott broke in. He was adjusting the set. The radio scanned the frequencies. There was silence across the spectrum.

Alex was devastated but his immediate priority was getting the craft on the ground. He prepared for the worst. His eyes scanned across the instruments. There was still time. For now, the craft held steady at twelve thousand feet altitude. Up here, the oxygen was thin, but not enough to pass out. His focus was on the computer panel displaying the onboard menu. Alex selected several function indicators. He verified the programmed heading. It indicated IAD. Elevation was set for 313 feet. They were headed for Dulles International. He'd have to deal with his daughter later. He could only hope she was all right.

Earlier, with Alex and Scott gone, in the cargo hold, Tracy had felt exposed. She was vulnerable. Left behind in the dark she could feel the chilled cargo air. She pulled the blanket tight around her shoulders and slid close to the crate. Her eyes tried to penetrate the darkness of the hold, but she could only make out empty spaces. Then, suddenly, she felt a lurch under her feet. She tried to steady herself on the crate, but could not find a solid grip. Her body was jerked off the floor. It took seconds to realize she was airborne. *Freefall,* her mind was screaming. It'd been many years since she had experienced the sensation. *Where was it?* Her mind tried to assimilate the information. *Flagstaff. Rollercoaster. That's it.* Her stomach was squeezing in on her chest cavity. She felt sick. Trying to latch onto something solid, her hands flailed through empty space. *Nothing.* She felt the oxygen level drop. Her vision became blurry. Her head turned dizzy. She blacked out.

Back in the cockpit, Scott had squeezed back in the pilot's seat. He fingered the radio set and found an active frequency. It was the time broadcast. Transmitted by NIST[65] radio, the WWV[66] call sign out of Fort Collins, it was a time code. Protected against cosmic rays, the atomic clock sent its steady signal into the ether. The receiver had picked it up. The craft's time zone was set to PDT. The craft's present location was three hours difference. He checked the fuel gauges. There was still time. They were about an hour's flight from Dulles. "Might just make it," he informed Alex, "if you can land this thing."

Alex focused on the computer readouts. He scanned through the many buttons on the cockpit screens. He pushed a button. It was for IAD OPS. The computer found the

---

[65] National Institute of Standards and Technology.
[66] Radio call sign broadcast globally by NIST located at Fort Collins, CO.

information. Data painted across the screen, containing major airport parameters. Another button brought up frequencies. "Try 122.775."

Scott made the selection on the radio gear. It was Dulles Operations.

"Mayday…mayday…" Scott operated the set. There was no response.

Alex scanned through the computer listing. "Try 120.250." It was the tower center. *Nothing.* "132.450." *Still nothing.* "Step through ranges 110 and 175."

"Roger." Scott made the selections. Precious minutes were ticking away.

"I can land on manual," Alex offered, "providing the ILS is working."

"If we can wake somebody up." Scott gestured at the ILS system panel. "How's this work?"

"Seems complicated," Alex explained, "but it's really quite simple." When on manual, the aircraft's transmitter shot out a narrow signal to the left, then the right, of the runway. The ground transmitter returned the signal. The onboard computer compensated for horizontal drifts. The same went for vertical glide slope. "Keeps the craft dead on course," he explained.

"What about the Autopilot?"

"Same principle," he explained further, "through GPS. But, with satellites out, ground transponders take over." The old system was still used as backup for just such an emergency.

"Dulles International…" The signal was weak. It came in barely audible. "Identify…"

"Need assistance," Scott shouted into the mic. "Urgent."

"Identify….identify." The request was repeated. Scott turned desperate. Neither of them knew the craft's identity. "Here." He tossed the receiver over to Alex.

"Check with Langley," Alex shouted. He was frustrated about yet another hurdle. He prayed Foster was able to patch the earlier call. It should give them landing clearance. *Then what?* Even under the best of conditions, he wasn't sure if he could pull off a landing. His eyes gauged the instrument panel. He could only guess at some of the functions. The craft held relatively steady. They were getting close to Dulles. "What's the radar status?"

"Out, but," the voice came back, "got you in sight." There was a pause. "You Bauer? Brooks with you?"

"Roger." It gave him renewed hope. They'd been notified. "Need your assistance."

"Pilots?"

"Dead."

"Who's flying?"

"Autopilot."

"You alright?"

"Terrorists on board."

"Will guide you in…SWAT is on standby."

"Okay…" Alex affirmed, "keep it simple."

"How's fuel?"

Alex checked the gauges. "Looks empty." A sickening feeling swept his stomach. "Better make it quick. What heading?"

"Straight north—outer runway." Coming from the west, the craft was flying crosswind. Alex made one major correction to get the craft on final approach. It was going to be rough with radar out.

"Check your altitude," the tower urged. "Too high."

The altimeter showed the craft at five thousand. The craft was ready for flaps. Alex pushed the button. His heart skipped a few beats. There was no response. Bullets may have damaged the instruments. He tried the manual lever. It worked. He set flats at fifteen degrees.

Eyes fixated on the distance, Scott stared straight ahead. Aiding Alex, his hands were steady on the controls. It seemed he was getting the feel of flying. Seconds later, he'd located the target.

"Almost there…I see the runway! Ten o'clock," he indicated to Alex.

"Auto off." The voice came from tower control.

Alex switched to manual. The full weight of the craft pushed on the controls. They felt sluggish in his hands. From here on, he was guiding the craft. They broke through a thin layer of clouds. Below, ten miles out, the final landing marker crept into view. Another minute, they should be on the ground.

"What the fuck?" Scott yelled out. "Up…up…pull up."

"Goin' to need a miracle." Alex's gaze was fixed on the runway. Sudden reality struck out at once. It required an instant decision. *Set down and crash, or pull up and crash minutes later?* Those were the choices. The sight ahead was a true reminder of the past few days. The landing path ahead was still being cleared by the salvage crews. Only two thirds of the way had been cleared. Being lighter in weight, that was sufficient for the WWII craft. They'd been using the short takeoff and landing markers, but it was different with the modern Airbus. It required the full length of the runway. It posed even more of a challenge. Alex came in hot. The craft had to clear what looked like a war zone. Piled in heaps of twisted metal was the wreckage of damaged craft that had crash-landed days earlier.

Alex couldn't see clear. Rivulets of sweat were streaming from the brows. Using his shirtsleeve, he wiped his forehead clear. The fabric was already soaked from sweat. *Don't lose it now,* his senses cautioned. There was no time to calculate the next move. Approach control made it for him.

"Switch to ground navigation"

"What?"

"TACAN[67] selector switch!"

"I see it."

"Reduce power…one third…forty degree flaps…landing gear."

Alex complied automatically. His ears followed the instructions. His fingers did the rest. "Done," he stammered. With flaps set, the craft responded instantly, but not in his favor. The flap acted like an air brake. Normal approach setting was ten degrees, then twenty for final. It felt like the craft went into a stall. The cockpit shuddered under the strain. Alex had a fleeting thought. *Tracy.* He prayed for her safety. Instruments had turned blurry from the vibration. He sought out the fuel gauges. Tank indicators were flashing at him. *Empty.* "I've got one shot!" he yelled into the mic.

"Don't worry." The voice had a calming effect. "We'll get you down."

Easy for him to say. Alex was sweating profusely. Scott's face appeared tense. One hand was clutched at the controls, the other on the radio. It was their vital link with the tower, their only link. Closing the distance had cleared the airwaves. Instructions now came in loud and clear.

---

[67] Tactical Air Navigation system used by military aircraft.

"Reduce speed 150...altimeter 313...runway, 'One Right'...final."

"Check." He'd been given the landing approach from the south, final approach.

"Slight bank right...hold it...hold...doing fine. Outer threshold reached...hold for touchdown."

Field glasses trained on the glide slope, the controller spotted the craft then shifted focus to the wheels. He was looking for the puffs of smoke the wheels gave off when touching concrete. "Not going to make it," he whispered. He had a sudden urge to yell out but kept silent.

Half a mile out, in the craft, ground effect took over. Alex felt it coming on. The craft sped up. Straight ahead was piled wreckage everywhere. His right hand gripped the flight controls. His left rested on the center bay throttle controls. "Scott!" he yelled. Alex shot him an alarmed glance. Both strained at the controls. The engines did not respond. A feeling of panic set in. He suddenly recalled that aircraft engines always lagged a few seconds. It took time for fuel to reach the burners. His tension relaxed. A second later, his eyes caught it. "Fuel's gone!"

The engines had gone dry. They stopped pushing. He felt the full pressure build up against his temples. His heart skipped again. The framework strained under the force. The craft dropped fifty feet.

His next action was more on instinct. In a last ditch effort, Alex reduced the flaps ten degrees. The craft responded. It gained momentum. It gained altitude, but not enough to clear the first barrier of wreckage. In a piercing crashing sound, the lower part of the fuselage plowed through the twisted wreckage. The sparks created by the impact would have ignited the fuel tanks if they had not gone empty.

From a distance, air traffic and ground control spotted smoke. It wasn't the sign for which they'd hoped.

Inside the cockpit, Alex and Scott fought with the controls. The wheels had just touched down on the runway. "Kill...kill engines," the voice commanded. Another command followed rapidly. "Brake...brake!" It was the final order by tower control. With their combined strength, both pushed down hard. Alex maneuvered the pedals to stay on course.

"Watch out!" Both sets of eyes spotted it. "More wreckage ahead."

Alex felt the brakes respond. The craft was slowing, but not fast enough. Relentlessly, the mass kept pushing forward.

"Running out of space," Scott called out in desperation.

Eyes fixed on the end of the runway, Alex yelled, "Push...push harder!" It was a desperate plea. Landing at maximum speed, they watched more wreckage by the end of the runway. The craft responded. It slowed, but not in time. A crunching sound tore into the fuselage, then the cockpit. The impact crushed the nose of the Airbus. The wheels collapsed. The craft ground to a halt. Then there was silence.

"Great landing!" The controller's voice came over the transmitter. On impact, the radio set had slammed against the instrument panel, but seemed still functional. Seconds later, a cluster of emergency vehicles swarmed in alongside the craft, accompanied by officials keeping up the pace. An exit ramp was pushed against the fuselage. The crosshatch popped up. The door sprang open. In swarmed the assault team.

SWAT patches prominently identified the detachment. Donned in the customary black assault garb, they wore goggles and protective masks. They spotted the two dead bodies by the galley. It's where Scott had dumped them.

"Pilots?" the leader asked.

Scott gave him a nod. "Brooks," he identified himself, "DELTA."

"Any others?"

"In back." Scott motioned to the rear of the craft.

"How many?"

"Don't know," he replied, "dozen, maybe."

The commander split the team. They took up positions—one defensive, the other offensive—advancing on the craft's interior.

Exhausted, Alex lingered in the cockpit. *Let them fight it out.* He was tired. There were shouts. Gunfire opened up seconds later. The sound came from the rear of the craft. The firing spread to the cargo hold below. He crouched deeper in the seat. There was shouting. There were screams. It shook him into reality. Then, it turned silent. "Tracy!" Alex yelled. He jumped to his feet. On unsteady legs he staggered through the galley but one member SWAT rushed him to the ramp. Below, the grounds were jammed with uniforms. His eyes frantically searched for any signs of her. She was nowhere in sight.

Then, seconds later, his face lit up. In the midst of the rush he spotted a friendly face. Flanked by Special OPS, Special Forces, and more SWAT, quickly headed his way with long strides, was Foster. It gave him hope. Hope for Tracy. She'd need it.

JIHAD ASSAULT TEAM

Earlier that day, when the Airbus had first landed in Denver, the New York cell didn't show. It'd missed the rendezvous. The Serpent had been furious. The plan was to unload the first cargo, then pick up the New York cell. Yusuf was supposed to continue on the flight to the West Coast to command the rest of the deliveries. He himself had planned to take control over the city, the new Jihad capital. With communication out, there was no means to contact the local team. It was the first mission error. He finally had to dispatch members from the flight team to deliver the cargo destined for Denver. "Damned neophytes," he kept cussing. "I ask for trained soldiers," he spat in disgust, "and what do they give me?" He'd kicked out violently. His boot connected with a comrade standing nearby. "Nothing but rabble." He made a mental note to enforce immediate changes as soon as he had complete command over the forces.

Sitting idle by the tarmac, two hours into the wait, he'd decided to take off. Any more delay would have impacted the schedule. He had no choice but take command. "San Francisco," he'd ordered the pilot. The craft departed immediately. The flight to the coast had been uneventful. The second drop went as planned, but there seemed a problem with the third stop. An alarm indication went off. There was a pressure drop, but a close inspection had revealed nothing. They were airborne again. It would be their last drop and final destination.

Presently, the craft was en route to Dulles. Taking the navigator's seat in the cockpit, he'd ordered full speed ahead to make up for lost time with the initial drop. Still furious at Yusuf for missing the rendezvous, he had to make the first concession to the plan, His Plan.

The jihad team had gathered in the back of the craft. It was not as spacious as up front, but provided room to accommodate the team. There was heated conversation. A dozen or more jihad was speculating. Rumors were prolific. None had a clue about the mission or destination ahead. There had been the unexpected change in Denver. Yusuf and his cell had gone missing. To their surprise, the mission went ahead as planned. Another surprise, nobody had expected the head of Jihad to be on board the craft. It was the first time anyone had ever seen him in person. The Serpent, up to this point, had been mostly an enigma. "Allah Akbar," one fighter praised. "We have a leader." The long-standing rumors were true. It caused great excitement.

Everybody was smoking. The cabin had turned hazy from stale fumes. Aside from consuming large quantities of daily tea, smoking was the team's singular past time. One hand held a cigarette tightly gripped between the fingers, the other balanced a cup of tea; it was intoxicating. Freshly brewed Oolong was percolating non-stop in the galley. The present heated discussions were centered on individual assignments after the last cargo was dropped off. What happened next would cease all conversation.

It came on unexpectedly. The craft, without warning, suddenly went into a steep dive. It almost inverted. Members of the squad were lifted off the floor. Bodies were sprawled on the ceiling, then, without warning, flung in the air, smashed against the rear of the craft. Spinning wildly, the craft plummeted toward the ground. At first, struggling against the force was impossible. It seemed minutes went by before the immense pressure lessened. Then, all of a sudden, piled on top of each other near the rear galley and toilets, the team landed back on the floor. Teapots, trays, and luggage had taken the same route.

Broken into many pieces, cups had smashed against the bulkhead. When gravity returned, the cabin was in disarray. Personal belongings, weapons, and luggage were strewn in every direction. Members hastily collected dropped assault gear and weapons.

The Serpent, after being identified by Alex as Hasan Hammad, with the craft headed for the ground, after one last shot had taken the opportunity to rush from the cockpit. To keep himself from flying across the bulkhead, he clutched at whatever hand hold he could grasp, his head still reeling from the unexpected encounter with his former contracting partner. *Out of all people, it had to be him.* Hasan Hammad had made a crucial error. "Stupid…stupid…stupid," he cussed at himself. *All because Yusuf hadn't shown.* He'd have to correct the mistake, immediately.

Somewhat recovered after the freefall, presently he was consulting with the team in the back of the cabin. Plans had to be made for the inevitable action that would follow when the craft landed, offensive or defensive. Either way, it'd be bloody. With the craft in the air, there was still time. Once they touched down, security forces would be swarming all over the place.

"Listen up." He was giving the final orders. The atmosphere was tense. The craft had been scheduled to land for a final delivery, but had failed. The plan had been disrupted. "We must expect resistance." It was then his eyes caught the reflection of something. It kept flashing. "We have an alarm," he alerted the crew. "Cargo hold. Now!" He ordered his most trusted lieutenants Rashid Abu and Shakir Murad to investigate. Seconds later, Murad came rushing back, gesticulating wildly for his leader to follow. In a state of heightened excitement, he blurted out, "We have captive." The jihad leader directed the others to stay then hurried to the cargo hold.

CARGO HOLD

Was it a dream? Or was it real? She couldn't tell in the darkness. It was pitch black. Her body had slammed against the bulkhead. Exerting great effort, without much success, she strained against the cargo wall. Then, all of a sudden, gravity returned. Tracy felt the full weight of her body slam back onto the floor. There were shadows reaching out. She felt around. Her hands touched solid floor. "What just happened?" Tracy questioned her consciousness. The craft's jets were screaming into her ears. Then, another force tore at her body. She was picked up again. Her mind did not have the time to analyze. There was freefall followed by intense pain. It had knocked the wind from her lungs. It was then that she realized the action was real. Her body was shaken. In the dark, she'd lost all sense of direction. With the last fall, the sound of the engines had turned normal. The craft seemed to stabilize. Tracy felt around. Her hands were fishing for the duffels. She needed a flashlight. It would make all the difference. There was a sudden sound. It came from above. Then, in quick succession, bodies dropped from the ceiling. Hastened shadows closed in on her.

Seconds later, a sudden grip tightened around her waist. She could make out features. They were strange faces. Arabian faces. Features she'd studied for years from surveillance photos. Then it dawned on her. *I'm in the hands of the enemy.* It sickened her. The feeling was overwhelming.

"What have we here?" She recognized the voice. It belonged to the commander of the cargo team. "Stowaway?"

She struggled against the tight grip on her waist. There was groping. Something slid into the back pocket of her jeans. It was a hand. It found the object of their search. *My wallet. My ID,* she groaned.

"Bauer?" The voice turned incredulous. "Tracy Bauer?" The shadow turned to his comrades. "We've struck gold." The voice turned triumphant. "She's our way out."

Tracy felt her body pushed to the floor. She struggled against the force, but was overpowered in seconds. She was no match for the assailants. With hands and legs bound, she submitted to the inevitable. Straps cut deep into her flesh causing red welts. The shadows were chatting in what she thought was Farsi. *Could be Arabic.* It didn't matter. They were ruthless people. Their methods were brutal. She dared not think further. She'd seen their video broadcasts recoded on YouTube, horrible scenes. Blindfolded captives, they'd chopped off their heads. The visualization reached her with full force. She shuddered at the thought. It shut her system down. Her body contracted. She went into shock. Tracy blacked out once more.

"You…you…you…" Hammad gestured. He was breaking up his fighters. One group, he dispatched to the cargo entrance; the other took position behind the remaining crate. They were guarding Tracy. The third, he ordered, "Follow me." In quick succession, they disappeared through the ceiling opening. Back in the passenger section, flanked by two trusted lieutenants, he took position in the galley. It was the best possible spot for defense. From there, he could cover the entrance and still be connected with his team below. His mind calculated the odds. He visualized probabilities from opposing forces. He and his team had dug in for whatever would be next.

He considered eliminating Alex and his buddy but rationalized against it. He could have easily taken them out but had no replacement pilots. He also knew Alex and Scott were fighters. They would not have relented. They'd rather have sought death than turn the craft over.

With a sudden thud, the craft landed. He braced himself against the braking force. One final time, he checked the team. They were in position. They were ready. He was ready.

There was sudden gunfire. It came from the cargo hold. He could make out the rapid recoil action from automatics. He could identify the weapons by sound. AK-47s. It was his team.

As soon as the craft landed, a ramp was pushed up against the rear passenger exit. Agents swarmed in by the dozens. Where the SWAT team focused on the passenger section above, the FBI headed for the cargo hold below. Orders were shouted. The fighting had begun. It shifted from the tarmac to the cargo hold, then to the cabin. In the forward galley, Hammad held his position.

On the tarmac, after the craft touched down, FBI agents took position. They met no resistance. Pressing on, they swarmed into the darkened cargo hold. The lead spotted movement by the cargo. He was covered by his team. He pushed on. He advanced deeper. Narrow beams from the many flashlights were darting from place to place. They barely illuminated the darkness. Close to the bulkhead, the cargo was spotted. The team headed for crate. The space appeared empty. "Secure," the lead announced.

It was to be his last command. A stream of bullets streamed his way. It sprayed down from the ceiling and found its target. Shadows appeared by the ceiling opening. Silently, in rapid succession, they dropped from above. The FBI retreated. Some sought cover behind the crate. Too late, they realized, they'd been trapped. There was more fiery exchange. Bullets ricocheted off the framework. Some penetrated the walls. Suddenly, much like an explosion, there was a crashing sound. It was the cargo door slamming shut. Darkness set in, illuminated only by a few narrow beams of flashlights. The craft had acquired additional hostages, the FBI.

Above, in the dark, the leader dropped from the ceiling. Another body followed. Deliberately, he pushed his way into the beams of light. Tightly gripped in his arms, he carried a shield. He held a shape. It was that of a woman. She looked familiar to the agents. And so did the assailant. The FBI was confronted by the enemy. It was an enemy that had escaped them for years. They had come face to face with the Serpent. It would have been triumphant if the circumstances had been reversed. The balance of power had shifted. It was in the hands of jihad, the enemy.

SHOWDOWN

There was confusion. There were shouts. The ramp was packed with agents shoving their up. A black-clad menace headed in his direction. He appeared to be the leader. "You Bauer?"

Alex nodded in acknowledgement.

"You're expected." Alex was shoved down the ramp. There, he spotted the familiar face. As soon as he set foot on the tarmac, Forster greeted him. He was accompanied by Jon Barrister, head of the DHS.

"You sure know how to pick 'em," Foster cut in. "Didn't know you flew big birds." There was mocking in his tone, but not without a hint of admiration.

"Only in emergencies," Alex grimaced, "ten-minute crash course."

"So I've heard…but," he demanded, "what's up? Where's the cargo?"

"Tracy's on board," Alex blurted. "Get her," he beckoned.

"The FBI," Barrister voiced, "will take care of it." He had assumed authority. He pointed at the cargo hold. "Jihad?"

"Back of the craft," Alex gestured, "doesn't look good." His face displayed grave concern. "Don't know how much time we've got."

"What?" Foster gazed at him. He was waiting for an explanation.

"You'll need a HAZMAT team."

"HAZMAT what?"

"West Coast, central, and east," Alex explained.

"Be more specific," Foster demanded. He was anxious to see the cargo.

"Tracked three drops." Alex was specific. "San Francisco, Chicago, and here."

Foster urged him toward the cargo hold, but was stopped by the FBI. There was gunfire coming from inside. Alex froze. "Tracy." He tried to force his way through the barricade. He was held back. He struggled free, but was detained with force. Several agents had a tight grip on his body. He could only watch from a distance. His heart reached out to his daughter. "Not again," he muttered. Visions from the last capture were still fresh on his mind.

"She'll be alright," Foster consoled. He motioned at the agents. "Let them handle it." He released the grip on his friend. "What about the cargo?" Foster urged again.

"Couldn't identify the contents," Alex insisted.

The general gestured in the direction of the terminal. "FBI will handle it." Agents were rushing across the tarmac. Multiple branches of the government were on the scene. Each branch was identified by the organization's colors.

"We don't have time to investigate." Alex was getting frustrated. *Politics,* he thought, *are not what we need.* "We're at war." This was a military issue. It should be dealt with by DOD and the NNSA. "Lethal substances involved."

His pleading fell on ignorant ears. The shooting had stopped. He was warded off the cargo area. There was much hurrying in and around the craft. Word leaked out. "Jihad issued demands." Negotiators were called in. As soon as the first arrived, he was ushered to the grounded craft. He was directed inside the hold. Tense minutes passed. He appeared once then was pulled back inside. Minutes turned into an hour. Rumors spread. "Negotiations failed." It'd turned into a standoff. He'd returned without resolution. Demands were evaluated by NNSA. Jihad demanded release of the craft. Word came back. "Demands denied—against hostage taking policy!"

Because of Tracy, however, the demands had to be reevaluated. Alex felt responsible. Aside from his daughter, several other lives were at stake, those of the FBI agents.

"Do something," Alex said. Every fiber in his body strained. He was torn between reasoning and compromise. The life of his precious daughter was hanging on a thread. An entire nation was in jeopardy. He almost couldn't bear the thought. His emotions were torn from fear to rage. The standoff continued. SWAT were given final orders. "Stand down."

Back at command, the FBI went into action. Law enforcement, at the cities indicated by Alex, was notified, but communications were still down. The confederate fleet was on standby, ready to take special units to dedicated areas. Special Forces were alerted. Military units were directed to search for suspicious cargo. Teams with radioactive sensors were tracing cargo and container shipments in and around the cities. So far, nothing had been uncovered.

An aide rushed at Foster. "They want you at HQ."

"In a minute." The general hesitated. He needed Alex to be there. There was information on the cargo only he could identify. "Let's go," he ordered. Alex was reluctant.

"I won't leave my daughter," he insisted. He was adamant. He felt sick at the thought, but also realized the need to identify the deadly cargo. *Sandia may have some answers,* he hoped.

"Nothing more you can do here," Foster insisted. "Three hundred sixty million people in jeopardy." His face changed from compassion to urgency. "They need you."

"FBI, DOD's on the case. Let them handle it." Foster took hold of Alex. He tugged on his sleeve to urge him along. It was then he realized the tattered condition his friend was in. He also reeked from sweat and body odor. "You, my friend," he insisted, "need a shower."

Alex replied, "I got news." He pulled his arm from the solid grip.

"What?" Foster demanded. He was annoyed about another delay.

"The Jihad leader." Alex momentarily paused.

"Go on," Barrister, standing close by with ears perked cut in.

Alex's eyes were fixed on the face of the DHS head. He did not want to miss the reaction that was sure to follow. After all, it was his people that had missed the connection with the jihad leader.

"Yeah?" Foster almost blew up from impatience.

"Serpent," Alex stressed.

"Spit it out," Barrister insisted. His face had turned red with impatience.

"Hasan Hammad!" He held his sight on the DHS. At first, the face appeared expressionless. *Either he knew,* Alex thought, *or he's playing dumb.*

"The subcontractor?" Foster reacted. "Serpent and Hammad! Same person?" His voice had turned incredulous.

"Same," Alex validated.

"How can that be? Impossible! What's your source? What's your proof?" Barrister fired questions at him to answers he should have known. "You gotta be wrong."

"He's on the craft." Alex was giving him the only fact that counted. "He killed the pilots."

There was an extended pause. The information changed everything. To imagine the leader of the jihad forces penetrating into the country was beyond belief.

New action orders were issued. They went out to every agency on the case. U.S. defense forces had to be mobilized. It was a national emergency. Responsibilities immediately shifted. "Elevate DEFCON," Barrister ordered.

"We need the FBI in on this." The general gestured in the direction of the tarmac.

"Don't have time to investigate," Alex objected. He became frustrated once more. *Politics,* he thought, *that's all we need.* "We're at war." This was a military issue. It should be managed by DOD and NNSA since it involved radioactive substances. Yellow tape went up around the craft. The FBI had taken control of the crime scene. DOD was taking action for the nation. Alex was directed off the cargo area. He was shoved from the tarmac by members of the local SWAT team.

"Come," Foster insisted, "back to HQ."

DULLES INTERNATIONAL

Days earlier, wrecking crews had been called up. They had faced the monumental effort of clearing crashed airplane wreckage left in the wake of that disastrous night. Whatever could be towed had first priority. Space had been set aside on the north end of the airport perimeter. Fuselages, twisted frames, and debris quickly followed. All runways would gradually be cleared. Although only on visual, the tower was back in partial operation. Takeoff and landings were spaced out to assure airport safety. Space had been cleared to set up mobile command posts. Tactical units from defense organizations occupied the stations. To expedite in and out traffic, each was identified by the appropriate office symbol.

Space within was limited. One end of a van housed an array of computers. The other would accommodate a small galley with restroom facilities. Units were setup for office desks, tables with chairs to host visitors, and cluster of comm gear. Alex was seated across from Foster.

He felt nauseated. He kept staring through the window louvers in the direction of the Airbus. The craft sat at the end of the runway where it had landed hours ago. "What's the city like?" He made conversation to occupy his thoughts.

"Martial law," Foster explained. Following the attack on the nation, the government immediately went into action. The city had been made off limits to all personal traffic. Only limited commercial vehicles were authorized to support military and National Guard units. To maintain civil order, local law enforcement went into action. Government units directed emergency and rescue. There was looting. Some elements could not be stopped. They took the chance caused by the chaotic conditions.

He thought he'd challenge Foster for his evasiveness days earlier. "Thought we had personal synergy?" Alex approached the subject. The last thing he wanted was to break off their long-standing friendship.

"Thing with the launch?"

"That's the one," he acknowledged.

"Sorry about that." Foster exhaled. He remained stern faced. Alex could see from his body language he'd touched a sore point. Foster was tight lipped, avoiding eye contact.

Putting personal feelings aside, Alex probed further. "I really needed your help back there." He wanted to justify the missile launch.

"I knew that."

"Overstepped my boundaries?"

"You did great."

"Then…"

"Look, Alex," Foster offered. His tone had softened. "There're things better left alone."

"You've trusted me in the past. What's changed?"

"It's not just a matter of trust. There're forces you don't know about."

"Like what?"

"Can't tell you."

"That's what gets me," Alex spat back. He tried to maintain his calm. "Always a one way street. Information's going in," he stressed, "but nothing's coming back out. How am I supposed to make an intelligent decision?" Lines of frustrations appeared across his forehead. "I've been struggling with that for years…kept in the dark throughout the entire cold war…I'm tired of this bullshit."

"You're a pawn," Foster explained, "just like me." He spoke in a halting voice. His gaze fell on the agents working nearby. Some had perked up to get a better listening position. He shot a warning sign at Alex. "Above everything else," he cautioned, "you should know, information's disseminated on a need-to-know basis."

"Thanks for reminding me." Alex understood the protocol too well. He suddenly realized Hank couldn't talk openly. *I'm such an idiot,* he thought. He immediately realized his failure to catch the subtle hints he'd been given. He glanced sideways at his longtime friend. In silence, he acknowledged the reprimand.

"What about Barrister?" he probed. "Can he be trusted?"

Foster briefed Alex about Barrister. He'd learned of his impressive career with naval intelligence, then as presidential appointee for central intelligence. It was this post that eventually earned him Director, National Intelligence, currently head of the DHS, in charge of this recently created organization.

Foster took the initiative. He was addressing Alex. "What've you got?"

"My assessment is a dirty bomb."

"I want specifics." Foster would not tolerate indecision, especially not today.

"For that we need Sandia on this." Alex voiced the only logical course of action. Everything else would only be guesswork. There was nothing else that could be achieved on the local level. They desperately needed a connection with the lab, but that could take days. There was no time. Lethal cargos had been delivered with target destinations unknown. Timed bombs were ready to go off.

"Take a break." Foster made the suggestion. "We'll handle it." He'd noticed Alex suppressing several yawns.

"Could use some rest," Alex responded. He felt drained.

"Let me take you somewhere." The Sheraton was the popular hotel. It was nearby. On shaky legs, Alex got to his feet. He stiffly followed Foster to the staff car. He flopped in the backseat. He strained to keep the eyes open. "It's only a couple minutes' drive," Foster encouraged a weary Alex. With a wink he dispatched the driver. "I'll send for you in a couple of hours."

"Right." Alex was glad to have some relaxing time before the mission went under way. After checking in at the Sheraton, Alex ordered a sandwich at the desk. He hadn't eaten all day and was famished. He just realized he hadn't slept in days. He was exhausted. He dragged his weary body to the made up bed. Plopped on top, his last thought was on Tracy. He immediately fell asleep, oblivious to room service delivery.

NSA HEADQUARTERS

For the past days Brian had been struggling. There was complete lack of direction. It wasn't only him. It was felt agency wide. Personal comments from other agents attested to that. For many years, the organization had operated like a well-maintained engine, much like a self-contained machine. With the satellites out, the heart of the system had broken down. NSA was kept in the dark.

With surveillance inoperative, NSA had become a wounded animal. *Dragon without its head,* he mused. It was no laughing matter. It was the reason for his frustration. Ever since the return from the recall, his efforts had been a total waste of his time. Presently, poised in front of his laptop, he hoped something would happen, anything. He'd been testing connections non-stop. He'd tried every conceivable link and database, but could not make a single connection. "Downlink Failure," or "Database Access Denied," were the responses returned from the various software applications he was using.

"What's the word with DSCS?"[68] The department director's voice was clearly discernible over the PA. His frustration was obvious. He'd been asking for status over and over as soon as backup power was restored. The world had been breathing down his neck for days. His tech team hadn't been able to get anything up. He'd hoped the Defense Satellite Communication System would give him coverage, but no such luck. DSCS, somewhat antiquated for its time was still kept up for emergency backups.

Sprawled across the desk, Brian stared at the space assets chart. *AEHF[69],* he thought, *my last chance.* The system provided coverage for U.S. forces and embassies across the globe. Most of it was hardened equipment. It should have shielded out the damaging rays.

It would be his last hope to get something going. He studied the charts again. He needed to borrow a unit from the southern hemisphere, or from European coverage. There'd be screams from those sectors, but it couldn't be helped. It would be months before new assets could be launched. He could only guess at their reaction, especially from NATO. "Unacceptable...not a chance..." Whatever the responses, it would be politically polite, but denied, nevertheless. In a way, he was glad communication was out. That way, he didn't have to take the verbal abuse that was sure to follow. *I need coverage now,* he resolved.

Although space surveillance was his responsibility, he did not have the authorization to move assets. That was handled at Schriever by SPACECOM and the GPS folks. They were the ones synchronizing the space vehicles. Unfortunately, he had not been able to get any cooperation from there. Organizations were self-protective, especially in times of crises, and especially when survival was at stake. But there were ways around that. He'd used them in the past. He'd have to break some rules. People did it all the time. *It was easier to ask for forgiveness than to get permission.* It'd been his "mode of operandi" for years. Act first and beg forgiveness later.

Brian was contemplating the moves it would take to redirect the satellite. *Re-home,* was the tech lingo. He sat quietly for a moment. In the background, he could hear the techs chatter. A team of analysis and tracking technicians were slouched over a cluster of monitors. Each had been assigned a specific sector. Their agile fingers were rushing

---

[68] The Defense Satellite Communications System provides the United States with military communications to support globally distributed military users.

[69] Advanced Extremely High Frequency is the military's most recent communication system.

across the many keyboards. To some, it may have been tedious work, but to these geeks, it was the only world they knew.

"Got something," one announced with excitement. The call was heard over the intercom. It would surely earn him an "Attaboy," and perhaps a promotion. "Getting data."

"Run it through analysis." Brian was on his feet. "See if it's valid, and," he stressed, "tune in video." The wall screen came alive. Distorted images reflected across the screen. Several more key strokes by the operator stabilized the images. He had a lock. What showed was a digital image fed by the unit's internal memory. It may have been stored from the last search before the system crash. Brian wasn't sure. He couldn't tell.

"Run an interface on both up and down links." *Maybe,* he thought with relief, *I don't have to do something illegal like breaking into unauthorized software.* Phones were already ringing. Word got out fast. "Everybody in the world wants pictures." Brian groaned. He also understood the urgency. The presidency relied on the daily briefs for making political decisions. Organization heads from the DOD, CIA, DIA, NRO, and NASA depended on it. Then there was weather, news, research, Google, and many others wrestling to get the latest images.

With an initial uplink established, online circuits were quick to overload. It was difficult to keep the link up. Brian reached for the yellow phone. Color coded devices had been implemented. Yellow took priority over everything with the exception of red. Red was reserved for the president and organization commanders at war. Its ring was persistent. *Who'll get first priority?* Somebody had already decided.

"Need a dedicated link on the Dulles grid."

"Still checking equipment," Brian apologized. "I'll let you know as soon as we're done."

"Now," Foster insisted. "I'll take my chances."

"I can't guarantee..." Brian gave in. "Just a sec." One hand over the mouthpiece, he muttered, "Biz as usual. Turn primary over to DOD," he called to a nearby operator. After days of wrestling with satellites and ground equipment he was finally able to relax. "Let them check it out."

"Right." Eyes were fixated on the wall mounted display; there it was, in plain view. Plotted across the monitors were familiar images of the eastern seaboard of the United States.

"Spectacular," Brian was awed, "NSA's got eyes again." Although the view was still blurred, it was a step toward pulling the nation out of darkness.

"General," Brian announced, "you've got your link." The pressure was off his back. Now it was up to the tech group to keep it up. "By the way," he hastened before the line went dead, "What's happening at Dulles?"

"Hostage scene."

"What?"

"Your friend Bauer and daughter." *Click.*

Brian stared at the receiver. He was still trying to understand the general's words. *Alex and Tracy hostage?* It took a few seconds to sink in.

"Get me a link with Dulles," he yelled to the tech crew. He couldn't wait. He rushed for the exit, destination Dulles.

DULLES SHERATON

There was persistent knocking. It finally woke him. He had been dreaming. He threw the covers off a sweat soaked body. Gasping for air, Alex sat up straight. He knew the feeling too well. He'd experienced it many times in the past, always connected with troubling events. It was a cross he'd bore since childhood. *My cross.* He felt like his body had been fighting battles for hours. It took a few seconds to calm his quivering nerves. They were vivid dreams, surfacing from a troubled mind. A mind reliving segments of reality merged with fractions of past visions. *Whose visions?* He didn't know. There was the knocking again, this time accompanied by a muffled voice. Wearing only shorts, he quickly strode to the door.

"Foster sent me." It was the general's personal aid. "Car's waiting, Mr. Bauer."

"Be with you in a minute." He closed the door on the driver who indicated he'd be waiting in the lobby. Alex took a quick shower, put his clothes back on, grabbed the jacket and headed for the door. On the way out, he grabbed the sandwich from the table. It only took him three bites to finish. Arriving downstairs, he checked out.

The bill had already been paid. *Foster,* he mused. With the nation's banking system disabled, credit cards wouldn't have worked anyway. Besides, he was short on cash. He thought of people entrapped in similar predicaments. *How do you pay when the cash runs out?* Barter. *Barter with what?* Most likely wind up in jail. *Who'd enforce the law?* There must be thousands of petty thefts happening across the nation.

Alex slipped into the limo. The chauffer shut the door behind. Surrounded by leather upholstery usually reserved for corporate executives and government officials, he sat in comfort. He was not surprised. Not all vehicles had been disabled, especially government and military. The driver was headed back to the airport. He'd been summoned directly to the DOD center. They needed answers from the research labs. Alex checked his wristwatch. It was an automatic motion. The time hadn't moved since the attack. The hour and minute hands were still locked in the same position. "Got the time?"

The driver stretched to reach into his coat pocket. Deliberately, he pulled out a pocket watch and read the current time. "Heirloom," he proudly announced. "Old fashioned, but still works." Three hours had passed since Alex had gone to sleep. He hoped the lab would have results. It would decide his next move.

Although his eyes were watching the scenery pass by, his brain was elsewhere. His thoughts were on the hostage craft. What a mess it'd turned out to be. His mind reached out to his daughter, the people, and the dead. Rage returned. The dead couldn't be helped. They were gone. Life cut short by the enemy. The people, the nation, his daughter, must be saved. Renewed hatred for the Serpent surfaced. "I'll get you," he muttered.

DHS HEADQUARTERS

"What's the verdict?" It was Barrister calling attention. His audience was the lab coats. The first satellite link had just been brought on line. The department was hurriedly connected with the tactical center at the Dulles airport. Primary was established with the national laboratories. Sandia scientists had assembled on the distant end. They were on hold for the head of the homeland department to come on line.

"Bad news," the speaker, head of Sandia was all scientist—all facts. His team had just finished the preliminary spectrum analysis from the enhanced photography previously sent on the wire. "It's a pathogen," he reported, "worst kind…waterborne protozoa family." It was critical information. It was alarming news. "New strain."

"What exactly is it," Barrister cut in, "we're looking for? How do we neutralize it?"

"Don't know. We're still working."

The laboratory's preliminary analysis had unveiled a waterborne agent identified as pathogenic microorganisms. Waterborne, if released, was directly transmitted into the body from contaminated drinking water. Alex drew a parallel from what he knew about biology with what the nation was facing.

A pathogen was a biological agent causing disease or illness to its human, animal, or plant host. Some pathogens, such as the bacterium Yersinia Pestis, which may have caused the Black Plague, the Variola virus, and the Malaria protozoa have been responsible for massive casualties throughout the ages.

In modern times, most people were familiar with the HIV virus, already infecting millions. Along similar lines was the SARS virus. Today, while many medical advances had been made to safeguard against infection by pathogens through the use of vaccinations, antibiotics, and fungicide, pathogens continued to threaten human life. No known preventative was available even though some antidotes had been developed.

"Foster?" Barrister called.

"Here," the familiar voice boomed from the background.

"Who's liaison with DOD and the labs?"

"Bauer," was the comeback.

"But…but he's civilian…" There were several objections. Most came from the military.

"I want him on the team, and," Foster insisted, "that's final."

"Don't like it." It was a disgruntled response from the CIA. "Only take orders from JCS."

"He'll be the Point of Contact for this operation," Hank held steadfast, "that's final…go ahead, Alex."

Alex was reluctant to accept the responsibility. A civilian in charge of government organizations spelled trouble. There were many agents in the field representing the various organizations—the FBI, CIA, DCA, DIA, and military Intel. Despite being forced to report to the DHS, many still struggled with internal conflicts. Putting Bauer as liaison would be difficult, but it'd get results. Foster trusted him.

Alex, notwithstanding resistance, had been volunteered. He didn't like it. He was never much for politics and power plays. He'd been successfully avoiding those through most of his career. *Why start now?* He'd only be miserable, but, because of the critical state the nation was in, reluctantly, he conceded. "How's the FBI doing?" He took a shot to test responses.

"Agents report suspicious activities on the West Coast, Sacramento." It was the head of the FBI. "Craft had other stopovers, right?" Based on the estimated flight pattern Bauer had reported, FBI analysis suggested Denver, but that hadn't been confirmed. Anti-terrorist teams had been rushed to the suspected sites. They were made up from various tactical defense detachments including the Air Force's AFSOC,[70] Navy Seals, and DELTA Force. Reports were still marginal. Communication was still out in many sectors.

---

[70] Air Force Special Operations Command.

TACTICAL ACTION CENTER

Dulles Airport had turned into the busiest place on the Eastern Seaboard. Mobile units had arrived from every conceivable division made up of military, paramilitary, patriots, and general citizen volunteers. Every effort was directed towards search and rescue, infrastructure repair, and communication restoration. Repair crews had been busy for days to get vehicles repaired. Emergency and mobile command had priority. Support teams were dispatched. More arrived by the hour. Temporary news feed gave coverage as well, although most had no links to the outside world. Relayed through repeater stations, much was transmitted via microwave line of sight from ground towers.

"They want Bauer." The call was relayed from the negotiation team. It reached the head of counter-terrorism, the CIA. "Where is he?" It was Harry Carter talking with the DI. His deputy for intelligence was on location. The order was issued by the jihad leader. He'd refused to negotiate with anyone else.

"What?" The backup line quality was poor. "Repeat." Most of the conversation was lost. It had to be repeated by shouting.

"Find Bauer…dammit!"

The space around the Airbus had been cleared. The order was "fifty meter" clearance. The demand was met, but not until threats were made to blow up the cargo. The threat was real. It not only would affect the people in the Dulles region, but D.C. and every other location in the wake of the contaminated cloud. Although the virus had been identified as waterborne protozoa, there was enough moisture in the air to release lethal dosages to the ground if the device was detonated.

Ten minutes earlier, Foster's staff limo was waiting by the Sheraton entrance. It took only minutes for Alex to reach the airport. Agents were expecting him. "This way." He was hastily guided to the Airbus and up the ramp. An agent banged on the door. It opened slightly. A face appeared. The gap widened. It was the jihad leader. Flanked by his lieutenants, he appeared in full view.

"Alex," he motioned with a royal gesture to his former partner, "step up."

Alex immediately spotted his daughter. She was guarded by the terrorist squad. Although her hands and legs were tied, she seemed unharmed. "Daddy," she stammered, "I'm sorry."

"Not your fault." Alex threw a warning glance at Hammad before rushing to her side. He was fuming. His eyes pierced into him. "If you harm her," he spat at him, "I will tear your body apart limb by limb." He'd seek the most extreme punishment. Killing was not in his character, but when pushed against the wall, he'd come out fighting. Obviously, based on the extremists' past, fairness was not on the jihadists' agenda. He'd seen enough decapitation videos of their many executions. Mercy killings they were not. She may have a chance as long as he held negotiations in a civilized manner. He went right to business. "What do you want?"

The demand was clear. "Fuel, food for my team, immediate release of the craft, and clear airspace."

"Can't guarantee it," Alex shook his head, "but I'll try." He did not have the power, or the authority. "I need time," he stalled.

"Time," was the resolute response, "is something you do not have." Hammad, halting and deliberate, spoke in a familiar oriental tone of voice. In a swift motion, the jihad leader activated a trigger. With the push of a button, the electronic circuit set in motion a timer only he was able to stop. "Thirty minutes."

Alex shot a pleading glance at Tracy. *Forgive me.* He didn't have to explain. She understood. He'd do his best to get her free. Automatic barrels pressed against his back, he was shoved from the craft. He was forced down the ramp.

The body of an FBI agent followed, thrown from the ramp. Medics were rushing up. It was too late to save his life. The agent had been dead for hours. Alex was surrounded. Members from every agency wanted to get briefed. The time allocated to organize the demands was impossible.

"Please hurry." Alex was facing Foster. If anybody could bring the demands together it was him. He had the power. He had the authority.

"Not up to me." Foster was stalling. Alex could see the man's thoughts grinding. Lives were at stake. On the one side were half a dozen hostages, on the other, a hundred thousand citizens, maybe more. It would be an easy choice in some nations. In nations where compassion was not high priority, the hostages could be sacrificed. Not here. This nation was built on democracy. And with it came benevolence, passion, and compassion for the human being. The forefathers saw to it with "Liberty, freedom, and preservation of individual rights for every citizen." It was guaranteed by the Constitution. The choice was clear and simple. "Defend, shield, and protect every living soul."

"Please," Alex urged, "time's running." Foster was interrupted by the head of the FBI. The man came to his rescue. He would share the responsibility he faced.

"You know the demands!" He was not a happy man. His face showed it. "What's keeping you?" He seemed a man of action. From his perspective, there was no option. The lives of his people were on the line. Every agent on his team carried its weight in gold. They knew it. They depended on him. There was a trust in the community. The bond reached through all ranks. From the new recruit in the field to the seasoned agent seated at the HQ's desk, they gave their unwavering trust to the shield. "Let's get rolling."

"Okay." Foster made the decision. His raised arm called for action. The motion said it. "Move out." He shot Alex a quick glance. A sign of empathy swept the eyes of the usually stern faced commander. His silent lips projected one word, "Tracy."

CONFEDERATE AIR FORCE

Wesley "Wes" Simmons sat in the cockpit of the Flying Fortress. The seat felt comfortable. It should. He'd sat in it for a lifetime. The worn leather had formed perfectly around his butt and back. The craft was on its return flight. He'd been flying troops and cargo to the coast. At the moment, he was listening in on his crew. They were chatting on the in-board "Birdman" frequency. Birdman was the assigned call sign for the fortress. The subject was about the mission just accomplished. To be heard, crewmembers had to shout over the steady drone generated by four Wright, turbo-supercharged radial "Cyclone" engines.

In today's flyer's world, this type of communication would be unacceptable. Pilot crews wore the latest head and radio gear technology provided. Sealed earpieces filtered out most of the engine noise. Frequencies were so sophisticated only the most sensitive equipment picked up the radio signals. It wasn't the case here. As a matter of fact, the crew still wore the traditional uniform and leather helmets from sixty years ago. Dictated by the code of honor, it was part of the legacy tradition.

Wes pressed his body into the contours of the chair. *Soon,* he contemplated, *I won't be around.* Getting high up in age, in today's world, he'd have been retired long ago. Over the past decade, most of his generation had passed on. Only a few diehards were left from the annals of World War II. "Hell," he muttered, "there aren't enough left to even hold the next reunion." Tears came to his eyes. He'd felt so lonely since Margaret went on. She'd been the cornerstone in his life. She was the reason he'd survived the big war.

A century ago, it seemed, flying non-stop missions over Germany's defense lines had taken its toll. Most of his buddies did not survive the daily grind of war. *Damned Messerschmitt and Fuckers had their field days.* The latter in actuality was a Focke-Wulf (better known as Butcher Bird), the most feared fighting machine for its time. It had been a game of numbers. Unfortunately, in the air, the odds were in favor of the enemy. The B-17 and B-24, flying in formation by the thousands, crossing into enemy territory like a cloud of migrating birds, were exposed to the fiery carnage of enemy fighters. If the crew got lucky, the armed cargo was dropped before the craft was shot out of the air.

For most of his buddies it was a one-way mission. Enemy fighters only had to come up from below to seek out their target. And the targets were many. Flying fortresses were vulnerable and exposed below the belly. On every mission, they fell out of the sky by the hundreds and with them, their crews.

He considered himself lucky to have survived and lived this long. Despite the constant danger, he missed those days. But that was long ago. The war was still vivid in his mind, but the details had faded into history. Hell, he couldn't even remember the names of his crew even though the haggard war worn faces were still imprinted in his mind. He inhaled deeply to shake the sadness from the memory. "What's the ETA?"

"Thirty minutes," his navigator replied.

The crew flying today was all new. Although they were from another generation, he had recruited them nevertheless. A generation to which he had a difficult time relating, they were dedicated to these dated birds. They were proud to be part of history, a history quickly waning. "What's gonna happen after I'm gone?" He'd asked the question many a time. *There's nobody left to teach new recruits. Probably junk the fleet.* Sooner or later, the old had to give way to the new. Even with him. *Handwriting's on the wall. Imagine,* the aging mind was jogging his memory, *Commemorative Air Force*. He was still furious about the name change.

In 2002, under much protest, the Confederate Air Force was forced to adopt a new name. Many outsiders felt the legacy name was confusing. It would not accurately reflect the purpose of today's organization. Fundraising efforts put on the pressure. Due to a move of political correctness, "Confederate" was considered offensive to some.

"Descending to ten thousand," the copilot announced. He'd reduced the throttle to accommodate the new altitude. The craft slowly descended to its final destination, Dulles Airport. Today was no different.

DHS HEADQUARTERS

"Let me get this straight." Even as callused as Barrister was, he could not believe what he'd just been told. He knew that all conversation, whether business or private, was recorded. To get the record straight he had it repeated. "Release the terrorists?" After all the damages they'd caused to the nation? "Let them go?"

"That's right," John Hanson, director for intelligence, NRO, emphasized once more. "Give 'em what they want."

"You can't be serious." He was baffled. "What about the policies...the ideals...national integrity?" He felt betrayed. No wonder the nation was in trouble. "Every Tom, Dick, and Harry can just waltz in and demand the sky." *May sound like a cliché,* he thought in retrospect, *but holds true to the bone.* "It's your ass on the line," Barrister threw back. He sure didn't want to go down. This was serious. His entire career, one he'd so assiduously dedicated to the defense of the nation, could be destroyed in an instant.

"I'm not making up the orders," Hanson insisted. "Besides," he stressed, "I don't have to sweat it."

"Right," Barrister agreed, "you people don't exist." The NRO was the nation's most obscure organization. A top-secret organization, it was uncommon knowledge to most citizens.

The NRO was a branch of the Department of Defense. The Director for the NRO was appointed by the Secretary of Defense. Traditionally, the position was given to either the Undersecretary of the Air Force or, in some cases, the Assistant Secretary of the Air Force for Space OPS. The majority of the work force was private corporate contractors, with a limited, but unaccountable, budget. To supplement the force, the NRO was also staffed by personnel from the CIA, NSA, DIA, and military services.

The agency had directorates for SIGINT,[71] IMINT, and Advanced Systems and Technology sectors. In plain English, the NRO designed, built, and operated the nation's reconnaissance satellites. NRO products, provided to an expanding list of customers such as the Central Intelligence Agency and the Department of Defense, could warn of potential trouble spots around the world, help plan military operations, and monitor global environmental changes. As part of the 16-member Intelligence Community, the NRO played a primary role in achieving information superiority for the U.S. government and Armed Forces.

"Get with the local SWAT to 'Stand Down,'" Hanson ordered over the radio phone.

Barrister leaned back in the leather upholstered, posh office chair. He wasn't about to jump on the order just given. He didn't follow orders easily. With him seated at the top of the Intel chain of command, although he'd been recent elected, it should be him dishing out commands. *But,* he rationalized, *everybody reports to somebody, even the president. By the way,* he surmised, *where is he these days? Should put the burden on him.* But, due to the immediate crisis on hand, Barrister thought better.

---

[71] SIGINT - Signals Intelligence is intelligence gathering by interception of signals. IMINT - Imagery Intelligence is an intelligence gathering discipline which collects information via satellite and aerial photography.

Presently, he fished for his mobile, but tossed it on the table with disgust after he realized that digital communication was still out. *Damned gadgets,* he thought with disgust. Instead, he reached for the radio receiver to call the crisis center. "Give me SWAT command," he bellowed into the receiver, demanding immediate attention.

He sat for a few seconds, waiting out the silence. When a voice appeared, he gave the order, "Stand down...repeat...stand down! Give 'em what they asked for, fuel, crew, airspace, and whatever."

DULLES INTERNATIONAL

The jihad force was stationed by the portholes, keeping watch. The lieutenants, Rashid Abu and Shakir Murad, were pacing the aisles. Hammad was seated in first class. He shot an occasional glance at Tracy. Bound by the wrists, she was forced into the next seats, as were the agents.

She could feel his piercing eyes. They were fixated on the contours of her body. "Your father has done well," the Serpent picked up the conversation. His voice was not without admiration. "It is only a shame," he patted her leg, "that he's on the side of the enemy." She lifted her head in his direction. It was done with deliberation. Her face reflected her present condition.

"If eyes could kill," his grin lingered on her, "I would be a dead man."

"You're already a dead man." Her eyes contained hatred. Projected at him, he didn't seem to notice. Aside from the current situation, Tracy had to admire him. He was not an unattractive guy. As a matter of fact, if it were not for the pronounced grin permanently carved into his face, he could be considered handsome. It was only now that she noticed the scar.

He slowly pursed his full lips in response. "Death, my dear," he accentuated, "is our savior." His eyes pierced into her. "It is not a sacrifice. It is the ultimate salvation for people like us." He paused expectantly. "Well?"

"Why would I talk to you?" She lifted her bound hands. "They hurt." Her wrists had taken on a purple hue. The plastic tie wraps cut into her flesh. She deliberately challenged his authority.

"If you promise to behave," he yielded, "I will have them removed." His hand went in the air. He snapped his fingers. A lieutenant rushed up. "Take them off." Finally, her hands were free. She rubbed her wrists profusely, feeling circulation rush back through her veins. "Tell me about Alex." He checked the time on his wristwatch. There were twenty minutes left in the ultimatum. He leaned back in the comfort of first class seating. "What makes him tick?" It was obvious he was expecting a response in return for freeing her bound hands. "I only knew him briefly through business. He is a worthy adversary."

"If I may correct you," she challenged, "in my country, you are the adversary."

"That is a matter of opinion…circumstances, don't you think?" His eyes were prying at hers. He went on to say, "My people have suffered for too long. They have been unjustly suppressed by your world. It was only a matter of time before we changed the balance of power. The day of reckoning has come. You are witnessing history being made. Now," he questioned her again, "what about Alex?"

"Dad," she said with great pride, "is a warrior." She flung a strain of hair from her face. "A warrior in his own way." She had admired him as long as she could remember. He had molded her in ways no mother could. He had shaped her life to be a reflection of his. Although he would never admit it, deep down, she felt it was a paternal desire to carry on the genes in a male offspring. "Your so called people," taking a deliberate pause, she shot a glance at the lieutenants, "were not the only ones experiencing hardship. Most nations, most people at one time or other, have." In her dad's time, he saw hardship for the Jewish people, the ally nations, as well as local citizens digging out from a world war, an unprecedented war. Since then, there had been many other conflicts, major and minor. With hardship, people endured. "Who're you to judge?"

"In all fairness," Hammad replied, "with him being foreign born," there was a quizzical look on his face, "how did he penetrate the inner circles of the government?"

She sensed he was prodding for information. "Don't know." *No way will he get anything out of me.* "You'll have to ask him." She shot him a defiant glance. "You'll get your chance." There was sudden chatter in the back of the cabin. Hammad was interrupted by a lieutenant. They were talking in a tongue she did not understand. It was alarming. She wanted to get away, as far away as possible. To be more comfortable, she propped her body up on the armrest. Her head rested against the bulkhead.

The cabin was doused in semi-darkness. At the onset of negotiations, window shades had been drawn by the terrorists. Hostages were kept purposely in the dark. It would provide leverage in favor of the attackers. Tracy edged her hand toward the lower end of the shade. She had to find out the conditions outside the craft. Slowly, she lifted the shade a fraction. It allowed enough of a viewing angle to see the tarmac below.

She got enough of a peek to assess the status. The tarmac was swarming with local law enforcement and anti-terrorist teams. She had caught a glimpse of uniforms identifying the various organizations. On hand were SWAT, the FBI, and DELTA. There was also, she assumed, Green Beret Special Forces. She thought she'd even recognized Brooks standing next to a familiar build. *Impossible!* Her heart began thumping wildly. *Could it be? It is!* In an instant she'd recognized the face of her life. *Brian.* Her heart skipped with joy. Her mind began churning with ideas—ideas to get away from here.

She caught a reflection in the window. It was an FBI agent behind her seat. He gestured at his bound hands. He knew her hands had been freed. She gave him a quick wink just as Hammad noticed the bright light beam penetrating the cabin. He shook his head at her. "Naughty, naughty," he said, then pulled the shade shut. She reclined once more.

Minutes later her thoughts were interrupted. There was knocking on the nearby exit door. Hammad jumped to his feet. He shot her a quick glance. She read the meaning. *Watch it. Don't do anything stupid you might regret.* He was followed closely by his lieutenants. Her spirits were renewed. With anticipation, her eyes rested on the entrance. The exit opened. Two uniforms were allowed in. From their appearance, it was a relieve pilot and copilot. *Dammed negotiators!* A silent curse escaped her lips. *Giving in to their demands.* Her spirits sank. The exit shut close. Two minutes later, the sound of jet engines filled the cabin.

The craft began to move. *Oh no!* She realized the ordeal was not over. The craft's departure clearance could only mean one thing: certain death, getting shot from the air. She was petrified by the thought. The farther away the terrorists got, the slimmer her, and the other hostage's, chances would be for rescue. *Do something*, she commanded herself. Her eyes rapidly darted around the space. She was searching for an object, anything with which to defend herself.

Hammad, in the wake of the pilots, had disappeared inside the cockpit. Tracy was counting the rest of his forces. Armed with automatics, they were pacing the aisles. She carefully opened the window shade again. It gave her partial vision of the outside. Down below, as the craft picked up speed, she watched the rescue force fall behind. Armored cars flanked the moving craft, trying to match the craft's speed. The Airbus approached the end of the runway. It slowed, then gradually moved into takeoff position. *Do something.* Tracy was furious with herself. No guards were presently in sight. She got to her feet. She checked the overhead bin. *Nothing.* Only a few pillows and blankets were tucked in one corner. *The galley.* If she could get there, she might find something, but what? A knife...coffee pot...bottles, anything to cut the plastic straps from the bound FBI.

Her gaze fell on the agents behind her seat. She was about to move when one shot her a warning, but strong hands forced her back into the seat. A jihad lieutenant had planted his body beside her. He forced her to strap in. Reluctantly, she relented. A sigh of disgust escaped her lips. She was angry with herself. *Missed my chance.*

She could hear it. The jet engines were winding up to full speed. The craft began to move. It gained momentum. The ground was rushing by at an increasing rate. In another few seconds it would reach takeoff speed. What followed was the familiar thump from multi-quad wheels leaving the ground. In an air of despair, Tracy slowly exhaled. Her mind sought out the distance ahead. She relinquished herself to her unavoidable fate, death.

FLYING FORTRESS

"Better call in," Wes instructed the copilot. The sprawling complex of Dulles International was panning into view. It would only be minutes before the flight would terminate. Crossing the continent in a super fortress was a day's work. Where today's jetliners would only require four hours from coast to coast, these prop driven craft labored many more hours.

"Birdman," he requested, "Birdman final approach." The radio dial was set at 120.250, the tower center.

"Birdman," approach control came back, "got you on radar." There was a short break. "What's your intention?"

"Request landing clearance."

"Switch to 132.450," the operator demanded, "hold flight path." It was standard procedure to switch from approach to ground control. Unusual was the holding pattern.

"Roger." *Wonder what that's all about?* "Put us on hold?" With squinting eyes, the copilot leaned forward. His fingers reached for the frequency dial. He twisted the old-fashioned selector knob to the designated setting. Then something caught his immediately attention. It'd turned silent in the cockpit. They all heard it. There was profuse chatter on the ground. Wes switched to onboard PA for the crew to listen in on. What they heard was not just the ordinary ground control interchange with other flights. It was command and control demands issued between law enforcement, airport control, and other authorities shouting orders. It quickly became obvious there was an unusual situation in progress.

Wes picked up the mic to reach ground control. After eight hours of flight time the fuel gauges were nearing empty. "What's the emergency?" He was concerned. With his craft put on hold, he needed status. "Running low on fuel," he checked in.

"Hostage situation," the operator reported. "Jihad has taken control. Terrorist craft on hold at end of runway." There was a brief pause, then the operator returned, "Do not approach runway…repeat, do not land."

"What's the nearest alternate?" Wes had turned to his copilot who'd already pulled the regional map from the case.

"National and Andrews," he replied. "Don't know their status." One was civilian, the other military. Chances were the military was in better shape.

"Try Andrews," Wes instructed.

He turned his attention back to IAD ground. It became clear to him that the airspace had been taken over by a hostile force. Apparently, a jihad group had taken command over a craft demanding takeoff clearance. *Imagine,* he contemplated in silence, *terrorists take hold of United States air space.* He could hardly fathom the possibility. Anger he hadn't felt for a long time welled up from the depths of his withered body. Last time, he recalled, had been during the final missions over Dresden when his convoy was attacked by the then dreaded Messerschmitt 262.

The ME-262 was the world's first operational jet-powered fighter aircraft. The craft, much faster than the Spitfire, their usual fighter escort, had appeared out of nowhere. With its superior flight and firepower, after eliminating the British escort fighters, it had had a field day with the Fortresses. He and his crew never had a chance to retaliate for or pay retribution to the many Army/Air Core buddies he'd lost in that battle. *Never again,* he'd vowed, *will I succumb to an enemy.* The rage he felt turned to fury. He couldn't help it. The feeling had been suppressed and pent up for too long. *What do I have to lose? They won't put an old man in stockade. Hell,* a possibility crossed his mind, *if I'm lucky,* he gloried, *I'll go out in flying colors.*

He gently squeezed on the flight controls. It let his copilot know he'd taken over the flight then pushed the talk button. "Smokey," he yelled into the intercom. A young airman on the crew jumped to attention. It was not often that the seasoned WWII veteran called on him. "Here's your chance."

"What, sir?"

"Take up position." Wes was serious. *I'll teach them!* "Lower dorsal cage."

The crew was seated in back along the catwalk, listening in on the pilot to ground dialogue. They could not believe their ears. All eyes focused on Smokey, the gunner. Sure, the fighting equipment had been kept operational, but only for show. It gave them bragging rights during visitor day. "This thing operational?" some eager youngster would ask. "Sure thing," would be the proud response by the tour guide.

"Gear ready?" Wes called back.

"Yes sir," a shocked Smokey replied, "but I've never shot it."

"Today," a proud Simmons informed him, "is your day."

Smokey shrugged his shoulders. He was unsure what to expect. "Must be a joke," he muttered to the crew seated along the catwalk. He jumped to his feet, his face showing a hint of fright. He had never been in a combat situation. He turned to his buddies for an answer. "You can do it," the crew chief, standing alongside, encouraged him. It was more of a gesture than spoken words. Smokey carefully pushed his way towards the lower dorsal turret. The hatch was located at the midsection of the fuselage. He opened the latches that kept the dome secure. Space was tight, very tight. He squeezed his lanky body into the glass-bottom cage and pulled the hatch cover over. He was on his own.

The steady drone of the craft suddenly took on a high pitch. The crew felt the immediate change in the craft. The fuselage strained hard under the immense pressure. Wesley Simmons had pushed the super fortress into a steep dive. Smokey took it as a cue. His hands tightened around the control arms. Finger on the triggers, he was getting ready to strafe.

AIRBUS A-330

Tracy's body was pressed against the backrest. She felt the g-force from the acceleration push against her back. Seconds later the craft left the tarmac. They were airborne. Leaving the hostage scene behind, they were allowed to open the window shades. The pilot took the craft into a departure turn then headed east. *New York's the final destination,* she guessed. The craft was steadily climbing. Seated next to her was the jihad fighter. He stirred. She sensed his eyes staring at her. He was mocking her. His body was halfway turned towards her. His head was facing her square on. Tracy avoided his stare. His eyes shifted downward to her breasts. "You virgin?" he prodded in heavy-accented Arabic.

Must be one of few phrases they learn, she guessed. "Not a chance." She pulled her blouse tighter across the shoulders. Her eyes reflected the repulse she felt. He only grinned and leered at her. His eyes pierced into hers. "We win," he jeered.

She tried her best to avoid his stare. Her eyes darted across the first class cabin. Only blank stares reflected from the bound agents. Then she spotted it. It appeared through the opposite porthole, slowly creeping into her field of vision. It started as a small speck. At first, she thought it was a bird. That's what her mind registered. Then, the analytical part set in. *Bird? Impossible. No bird,* her mind rationalized, *could keep up the speed.*

The speck changed direction. It rapidly grew in size. It came directly at them. She recognized the object. It was a super fortress bearing down on them. Her eyes widened with surprise. The object grew to immense size. It filled the entire porthole. She turned to face the terrorist staring at her. "You lose!" she spat out triumphantly just before an ear-piercing impact.

Moments earlier, the jihad fighter had caught the sudden change in her expression. He watched her shrink into her seat. Her body was pressed against the cabin wall. At first, his eyes reflected puzzlement then turned to alarm. He had sensed something was about to go terribly wrong. And that something was behind him. He broke his gaze from hers. He tried to shift his body, but froze in midair. A hail of .50 caliber bullets slammed into the side of the craft. It sounded like the craft had hit a wall of ice pellets.

With piercing force, a tracer bullet found its target, a soft target. It'd entered his back. Almost instantly, it was followed by a live round. When it broke his skin, the shiny metal tip from a fifty mm shell tumbled wildly through his body. It cut a deadly swath through organs, muscles, and tissue as it came to rest against his sternum. The live target suddenly contracted. Blood welled up in a sudden gush of red liquid. There was a violent cough. It was followed by a stream of blood squirting from the fighter's throat. It splattered across Tracy's face. She raised her hands to protect herself. His upper body slammed into her. His back was arched in pain. A trail of phosphorous smoke slowly curled up towards the ceiling. His clothes had caught on fire, filling the cabin with caustic smoke. An alarm went off. It added to the confusion. The fighter's body, in a silent cry for victory, collapsed on itself. His spirit left the dead body. Only Muhammad would know its final destination.

FLYING FORTRESS

Back at the super fortress, Wes was elated. For the first time in years, he couldn't recall how many, he was filled with the immensity of the fighting sensation. A surge of adrenaline rushed through his aging body. He felt alive. He felt reborn. His eyes swept across his hands tightly gripped around the controls. He could almost see the skin glow. They then shifted to the horizon. They were seeking out the enemy. There, five thousand feet below, the Airbus was just leaving the ground. After takeoff, he watched it pull into a tight turn. His mind registered, *There's my chance. Flank's exposed.* He pushed full throttle. He aimed the fortress for the exposed flank. It rushed in at full speed. "Smokey," he yelled into the intercom, "take 'em out."

His heart jumped with joy when a stream of tracers left the dorsal dome. It missed the target. "Get focused," he yelled into the headset, hoping Smokey would hear. He was rapidly closing in on the enemy. Fractions later, there was a second burst. This time, a stream of bullets slammed into the target. Wes aimed for the craft's midsection. "You won't get away," he yelled, "not this time!" His mind fixated on one thing. *Get the enemy.* Seconds later the super fortress rammed the Airbus. It'd missed the exposed flank by a few feet. Instead, the fortress skidded over the top of the Airbus.

The force tore the dorsal off its mountings. The next second, the turret was torn from the fortress. It spun wildly through the air. Smokey held on to the control stick, finger locked on the button, firing. The world outside was spinning out of control. He stared straight ahead. The last vision in this world, for Smokey, was the stream of .50 caliber rounds drilling into the enemy. A broad smile was carved into the usually serious face. He died knowing he'd accomplished something extraordinary serving the country.

Wes was shaken back to reality by the crushing sounds of metal. *The crew!* It suddenly dawned on him there were other lives at stake. For him to end this way was one thing, but taking with him an entire crew was not fair. Most were young lives. To clear his head, he slapped hard against the side of his leather cap. It cleared his vision. He watched the ground rush up. In the spirit of the fight he'd completely forgotten about the copilot. He shot a quick glance at him. A pleading face stared back at him.

In one swift move, Wes cut the power on all four engines. Under combined strength, pilot and copilot pulled hard on the controls. The craft responded ever so slowly. There was no second chance with the tail torn off. The craft's body strained hard against the forces of gravity. The nose slowly inched up. Ahead, the blue horizon crept into view. It would be a straight shot.

"Brace for impact." The crew heard him yell out. In a last ditch effort Wes pushed down hard on the flap lever. It was enough to give the heavy body a few feet clearance. Seconds later, the craft plowed into the ground. The impact tore away wings and engines. There was no explosion. The fuel tanks had gone dry. In the midst of the green, lush countryside outside of Dulles, the craft slithered to a rest. Seconds later, a hundred yards out, still spewing bullets, Smokey's spinning wheel crashed into the field. Wes thought he'd spotted the young soldier's broad smile as he still gripped the firing controls. He was immensely proud of the young fella.

AIRBUS A-330

After their departure, Hasan Hammad had slid his frame back into the navigator seat. From this position he had complete visual and command over the pilots and craft. He was watching the pilots' every move. He knew enough about flying to recognize proper execution of instruments and controls. Departure had gone well despite the unforeseen delays with the hostage situation. "Just part of battle," he'd told his stressed lieutenants. "You must adapt to changes."

The American authorities had complied with his demands on all counts. *Life is good.* He could continue with the mission as planned. His timepiece registered a three-hour delay. *Not bad for a hostage scene.* The altimeter recorded two thousand feet and climbing when the alarm went off.

"Air leak in the cabin." The copilot reacted to the alarm, pushing the reset switch. No change. The indicator kept on pulsing. Fractions later, there was a sudden rush of air escaping the cockpit. A bullet had penetrated the left side of the cabin. It left a jagged hole just below the windshield. From there, it'd continued on its destructive path into the pilot's chest. It left a gaping exit wound. Minute traces of blood droplets splattered through the cockpit. The force of impact jolted the pilot's body from the seat. Hammad's eyes followed the trail of destruction.

Next, he felt the full force of the impact. He was too stunned to react. It came in the form of a gigantic shadow, much like a killer whale on its final kill. It bit off the tailfin. The super fortress had just torn into the Airbus. The cutting force felt horrendous. The craft shook violently. Its path was forced downward.

"Control's gone," the copilot, who'd noticed the pilot slump into the controls, shouted. Taking control, he'd realized the tail rudder was out. From here on out, to steer the craft would have to be through engine controls. To his luck, the horizontals still responded. "We can make it down," he yelled to the back of the cockpit.

"Keep flying," the voice responded. It was direct. It was a deadly command. The copilot could not believe his ears. He tore his view from the instruments, spinning around to face the terrorist. He was staring at the barrel end of a semi-automatic. *I'm dead,* his mind registered. His eyes touched on the dead pilot. He knew the faith of the previous flight crew. "Controls are out!" he yelled. "Don't you get it?" His face was contorted in defiance.

"Keep flying," a grim face insisted.

The copilot saw no option. No way out. The opening of the barrel was pressed against his left temple. "Fuck you," he lashed out, "damn foreigner." *I'm already dead. What difference does it make? I won't beg.* With a sudden move, he cut the engine power and forced the nose down. His focus shifted to the emergency landing ahead. Ignoring the menace in back, he decided, "To hell with you." Pushing down hard on the right rudder, he tried to make it back to Dulles Airport, but there was no response. Then it struck him; in an instant he realized, "Tail rudder's gone." Frantically, fumbling to reach the checklist, a second later he changed his mind. There was no time to read. He'd have to rely on his memory. From here on out, his every move had to be by the book, as he'd learned and practiced it on the simulator.

Left hand clutching at the controls, he had to make all the moves alone. *Reduce engine power, right side.* "Come on, dammit…come on…." With only one hand available to move two sets of control levers, he applied power to one engine first then compensated for lateral drifts with the other. The craft finally responded imperceptibly slow. His eyes frantically followed the banking instruments. 180 turn—"Done." *What's next? Elevation trims.* "Done." The craft's nose responded. Unstable as it was, the nose rested on the distant target some miles ahead. *Next? Reduce left engine power.* The transponder reacted. The craft's nose finally stabilized. Through the distant haze ahead, he could make out IAD. Ever so slightly, the airport complex crept closer.

Next, his eyes sought out the landing gear. He pumped the manual lever. Seconds later, he felt it respond. It put too much drag on their speed. It slowed the craft into a stall. *Reduce flaps.* His heart was pounding, waiting. It took seconds for the craft to react. *There it is.*

Two minutes later the nose crossed the threshold. "Power." It was the signal to pull back all console levers. With both hands trained on the controls, he pulled hard. The two engines responded. Four sets of tires scourged the concrete. The craft sat down hard. It left a trail of burnt rubber smoke in their wake.

"Brakes." The craft slowed to a halt just short of the end of the runway. Spearheaded by a cluster of mobile defense forces, ground control and emergency vehicles were swarming in on the Airbus. Exhilarated, the copilot inhaled deeply. *Made it!* His body swelled with pride, short of self-indulgence. Uncertain what to expect, he slowly turned to face the enemy. The spot was vacant. The jihad leader had rushed from the cabin. The copilot exhaled with tremendous relief. What followed would be out of his hands.

Back in first class, with the assault from above, air masks had dropped from their restraints. They were not needed. Cabin pressure had already equalized with the outside air. The dead body rested heavily on Tracy's chest. Something was poking into her ribs. It was his combat knife. She quickly pulled it from his belt and pocketed it, then used every ounce of energy to push his body off of her. The dead body's hands released the grip it had on its weapon. Tracy tried to catch it. The AK-47 landed on the carpet by her feet. She rushed for the weapon. First time with her hands on an automatic weapon, she fumbled with the safety latch. "I can do this," she mumbled then rushed up the aisle, clutching the weapon. Her eyes caught movement ahead. She leveled the barrel and released a burst. The metal stock slammed hard into her right shoulder. The recoil forced the barrel upward. "Dammit!" She'd missed. The target had sought cover.

Her eyes caught a motion to her right. It was the FBI. An agent had rushed up to her. His hands were bound. She quickly cut the tie wrap with the knife she took from the dead jihad. His hands were free. There was an unexpected jolt. It knocked her to the floor.

The hard landing had ripped the knife from her hand. She grabbed a hold of it and tossed it to the agent. He sprang into action, freeing the rest of his force. They rushed for the passenger section. Their aim was the assailants gathered in the back of the craft.

A sound from the cockpit reached her ears. She turned in the direction. There, six feet away, poised in her direction, she came face to face with Hammad. He had pulled his semi. His aim was direct. It was leveled at her heart. Her eyes shifted from the barrel to his face. In its sphere was the frozen grin. She recognized the expression. It held one word. "Reckoning."

It was the gleam of recognition. She followed his facial expression. It happened in a split second. It'd changed from aspiration to respect to hatred, then quickly shifted to survival mode. He pulled the trigger. She expected an explosive sound. *Nothing.* The semi had jammed. It took seconds for Tracy to realize the misfire. Now, it was her turn to take a life. She was about to pull the trigger, but was stopped by the FBI. "Tracy," one shouted, "we need him alive!"

Her mind raged for vengeance. *Not fair!* The message reached her conscious state. *I want revenge.* In a split second, she evaluated the odds, and the consequences. Reasoning won. *Where's justice?* She slowly leveled the weapon at the floor. The agents rushed in, ready to kill.

Hasan Hammad, now identified as the Serpent, raised his weapon. He was uncertain. Facing multiple enemy weapons aimed at him, he quickly evaluated his options. It was not the reasoning for survival that won out. It was the cause for his people. In a halting motion, he handed over the weapon. Defeat projecting from the lean body. The glimmer in his eyes told another story. They were filled with hatred—hatred for the free world, hatred for the unjust, and hatred for his failure.

Greatly defeated, his pupils contracted into narrow slits, but not without the glimmer of hope. For the present, he succumbed to the inevitable, imprisonment, followed with torture, perhaps even death. His heart was filled with rage. His mind felt regret for his fallen comrades. *Allah,* in the midst of the ensuing turmoil his mind silently screamed out, *Insha'Allah!*

DULLES INTERNATIONAL

There was much haste in and around the craft in the following hours. Alex was among the first to board. His daughter rushed into his arms. She did not have to say much. Her looks told the story. He held her tight. He could feel her body shiver from her shoulders while his eyes absorbed the surroundings. They captured the bodies, the dead and the live then locked on the object of the search. *There he is. The Serpent.* He locked eyes with the captured, but they returned only an empty stare. "Come," Alex gestured. He pulled her from the carnage. "It's over."

Bodies were removed. Cargo was unloaded. With hands tied in back the captured were escorted to a waiting vehicle. Heavy-duty tie wraps were used. They were the preferred method to restrain a prisoner. It was an effective method. They were cheap. Despite being light in weight, they were secure.

"Which one's the Serpent?" Foster was curious.

"I'll give you one guess."

"One staring you down?"

"That's the one." It was still difficult for Alex to grasp his encounter with Hammad, former partner turned killer. *How can anyone turn this ruthless?* He glared at him. A stone cold stare was returned. "Wishes me dead."

"Formidable character." Foster shook his head then motioned Alex to follow. "Command center."

Earlier, speeding towards Dulles, Brian had just entered the toll road. The booths were empty. A few minutes more and he'd be at the airport. Up ahead his eyes caught movement. He had to squint against the bright sun. It was a magnificent sight.

He recognized the two craft. A B-17 was one, an A-330 Airbus another. "What the fuck?" He was stunned. *Dogfight?* He couldn't believe his eyes. Awe struck, he determined, "It is." He watched in fascination as one body chased the other with fiery streams of tracers leaping out. Then a second pass, another hail of bullets, quickly followed.

Spellbound, he slammed on the brakes and jumped from the vehicle to get a clear view. Just then, the titans clashed. "Another 9/11?" It was incredible. Visions of past images crossed his stunned mind. He jumped back in the vehicle and sped on.

He just witnessed the fortress slice through the Airbus. A shiny object tore from the first craft. Another broke loose in the second. He watched the turret spin through the air. The tail rudder followed. The guns were still firing. Tracers spiraled out in all directions.

Brian watched the pieces until they disappeared below the horizon. He had no clue Tracy was onboard one craft. The fortress hit first. Followed closely in its wake was the tail of the Airbus. It was carried by the wind much like a leaf in the autumn breeze. Last was the spinning cage skipping across the open field still spewing tracers and bullets. Brian had arrived at the Dulles Airport just as the Airbus landed. Without the rudder, it fishtailed wide, but made the ground short of a crash.

The tarmac was crowded with emergency vehicles and rescue people. He spotted the command center and head for it. Right away there were familiar faces.

"Brooks?" Brian acknowledged the DELTA fighter. "You here?"

"Everybody's here."

"Where's she?"

Brooks gestured in the direction of the Airbus. "Follow me." Both headed in the direction.

Brian was petrified. He had an ominous feeling. *Tracy?* He picked up the pace and rushed to the crash scene. Two emergency ramps popped from the craft. Agents jumped the slides. A mobile exit ramp had just arrived. It was pushed against a front cabin exit. Brian rushed up the steps. He was bumped upwards by a stream of search and rescue workers. He halted by the entrance. *There she is.* He spotted the face he'd missed so much. She was surrounded by agents. Her eyes darted from one to the other, then to the exit.

She'd spotted him. She tore away from the group. "Brian!" she yelled. Tears of joy were rolling down her cheeks. A second later they were clutched in each other's arms.

Over her shoulders, Brian spotted Alex. They acknowledged each other. "Good to see you." He allowed them the time, but was anxious to exit. He tapped Brian's shoulder. "Time to go."

Tracy wiped the tears from her face then opened her eyes. Through teary eyes, she made out her dad standing beside them. "Dad," she wailed, "I'm sorry."

"You're safe," he muttered, "that's all that counts."

"Seems like," she sighed, "every time I see you, I have to say 'I'm sorry.'"

"Come," he urged, "we have things to do."

Duffle slung over his shoulder, they met Brooks by the ramp who seemed anxious to depart. "Where're you headed?" Alex asked.

"The Fort," Scott made reference to Fort Belvoir located nearby, "as soon as transportation gets here." Supporting beltway operations for the government, mostly DOD, the Fort was a defense-related complex. It was home to many military and defense detachments. It coordinated mission deployments, operations management, and more sinister functions. Scott Brooks had been put in charge of leading the defense forces. He'd earned it. *What's the quickest way to gain recognition?* he'd say with a notion of self-indulgence. *Front lines.*

Soon, manned by a local guards unit, seemingly heavily armed, a light armored truck pulled up. Aside the standard side arm, additional armament issued these days was the M-16. An equal to the AK-47, it was the military's preferred weapon for assault operations. A cargo crew was busy loading the radioactive crate onto the truck bed. "Careful," the chief shouted more than once.

More commands were issued. The Sandia team had identified its contents. The defense team was alerted. "Relatively safe as long as the cylinders are intact." Technical explosive experts had assembled at the Fort. Minutes later the cargo was on its way. A team of chemical experts was on standby to receive the cargo. It was up to the NNSA team to neutralize its contents.

Alex, Tracy, Brian, and Scott had been standing near the command center. At the moment they were uncertain what direction to take. The center was busy with the detainees. The threat was eliminated. Everybody dear to him was safe.

"What's next?" Brian and Tracy were preparing to leave.

Scott just reappeared. Alex waved him over. He may have some news on the current conditions. "Prisoners?" Alex raised a concern. He hadn't seen any since they left the craft.

"Transport's on the way," Scott said. He was impatient as well. "What's keeping them?" There seemed to be a shortage of vehicles.

"Only been a few days," Brian reminded them. Vehicle repairs were slow, but well underway. Transportation finally showed. Two semi-trucks had just arrived. Orders were shouted. "Let's go…get hopping." Energized guardsmen jumped from the truck bed. Prisoners were hoarded onto the vehicles. The plan was to get them to a secure place.

"Bauer," a voice shouted. It was Foster rapidly approaching. Both Tracy and Alex turned towards the booming sound. "Need you." A few more strides brought him close. He spotted Tracy. His eyes brightened. He reached out to give her a hearty hug. "Glad you're safe." He quickly let go to face Alex. "Come," he ordered. "Debriefing."

They hastened for the mobile OPS center. Facing her, Foster indicated Brooks. "You go with him." She understood.

Tracy hopped into the cab of the trailing vehicle. Scott was driving one of the vehicles. The convoy was on the move. They were headed for the Fort. A sigh escaped her lips as she finally relaxed. Under Scott's protection, she would be in safe hands. *Only a few more hours,* she thought. She was longing for time to spend with Brian. She promised to make up much wasted time later. *But a shower first and something to eat.*

They entered the Dulles toll road. They were headed towards the beltway, and on to Belvoir, thirty some miles east.

CONVOY

"D.C. Tactical." It was his call sign. "Come in." Tariq Amman, First Lieutenant, mission coordinator for Jihad, cell D.C., had been monitoring the ether for days. Scanning the 1.6 through 30 MHz range of frequencies, an HF-SSB base station relentlessly searched the airwaves. The equipment was sophisticated and the latest on the market. It was a critical element to the mission. What made it so vital was the MILSPEC components used to harden the equipment. Being hardened made it not only durable against vibration and shock, but shielded the unit from destructive gamma rays. Developed for the U.S. military and law enforcement, sales for the units were closely monitored by the government, but there were ways around that, if you had the money. And money was no object for their cause. D.C. Tactical was not the only station operating the equipment. There were many more located in and around the United States.

"D.C. Tactical," Amman acknowledged. "Go."

"Freedom Base Alpha," the distant end responded. It was the code for Al Qaeda's global command base. With primary communication disabled over the U.S., the signal was relayed across a number of hops. Al Qaeda command and control operated with the complexity equaled only by the United States, Australia, Israel, and other modern defense systems. Today, the command data stream was routed via southern hemisphere satellites still in operation, relayed through Mexican ground stations, and then shot across the border on microwave.

"Mission urgent...action immediate...mobile dispatch..." the voice commanded. "Support units to IAD...intercept convoy. Liberate supreme commander." Amman could not believe his ears. *Head of Jihad penetrated the United States? Incredible!* But coming from the base, the order was specific.

"Roger." The local cell leader responded. His voice quivered with exhilaration. "Will do." His orders were immediate. The mobile response force was dispatched within minutes.

Fifteen minutes into the trip it happened. The convoy's lead driver yelled out, "What the hell?" His voice sounded more surprised than alarmed. It came on unexpectedly, but developed in rapid sequence. The incident was over in only minutes. The plot was carried out with military precision. It had been executed by the book.

The convoy had just approached the 45-B exit sign. A relatively tight turn, the lead driver had slowed to 35 mph to negotiate the McLean off ramp. The driver planned to turn south on 495, the Capital Beltway. They were waiting. Beneath the under pass, blocking the road, were several vehicles. In the lead was a light armored assault type vehicle armed with twin turret mounted machineguns. Several support vehicles swarmed in from the flanks. The approaching convoy was boxed in.

Rapid gunfire opened from both sides. The convoy was an uneven match for the top mounted machine turret perched on the armored vehicle. Guardsmen jumping from convoy trucks collapsed as soon as they hit the ground. Groaning bodies were sprawled across the concrete. Red puddles of blood collected on the road. Streams of bullets ricocheted off the concrete walls. Many found their targets.

At the onset of firing, the prisoners crouched low, hugging the truck beds. The driver of one vehicle was killed almost instantly.

Brooks had jumped from the cab of the lead van. He sought cover behind the carrier. Tracy crouched low in the seat of his vehicle. She had no weapon to defend herself. She witnessed the unfolding scene ahead. National guardsmen seeking cover were gunned down by hails of bullets. Then suddenly, the passenger side door was flung open. A face popped into view. It was the face she detested most.

"We meet again." It was Hasan Hammad grinning at her. He shoved a semi into her face.

"Not again," she groaned. "Didn't you get enough of me? I hate you!"

"In time," he scoffed with a foreboding grin, "you might begin to like me."

"There aren't enough days in the universe for that to ever happen." She glared at him.

"Out," he ordered her from the vehicle.

Tracy was shoved in the armored car.

"Move out," Hammad ordered.

The path ahead had been cleared. The driver stepped on the accelerator. The convoy with the armored escorts in the lead pulled out. The vehicles sped off, headed south on I-495. Left behind was Brooks in the company of the dead and the wounded.

Tracy took stock of what just happened. Scott was nowhere near. Even though she was skeptical of the man, he seemed to be of righteous caliber. *Could be on the convoy,* she hoped. Tracy was fuming with renewed rage but kept silent. She was sandwiched in between the attackers. She suspected the attackers were a local jihad cell. *Well organized,* she deduced. *Pull off an assault in the midst of the capital. Incredible.*

The hijacked convoy rounded the southern stretches of I-495. From there, it headed east. Springfield lay just ahead to the right. Minutes later Alexandria passed to the left. The lead vehicle prepared for exit. There was no one in pursuit. Communication was still sparse, and so was traffic. It was possible that neither military nor law enforcement had been alerted. Tracy faced a future of uncertainty again.

Ahead, parked off to the side, into view came what looked like a sixteen wheeler. The truck showed no markings. It was a standard interstate transporter for hauling containers. She watched the loading ramp being lowered. The armored vehicle containing Tracy and the lethal cargo was quickly guided up the ramp. The gates shut with a clang. Darkness fell over her. "Damn you," she spat into the silence. "I'll get even." With that, her thoughts were on the future with a promise to herself to never let her present situation be repeated.

She vowed revenge on every adversary trying to bring harm to her, to the citizens of the country, and the nations of the free world.

EGLIN AFB

"33rd Fighter Wing." The operator sounded harried. Ever since she arrived on the job this morning, the switchboard had been overloaded with calls. Nearest neighbor to Cuba, for SOUTHCOM, Eglin was the first line of defense. Its main mission was train, maintain, and support Air Force, Marine, and Navy pilots.

The 33rd, known as "Nomads" for its constant travel throughout the world, had a long and distinguished history. First activated at Roswell Army Air Field, New Mexico in 1947, the unit had served many conflicts. Most recent campaigns had been Desert Shield, Desert Storm, and the deployment to the shores of Egypt and Libya.

"Get me the squad commander." Tucker decided to check the current operational status of the base's fighting assets. To his dismay, he was told, "Nothing's flight worthy since the blackout." Electronics and aviation instruments were fried. Most craft had been dead-lined for maintenance and repairs. Replacements had been promised from Canada, but hadn't arrived yet.

"Can't help you," he was told in no uncertain terms. "Check with AAC."

Also headquartered at Eglin was the Air Armament Center. It had the ultimate responsibility to account for the base's flight and armament resources. With the air fleet grounded, so were the weapons systems. Maintenance crews were busy testing armament losses. When the EMP went off, it had triggered a pile of air-to-air missiles on hold for training deployment. Most of the ammo dump nearby went up into smoke including some HARM systems, air-to-surface missiles, miniature air-launched decoys, and sensor fused weapons. Small diameter bombs and high-speed anti-radiation missiles had been spared.

"Better get something in the air," Tucker ordered, "and fast." He was furious. His fury wasn't solely directed at Eglin, although he felt somebody was passing the buck. He realized the gravity of the situation after the attack on the nation's defense system, but this was ridiculous.

"What'd you want me to do?" the commander fired back. "Shit up craft?"

"No need to get vulgar." Tucker realized he was pushing, but what the hell; he had a situation on his hands. "Enemy's on the doorsteps and I got nothing to fend off."

"Sorry," the commander gave in, "we can't help you."

That's it? One attack on the nation and the rest of the world can waltz in just like that? "We'll see about that." Tucker slammed the receiver so hard it chipped the earpiece.

He was resolved to do something even if it meant taking up arms himself. He could feel the old fighting spirit well up within. *Why's everybody so complacent?* He was shaking his head in disbelief and grabbed the phone back. He wanted facts. He needed status. Foster came to mind. He dialed the Pentagon. The earpiece made a cut into his earlobe. He felt a warm trickle on his cheek. He wiped one sleeve across the face. He spotted the red droplets on the shirt. "First battle wound," he muttered, shaking his head.

THE PENTAGON

The switchboard had been swamped ever since he arrived at the office. Most calls came in from SOUTHCOM. *Tucker was right,* Foster concluded after getting continuous feedback, mostly from Air Force Intel. Fed by agents staged around the southern perimeters, Central America, and the Dominican Republic, information was coming in over the wire non-stop. "Big push out of Cuba," was the common consensus. It did not take much intelligence to realize their intention when the puzzle was pieced together. It was plain and simple. "All-out assault on the United States."

It may have sounded ludicrous to any command on U.S. soil, but to a nation desperate for economic survival, it was a clear choice. *They have nothing to lose. It's a one-time opportunity,* were some of his private thoughts about the facts when he picked up the call. He recognized the caller on the ID signature.

"Okay." The first thing out of Tucker's mouth was, "We're fucked."

"Not necessarily." Foster had an idea. It may have been a presumptuous thought, but it might just work. He clearly recalled prior talks he had had with Alex on the subject of transportation. When everything else had failed, it was Alex who brought it to his attention. *And look where we stand now?* It turned out to be the backbone during the worst crisis the nation had seen. "Confederate Air Force."

"You kiddin'?" Tucker fumed. "They'd been mothballed ages ago. Museum pieces," he bellowed, "that's what they are." He couldn't believe his ears; to even suggest such was an insult. "You lost your marbles?"

"Pay close attention," Foster demanded, "it's our only chance. You get in touch with Simmons and work it out. He'll know what to do." Foster was eager to hand off some of the burden. He'd been bombarded with grievances and criticisms from every idiot in the field. Sentiments back at command weren't much better. *I'll put a stop to that.* "Just do it!"

"In case you don't know," Tucker objected, reminding him one last time, "Confederate fleet no longer exists. It'd been decommissioned a decade ago to 'Commemorate' heritage." He laughed out loud at the thought of having WWII craft considered a defense force. "Idiots," he spat at Foster.

"We'll see about that." Foster was furious at the insult. He was also angry at Congress for letting political influence push aside a force that had once had saved the globe from the Nazis. It was about time these veterans got recognition. *I agree, there isn't much left of the once proud fighting fleet, but the fighting spirit is still very much alive. Past weeks have proven that.* "You work it out with Simmons," he insisted, "and don't give me anymore crap."

CONFEDERATE AIR FORCE

Wesley Simmons had partially recovered after the ad hoc Airbus encounter followed by the unceremonious crash of his B-17. He was walking with a limp from the injury he'd received. His fractured right leg had been set in cast from the knee down. Doctors warned him about keeping the weight off his legs. "Humbug," was all he said. He'd refused convalescence time. It slowed his aging gait even more, but otherwise, he was okay. His spirits were high. He was ready getting involved again.

"The nation needs you," Foster had insisted. There was much to do on such short notice. His fleet had to be organized. Resources identified. Pilots commissioned. Repairs made wherever craft could be located. Once word got out of an impending invasion, volunteers showed up by the troves. Farmers, crop dusters, private pilots, wannabe pilots, and WWII enthusiasts readily chipped in.

Wes knew his flying days had come to an end. After sixty some years of active and reserve duty, they were finally over. He had a good run. Not just a career, but a whole lifetime of flying. Not many could claim such a feat. But, as he'd confessed to Foster, "It doesn't mean I can't fight."

Presently, he was on his way to Midland, Texas. Confederate management decided on this airfield because of its open terrain. Fort Worth, some two hundred fifty miles to the east, may have been a better choice, but it did not have the open space needed to accommodate the vast number of crafts expected.

From Midland, home of the Confederates, he would be able to effectively command the fleet. The airfield had already been alerted of his arrival. He was traveling on a B-25 Mitchell, his lofty and temporary home. It would be his airborne command center for what he'd planned. The plan was formidable if he could pull it off. It would require all of the resources he could muster: pilots, crafts, munitions, logistics, and more.

The craft had just touched down and slowly rolled to a stop near the tower. Wes carefully clambered down the bomb bay. He stepped on the steel frame ladder extended from the fuselage. Despite the cast on his right leg he managed. He touched solid ground beneath his feet once more. He took a few paces toward the tower building, and then the full extent of his fleet came into view. The field was busy. Craft continued to arrive, almost non-stop. Ground crews had their hands full with shuttling and shuffling arrivals. His eyes absorbed the wide range of craft at his disposal.

There were the Boeing, Curtiss, Douglas, Grumman, and the North American. Manufacturers represented celebrated makes and models such as the Avenger, Wildcat, Hellcat, Helldiver, Bearcat fighters and dive-bombers. Off in the distance easily identified B-17s, B-24s, and B-29s, in their majestic presence, towering over the field were the super fortresses. The fleet not only contained American makes; still arriving were foreign models acquired by flying enthusiasts such as the Japanese Zero, Russian Migs, German Junkers, Messerschmitt, and more.

By now, many in the nation had managed to come up with some form of communication. For most it was the HAM radio. There was a time when this radio gear was popular in the nation. Everybody got a license and learned the Morse code. When back in the 50s and 60s the technology just emerged, many acquired it induced by fear from an atomic attack. None came. Most of the gear was stored in attics and basement thereafter.

Today, when word got out about a possible assault on the nation, pilots dropped whatever activities they had been involved in at the time and bade their goodbyes to family and friends. Representing squadrons and wings, they came from every corner across the nation. There were the Arizona Wing, Dixie Wing, Great Lakes Wing, Jayhawk Wing, Mississippi Wing, Memphis Squadron, Golden Gate Wing, to name a few, and, of course, Texas' own many squadrons and wings. Close to a hundred and fifty craft had already arrived. The airfield was bustling with pilots and maintenance crews making last minute adjustment for what many hoped was a solid stand by the nation. Many had no real idea what to expect. They came just on the basis of rumors circulating the airwaves. Word was passed around that a meeting was scheduled within the hour. It was to be hosted by the head of the Confederates, Wes Simmons, who most of the pilots knew from the annual air shows, held across the nation.

The Midland administration building was located in the main airport complex. The media conference room had been set aside for the upcoming meeting. The room had filled up quickly. It was overflowing with flight crews who were anxiously awaiting true information, rumors put aside, for possible orders on a plan of attack.

As soon as Simmons entered, the room fell silent. He solidly planted his withered body on the pedestal. Despite having lost a couple of inches in height due to the aging process, Wes Simmons still towered over most of the attending crowd.

"I'm thrilled," he opened the assembly, "as many of you showed up as did on such short notice. It shows the true spirit of the nation." He briefly touched on the current state of the nation. He then went on to the real reason everybody had been called up. "We believe," he elaborated, "that the nation's under imminent threat from an all-out military assault." His eyes skimmed over the sea of covered heads. Most wore baseball caps, the preferred head cover of the day. "Attack's gonna come from Cuba. Intel indicates an attack from two fronts. Assault by air," he took a short breath, "followed with ground troops dispatched to the Eastern Seaboard."

Simmons continued with additional specifics he had on hand. "Air assault will be carried out by Cuban's air defense forces. We know," he emphasized, "that their air force's been deteriorated in recent years, mostly from lack of funding and the economic depression that's plagued the nation. Nevertheless," he further emphasized, "their flight assets contain modern day jet fighters obtained from the former Soviet Union." There were immediate objections from some of the pilots. Simmons knew it would happen. There were shouts. There was yelling. But in general, the crews were well behaved. It took a few minutes to calm the crowd. Many were seasoned pilots, quietly evaluating what they'd just heard.

"Propeller driven WWII craft pitted against modern day jets? Impossible! Maybe…doable," were some of the concerns expressed among the pilots. Emotions were mixed. Some of their facial expressions ranged from apprehension, to anxiety, to worry. The majority projected an overwhelming sense of elation. It was those who would lead the strike force. It was a monumental decision. *A gutsy move.* Although the odds were in favor of the enemy, most were a hundred percent behind defending the nation. The die had been cast. It was up to the individual to commit and combat the enemy. But first, an overall battle plan had to be developed. And that was Simmons' strategy.

He pulled the most qualified pilots aside. He knew them well from the many air shows they'd performed in. These would lead the battle. They would be assigned wing commands. They didn't need to be persuaded about the balance of forces or, more appropriately, imbalance. They knew they could do it. Not so much from the limited assets on hand, but through a fighting spirit. Many were daredevils, acrobats of the air, aces in space. They had what it'd take to win, despite the technological advantages presumed by the enemy. The plan was set in motion. The crew was ready for battle. Presently, they were awaiting final orders. There was one more thing he had to do.

"Commercial Aviation," the operator acknowledged his call.

"Get me the chief." Simmons needed to speak with one specific individual. And that was the man in charge of the commercial stunt pilots contracted for the annual air shows. Annual, in this case, did not mean a once a year event. Air shows were performed almost weekly at one place or another throughout the nation, especially during summer months. Shows were scheduled a year ahead to commence in early spring lasting through late fall. Shuttling craft and supplies from place to place week after week, the schedule was hectic. It embraced many cities and towns from the Eastern Seaboard to the Pacific out west and everything in-between the Mexican and Canadian boarders. Kicking off a show was the usual stunt crew entertaining the crowd with their well-rehearsed, but risky, maneuvers, while visitors could tour the Confederate fleet on display. Throughout the day, one Confederate squadron after another, to the delight of the spectators, would take to the air. Spellbound and awestruck, the crowd would crane towards the skies for an everlasting impression of the once, and still, glorious fleet.

"Mitch," a voice answered the call seconds later.

EGLIN AFB

"You out of your mind?" the crazed base commander screamed into the receiver. "What the fuck are you doing to my base?"

"Now," Tucker was trying to pacify the irate commander, "calm down, will ya?" He'd been on the phone half the night taking instructions from Simmons about the air defense strategy the seasoned WWII veteran had applied to the anticipated invasion. After that, he had alerted Eglin and instructed the base and wing commanders on their part in the mission. Tucker had to agree that, to the uninformed, the overall plan must sound ludicrous. "It's the only thing we've got," he reasoned. A brief explanation about using the airbase as a staging field was refused by the wing commanders as completely idiotic. But after listening to what he had to say, there were sounds of approval.

"Plan may just work," the commander admitted.

Tucker immediately set out to contact Simmons who'd been on standby.

"Be there in a couple of hours, work out the details," Simmons advised when Tucker gave the go signal.

"Let's make it sixteen hundred hours," he was informed by Tucker.

Simmons took off from Midland shortly after. He was on his way to Eglin to brief the team. He called it "His Team," rather than his forces. After all, it wasn't much of a force. His combatants were untrained, they were undisciplined, but they sure had the fighting spirit. "That's all I need," he assured Tucker, "for a fighting chance, especially with the enemy at the doorstep."

At the designated hour, the Eglin wing commander and his fighter pilots had assembled at the mission command center. The clock showed a few minutes short of 4:00 PM. The intercom suddenly came alive. "Simmons just touched down," they were informed. As promised, he'd arrived in a B-25 Mitchell. His flight team had been patiently waiting. Most pilots were busy with last minute flight checks. Unlike modern preflight tests by computers, maintenance was mostly performed manually on the legacy fleet via visual checks.

Eglin's fighter pilots were largely kept in the dark about the upcoming mission. Fighter crews had been grounded until the F-15s were flight ready. That could be weeks away. Electronics and computer parts had been located with allied nations. Unfortunately, they were not giving up their spares with the uncertain world situation. For now, the pilots were grounded.

Some sounded off with smart comments like "gonna fly crop dust over Cuba" and "happy kite flying." The entire affair was a joke to them. Who'd ever heard of prop-powered craft going against modern day jet fighters? It was a crazy idea, but nobody had come up with a better plan.

Dressed in his customary dated and well-worn WWII attire, Simmons showed up right on time. The tall, somewhat frail appearing eighty-some war veteran looked withered over with age. People who saw him for the first time looked at him with doubtful eyes. "Him, the head?"

"Lieutenant General Wesley Simmons," he was welcomed by the base commander. Despite the showing age he carried himself with great pride. Taking long, steadfast strides he was ushered to the podium. There, in full view, with a nod, he acknowledged the assembly and took charge with, "Got a lot of ground to cover and don't have much time." He came right to the point. "Here's the attack plan."

Over the next few hours he laid out the details of the battle strategy. Laser pointer in one hand he gesticulated, wildly at times, across the width of the regional map fastened on the wall. He described the specific functions, in detail, that each squadron had to fill.

"To begin," he explained, "I will be flying a command post at fifteen thousand feet. Think of me as an E3 AWACS. For those who aren't familiar with WWII craft, the Mitchell's a B-25 medium bomber. Aside from being the command sentry, the craft's fully armed with a half dozen .50 in caliber machine guns. If the enemy makes it up this high," he promised, "I'll take care of it myself. By the way," he further informed the crews, "every Confederate craft, fighter and bomber is fully armed and combat ready, fitted with machine guns and in-board cannons. The fleet's on its way from Midland as we speak." He took a brief pause to collect his next thoughts.

Determined, he continued, "I must remind you that enemy's got the advantage in speed, but we've got maneuverability on our side. Try to keep the battle," he warned, "below fifteen thousand. None of our craft have workable oxygen." Simmons granted a fifteen-minute break. It gave the battle team a chance to adjust to his plan and make notes.

"Attention…quiet please," Simmons was ready to detail the tactical strategy. He whacked the pedestal a couple of times with a gavel. The room finally quieted down enough for him to commence with the most important phase. This would be the make and break maneuver. He had it all worked out in his mind. It was time to share it with his team. He liked what he saw. They were a no nonsense bunch of flying enthusiasts one could only hope for. Great expectation was edged into the many faces. "According to Intel sources," he projected, "we expect the enemy strike first thing in the morning, dawn." Both hands propped on the pedestal, he took a long-drawn breath of air then went into specifics.

"You all know football." He wasn't expecting any responses other than nodding confirmations. "Think of the battle plan as two teams," he continued. "At the onset of the battle, the ball's gonna be in the visitor's court, the enemy's. They'll be headed for their respective goals…targets, Norfolk and D.C."

"Why there?" He'd anticipated the question. Many hands went in the air. He didn't want to engage in lengthy debates and went on, "Shipyard and the nation's capital." Covered by their air force support, Cuban ground forces were expected to land in Norfolk and Annapolis.

"From those two points, they'll converge on the capital. We can't let that happen. So," he emphasized, "here's the plan." Just like at the games, Simmons laid out several football scenarios. He had assigned call names to each attack and maneuver. He would exercise and call the specific strategies as he saw the battle develop from above. It was up to the teams to carry them out. "Hope you all remember football." It was important for the pilots to respond on his calls.

"Our counter force, made up of military pilots and civilians alike…"

"Wait a minute," someone interrupted. Every face shifted in the caller's direction. "I'm not trained to fly those old clunkers." Raised the concern was a young face most recognized as a hotshot F15 pilot.

"Then wing it," Simmons shot back. "Just like driving a Model "T" mobile."

He was slightly annoyed at the interruption but continued. "As I said, we split into two wings. Red Wing—Norfolk, and Yellow Wing—Annapolis." He had picked the two colors on purpose. The majority of planes on the aerobatic stunt teams were generally painted one of the two colors. "Tomorrow morning," he went on, "the two teams will be sent out as decoys. What I mean by that…" He paused, waiting for the room to quiet down. There were yells and calls from the crews wanting to know what and why.

"Let me explain," Simmons clarified, "the two wings will be made up of the fastest stunt craft we have on hand. Mitch here," he turned to the man standing next to him that everybody in the room knew and deeply respected, "will lead the enemy into a trap. Mitch," he gestured to close his deliberation, "will take it from here."

Mitchell "Mitch" Kelley was well known in the stunt flyer community. He was one of those few daredevils that excelled to tell, live, and reap its rewards. Retired from actively flying annual stunt shows and exhibition flights, he'd decided to give it one more shot when Wes approached him the day before with the proposal. After Wes sketched out the tactics, he was jazzed about the plan. The old flying spirit surfaced in all of its intensity. He couldn't wait to get back into the seat of his well-worn but reliable and flight worthy Jaeger, the label he'd given his flying arrow for the German-named WWII sky hunters. He'd be on the frontlines one more time to lead his interceptor assault wing.

"To avoid radar detection," Kelley explained, "the air assault's expected to arrive at low level from the south. Wings Red and Yellow will be waiting at the Florida Straits at ten thousand ceiling. We'll be the decoys, splitting the advancing force into sections. It will be," Mitch turned dead serious, "your job to stop the invasion."

He went on to further describe the battle scenarios. The two wings, at high speed, would draw the enemy into two separate battle groups. Between five and ten thousand feet was the field designated for battle zones red and yellow. "Once the trap is set, Wesley's fighters and bombers will swoop into action." It was anticipated that the majority of the Confederate fleet would survive and make it to Norfolk and Annapolis, if necessary, to ward off the shore invasion. "With that, I'll turn the floor back to Wes." He stepped aside to make room for Simmons and terminated his delivery.

"My primary objective," Simmons picked up as he stepped up to the pedestal, "is to engage the enemy in battle to deplete their fuel supply. We must prevent them from ever reaching the Virginia shores." The invading combat forces were expected to fall short for the eight hundred plus miles flight distance to the north only if the force could be distracted and detained above Florida waters.

In case the air battle was unsuccessful, the only hope left was for submarines to block the landing, but in view of present conditions, that was not considered an option. There was no guarantee any of the deployed sub forces were aware of the present state of the nation, since the communication infrastructure had been destroyed.

Stepping aside to give him room to maneuver, Simmons motioned. "Questions?" As expected, there were many questions. For that, he stepped up to the map.

The room had come alive. Questions were flying at him like rapid fire. "What's the battle zone? What're the characteristics…performance…armament?"

"Let's take it one at the time." As always, he made a logical suggestion. *Keep the focus on one, and only one, target at a time.* Just like in battle. In battle, airmen cannot be distracted by multiple objects advancing from different directions. That was for computers to plot and figure out. In this case there were no computers. There was only visual recognition, assessment, reaction, and response. *In that order.*

"Battle zone," he said, extending the laser pointer. With a competent arc he motioned across the highlighted points traced out for the battlefield. He picked the first point. "Havana to Miami, approximately two hundred miles." Then he traced to the second. "Miami to Nassau, another two hundred." From there, he traced to close the triangular loop. "Another two hundred miles back to Cuba. Six hundred mile triangulation or," he quickly calculated the area, "twenty thousand square miles."

"Lot of square miles," one pilot yelled from across the room.

"Seems that way," Simmons replied. "But, in actuality," he was directly addressing the pilot, "with the numbers of craft and speeds involved we'll need the space."

"Looks like the Bermuda Triangle to me," another pilot readily suggested. The statement immediately silenced the room. Haunting memories of a distant past got everyone's attention. Even Simmons paused.

"You're right," he admitted. His gaze lingered on the map. "Let's call it the Bahaman Triangle," he suggested. "May just get written into the history books as such." He dared not even think about how many of his craft would perish in the depths of those waters. "Here," he gestured, "pass it out." He reached for a stack of folders. Each contained the specific characteristics for what remained in Cuban's air defense forces anticipated in the assault.

He spent another hour with the questions the pilots had. "And remember," Simmons put strong emphasis on the most important concern, "eliminate one target at a time." Simmons concluded the briefing. He put the pointer aside. "Good luck to all of you," was his departing wish, "and make your flag proud." Despite the cast, he left the room with his customary solidly grounded strides.

CUBAN AIR DEFENSE FORCE

In the sky, daylight had just set in. Bright yellow streams of sunrays gradually broke over the eastern horizon. The edge of the sun was still hidden below the curvature of the earth. Below, the gentle swells of the Florida Straits were doused in the blackness of night. Cloaked by darkness, they came as expected. Ghostly specs of grayish dots skimmed low above the white crested swells. A menace headed into U.S. territory, they rapidly advanced on a northerly course. Miles to the left of the formation, Florida's southernmost island zone, Key West, panned into the enemy's field of vision. Advancing into enemy territory, the 21s, 23s, and MiG-29s held a tight formation. The attack front had one thing, and only one thing, in mind: head for the Virginia shores as fast as possible. Low formation was held to avoid enemy radar. As long as the formation stayed on a direct course, fuel capacity was sufficient to reach the destination. Since the U.S. Air Force was grounded by the blackout, Cuban command intelligence was confident there would be no resistance. Northern airspace had been cloaked in silence for days. Intel had it the United States had been under attack, but that had not been confirmed due to the lack of embassy communiqué.

The advancing force was formidable under any circumstance. Nevertheless, there were two interdependent flaws with the basic assault strategy. One, Cuba had no aircraft carrier in its naval assets, which made it a one-way flight. Two, no landing sites had been assured. Naval commanders realized their grave position without off shore flight support, but with a onetime military opportunity available only on such short notice, alternative sources had to be sought. There were none. For all practical purposes, this was a one-way mission. The pilots knew it, and so did the commanding general. The craft had to land in enemy territory. Ground assault forces staged in the northern waters were to guarantee safe landings. "Viva la Cuba," was the battle maxim swelled at departure.

Ground assault forces had been dispatched thirty hours ago when the naval exercise was launched. There had been no prior military-collaborated statement to an exercise, as dictated by international agreement, to alert neighboring nations. Thanks to the communication blackout across the straits, the attack would come as complete surprise. Cuba had not been affected by the EMP because its position was just below the horizon, out of reach from damaging X and gamma rays. The deadly barrage of neutron pulsing was ineffective over the horizon. In case the assault turned to failure, in front of the United Nation's courts, the blackout would legitimize an excuse for the island's martial exploits. Failure, however, was not an option. It was a one-way make or break mission.

Cesar Romulus, lead wing commander for Cuban forces was trying to hold a tight formation. Between checking the flight instruments and casting hasty glances over his right and left shoulders, he had a busy time keeping the wings in check. Ever since the force had left home base, "Close up, 23…and throttle back, 29," were two frequently used instructions. Since it was the slowest of the jet force, the MiG-21 was used to fly lead wing. It was pacing the rest of the formation. The compass heading was set for 14.85 degrees NNE, bearing in on Washington D.C. With a distance of 982 nautical miles, at the present cruising speed, the flight should take about an hour to reach their destination.

The space ahead appeared wide open. Skimming along ten miles off shores the eastern coastlines, the lead commander judged, *This is going to be a breeze.*

Seconds later, Romulus' vision was slightly distracted by what appeared to be a peculiar cloud formation just above the horizon. Squinting, he tried to penetrate the cloud, but the brilliant morning rays radiating from the rising sun impaired the commander's vision. He couldn't quite make it out, but kept his focus on the front. Just in case, he flipped his helmet visor into position. It helped filter out the glare, but did nothing to enhance the field of view ahead. "Hold formation," he commanded the wings. He'd been listening in on the rapid chatter of his pilots. Despite the strict radio silence orders, pilots and crew disregarded the command decision. The event was too monumental for anyone to maintain silence. There was a certain enthusiasm in the voices. He felt elated at their eagerness, and to no surprise. It had been ages since the last combat mission. The pilots were highly energized for what lay ahead in an hour's flight time.

Minutes later, totally unexpected to the advancing party, it came on like lighting. From twelve o'clock high, in speeds to match the attacking force, amid the lead wings, red and yellow flashes appeared out of the skies. The forward pilots were jolted out of the morning calm. Alert eyes traced the sudden strikes from above, not comprehending the true gist of the immediate menace. The close circuit comm chatter had gone silent. It was thought the strikes had come from the cloud formation ahead. "Thunder and lightning," the commander muttered incredulously. Unsure what struck his forces, into the headset he yelled, "Keep formation!" He needed time to organize his thoughts. *Could it be? Not likely.* He dared not think the unthinkable. "An enemy strike?" He shrugged his shoulders in disbelief, hoping it truly was a lightning strike.

Aside of the steady whine from engines flying close to Mach one, it was silent within the plane's canopy. Suddenly, there it was again. More red and yellow strikes from above. In contrast to the first strike, this time, the wing lead caught a clear vision of the objects. It made no sense. "Stunt craft?" Daze changed to astonishment. Bewildered, he shook his head. It did nothing to clear his mind. There was no mistake. He could hear the keyed up responses in the headset. Others had acknowledged the strike as well.

"Wing leads 23, 29," he ordered, "investigate." From his field of vision he could follow his wingmen peeling off to give chase. *This is crazy,* he thought about the situation, *makes no sense.* There was nothing in textbooks. It was not part of any battle plan. He could only equate it to bugs attacking a flock of birds. He wasn't worried. *Guess who'll be eaten alive?*

"What's the status?" he queried the wingmen.

"In pursuit," one hastened back, "heading west."

"Negative," the commander bellowed, "return to formation!" He could not allow any diversions from the mission. Factors were too time critical for any interference or distraction. Providing air cover for the advancing marine force offshore Virginia waters was his primary focus, not to speak of the fuel limitation. No sooner had he finished the thought when the canopy on his MiG-21 was fractured. Several holes had appeared in rapid succession. The cracking sound of fractured glass followed. His eyes gleaned the circular openings across his field of vision. His ears took in the impacting sound from .50 caliber slugs penetrating into the instrument panel. His muscles instantly reacted. His body contracted with fear. Torso firmly pressed against the seatback, he tightened his grip on the controls. He lingered in this position until his mind caught up with reasoning.

"Do not pursue…repeat, do not pursue…stay on course!" It was more of a plea than an order. His mind was confused. *Follow the intrusion or stay on course.* He momentarily struggled with the notion, but the decision was taken from his hands by the rapid events that followed. They would wholly occupy the mind and the body.

What had appeared to be a cloud formation in the distance a minute ago now had transformed itself into a solid bank of steel in motion, headed in his direction. There was no mistake this time. Bewildered, he struggled with reality.

"Twelve o'clock high," a frantic voice yelled from the intercom. He realized it was his own. He could not restrain himself any longer. His eyes saw flashes of red and yellow shoot from every possible direction. It would be moments before he realized the colors were the results of his own fury and rage, rather than fuselages painted in customary WWII colors, olive drab. The battle had begun before he even had a chance to make a conscious decision. His air fleet was being sucked into the rapidly advancing cloud of propellers and steel, spitting hails of bullets.

"Attack!" he yelled into the intercom. It was more a cry for help than an order.

AWACS COMMAND

"Sector status?" Wesley Simmons was circling the skies overhead at close to fifteen thousand feet. The air had grown thin without an oxygen tank, but he'd expected that. It was okay as long as you didn't exert yourself. He felt lightheaded, but otherwise was okay. The only moving parts of his body were the eyes. And that didn't use up much energy. He was more aware of the freezing cold despite the compact heating unit purring away behind the seat. The blower put out barely enough thermals to warm the cockpit space. Whatever little heat it put out was quickly sucked away into the lofty fuselage.

Planes built for the war back then were nothing like planes these days where everything was airtight. They had been manufactured on assembly lines hurriedly put together. Quality control was not an industry standard yet. That would become part of the future. Whatever was built would be temporary, expected to only last a few missions, if at all. The ravages of war would see to that regardless of how much material was produced by the human assembly lines. "Gotta give them credit." Simmons had a nostalgic moment whenever his thoughts touched on "Riveting Rosie" and all the other women work forces called upon under the once so proud slogan, "We Can Do It." *Wonder how many of them are still left?* "This one's for you, gals!"

"You got control." He watchfully motioned to his copilot. "Hand me the glasses." The ballgame was in his hands now. From here on out he would direct the battle from the cockpit of the Mitchell AWACS. The mental picture for game calls he'd worked out the past few days was vividly ahead. All he had to do was put it into action, just like on the field. If all went well, it would be defense followed by offense calls no matter how many plays it would take. The binoculars were trained on the field ahead. At six o'clock below, the rapidly advancing MiG formation was panning into his circular vision. "Here they come," he yelled over the drone of the engines, "right on time." From his vantage point he could easily direct the battle.

Clutched tightly between his stiffened fingers, Wes firmly kept the glasses trained on the space some five to ten miles ahead and below. He mentally superimposed the space onto a football playing field. The only difference was that his game was played out three dimensionally. *What a concept.* Chest inflated with conceit, he felt like a super coach. *Wish they could see me now.* He was referring to his combat buddies back in England, then flying nightly missions over Germany. Momentarily, he was saddened by the thought of the distant, but still vivid, epoch clinging to his mind. He was the only one that remained. The others were all gone now, dead from old age years ago. A sudden chill moved through his withered body. He felt lonesome. *Before long,* he consoled himself, *I'll join you guys wherever you are.* He knew his time would be up soon.

"On the way," the copilot urged. Keyed in to receive running flight instructions from below, he sat motionless next to Simmons.

Simmons had turned all business. He mused as he watched Mitch's red and yellow stunt planes make the initial strikes. They cut down almost vertically across the front of the advancing field. He expected an immediate reaction from the advancing force. *Nothing!* He was getting nervous when the second wave of aerobat struck. *Still nothing.* The next strike seemed to change the playing field. From the AWACS loft he followed the enemy wingmen giving chase. "That's it." he could make out Kelley's and the stunt pilot's energized chatter from below. "Battle's on." The enemy took the bait. Wes watched in fascination as the stunt craft drew the MiG's into battle. "Follow the plan," he shouted into the mic, hoping the stunt pilots would pick up the action plan.

"Got the game," a voice bellowed into the mic. It was sector Alpha taking the first play. Circling at ten thousand feet, three B-17 flying fortresses were controlling the sector spaces. They were the linemen reporting to Coach Simmons above. Each of the linemen had linebacker support from a fleet of fighters and dive-bombers. Defensive backs were also many. Towering over the fields near the rear were the B-24 liberators.

The three dimensional field, segmented into three sectors close to fifty miles wide, was complete. It solidly blocked any intrusion from fifteen thousand feet high down through the three-dimensional space to ground level. From here on out, it would be up to the individual players, one hundred fifty strong, to tackle, defend, and take down the enemy. Although the speed advantage was with the enemy and its fleet of fifty some MiG fighters, the defensive play had home advantage in maneuverability, rehearsed strategy, and numbers in its favor.

Up front, at sea level, were the decoys, Kelley's stunt pilots, the linemen splitting the enemy force apart. Close behind, at the five thousand foot level, taking on the brunt of the defensive play, were the linebackers and defensive backs stacked up to ten thousand feet. Three sector coaches, Alpha, Bravo, and Charlie, in their B-17s reported the individual processes to Simmons directing the play from high above. For now, it was pure defensive strategy, but Simmons, in due time would change the game plan in his favor. The battle in the Bahaman Triangle was on. It would be a battle over the life and death of two neighboring nations. One was fighting for a free and safe democracy, the other clung to the remnants of communism. Worse yet, there was one more contender. And that one was serious. That one, waiting in the curtains of silence, was fighting for world dominance.

CONFEDERATE AIR DEFENSE

From his loft, Simmons had a plain view of the battlefield. He could clearly identify the wing formation he had designed with the limited resources available. At first, there had been fierce opposition from his squadron leads. "Uneven match…too few resources…dated equipment…and insufficient ammo," were the many objections. It had taken quite a bit of persuasion to arrive at a common consensus. In the end, it was settled. With resources just right, the game plan would work. Although they dated back many decades, he'd stressed all points of arguments were based on personal experience. Final battle design would be the standard Air Force flight configuration proven effective in many air battles.

Flight configuration called for one wing, two battle groups each containing five flights, with three squadrons each configured for five craft per squadron, totaling approximately one hundred fifty craft. "Perfect." Simmons had been pleased.

His current focus was centered on the battle group closest to the advancing enemy. The squadrons and flights were spread out over at least five miles to allow sufficient fighting room. Some flights just engaged with the advancing lead formation. It was still unclear at this point if the enemy would keep formation and move on or, as he hoped, fan out and pursue Kelley's aggressively buzzing stunt craft desperately trying to break up the enemy forces.

"Squadron One," Simmons called out a warning, "watch your back." Several of the enemy craft had broken away to give chase. "Squadron Two," his next command sounded, "engage." Squadrons two and three were staged several thousand feet apart, each in their own layered space. He wanted to keep squadron three and its five flights in a reserve position to fend off anything that got through the first defensive line. "Enemy's engaged," Simmons informed his group commanders.

From here on out it would be up to the group commanders to call the home plays. All he could do was keep his eyes trained on the battlefield to assure the formation of the players, as rehearsed. It had worked on the wallboard. *Why wouldn't it here, real time, live?* For now, it appeared his commanders had their flights under control. Most importantly, none of his craft had been eliminated yet, but he, as well as his team, knew it wouldn't stay that way for long. There were going to be casualties. There always were in dogfights, especially when the fight was an all-out battle for the win by either side.

Simmons took a deep breath. He sat back to soothe his nerves, on edge since early that morning. He needed a clear mental picture while listening to the play calls as they unfolded several thousand feet below. He knew the plays well. There was the "3-3-5," the first call. Translated into action, the formula called for a number of linemen followed by linebackers then defensive backs to take on the brunt of the first assault. The present field was staged purely in a defensive posture that would change as soon as there was an opening for a counter strike. And here it was, "Shotgun." Squadron two command had made the call based on an opening left by squadron one. It was a popular play call. Here, the formation offered an immediate advantage. The offensive flight had room to penetrate behind enemy lines and form a tight, cohesive "pocket" to maneuver within and take down the sector. The action spread immediate confusion within the advancing forces. It broke up the tight formation the enemy was so desperate trying to hold.

"It's working," Simmons yelled out over the drone of the props. He was elated. The battlefield was breaking up into sections. The enemy was pushed out of formation. *Major mistake,* he opined, *poor bastards.* That was one thing why his WWII bombing runs were so successful. "Keep formation no matter what." Sure, there would be losses. It was expected with any conflict, but could be minimized through ironclad discipline. And that had to be drilled into each soldier before going into battle. "Keep formation. Keep pushing ahead. Penetrate." Once there was a fracture in the formation, it had to be quickly closed up and filled in from the rear. The same strategy worked for the game, here and now.

The fighting had begun only minutes ago. Now, it was in full swing. It wasn't going to be an easy win for his fly-by-cable dated craft pitted against modern day, computer controlled fly-by-wire jet fighters, but it was all he had to fight off the offensive. All he could do was hope to take down as many jets as he could. *Winning?* That would be for the annals of history to decide. *Wishful thinking, who knows? There have been miracles before.* And a miracle he and his team desperately needed. Orders were issued on the fly.

"Watch your flanks…"

"Close up…"

"Hold formation," were some of the directing calls heard over the ether. The well-rehearsed play, regardless of battle formation, had become personal. In response, other, not so pleasant calls came through the headsets.

"I'm hit…"

"Breaking up…"

"Going down…"

"Shit!"

"Gotcha…"

"One less commie…"

"Where'd he come from?"

In the midst of the calls of desperation, euphoria, and jubilation, the battle raged on.

CUBAN AIR OFFENSE

Cesar Romulus made one monumental effort to stay on course, to refrain from breaking formation. It was useless. Directly from above, unobstructed, his fighters were getting cut to pieces by the red and yellow thunderbolt strikes bearing down on his task force. The last strike had taken out three of his fighter craft. Disabled from leaking fuel tanks after getting hit by .50 caliber bullets, they were headed back to the island, hoping to make it to the nearest landing strip. Those were the lucky ones.

Presently, he had just issued the order to attack. It was a difficult choice he had to make, to stay and fight. He knew it would eliminate his primary objective, reaching the Virginia shores. The sea and land assault would be without the desperately needed air coverage he'd promised to uphold. It couldn't be helped. What he faced was a much larger threat. It had appeared out of nowhere, suddenly. It had not been accounted for in the battle plan. *Unexpected.* He had to deal with it now.

"Shoot at will." It was the only sensible order to execute. Immediately, his tightly kept air formation split apart. Unprepared and unrehearsed, his fighters gave chase. Each on his own, they were being engaged by what appeared to be a well laid out assault strategy by this bizarre, and rather outlandish, attack force. Romulus was enraged. To keep the canopy from breaking up he throttled back to almost stall speed. It was barely enough power to keep his craft in the air. He became a vulnerable target. To bail out was not an option. It would mean certain death. He knew how shark infested these waters were off the Florida coast. Squinting through clenched eyelids, he could barely make out the stream of tracers coming his way through the broken windshield. The air was tearing at his face. There were more impacts on the fuselage. He needed to get the piercing sunrays out of his face. He peeled off to the right. *That's better.* At least he could see with a clear vision.

"General." He barely made out the warning call. "Watch your back." There was so much chatter in the air, both in Spanish and in English. Both sides were tuned in on the same frequency. Romulus had given the order deliberately. Many of his fighters understood the English language. They may not have spoken it fluently, but, in general, most of the educated understood the neighboring language. His ears were tuned in on the American pilots. Shaking his head, he was unsure what was being said. There was something oddly familiar, but yet unrecognizable, in what he made out as battle calls. "3-3-5…4-3" and "3-5-3" were some of the calls. Then it struck home. "Football strategy!"

He would have kicked himself in the butt if he wasn't strapped into the seat. "Of course!" *They're using game calls.* Suddenly recognizing the strategy, wildly shaking his head, he yelled out, "Son of a bitch!" Many years ago, when the nation was still broadcasting American football, he used to sit in front of the television and watch. It had been fascinating to see these giants clash with unrestrained force, slamming against each other to take down the pig skin, but that was long ago. With national censorship tightly enforced since the move to communism, the only sports on the air was the national's favorite, Fútbol.

He tried to linger on the moment, but his thoughts were torn from the pleasant, yet long forgotten, memories of his youth. It was useless. He could not remember the calls. Instead, he was awed by the disciplined formation with which the enemy bore down on him and his comrades. "Gotta gain altitude." He forced himself into action. It was up to him to take charge of the battle. He could not permit this archaic task force get the upper hand. That would be ridiculous. He could not imagine going down in history as the "commander who lost the battle to toy soldiers." He would rather perish in the glory of battle. With recharged energy, he increased power to the afterburners. He broke free from the engaging field. It took him to new heights. At fifteen thousand feet, he had clear and unobstructed vision. He leveled off. Below was the raging battle taking hold. In the distance, he could make out one lonely craft, a dated yet majestic-looking bomber from an epoch long ago.

Curious, he headed directly for it. *What's a single bomber doing at this altitude?* He took his MiG-21 into a wide turn then buzzed straight across the nose to get a clear view into the canopy. In an instant, both pilots' eyes made contact. The split second it took for the flyby was enough to assess the rank, position, and status of the pilots.

"I'll be damned," Romulus called out, "Wesley Simmons." He'd come face to face with his adversary. He clearly remembered the earlier encounter he had with him. It was during the Cuban missile crisis in '62. Being a hotshot combat pilot back then, he dared the American pilots on flyover surveillance missions, in open air. Unknown to the world, he and Simmons were battling out their differences, he for the cause of communism, the American pilot for democracy. The dogfight did not last long. He was unrepentantly recalled back to base. Later on, he found out that the two nations had come to some agreement averting a war in the last minute. Backed by the Soviets, it was the closest his nation came forcing a nuclear war. Although it was long ago, he never forgot a face.

He would have to wait. "I'll deal with you later." For now, Cesar had a more pressing need, to return to the battlefront. And that, he knew, was some five thousand feet below. A tight loop brought him right on top of it.

AERIAL BATTLE

"Plan's working." Simmons had the strategy well in hand. His field of vision was momentarily distracted. A MiG-21 came out of nowhere, buzzing the cockpit. They made eye contact. He recognized the pilot immediately from an earlier encounter. *Cesar Romulus, head of the Cuban air defense forces.* As quickly as he had appeared, he'd disappeared. *Good.* He'd face his adversary when the time came. He focused on the field below once more.

From his vantage point he clearly made out the fighting fronts. His vision embraced all three squadrons. At this moment, flights One and Three were on the defensive. Although in constant motion, he could make out the defensive formations. In tight pattern, fending off the advancing MiG's, were the linemen up front. It was a joy to see the F-4 Wildcat, F-6 Hellcat, F-8 Bearcat, British Spitfire, Mitsubishi Zero, and the North American P-51 Mustang swoop down on the enemy. "WWII all over again," he said approvingly.

Followed tightly were the linebackers, the second line of defense. They were made up from the Curtiss A-25 Helldiver, P-40 Warhawk, Douglas A-26 attack craft, and the Grumman TBF Avenger. From an inventory perspective, the Grumman's trainer/bomber/fighter combination craft "Avenger" were the most prolific in numbers. *Probably,* Simmons surmised, *the result of the loss of one entire wing in the Bermuda Triangle back in '45.* The infamous loss of Flight-19 had gained much popularity among WWII aficionados.

Defensive backs brought up the rear. A cluster of straggler craft—latecomers, not necessarily configured for direct assault tasks but effective, nevertheless, for fending off the enemy—closed up the back. It was up to them to pursue breakaway fighters.

Squadron Two had taken the brunt of the initial attack wave. At this moment, it was deeply involved in an offensive strike. The tide was shifting back and forth between offensive and defensive plays. Well-defined offensive calls Simmons and his three squadron leaders applied were Shotgun, Wishbone, Wildcat, Pistol, and Single wing set back, executed as they saw fit. They had been proven on the ball field; they worked well in space.

In between battle commands from above, fearful screams, cries of desperation, and panic calls could be heard from pilots in trouble. Many called in status and final position before going down or bailing out. A fleet of rescue vessels was on its way. They'd been dispatched from various shore points off the Florida coastal harbors. The Coast Guard had been on standby since the early morning hours. Once the battlefront had been established, the fleet was directed to the area to rescue downed pilots.

Forty minutes into battle, there had already been heavy losses on both sides. Downed American pilots were easy to spot as they clung onto their floating craft. Cuban pilots were not so lucky. Their jet-powered aircraft, once the fuel ran out, went down much like a rock. When the mass of metal hit the waves it just kept on going into the depths of the oceans. Some pilots ejected. They made it out on parachutes. They were picked up by the rescue vessels just the same. American recovery teams adhered to the Geneva Convention, the rules of war. It was the democratic way. It was the humane way, regardless of the enemy's intention.

In the space above, fighting continued. Below the surface, the downed pilots faced a new enemy. *Sharks!* They came in troves. Homed in by keen predatory senses, they were attracted by the many splashes of spent metal and bodies. Screams and cries of terror continued to be heard as ferocious predators sought out new prey as it fell from the skies.

"3-5-3, HUD." Group commander, squadron One, just implemented the next defensive call. He coordinated the play with squadron Three, who confirmed his response with "3-5-3." The result was more craft downed with sheared off wings, disintegrated tail rudders, fractured canopies, exploded fuel tanks ignited by piercing bullets, mid-air crashes, and pieces of fuselages propelled wildly through space, only to cause more inflicting damages to craft and bodies.

"I'm hit...I'm hit." Two F-6 Hellcats had just been destroyed by the enemy. The pilots were able to bail out even though both craft were burning up. What awaited them in the seas below would be anyone's guess.

"Going down." Three more calls of desperation followed in short succession, initiated by pilots from an F-4 Wildcat, an F-8 Bearcat, and P-51 Mustang.

"Bailing out." There were many more calls each time the battle shifted from defensive to offensive, and back to defensive formation again and again. The Grumman, Curtiss, Douglas, and North American assets were dwindling at an alarming rate.

Many more cries went silent. They went unheard. They were lost in silence by dramas played out within the cockpits. There was metal, fabric, and flesh torn to bits with blood gushing uncontrollably through the interior, painting much of it in scarlet red. Penetrating bullets from lead-spitting cannons cut through the fuselages like a crazed logger cutting through a tree trunk. Everything in the way of sprayed bullets either quit functioning or fell apart in pieces. Cut limbs, with steering controls clutched between cramped fingers, were still holding on for dear life while flying through the air. Feet and legs severed from bodies lay twitching on the cockpit floor with muscles groping desperately for the detached limbs. The brain did not know. It sent out commands to the extracted limbs until the craft incinerated or hit the ground. Damaged craft spun through the air much like tumbleweed bouncing across the desert sands in an autumn storm. Such was the call of war.

Simmons watched his fleet dwindle rapidly while the battle swayed back and forth. There was one difference. Where a player on the field would be retired after an injury, here, in space, there was no option. An "out" was permanent. His calls filled in the gaps wherever there was an opening or exposed flank. Losses mounted. Much of his fighting force was gone. Many on his team were forced to bail out. Some lumbered back to land in their shot up craft as long as the fuel lasted and the plane held up. The playfield had been narrowed very much. It was down to one remaining team. Likewise, not much remained from the enemy. The MiG attacks, with barely enough fuel left to keep aloft, had slowed to a few persistent fighters. What players were left gave it one final assault.

"I'm hit...I'm hit." It was a voice everybody recognized. It was the voice of Mitch Kelley. His craft, after chasing after one of the few remaining MiG's, had just taken a series of .50 caliber bullets. When the slugs cut across the fuselage, it sounded like a buzz saw in action. Almost at the point of getting cut in half, Mitch tried to outmaneuver the Cuban pilot giving chase. The craft, his beloved Jaeger, did not respond. It was mortally wounded. None of the controls worked. Mitch knew it would be the end. He'd had enough close calls in his career to know the results. "Bail out or perish," were the two options. He had to make in a split second decision. Over land, he may have saved the precious craft, but out at sea, the chance of saving the craft was almost none. It would sink the minute a wave washed over the body. The sheer weight of the engine would pull the rest of the craft into the deep.

Hurtled into a dive, watching the white crested waves rush in, Mitch popped the canopy. The negative pressure sucked the air from his lungs. In a last-ditch effort, trying to alert his crew and rescue party, he cried, "Bailing out…bailing out," and jumped. As soon as he pulled the ripcord, his body slammed tight into the security of the chute. Drifting slowly towards the water, he watched the few remaining enemy craft engage in one final fight, then, giving up the battle, turn south to head back home to Cuba. He was safe.

Simmons had to make one final stand. *Time for a blitz.* After this, there wouldn't be enough resources left to ward off the remaining MiG's. Determined, he issued the final play call. "Squad Two 4-4…Fire…Ringo…Loop…Sam." *This is it.*

His focus, trained on this last play, was suddenly distracted. He could hear it loud and clear. It started at the rear of the tail section. It reminded him of a jackhammer breaking into a slab of concrete. The ominous sound rapidly advanced. It cut through the fuselage into the cockpit. The sound was accompanied by a sudden jolt to his back. That's where it stopped. The .50 caliber bullet took his breath away. There was no pain. Another round slammed in from the far side of the cockpit. He watched his copilot slam forward. His lifeless body landed against the controls.

The craft, the majestic B-25 Mitchell, slowly slipped forward. The nose gently edged down towards the swelling seas. The weight of the copilot's body pushed against the flight controls. Simmons tried to steady the craft. His body did not react. He struggled to gain control…again and again. But there was no reaction. He could move his head sideways, up and down, but not the rest of his body. *What happened? What's happened to me?* He stared at the instruments. The craft was picking up speed. There was nothing he could do to slow it. No matter how hard he tried, he could not pull up the nose. The pitch of the engines was accelerating. In an instant, he realized, *This is the end.*

When he realized he'd been paralyzed from the chest on down, a sudden calm came over him. His eyes wandered from the instruments to the vision ahead. His body weakened. He could not see the stream of blood oozing from below. It was running down both legs onto the metal floor. There, by force of gravity, it slowly collected toward the front of the craft. His eyes took in Earth's beauty below the horizon one last time when a gently flowing object entered his failing vision. It inched its way ever so slowly from the corner to the left. Beautiful, gray, huge in size, it was the soaring shape of a bird. It nudged into full view. His weakened gaze reflected on the bird. Simmons' face changed to puzzlement. The bird took on the shape of a face. It was a familiar face. There was eye contact. The face held a solid salute. Salutation from one fighter to another, it was filled with respect, admiration, and wonder.

Cesar Romulus bade goodbye to the enemy. It was a formidable enemy. It was a salute to Wesley "Wes" Simmons, heralded warrior from another epoch. "So long, my friend." Romulus checked his fuel gauge as he peeled away from this once proud WWII bird with one thought in mind. *With luck, I can make it home.*

Simmons, clinging to life, had one final thought before his brain completely drained of blood. "I'm coming home." It was his last thought. It was a pleasant thought. His buddies were waiting by the divine gates of eternal bliss.

END GAME

The battle over the Bahaman Triangle had lasted close to two hours. The toll was heavy with many losses of lives on both sides. After the numbers were counted, there were no victory calls. In the hearts of the American people, only silent triumphs endured. Their livelihood had been protected by the sheer courage of the dedicated WWII buffs. About two dozen craft were still intact. Wounded, but alive, their pilots had made it back to home base. It would take some time, but the damaged craft would be repaired and eventually restored. Others had found their graves in the depths of the sea. Some pilots, after ditching, made it out alive. They had been picked up by the rescue vessels steaming back and forth to collect the downed and the injured.

Some pilots, trapped within their cockpits, unceremoniously drowned. Strapped forever within the restrains of their seats, they went to their graves. The rest, it was better not to think of their gruesome fates. Presently, on their way home with sustained injuries, each bestowed with a sense of great pride, in total, fifty-six pilots were rescued. Their names, as well as the names of the perished, would be recorded into historical archives. Much literature and many books would emerge from today's heroic events. Some would be analytical in nature. Others would turn into romantic novels. More would describe the accounts from a military and political perspective. All in all, the day would deserve a place in history.

Enemy losses were equally heavy. Only a total of five craft and pilots survived to live another day. Their fighting days would be over. What little remained from the air defense forces would probably be retired. Without the necessary funding, nothing would remain to even be considered a wholesome fighting force.

Destined for the retirement guaranteed to follow after failing to succeed but having had one last chance to fight in battle, Cesar Romulus had mixed feelings. Although he was beaten, he was proud, nevertheless. At cruising speed, to stretch what little precious fuel was left in the tank, he presently was headed south to his beloved Cuba. On the one hand, he was proud of his comrades to have fought one last time for democracy, as misguided it may have been; on the other, he was sad at having lost that chance. Headed for home base, unsure how to face the ministry, family shame, public humiliation, and, most of all, the dreaded press, he decided, "I should end my life here and now." Hands lightly shaking from the inevitable, fear seeping into his brain from the unknown with an aging body strained forward to reach the panel, his index finger rested on the power switch. He hesitated one moment to consider the steps he must take before executing the final act in this life. "Shut off the engine…push down on the nose…focus on the blue waters rushing at me." It would be easy. He'd never feel the impact. He'd be heralded as a hero.

About ready to execute the final thought, he suddenly changed his mind. A string of images, notions, had come across his field of thoughts. "They need me."

What changed his mind was the freedom he felt soaring the air currents, fighting for independence, and the hope, as little there was, for a free nation. He had suddenly realized how important it was for him to carry a message to the people, his people; a people that had been struggling with poverty, misery, and suppression for too long. "I must free my people," was the self-induced message. With this glimmer of hope, Cesar

Romulus, determined to keep on fighting this time, would fight for a worthy cause. Settled back into his seat, he headed for home, praying the fuel would last.

Two hours earlier, in the twilight of dawn, the captain, Cuban naval armada, stood on the bridge of the lead vessel and ordered, "Half speed, dead ahead." To inform the other ships in the armada of the speed change, the command flag was hoisted. He was squinting into the horizon ahead. He was looking for a shoreline. He knew it would be there. The radar instruments had announced the land before anyone on the bridge could spot it. He was searching for something else. The something that should have already been here, waiting. Quietly, he whispered his concern. "Where are they?" It was a question posed more to himself than his commander close by. *Where's my air support?* Both pairs of binoculars were trained at the horizon ahead, scanning and seeking. "Try naval headquarters again."

"Nothing," was the report. Ever since the fleet had left the Cuban shores, radio silence had been strictly enforced. It was to be a surprise attack on their American neighbor. There had been enough chatter already on the island alerting foreign intelligence that something urgent was up without giving away the position of the fleet through added communication. Tension in the ether had been building for days. Under normal conditions, high-speed computers at the U.S. naval intelligence offices would have already keyed in to process real time data streams received on wireless channels. But conditions today were not normal. They hadn't been normal for days. And, under those conditions, anything could slip through the nation's security fences, no matter how sophisticated listening devices might have been.

The captain in command for the assault armada had decided to wait another thirty minutes. He desperately needed air support. *Where are they? Has something gone amiss?* He dared not think about it. For him and the flotilla to succeed, he needed the combined strength of the Cuban defense forces: the army, the air force, and his navy. A feeling of desperation came over him. He shifted his focus south, the direction they'd come, to the full force of the armada. Looking over the fleet, his heart sank to its lowest level. *What has happened to us? Where is the nation's pride?*

Both hands propped against the bridge rail, he steadied his body against the gently rolling swells off the Virginian shores. He did not need the binoculars to assess the dwindled inventory under his command. His vision took hold of the aging skin stretched loosely across his bony fingers. What used to be a healthy pair of strong and powerful hands now was lined by protruding blood vessels laboring to get blood to his extremities. *Where has the time gone?*

Heavy hearted, his gaze struck what was left of a once proud fleet. There were not many ships above the water line, or below. Commissioned had been everything in Cuban's naval inventory[72] that could be of use for the assault. Most were used to carry troops.

---

[72] Cuba's naval forces: Two Koni class frigates, five Osa and Pauk classes with Styk anti-ship missile-topped assault boats, Polnocni amphibious carrier with a dozen troop manned with Cuban combatant forces, barely 15,000 men to support the impending assault. One Polnocni class amphibian warfare vessel. Aside from being able to carry eight armored personnel carriers or similar payload in its belly, it was armed with four Strela surface-to-air missile systems, four twin mounted 30 mm AK-230 air defense guns, and two 140 mm Ogon 18-barreled rocket launchers.

Below the surface, a couple submarines from the Russian Foxtrot class were running flank safety for the fleet. Once the assault orders were issued, landing support would be provided by Cuban-built Bandera VI mobile launchers, mounted on amphibious landing boats. Although sturdy by design, they had barely kept up the journey to these waters at a pace of thirty knots. They had come on a one-way mission. *I must succeed,* was the captain's major concern. *There's no turning back.* He was contemplating what action to take if the air force hadn't showed up in—he checked his wristwatch—twenty minutes. By now, the shoreline had crept into full view. In the distance he could discern small craft. "Fishing boats," the second mate reported. He'd been tracking their approach closely. There seemed to be no alert out on their covert approach. Aside from what appeared to be local fishing vessels, the shores seemed calm. *Surprise could be on our side.* "But where're the MiG's?"

The captain checked his timepiece again and again. "Ten minutes and still no planes." His weary eyes sought out his second in command. "Guess," he wagered, heavy hearted, "it's up to us. They're not coming." His gaze was on the timepiece, watching the last seconds tick away. At time zero, he made his decision. "Full steam ahead!" He picked up the field glass to verify the command being propagated through the fleet. "Flag's up." At full speed, the armada was headed for the shores some twelve miles distant. In fewer than fifteen minutes, the landing would take place.

Once again he shook his head. "What's happened to the promised air support?" Frustrated, he kicked the rusty rail with his right boot. Dry paint flaked off in penny-sized chips. He watched them be carried away by the passing breeze. Again, he watched the skies for activity. *Anything?* Any activity would have lightened his heart. Another ten minutes and he'd be in position for the attack. He would command the land assault from three miles out, the safety margin not to run aground and the maximum effective range for his armaments. It'd give the Koni-class frigates the best chance to effectively use their turret guns. Distraught, frustrated, and disappointed, he scanned the airspace to the south. *Nothing.*

"Dead stop," the captain ordered, "flag's up." The armada had arrived. Without propelling force driving the vessels ahead, the Cuban landing force slowed its forward momentum only to float in the gentle swells of the Atlantic waters. Still no signs from above, extremely frustrated by now, the captain muttered, "Where's the air cover, dammit?" Spitting over the rail in irate disgust, he cussed. *Better get here soon,* he threatened in silence. He shook his head, wiping spittle off his face where the wind had blown it back. *Or there'll be hell to pay.*

He wasn't about to quit. He wasn't about to turn back, not after coming this far. Five minutes went by, then five more. After fifteen more minutes, with no air cover in sight, he desperately scanned the southern horizon. *What'll I do? What should I do?* Undecided, feeling completely abandoned, he viciously cursed, "Fuck the air force. Fuck the damned lot…" he cursed over and over when he realized he was stood up. Unable to wait any longer, subjected to the strong ocean currents, his armada was drifting off, away from the shores. Totally disgusted, but determined, he finally decided, "It's up to me."

From here on it would be up to his ground forces. Another flag was hoisted. In plain view for all to see the flag was raised. "Attack!" Scanning the horizon one more time, he muttered, into an uncertain future that was sure to follow, "May God be with us. Full steam ahead," he ordered his commander.

No sooner had the words left his quivering lips than his eyes widened in shock. They took on a look of absolute astonishment. His mind could not register to react. He, as well

                    T. RANDALL

as his assault commanders, was stunned. Bodies frozen with shock, Cuba's assault forces came to an immediate halt. What they witnessed was uncanny. There was nothing like it in textbooks. Never before in naval history had something like this occurred. A solid wall had grown out of the seas below, blocking the armada's way to the shores. It was a stunning blow.

Days before, the captain, U.S. submarine forces Atlantic fleet, had become alarmed by a persistent radio silence from command headquarters. The super low frequency usually emanating signals from Chequamegon National Forest was absent. At frequent time intervals, it should have transmitted instructions carried through the oceans to let the submariners know when and where to surface for instructions. Since none came forward, the monitoring crew had become alarmed. Based on fleet directives, in scheduled intervals, the sub spooled out its trailing antennas to receive further orders from above. Unknown to the underwater fleet was that the nation's satellites and ground communication had been destroyed. A command decision was made to surface.

No directives were received from U.S. satellites. On board SIGINT, eventually picked up and deciphered intelligence from foreign language sources. In addition, VLF and ELF on low frequency surface waves from other subs supported a heightened state of alert condition on the Eastern Seaboard. Coded communication received from subs stationed near the island of Cuba indicated a war party headed north. Since no war games had been scheduled, the action demonstrated signs of aggressive behavior. A command decision became necessary to block the advancing, and possibly hostile, naval fleet. It was the coordinated effort of the combined U.S. submarine fleet patrolling the Atlantic waters to ward off the war party.

In response, the sub fleet surfaced. What followed was a solid barrier the foreign vessels dared not penetrate. Any aggressive action would have meant absolute suicide to the advancing fleet. Launch pads poised with Tomahawk missiles and surface torpedo pods were pointed in their direction forcing a standoff...for now.

The blockade dispatched a landing party to the Cuban command ship, the frigate, to investigate the enemy's intentions.

Unremitting terms were clearly identified by the sub commander. "Return to your bases," was his order, "or face the destruction of your naval fleet. Those are our terms." He gave no options. The choice was theirs. The captain was allowed one hour. "Spend it wisely," he was advised.

It was clear from the faces of the sub crew that they would welcome an opportunity to test out newly commissioned weapons on live subjects. In anticipation, they waited.

It took fewer than twenty minutes to receive a reply. "We concede."

"Well," addressing his exec, the sub commander affirmed, "we've lost another opportunity." Because of the international ban on nuclear and weapons of mass destructions weapons testing, above and below the earth's surface, the commander felt he'd lost what could have been an opportunistic and very valuable practice, testing out new weapons carried onboard.

Years would go by for the Confederate air force to regain its former status back. It would be recorded in history as the "Last Stand of the Leather Heads." The credit to these unselfish fighters clad in the dated, but well distinguishable, leather caps worn by flyers during the two world wars was well deserved. It identified a warrior, at times underappreciated and taken for granted as "collateral force," only to emerge with full glory, saving the grace of a once proud and powerful force. Eventually, time and history would tell the outcome of an unnecessary conflict instigated by greedy and ambitious rulers, trying to extend and expand their reign for dominance and supremacy. It would not be the last time. Unrest was in the nature of human kind. One thing would be certain: the glory of what had been degraded to a Commemorate air show unit, the once superior air force fighting two world wars, would be restored. It would regain full recognition, once more to be recorded by historians as "Confederate Air Force."

RUSSIAN FEDERATION (Ministry of Foreign Affairs)

"Please." Vladimir Potempkin invited the minister of defense to join him on the park bench. Potempkin had purposely arrived earlier. It gave him an opportunity to spend some time at his favorite place, the Square of Europe. He'd been seated in the quiet of the dark by the Moskva River that, at this location, embraced some of the city's more historic places. Located just outside the Garden Ring, bordered by the Rail Terminal on the one side, with the House of Government on the other, it gave him a clear view of the city. It may seem peaceful at the moment, but the place had seen much turmoil in Moscow's colorful history. He vividly recalled historic events that took place within his lifetime, culminating into chaotic consequences people dared not openly discuss.

Here, today, in the calm of night he felt privileged to still be alive to enjoy this great city. Where many of his colleagues had succumbed to ravishes of war and purges by past regimes, he had survived. He savored every moment. And, for the moment, he was only vaguely aware of his late evening guest seated beside.

His mind was absorbing the present to its fullest. Not in his wildest imagination, not so long ago, could he have foreseen the turn of events his nation had taken. Images of tyrannical leaders like Stalin, Khrushchev, and more recent leadership figures were passing silently across his vision. It still gave him chills thinking of that violent past.

"Peaceful. Da?" He casually opened the conversation.

"What have we become?" Almost inaudible, the minister of defense dared his private thoughts. "A nation of democracy," he pointed out, "we once hated so much. Look at this now." He gently waved his arm across their field of vision. His eyes were fixated on the distance. Tall skyscrapers, majestically topped by gigantic cranes intensely illuminated by floodlight, cast their ominous shadows on the grounds below. A sign of the present, it was the product of prosperity. "Are we better off?"

"Between you and I," Potempkin volunteered, "No. We both have lost our power base, but," he carefully weighed his words, "we live in peace, and that, my friend," he let the thought sink in, "is priceless." He purposely used the familiar label of *friend* to address his equal yet superior opponent seated aside him. In the not too distant past, he would have addressed him as comrade. In the political and economic trends of the present, all references to the turbulent past had been eradicated from the daily language. Only written accounts archived in museums and the many historical monuments once damaged by war, but restored to their present splendor, had been left to remind the public of a confusing past. *Or was it?*

Potempkin threw a quick glance at the minister. He tried to gauge the man's inner secrets. The contours of the party-hardened face revealed nothing. It held no signs of emotions. *Why do I feel so suspicious?* He asked himself that question each time he had to face an important functionary. *Distrust,* he finally concluded, *must be a fallacy of my generation.* And he was right. After all, this was a clandestine meeting.

"I envy you," the minister of defense said, "you've arrived at the end of your career." He acknowledged the retirement announcement made official earlier the day. Potempkin had been retired. It had been done with dignity, but everyone in the committee knew it was the result of the failed Cuban crisis. Somebody had to be sacked, the protocol with every failed attempt. Today, it was him. It had not come as surprise. He knew how the system worked. All that was left for him was to voice his own justification. There was no feel for vindication. That time had long since expired. There was no remorse. Only a hint of sadness remained in his chest.

"You think I did the right thing?" Potempkin waited. There was no immediate response. He needed to know. He needed to know the direction the new regime, the so-called Democratic Party, would take. *And that's,* he suddenly realized his predicament, *where the infernal distrust comes into play.*

"We have missed a great opportunity." Haltingly, the minister of defense spoke. He deliberated every word. "We have become one of many nations." He took his time to express the current sentiment of many of the members. "We have lost our inherited birthright." There was a profound sadness to the voice, a certain melancholy. "We have lost our superpower status. We are nothing."

"I did what I could," Potempkin tried to justify his position, "on such short notice." He was in the right, he felt. There had been no time to prepare for a strike on the United States. Today, in a world of trivial negotiations, there was no room for political exploits, let alone military action.

"The United Stated is not our enemy anymore." There it was. The minister had spoken the truth out loud that everyone else was thinking only privately. "You may be right." There was a hint of a sigh in the reply.

"If you don't watch out," Potempkin was sincerely warned, "you will lose your nation altogether." Both were well aware of the silent threat emerging across the international horizons.

"I will let the Americans deal with it." It was an unspoken reference. There was no need to identify the new enemy. Both knew too well who that was. It was a threat that would bring the United States to its knees and their nation as well. The window of opportunity had opened and closed. It had shut as quickly as it was opened. Pursuing their own private thoughts, both sat in silence for some time.

It had turned late. The sound of a distant clock announced the hour of midnight. Potempkin checked his watch. He was in no hurry. There was no one waiting for him. With deep regrets, he felt the loneliness sink into his life. A sigh escaped his lips. Moments later, the functionaries got up and hurried on their own ways: one back to an uncertain future, the other into a lonely, but well deserved, retirement.

STATE OF THE NATION

"Citizens of the United States," the president was addressing the nation for the first time since the attack, "you all know by now that the nation had been under attack. First," he went on to say, "let me assure all of you that the government of the United States, the military, and the defense forces are still in command and will stay in command to hunt the responsible parties down until the last of the criminals are brought to justice. The attack was deliberate. It was an attack well planned out and executed with one purpose, and one purpose alone, to undermine the nation's communication and finance infrastructure; to destroy, or at least disrupt, trade, commerce, and, most importantly, the security of the nation and the free world. What followed immediately after was an act of utmost violence in the form of a nuclear assault on one of our nation's most treasured cities, San Francisco, and its unsuspecting citizens. It was the most cowardly act an enemy could afflict on another nation and its people." The broadcast went out over the airwaves anticipating to be heard by the fleet of HAM operators. Word would spread quickly by word of mouth to the local population.

"Let me assure you," he went on, "I, with the full support of the government, the military, and the defense forces, will do my utmost to bring the nation back to an even stronger state of wellbeing. Sometimes," he expanded, "it takes an act of defiance to realize the weakness and vulnerability for a nation, to force it to wake up and take stock. As you can see, communication is slowly being restored. Rebuilding San Francisco is yet another task. I, on behalf of the government, am extending our most sincere sympathies and condolences to the survivors of that once so beautiful city.

"In summary," he continued, "damages afflicted to our nation are as follows: infrastructure, power grid, satellite, ground communications, air and ground transportation, banking and finance systems, backup and emergency services, and commercial business and government services."

There was much more damage ranging from major enterprises to local grocery stores. All had been affected in one way or other. Barter had become the means for trade. Gold and silver coins were in use with whoever had this precious commodity. Paper currency and cash was in use, but only with limited access. Banking facilities closed as fast as they had opened. That was true for supermarkets, stores, and shops. Objects of value could be traded, but most businesses did not bother. Many did not know the value of bartered items.

"I must strongly emphasize," the president went on, "that the danger is not over yet. There are indications that more cities are being targeted by the enemy in an attempt to disrupt and destroy us even more. Our defense forces, with the support of every law-enforcing agency, are currently doing their best to identify the threat and bring its perpetrators to justice. My promise to you, citizens of the United States, is that this act of cowardice inflicted only a temporary setback and we will do our best to reestablish a stronger defense grid to prevent another occurrence of similar acts of destruction.

"We have taken measures of retaliation against the enemy by annihilating their foremost place of commerce, namely the capital city of North Korea, Pyongyang. We have inflicted severe damages to the primary enemy of the free world in measures yet to be established. Assessments have been slow to arrive because of the disruption to our communication and surveillance systems. But, let me assure you, these systems are currently being repaired and will eventually be replaced with the aid of our allied nations that have promised to extend their full support.

"However," he expounded further, "there are enemy forces infiltrating into the United States that are much more dangerous. Warnings have been sent to the potential cities targeted for destruction. The National Guard, defense forces, local law enforcement agencies, and the FBI have been deployed to the following regions: the Pacific Coast, Denver, Chicago, and the Eastern Seaboard.

Furthermore, the nation and the District of Columbia are presently being held hostage. With the defense shield down and surveillance disabled, it is difficult to assess the size of the forces and intentions from a yet unidentified assailant. We are negotiating with the head of the Islamic forces for the release of the hostages and to prevent any further acts of aggression. Let me point out," he concluded, "that there is no guarantee on the success of the negotiations, but let me assure you, the enemy will be brought to justice. My promise to you, citizens, is that the forces that are undermining the nation and the free world will be dealt with in the most severe manner. The punishment will be severe to bring the responsible to justice, but, the end will justify the means. That's my promise to you. May God bless all of you and protect this beautiful nation of ours."

TACTICAL ACTION CENTER

It appeared communication in the eastern sector of the nation had been reestablished, if only within the intelligence community. It had taken all available resources on hand to achieve that. National security was given first priority. Commercial, business, news, and the other services had to wait. After all, national security was at stake. The threat was still alive and real. "National security" was the new buzz phrase. It had gained a new level of importance. For government and military alike, it was a license to steal. Not that a license would be required. It was a barter system solely based on promises. Let the economists resolve the finances and reserves when the time came to collect. National debts to the tax payers would be long lasting. It wouldn't be a first time.

At the moment, the monitors were tuned to the speaker. The DHS tactical center was setup to serve as primary command and communication center for the nation. Live information kept streaming in from the field. Microwave towers were hastily connected to link up mobile action teams. The towers, although not an ideal solution, provided a direct line of sight link. It'd have to do until new satellites were placed in orbit. The technology was ancient but it worked. It had been used effectively for fifty years following WWII. The only drawback was that transmit line of sight could not be obstructed.

The room was packed with reps from the NNSA, FBI, and DOD. Data just received from Sandia caused an immediate stir. "According to the lab coats," Barrister, whose image appeared in full width across the monitors, was saying, "we're dealing with a biological agent." His voice was disrupted by intermittent breaks in line quality. "Any comments?" Alex had been called to the center. He was watching tight-lipped.

The monitor kept switching between speakers. "Let's look at the craft's flight path again," the Deputy Director, FBI, suggested. His voice disrupted the current speaker. He gestured to the wallboard. "Alex, if you please."

Alex had been anxiously waiting his turn. When it came to meetings and conferences, his general attitude was, *let the power brokers do the talking*. Today, he couldn't wait for the analysis to be over. Laser pointer firmly planted in one hand, he traced the light beam across the wall-projected U.S. map. "We know the first crate was unloaded in San Francisco." He recapped the flight path. "Next drop was Chicago. Last and final stop," he briefly paused to collect his thoughts, "well, the last payload's been conveniently lost." He was still furious. *How could this happen? The convoy was heavily protected.* His focus was momentarily distracted. "Bauer," Barrister boomed impatiently, "please continue." There were a number of speculations on the whereabouts of the lost container. Alex had his own ideas.

"Where does that leave us?" One agent posed the questioned.

"I'll come to that." Alex ignored the caller. He realized the pressure the agencies were under, but wanted to lay out his own theory. "We have payloads delivered to three potential targets." The means to which the viral agents would be released had not yet been established. It could be by ground, by air, or by water carriers. "We just don't know. It's up to your people. Let me remind you," he urged, "that we don't have much time."

"Suggestions?" It was the Deputy Director for NNSA. He sounded edgy. He was waiting for responses. None came forward.

"Let's look at the flight pattern," Alex picked up. "Because of the limited nuclear capability of the nation we're dealing with, we can rule out radiation hazards. That leaves two alternatives, namely, biological and chemical. Get me a meteorological overlay for the U.S. map," he ordered the video operator. He planted his body in front of the camera. It momentarily cast his shadow on the screen. Using markers, he delineated three possible drop zones. "What's common to all points?" he asked, stepping back.

"Air movement…jet stream…weather dissipation…" were some hesitant responses posed by the teams. "It'd make sense for air currents to carry the contaminants."

Alex quickly countered, "That would affect only a narrow belt across the northern perimeter."

"Wait a minute," a scientist from the Sandia lab cut in.

"Go ahead." Alex was annoyed but allowed the interruption.

"From the chemical composition of the substances we analyzed," the scientist deducted, "delivery by air would be ineffective."

"Please explain."

"Pathogenic microorganisms such as the Protozoan family we detected can only proliferate in water."

"Then it's agreed," the director of NNSA proposed without anticipating further objections, "the probable delivery will be by water carrier."

"But," a voice came forward, "with the size of our major waterways, it'd be impossible to poison a large body of population effectively." This made sense considering the relatively small amount of poisonous agents released in comparison to the massive amount of water flow.

"Rationale's valid but inconclusive," Sandia cut in. "Consider the common cold virus," he enlightened the speaker, "carried across the nation spread over a vast geographical body of air." The virus carried around the globe by the jet stream affected the masses with each seasonal wave. "It only takes a few spores to affect a new host." It made sense. Many agreed.

"Could we have a map of the major rivers?" Alex requested. He wanted to make sure he did not overlook anything. He studied the map again. "What water ways are common with the flight path?" He stepped back to allow everyone full view.

"There are the Sacramento, Colorado, Illinois, and Hudson rivers," someone pointed out.

"Doesn't make sense," another observer interrupted. "Sacramento feeds west into the river delta by the Bay. Why contaminate San Francisco when much of the population's already annihilated?"

"Makes sense," most agreed.

"Then let's start from the backend." Alex scribbled on a notepad. He slid the paper into the image reader. "Following river sources are suspect: New York - Hudson and East rivers; Chicago - Illinois and Mississippi; Denver - Arkansas, Platte, Colorado, and Rio Grande; California - Sacramento River."

"Interesting," muffled voices rumbled through the action center, "all rivers leading south."

"We have a pattern," Barrister cut in, "but it doesn't explain the West Coast."

"Wait a minute." Alex paused. He just recognized the obvious. There was a halting silence. He had finally gained the respect he'd deserved. People listened, and they listened to a civilian. "Some of you Easterners," he spoke with full confidence, "may not realize this, but there's an aqueduct cutting across California." There were several confirmations from the audience. "Channel extends from Sacramento clear across the state feeding the entire southern region."

"What do you mean?" Not everybody in the nation had come across the channel visible only on close up.

"Pull it up on the monitor," he ordered, "let's see." There it was, for all eyes to see, the aqueduct system, hundreds of miles in length. A brief text description indicated it had been built in the early part of the 19th century. Its sole purpose was to carry water from Northern California to the south. The waterway was a concrete-lined channel with basic measurements of 40 feet at the base by 110 feet width at the top, with a general depth of 32 feet.

The aqueduct started in the San Joaquin-Sacramento river delta at the Banks Plant where it pumped water in from the Clifton Court Forebay. From there, water was pushed to the Bethany Reservoir, which, in turn, served as a Forebay to the South Bay pumping plant for final distribution in the south.

The general design and construction of the waterway was simple. For the water to flow, the canal was built at a slight grade and, when it arrived at a pumping station, was pumped back up where it would gradually flowed downhill again to the next station, eventually feeding the San Luis Reservoir.

"Think we've got something," Barrister agreed. "We..." he was about to make an assessment, but was rudely interrupted by a face on the video screen which everybody recognized.

"We've got a situation." It was the head of the CDC. People in Chicago are getting sick by the hundreds. Denver reports similar alerts." He paused a few seconds to allow the assembly to calm down. "The sick," he conveyed, "appear to have symptoms related to severe viral infections."

"I need specifics," the principal scientist from Sandia demanded. He was visibly shaken.

"Fever, chills, coughing," was the grave response, "muscle aches, nausea, vomiting, and diarrhea, and that's just the initial stage. We don't know the final effects."

"How soon will you know?"

"When blood shows," the CDC spokesman stated. "Could be hours, could be days."

It was a clue Alex needed. His expertise was needed elsewhere. It was time for an action plan. *My action plan.* For that, he'd need transportation. And there wasn't any. Two days earlier, orders had come in for all assets to be turned over to the Air Force, immediately. Craft attached to rescue and support missions were seized and recalled to Midland. "Something's up." Rumors were prolific. The entire nation had been caught off guard.

Word eventually got out about Cuba's assault on U.S. soil. Nobody saw it coming. It was a fretful two days waiting for the outcome. Then word arrived. "Confederates won." The news immediately lifted the spirit of the people. Despite the current biological threat, there was renewed hope.

The results were very much visible. Wings and fuselages wore telltale signs of air battle. They were riddled with bullet holes. "Repairs have to wait," the pilots had been told, "'til after the hostage rescue." Alex was released from his tactical responsibilities. His liaison was turned over to the head of DHS.

"One person's happy," Alex remarked to a nearby functionary now that command had been turned back over to military OPS.

"Not to mention the Air Force," was the comeback.

"Gotta get a move on," Alex urged himself on as he left the center. "We've already lost too much time." He needed air transportation. He needed it now.

AERIAL PURSUIT

There were crisis issues at hand. Alex couldn't waste any more time. At the far end of the hallway, on the way out, he passed the OPS center. Brian was waiting. Taking Alex's cue, he fell in with his footsteps. Alex suddenly stopped in his tracks. Startled, Brian bumped into him. They had spotted Brooks driving up. "What are you doing back?"

"Convoy's been ambushed," he blurted out. "Enemy forces were waiting for us." He briefly illustrated the attack. "Don't know where they get their weapons. Ambush was over in a couple minutes."

"Tracy?" Alex challenged him. She had been put in the man's trust. It was his responsibility to get her safely to the destination. He had blown it.

"We'll get her back," was all he said. There was no need to further expand on the situation. They were men of action. No excuses. No delays. The time to act was now. Scott gestured for Alex to follow. He was already headed for an assault vehicle assigned to the CIA. He took possession. "Where to?"

"Andrews," Alex ordered. The vehicle was already in motion. In back, Brian worked the tactical radio. He was trying to raise NSA OPS when the vehicle came to an abrupt halt.

"Where're you goin'?" Foster yelled. He had intercepted the vehicle. Grim faced, he waved them to a stop. When he saw Alex leave the tactical center with his party in tow he knew something was up. He'd rushed to catch up.

Alex was fuming. He couldn't afford more delays. He urged Scott to step on it. But Foster didn't budge.

Alex turned to face his long time general friend. "You know where I have to be."

"I need you here," Foster insisted.

"But," Alex resisted, "my daughter."

"Nothing your friends can't handle." He gestured at the two. "I've got bigger issues." He didn't have to spell it out. The nation was in peril. Foster opened the door for Alex who reluctantly stepped out. He then waved them off. Scott and Brian, for whatever turned up next, would be on their own.

Inside the assault vehicle, Brian waited for NSA OPS to respond. "Sparky," he recognized the voice, "satellite status?"

"We've got control."

"Get a trace on I-95."

Sparky entered the coordinates. A string of commands went up in orbit. It was received by the satellite. Some 250 miles up, the space object reacted. It immediately sought out the new target. The rotation locked in on the eastern sector. Its receiver dish traced a path along I-95 east. Dynamic images painted across the ground based monitors.

"What are we looking for?" Sparky asked.

"Transport vehicle," Scott answered. Brian repeated the message in on the mic. "Freight truck…no markings…destination…Big Apple."

"Standby."

"What's next?" Brian posed the question. "Got a plan?" He had a foreboding feeling about what would come. Pursuing the hijacked convoy via this vehicle was worthless.

Too much time had elapsed to give chase. The only alternative would be by air. Andrews was thirty minutes away.

"Alert Base OPS," Scott ordered. Brian tuned the receiver. He notified Andrews of their impending arrival.

Twenty-five minutes later the base was in view. Gate security had already been alerted. They were waved on to the departure building. The AFB, it seemed, was operational. Although crippled in appearance, some of the Confederate craft had been salvaged. They were back in use waiting to depart. Where the sound of jets used to fill the air, today it was propellers. The confederates were providing transport. It limited the team's choices. They had to be in the air quick. The most likely craft would be a chopper. Scott and Brian approached the crew chief. He shook his head when asked for transport. "Not possible."

Not taking no for an answer, Scott held his ground. "What?"

"Nothing's flight worthy," was the reply, "need maintenance." What they needed was an attack craft. It'd give them the speed and power to catch up. Apache, Blackhawk, and Kiowa needed computers to fly, but those were grounded by the EMP burst. Stacked with sophisticated software, they needed computers to navigate.

"Wait." Brian had a thought. "Any chance a legacy chopper in-house like attack, assault, or gunship?" Those heavy-duty workhorses, officially decommissioned decades ago, were still used for special OPS. If he could get his hands on one it could carry them the distance.

"Hangar," the chief gestured in the proper direction. "The maintenance chief, buddy of mine, may have something."

There were several hangars on the field.

"Big one," Scott asked.

"No," the crew chief corrected. "Stores Air Force One." The hangar he indicated was farther down the base. Craft of various types were being worked on. Maintenance staff had been busy for days, trying to salvage anything flight worthy.

The maintenance chief sauntered over. "Impressive," he said, motioning at the tarmac, "right?"

"Looks like WWII," Brian replied.

"That's the idea." He was sizing up the two visitors, one in a combat outfit the other in flight jacket. He inspected the office symbols displayed on their lapels. "DELTA," he cut a grin, "NSA. I'm impressed."

"We need your help," Scott cut in.

"Let me guess." The chief grinned. "Chasing bad guys."

"Listen," Scott urged, "we need something fast." He looked around the maintenance hangar. "What have you got?"

"What can you fly?" The chief shifted his gaze to Brian. "Veteran?"

"You got it," Brian said with pride. "Gulf War."

The chief was a Vet himself. It seemed he'd appreciate anyone with like history. The war...the action...death counts...followed with a few days R & R. Brian could read passion in the man's eyes.

"Follow me," the chief gestured. He waved them into the far recesses of the hangar. A tarpaulin partially covered the craft. He pulled it off with a snap.

"That's it." Brian recognized the craft. "Cobra. Incredible." The Bell AH-1 Huey Cobra was his favorite flying machine. He felt elated.

They were staring at what appeared a modified combat version of the once popular gunship. It had been outfitted with new electronics. Frame and pods had been refurbished to carry new ordinance. At one time, the Cobra was the military's infantry workhorse, but it had been decommissioned after the Vietnam War. Re-commissioned again for the Gulf War in the early '90s, it had gained tremendous popularity, especially with the NATO alliance. Retrofitted, it could be obtained relatively inexpensive. Foreign nations jumped at the opportunity. Military factions from Japan, Korea, and Israel acquired everything from U.S. arsenals they could get their hands on. The U.S. military retained some of the units to support hot spot special operations. Most of those were obscure missions executed for Intel services. The refurbished units contained the latest in sophistication from FLIR to hellfire missile mounting pods. The forward-looking infrared system had night targeting sensors so sensitive they were able to spot a small rodent hiding under the brush.

"Looks awesome." Scott made the comment. He'd seen these killing machines, but never up close.

"What'll it take to get this off the ground?"

"Whatcha got in mind?" The chief wanted to know.

"New York City," Brian replied, "and fast."

"Hey." The chief yelled in the direction of the chopper. "Get your ass down here." He waved at one of the maintenance crew working inside the cockpit. A lanky fellow hopped off the craft. The young soldier approached his boss. He stood at attention. "Relax," the chief ordered. "What's the status with the craft?"

"Basic instruments are working," he reported, "compass, altimeter, fuel gauge, speed indicator. Just put in a new FLIR module. The rest is still down." He shrugged. "Waiting for replacement parts."

Scott was curious. "What's the speed and radius?

"Modified version," he said, "275 nautical mile range…maxed at 175 knots."

Scott calculated. He approved with a nod. "It'll take us there."

Brian was also satisfied. The flying distance to New York was just under 230 miles. There was plenty of fuel. "Let's talk turkey," Brian turned factual.

"Don't suppose," the chief speculated, "you got orders?"

"These times?" His response was suggestive. "Tell you what," Brian made a proposition, "I'll square with you when we get back. You won't be sorry."

"Good enough for me," the chief replied. He quickly headed up the ramp. The controls checked out fine, and, after an engine test, so did the power plant. The chopper was flight ready minutes later.

NSA HEADQUARTERS

This was action he liked. It was what Sparky needed to make the job worthwhile. There had been no shortage of it the past weeks. Things were looking up. Space assets were getting repaired. He was getting his tools back. It was what he'd signed up for. Test and diagnostics weren't his preference. *Give me a mission, anything, I'll track it down.* A miniature joystick projected from the command platform. With a caressing gesture, he let his fingers glide over the controls. "Extension of manhood," he chuckle. He'd grin when he was teased by coworkers. "On the job only," he'd reply. The stick was his link with the target. *Any target.* It didn't matter where on the planet, he'd find it. It could be hidden beneath brush, blend in with surrounding terrain, or be obscured from sight, and his eyes would spot it.

The other connection vital to his job was the headset. It was the link with the source. Technology had not yet advanced enough to have a direct connection from the brain to the target. "But," he'd assured his coworkers, thinking of miniature implants into the brain, "it'll come." It was only a matter of time for thought control to emerge as a technology.

For now, it was up to him to provide the link. "Roger," he acknowledged Brian's call. The satellite in his control was much like a video game. As a matter of fact, video games he played at home on his Xbox were much more sophisticated. Here, on the job, it was mostly about resolution rather than action, with KH, anyway. It was different with the kinetics. Working those was more like Star Wars. *You could intercept to shoot an object out of the sky.* But he couldn't talk about that. That part of his job was off limits to the outside world.

For now, today, the job was tracking I-95. Gradually, Sparky traced the crosshairs on the miniature screen along the interstate. It was amazing how clear the ground-based objects came into view with infinite zoom. Color, make, and model could easily be identified. What made it even better these days was the sparse traffic. Traffic on the road was mostly dispatch vehicles to aid road services. Home or garage calls had the lowest priority or none at all. America's workforce was practically stranded at home. Many were looking for things to do. Neighbors, once strangers to each other, now connected. Ideas were shared, advice given, and social bonds established. Items such as wine, beer, and spirits were in high demand. Citizens had time on their hands to enjoy leisure. Some enjoyed the idle time. Many reevaluated their lifestyles. Others made use through ingenuity. Crafts, skills, and creativity were put to use. Ideas and resourcefulness were flying high. People talked to each other. People learned to trust. Every human quality was explored. New values were forged to shape a new dawn.

Corporate business was idle. Most industries had been crushed. Although infrastructures were still in place, they had no input sources. Power, communication, and physical resources were shut out. Shops, while open, were only selling canned goods and other nonperishable items. The nation had been caught up in a state of economic meltdown.

It did not take Sparky long to identify the ambush vehicle. "Got 'em," he shouted into the mic.

"Keep a lock on the target," Brian advised, "we're closing in." In the distance, the New York City skyline slowly emerged from the horizon. He flew high enough not to be spotted but low enough not to lose sight.

Scott kept silent. He seemed to ponder deep thoughts. *Wonder what's on his mind?* Brian dared not imagine.

NEW YORK CITY (Port Authority)

Central New York, city of contrast, culturally and otherwise, usually brilliantly lit from millions of light sources, tonight, as it had been for almost two weeks, was bathed in darkness. Stores had been emptied days ago. There was nothing to be had. Most dwellings stood empty, vacated by the occupants in search for food. The other half had nowhere to go. The ones remaining were mostly scavenging garbage dumps and sewage canals. Martial law had been declared soon after the initial attack on the nation. To protect the core of the city, National Guardsmen and law enforcement elements were taking a stand against criminal elements. For the first time in modern history, the city gave its population a break. It had shut down much like computers, banks, businesses, and every other facility dependent on power. Despite the darkness and the lockdown, there was some activity. Maintenance crews, under the protection of the law, had been dispatched by the city to salvage generator and power sources wherever they could be located. An enormous effort was underway to build a temporary infrastructure to prevent the city from complete collapse.

Some yellow cabs, aside from crew vehicles repaired days ago, were the only transportation available to shuttle crews up and down major city links. The occasional sound of a car horn announced their presence. Other sounds came from portable generators needed to feed the fleet of maintenance vehicles. Every conceivable pothole was occupied by the crews. Repairs were well underway to repair damaged power cables and comm lines. The city was fueled from emergency resources kept in storage tanks across the rivers.

One taxi was trying to beat out the others. It was weaving in and out of traffic inching its way ahead. The only passenger was late. "Stop," he called out, "let me out here." Slamming on the brakes, the driver was shaken from his private thoughts. The hurried passenger dislodged. The cabby's hand extended from the window, demanding fare. He was palmed a large bill.

"Don't got change." He had plenty of bills, but tried to manipulate a sizable tip. He only took fares with cash. He had no interest in barter. His cab wasn't large enough to accommodate the items offered by some. It was either cash or no ride.

"Keep it."

The driver stepped on the accelerator to fetch the next ride. "Thanks, buddy," were his trailing words.

With no one in sight, the passenger gave a sigh of relief. Ten minutes into the wait, he began pacing the sidewalk. Another ten, he was cussing. Agitated at first, he soon turned worried. He speculated about a possible no show. Without a phone there was no way of making contact. Finally, a set of headlights emerged, moving in his direction. It was the van he'd been expecting. "You're late," he spat at the driver. His impatience had turned to anger. "Where the f..." he was about to release a string of pent up curses, but instantly held back. He bit his tongue to prevent the swearword from slipping through his lips. His angry face had turned to surprise. In an instant, he'd recognized the party. Sitting in the passenger seat was the head of the jihad, flanked by his lieutenants. "I have to get back to my desk," he whispered, "they're already suspicious."

"This won't take long," the leader responded, jumping from the van, quickly followed by his lieutenants. The leader took a few seconds to assess the present environment. "You ready?" he addressed the local contact.

"Hurry up," the contact affirmed without waiting for a response. "Please." He was already in motion. He gestured for them to follow then promptly disappeared into the darkened complex ahead.

"Hillview Pump Station," the sign proclaimed. The visiting party followed the man inside.

The complex was Manhattan's lifeline. Without it, the city and its outlaying boroughs could not exist. It currently supplied eight million people, increasing to twelve million during daytime, with an insatiable demand for water and disposing waste.

As usual this time of night, slouched comfortably in his chair, the watch guard was eating his dinner. Today, it was a sandwich. The maintenance team working on the pumps and generators had left for the day. Where normally the small TV screen would keep him company, it was quiet. The emergency lighting, fueled by an auxiliary generator, barely illuminated the office. The only sound was him munching on the sandwich. "Another long night," he grumbled. About to take another bite, he was distracted by some commotion near the entrance. Alerted, he put the sandwich aside. About to get up, he froze in motion.

A squad of intruders rushed in without warning. He fumbled for the gun in the holster but then relaxed. He'd recognized a former coworker. "Jim," he faltered, "what's going on?" He was surrounded by several toughs jabbering away in a foreign tongue.

"Not your concern." It would be the last words he'd hear in this world. He felt the impact of a single bullet fired into his forehead but never heard the sound. His body went limp. One final breath escaped his lungs as a dependable, but boring, life was cut short.

"Pull up," Hammad urged Rashid Abu and Shakir Murad, his principle lieutenants, who unloaded in haste. "Careful," he shouted, striding toward the service elevator, shoving a struggling shape ahead. It was a woman. She was blindfolded.

The team was ready to load the dolly, weighed down by a heavy crate, into the service elevator. Somebody pushed a button. "Nothing." There was no power. The cargo had to be moved down the stairwell. It would be several levels down. "Move it...hurry up..." Hammad kept urging. It took precious time and effort to deliver the cargo to the sub-terrain level.

"Where are we? What are you doing?" It was the woman's voice echoing eerily through the underground station. "Bastards," she shouted into the hollows of the building.

"Shut up." The others watched the leader slap her hard across the blindfold. "Get her inside."

"You'll pay for this," she spat at him. Her voice resonated between the walls. "My dad will hound you forever." She hoped he'd be on their trail. *But is there time?* Despite the repeated beatings she'd taken she wasn't ready to succumb to the inevitable. Her legs struggled to keep from getting dragged along in the darkness. *We're close to the destination,* she reasoned. She was keenly aware of the harried tension. *Is this the end,* she questioned herself, *after all I've been through?* "Watch out, you imbecile," an angry voice demanded, "don't break the crystals."

Crystals what? Feeling helpless, Tracy tried to assess her predicament. An ominous feeling welled up in her mind. *No help is coming.* Her life would soon be over.

In the depths below, the team was busy shutting off valves, bypass conduits, and making connections into the main water distribution system. The BIO canister was ready to be mounted. "Over here," a voice ordered. She felt her body lifted, then slammed down hard. Groping hands reached for her struggling limbs. Her body was forced onto a solid object. Straps were stretched around both wrists and ankles. She strained, she struggled, but was unable to move. Beneath her back, she felt a hardened contour. It was an uneven surface. In her desperate struggle to resist, Tracy was rewarded with more blows. She screamed at her attackers. It did not help, but strangely enough, relieved some of the tension from within. Minutes later, her body was firmly restrained. She was unable to move. Not even her head.

Where one team struggled with her, another was busy making the final connections to the city's water mains. The men had been busy mounting the glass containers into the duct bypass. Only one task remained, releasing the valves. The group was anxious to get going. They watched with apprehension as the colored contents from the glass cylinders seeped into the water system, releasing a lethal substance. It was well on its way to massive destruction.

"Let's get out of here," Tracy heard the trailing words. Hurried footsteps disappeared toward the far entrance. An eerie silence fell over the cavern. Tracy was alone. She was left to her own thoughts. *There it is again.* Her ears caught a faint click. It seemed to originate from close by. "Who's there?" she called out. There was no answer. There it was again, the click. She tried to analyze the sound.

Watch...clock...timepiece, her mind registered. After a few more clicks, it suddenly dawned on her. *Timer...bomb!* At the realization, sheer panic set in.

Tracy tried to arch her back to shake loose from the restraints. The twisting wrists and ankles only caused the restraints to tighten more, causing more stinging pain. Her mind struggled for a way out. There wasn't any. "Don't let me die," she pleaded. "Not this way." But no one listened. Facing the inevitable, her mind struggled for inner peace. Images rapidly passed across a desperate mind. Time spun backwards. She returned to childhood, but there was no solution, only desperation. "Michael," her mind screamed into the silence, "help me!"

Tracy was not a religious person. While she had been brought up Catholic as child, she'd since dropped active participation in her faith. The demand for a promising career had taken over her life. "But," she clearly recalled her dad's ardent advice, "if you ever get in trouble," he'd suggested, "where there's no way out, call on the angel. He'll hear you."

Back then, she believed the advice was based only on notions of faith. Today, in desperation, entrapped in the darkened abyss, awaiting the inevitable in silence, her prayers were sincere.

There have been many accounts of miracles where the archangel Michael came to the rescue. Within Roman Catholic teachings, the archangel had a specific role. Chief opponent to Satan, the role called for saving the soul at an hour of extreme desperation.

MANHATTAN DIVERS (Skydiving club)

Earlier the same evening, at the other end of town, well toward the center of Manhattan, a group of youngsters, casually dressed in sweatpants, sweaters, and hiking boots, weighted down with jump packs and gear, climbed their way up a series of seemingly endless steps within a tightly packed stairway. "How much more?" a girl in her late teens, short on breath, puffed at her partner as she pushed her body up the stairs.

"Fifteen minutes," her companion guessed, also huffing for air, "maybe less."

"Let's rest a minute," the lead member in the group, obviously in better shape, suggested.

Almost thirty minutes ago, the sign had proclaimed "Emergency Exit" when the group entered the building. Behaving stealthily, almost to the point of covertness, their act was an unauthorized one. They all were aware that it was an illegal entry. It was this daring act that made the journey worthwhile. Otherwise, any one of the covertly acting members would admit, "What'd be the point?"

In the hollows of the shaft, presently taking another break from climbing the steep ascent, the group, a local sky jump club, also well known to the city's law enforcing agency for making daring jumps off tall structures, made their entrance through one of the emergency exits left unlocked.

Several in the group were newcomers dared by the seasoned members to encourage a first illegal jump. Under normal conditions, prior to the all-consuming blackout, because of the illegality of their acts, the tension would be high. Well on their way up the high-rise, this evening, within the semi-darkness of a few beams of darting flashlights, it was mostly a feeling of heightened anticipation. Falling a thousand feet in freefall, the upcoming event scheduled at sunup, would be thrilling to say the least. It was this thrill that kept pushing the members upward toward this evening's target, the upper deck.

It took another twenty minutes of grunts and sweat for the group to finally reach their goal. They quickly settled into one of the offices on the uppermost floor to wait for next morning's event. In the meantime, jump packs downed, gears stored against walls, blankets unwrapped, a bottle of whisky made its appearance to be enjoyed by the newcomers into the wee hours. That was the plan.

AERIAL PURSUIT

Brian was strapped into the front seat. The contours of the seat, shaped from many missions wrapped tightly around his back. Making his way north at ten thousand feet, he felt elated once more. The view was spectacular. The Cobra was a tandem two seat craft: pilot up front, gunner/navigator in back. Scott had the gunner's position. Both were listening through the headset. Sparky was giving directions. The satellite link, two hundred fifty some miles out, had a lock on I-95 traffic.

Orders issued by Foster were simple. "Shoot to kill." It would have been an easy task were it not for Tracy. For now, he kept pace with the moving vehicle. The craft had left Baltimore and Newark in its wake some time ago. Ahead, a cluster of shadows gradually moved into view. "What's the time?" Brian shouted to the back of the cockpit.

"Thirty five minutes out," Scott shot back.

Twenty minutes later, the Manhattan skyline came into view. Darkness had settled in for the night. The sight was an eerie one. If it wasn't for the moon, navigation would be impossible. The skyline rose up hundreds of feet in gigantic silhouettes. With skyscrapers reaching for the skies, the scene looked like an invasion of giants from another planet.

"Time to get on deck," Scott urged from the gunner seat.

Brian reduced the throttle of the gunship. From here on out it would be a close up chase. They had followed the speeding truck up to Jersey City then cut across on I-78 toward the Holland Tunnel. There, they abruptly lost sight of the vehicle. The truck had sped into the tunnel entrance. Giving chase, Brian pulled up close. He was about to charge into the tunnel, but at the last moment pulled up hard.

He'd gauged the clearance. "Won't make it!" he yelled, aborting the chase. "No clearance." The craft almost clipped the tunnel entrance. "Dammit." He spun out, headed across Hudson River. "We lost them."

"Now!" One mile into the tunnel, the driver slammed down hard on the brakes. The truck skidded to a sudden stop. "Switch vehicles!" Hammad gave swift orders for Abu and Murad to unload. It would allow him to escape pursuit. Two ramps were extended from the truck bed. A driver backed out the van. The rest of the squad remained on the truck. Hammad issued more orders. The truck sped off towards the Manhattan exit. It'd act as decoy.

The decoy seemed to work. At the Manhattan tunnel exit, the Cobra hovered, waiting. Brian and Scott were in position. And so was Manhattan law enforcement. The speeding truck was spotted. The chase was on.

Seconds later, the van emerged. It left unobstructed. It sped ahead. A cluster of street signs came into view. Several roads converged from different directions. "9A," Hammad instructed Murad, currently driving, "north." The van swerved its way along the eastern edge of Hudson River. Complete darkness embraced the occupants. Only the skyline silhouettes caused by the moon were cast onto the slow flowing body of water below. A few miles west, the New Jersey shores were doused in complete darkness.

"What's he doing?" Sparky called out. Since the 9/11 attack on the trade center, tight restrictions on eastbound tunnel traffic had been in place. A ban on commercial traffic was strictly enforced. On the remote monitor, he watched the speeding truck enter the tunnel. "Great," he breathed a sigh of relief. It'd mean certain capture. In the next minute, the chase could be over. Law enforcement was waiting at the exit.

Sparky had a lock on the target when it entered the tunnel. He adjusted the joystick. He let the crosshairs glide across the Hudson River. Panning ahead, he located the tunnel exit. He centered on it. Below, his eyes caught a fleet of shadows. A grin swept across his face. "The law." He zoomed in on the ground then spotted the sign. "Canal Street," it said.

What's keeping it? He'd been mentally calculating the time for the vehicle to exit. There was no truck. He was about to call the gunship when it finally surfaced. "About time," he exhaled and reacquired the satellite lock. The moving target changed direction, heading south. What he missed, seconds later, was a commercial van emerging the tunnel.

"Heading," Sparky's voice alerted the Cobra, "south, possible 'Trade' grounds."

Two hundred miles southwest at the Dulles command center, fed by the FLIR, a team intensely followed the surveillance on the display monitors. The forward-looking infrared camera mounted on the gunship pod sent dynamic data streams over the satellite.

"NY-9A south," Sparky's metallic sounding voice came through.

Brian gave chase. He struggled to keep track of the speeding truck. His eyes strained through the darkness. He could barely make out the twin road leading south. Up ahead, the infamous 9/11 landmark crept into view. Brian caught sight of it. Although sparsely illuminated, construction for the new complex was well under way.

At central command, a team of technicians was feverishly at work. They needed video and voice to make decisions. From their back office position, DOD battle strategy and command directives would be essential.

On the frontline, the chopper hovered. They waited. The semi had reached its destination. An armed squadron jumped from the truck bed. Their aim was the new freedom towers.

"Such a disgrace." Brian noticed the empty spaces where the once prominent Trade Center towers had stood. "There'll be justice." It was a promise he'd made years ago. "Today's it."

"Won't be long before Freedom Tower's up," Scott shouted over the chopping sound. "Only a couple more years. Watch out!" He gestured wildly.

Brian acted on instinct. He took the craft into a tight turn. At the same time, he pulled back hard on the controls. The chopper almost stalled out. It had drifted with the air currents and nearly got clipped by a tower.

Scott's legs pushed against the G-forces. "You keep this up," he scoffed, "and my feet are gonna punch through the floor." A cowboy at heart, he totally enjoyed the ride.

"Target's in sight," Sparky reported back, "ground action below."

"About time," Brian echoed. He was ready for action. Many years had passed since he'd seen battle. He was ready.

"…ck …ll."

"Repeat…repeat, please." He'd missed the command. "Losing signal," he said over the channel.

"Attack," the voice repeated, "at will." Signal strength was back. Orders issued by HQ command were clear. Brian was ready. And so was Scott.

Brian pushed on the controls. The craft responded. He forced the nose forward and down. The gunship picked up speed. He made a wide turn over the Hudson. Just short of the water, he flared out and headed for shore. The target was in view, clearly visible on the infrared. In a stealthy approach, he inched the craft forward counting a dozen heat signatures in motion.

"Let's see if these work." Scott's moves were deliberate. He was the fighter. He wanted control. The Cobra was fitted with dual controls. Identical, there was primary with secondary backup. Perched in the gunner's seat, he showed extreme determination. Right hand on the control stick, using his thumb, he flipped the safety switch. Onboard weapons went hot. His index fingered the red-colored trigger.

"Hang on," Brian shouted to warn Scott. He knew what would be next. "Whiplash."

Scott squeezed the trigger. "Dammit!" he exclaimed. Something took his breath. The Cobra reacted. The forward motion decelerated to an instant halt. It was the recoil action from twin Gatling guns mounted on both sides of the fuselage. It'd not only snapped the craft into a dead stop. Much like a cannon turret, the gunship violently kicked back several yards. Stunned by the recoil, Scott shouted, "What was that?"

Much like a fire hose at full force, a swooshing sound was caused by projectiles speeding through air at supersonic speed. At the target, a wall of bullets struck home with explosive force.

A hundred yards ahead, the truck disintegrated in a hail of fire created by twin XM-18 mini guns, rotating at a hundred rounds per second. "Like it?" Brian carried a grin. It said it all. "Sanctions for casualties from years ago." Justice had finally been served, although only in part.

"Didn't know what I've been missing," Scott shouted back. He felt ecstatic by the unexpected experience. "Let's do it again."

"HUD," the switch indicated. Brian flipped the switch to activate the heads up display. He took control. "Watch the wall." He pulled the craft into a tight turn then gestured ahead. There were figures. They were running. Some had escaped the inferno. They sought cover. Some scrambled up an embankment. It was a newly constructed wall. It was the foundation for the Freedom Towers. Swooping in low, Brian steadied the craft then pulled the trigger. The hail of bullets was deafening. Much like a searchlight, the horizontal stream illuminated the night. Again, a solid wall of bullets rushed towards the targets. Instants later, several figures tumbled over like miniature figures in a shooting gallery.

"Why," Scott shouted, exhilarated, "it's a turkey shoot." They watched figures drop off the dark side of the wall. "Let's move in," he ordered. This was his show. He was ready for combat. It'd been years since his last face off with a combatant. Already on the skids, he jumped before the chopper touched ground.

Brian sat the craft down and killed the engine. The rotors were still churning when he jumped, rushing after Scott.

Illuminated by construction lighting, yards ahead, Scott clambered up a wall. One target desperately clung to the edge; others lay wounded. Scott stooped down. He screamed with rage, "The girl?" There was no answer. He shook the assailant repeatedly. Even applying force he did not get a response. Bullets had penetrated the man's chest. He was wheezing. Blood splattered from the lungs when he tried to talk. Scott pressed both hands on the oozing wounds. The injured was unable to bear the pain. Both palms up, just before passing into eternity, the jihad gestured toward the sky.

Brian watched Scott trying to get information. Refusing to answer even under extreme pain gave Brian an idea. He rushed to the vehicle they'd been chasing. He checked the inside and the trunk. It was empty. They'd been chasing a decoy. There was no time to waste now. Turned desperate, he recalled the DELTA warrior. They rushed back to the helicopter.

"Sparky," he yelled into the mic, "need your help."

"Like what you did back there," his voice replied over the headset. "What's up?"

"Been chasing a decoy," Brian explained. "Delivery vehicle's been inside the truck. Please tell me you've been recording."

"Stand by."

GROUND PURSUIT

"We're screwed," Scott grunted. He shook his head. "We wasted too much time." As a man of action, he was frustrated. "Give me a battlefield," he said, "or ground mission anytime. But this," his fist hammered on his right leg, "is bullshit." He was displeased with the mission. He'd have preferred taking out the truck when it was still on the interstate, but Brian fiercely objected. He'd been concerned for Tracy's safety. There was no guarantee that she'd come out alive. The mission's main objective had slipped through his hands. The Serpent was still on the loose.

"Just wait." Brian sensed his frustration. "Surveillance will get back."

At the NSA HQ, Sparky acted. He'd know what to do. He was still puzzled, but his subconscious had registered the slight time lag when the truck made its tunnel exit almost an hour ago. At the time, he'd ignored the lapse. Only now he realized it could have been the place for a switch. It was worth investigating.

He called for a trace to the tunnel. His team already analyzed the recorded data. A dozen eyes were penetrating dark ground images. Apparently they'd missed a second shadow emerge. It appeared from the tunnel exit just seconds after the decoy. Where the truck had turned onto West Side south, the shadow sped north. "Got something." Sparky's voice broke the silence. He sounded elated.

"Shoot," Brian acknowledged. He and Scott were ready to give chase.

"Standby," Sparky wavered, "awaiting confirmation." The Cobra was put on hold. Two hundred miles southwest at the tactical center, FBI agents were launching an offensive. Key elements to an effective countermeasure were still missing and vague, to say the least.

At the command center, Alex and Foster had followed the chase on the monitor. At this moment, the image was frozen on Manhattan. The chase was put on hold. "What's up?" Foster demanded on the radio with the FBI. He listened intently then shared the information with Alex.

"Manhattan, North End?" Alex tried to rationalize the information. "What's up there?"

"Here." Foster handed him the receiver. It was the director, FBI, Manhattan regional office, on the line.

"What exactly is it you want?" an irritated director demanded. He'd already been in bed when the D.C. office called.

"Map on New York," Alex was annoyed, "water supply system."

"Don't have that info," the director shot back, "not here, not now, not at the home."

"At least," Alex pleaded, "give me an idea…a general outline."

"If you insist," the director replied. "There's Catskill Aqueduct, Delaware Aqueduct, Croton Aqueduct, and Kensico Reservoir." Following a brief pause, he added, "All feeding Manhattan and New York boroughs."

"Different systems," Alex felt a sense of hopelessness, "four in all? He was looking for a central point. With time running out, there was no hope even to make an attempt to stop the assailants.

"Three separate tunnel systems," the director corrected him, "built last century."

"Is there anything," Alex was almost begging, "anything common at all?"

There was silence at the distant end. Dismayed and hopeless, Alex shook his head. He waited anxiously for the response. "Well?"

"Actually," the director hesitated, "there is. Hillview Reservoir, Yonkers," he explained, "collection point just north of the Bronx." The water supply system originating north in the Catskills was not limited to Manhattan Island. The city was only a minor sector. Most of the population in the region was located in the four outlaying boroughs, Bronx, Brooklyn, Queens, and Staten Island, with a total population of over eight million. The Hillview reservoir channeled water to all.

"That's got to be it!" Alex was ecstatic. "Sparky." He was already on the NSA link. "Hillview Reservoir," he relayed the information, "Bronx, north end." Immediately, the satellite went into motion, as did the Cobra.

"Did you get that?" Sparky's voice redirected at Brian and Scott hovering above lower Manhattan.

"Roger," Brian responded, "on the way." Sparky was guiding the craft to the new heading. They sped north along the West Side highway, then cut east over Riverdale, and, from there, connected to Central Park Avenue. In the distance, they could make out the reservoir panning into view. "Need new coordinates."

"South end." Sparky was on top of it, literally. The satellite dish was pointing almost straight down. "Intersection Hillview and Kimball," he corrected, "I've got you in sight."

At the tactical center, many eyes were centered on the dynamic images panning across the monitors. Although the darkened shadow of the reservoir was barely visible, the Cobra in motion was. The port and starboard lighting identified the craft's position. "Pump station…van…rear parking lot."

"Got it," Brian shot back, "goin' on deck." Scott was already on the skids. Emerging from the shadows, there it was, sitting alongside the Hillview pump station: a black van with its engine idling.

Scott took fire as soon as his feet touched ground. He saw the flashes before the projectiles ricocheted off the fuselage. The fire came from the building. Bright flashes exploded from the dark recesses by the entrance. "Take cover!"

Brian took cover at the first sound of the incoming round. His body was dug in. He didn't have to be told. Projectiles hitting metal sounded too familiar. He'd heard it many times in battle. *Afghanistan,* it was, *ground fire.*

Scott moved first. "Cover me." His voice faded with distance. Scott was headed for the van. Watching him close the distance, Brian gave cover. He pulled the release then aimed at the building entrance. Automatic clutched between his hands, he pulled the trigger. An instant later a stream of tracers hit the target. The AK-47 he'd taken from the dead terrorist at the trade grounds pumped bullets until the magazine was empty. He watched the end of the barrel turn red from friction heat.

Fire from the building was returned with equal force. Brian felt gravel and dirt hit his face. Then the grounds ahead suddenly lit up. A blinding flash came from the direction of the van. The vehicle lifted up with tremendous force. So did Scott. The fuel tank had exploded. A fireball engulfed the tumbling vehicle as it crashed back down. Scott's body landed nearby.

Momentarily stunned, seconds later, Brian rushed to his aid. Scott appeared dead, but moments later he stirred, then opened his eyes. He appeared disoriented. Brian reached for his arm to help him up. On shaky legs he stood for a moment. Otherwise he seemed okay.

"You okay?"

Dumbfounded, Scott stared at Brian. His face turned puzzled. He gestured at his ears. The explosion had caused a terrific case of tinnitus. He rubbed his ears to clear the noise. Both hands came off smeared with blotches of blood. He shook his head repeatedly.

"Busted ear drums," Brian said, looking at the fighter. He knew the symptoms. He'd experienced it on more than one occasion. "Let's go," he urged. They headed for the station entrance. It'd turned silent.

Scott quickly recovered. With weapons drawn, he advanced into the dimly lit entrance. Brian followed. The emergency lighting barely illuminated the hallways. A steady hum was present. He felt it vibrate through the concrete floor.

"Generators," Scott shouted into the dark, "hydro-electric." The service elevator lay just ahead. The doors were shut. Scott pushed the buttons. *Nothing.* "Service's out." He spotted the emergency exit. "We'll have to take the staircase."

Forcefully, but with caution, he pulled the handle. The steel gave way. The door popped opened. Pupils dilated, it took seconds for their eyes to adjust. There were shadows. There was motion. Scott acted on instinct. He dropped onto one knee, aimed, and released the trigger. Brian, a few paces behind, almost walked into a hail of bullets streaming up from the dark. Exploding tracers cut fiery streams through the hall. They had come from different directions. Wedged between the staircase below and the elevator shaft above, Scott shouted, "Trap!" The escape route had been cut off.

Undecided on their next move, both Scott and Brian hesitated in silence. Then, a voice emerged from the dark. "Lose the weapons... drop 'em...drop your weapons...now!" The command was clear. Issued with authority, it was deliberate. It came from above. The fiery streams of bullets from below had stopped. Only harried breathing was perceptible, originating from the dark. There was a blink in Brian's eyes. He nodded at the darkened space above. Scott understood. Shifting his gaze upward, he saw standing there, at this full height, the enemy..." String down at him was the Serpent.

They were trapped. There were only two choices: shoot it out or give up. Knowing the enemy, either way they were destined to die. Scott's instinct said shoot, but his rational mind dictated otherwise. He lowered his weapon. Brian followed suit but held a firm grip on the shaft. Both conceded to the capture indicating, "You win."

Brian spoke. He demanded, "Where's Tracy?" His eyes reflected the state of his mind—fury.

Scott's manner was pure soldier. His mind was calculating the odds: *The more dialogue, the better our chances for survival.*

"Safe," the Serpent returned, "for now." Although his eyes projected fury, there was a hint of admiration in his voice. "Sizable adversary," he motioned with his thumb at the station, "that one." The words were spoken by someone used to dealing with men only. To him, the woman was an object of subservience, a subject of pleasures.

"You don't get away." Brian was unwavering.

"Look around." The jihad leader's response was unfaltering, steadfast. "Count the odds." Aside from the impatient scuffing of boots, the stairway had turned silent. From below, the squad of fanatics still had their weapons trained on the two targets. The Serpent had closed the trap from above. For Brian and Scott there was no way out.

Time was short. It was running out. Both Brian and Scott knew it. Further dialogue would serve no purpose. It was decision time. Three pairs of eyes were locked in a deadly embrace. Others followed from below. *Who'd flinch first?* Scott was about to raise the weapon, then froze. Brian shot him an alert. There was a crackle. It came from the depths of the headset. A clear voice followed—Sparky's voice. "Lose the steel…repeat…lose the steel."

Slightly bewildered, Brian dropped his weapon. Scott saw a warning in his eyes. At first, he hesitated but with a nod from Brian he followed suit. He slid his weapon strap from his shoulder. It slowly slid from his arm then, with a metallic clang, landed on the concrete floor. Both had rendered their fates into the enemy's hands.

The Serpent, poised on the stairway above, reacted accordingly. The jihad leader visibly relaxed. The killers below did not. It was their chance for a kill. And the chance was now. Their edgy fingers tightened on the triggers, but relaxed with the next command issued by the Serpent. Weapon tightly clutched in hand, arm raised high above his head, he demanded their attention. He'd realized the tremendous advantage he'd just gained. "Hostages!" he shouted into the dark below.

He'd just been handed a way out of enemy territory. Immediately, he gave orders to stand down, but the standoff would not last very long. Another decision would quickly follow. It would come from above. Way above. It would come with unexpected force. It'd break the deadlock.

STEALTH OPS

"Gotta get to somebody," Sparky hurried, "and fast." Using quick strides, he was moving to the OPS center. When Brian took the chopper on deck, he'd listened on the comm, but not for long. The signal faded quickly when they entered the building. He maxed out the volume to get an audible, but the dialogue only turned into static bursts. Just prior, there was something that alerted his senses, something familiar. He went to work on the computer to load the pattern analyzer. He initiated the pattern search. It did not take long. The software came back with a match. Voice patterns identified Scott and Brian, but there was also someone else. "Can't be," his mind screamed at him. "Serpent? Here on U.S. soil?"

NSA had been tracking the voice for quite some time. They could never get a match on an individual. It had been elusive until just now. "The Serpent?" he questioned again, "incredulous!" He was shaking his head in disbelief. There was no time to waste. Sparky needed a decision. It had to be now. To report his find up the chain meant wasted time. There would be delays, queries, and possible loss of lives. "Who'd be the best contact?" he asked himself. "Foster." He was the one spearheading the current chase.

He switched to Dulles tactical. "Get me Foster," he demanded.

"Who wants him?"

"NSA."

"Standby," the response was clear. He'd been put on hold. Sparky was frustrated. He'd just been sidelined. *I'm a Nobody.* He was about to seek alternative contacts when a voice picked up. It was a booming voice. "What?"

"General Foster?"

"Shoot." Foster was as abrasive as ever.

"Sir..." Sparky gave him a brief description. He informed the general of the encounter and the current standoff at Hillview. "Please hurry," he urged.

Foster needed action. He struggled for options. There were none. It was a decision he couldn't make on his own. It required approval from JCS. It required the military. It would mean delays and more delays. There was no time for that. He needed the weapon now.

He was switched to secure. He dialed. It was the Intel's highest priority line. He'd accessed the SCI net. Dulles tactical was connected to a complex network of command and control centers isolated from the rest of the world. It was the community's own secret world of highly sophisticated and classified communication. The system was secure to level A-3. It meant equipment and personnel were cleared to the highest levels of clearance. The link was established without delay.

Within seconds the distant end responded, "Fox One." Foster was connected with the most outlying reaches in U.S. territory: the borderlines of Alaska and the Yukon.

Foster identified himself then. "Base commander," he urged. He needed the top man.

"Standby."

"Foster?" The commander was on the line. "What's up?"

Foster had dealt with him a couple of times before. *Straight shooter...tough as they come.*

"Listen," Foster urged, "I need your help and I need it now." He briefly told the man the predicament he and the nation were in. With most of the defense systems disabled, he had no other options available.

"Can't do it," was the negative response. The man held steadfast. "I need authorization." He wouldn't budge. "Highest level."

"I am your authorization," Foster shouted. He'd dealt with many stubborn uniforms during his career. He wouldn't let this guy put him off. There was silence. "Well?" he pressed on.

After an extended pause, the man replied, "Gonna be your ass."

"I'll take responsibility." Foster had won this round. *Now the tricky part...the task.* "What'd it take?"

"What?"

"Fire up."

"Have you gone mad?" The response was clear. "You insane?" He sounded enraged. "Authorize a weapon that doesn't exist?"

"Do it." Foster could force the order. He didn't need the man's cooperation. He outranked him by several grades. The problem was national security. For that, JCS had to get involved, purely for political reasons. "How much time we've got?"

"Two minutes." Foster got his way. "What's the target?"

He pulled a well-worn map for the eastern sector from the pocket of his fatigues. "40, 54' 26 North, 73, 52' 07" West, and," he paused to let the full extent sink in, "initial blast twenty-five...follow with flash bursts at seventy-five...below ground." He knew the weapon's power and capabilities. The parameters would be sufficient for the task.

Foster knew he'd be in deep water if he failed. It wasn't the first time. Right now, he could care less. Friends were in trouble. The safety of the nation was on the line. Depending on the outcome, he'd either be the hero, or, if things went bad, the villain. Foster had just petitioned the military's latest defense weapon. Officially, it didn't exist. Each time the issue came up with the public, the Pentagon had denied its existence. And, in recent years, it had come up more frequently. Conspirators and activists made sure of that, but today, justice would be served.

The weapon had been conceived by DARPA decades ago. It began as a conceptual design that grew into a powerful defense system. It'd eventually replace ground-based weaponry. From an experimental position, it was a scientist's dream. As a weapon, it still had its challenges. Simulation tests were still being performed. The results were uncanny but still needed more accuracy. At present, most tests were concentrated to the northern hemisphere, localized to unpopulated regions.

What Foster needed most was surgical accuracy. On top of it, it would be in a heavily populated area.

"Good luck." The base commander sounded off. "Wouldn't wanna be in your shoes."

"Just get the damned thing ready," Foster insisted. "Now!"

NYPD

"Get something in the air," the mayor ordered, "anything." The chief of the New York City police department was furious. He'd just taken major heat from the mayor. Neither was happy. Labeled a hothead, his men tried to avoid him whenever possible. They knew his ability in handing down the bat, the baton of fury. Somebody had to take the blame. Someone always did. With him on the loose, the uniforms looked busy. Some were hiding in paperwork; others rushed for the exit.

"What's the status with the chopper?" he yelled at the division chief. He felt trapped in his own domain. He'd just learned about the attack on the city's water supply system. "Jihad," he muttered, "out of all people." It wasn't enough that crime had skyrocketed with looting, burglaries, and break-ins. "Now this," he fumed, "city's been taken hostage." He couldn't fathom the nation's largest metropolis under siege. "Who's responsible for the fuckup?" He was cussing out every government department in the nation for letting this happen. "Where's the FBI, the CIA, when you need them?"

Stomping through the halls, he was calling names. He had to get his men together. He needed a team. He needed it now. All able squad cars had been dispatched. Many were still dead lined. Most were busy at the south end. The tunnels had been blocked. Exit ports were on alert. He needed to be on location. Now! Ground transport would be too slow to get him up to Hillview. He needed airlift.

The SWAT team had been alerted. They were on the way. "Sir," the department head rushed in, "chopper's waiting." The chief was already out the door. He was closely followed by his team. Minutes later, he was in the air.

"Pull in all available units," he urged, "from the boroughs, if you have to."

Dispatch was already on the air. Orders were issued. "Code 2, Code 11, Hillview Reservoir…10-79 all units."

"What's the code for 'Hostage…Hazmat…BIO Agent'?" the chief yelled over the sound of the engine. He was frustrated. "Anybody?"

"Gimme the mic." He snatched it from dispatch. "Patch me in with tactical." It was a call for immediate action. He didn't have enough resources to handle an attack on the city. He needed help. And fast. What he needed was a direct link with defense out at Dulles. They'd know how to handle the threat. They were the experts.

The craft was on its way. They were headed north. The craft felt sluggish. It was loaded down with the department's heavies. "Five more minutes," the pilot announced. Thanks to the full moon he could see the outline of the tower in the distance coming up. A few minutes later he sat the craft down on the Hillview grounds, spilling out its occupants.

"What's this?" He noticed another craft on the ground. "Military? Strange looking beast."

"Gunship," an ex-combatant explained.

The chief had never seen one up close. His name was called. An agent rushed in. He was handed a receiver. Dulles was on the line. "Do not," the voice warned, "repeat…do not enter the building…stay clear."

"Huh? Who'd they think they are?" The chief was furious. "Nobody's telling *me* to stay clear. It's my city. I do what *I* want." He was on solid ground. It was his responsibility. "Where are they," he huffed, "if it's that critical?" The chief's ego had been touched. He didn't like it. "It's my call." It was his collar, so to speak. He decided not to wait. God only knew when reinforcement would get in from the Burroughs. He stepped out front to give the order. "Advance."

STEALTH OPS

Trapped in the power station, Hammad realized in an instant that years of careful planning and concealing identity were gone; he'd been compromised. He couldn't let that happen. There was only one way to save his cover. Eliminate the two adversaries. It was that simple. Trapped on a flight of stairs below, they were weaponless. He'd rendered them defenseless. His stare was locked on Scott. He despised black OPS. Especially DELTA, the enemy's prestigious fighting elite. He could have spared Brian. Hammad had great admiration for people with special skills. And that one definitely had what it took. He was waiting for the special OPS to flinch, to pull the trigger. His right index finger moved ever so slightly. It tested the steel. His pupils contracted to a squint. He'd already made the decision. Another second, he'd pull the trigger. Just then, the two fighters put their weapons down. Puzzled, Hammad removed his trigger finger.

Then he felt it. At first, it was only a slight burning sensation. He'd been around weapons much of his career, especially during the Afghan war. He recognized the heat signature from an overheated gun barrel. He felt it on both hands. Dumbfounded to the core he stammered, "Allah…what?"

Immediately after, his gaze shifted to his hands. In disbelief, he stared at the skeletal outlines of his bones. "X-ray vision?" For a second he questioned his sanity then, in a sudden reflex action, unclenched his fingers. The skeleton images matched the motion. It was then his mind registered. *Something's wrong.* In a swift reaction, he released both hands from the blue steel, but they wouldn't budge. They seemed frozen to the gun. Violently, he shook both hands to free his grip. Finally, they came loose. With a hollow clang, the automatic tumbled to the concrete floor. The sound reverberated in the stairwell. His gaze struck both palms. The skin had torn from the flesh. In strands it'd stuck to the steel. Trying to understand what had just happened, feeling intense pain shoot though his hands, arms, shoulders, and chest, he shook his head in utter disbelief.

It took him several seconds to catch his composure. Then his gaze shifted to the adversaries poised below, who seemed all right. There was no reaction from them. Several flights below them, intense yelling and screaming echoed through the stairway. The cries came from his attack force. Then it struck him. "Pulse weapon."

To live, he realized on impulse, he had to get out. Get out fast. On that thought, he jumped for the nearby exit, lunging for the steel bar but retracting instantly. The door handle felt hot, sizzling hot. Using his boot, he kicked it open with a crash. He threw his weight through the exit. Taking in the scene ahead with a vision turned blurry, he saw that dozens of automatic weapons were aimed at his body. The Manhattan police force had arrived.

Flying through the air, giving in to the inevitable surrender, with a halting thud he landed hard on the concrete.

"Hold your fire." It was the chief shouting the command.

Inside the stairwell, Scott was squatting. Brian was by his side, facing the attackers below. Scott reached for his right boot. His gaze was focused on Hammad. He felt for the knife, finding it immediately. The skin on his hand and leg was heating up. It seemed to emanate from the knife. He tossed it away, his eyes never wavering from the enemy whose body remained frozen. There was one thing he'd noticed. Hammad's pupils went through rapid changes. They'd turned from surprise to recognition then astonishment at the unfolding scene. Then, without provocation, the fighter dropped his weapon, taking flight toward the exit while intense shouts and screams came from below. For a second, Brian was fixated on the cries.

Scott, poised on his side, followed his gaze. Beyond the screams, there were additional sounds emanating from above. It sounded like concrete breaking up. He shifted his gaze up. The ceiling began to buckle. Cracks rapidly appeared. The color changed from the customary gray to a dark brown, then began to smolder. The concrete, in front of his eyes, incinerated from the intense heat. Pulling hard, he took hold of Brian's arm. On the heels of Hammad, both took three steps at a time then tumbled for the exit with both landing alongside the building.

Their bodies landed hard. Scott acted first. He saw the astonished look in Brian's eyes. But there was more. He faced an entire police force ready to shoot. He yanked his ID from his jacket and held it up high. "Don't," he yelled. "Don't shoot."

Brian copied the motion. Commands were shouted. There was confusion. Then, directly in front of them something unusual took place. The uniforms abruptly sought cover. They sought cover behind police and rescue vehicles. Spotlights were trained on them. The forces seemed suspended.

"Hold your fire," the chief shouted.

Brian could feel heat. It grew in intensity. It wasn't the spotlights. The heat came from above. It seemed the night had come alive. Darkness turned to light. It started with a bright spot in the far reaches of night. All the eyes shifted to the sky. The dark gave off what appeared a beam of light. A luminous shaft reached for the ground. It touched the building they'd just left. Darkness turned to full brilliance. Like an exploding star, a supernova, with unequaled intensity, the beam released its concentrated energy. It hit the power station's roof. From there, with lightning speed, the energy traveled down the stairwell shaft, leaving the ceiling exposed to the night. Muffled screams seeped up from the stairwell. Then it turned quiet. It was over in two seconds.

"Particle beam weapon," Brian hissed at Scott crouched by his side.

"What?" Scott looked dumbfounded. There had been rumors for years about some new super weapon being tested by DARPA. However, he'd never given them much credence. He'd have to see it with his own eyes. And now he had.

Brian had known about it for some time. Rumors, over the years, had surfaced. Besides, on a couple occasions, Alex had mentioned it after talking with Foster. One time the general had mumbled something about "HAARP."[73]

When the NYPD finally entered the well shaft, only the remains of incinerated bodies were left. Skin and tissue had been burned off the terrorist's bodies, leaving only charred bones scattered along the concrete floor. Some skeleton hands were still

---

[73] Officially, High-frequency Active Auroral Research Program (HAARP) is an ionospheric research program jointly funded by the U.S. Air Force, the U.S. Navy, and the University of Alaska in collaboration with other universities and the Defense Advanced Research Projects Agency (DARPA). Its purpose is to analyze the ionosphere and investigate such for radio communications and surveillance purposes (missile intrusion detection). The HAARP program operates a major Arctic facility, known as the HAARP Research Station, on an Air Force-owned site near Gakona, Alaska. Other facilities are being built around the globe by various nations. Under the disguise of DARPA, rumors have it that HAARP may be associated with a newly developed space-based superweapon.

clutching the triggers of twisted steel that once were automatics. It seemed an entire terrorist cell had been eliminated. Unfortunately for the law, there wasn't much left to identify the victims.

RESCUE

Tracy, was Brian's first thought. Her name lingered on his lips. His body was still frozen. A shadow hovered over him. It was Scott. He was ready to move.

"Come on," he urged.

"Serpent?"

"Forget it," he said, "let the law worry about him."

Scott pulled on his arm. He practically dragged him inside the building. Hammad was nowhere to be seen. *Escaped again,* Brian came to realize. His eyes caught the sea of uniforms. Like he, they struggled to make sense of what'd just happened. Whatever it was, particle gun, pulse weapon, microwave beam, it'd proven effective. Success was obvious. The spiral staircase had been twisted out of alignment. The handrails were warped. Amid the debris of twisted weapons, the platform and stairway below were piled with charred bodies. Scott pushed his way down the stairwell. Brian followed.

At the ground level, they were confronted by more twisted steel. The fire door had melted from its hinges. They kicked it aside. The entrance opened into a giant cavern. Across the threshold, they cautiously stepped into the gigantic pump station. With every step, the sound of a steady hum increased. It must have exceeded 120 decibels. Not an unpleasant sound, it was the pulse of the system. Fed by diesel fuel, the pumps were driving a cluster of generators partially hidden by the underground recesses. Bright polished brace shafts were spinning at a high rate. It was these that pushed the water through a cluster of canals feeding the Manhattan water supply.

The place felt overwhelming. Banks of LEDs and control switches were mounted on complex panels, each controlling a water supply sector. "Let's split up. You," Scott gestured, "over there." Both headed in different direction to canvas the grounds. It was a series of caverns each stacked with generators, piping, and valves. The initial search revealed nothing. Deeper in the recesses, Brian suddenly spotted something. It was a contour inconsistent with the rest of the layout. "Over here," he yelled. What he spotted was the form of a human body strapped onto a gigantic pipe. Scott rushed to his side. They'd located the object of the search.

"Careful," Scott warned. Brian was already inspecting the contours. It wasn't moving. "Could be a trap."

With deliberate caution, Brian removed the canvas that held the body. It gradually revealed the face. It was Tracy. Her body was strapped firmly to the delivery device. His fingers went for her neck, checking for a pulse. "She's alive." He released a sigh of relief. "Hang on, girl."

Scott tossed the duffel to the floor. It freed his hands to inspect the mechanism. Two of the crystal cylinders were connected to the central water supply intake. A third was centered on her face, touching her lips. He spotted the tiniest motion. A plunger was moving ever so slightly. The contents were being released from the glass vial.

There was a sudden twitch on her face. Her eyes opened. She recognized the faces. "Don't move," Brian whispered. Tracy had gained full consciousness. Eyes widened, she recognized the cylinders. Her eyes revealed terror. They were fixed on the cylinders.

Scott was working the device. He spotted the trigger. The timer was ticking toward the zero point.

Brian gently pressed down on her upper body. "Keep still," he cautioned. He watched the man in action. Scott seemed calm. It was his world.

He studied the wires. There were many. "Doesn't make sense," he muttered into the silence. Some seemed decoys, others live connections.

Brian kept his eyes on the timer. "There's no time." He was frantic. "Do something!"

There's got to be a sequence. Scott had an idea. "What's the color code?" He was referring to the old timer's color charts used for electrical installations. A code designed by the industry many decades ago, it was to guide electricians through the maze of interconnecting wires. "Quick."

"Don't know." Brian desperately tried to remember. *Who could think under so much pressure?* He shook his head to clear his mind. "Wait." His face lit up. It came back to him. "Of course." He recalled the code he'd learned during basics. "Color code."

"What?" Scott thought he'd gone mad.

Brian thought better. "Here's the colors," he yelled. "Black…brown…red…orange… yellow…green…blue…" It was the standard color code every electronics technician was familiar with.

"Hurry up, dammit." Brian was frantic now. He watched the timer. It was relentlessly ticking toward the zero count. Above, the vial kept compressing. The cylinder's contents were slowly seeping toward her face. He tried to locate an object to cover her mouth. *Anything.* He used his hands. "There's no time," he shouted. "Hang on, baby." One more turn on the dial and life would be over for her. And so would theirs. He was ready to tear Tracy from the entrapment. Her body was strapped to the timer.

Scott threw out a warning. "Don't." His hands were busy with the wires. He was counting the colors. His face showed a glimmer of hope. He glared at Brian. "Give me a second." He fished for a pair of pliers from the bag. "The codes," he called out, "again!"

Brian repeated the codes. His gaze shifted from the timer to Scott and back again as time ran out. Scott cut the wires in a precision sequence. He'd mentally selected the wires. Power function: black, white, red (*ground, neutral, hot*). Then, timer signals: red/yellow, blue/white, and green (*hot, feed, return*), followed by the substance controls: *green, white, blue (ground, neutral, active)*. It'd made sense. He paused, then cut the last wire. There was an imperceptible click. The ticking stopped. The timer had halted, and so had the cylinder motion. "Think we'll live." Scott exhaled with an audible sigh. The release mechanism had stopped. The lethal substance was contained.

Brian tore the cylinder from Tracy's face. He cut the restraining straps from her body. Tracy had gained full awareness.

"Michael," she called out, "you came."

For a second, Brian looked bewildered. "Michael who?"

"Never mind." Tracy was shaking her head. She seemed absentminded but recognized Brian.

"You all right?"

"Never," she reached for him with outstretched arms, "leave me again."

"Welcome back to the world." He beamed.

They were the most precious words she'd ever heard. Her eyes caught Scott moving nearby. "Where's Dad?"

"Safe," she heard him say. "You hurt?"

"I don't think so," she said. Brian stooped over her. He gently reached for her shoulders. Scott supported her torso. Together, they lifted her from the deadly device that had almost cost her life, theirs, and millions of other innocent people. She reached up with both hands to pull his face down. She planted a kiss on Brian's lips. Her eyes sought out Scott. "Thank you," she said. They were sincere words.

He returned the gesture with a wink of an eye. "Let's get out of here." He was already on the move, heading for the exit.

Tracy's body felt stiff. Her legs were shaky. She held onto Brian. She shot a worried glance at him. "Serpent?"

"Escaped." Brian watched her face change from disappointment to disgust, to anger, and then to rage, but she kept quiet. He wondered what was on her mind. "Let's get outta here," he urged, "your dad's waiting."

"All LM units…code 30…possible 51-Bravo," the metallic sounding voice crackled over the ether. Coded orders were sent. They were police broadcasts. Police units from several districts were on alert and were quick to respond.

Ever since 9/11, the Lower Manhattan emergency response teams had been drilled for potential emergencies such as tonight. "11-54…901S," the call went out. Where there had been periodic exercises in the past, this call was critical. It called to block all tunnel exits.

ESCAPE ONE

Hammad landed on the concrete. It was a hard fall, knocking the wind from his lungs. It'd stunned him for only seconds. Pushing up with both hands, he forced his body off the ground. "Ouch." There was intense pain. He disregarded it for the moment distracted by temporary blindness from the many searchlights. Dozens of police cruisers and emergency vehicles illuminated the Hillview grounds. To get focus, he raised one hand to shield his eyes. Then he spotted it. Between his stretched out fingers, an immense force confronting him. He calculated. His mind resisted. *Is this how it shall end?* He slowly propped up on one knee. Right hand wiping across his face to clear his vision, he noticed something odd. Faces were directed up. The entire force appeared frozen in time. They were watching the sky. He did not bother to check the object of their attention. All he saw was the chance for escape. And he acted accordingly.

He couldn't believe his eyes. "A chopper?" He spotted the craft sitting at the edge of the grounds. The blades were slowly turning. *Ignition's on,* his trained mind registered. He slid sideways to escape the spotlights. He encircled the army of law-enforcing agents. Getting to the craft in the shadows of night was not difficult. Although some members of the defense forces noticed him, they did not act. The spectacle unfolding from above captured everyone's attention. The brief glimpse his eyes caught was of a beam of energy pulsing the building. He jumped into the cockpit. His escape was set. He'd barely noticed one other craft stationed nearby sitting idle in the dark.

The Serpent had lucky out once more. He'd escaped again. "Insha' Allah," he shouted over the roar of the engines as he pushed the accelerator to the maximum speed. He was thrilled by the means of which he'd escaped. What puzzled him was the weapon that had wiped out his force. *What was it? Where did it come from?* In an instant, his team was gone, obliterated. No way could anyone have survived. As for him, it was divine intervention.

"I need this weapon…gotta have it." It was a promise. "But first," he muttered, "I must get out of here." The devices were delivered. He'd accomplished the mission. Many would die in the city, many more in the country, thanks to his cells and the BIO deliveries.

Hands tightly gripping on the flight controls, he cried out, "Ouch!" Clenching his teeth in pain, he inspected one hand, then the other. They were throbbing. It was then he realized the extent of the burn. It'd taken the skin right off the palms. Raw flesh was exposed. He tore off one sleeve from the shirt he wore, then the other. One end clenched between his teeth as he kept an eye on the darkness ahead, he was able to wrap the fabric around his hands. It was a temporary fix. The bandage would keep his palms from sticking to the controls. "That'll do…for now."

He pulled for vertical lift. The helicopter shot off the ground, gaining altitude and speed with every second. He headed directly south.

Instruments barely visible in the dark, he squinted to check the gauges. The altimeter indicated fifteen hundred feet with the fuel gauge reading full. *Time to level out.* It'd be enough to clear the skyscrapers that he knew lay ahead. Gazing into the dark, he could make out the outlines of central Manhattan. With the chopper headed south, it'd take him directly to the Virginia shores. There, days before, he'd made arrangements to meet up with the Cuban ground forces which, he hoped, would be well on their way for an all-out assault on the nation's capital.

Hammad wasn't out of hot water yet. There was the new weapon he'd have to consider. If they got a fix on his craft, it'd be curtains. In addition, there was the Miami coastal guard and the U.S. Naval forces he possibly had to confront. He could only hope that their air and sea transports were still disabled. But there'd be no guarantee. For now, he was content with his escape. He was about to adjust the compass for a 210-degree west correction when a sharp ping in the rear of the cabin got his attention. *I'm being pursued.* He reacted on instinct. With his left foot, he slammed the rudder controls followed by a tight jerk on the controls. The chopper's blades strained under the sudden pressure but held. He'd pulled the craft into a steep turn to get a fix. "Damned infidels," he cursed into the dark. "Where are you?" Then he spotted it.

RETRIBUTION

Agonized by the very thought, Tracy yelled out, "What, escaped?" It was inconceivable to her how anyone could get lucky enough to escape time after time. Partially lifted, partially dragged, supported by Brian and Scott on either side, she was rushed from the cold of the caverns to the exit shaft. After a brief pause to catch her breath, they hastened her up the stairs.

Stopped suddenly short in her footsteps, Tracy, tripping over bodies, was sickened by the sight. Her hands flew up to her mouth then gestured at the burnt corpses strewn across the stairs. "What's this?"

"What's left from the hostage party," Brian replied. Flashlight beam darting over dozens of bodies, he briefly explained the standoff followed by the beam from the sky.

"What beam?" Tracy wanted to know. EMP, satellites, nuclear attack, the chase, hostage taking, chemicals—it didn't make sense to her. Too many pieces were missing for her to get a clear picture.

Pulling her by the arm, Scott urged, "Later. Let's move it." He took the lead up the stairwell. "We've got one more job." He'd been so close to the enemy. Slightly short on breath, resolute nevertheless, Scott vowed, "This time, he won't get away." He wasn't going to let the Serpent slip through his hands again.

Hurried up the stairs, close to exhaustion, Brian suggested, "Let the law take care of it." He needed a break, and Tracy did as well. "Don't you ever rest?"

"Not until we get him." Half way up the stairwell, around the next bend, they ran into a solid wall of resistance. Assault rifles aimed at them, laser points darting across their chests, someone yelled, "On your knees!" Clad in black garb, visors over their faces, ready to kill anything that moved, the SWAT team intercepted them.

Hesitating, reluctant to comply, shielding Tracy, Brian muttered, "Not again." He was getting sick being told what to do.

"Hold your fire," Scott yelled into the streamers of beams, "CIA." He'd already flashed his badge. Brian pulled his. Tracy, arms raised, held steadfast.

"You…you," the squad leader said, motioning to a couple of team members, "take 'em." The squad leader hurried down the stairwell, followed by his team.

Scott, Tracy, and Brian were hastened up the stairs to meet up with Manhattan law enforcement. Put on hold while the chief was busy doling out commands, Scott hissed, from between clenched teeth, "Gotta get outta here." He shot a quick glance at Brian who nodded in agreement. Motioned ahead, what got his attention was the chopping sound of blades. Across the field, amid an army of busy law enforcement agencies, a helicopter was taking off. It was the craft the chief had used earlier to respond to the scene. Both recognized the profile behind the controls.

Brian nudged her in the side to get her attention. "Tracy," he whispered, "take charge." He motioned at the craft gaining altitude. "Serpent." She took the cue. Planting herself in front of the chief, she said, "I need water." It was enough to distract him for the moment. When he turned back, Brian and Scott were gone. The chief shrugged and went on with police business. Tracy watched in anger them disappear into the dark. She wanted to come along but also realized the Cobra was too tight. There were only two seats. Front for the pilot and rear for the navigator.

As soon as the craft lifted off, Brian was on the radio. Above the roar of the ascending turbo engine, he shouted, "OPS, come in!" He was pinging Sparky. He needed eyes in the sky, infrared, and fast. The ground below, illuminated by the rescue vehicles, slowly faded into the dark. Ahead, pitch black awaited them. Gaining altitude, darkness was closing in fast.

Seconds later, Sparky's voice popped in. "What gives?" He'd been on break when the call came.

"Need sky support," Brian urged, "now!"

Sparky was already panning the satellite's infrared sensors to get a lock on the craft as he watched vague images of the Manhattan skyline paint across the monitor screens. "Target?"

"Chopper," Brian reported, "headed south." He thought a moment then suggested, "Freedom Towers." He kept the dialogue brief. *This is my mission.* No way would he get authorization for what he had in mind.

"Heading," Sparky came back, "210 west…got 'em in sight…couple minutes out."

"Roger that," Brian responded. His eyes slowly adjusted to the dark. To the right, he spotted the narrow band of water snaking down from the north.

"West Side," Scott acknowledged. It was the city's high-speed commuter link running alongside the Hudson River, connecting the north with the south.

"Follow it," Sparky cut in. The radio was quiet for a few minutes.

Brian was straining his eyes. Below, the ground was illuminated by the moon's reflection on the river. Aside from the Manhattan skyline, the airspace ahead seemed clear. To the right, a dark shadow was slowly panning into view: George Washington.

He spotted the bridge. "Got it," Brian acknowledged.

"New heading," the voice shot back, "South, 9A."

Aside from utility vehicles speeding up and down the major link, traffic on the West Side Highway was sparsely populated. Brian kept the craft at two thousand feet. At this elevation, he'd just stay clear of skyscrapers. Minutes later, to the left, Central Park crept into view followed by the Empire State Building.

"Target," Sparky broke the silence, "should be in view."

Craft giving chase, two pairs of eyes were straining through darkness. "There," Scott signaled, "ten o'clock." With speed maxed out, with the World Trade Center gone, barely missing the Empire State Building, Manhattan's tallest building once more, he intercepted. They were closing in fast. Brian reduced the throttle and slightly pushed the controls forward. The Cobra responded. It dropped its nose.

A thousand yards ahead, the shadowy target came into view. Giving chase, right hand on the control stick, he flipped the switch. Immediately, the weapons went hot. Brian checked the HUD display for weapon select. He chose the on-board cannon. In contrast to the rapid-fire mini guns, this weapon was more accurate to single out a moving target. Brian had a lock. His thumb held firm on the firing button. "Take that!" he yelled.

Much like a bucking bronco, with each burst from the center mounted onboard cannon, the Cobra kicked out. A stream of tracers provided an instant visual to the target. Up ahead, the impact was obvious. In the dark of night, like fireworks, sparks bounced off from projectiles hitting metal against metal.

Flying at all out speed, Hammad felt the impact and sound like a sledgehammer tearing into concrete. He was stunned. He whipped the craft into a tight turn to the right to get a fix on whatever had hit him. A 180 gave him the answer. *The dreaded Cobra.* Immediately, he cut to the left. Frantic for cover, five hundred yards out, he aimed for the Empire State Building. It rushed in. "It's my only chance." It'd give him cover.

A quarter mile back, Brian gave chase. "Take this!" he yelled with each push of the red trigger button. "And this!"

Both craft were in a ride only a hardened pilot could endure. G-forces exerted on the craft were incredible. Broken up by tight banks, up and down the craft went. Whatever direction the Serpent aimed at, Brian was right on his tail. No way was he going to lose the target. "Not gonna get away this time," he vowed.

Scott, right hand clutched on the door rail, with the left fumbling for a hold, any hold, was jolted back and forth. Despite the jerky motion immediately followed with added Gs, he totally enjoyed the thrill ride. At the moment, there wasn't anything he could do to contribute to the chase. *My time will come,* was the promise. For now, he let his buddy do the fighting.

His enemy closing in, now a hundred yards out, speeding ahead, Hammad promised, "No way am I going to get caught, not this close to freedom." To get away from the pursuit, the Serpent did the best he could, but could not match the engine power of the Cobra. "Gotta outmaneuver them." He calculated that it was his only chance. Based on the distance the Cobra had flown from D.C., he figured, "Must be flying on fumes."

Ding...knock...ding...knock. In rapid succession, the sound of tracers intermixed with the sound of exploding 30 mm shells from the twin-mounted fuselage cannons. He'd just taken more hits. He flipped his head to the left and right to check for damages. *More holes in the fuselage. Not a big deal,* he thought. As long as there was no smoke, no vital parts were damaged. Twisting and turning the police chopper into daring spirals, a dark shadow just caught his eyes. It appeared straight ahead out of the dark. *High-rise,* his brain registered. Another quick reaction pulled the craft into a steep climb. The motion was almost too violent for the craft. It spun the chopper into a tight spiral, barely clearing the rooftop beneath, then, just as quick, he aimed the nose for the ground after clearing the top. For the moment, the impact of bullets had stopped. In the wake of the high-rise, he dove for cover.

Brian had the chopper in sight directly ahead. Despite Hammad's rapid maneuvers, the HUD's infrared was locked on the target. Ready to fire at any moment, Brian said to Scott, crouched in the gunner's seat, "Wish I had a missile." Brian shot another glance at the overhead HUD display. He had visual on the rocket pod configuration, but at this time indicated empty. Finger on the trigger, he thought, *Cannon will have to do.*

An instant away from the kill shot, the unexpected happened. Although seasoned pilot he was, something extremely bizarre was about to take place. What followed was an act of desperation. In order to survive the next maneuver, primal instinct took hold of his mind and his body.

Giving chase at maximum speed, target locked in the crosshairs, an instant later, with the next pull on the trigger, Brian knew the so elusive adversary would be history.

Watching the scene ahead unfold, bracing his body for what would come next, Scott shouted, into the eerie darkness, "Get 'em!"

Grinning with delight at the final act up ahead, but momentarily distracted from the target, Brian shot a quick glance at the DELTA warrior. It was during this unfortunate distraction when the unexpected happened. A hundred yards ahead, to clear the high-rise coming up fast, Hammad had pulled the chopper into a steep climb, barely missing the building's rooftop. Although only a fraction of a second went by, what Brian had missed altogether was this daring maneuver.

His face still set in a grin; Brian threw his gaze back at the HUD. Straight ahead, lit up by the reflection of the moon, closing in fast, he thought, *There it is.* What his mind registered was the fast moving target. What he failed to do was check the craft's configuration closing in at him. An instant later he realized the gross mistake, but it was too late to avoid colliding with the high-rise directly blocking the Cobra's path. With the AH-1 at full throttle, a solid wall reflecting the contours of his craft, the building ahead rushed in at them. There was no avoiding the inevitable. It would mean a crash. It would be imminent death regardless at their lofty height.

Scott realized he'd made a mistake by distracting Brian from the chase. To correct his mistake, he did the one thing he was good at: fight. Fighting his way out was his only natural act, and that was without thinking, without planning, without preparation; it was purely on instinct. Facing imminent death form a direct impact into the face of the glass-encased skyscraper, he yelled the one thing his mind could muster up. "Minis!"

Brian, ears subconsciously taking in the sound waves created by Scott, did not have time for a conscious act. In one swift motion, his index finger flipped the safety off the miniguns, sought the trigger, and fired. Facing momentary death, aiming the weapons straight ahead, in one continuous hail of .50 caliber bullets, the miniguns incinerated the wall ahead cutting a tunnel clear through the building. Glass panels, load barriers, ceiling, office walls, furniture, and other materials holding the floor and ceiling together were cut into pieces much like a wood chipper mulching down a tree trunk. All the material in the chopper's path was incinerated, leaving a tunnel for the Cobra to ram its way through from one end of the building out the other. Between skirting along the floor and bouncing off debris, the frame of the craft held steadfast. Clearing the ceiling only by inches, the rotor blades kept chewing their way through a path of fiery destruction, flinging particles outward much like the metal projectiles emanating from the rotating barrels of the twin Gatling guns.

What Brian and Scott experienced was the true force of the Cobra's firepower. The path the guns opened up was the result of two continuous bursts of energy with two hundred copper slugs a second, converted into one cutting force not even the well-seasoned Brian had ever imagined possible. The quick reaction, in a last act of desperation, as daring it was, saved both of their lives. The Cobra, fuselage dinged and dented by projectiles, but otherwise flight worthy, emerged at full speed on the far side of the high-rise just in time to meet up with Hammad's craft.

Eyes widened with dumbfounded surprise at the emerging Cobra off to his right, his first reaction was, "Impossible...can't be...nobody's this lucky." But there, in full view, unlikely as it may seem, he was being chased again. "Damn the infidels," he yelled into the dark, taking his craft into another dive, hoping to shake his pursuers one final time. Hope, while speeding towards his point of rendezvous, however, would not come without its dues.

Yards behind, Brian and Scott, desperately trying to catch the enemy once and for all, continued the chase. Battered, but otherwise not severely damaged, the Cobra's turbo, by the second, kept inching them closer to the enemy. He was just about to aim and fire the on-board cannon when all of a sudden the engine quit. For a second, it turned dead silent. Caught up in battle, Brian had failed to check the fuel gauges. He'd pushed the craft dry. *Out of fuel,* his mind screamed out. An instant later, the controls turned sluggish. He'd just taken the craft into a steep climb when it happened. "We're in trouble."

Scott shot a glance at Brian. The expression on the man's face said it best. "Live and let die."

Without power, rotor spinning freely, the Cobra hovered for a few seconds. Frantically, eyes darting between instruments and ground, Brian shouted, "Five hundred! Going down!" It was the command no pilot ever wanted to give, and no passenger would ever want to hear. It meant free fall, controlled crash, under ideal conditions.

Scott's head was clear. If there was a time for panic, that time was now. Too much of a fighter, he wasn't going to let that happen. However, he wasn't in control. It was up to his buddy to make it right. Aside from a whistling sound made by the overhead blades, spinning freely connected to the turning rotor, it'd turned dead quiet in the cockpit. On instinct again, Brian reacted. Theory was something the books taught, but this case called for experience. Experience in freefall? Nobody had any.

The blades were spinning wildly with the inertia. It was the pitch that kept the craft stable, but that would only last a few more seconds.

Brian's mind raced through long forgotten memories. He'd faced the peril once before. It was chasing the Taliban. Long time ago, he vaguely recalled it. His brain assimilated. It became clear. He'd know what to do. "Hang on," he yelled at Scott and disengaged.

For a second more the craft hovered and then dropped straight to the ground. Rotors spinning one way, from opposing forces the fuselage began rotating in the opposite direction. With the ground rushing up fast, the horizon in the distance was also spinning, slowly at first, then ever more. To keep from getting dizzy, Brian had his eyes fixed on the altimeter. With increasing speed, the needle dropped toward ground zero. "Four hundred," he called out. Three hundred…two hundred…fifty…forty…thirty. He needed at least twenty-five feet clearance from the ground. Then, in a quick motion, he threw the pitch control in reverse.

The strain on the blades was terrific, bent almost to the breaking, but they held together. With blades rotating for lift, under tremendous pressure the craft's body slowed from ten Gs to one in less than two seconds. A fraction later, it slammed into the ground. The skids bent under the impact but the cabin held. Shaking and twisting violently from the gyro effects, however unstable, it remained upright. The top rotor blades ripped from their mountings, spinning wildly through the air. Pieces of metal torn from the rear blades sliced through the fuselage. Others cut through the air, turned into lethal projectiles.

On impact, Brian's body compressed deep into the seat. The shock traveled up his spine. It was a sickening feeling. He almost blacked out. "Damn you," he heard Scott shout into his ear, who then punched the exit door. It seemed jammed tight. He kicked the window. It splintered. It gave an escape. He crawled out.

Knees jammed into the instruments, both legs stuck beneath the panel, Brian was moaning. Scott saw Brian in trouble. He hastened to the other side, tore the gate off its hinges, and pulled him from the wreckage.

As Scott inspected Brian's injuries, an unexpected voice echoed from the dark. "Drop your weapons." It was an infuriated voice. "On your knees." The shout came from the dark recesses of the grounds. They'd been waiting.

Still dazed from the impact, Scott muttered, "Here we go again." He spun around to face the caller. He recognized the law. Unknown to them, local law enforcement had followed the aerial pursuit, but did not know who had landed. Fuming, Scott reached into his pocket for his ID.

Perched on the wreckage, Brian, rubbing his damaged knees, was stunned. "Idiots," he muttered. It was all he could muster. In his present condition, he presented no threat to the law.

Weapon leveled, an agent inched his way forward. He recognized Brian from the earlier encounter. "Lucky bastards," he proclaimed, not without admiration, "the both of you."

"Fugitive." Brian gestured upwards.

"The Serpent?" FBI agents had followed the aerial battle on a dedicated comm link.

"The one!"

"Take a break," the agent suggested. "We're on it." He jerked his head at his team and stormed off.

Brian took the advice. Although his mind was filled with rage, he had no choice but to rest. His legs were killing him. "Get me a mic," he ordered a nearby uniform. He was dying to talk to Tracy.

Scott, coming out practically unscathed, immediately teamed up with the law. Furious, but otherwise unharmed, he still hoped to catch up with the fugitive.

MANHATTAN DIVERS

In the briskness of a crystal clear sky, on top of the tallest high-rise, the Divers, Manhattan's finest skydivers had settled in for an evening of drinking and telling stories. As with numerous occasions before, this was going to be one fun night. Unlike the past, today, in the wake of the blackout, would be a relatively calm evening. There was no law expected to chase, incarcerate, and fine the paraglide enthusiasts. With the nation's flights grounded for God knew how long, daring as it was, they found the only alternative available to pursue their hobby. And that was Manhattan's skyline.

Telling another of his tall tales, the team lead, slightly inebriated like everybody else, suddenly turned silent. Now, all could hear it. It was the chopping sound they all were familiar with. It was the sound of rotating blades cutting through the night. And the sound came their way. Seconds later it was on top of them. Led by a tremendous pressure wave, what appeared a NY City police helicopter was rapidly swooping in on them.

Unexpected as it came on, the divers, on unsteady legs, staggered for cover, grappling for their gear. Each made an attempt to escape the law. Barely clearing the upper building level, to the surprise to all, the craft kept on going. It disappeared into the darkened night as rapidly as it had appeared. With mouths gaping wide open, most of the team was stunned. There was no time to rationalize what had just happened. A second later the same pressure hit their bodies once more. This time, the sound waves broke with a lower pitch, but with much more force.

Unlike the first craft, this one did not clear the top. It came directly at them. One second they were hiding under desks and tables from the first encounter, the next second, death and destruction was upon them. In shock, on the brink of sheer panic, the newcomers, for what came next, froze in whatever position they found themselves.

There were no words to describe the demolition other than two solid, circular firewalls rushing in at the divers, compressing the air ahead. Everything in its path incinerated into dust and debris. Looking on in sheer horror, holding on for dear life to whatever objects were nearby, the team watched as the AH-1 sliced its way through offices and hallways one by one to exit at the far end. Leaving a deep vacuum from the fire-spitting guns in its wake, with a sucking sound and tremendous force air rushed into the building, sweeping the team out the far end of the high-rise into the Cobra's wake.

Tumbling wildly through the vacuum left by the chopper, the diving team, clutching their backpacks, desperately clung to the only object that could save their lives—the parachutes.

ESCAPE TWO

Two miles out, thirty seconds later, barely escaping the pursuit, Hammad watched as the Cobra first blasted its way out of the skyline, then, seconds later, halted in midair only to plummet to the ground. Thinking it was the end of a couple more infidels, he was truly elated. Not waiting around or inspecting the crash site, pulling the craft back up to twelve hundred feet flying altitude, he sped off to the south. Maxing out the speed, checking the fuel gauge and compass, he tried to make up the lost time. Compensating for wind drift, headed at a steady 210 degrees, he hoped to still make the rendezvous some two hundred eighty miles out. Body leaning into the craft, eyes watching the ground, cruising at maximum speed, he figured, *Should be there in an hour.* Keeping an eye on the shoreline, his direction reference, he calculated that it'd be an easy flight as long as there were no more obstacles in the way.

Almost an hour into the flight, the Norfolk shores approaching in the distance, Hammad prepared for the landing. Scanning the horizon, then the instruments, his eyes kept darting to the fuel gauge. "Empty," the gauge read amid the flashing alarm.

Expecting some activity by the shores, he pulled a map from his pocket. Unfolding it, he checked the contours against the shoreline. They matched. Flying into darkness, he expected the shores to be illuminated by the landing forces which, he knew, should be moving inland by now. There was no ground force in sight. Not even a dim light. "Nothing?"

He was completely perplexed. Undecided what direction to turn, staring into the dark void, out of the distance some five miles out at sea appeared what he made out a floating barrier. Changing course, he headed there. Keeping an eye on the fuel gauge, he desperately sought a landing spot. "Not gonna make it," he muttered hopelessly. Descending on what appeared to be half-submerged vessels, he suddenly yanked back on the control stick. "What the fuck?" At the last second, he recognized the blockade. "Subs?"

Almost on deck, to the shock of all times, he'd identified the insignia, "USS." He had to make a split second decision—land on the nuclear powered submarines, or ditch in the open ocean. He chose the latter. To gain distance from the enemy fleet, by now flying on fumes, he gave it one last try. He pulled up, out of the immediate danger zone, and headed out to sea. Five hundred feet up, he spotted more objects ahead. From the distance, he recognized what should have been the rendezvous point. Steering directly for it, he spotted the dated, but floating, platform he identified as an amphibian carrier, most likely landing spot for the Cuban navy.

Draining the last drops of fuel, he sat down hard on the ancient deck. Ground forces, idling on deck, dejected about a war lost before it even began, maddened at having to return to Cuba, had been expecting him. Words he didn't understand flew at him from all directions. Three sailors approached in hurried strides. *Landing party,* he assumed. They hastily led him up to the bridge. "Tower." He understood the word.

The captain, dressed up in a formal naval uniform, insignias proudly displayed on his left chest, extended hand stretched out, addressed the visitor. "Hasan Hammad?"

Semi-sarcastically, Hammad replied, "You're headed in the wrong direction." Something must have gone wrong. He was fuming.

"Naval blockade," the captain explained, "must have monitored our communiqué."

"What's your plan?" Hammad could not fathom anything but an alternative tactic.

"No plan," the captain responded, "going back to Cuba."

Getting angrier by the minute, disrespecting such infantile behavior, Hammad ordered the captain, "Listen, you get me to the Pacific Coast."

Taking on a perplexed expression, the captain wondered, "What's out there?" For all practical purposes, the United States of America, in the dark for almost two weeks, had been immobilized, especially the western part.

Ignoring the captain's query, Hammad insisted, "I must get there. What's your armament? What weapons are onboard? Any craft?"

"Follow me." The ship captain led the way across the flight deck. From there, hastening for the platform elevator, closely followed by an inspection party, he ordered a descent. Passing through several levels of platforms, maintenance and storage mostly, close to the watermark they stepped out. "There," he gestured towards one end of the floor, "take your pick."

Hammad, to his amazement, stared at what he made out as one of few remaining Russian air force assets left on Cuba after Nikita Khrushchev, then Soviet Premier, ordered the humiliating removal of his military and missile forces back in '62. Straight in front of him, tied to the iron platform, was the most feared helicopter in the Russian military arsenal, the missile spiked, long-range attack helicopter, the MI-24 Hind. Taking notice of the many rusty patches on the aging craft, feeling the cool touch of metal, Hammad, joyously hurrying up the ladder, eyed the captain. "Get me to the coast," he ordered once more.

"Get it ready," the captain gestured at the nearby crew. "Follow me." He motioned Hammad back to the bridge.

Shaking his head at the visitor, he offered, "I can take you as far as Corpus Christi." Curious about his sudden appearance, the captain could only speculate on the plan the unexpected visitor, head of the terrorist forces, had in mind. He couldn't care less. Without air coverage, with aging vessels, a lack of mission backup, and an enemy alerted and in offensive naval posture, his mission was over. Enemy naval forces, he'd bet, were surely coasting below the surface, escorting his fleet back to Cuba. Let Al Qaeda, or whatever other aggressive faction was on America's doorsteps, deal with the ravaged nation. Moving ahead at full steam, he ordered his first officer toward the American/Mexican coastal waters.

Hammad Hasan, renewed hope at the doorstep, again, could not believe the luck destiny had just awarded him. As soon as his eyes struck the Russian craft—rusty, tarnished, and dated as it was, but nevertheless flight worthy—his heart had leaped with joy. Fond memories came back. It energized his body for what lay ahead. He'd flown one of these craft during the Afghan war against Russian forces, then the enemy.

Under full power, steaming towards his goal of the Mexican shores, he could feel the choppy swells slapping against the bulkhead. After an invitation to join the captain at a late evening meal, Hasan formulated a new attack strategy. "This time, I shall succeed," he boasted, calculating out odds for an attack from within the nation.

NAVAL BASE (Guantánamo Bay)

"On your feet," the warden ordered. New detainees had just arrived. Gloomy faced, most stared straight ahead. Others had their eyes averted at the floor. He could always recognize the troublemakers. Swelled with pride, defiance cut across their faces. *Getting younger every year,* he thought. He found it pathetic to see these young kids beaten and bound, lined up against the wall. Head of the interrogation team, it was his job to break what was left of the spirited, misguided fools. He could never understand what drove this lot to end a youthful life.

His job used to be clear-cut: beat information from the captured. These days, with the camp on the political chopping block, he was treading on eggshells. He hated it, public spotlight and all the political crap. "By the book," he'd instructed his team. New order was to obey rules. He couldn't afford any more publicity. His job was on the line. There was enough press about this place without creating more political tension.

He'd been at Camp X-Ray for most of his career. Over the years, he'd seen countless political changes, as well as cultural ones. Inconsistency was the name of the game. Things seemed to change with each new administration. During the early days, almost all detainees were criminals and thugs expelled by Castro and other Central American dictatorships. Over the years, many of the radicals had aligned with economic development. Their focus had shifted from political to commercial.

Today, new inmates were a much different breed. Aside from being younger, they didn't have the tough core characteristics. These were kids, children, brainwashed and deployed out of desperation. Suicide missions, that's what they were. Empty promises in the name of Allah.

He could never understand how anybody could spend hours of each and every day kneeling, stooped over chanting in prayer. *What a waste of time,* he thought. *No wonder their economy is in such shambles.* He, like his soldiers, had been forced to adapt to the new breed. Continuous amendments were shoved down their throats to comply with an ever-increasing challenge. He did not hold a crutch to this breed. Theirs was a cause for justice. *We have ours. They have theirs.*

Slightly disheveled, grimy yet defiant, the kid stared across the desk. He wouldn't get much out of him, if anything. From his demeanor, the detainee would rather die than disclose information about his mission. *Hell,* the warden pondered, *probably only knows one piece of information... his target for destruction.* If that didn't work, he'd blow himself up into the promised abode.

He scribbled on the paper, "Done." He'd finished recording the profile in the inmate ledger. "Get him out of here," he ordered the MPs guarding the prisoner, then watched him being dragged away to the next round of interrogation. Hands crossed on top of his belly, he leaned back in the comfort of his chair.

Reminiscing, it seemed a lifetime ago, the day he'd arrived on this island. Conditions at Gitmo then were much different. They'd been inhumane. Today, aside from political pressure, life was easy. It was all psychology to break a prisoner. Even the camp administration had changed. It was much different now.

Guantánamo, established at Guantánamo Bay's Naval Base, Cuba, held political prisoners accused by the United States government of being terrorist operatives. The camp grew from the need for politically defined policies. Today's typical inmate was considered a war criminal or enemy combatant. He was a subject without a nation. With political elements created out of factions such as Al Qaeda, Taliban, and Jihad, no nation was willing to provide shelter for them. To isolate the various factions, a number of detainments were created on U.S. soil consisting of Camp Delta, Camp Echo, Camp Iguana, and Camp X-Ray.

Since the beginning of the Afghan war, more than 775 detainees had been brought to Guantánamo, of which approximately 420 had been released. As of today, only 355 detainees remained. More than one fifth was cleared for release. Others had to wait months or years to be released or relocated. It became increasingly difficult for U.S. officials to line up places for a new home.

Detainees were categorized. Camp X-Ray, for instance, U.S. government officials had classified as enemy combatants rather than prisoners of war. It'd justified this designation by claiming that they had neither the status of regular soldiers nor that of guerrillas and were not part of a regular army or militia. In contrast, Camp Iguana was designed to house juvenile criminals to keep minors away, for their protection, from aggressive adult prisoners.

Kept on day and night, in the midst of floodlights, prisoners were held in small mesh-sided cells. Aside from that, detainees were treated with fair credence, as long as they behaved within the constraints of the law. They were given rations similar to those of U.S. forces, with special consideration for Muslim dietary needs. Blindfolded when moving within the camp and forbidden to talk in groups of more than three, detainees were kept in isolation most of the day.

In recent years, the use of Guantánamo Bay as a military prison had drawn fire from human rights organizations and other critics, who'd cited reports that detainees had been tortured or otherwise poorly treated. Supporters of the detention argued that trial review of detentions had never been afforded to prisoners of war, and that it was reasonable for enemy combatants to be detained until the cessation of hostilities.

"Place's gonna swarm with arrivals," the chief of interrogation, wiping beads of sweat from his face, remarked to no one in particular. Ever since communication had come back, he'd closely followed the sporadic news broadcasts, if only marginal.

"Wonder how the mainland's doing," one soldier queried.

"Haven't heard of anybody declaring war," the chief countered.

CASTLE ROCK

It was early morning. Both were watching sunrise over the Kansas plains. Her torso was nudged against Brian, Tracy said, "It's great to be back."

"Thought we lost you," he replied, "the morning you'd disappeared. Thought you'd gone out for an early jog."

Angered, Tracy grumbled, "Don't remind me. I still don't know why I was captured, who did it, or why they let me live."

"As far as I know," he hinted, "from what your dad said, you were a political pawn."

"What?"

"They," Brian paused, "wanted your dad's full cooperation." Explaining further, he said, "Since he's the only one that knows a bypass without political protocols or possible diplomatic intervention to a counterstrike…and a strike had to be initiated. You were the guarantee."

"But that was before the nuclear strike."

"Goes to show you," he implied, "somebody had it already planned out."

"When I was locked up," she admitted, "I tried to reason it out." "Couldn't come up with an answer either. What a strain it must have been on him." Her face reflected on the pain her dad must have felt.

Watching her discomfort, Brian confessed, "I'm sorry that I wasn't there for you." His voice was inflected with remorse.

"I'm here now." She gently reached for his hand. "That's all that counts." There was forgiveness in her voice. It'd just been yesterday—the ordeal, the trauma, the rescue, but the threat to the population still existed.

Alex walked up, joining them on the deck. Tracy felt his presence. She turned to him. Lines of concern cut across his face. "Dad…you're here? Didn't hear you get in. Thought you were with Foster."

"Got in late last night. Crisis developed. I'm headed for the west coast."

"When?"

"Next hour."

Although the traumatic events were still vivid in her mind, Tracy seemed to have recovered from her ordeals. They would probably remain with her for some time, if not forever, especially the nightmares. Following the rescue, there had not been time to discuss personal issues. Most of the time was spent in debriefings.

"Dad," Tracy beckoned, "give us a moment."

"Make it quick."

She led Brian to the guestroom. "See this?" Her hand waved across the room.

He followed her gesture. He knew what she needed. Peace and quiet for a change, convalescing time, a chance to recuperate. He studied her face. It reflected the recent traumatic events. The past week had been chaotic for both of them. She turned toward him. "What do you think?"

"I think you've had enough adventure for one lifetime." It was more of a statement than a question. The choice would be hers. His body felt warmed by her presence. He liked the feeling, but there was unfinished business they had to face. He'd be at her side no matter what.

"We ever get to spend time together?" She regretted the words as soon as they'd left her lips. Brian kept silent. It wasn't fair putting her personal weight on him. She knew he was on a mission. They all were. "Am I being selfish?"

"Your choice," he said, almost inaudible. He could not influence her. He knew what had to be done.

She silently recaptured the past few weeks. There was adventure, no doubt about that. In hindsight, she relished that. She had to admit that most people would not experience that much action in a lifetime. It'd made her a much stronger person. Despite the trauma, she came out unscathed. With the danger and excitement and all, no vacation could ever come close to what the past days had given her. "Promise not to leave my side," she said, "ever!"

"I give you my word," he reassured her. He was deadly sincere about it. "I'll never forgive myself," he promised, "if anything happens to you."

Working as team, each had gained new respect. "Okay." She was reassured once more. She'd be safe. "How about it?" She'd sidled up to him. "You ready?"

"Been ready since the first day we met." A sly grin had swept across his face. He pulled her close.

"I mean," she beamed back at him, "the mission." She felt the warmth emanating from his body. She also felt the strength of his manhood press against her. "Later," she hinted with a promising nod. Her smile held steadfast with unspoken passion and romance.

"Promise?" He was reluctant to let her free.

She pulled him close for a tender kiss then briskly broke away. "Dad's waiting."

Despite the lack of military time, battle experience, or combat training, Tracy felt she could hold her own. With all that was going on in the nation, she felt she'd be able to contribute more on the frontlines than just sitting back in the home office and chasing cybernetic attacks. Something had been missing in her life, she suddenly realized. It was the excitement, the exhilaration, and the feeling of thrills. The last couple of weeks, in the wake of the attack, she felt she'd found a new direction.

The previous days, Alex and Foster had received continuous reports from the field. Reports indicated foreign agents near Chicago had been captured. New York cell had been eliminated as well. In addition, FBI agents were closing in on the Denver cell. It'd be only a matter of days, perhaps hours, before they'd be in custody as well.

Alex needed a timeout. He hoped the general would dispatch a team from the defense department or military, but Foster wouldn't have it. "I want you out west!" It was a direct order. "Hook up with the FBI."

Presently, Alex rejoined them both on the deck wearing a fresh set of cloth. "Gotta go. Plane's waiting at Pete field."

"Want our company?"

Somewhat surprised, he wondered at her determination. Then a proud smile appeared on his face, "Only if you feel up to it."

"Where we headed?"

"Travis," he said. Tracy and Brian closed up to join him.

"When?"

"Now," he urged, "get your things ready." There was more to the story than he let on. Foster must have briefed him on specifics he'd promised to keep secret.

Brian shot a gaze at Tracy. He'd detected danger in what Alex had just said. She returned his gaze and shrugged her shoulders.

"Hurry up," they caught his voice disappearing in the direction of the hall. "And," he yelled, "bring your skates along."

"Skates?" Tracy was startled.

"In-lines," his voice trailed, "roller blades, you know, and get Brian my spare set."

Tracy got busy in the den then became aware of a grinding sound emerging in the distance. It was a familiar sound. It was the chopping blades from a helicopter sent to pick them up. It'd take them to Pete Field. Foster had already booked seats on the next Confederate flight out to Travis.

FT. KNOX

By now, Knox Commander Wendell Nelson, Sergeant Major Brodie Elliott, Patriot leader Rusty Norton, First Lieutenant Duke Wheeler, aka Bad Man, the remains of the mechanized infantry force, immobilized by the Patriots, and everybody else realized no help from the former government or military was forthcoming. *Word just couldn't get out,* was the general consensus. It seemed the world, the ether waves, had turned silent. Satellites, ground communication, mobile equipment—nothing responded to queries and calls. Presently, at the Fort and the surrounding area, nobody had an idea about the state of the nation. It took days for word of the attack on the nation to reach Knox command. Eventually, spread by ships coming up the Ohio River, news slowly filtered in.

"West Coast's been nuked…Government's relocated…Military's out of commission… Economy's collapsed…Riots everywhere"—rumors were prolific. Unbelievable as it may have sounded, based on local conditions, Norton reasoned, "Rumors may just be true."

Where days ago his plan may have been mostly wishful thinking, Rusty Norton, convinced by the reports, was solidifying his plan. He was forging ahead with full speed.

Wendell Nelson, potential threat and uncooperative as he was, had been put under confined Knox arrest by Norton. Brodie Elliott, popular as he was, took full reign over the Fort. Duke Wheeler, known to most as Bad Man, backed by the former prison gang, now consolidated into the forces reclassified as Patriot fighters and, for all practical purposes, became the enforcer of law and order.

In the midst of the reformation, using the words of the original document a new constitution was created with new articles declared effective immediately. The new constitution, or, rather, the laws of the new republic replacing the constitution, as crudely as it was written during this early phase, taking into account a new dawn for the continent, was hammered out by day and by candlelight.

The U.S. dollar, the monetary system as it had existed up to now, with all of its depths, inflated values, and unprotected assets was removed from the economy. Until a new currency could be established, for all practical purposes the bartering system would be in place. Coins, gold in the hands of individuals, wherever available, could be used at their current values. No currency printing, no coining, no promissory notes of any kind were allowed as purchasing power.

Norton, elect leader for the republic, took firm reign over the new land. With a slightly inflated ego, cheered on wherever he walked for having taken such a bold move as creating a new government that, however, still needed to be defined, had a difficult time keeping his feet planted on solid ground. As unbelievable as it appeared, he'd pulled off the impossible. "Spread the word, meeting in one hour," he ordered his lieutenant, who was always at his disposal, "all hands."

"What's up?"

"New constitution, and…" he added, on a second thought, "see if you can rustle up a copy of the Declaration."

"About time," ready to alert the section heads, Bad Man approved. "Hey," he called out to his section heads busy at work gathering the crowd for a first, and most historic, congressional assembly, "anybody know the Declaration? And get me a scribe!"

"I know," one caller, hands raised to indicate to his location, readily boasted, "where there's a copy."

"Go, get it."

The caller quickly disappeared, headed for the historical archive section in the Fort only to return minutes later. Handing Norton the copy, he proudly replied, "Here it is." Norton, ready to address the assembly, gazing at the nation's most revered historical document, kept shaking his head. For the first time in his life, he actually took the time to read the constitution. Laid before him, in its full glory, it read:

IN CONGRESS, July 4, 1776.

The unanimous Declaration of the thirteen united States of America,

When in the Course of human events, it becomes necessary for one people to dissolve the political bands which have connected them with another, and to assume among the powers of the earth, the separate and equal station to which the Laws of Nature and of Nature's God entitle them, a decent respect to the opinions of mankind requires that they should declare the causes which impel them to the separation...

There was more, much more to the text eventually signed by representatives from the original thirteen states. "This is good," Norton said, tossing the pages aside and finally looking up from reading the document, "but needs a lot of rework," he decided.

And, along with its struggles to uphold the new congress, new declaration, and, most of all, new government, a new dawn began. But this time, it would be managed "By The People...For The People."

SACRAMENTO RIVER DELTA

With SFO still in shambles, the San Jose and Sacramento airports not much better off, Travis AB had grown tremendously. It'd become the major hub on the West Coast. Located forty miles west of Sacramento, the state's capital, Travis had also become headquarters to FEMA and other support agencies. In addition, CDC had staff on hand to cope with infections and diseases from the decaying bodies. The sounds form propeller-driven craft was in the air day and night. Commercial jetliners were still disabled, grounded for repairs. Public travel was immobilized for the same reasons. Most airports around the nation had been shut down. Only emergency travel was authorized. Special government orders were required to get to any destination.

Martial law had been declared by Mount Weather and was still in effect. National Guardsmen, wherever called into action, were immediately transported to the central region. Rumors had it that a new faction had taken over not only in the central region, but was advancing on the D.C. as well, seizing every state in between. Apparently, growing by the day, it'd become a major resistance force.

Only minutes ago, Alex, Tracy, and Brian had arrived on a B-25 Mitchell. They were met by the head of the FBI, who'd been informed of the team's arrival. Alex, liaison with the Pentagon, was given free hand in coordinating the effort. Presently, he was getting an initial status. "Casualties have been identified in Stockton and Merced," he was informed, "disease is rapidly spreading south."

"Don't have much time," Alex urged. "Bakersfield and L.A. basin are not far off. Who's spreading the contaminants?" He wanted to know. He had an idea, but getting ready to track the infiltrators, he needed specifics.

"Cell West," the agent confirmed, "been dormant for years waiting for a chance to surface." It was the same terrorist group Alex, Tracy, and Scott had encountered at SFO a week earlier.

"What's the condition from above?"

"My people," the FBI chief indicated, "are giving chase. Got choppers on their trail. Pilots use spectrum analyzers." To track and identify the deadly spreading agents, spectrum analysis was used to spot color changes in the water.

"Stay with it. Keep the line open, and," Alex, since he'd been put in charge as liaison, wanted assurance, "stay on the same frequency, all your agents."

"Will do."

Earlier, Alex had been briefed of Foster's tentative attack strategy. The mission, highly classified, supposedly a reprisal action, was all Alex got from him. It'd involve heavy asset support from the Air Force. Although Foster hadn't been sure of the flight's conditions at the moment, he promised to get back with him within the hour. The Castle Team would be provided air support.

Old faithful, the AH-1 Huey Cobra,[74] despite being slightly damaged after the freefall the day before in New York City, was supposedly on the way. It'd been picked up

---

[74] General characteristics
Type: AH-1G, Huey Cobra
Crew: 2 in tandem, one pilot, co-pilot/gunner
Length: 53 ft (with both rotors turning)

and transported out here on a Confederate cargo craft scheduled to arrive shortly. The team was awaiting delivery.

The immediate plan was to head south, intercept the jihad cell, and isolate the virus contaminants speeding toward Los Angeles. How that would be accomplished, at the moment, no one had a clue.

Rotor diameter: 44 ft
Height: 13 ft 6 in
Empty weight: 5,810 lb.
Max. takeoff weight: 9,500 lb.
Powerplant: 1 × Lycoming T53-L-13 turboshaft, 1,100 shp (820 kW)
Rotor system: 2 blades on main rotor, 2 blades on tail rotor
Fuselage length: 44 ft 5 in
Stub wing span: 10 ft 4 in
Performance
Never exceed speed: 190 knots (219 mph)
Maximum speed: 149 knots (171 mph)
Range: 310 nm. (357 mi)
Service ceiling: 11,400 ft
Rate of climb: 1,230 ft/min
Armament
2 × 7.62 mm (0.308 in) multi-barrel Miniguns, or 2 × M129 40 mm Grenade launchers, or one of each, in the M28 turret. (When one of each was mounted, due to automated ammo feeding problems, the minigun was mounted on the right side of the turret.)
2.75 in (70 mm) rockets - 7 rockets mounted in the M158 launcher or 19 rockets in the M200 launcher
M18 7.62 mm Minigun pod or XM35 armament subsystem with XM195 20 mm cannon

STRATEGIC AIR COMMAND

"Offutt," Hawkins growled into the receiver. He was connected with Foster's office. Although the secretary had put him on hold, he was relieved that communication was back. In the past days without electricity and phone, he'd felt helpless. Sure, there was the emergency HF and UHF radios, but those were only for mission commands. Family and personal calls had been restricted to zero. The wife worried every time he'd left the house.

"What's the B-2 status?" Foster's voice boomed at him.

"Foster?" He affirmed.

"Right."

"What a mess we're in."

"You know it." Foster was in total agreement. "Listen," he demanded, "I need four Spirits in the air. Immediately!"

"Doubt," he countered, "anything's flight worthy."

"Damn, Hawk," Foster wasn't about to get pushed off. "Don't give me any crap." He wasn't born yesterday. He knew too well those birds were hardened, EMP protected. They'd been built to "defend and retaliate" against airspace intrusion. They were the modern man's answer to Airships from the first world war and Flying Fortresses from the second.

"What's the mission?"

"Classified." The response was firm. It was final.

"I need to know the mission," Hawkins demanded.

"Can't tell you," Foster insisted. "Highest orders," he persisted. "Call me back," he commanded, "as soon as they're airborne."

"Roger," Hawkins fired back. He was not only annoyed, he was furious. "Always the last to know," he grumbled, but reached for the mission phone. It was the direct connection with the 509th bomber wing at Whiteman.

"What's the status on our B-2s?" he demanded as soon as the voice cut in.

"Down for maintenance," was the response. "Check with Nellis or Edwards." *Click.* He got the same rejection from Nellis but lucked out with his next call.

"Edwards," the caller identified the command. It was the Air Force's most obscure airbase. Located ninety some miles out of San Bernardino, this historic test range was located in the midst of the Mojave Desert. Surrounded by white sands in the middle of bluish jagged mountain ridges, the base was a jewel. Held classified for decades, it gained notoriety in the early '80s with the disclosure of Lockheed's F-117 Stealth.

After ten minutes of pleading followed with threats, he finally reached the right office. Hawkins lucked out. AV-1 and AV-9 were flight ready, he was told. That wasn't enough for the mission. He got kicked back to Nellis once more. After exerting more threats, AV-3, 6, 12, and 15 could be ready within a day, he was assured.

Satisfied, the strong urge to smoke overcame his senses. From the desk drawer he reached for his Lucky pack. He'd saved the last cigarette. It was a symbol of a lifelong habit. *Should I?* He wavered a few seconds. *Better not,* he decided. He'd promised the wife not to smoke again. With jittery fingers from the lack of nicotine, he placed the next call.

"Standby," the DOD operator responded. *Put on hold again.* It gave Lewis Hawkins time to reflect on the AV symbols while he waited. *Spirit of America, Spirit of California, Spirit of New York, how appropriate.* The world's most sophisticated bombers had been designated in honor of the nation's states.

"This is your lucky day," he proclaimed when Foster picked up. "I got your Wing."

"Took your time," Foster replied, "didn't you?"

Hawkins wasn't happy with the response. He felt like letting off some steam but thought otherwise. *Not worth it,* he'd decided. Besides, he needed additional information. "What's the mission?" he demanded again.

"Top secret," Foster insisted, "SCI."

"Aren't they all," he barked into the mouthpiece. Annoyed at first, now he was enraged. "Need to know the payload."

"Listen," Foster shot back, "you'll get your orders after the flight's in the air. Just make sure they're topped off and armed with Paveways and GBU-28s."

"Wow," Lewis grunted. He was stunned. *Big ones...must be going deep.* He knew from previous missions that the GBU series were the arsenal's ultimate.

"Also," Foster ordered, "alert refueling stations in Alaska and NATO Europe."

"Will do."

"Call back when the Wing's ready." Foster terminated the call. What he kept from the SAC commander was, *We're launching a WMD offensive.*

Wonder what's up, Hawkins speculated. Somebody had really pissed off the Pentagon. "Weapons of mass destruction?"

He sat in awe for a few minutes staring at the opposite wall. Pictures from his past accomplishments were facing him. It was a series of framed photographs he once commanded. It was just before he'd been assigned this desk job. It seemed so long ago. He was still furious the day he was forced to turn in his command. "Next generation," he was told. "You know the policy." He'd been desperately fighting to keep the command, but knew the outcome.

SAC had been his calling. He'd given forty years of his life to this command, but had stepped down with the promised promotion to Brigadier General. "What good's a rank without a life?" he'd stated to the wife.

"You got me," she'd reminded him. Not on only one occasion did she remind him of his family obligations. "Vacations, visits the kids, recreation," were her usual comments.

All that's left of a career, he thought, bittersweet, *is watching the birds take off.*

Depressed, feeling melancholy, he reached in the desk drawer. With careful deliberation, he pulled out an album. "SAC," the cover proclaimed, "My Life."

It was a personal treasure. One by one, he slowly turned the pages. As he had many times before, his gaze lingered on one specific photo, one of the most magnificent craft ever designed, the Northrop Grumman B-2 Spirit. Designed with the world's most technologically-advanced defense shield, detection equipment, and armament, the B-2's stealth technology was intended to aid the aircraft's penetration role in order to survive extremely dense anti-aircraft defenses considered impenetrable by other combat aircraft.

He specifically remembered the last mission. It was a special missions launched from Whiteman Air Force Base, MS, resulted in flights in excess of 30 hours, with one specific flight lasting over 50 hours. It was this flight in the picture that gave him pleasure. It was an extended flight he and his team had endured between drops, refueling, and catching naps home on autopilot, only to load up again for yet another run. Soon, the album would be the only treasure remaining after he'd retired.

SACRAMENTO RIVER DELTA

The Cobra, undercarriage and skids damaged days earlier, had finally arrived. The craft, hastily repaired, partially restored to flight condition during transit also sported a set of new blades. Presently in the air, they were making good time. Thirty minutes out from Travis, flying at five thousand feet, Alex and Brian were headed on a southeasterly course. Focused mostly on the ground below, headed towards Stockton, their eyes were feverishly searching for landmarks. The immediate plan was to intersect with I-5 out of Sacramento. It'd take them to the aqueduct structure. Since the Huey was only a two-seated craft, Tracy, amid furious protests, was forced to remain behind. "We'll get you," Alex promised.

"Hell," she'd made one final attempt, "I'll ride the skids."

"Not this time." Brian had used his charm to make her understand. "Work with the FBI," he offered, "we'll be in touch," and off they went.

The craft had just left the Sacramento River in its wake. Up ahead, the San Joaquin river delta, California's breadbasket and nation's fruit bowl, was panning into view. It was their point of rendezvous with the aqueduct. "What do you think?" Brian, steady at the controls, asked.

Craned out the window, Alex recognized a landmark just ahead. "Discovery Bay." He knew the area well. He'd been this way on numerous occasions. The landmark was easily identified by the thousands of wind turbines spinning on nearby ridge tops. Wind farms like these were the region's trademarks.

"Think that's it?" Brian gestured in the direction of a sizable body of water. Alex, reaching for the pair of binoculars he'd packed, had it trained on a concrete building complex by the southern edge of the waterfront.

"Don't think so," he said skeptically.

Undecided, Brian hovered at an intake of the California aqueduct. In fact there were two. It appeared that both channels were fed by the Clifton Court Forebay. From here on, both channels independently ran in parallel alongside I-5 winding south. "Doesn't look like a pump station."

Eyes darting back and forth, Alex scanned the horizon. Unsure, he gestured a few miles ahead. "Over there."

Brian was already headed in the direction. A minute later he flared the craft out alongside the admin building by the Forebay. Exercising caution, he hovered, then gradually settled the chopper down on the vacant lot. The place appeared vacated. There were no jihad infiltrators in the area.

The station was enormous. The sound of pumps droned over the idling chopping blades. What they heard was water getting pumped uphill through a cluster of huge pipes. A half a mile farther, a series of five channels fed the next segment of the aqueduct. The mission was to shut down the pump stations, but how?

It was the team's task to find out. What they faced seemed to be a self-maintained station. During normal operation, incoming electricity would drive the turbines, but with electricity still out, in many instances, backup generators had taken over. Thus, pump functions were self-maintained. Deliberately engineered this way, in case of a catastrophic event, it was a failsafe system. The team tried to gain entrance, but without electricity there was no way in. The electronic locking system was disabled. The system had defeated itself.

"Let's get a water sample." Alex was already by the water's edge. To the eyes, the sample appeared clear. When he broke the chemical analysis capsule it revealed a different story. The water was heavily polluted, not only from dust particles picked up from the air, but also by the deadly protozoa. "Somebody was already here."

"Don't get any liquid on you," Brian cautioned, "there's no water to wash off."

"Right." Alex hesitated, evaluating the next step.

"What's the verdict?" Brian had the rotors run idle. "We don't have much fuel left," he warned.

"Can't do anything from here," Alex agreed, "better get goin'."

Back inside the idling craft, Alex studied the map. Forehead furrowed with deep concern, he said, "It won't be any different ahead. We're in trouble."

"Let's go." Alex was already climbing into the craft. "Farther south." Seconds later they were airborne. According to the map, Bethany Reservoir was only a few miles ahead. It came into view as soon as the craft gained sufficient altitude. They quickly learned, again, that there was no pump on this body of water. The aqueduct fed the lake from one end and drained out at the far end. The flow of water was by gravity only. There was one more alternative, the San Luis Reservoir. Sixty miles farther south, it was the next pump station, and it would also be the last.

Fifteen minutes into the flight, the gigantic San Luis body of water came into view. Flying low, searching for activities, Brian skimmed the water's edge. He could clearly see the aqueduct enter the north end. "Where's the exit?"

"Wait." Alex spotted what could be a pump station. "There," he gestured east, "O'Neil Forebay." Merced was a few miles off to the east. Just to the west was infamous Hollister, the state's earthquake center. The faulty ridge running south to north was clearly visible from the air.

Brian sat the craft down in a nearby field. The station seemed identical to the last one. Again, there was no access to the complex. It was operating on backup power as well.

"What?" Brian straightened up.

"Next pump," Alex warned, "aqueduct's going to split." The map clearly identified the downstream segments. A split occurred just before the Tehachapi Mountains. "Distance's a hundred seventy five miles." Beyond, it would be impossible to neutralize the water. The aqueduct split into three segments: Santa Barbara, Los Angeles, and San Bernardino.

Brian, with fuel running low, again voiced concern, "We need help." Brian had already lifted off, headed south toward the next destination.

Alex agreed. "I'll try Foster." It would be their only option.

Alex was on the HF transmitter. He dialed the frequency then repeatedly flashed the Talk button, but the radio kept silent. There was no response from Dulles tactical. "No transmission." The distance was ineffective at ground level.

"Need altitude," Brian suggested. "I'll take it up a thousand." Ascending past the one thousand foot level, Alex tried again.

"Cobra One…Cobra One," Alex repeated in periodic intervals.

Minutes of precious time went by, then all of a sudden there was a faint crackle quickly followed by an audible, "Identify."

Alex, anxious for a connection with the OPS center, responded, "Bauer." There was no need to identify any further. The defense agency was on high alert. They were closely following the mission. They'd been waiting for the call.

"Foster?" Alex shouted over the pitch of the rotors.

Seconds later, the familiar voice boomed from the ether, "You on secure?"

"Can be—just a sec..." He turned the selector knob to Secure Voice. "Shoot."

"Here's the mission," the general firmed up. "You take care of California," he stated, "I do the rest—confirm."

"California, my call," Alex repeated, "outside the borders, yours."

"Roger that. Spirit of California's on the way."

"How soon?"

"Thirty minutes," Foster affirmed. "You're forward spotter. Good luck."

"Thanks," Alex replied, "we'll need it." The headset clicked off. There was no glory being volunteered Forward Spotter. It meant focal point on the target. In other words, the Cobra was dedicated to identifying the precise location of the target for the B-2 to pinpoint with accuracy. For Alex and Brian, it would be a close call either way.

He motioned to Brian. "Crank it up." Then he reached in back for the duffle. Groping inside, he fished for his mobile. It wasn't a signal he needed. Satellites were still out. He flipped the cover then pulled up the Tools menu. He needed the calculator. Hastily punching in numbers, he calculated distance and time. Fewer than a hundred miles out, their arrival would have to coincide with the Spirit of California, infamous but deadly, B-2 stealth bomber headed that way. "Max it out," Alex urged, "don't know if we can make it."

The plan was simple. Seek out the enemy, the ones poisoning the waters, then knock out the pump station. It would be their last chance to save the population in the state's southern regions.

Fifteen minutes into the flight, Brian called out, "Bakersfield's coming up." He hadn't bothered to gain elevation. It'd take too much time and fuel. The terrain ahead was pretty flat. "Ten more minutes." It'd be the time for the call from above.

Bakersfield slowly passed to the left. "Poor folks," Brian remarked. "We need a refueling stop."

"No time for that," Alex objected, "bomber's on the way."

For the city, there was not much hope left. Contaminants had already reached the city and surrounding towns. Straight ahead, still in the distance, the hilly ridges of Tehachapi Mountain Range slowly crept into view. The Edmonston pumping plant, primary distribution point for the entire L.A. basin, would be at its base. From there, water was pumped 1,926 feet up and over the mountain range. Once the contaminants reached that segment, it would be impossible to save the L.A. population. Millions of unsuspecting people would perish.

"What's the plan?" Brian was praying for information.

Alex had been tightlipped about Foster's plan. "You know the policy." He wasn't about to compromise anyone's position.

"Yeah, but," he complained, "I'm part of the team."

"That's true," Alex admitted. "I suspect you've already guessed what's waiting above?" Not wanting the rest of the world listen, he removed his headset.

"Mass destruction?" Brian always feared one day a nation would use this ultimate weapon. *But the United States? My country? Most peace-loving nation on earth? Impossible.* The thought alone weighed heavily. "Today's it?"

Alex made no comment.

Brian reclined in the seat, waiting out the inevitable. There was not much he could do. He'd served through several combats. The excuse politicians used was always the same: lateral casualties.

Minutes later they arrived. Brian slowed the Cobra into hover mode. The mountain range was straight ahead, only hundreds of yards distant. The pump station was in full view below.

Binoculars trained on the grounds below, searching for activity, Alex spotted something. He made out what appeared human bodies hastening for cover. "Enemy below," he shouted, "Take it on deck."

Brian reacted. He pushed the nose of the craft towards ground.

Selecting the appropriate weapon for the moving targets, Alex warned, "Miniguns, hot." Packed into the gunner's seat, sweaty body scorching from bright sunlight burning through the bubble, within the safety shield, Alex had a tight grip on the turret. Eyes searching for the target, finger on the trigger, he was ready to fire, but there was no target in sight. "Get me closer," he yelled at Brian. The foreign fighters had disappeared into the pump inlet system.

Then, suddenly, both saw it at the same time. To their right, over the top of the ridge ahead, like a biblical monster, it bore down on them. Sliding into view was a dark shadow—a shadow of what appeared to be a combat craft, an attack craft. Stunned by the sudden appearance of the once dreaded craft on a collision course, Alex yelled, "Watch out—Russian Hind!"

Brian, immediately taking evasive action, spun the Cobra around, maxed out the speed and dove for cover toward the ground, hoping to escape in the valley below. Immediately, from the corner of his eyes, he could see the Hind give chase. "Not good," he shouted, gasping for air, at Alex who, at the moment, felt defenseless. There were no rear-mounted weapons onboard the Cobra. Unlike at the craft they'd just confronted, there were no side mounted turret guns either. Brian, with the Hind in pursuit, was on the run.

AIR BATTLE

Earlier that day, the Cuban armada, after a forty-eight hour voyage at full steam ahead to cover the sixteen hundred miles distance, arrived at the eastern Mexican shores in the early morning hours at Port Isabel. How they made it past the Bahamas, Florida Straits, Cuba, and Cancun without getting sunk by the American submarine fleet was a miracle. Some invisible power must have recalled the ever watchful, nuclear fueled, tactically submerged enemy fleet. *Allah*, the Serpent marveled, once again had been on his side.

Hammad, currently at the flight controls of the dreaded Hind, Russia's capable equivalent of the American Huey AH-1 Cobra, after lifting off the carrier, headed for the rendezvous point in the southern regions of California with the longtime inactive, dormant Cuban Cell in back of the craft staged for an attack.

Cell U.S. West, California's tactical jihad team with Muhab Sadek in command, until now active at the northern perimeters, had received new orders via HF radio. Presently dispatched along the aqueduct channels, Hammad planned to merge both teams. He needed an effective fighting force to take the U.S. continent by surprise, as long as the nation was still in disarray. Once the American forces, the enemy, were able to restage and reorganize, with the combined strength of military, National Guards, and law enforcement, the task would become impossible. The Plan, his long sought out solution for world dominance, would become obsolete.

At present, airspeed at maximum power, Hammad had to hurry rushing into the unknown. Following two refueling stops, one in Chihuahua, in the central regions of Mexico, and another in Mexicali, the last town near California's southern border, Hammad was close to the destination. Passing one last barrier, the Tehachapi Mountain Range the map indicated, he was well on the way to meet up with U.S. Cell West.

To his surprise, he had not run into any kind of resistance. It almost seemed like the entire nation was asleep. Racing north, barely skimming the mountain range, Hammad, following the contours of the hilly terrain, pushed the nose of his craft into the vast valley immediately ahead. From this height, with an immense view into California's San Joaquin Valley, he promised himself that this would be the new nation's paradise, his and his people's paradise. Awestruck by the vastness and taking in the magnificent view, he shouted, "Insha' Allah!" Reluctant to break away from the awesome, breathtaking landscape ahead—so different from the Arabian deserts—Hammad headed toward the valley, the new nation, his nation, the Promised Land.

It was then, racing across his visor that he spotted the craft only yards ahead skimming along the mountain tops. On imminent collision course, he instantly reacted. Banking steep and fast he barely clearing the oncoming craft's rotors. Flying for hours, throat parched from lack of fluids, all he could gather was, "Cobra!" It was an involuntary shout escaping his lips. His nerves immediately tightened to the bursting point. He could feel the adrenaline pump into his chest, throat, and temples. He even heard his heart pound inside his ears. It'd tripled from excitement within a few beats.

Comfortably seated in back of the craft, anticipating disembarking soon at their destination, the intercom suddenly sprang into action, "Alert...Alert...Alert." The combat crew, eight in all, grabbing helmets, immediately jumped into action. Each rushed for a pre-assigned battle station. Already armed, hanging onto steel, fingers on the triggers, they waited for a target.

Hammad, in front, eyes darting between the HUD display and horizon ahead so as not to lose sight of the Cobra, pushing the throttle to maximum speed, gave chase. On the last sighting he had on the AH-1, it was hugging the terrain, headed for the valley.

At present, diving at maximum speed toward the valley, utterly stunned after the unexpected sighting, Brian and Alex attempted to recover from shock.

"Russian forces!" Brain exclaimed. "Here, on U.S. soil?"

Charging to call for immediate support, Alex almost ripped the mic cord from its mounting. "AV10...AV10...come in...come in...Code Red...Code Red!" Never before had he had to resort to this kind of alert. To call on air support, the Air Force's most advanced and sophisticated stealth bomber, was a call of extreme emergency.

Within seconds, a metallic sounding voice responded, "Cobra One, what's your status?"

"Extreme conditions." Alex cautioned, "Russian attack force. Need assistance...San Joaquin Valley," he shouted into the mic.

"Sorry," the pilot shot back, "no defense weapons on board."

"The one time I need air support," Alex gasped, "they got nothin'." Then it dawned on him. He'd just remembered the mission—penetrating buster bombs. There was no use dwelling on their present, almost impossible situation. "Gotta fight," he instructed his buddy, "you ready?"

"Cobra's no match for the Hind," Brian, not yet completely recovered from the utter surprise of less than a minute ago, snapped back. It was clearly an uneven match. "Can't match speed and weapons," he panted.

Frustrated at not being able to help, Alex struggled for a secure hold on what would come next. For now, for whatever was in store, he put his life in his buddy's hands. Succumbed to the inevitable, the warrior he was, he let out a ferocious scream, "Go...get 'em!"

Tightly strapped into the seat, after the brief glimpse at the gray-colored menace seconds ago, Alex tried to recall the attack craft's parameters.

Most Probable Armament:[75] MI-24 HIND D, Turret-mounted 4-barrel 12.7-mm Gatling type machinegun, Twin, 4 each 57-mm rockets.

---

[75]

Aircraft Type	Hind D
Mission Role	Assault, gunship, antitank
Crew	Two (pilots in tandem cockpits)
Combat Load	8 Combat troops
Similar Aircraft	AH-1 Cobra, UH-60 Black Hawk, AH-64 Apache, Mangusta A129
Fuel	Internal: 486 gal
Internal Aux Tank	In cabin: 324 gal
External Fuel Tanks	2 x 132 gal each
Engines	2 x 2,200 hp Isotov, TV-3-117 turbines
Maximum Speed	168 mph
Range	With Aux Fuel: 590 miles
Service Ceiling	13,500 feet
Vertical Climb Rate	45 ft/s
Armament	Armored cockpit
	12.7-mm 4 x Barrel Machinegun: Range .9 miles, Rate of Fire: 2,600
	30-mm Twin Barrel Cannon: Range 2.4 miles, Rate of Fire, up to 2,600
	2-12 - AT-2C or AT-6C Spiral Anti-Tank Guided Missile (ATGM)
	2-4 - 80-mm S-8 rocket pods (20 ea.)
	2-4 - 57-mm S-5 rocket pods (32 ea.)
	940 - GSh-23L twin 23-mm Machine Gun (MG) pods

Brian had both hands clenched around the Cobra's control stick. His eyes were dead set on the terrain rushing past the craft a few feet below. Flying this close to the ground he knew was dangerous. Flying the craft, the choice was limited to either high up in the air, or flying low just in case they'd have to bail out fast. For now, he was hugging the ground as close as he possibly could. Then they heard it, in rapid succession, a hail of projectiles—"thud…thud…thud," the sound every pilot who'd ever been in combat dreaded. It was the sound of heavy caliber from a nose-mounted cannon tearing into the fuselage.

With Brian at the controls dashing in and out of ground covered tree and brush vegetation, Alex kept checking for the smoke that he suspected was imminent at this rate of fire. At the moment, they were the prey, but that would have to change if they wanted to stay alive.

In every battle scene, every fighter knew that the advantage was with the attacker. He needed to turn the tide in their favor. And that, he was fully aware, was not an easy task with what was chasing them. More thuds and pings followed. In fact, Alex was astounded that the Cobra, after the stream of almost continuous hits, was still fully intact. *No wonder.* A fleeting thought crossed his mind. Unofficially, back in his early fighting days in Vietnam they used to call it the "Killing Fields," capable of mowing down structures, buildings, and everything inside within seconds with the twin turret mounted Gatling guns. There wasn't much left but kindling wood.

Not even considering the pod mounted armament, multi-staged missiles, and rockets in the Hind, if they weren't able to get away from the constant hails of bullets, the chase would be over in another minute. "Get us outta this," he yelled at Brian.

There was one advantage the Cobra had over the Hind, and that, Brian knew, with speed between the craft almost evenly matched, was maneuverability. The MI-24 carried a much heavier load with a weight difference of 16,000 pounds in the Cobra's favor. The firepower was a completely uneven match in the Hind's advantage.

Somehow, he had to take advantage of it. And he did after the next hail of bullets. Pushing the throttle to max power, with a rate of climb almost double that of the MI-24, he took the Huey into a steep ascent. The two-bladed main rotor, both he and Alex could hear, strained to its limited design capability. Brian had to use all of his skills to keep the blades from snapping into pieces. He'd applied what's known to fighter pilots as air brakes.

Weaving the hull from side to side during the pull, craning out the side windows, both Brian and Alex spotted the Hind shoot past almost dead center below. In an instant, the tide had turned. Now it was Brian giving chase. Brian, pushing the craft's nose towards the ground, quickly closed up the distance. Fingers already at work, he flipped

---

	4 each 250-kg Freefall Bombs (FAB)
	2 each 500-kg Freefall Bombs
Sensors	Forward Looking Infrared Radar (FLIR)
	Radar Warning Receiver (RWR) laser designator
Avionics	Low-level light TV
	Laser designator, FLIR, air data sensor, missile guidance transmitter
	Infrared signature suppressors mounted on engine exhausts
Radar warning	IFF, Infrared jammer, rotor brake, chaff and flares

the safety off, aimed the twin guns at the target, pushed the trigger, and let go. "Take this!" he shouted. Simultaneously, from twin miniguns, the two solid streams of fiery lead hailed towards target ahead.

During past wars, battles, and encounters, what made the Cobra so effective was the firing power from the GE manufactured M134 model, 7.62 mm, multi-barrel (6) miniguns with a 6,000 rounds per minute rate of fire, employing Gatling-style rotating barrels with an external power source. Shooting out a solid wall of lead from the two miniguns at two hundred rounds per second, the Cobra came to almost an immediate halt, falling back a hundred yards. The results were immediately visible. Two gigantic holes had appeared in the Hind's fuselage, torn open by the deadly onslaught.

Not used to swearing, in the height of battle, subjected to extreme maneuvers, almost out of breath, Alex managed to call out, "Dammit!"

Brian, to keep focus, to be effective again, had to close the distance. The Hind forged ahead at full speed toward whatever destination it was seeking, most likely the state capital. Brian gave chase.

In the Hind, Hammad, hundreds of yards in front after the change in battle posture, infuriated for not anticipating the AH-1 pilot's clever maneuver, was taking advantage of the widened gap in the chase. He knew, if he wanted to reach his destination without another confrontation that he had to ditch some weight. Gaining almost a mile distance, it gave him time for the next move. Without slowing down, he jerked the controls to the right into a 180 turn, watched the incoming Cobra, who, to avoid colliding, immediately slowed into a defensive position, and shouted, "Take that you fucking infidels!" He let go a series of S-5 pod mounted, 57 mm rockets. Thirty-two in total, he could afford to hold the trigger until a hit would be confirmed.

Suspecting it was the same pilot that had attacked him in New York the previous day, Hammad, despite his rage, gained new respect for the American's flying skills. The scene immediately developing from both views, Hammad's and Alex's, was incredible, almost an impossibility.

In the Cobra, from the corner of his eye, Brian immediately acknowledged the flashes launched from a series of deadly missiles. "Incoming!" he yelled as the silvery streaks, with tremendous speed, flashed by the fuselage, engines, and undercarriage.

On the opposing battleground, closing in fast, complete focus on the enemy, anticipating the Hind pilot's intended maneuver, Brian shouted, "Hang on!" and snapped the Cobra into a horizontal barrel roll, immediately followed by a similar vertical maneuver. He'd executed a perfect three-dimensional figure eight. The motion was seamless. Up, down, in, out, that simple, but in reality, the few seconds it took to execute, his brain could hardly comprehend the maneuver. It had to rely on pure memory. Whether through simulation exercises or from prior experience, it was, nevertheless, a most daring tactic not even a stunt pilot would consider.

Brian shot a fleeting glance at the Hind. Due to the enemy's mounted arsenal, he anticipated another attack. On extreme edge, Brian let out another yell. "Here they come!"

"When will it end?"

Alex saw what Brian had initiated. In a reflective defensive action, feet strained against the floor to stiffen the body, grip tightened on the cabin hold, "Good God," were the only words to escape from his lightly clenched lips. The next second he was upside down again.

Brian, focus on the fast approaching Hind, gauging when to maneuver next, reacted. Right hand griped firmly around the control stick, he pulled back hard. Fist white from being clenched around the shaft tightly pressed against his stomach, Brian held firm. The Cobra went into a forced climb. He held it there until the craft began to stall out.

About ten feet below, almost scraping the Cobra's skids, at full throttle, the MI-24 Russian-built Hind shot right past the vertically ascending Cobra. Again, due to a maneuverability advantage, Brian managed to avoid direct hits from another salvo of S-5 deadly aimed, laser guided missiles. This time, by not repeating the same move as executed just a minute ago, he planned to outsmart the Hind's pilot once more. Craft in steep ascent, when the forward momentum stopped, Brian pushed the controls hard forward and to the right. The craft responded immediately. Nose directed toward the ground, the Cobra went into a vertical spin. The acceleration was insane, and so was the seemingly out of control craft spinning towards the ground.

Just before impact, Brian pulled out and leveled off. The Cobra flared into a leveled flight, once more speeding ahead. A quarter mile out, the Hind had just made a tight turn facing Brian and Alex head on. What was ahead would be the most daring move two opponents could execute. The move was known as playing "Chicken." Only the most daring pilots would ever make such an attempt. The end result was clear. At least one of the craft, if not both, was destined to perish.

"Hang tight," Brian let out a final warning. He didn't have to explain. Alex knew the endgame. It was either him and Brian, or them winning out. Hovering, barely clearing the ground, suspended a mile apart, the two craft were pitted against each other for one final thrust. Due to the distance, both pilots, at the moment unable to check the other's immediate intentions, nevertheless expecting one final clash, almost simultaneously pushed their respective craft into full power. Gaining speed to maximum flight, the Cobra from one end with the Hind approaching from the other flew toward each other. The combined impact would be in access of three hundred fifty miles. At that speed, it would almost be impossible to avert the craft from the collision course.

Much like two knights in fully clad armor, rushing into each other, releasing all remaining weapons and ammunitions at once, the two craft closed in at an alarming rate. "One thousand feet," Brian called out the estimated distance, "five hundred…two hundred…one hundred…fifty…impact."

Fractions from impact, almost like a rehearsed play, both craft, on the brink of falling apart from immense strain, abruptly pulled off to their respective rights. In a last desperate effort, barely clearing each other, both craft sped out into opposite directions creating sounds much like explosive thunder. Both craft had received severe damages from an all-out onslaught of bullets, exploding shells, missiles, and rockets slamming into each other, bouncing off fuselages, and penetrating metal. Both craft, miracle as it was, had survived the inferno. In the split second that followed, there was recognition. Brian, as well as Alex, in an instant had recognized the attacker flying the Hind, "Hammad!" As unbelievable as it sounded, they had to deal with the facts. "Enemy still on U.S. soil."

Hammad, in a last ditch effort to save the craft, the crew, and his life, pulled up. An instant later, he recognized the Cobra crew, "Bauer? Harris?" As incredible as it was, he had to deal with it. With the attack just executed, the HUD alerts blinking at him indicating "Weapons spent," he had no choice but to avoid further confrontations with the Cobra. He cussed at himself for being so foolish expending the entire arsenal with the last maneuver. The only recourse from here on out was flight, getting back to the original mission. "Taking possession of the State Capital." Immediately, he changed directions to head for the destination.

To his surprise, the Cobra did not pursue. He still could not understand how his adversary anticipated yesterday's ad hoc decision to target southern California. "The man must be psychic," referring to Alex, was the only conclusion he could come up with. Greatly relieved, to finally proceed to the immediate destination, he focused on the mission that lay ahead.

During the evasive move, body forced against the seatback, with facial features contorted from the impossible Gs, voice distorted from the vibration, Alex let out a primordial yell while he watched the cluster of blazing missiles streak past only to wing up wildly spiraling into the space ahead. "Jeeesus!" Because of the craft's design, extreme G sustainability combined with fantastic maneuverability, which Brain had tested and experienced on numerous occasions, he had the best helicopter ever designed in his control.

Brian had just pulled out when Alex, not only utterly impressed by his buddy's deft flying skills, but also with the coolness that he'd executed the split-second evasive maneuver, stammered, "Hot damn." No words could describe the controlled, repeated stunts he'd just experienced. Leaning back in the well-worn but firmly anchored gunner's seat, Alex, still letting his mind process the feel of exhilaration, was shaken into reality.

Apparently the enemy, after just executing an impossible evasive maneuver, took immediate flight, headed north.

Alex, not expecting his buddy's maneuver, totally breathless, unable to securely hang on, shaken to the very core, heard himself shout, yell, and curse at the same time. Being steadfast in character, under normal circumstances, he'd be ashamed to repeat any of it. "Catch 'em," he yelled, but his wish was intercepted by an unexpected call.

"Cobra One...Cobra One." The radio cracked like a whip into the battle fifteen thousand feet below. Body tensed from the encounter, nerves on edge from the rollercoaster ride, Brian's heart almost leaped from his chest. He had completely forgotten about the mission from above. "Come in...come in," the voice demanded.

"Thank God," Alex shouted above the battle scene, "'bout time!" All he wanted was to get out of this unevenly matched battle.

For the next mission to be effective, he'd have to be guide for the downlink laser lock. He knew what to expect. It wasn't going to be a joyride. "Cobra One," he responded, "what's your position?"

"Twenty miles east of Mojave," the voice reported, "need final coordinates."

Alex, trying to steady his slightly shaking hands, leapt for the map. He needed to confirm the coordinates. Clearing his throat to steady his voice, he called off the parameters: "34°56'40.17 N...118°49'29.61 W...elevation...1,226."

"Will be on top in," the pilot calculated, "three minutes." From here on out, laser, computers, guidance systems, and software would do the rest. The plan called for tearing the pump station apart. It'd stop the flow of water but would also poison the surrounding valley. The fertile farming fields of the San Joaquin Valley and nearby Bakersfield would be affected. It'd also mean the end of the nation's lush and fertile breadbasket and fruit bowl for years to come. It'd still be a better choice than killing off the entire population in the south.

"Got you on radar," the voice cracked the silence again. "Ten seconds...take cover."

"What cover?" Alex yelled, "This is flat land."

Brian checked the altimeter. *Way too low.* He'd have to get the hell out of the blast zone. "Hang on," he shouted. The laser was locked on the target. He had to gain altitude fast or get shredded to pieces. Using all his energy that remained from the battle, he forced the craft into a steep climb. The ensuing G-forces strained heavily on their bodies.

"Not gonna make it," Alex yelled, knowing the magnitude of the weapon about to be released, "we need more altitude."

"Five seconds to impact," was the final warning from above.

Brian, straining for more altitude, kept pushing the craft skyward.

Alex was counting the seconds. "Four...three...two...one." He reached count zero. "Now." The payload had been released. Twenty seconds later, still climbing to clear ground, without any visible indication, the craft shook violently. With explosive force, the Cobra was lifted and tossed upward. Clumps of dirt and concrete shattered against the fuselage. Alex, not used to that much violence, watched in horror as smoke and fire shot past the window. Accompanied by the nasty sounds of metal biting into metal and dinging rotor blades, the craft became engulfed in smoke.

Brian had lost control. "Going down," he shouted in desperation. Attempts to steady the craft proved futile. Huey bucking wildly, spinning out of control, instruments out, flight controls not responding, black smoke trailed the cabin, he barely managed, "Fuel line's cut." The spray of fuel had caught fire; the spinning blades, in the crew's favor, kept the flames from reaching the fuel tank. No matter how hard he tried, Brian could not steady the craft. "Cutting rotors." Seconds later, just like the previous day over Manhattan, the craft went into freefall.

Alex felt a sickening feeling rise from the pit of his stomach. His body lifted from the heavy steel drop out beneath.

"Brace for impact," Brian yelled over the roar of the engine. With rotor blades stopped and no forward momentum, for a fraction of a second the damaged craft hovered, then, with an ever-increasing whine, plummeted toward the ground. With blades spinning at high speed, Brian watching the ground rush in, threw the blades' pitch into reverse. The craft, straining against gravity, immediately slowed to a dead stop, only feet from the ground.

"Jeeesus," Alex moaned. Six Gs pulled on their bodies just before the chopper hit ground.

Less than a second before impact, Brian, as he had done the day before, engaged the rotor. It'd turned into an air brake, but the altitude was too low. The ensuing impact was jolting. The craft bounced a couple of times but was held upright by the spinning blades. The rotor still functioned. With a flip of a finger, Brian killed the ignition. The craft, groaning from strain, settled down with one final bounce. Alex had already jumped from the craft. Brian quickly followed.

"You guys okay?" It was the metallic voice from above. Mission accomplished, the bomber was already headed for the next destination. Looking up, lingering in the wake of the bomber, Alex and Brian could make out a couple of waning contrail streamers.

"Shaken," Brian reported, "but alive."

"Sign off," was a final call by the pilot.

The bomber had done its job. The pump station, torn into countless pieces of debris, was completely destroyed and, with it, the main force of Cell West. The instant the bomb hit the station, the generators quit pumping water. With the immense pressure flow released, a column of 1,200 hundred plus feet of water came crashing down. Rapidly spreading out toward Bakersfield, it drowned the enemy forces but instantly flooded the valley.

"Let's get outta here," Alex urged. "There'll be a lot of angry farmers."

"Can't," Brian cautioned, "fuel line's busted."

Alex inspected the tear. "I think I can fix it." And he did. "Duct tape works miracles."

"Gotta get fuel."

"Let's try Bakersfield," Alex gestured. From their vantage point, the city outline was visible in the distance. It was a straight shot along RT-99 for a fuel opportunity. "City's built on oil."

"Yeah, but," Brian objected, "the Serpent's escaped again."

"Don't worry," Alex said, equally disheartened but tired from the constant chase, "we'll get 'em next time." Collecting his thoughts, "And," he emphasized, "there will be a next time." Alex sauntered into the sudden silence.

Brian settled the craft on the ground to inspect the damages. Stunned at the shape the craft was in, repeatedly shaking his head in disbelief, all he could do was force his face into a broad grin. "We'll make it," he'd decided. "Let's get Tracy."

SAN JOAQUIN VALLEY

Despite the heavy damages to the craft, minutes later Brian lifted off. Gaining altitude to inspect the terrain, the Hind was nowhere in sight. They could make out the damages caused to the pump station below.

Headed east in the direction of Bakersfield, the team was ready for a break. Brian had been behind the controls since early morning. Making the call, Travis Central patched the call right through to Tracy.

She sounded worried. "Where've you been all morning?"

"Get a flight out to Bakersfield," he replied, "we'll be at the south end of town."

Ten minutes later, on an airstrip south of town, Brian settled the ailing craft down. Fuel was available but had to be pumped manually. The airfield operator was on duty. Alex urged him to call the authorities about the water pollutant coming his way. He immediately jumped to it. A local shop dished out hot coffee and sandwiches.

While waiting for Tracy to arrive, they had a well-deserved lunch.

An hour later, Tracy arrived. She'd been shuttled in on a C-130 that had just touched down. Filled with joy, the Colorado team united again, she gave Brian a hug. "What's next?" Tracy wondered.

"South."

"Hop on in," Alex invited her to join him. "Gonna be crowded."

Minutes later, seated in tandem, with Tracy sandwiched into the gunner's seat, the Cobra was airborne again. Gasping for breathing room, she complained, "It's tight," she complained.

Headed for today's final segment, Alex assured her, "Won't be long, just sit tight."

"South," he motioned to Brian as he checked the map, "across the San Gabriel Mountains and keep it above twelve thousand."

"What's the distance?"

"Uh," Alex took an educated guess, "hundred twenty miles, more or less." He couldn't quite recall the driving time, let alone the flying. Ten minutes later they'd reached cruising altitude. Despite the crammed conditions for Tracy, the flight was breathtaking. Brian followed the general path along I-5 south. Not long after leaving Bakersfield, the Golden State Freeway cut into the mountain range. Antelope Valley lay to the far left. Thirty minutes later, Burbank came into view and, a few more miles ahead, Glendale. The sprawling landscape of the City of Angels was already visible in the distance. "Better find a landing strip." Brian changed the pitch of the craft. It slowed to a descending path. "What's that below?"

Alex checked the map. "Equestrian Center."

"Looks like a race track," Tracy said. "Look," she pointed nearby, "the L.A. River Basin."

Alex verified the map. "That's the place. Take it down." Minutes later, the craft settled down amid the deserted racetrack.

"Duffel," Alex gestured to the rear of the cabin. He'd already stepped off.

"What?" Tracy reached for the bag.

"Skates."

"Skates?" She'd forgotten.

"Promised you the thrill of a lifetime," he said, "didn't I?" He'd already clambered up an embankment. Brian and Tracy followed close behind. Directly below was what used to be the L.A. River. The bed was dry now. It'd been this way for decades. When settlers had first arrived here two centuries ago, it used to carry water, but with the rapid population growth that followed, the bed had quickly dried up. It became necessary to construct the aqueducts bypassing the river bed. Encased in 45-degree sloping concrete, today it served as flood canal.

"Gotta be kidding," Tracy called out.

"You'll like it," he assured her.

"What? We supposed to skate the walls…are you crazy?"

Alex laughed. He was busy strapping on his skates. He was dead serious. "Let's get goin'."

At first, Tracy and Brian were reluctant, but then they quickly followed his example. Unsure what would come next, both stared at the path ahead. Ahead lay a seemingly endless corridor snaking its way through the countryside. "Ready?" Alex shouted. He was checking out both their skating gear.

"Lead on," Tracy yelled. She gave Brian an encouraging hug then jumped down the sloping wall.

Alex led the way, his skates picking up speed. "Geronimo," she heard his voice trail off in the distance. Brian closed up right behind.

With Dad ahead, Brian in back, Tracy had not felt this exhilarated since childhood. Legs busy adjusting to the changing slopes, her body skimmed across the smooth concrete surface of the aqueduct. Rushing down one side, across the dry bottom, and up the opposite wall, steadily picking up speed, the team headed south. Along the way, still on somewhat shaky legs, Brian caught up.

"What gave you the idea?" she yelled after her dad.

"Used to skate flood canals," Alex replied. He always wanted to skate the ultimate ride, the L.A. River basin. He seemed pleased. The ride was thrilling. Waving both arms, Alex shouted into the sundown. "Hollywood!" Holding hands, Tracy and Brian promptly chimed in, "Here we come."

FINAL MISSION

It was a majestic sight—three stealth bombers pulled up in close formation. "Ghostly," would be a more suitable description for these streamlined contours tearing through the atmosphere. At their assigned altitude, the blackened radar-absorbing skins made each wing invincible. Enemy ground radar might detect the flight, but would log it off as just another flock of migrating birds. They were cruising at 50,000 feet. Protected from cosmic and other damaging rays by coated visor shields flipped over hidden faces, the pilots, since reaching altitude, waited for orders. At its best when talking air to air or air to ground, the built-in comm equipment presently remained silent.

Into the silence of space, there was a sudden crackle. Received just prior to takeoff, the wing commander alerted his crew. "Mission assignments." Instructions were to "Take the wing east across the Atlantic."

"Gonna be a long haul," he explained.

"About time," his right wingman voiced over the intercom. "I'm dying to learn the targets." It was the first active mission for most of the young crewmen. Only the wing commander had seen live action. But it'd been years. Since then, only action had been simulator training with an occasional demonstration run over the Air Academy and other prominent bases. Now, today, being seated in front of the constellation of instruments was exhilarating.

Embraced glove like, the flight commander's body was fully clad in the pressurized, computer-controlled G-suit. In heightened anticipation, he reached for the sealed envelope labeled Top Secret then read the brief mission orders in silence. *That's what I'm talking about.* The orders were direct and precise. The present text revealed only the flight's outline. Detailed instructions were stored in onboard computers.

The flight commander, a Texan, in a deliberate gesture articulating his inherited demeanor, flipped the selector switch to "Talk," momentarily alerting the crew. "Heah it izz," he announced in his haltingly southern slang, "youah aohdas." Already he envisioned the chuckling cheers by his crews. He was prone to their joking about his accent.

"AV-1...Zone Papa; AV-3...Indigo; AV-6...Kilo." He briefly paused to let the instructions sink in. "Check youha respective flight greedz." The pilots, despite the southern drawl, immediately recognized their respective mission assignments.

"What's the drop sequence?" one pilot, this being his first active mission, asked. There was a brief pause. Then the commander clarified the individual instructions:

"AV-1 fly zone: U.K., Germany, destination Iran. AV-3 fly zone: U.K., Russisa, destination Pakistan. AV-6 fly zone: Polar, Iceland, Siberia, destination North Korea...my route. Drop point's on computah when you reach youah zone."

At this point they did not know their specific targets. Data programmed into the onboard computers was accessible only upon reaching the destination. Set by SIOP as a safety measure, the precaution was to prevent compromise of the combat mission. When the computer received the final data from mission command, it was matched with the in-flight world map database, letting the software select the final targets.

"Might azz wehl get comftable," was his final remark to the wing. The commander craned out the window to check the general region. They'd just left the continent behind. To get full visual from the cockpit, he adjusted the seating. In view directly below were the deep blue waters of the Atlantic. Complete silence embraced the crews. Flying at supersonic speed, the engine sound was left in the wake of the craft. Inside, hardly a ripple was felt at this altitude. The air was too thin to cause turbulence. Besides, each move was immediately corrected by the onboard flight computers.

He reached for the logbook to make the periodically required entry. Final orders were pending until he'd reached his zone. Once that was done, to occupy his mind, he pulled up the computer menu and checked the craft's characteristics on display.

Despite the training and flight experience, the wing commander still had a difficult time converting to metrics. He was shaking his head to ward off drowsiness. Most of it was highly classified. It still amazed him, at his young age, to get a command assignment on this multi-billion dollar fortress. With the rank of captain, he didn't expect to fly this craft until much later in his career. That prestige was generally reserved for the rank of full-bird. *Novelty must have worn off,* he deduced when handed the B-2 commission.

In reality, once a critical mission had been tested and implemented through a high-ranking grade officer, the rank was gradually lowered to meet budget restraints and cost effectiveness. Such was the case with any military assignment.

LOS ANGELES

The phone kept ringing. Alex ignored it. He thought it was in the dream. It did not register for some time. He hadn't heard the sound in days. His eyes gradually opened. He blinked a couple of times to clear his vision then reached for the cradle. He found himself in unfamiliar surroundings. Sure enough, there actually was a phone on the nightstand. The ringing had stopped. He forced his body upright. Sitting by the edge of the bed, looking out the window it slowly came to him. He couldn't help but grin at the view. After checking into the motel he must have fallen asleep from sheer exhaustion.

The phone rang again. This time he picked up. "Bauer," he answered.

"Where've you been?" It was Foster's familiar voice on the line, demanding as usual.

His eyes rested on the world famous amusement park across from the window, "Disneyland." He couldn't resist the bit of humor.

"Get serious." Foster wasn't up for the personal joke. "Where are you?"

"L.A.," he said. "Any word on the Serpent?"

"You on secure?" Foster wanted to know.

"You kiddin'?" he said. "Nothing here's secure. It's California." It was his way of making a witty statement.

"How soon can you get to a Skiff?"

"Gotta check." Alex knew that local FBI offices usually had a skiff.

"Call as soon as you get there." Foster hung up.

Alex hurried to the bathroom. About to turn on the shower, he was interrupted by a persistent knocking from the hallway.

He opened the door. It was Tracy. "Morning, Dad," she said, and cheerfully planted a kiss on his cheek. "You need a shave."

"That's not all." He felt the two-day-old stubbles on his face and body odor emanating from his armpits; he desperately needed a shower. "I've been on the phone."

"You ready for breakfast?" Brian stuck his head in. Both were dressed for the street.

"Wish I could," he said with a hint of disappointment. "I've got a conference. Foster wants to talk. You go ahead. I'll catch up."

Thirty minutes later, Alex arrived at the local building. He was led down a hallway. The place was impeccably clean. There was nothing tactical about it. It was the FBI headquarters for the Pacific sector. The neatly dressed agent gestured, "Here's the Skiff," and handed Alex a temp ID. "Don't forget to drop it off," the agent advised, "when you check out." He left and closed the door. Alex gave him a quick nod.

"Let me fill you in," Foster stated on secure. "We've captured two Al Qaeda teams."

"Where?"

"Central Colorado," he was informed, "and the Chicago outskirts."

"Great." Alex sighed with relief. "What about out here?"

"You took care," he was assured, "of most of them. Appears," Foster continued, "we've foiled a major push," he briefly paused, "before it was carried out."

"What about the counterstrikes?"

"Strikes have been successful," he was informed. "All targets been taken out."

That was great news. "Maybe," Alex hinted, "there'll be peace for a while?" He hoped so much for a change, a peaceful time.

"Doubt it." Foster was his usual pessimistic self. "Okay, what have you got? It's your turn."

"You promised to listen," Alex stated. He wasn't going to be put off any further. He needed to clear his head.

"That I did. Shoot."

"Following current events," Alex proceeded, "something doesn't add up."

"Keep talking."

"Seems," he was careful to explain, "we're being sold out." He was hoping not to appear like a lunatic. He'd always kept a clear head. He never gave in to rumors and conspiracies and wasn't about to start, but there were clear signs that something was up.

"What gives you that idea?"

He did not like the response. *Could I be wrong about Hank?* Doubt crept into his mind. "Information I came across," he cautioned, "data I've compiled."

"Give me specifics," Foster demanded, "and make them facts. Don't want hunches."

"This one's tough to prove from the bottom up," Alex admitted. It was a sensitive issue. He approached the subject with caution. "I'll have to let one former president speak for himself." He explained:

The Federal Reserve was a creation of the Federal Reserve Act, signed into law in 1913 by then President Woodrow Wilson. Shortly after, and due to immense pressure by international bankers, Woodrow Wilson signed away the freedom of America. Acting on behalf of its own private interests, the Federal Reserve, by this act, had turned into a private corporation. Wilson had this unfortunate realization a couple years after the signing of the act as he wrote:

"I am a most unhappy man. I have unwittingly ruined my country...The growth of the nation, therefore, and all our activities are in the hands of a few men. We have come to be one of the worst ruled, one of the most completely controlled and dominated Governments in the civilized world, no longer a Government by free opinion, no longer a Government by conviction and the vote of the majority, but a Government by the opinion and duress of a small group of dominant men."

"Where did you get this?" Foster's voice carried an alarming overtone.

"Freedom of Information," Alex stated. It was just one of many classified documents recently made public.

"So," he countered, "what're you implying?"

"That's not all," Alex continued. "There're rumors about someone taking over the nation." He paused to let that sink in. "Hear of the Badlands?"

Following a conscious pause, Foster replied, "Maybe." It was all he'd admit.

"Just watch your back," Alex cautioned his longtime friend. "The government may not last much longer."

"That's it?

"For now," Alex insisted, "but there's more...much more."

"You're getting paranoid."

"See what I mean?" Alex stated. "Nobody takes this stuff seriously."

"Don't get me wrong," Foster pacified his friend. It sounded like he was trying to appease his concerns. "These are serious issues," he insisted, "but nobody's going to stick his neck out without concrete evidence."

"I've got the proof," Alex insisted, "but..."

Foster cut him short. "Tell you what," he said, "drop by the office next time you're in town." It was a weak consolation. "Maybe we can do something about it."

"Count on it," Alex said with finality. Foster had hung up. It left him with more questions than answers. *No justice for the common man.*

"Whatcha been doin'?" Brian greeted Alex when he showed up at the park. "Missed a good meal."

"Talked with Foster."

"What about?" Brian inquired, curiosity stirred.

"Oh, something that's been bothering me."

"What?"

"You know," he went on, "globalization…government takeover…civil war…and such."

"Any support from the Pentagon?" he queried.

"He thinks I'm paranoid."

"My office thinks I'm insane," Brian responded.

"If you don't watch out," Tracy added with a grin, "you'll both wind up in the nuthouse."

THE SERPENT

The store clerk was facing the hurried looking customer. "That'll be $2,675 dollars."

"Take cash?"

Face set in a friendly smile, taking the hundred dollar bills neatly counted out, she replied, "Nothing but."

"Thank you—come again." It still puzzled her that anyone would spend money on computer or electronic equipment. With power and communication still out, for who knew how long, she wondered, "Who'd be this stupid to spend thousands on useless equipment?"

Anxious to get out of there, he hastily accepted the change back. Tightly clutching the package, he quickened his paces then hailed a taxi. The Serpent was still furious at losing his principle cells in the country. Seated in back of the cab, he tried to relax. *How did they track us down? New York cell's gone Chicago, Denver, and Pacific as well. Got to start all over,* he resented. Forcing his mind off the problem, he pulled the laptop computer from its package.

He briefly stared at the brightly polished cover. Shaking his head, he wondered about the partially eaten apple symbol in its center. *How could a computer and a city be named after a fruit?* Leafing through the PC booklet, he tried to get a handle on the Apple jargon. The puzzled look he had on the face just seconds ago gradually faded.

The cab pulled up in front of the safe house. *At least,* he sighed, relieved, *this place's still here.* He paid the cabby and briskly entered the lobby. The desk clerk handed him the key. He couldn't wait to test the purchase of his computer.

"Very nice," he muttered, watching the Windows software load into memory, pleased the battery had been charged. With power out, he wasn't interested in connecting to the internet anyway. All he wanted was test the newly acquired application. "Next?" His gaze shifted to the neatly printed box top. Its label identified the application. "Packet Trap." It was the reason for the PC purchase.

He'd known about the software. The command center had a copy. Squinting at the fine print, he read on, "Network and Protocol—Analyzing Software," used to intercept and log digital network traffic. "Sniffer software decodes, captures, and analyzes packet traffic and its contents," it claimed, "in accordance with RFC or similar protocols. Depending on the network structure (router, hub, or switch), it captures traffic on all or parts of the wire using ARP." Address resolution protocol spoofing, he knew, allowed the user to read the data frames, modify, or trap network traffic. He also tested the "Crack" parameters that decoded stored passwords and account numbers.

He was aware of the principles of ARP spoofing to send fake messages over the Ethernet. "Hmm…denial of service attacks…spoofing…exactly what I need." Grinning with delight, he kicked back and studied the package: *may take some time to master the program to stay ahead the detested CIA.* "Never," he vowed, "will I get caught off guard again." It did not matter to him that power and electronics were still out in the nation. He'd spend the future at his new domain, Palm Jumeirah, his domicile waiting to be occupied. Problem was getting a flight out of the city. Completely satisfied, he shut the case, got up, and reached for his coat. With a grin on his face he left the apartment. "Think I'll take me a virgin." With a quiet promise he slipped out the door. "Why wait for the afterlife to get this exalted pleasure," he muttered in anticipation, "when you can taste it while alive?"

RISING NATION

George Wilmot, president of the United States, was giving another speech. It would be his last. Presently on the air, using HAM and HF, the nation's current broadcast media, from the security of Mount Weather's command center, he was addressing the people.

Listeners across the nation tuned into the channel could almost feel the heavyhearted voice of the president.

"My citizens," he began, "this isn't the first time a nation's been subjected to annihilation. Going back in history, for thousands of years, there were countless examples. Biblical accounts provide ample proof for that. One," he paused to collect his thoughts, "does not have to go back far into history to get a taste of turmoil. There's not one generation that has lived that hasn't experienced conflict, destruction, and, even worse, extermination to some extent. One only has to be reminded of war torn places such as the Gulf, Iraq, and Afghanistan, to name a few. Those," he stressed, "were recent events within our present generation.

"Closer to home," Wilmot went on, "we, the United States, have had our share of conflicts, especially in the early days of settlement. In those clashes, we think of human beings fighting other human beings, where inflictions were assessed by body counts. In today's world, however, we only need one demented individual to trigger an argument potentially escalating into a major conflict that could force a nation to its knees. There's one advantage the United States has over a more oppressed culture," he explained, "and that's the uniting following a conflict. We," the president continued, "as a nation, do not let cultural and religious differences keep us apart. No matter what the severity, we stand united against any and all enemies. Such is the case today, here, and in the future. It will take some time before our nation will be back in full swing.

"Leading up to the attack, there had been countless signs of an aging and fractured infrastructure. Primarily affected were power and communications. The effects will have far-reaching consequences for years to come. Banking records, trading data, health, commerce, personal, political, and economic parameters are all affected. Much historical data stored on electronic archives is lost. Intellectual wealth, as well as technological achievements, must again be researched, recovered, and rerecorded. That alone will create an entire new industry. There are, however, many more efforts emerging that are just as important.

"The attack satellites have caused enormous damages. Wall Street, along with banks, ATMs, post offices, and other capital accounting and distribution systems, is shut down. Hospitals, emergency care, and medical centers are disabled, or, at best, running on backup generators. Commercial air traffic's grounded in its entirety. God only knows," he expounded, "when that's coming back.

"In the midst of the turmoil," Wilmot further explained, "there is one positive element. For some unexplained reasons, outdated communication systems such as undersea cables, microwave towers, and antiquated radio gear have remained in place. What really saved the nation was the Confederates previously only looked upon as a legacy air fleet providing recreational services in the form of annual air shows. It was the ingenuity of a few that prevented the total collapse of the world's most advanced nation.

"Slowly," after a halting pause, the president went on, "one by one, command and control organizations, limited as they are established communications. NORAD, the nation's command center," Wilmot stressed, "despite prolific rumors to the contrary, is still in operation. Emergency shelters are up in every part of the northern part of California. It's San Francisco, the City's East Bay, that took most of the horrendous devastation. The piers, sandwiched between both bridges, the Golden Gate and Bay Bridges, that's where 'Ground Zero' took place. Devastation reached as far as Treasure and much of Yerba Buena Island. Also gone are the city's financial district, Market Street, Paragraph Hill, Russian Hill, Mission, Castro, Pacific Heights, Union Square, and other well-known landmarks. In all," he paused again, "every high-rise around the eastern slopes of the city hills, and many dwellings in-between, were leveled. Regions to the west were not affected to the same extent, because the blast carried out and upward from the epicenter. Most of this region was protected by the many hills of San Francisco.

"In other parts of the country, along the Eastern Seaboard, the D.C. area, and the central U.S. where people have lost power, communication, and economic support structures, emergency shelters have been setup. Once air transport, Confederates, was reestablished, HAM operators, Red Cross, and FEMA were quick to respond through the coordinated efforts of the National Guard and DHS. Already," Wilmot further indicated, "workable equipment is being distributed by the Army out of Ft. Monmouth, NJ, where tons of equipment is kept in storage."

Being the military's major storage facility, housed in a cluster of buildings a quarter mile long, manual operation quickly took over the usually computerized and automated storage and retrieval system. Equipment from every battle and age dating back to the Civil War was available. Entire mainframe computer systems, alongside comm and radio equipment of all sorts used for backup and potential replacement parts, were in storage, waiting to be deployed.

"Aside from complete destruction of the San Francisco city center, thanks to the patriotic responses of Alex Bauer and others," Wilmot further explained, "and their quick response to prevent a nuclear counterstrike by North Korea or another hostile nation, collateral damages have been kept to a minimum. As result of the first strike, every piece of household electronics, communication, and PC system is in need of repair. In the business world," he went on to say, "desktops and computer servers, data banks, and archived storage was incinerated, taking with it banking accounts, personal records, proprietary information, and classified data, unless it'd been isolated through shielded vault.

"People of the United States," the president concluded, "I don't need to stress that I, with the support of you citizens, will do my utmost to get this nation back on its feet. I just want to mention one last thing," he deliberately paused for a final time, "my sincere thanks to all of you taking pride in protecting this nation and your government from total takeover by forces that still have to be identified and dealt with. May God bless all of you."

NATIONAL SECURITY COUNCIL

"What's your plan, Mr. President?" The JCS secretary was saying. His tone was courteous but firm.

"Let's keep pushing forward."

"I meant the NSC policies." It was a reminder of the earlier topic. It may not have been of importance for the head of the nation to rework records for the historian; however, it was a vital piece of accountability. It documented each president's term in office. It would retain the link to the next elect and serve the public as an important legacy.

With a brisk move he waved him off. With indifference, the president said, "Forget that, I'm not interested."

"We don't have much time left." The secretary indicated the president's term in office would soon come to an end.

George Wilmot got up from the chair, shrugged his shoulders, and briskly headed back to the private chambers. "Let others take care of it," he muttered on the way out. By "it," he made reference to the Presidential Archive reports. "We've got more important issues at the moment." Rumors had been arriving daily about a certain "Badlands," a republic force gaining hold of the Plains out west. What bothered Wilmot the most was that the rumors might be true. Hastening back to the command center with worries about his family, the nation, and his dwindling defense forces, he muttered, "If that'd be the case, God help us all."

RUSSIAN FEDERATION (Former Politburo)

They were assembled in the crowded, smoke layered assembly room. Energized voices reverberated from the barren walls. The situation was tense. One could even assess it as chaotic. The policy makers for the new Russian Federation wildly gestured their personal opinions on the critical world situation recently caused by the Americans.

"They cannot be trusted," the assembly secretary for the RSFSR voiced his personal concerns to the member seated next to him.

"Let us face it," one member stated, "we do not know anymore who our enemies are." What used to be the Central Committee before the breakup of the USSR now had become the new Parliament. "We cannot even trust our former allies."

Seated at the immense table, the assembly secretary could identify only a few seasoned members. Most were new faces to the party regime. He clearly missed the days of the KGB with Andropov in charge, and Khrushchev pounding the table.

It was time to begin. "Order, please," he demanded. At once, the voices toned down. *At least I am still respected.* "We have a serious situation," he briefly paused to collect his thoughts, "we believe," he continued, "indications point to a nuclear exchange between North Korea and the United States of America." He stiffly turned to the head of the Federal Security Service, formerly the KGB, who was seated close by. "What is their present alert state?"

"We have nothing," was the response. "All communications to the Pentagon and the White House are out. Our satellites over the American continent are not reporting. Sensors from the other satellites indicate two nuclear explosions approximately forty minutes apart." The room exploded with expressive sounds like "impossible…preposterous…outrageous."

"Silence…silence, please." The secretary was pounding the table with his fist. It took minutes to quiet the assembly. Disbelief read in many of the faces. "We must assume North Korea initiated the exchange."

"What are our opportunities?" one party member demanded. It was the head of the Federal Security Service.

"We do not know," the secretary replied. He was as dumbfounded as the rest of the assembly. They had all been taken by surprise. He'd hoped the tension from North Korea had been only another power play by the nation's ruler, but they were proven wrong. He had pushed the free world capitalists too far. Retaliation came with unexpected furor. "For all practical purposes," he continued, "Russia is an isolated nation." Most of the former Soviet Union members, for economic gain, had joined the E.U.

"What are the probabilities of the European Union backing us?"

"It is too late. The Germans have taken command."

"We are on our own?" he screamed, red faced.

"Yes, Mister Secretary," was the pathetic reply.

His face had turned purple. He gaze shifted to the secretary of the armed forces. "What are the target points for our ICBM missiles?"

"We are programming new impact targets," was the response, "but that will take days."

"You mean to say," he hissed at his rival, "we have missed our opportunity?"

"It is not our fault," the officer defended himself. "All we can do is," he paused to let the assembly quiet down, "wait for what the Americans will do next."

He was outraged that his "Mother Russia" had been sideswiped. The government had been blinded by recent economic successes preventing any possibility for aggression. He vowed not to let it happen again. The secretary quickly adjourned the assembly.

PARTY HEADQUARTERS (Republic of China)

The secretary for foreign affairs reached for the gavel. He was just about to demand the assembly to order when an aid rushed in to relay an important message just received from International News sources.

The secretary stared at the text. His hands were shaking. He could not believe what he read:

"…preliminary reports indicate the capital city of Pyongyang, North Korea has been the target of a nuclear attack leaving uncountable victims in its wake. The apparent source is indicated to be the United States of America. No details are available at this time other than the confirmation of this report to be authentic."

Immediate pandemonium followed. For the first time since the end of the Cold War, the sound level exceeded one hundred decibels. It took minutes to calm the assembly.

"Order…order…order, please," he demanded. The gavel came down violently on the table. "Let us not jump to conclusions. We do not have all the facts. I propose today's session be adjourned until further notice." He briskly got up and waved the heads of his military forces into private chambers.

"What do you make of this?" he demanded and handed the message to the head of his defense forces.

"This will change our posture with the western world," was the response.

"Close our borders immediately," he ordered. "No travel authorized. Anybody!"

"Yes, Mr. Secretary."

"Nobody crosses the borders. Ground all air and sea transportation." He continued giving orders. "I want an assessment of our state security from the Second Party Department and foreign intelligence from the Third Department. Also, give me the present state of our retaliation assets from General Staff Headquarters."

"Yes, Mr. Secretary," the leader of the defense forces responded. "What else?"

"Get in touch with the Russian embassy to confirm the attack and assess their action plan. It will greatly affect our economic and international relations. Also, contact our members with the U.N. and confirm their positions.

"Yes, Mr. Secretary."

"The leaders of our nation," he roared, "must be disciplined." The nation had become complacent. It had been overtaken by an economic boom never seen before. The nation had become absorbed by a newly acquired prosperity. Focus had shifted from the old solidarity into new horizons of untold wealth. The State had become vulnerable. "We must protect the nation," he demanded, "against all possible interferences." Only he and a few trusted from the inner circle knew the true plan for their long-term global goals.

BAUER HERITAGE

Alex Bauer

Putting recent incidents behind, Alex experienced immense guilt from his almost total annihilation of an unsuspecting nation, that of North Korea. To cope with the guilt, he immersed himself in work. Pursuing consulting, his focus was directed at commercial projects, with an assurance for protection against future EMP vulnerability. Before long, his business thrived with built-in protections to commercial computer and communication equipment in the hope that there may never be a need to unleash the technology. Nevertheless, knowing mankind, that was only wishful thinking.

Weeks into the endeavor, he'd almost forgotten an incident at SPACECOM. He looked up a name in the base locator then dialed the number.

"Hicks," the soft voice answered.

"Hello Rhonda, it's Alex…remember me?"

"I wondered," she rejoiced, "if you'd ever call."

"Could we get together for lunch?"

"Of course," she said in a firm, but promising tone of voice. There would be hope for her future after all.

Tracy Bauer

Tracy met her ultimate challenge, Brian Harris. Mutually enjoying work and personal lives to the maximum, both arranged for a workable compromise. Where Tracy continued working many hours between her organization and the Pentagon, whenever possible she allowed time to accompany Brian during his travels on whatever assignments. Working out upcoming space asset issues matched to inter-organizational policies, they made an effective team. Hoping they'd eventually have the time to raise a family, she readily accepted the personal partnership with Brian. Unknown to both, in the not too distant future, destiny, would take a much different turn. Tracy was destined for challenges even she thought impossible.

Brian Harris

Brain continued a fast-paced career with the NSA, but many times in the company of Tracy whether in person or in spirit, depending on situation crises. Traveling together, wherever the opportunity was presented, they had the greatest time exploring famous spots along with popular tourist sites. They learned to coexist in an environment of hectic work schedules and personal leisurely life.

Lisa (Liz) Bauer

Liz continued giving her body and soul to the survivors of the San Francisco bombing. Through this, she found the ultimate purpose in dedicating her life to the cause of unfortunate victims. In times of crises, she'd visit many troubled sites to help arrange local support with the aid of organizations such as the Red Cross, UNICEF, and other world relief organizations.

The Serpent (aka) Hammad Hasan

The world's most renowned and feared adversary, despite the mission failure, had gained respect from many terrorist factions. Pledging vengeance, he was striving to achieve global supremacy over the free world. To thrive yet another day, he continued to successfully avoid the far-reaching tentacles of the world's intelligence systems. His goal was to gain world dominance for the Islamic nations whether by diplomatic accesses or through divinely-inspired guidance by Allah.

"Our time will come," was his passionate promise to his people. For now, he was enjoying the luxury of his newly acquired domicile, the stately estate especially designed to house his command headquarters: Palm Jumeirah, the seat of Jihad, powerbase for a new world order, Islam.

AFTERWORD

PENTAGON'S HAMMER is about the vulnerability of the Unites States of America as subjected to global manipulations from the world's foremost power brokers. The premise of the novel is based on Electromagnetic Pulsing (EMP) and our nation's defense infrastructure's vulnerability to it. To guard against such vulnerability, the novel describes, in detail, the weaknesses and shortfalls of the many safeguards in place, at times, strained by budget cuts, consequently affecting the many Intel and government organizations' ability to be effectively proactive.

Perhaps it is not too late to educate aggressive nations and their leaders to join a free world, a world of opportunistic, but frail creatures, The Human Being, in trying to create a peaceful coexistence on a vulnerable, but otherwise beautiful, Earth. As far as we know, it is the only populated globe in a cosmos of unlimited possibilities and should be treated as such.

The story illustrates the probabilities of potential threats by air, sea, and land that could cause severe economic disruptions to the nation and the well-being of its citizens. Where the major segments of the events have already been staged by unsympathetic forces to the free world, the remaining fictional accounts offer a potential futuristic possibility, by which, if left unchecked, fiction could become reality. The contents of this novel shall serve as warning to nations with the intention of causing harm to the people of the United States and its allies.

With the end of the Cold War, major threats of nuclear attacks diminished—so we thought. PENTAGON'S HAMMER, however, represents an alternative scenario. Because of what we are, mankind will never be at peace for very long. Whereas many nations continue to strive for a lasting peace, others will never align. Struggle for survival will continue as it has for eons. Globally, where one nation fights for more space, others will for ideology or, worse yet, for the religious cause. Closer to home, with the many beliefs and faiths inherent to the nation, Americans living in a democratic nation have learned to live side-by-side. We have demonstrated to the world that it is possible for many factions to coexist with each other.

The reason our democratic nation has thrived is because of this simple rule: church and state are kept separate. Where the state is run by government and politicians, politics, for most part, is not greatly influenced by religious orders. As founded by our forefathers, it is our privilege to live in a paradigm based on the principles constituted by the Bill of Rights for liberty, justice, freedom of speech, and freedom for all.

For this reason, contemptuous nations should study the constitution of the United States to learn what it takes to coexist among a world of diversified faiths and cultures. There was a strong reason why this constitution was created. After all, the nation's founders created the new nation to escape persecution from dominant religious factions themselves. This nation, culture, border and its people are of the utmost importance, to be protected regardless of political makeup. In collaboration with likeminded nations, with the help of science and technology, we can only hope to control and manage future acts of aggression.

There may come a time when all nations will be united under one global government with the purpose, in mind, to effectively manage violence, crime and aggression, but in the process they will also lose their inherited identity. For this reason, it is important to protect the nation's borders even though it may cause the occasional conflict. As with crime, prosperity, and population growth, terrorism is expanding, and it's here to stay. The only recourse we have is to manage its means effectively. With the expanding threats, entire new industries have been created, demanding great resources in manpower and expenditure. The cost of freedom, however, is high. To keep this freedom, we all have to share an ever-growing awareness for the preservation of the free world.

Within the confines of this novel, where public awareness does not generally include national intelligence knowledge, PENTAGON'S HAMMER demonstrates elements required to effectively manage a national defense system. There are many elements needed to accomplish this objective. Some of these include satellite surveillance, sensitive organizational policies and procedures, interoperability, common picture elements, complicated emergency plans, and sophisticated design, specifically in science and technology for nuclear, computer, and satellite and communication systems, on top of personal commitment and dedication.

Organizational readiness should be the nation's highest objective to protect against terrorism, as well as hostile aggression and crimes against humanity, but cannot always assure success. We can only hope that in cases of aggression and emergencies, whether created by natural causes, hostile acts, or radical factions, effective crisis management will take over to resolve the situations. Effective management may not always work with the nation's infrastructure destroyed, as depicted in PENTAGON'S HAMMER. The end result may be a much stronger nation that emerges from the rubble because the American people are of resilient stock with an inherent pioneering spirit that allows them to forge ahead and succeed, no matter what obstacles are thrown across their paths. It is this spirit that will prevent the nation from ever getting annihilated.

T. RANDALL